Catherine Aird has served both as Vice-Chairman and as Chairman of the Crime Writers' Association and is the author of some fourteen detective novels. She has also written a *son et lumière* and has edited a number of parish histories. In recognition of her work she was awarded an honorary MA degree from the University of Kent and was made an MBE for her services to the Girl Guide Association. Though she has lived in Kent for many years, she was brought up in Huddersfield.

Also by Catherine Aird in Pan Books

The Body Politic

The
Catherine Aird
Collection

Three Sloan and Crosby novels

His Burial Too | Last Respects | Harm's Way

Pan Books

His Burial Too first published 1973 for the Crime Club by Doubleday &
Company, Inc., New York
First published in Great Britain in this edition 1993
© Catherine Aird 1973
Last Respects first published 1982 by Doubleday & Company, Inc., New York,
and simultaneously in Canada
First published in Great Britain in this edition 1993
© Catherine Aird 1982
Harms Way first published 1984 by William Collins Sons & Co. Ltd
First published in this edition 1993
© Catherine Aird 1984
This combined edition first published 1993 by Pan Books
an imprint of Macmillan Publishers Ltd
25 Eccleston Place, London SW1W 9NF
and Basingstoke
Associated companies throughout the world
ISBN 0 330 32645 7
Copyright © Catherine Aird 1973, 1982, 1984. This collection Catherine Aird 1993
The right of Catherine Aird to be identified as the author of this work has been
asserted by her in accordance with the Copyright, Designs and Patents Act 1988.

9 8 7 6 5 4 3
A CIP catalogue record for this book is available from the British Library.

Typeset by Cambridge Composing (UK) Ltd, Cambridge
Printed by Mackays of Chatham PLC, Chatham, Kent

Contents

The
Catherine Aird
Collection

His Burial Too

For Jennifer, Peter, Jonty, and Elizabeth, with love.

The chapter headings are taken from the plays of John Webster and Cyril Tourneur.

Who has his birth day, has his buriall too;
As we into the world come, out we goe.

Epitaph in Crundale church

Men oft are valued high, when they're
most wretched.

1

It was the knocking which woke Fenella Tindall.

Not the first time it happened.

The first time the knocking came she was dreaming so deeply that she didn't even hear it. In her dream she wasn't tucked up safely at home in her own bedroom in the English village of Cleete at all. She was miles and miles away. In her dream she was in Italy. In Rome, to be exact. Walking down the Via Veneto with the two young Trallanti children.

It was in her dream as it had always been in real life – the pudgy little Nicola hurrying along beside her, her chubby hand tightly clutched in Fenella's, and the older and more adventuresome Giovanni skipping ahead of them both.

Nevertheless the knocking must have begun to register on her mind because her dream changed gear slightly.

She was calling to Giovanni now, telling him not to go too far ahead on his own. She had spent a lot of her time in Italy with the Trallanti children doing just that. She doubted whether in the long run anyone – anyone at all – was going to be able to keep Giovanni back. Already the boy was slim-hipped and handsome, and as lithe as quicksilver. And some-day, too, not so many light-years away, his sister Nicola, dark, slow, and almost insultingly good-looking, was going to break a heart or two.

Not that that was Fenella's problem.

Her problem had been teaching them English.

Fenella's own Italian was good – that had been how she had got the job in the first place – but she always spoke to the children in English. That was what their mother, the Principessa, wanted. That was how the English Miss Fenella Tindall of Cleete had come to be in Italy at all. To teach English to the Trallanti children.

'So that it is their second tongue, Miss Tindall,' their mother had said firmly. 'That is what I want.'

And even that wasn't Fenella Tindall's problem any more. Not now.

Not since she had had to come back to England again . . .

The knocking came again and this time it did reach her bedroom. The Italian dream faded. Her sleep-soaked mind forgot the Principessa and – in the infinitely accommodating way of dreams – tossed up an association to match the extraneous noise.

She was hammering away at something now – she wasn't quite sure what.

But urgently . . .

Now another figure appeared at the edge of her dream. A man, this time. She couldn't see him very clearly but again in the way of dreams she somehow knew who he was. Guiseppe Mardoni . . . She was aware of him there . . . small, dark, and engaging – and on the fringe.

There was another bout of knocking and she came one stage nearer true wakefulness. Another thought flitted through her mind.

'Wake Duncan with thy knocking . . .'

Then the sound – the real sound – came again and all the layers of unconsciousness were stripped away. She opened her eyes, admitted the world, and was properly awake at last. The Trallanti children, Macbeth, and the insubstantial Guiseppe were all thoroughly banished by the present.

The present apparently consisted of someone knocking at the front door.

Fenella struggled out of bed and snatched at her dressing gown. It was a beautiful dressing gown – one which she had brought back with her from Rome and really cherished . . .

She stopped suddenly. As she had been feeling about for her bedroom slippers her eye had fallen on her little bedside clock.

It said half-past eight.

She blinked.

It couldn't be as late as half-past eight.

Not half-past eight in the morning.

What about breakfast? What about getting her father off to work in Berebury? She shook herself. This wouldn't do at all. After all, the whole idea had been that something like this shouldn't happen. This was what she had come home from Italy for. To look after her father. She didn't seem to be making a very good job of it this morning.

She opened her bedroom door and shot along the upstairs landing. She called out to her father as she hurried downstairs to answer the door. Even in her present rush she was vaguely surprised that he wasn't already moving about. It really wasn't like him to sleep in quite as late as this – whether or not she was there to give him a call.

The knocking was coming from the front door all right. A renewed bout of it settled any doubts about that.

Fenella unlocked the door.

'Couldn't make anyone hear at the back,' announced a short dumpy woman equably, 'so I came round to the front.'

'Oh, it's you, Mrs Turvey.' Fenella pushed her hair back out of her eyes. 'Come in. Thank goodness you woke me. We must have slept in.'

'Happens to us all, miss, some time or other.' Mrs Turvey lived farther down Cleete High Street and 'did' for the Tindalls. She came in for a few hours every morning.

'I'd no idea it was so late . . .'

'Shouldn't be surprised myself if it wasn't the heat,' said Mrs Turvey, stepping into the hall. 'Ever such a hot night, it was. Not that it'll have seemed all that hot to you, miss, I expect. Not after that Rome.'

Fenella smiled faintly. 'No, it was just about right for me. What I remember of it.' She had only been awake a matter of minutes but already she would have been hard put to it to say what it was that she had been dreaming about.

'Hot enough to make anyone oversleep in England, anyway,' reaffirmed Mrs Turvey.

'You could be right about that – my father doesn't seem to have woken yet even,' said Fenella, going back towards the stairs. 'I'd better give him another shout now in case he didn't hear me come down.'

'And I'd better put the kettle on.' Mrs Turvey started off in the direction of the kitchen. 'He can't go off, not without something inside him. Not even if he is late.'

Fenella paused with one foot on the bottom step of the staircase as a new thought assailed her. 'Mrs Turvey, you don't think that he's just gone out on his own without waking me, do you? You know, made his own breakfast and gone . . .'

'Well, it would be for the very first time, if he had, wouldn't it?' answered Mrs Turvey, not without spirit. 'Had to be here b'half-past seven sharp, I did, until you came back home, miss. Every morning.'

'That's true.' Fenella nodded. No one could have called her father domesticated. Clever, good at his job, admirable and devoted parent – all of those things.

But domesticated – no.

That was the whole trouble. That was why she had come back home from Italy. She had been perfectly happy with the Trallantis in Rome but her father had been lonely and sad in England. She hadn't been able to bear the thought of him leading a solitary existence in Cleete . . .

'There's another thing, miss,' said Mrs Turvey, rapidly unrolling the apron she had brought with her, 'if he should happen to have got himself off on his own for once in a while . . .'

'Yes?'

'Then he's gone and locked all the doors behind him – which he wouldn't be likely to do seeing as how he knew I would be coming round soon the same as always.'

'How silly of me,' conceded Fenella quickly. 'I hadn't thought of that.' She turned and ran upstairs and then hurried along the landing to her father's bedroom. She tapped on the door.

There was no reply.

She knocked again.

'I'm afraid it's awfully late,' she called out. 'We've both slept in this morning.'

There was still no answer.

She put her hand on the knob and opened the door. The bedroom curtains were still drawn against the light but the morning sun beyond them was coming in strongly enough for her to see quite easily that the bed was empty.

Not only empty but still made.

There was no sign whatsoever of her father in the room. More importantly, there was no sign whatsoever of his having been in there at all overnight. Everything was just as it had been when Fenella had gone in during the evening before to draw the curtains and to turn down the bed.

She took a second swift glance round the room and then went back on the landing and called down to Mrs Turvey.

'He's gone.' She swallowed. 'At least, he's not here.'

Police Superintendent Leeyes landed the problem of the absent Mr Tindall of Cleete squarely on the desk of Detective Inspector C. D. Sloan (Christopher Dennis to his wife and parents, 'Seedy' to his friends) not very long after that hard-working officer reported for duty at Berebury Police Station that morning.

The Thursday morning.

The Thursday after the Wednesday.

Everyone was to remember Wednesday, July 16th. That, at least, was one thing which helped the police. Wednesday, July 16th, was one of the hottest days in living memory in the county of Calleshire and it wasn't forgotten for a long time.

It had been really hot. Not just the ordinary warm weather which customarily passes for summer in England, but hot.

Workers in chocolate factories had had to be sent home because the chocolate was unworkable. Sales of ice cream had soared along with the thermometer. By the middle of the afternoon it had been so hot that – over in the south-eastern corner of the county of Calleshire – a fat man had attended a funeral without his jacket.

This particular disregard for the proprieties so incensed a retired major general (who didn't know what things were comin' to) that he wrote an indignant letter about it to the editor of one of the local papers – the *Calleford Chronicle*. The police later read this in their patient attempt to build up a complete picture of the day in question.

The letter, predictably, triggered off an energetic correspondence which only finished – weeks afterwards – with a spirited letter from another mourner at the same funeral, who wrote that he was sure that the deceased would have been sympathetic towards the shirt sleeves (he was about to be cremated anyway) – and with a terse note from the editor of the paper saying 'This correspondence is now closed.'

By the time that happened everyone in Calleshire knew the name of Richard Mallory Tindall.

The Criminal Investigation Department of Berebury Division, of which Detective Inspector C. D. Sloan was in charge, was small – all matters of great criminal moment being referred to the Calleshire County Constabulary Headquarters in the county town of Calleford. It did, however, collect – much to Sloan's regret – all the odd jobs.

This, it seemed, was one of the odd jobs.

'Man missing,' announced Superintendent Leeyes briefly, waving a thin message sheet in his hand. 'Seems as if he didn't go home last night.'

'Can't say I blame him for that, sir,' rejoined Inspector Sloan, fingering his collar. 'Thank goodness it's better today.'

The Thursday, as everyone – but everyone – remarked, mercifully was cooler than the Wednesday and almost everyone was relieved. Even those who had begun by lapping up the heat of the day before with a certain atavistic voluptuousness had ceased to wallow in it and begun instead to weary of it by evening. Hot nights were for sub-Mediterranean type peoples, not the English.

Superintendent Leeyes, who never admitted to changes of temperature on principle, grunted.

'Much too hot for sleeping in a bed,' continued Sloan firmly. 'I shouldn't have minded staying out myself last night, sir, come to that.'

Leeyes glared at him. 'Supposing he was that daft, too, and went down to Kinnisport for a swim in the moonlight or some such fancy carry-on in the dark then neither his clothes nor his body have turned up . . .' He paused and then added lugubriously, '. . . yet.'

'He just didn't go home, sir?' enquired Inspector Sloan. 'Er . . . is that all?'

The missing man – if he was missing – was by no means the only problem to fetch up on his desk. Like beachcombings washed up by the tide, other worries were stranded there too. There was a nasty little outbreak of anonymous letters over at the village of Constance Parva to be sorted out – to say nothing of the mysterious behaviour of the Berebury mayoral car. The funniest of things kept on happening to that – and always when the mayor was sitting in it.

'That's all,' responded Leeyes flatly. 'He just didn't go home.'

'But it's not a crime, sir,' ventured Detective Inspector Sloan. For all that he was the titular head of Berebury's tiny Criminal Investigation Department Missing Persons didn't usually come within his province. 'Not to go home, I mean.'

'I know it's not,' snapped Leeyes, 'but he's officially been reported missing and we can't just write it down and forget it, can we, Sloan?'

'No, sir, but . . .'

'And what with your friend, Inspector Harpe, grabbing everyone on the strength of who's capable of waving his arms about – and some who aren't – for his blasted traffic problems . . .'

'Yes, sir, but . . .'

'Not that a collection of scarecrows wouldn't do the job just as well for all the good they seem to do . . .'

'Quite, sir,' agreed Sloan with feeling. Berebury's traffic jams were a byword in the county – and classic textbook in origin. A medieval town plan surrounded by twentieth century urban sprawl, the experts said. The police had a pithier way of putting it.

'That means,' said Leeyes, coming triumphantly up the straight, 'that there's only you and Detective Sergeant Gelven left not trying to sort out motorists.'

'Yes, sir,' repeated Sloan, subconsciously noting that even at a time like this the superintendent didn't think Sloan's own most junior assistant, Detective Constable Crosby, was worth a mention. Those were Sloan's sentiments, too. The defective constable was what they called him at the station . . .

The superintendent threw his pen down on to the desk. 'That's what police work's been reduced to, Sloan. Caning the motorist. Motoring law and motoring order. That's all anyone cares about these days. I never thought I'd live to see the day when . . .'

Detective Inspector Sloan cleared his throat and tried valiantly to get back to the point. 'This chap, sir. How did we hear he was missing?'

'What? Oh, Police Constable Hepple told us. You know him, Sloan, don't you? He keeps everything nice and quiet down to the south – Larking way and round there.'

Sloan nodded but said nothing. Her Majesty's Inspector of Constabulary might not define the duties of a police constable as 'keeping everything nice and quiet' but it put the situation in a nutshell as far as the superintendent was concerned.

'Hepple's stationed at Larking,' the superintendent was going on, 'as you know, but he covers this little village of Cleete as well. And half a dozen others.' Leeyes grunted. 'Seems as if he bicycled over there this morning to pin up a notice in the church porch about warble fly . . .'

Sloan kept his face expressionless. Somewhere he had once read that there were really only half a dozen original stories in the world. He knew that Cinderella was one of them; the woodcutter's son and the Princess was another and – going back aeons before Aesop – the eternally fascinating tale of the Town Mouse and the Country Mouse.

He sighed.

Bicycling to the church to put up a notice in the porch about the dangers of warble fly to sheep was about as far removed from town police life as it was from the planet Mars. And being late with it into the bargain, thought Sloan suddenly. He might work in the town but he'd been brought up in the country. You dipped sheep earlier than this.

'The church porch?' he echoed dully.

'That's right. And that's where this chap's daily woman nabbed him with this story about her employer being missing.' The superintendent peered at the message sheet again. 'The woman's name is Mrs Turvey. Apparently she went to the house this morning at eight thirty like she always does and . . .'

'No chap?'

'Exactly.' Leeyes grunted again. 'Bed not slept in . . .'

'So it doesn't happen often then,' deduced Sloan intelligently.

'Never before, apparently. Not without him saying. That's what's making her so worried. If he's ever delayed anywhere he always lets them know?'

'Them?'

'There's a daughter.' The superintendent flipped over another sheet of paper. 'Funny name she's got . . . here it is. Fenella.'

'Fenella.' Detective Inspector Sloan wrote that down in his notebook.

On a new page.

Every case had to begin somewhere.

Usually with a name.

'Anyway,' persisted Leeyes, 'Hepple says this Mrs Turvey told him that when Miss Fenella saw that the master's bed hadn't been slept in . . .'

Sloan kept his face straight with an effort.

It *was* different, all right, out there in the country.

'. . . she called her upstairs and they both had a look for him. The daughter didn't know he wasn't in the house. She was expecting him to have come home after she'd gone to bed.'

'I see, sir.' He didn't see anything yet but he would. In time.

'That means you'll have to find him, Sloan, whether you like it or not.'

'Yes, sir.' Sloan cleared his throat and said, 'But what about whether he likes it?'

'What's that? What did you say?'

'Can we be sure that he wants to be found?' That might make a difference. Sloan himself wouldn't have wanted to have been restored to the bosoms of some of the families he had known people have.

'Why not?' demanded the superintendent, who was not given to finer family feelings.

'Like I said, sir, it's not a crime not to go home for the night.'

Superintendent Leeyes looked quite blank.

'I mean, sir,' amplified the inspector patiently, 'perhaps he's left his wife on purpose and doesn't want her to know where he is . . .'

'No,' declared Leeyes triumphantly, 'it isn't like that at all because he hasn't got a wife.'

'I see, sir.'

'Constable Hepple said so. And he knows everything about them all out that way.'

Sloan nodded his understanding. This was what made Hepple a good man all right. They said that knowledge was strength. That would be how the singlehanded Hepple was able to keep everything nice and quiet in his own little territory to the south of Berebury.

'She died a few months ago,' went on Leeyes. 'Hepple says he's only got a daughter. Fenella. Miss Fenella Tindall.'

'Tindall?' exclaimed Sloan suddenly, hearing the surname for the first time. 'That rings a bell. Sir, would that by any chance by anything to do with that rather odd firm, Struthers and Tindall?'

It was the superintendent's turn to nod.

'You know,' went on Sloan hurriedly, 'the people who have

that works down near the Wellgate here in Berebury who call themselves something funny . . .'

'Precision, Investigation, and Development Engineers,' supplied Leeyes.

'And who are always asking Inspector Tetley for extra security without wanting to tell us why?'

'Everything to do with them,' said Leeyes neatly. 'That Tindall.'

'Oh, dear.'

'Exactly.'

Unequal nature, to place women's hearts
so far upon the left side!

2

Busier by far than the Dower House at Cleete and a good deal
noisier than the police station at Berebury were the works of
Messrs Struthers and Tindall near the Wellgate in Berebury. It
was a long low building, all on one floor and as orderly as a
beehive. The perpetual hum which could be heard even from
the outside carried the similarity still further. The resemblance, though, ended at the laboratory door. Bees lived by
instinct. They didn't do experiments.

Miss Hilda Holroyd, private secretary to Mr Richard
Tindall, replaced the telephone receiver on her desk in the
office with a visible frown.

She thought for a moment and then went and tapped on the
door of the combined office and laboratory of Mr Tindall's
second-in-command. That was Mr Henry Pysden, who was
the deputy general manager and also head of the scientific side
of the firm.

Reluctantly.

Mr Pysden made no secret of the fact that he hated being
disturbed when he was working on an experiment himself and
she had been in to him twice this morning already. The first
time had been to enquire if he had had any message from Mr
Tindall to say he wasn't coming in which hadn't reached her.

He said he hadn't.

The second time had been to ask him if he would see an
importunate visitor, Mr Gordon Cranswick, who had arrived

on the doorstep and who was showing signs of not wanting to be fobbed off by her.

He said he wouldn't.

And had added: 'If it's about the last batch of tests we did for him, tell him to see Paul Blake or one of the metallurgists. If it's anything else he'll have to wait and see Mr Tindall when he does get here. Or make another appointment.'

'I've just rung Mrs Turvey at Cleete,' she began this time.

'Turvey?' Henry Pysden's voice sounded quite blank. He lifted his head – it was dome-shaped and almost bald – and peered at her through his thick-lensed glasses. 'Turvey? I don't know anyone called Turvey.'

'Mrs Turvey is Mr Tindall's daily woman at the Dower House,' explained Miss Holroyd patiently. 'She says he's not there either and she's told the police that Mr Tindall's missing.'

'Good idea,' said the deputy general manager warmly.

Miss Holroyd looked distressed. 'But something quite ordinary might have happened to him.'

'And it might not.' Henry Psyden tapped his pen on the desk. 'I can't go looking for him, Miss Holroyd.'

'No, Mr Pysden, of course not.'

'Besides' – the man essayed a faint smile – 'it's much more in their line than in mine.'

She smiled back. 'Yes, Mr Pysden.'

That was very true. There was never any point in getting the short-sighted Mr Pysden to help to look for anything.

'If there is an expert,' pronounced Mr Pysden, 'I say get him. I always tell people that, Miss Holroyd.'

'Yes, Mr Pysden.' Miss Holroyd nodded. That was true. She had often heard him say exactly that to clients.

Just as often, in fact, as she had heard Mr Tindall say the exact opposite to the same clients.

With him it was definitely the other way round. He positively favoured the amateur approach. 'Your amateur's not cluttered up with academic prejudice, Miss Holroyd,' Richard Tindall was fond of saying. 'He hasn't read every single thing that has ever been written on the subject. The amateur sees a problem in its simplest form and it doesn't occur to him that it's insoluble.'

'He'll turn up, I expect, soon enough,' Henry Pysden was saying easily. 'I shouldn't worry too much if I were you, Miss Holroyd. It's quite early still, you know.'

'But it's not like Mr Tindall,' she persisted.

'He was late yesterday morning,' pointed out Pysden.

'That was the road works.'

'Well, then . . .'

Miss Holroyd shook her head. 'No. They're all finished now. I checked.'

'The devil you did!' exclaimed Pysden. 'Do you ever overlook anything, Miss Holroyd?'

Her expression was austere. 'Not if I can help it, Mr Pysden.'

'No, of course not,' he said hastily, seeming somehow to retreat behind his glasses. 'I am sure you don't. By the way, Miss Holroyd, now that you are here I wonder if you would let me have the office patent register? I need it for the Galloway contract.'

'Certainly, Mr Pysden. I think Mr Blake is working on it this morning. I'll get him to send it along to you.'

'Blake?' said the deputy general manager sharply. 'What's he doing with the patent register?'

Miss Holroyd frowned. 'I rather think he's working on the Harbleton Engineering problem.'

'Not United Mellemetics?'

'United Mellemetics?' Miss Holroyd looked up. 'He can't be working on that. Don't you remember? You've still got the United Mellemetics file, Mr Pysden.'

Henry Pysden shook his head. 'No, I haven't, Miss Holroyd. I gave the file and the report back to Mr Tindall yesterday morning. When we had our coffee together. I'd finished with it by then.'

'That's funny.' Miss Holroyd looked puzzled. 'I'm sure it's not in the safe . . .'

Mr Pysden stared at her.

*

There was a tiny tinkle as Mrs Turvey replaced the telephone receiver in the hall at the Dower House at Cleete. Then she hurried back to the kitchen.

As she bustled along she called out urgently, 'The milk, Miss Fenella. Do catch it before it boils over.'

'I did,' said Fenella Tindall.

She was sitting now at the kitchen table, both hands clasped round a cup of coffee, still in her dressing gown. It was an Italian dressing gown, rich in all the colours of the Renaissance. Her mind, though, was not on clothes. She looked up anxiously as the daily woman came back into the kitchen.

'That wasn't my father on the telephone, was it, Mrs Turvey?'

'No, miss, I'm afraid it wasn't.'

'Oh . . .'

'It was Miss Holroyd from your father's works. She was wondering why he wasn't in this morning yet.'

'Oh, dear.'

'He didn't go off early after all, then,' said Mrs Turvey, 'that's one thing for sure.'

'No.'

'Not that I thought that he had done, I must say. He's not an early bird, your father. Never 'as been, not since I've known him.'

'No,' absently. Fenella frowned. 'And that means he didn't stay the night there either.'

Mrs Turvey's square kindly face registered concern. 'Doesn't look like it, miss, though I'm sure there's no call to get that worried . . .'

'What did you say to her?'

'That he wasn't here and that it didn't look to us as if he'd been home at all last night. Do drink up some of that coffee, miss. There's never any good worrying on an empty stomach, that I do know.'

Fenella obediently took a sip of coffee. And then another. She was surprised to find how thirsty she was.

And puzzled.

She had been back home long enough to know her father

didn't make a habit of staying out all night without saying anything to anyone. Besides, he was very much a man who liked routine; everything at its proper time and in its proper place. This behaviour just wasn't like him.

'Poor Miss Holroyd,' continued Mrs Turvey. 'She said he's got someone there now who says he's got an appointment to see your father and she was beginning to get worried, too.'

'She'll cope,' said Fenella decidedly. 'My father always says Miss Holroyd can cope with anything.'

'That's as may be,' said Mrs Turvey enigmatically.

Fenella, undeceived by this, grinned. She knew all about the perpetual state of rivalry that existed between Mrs Turvey and Miss Holroyd, both as jealous as Malbecco. Fortunately each felt superior to the other – Mrs Turvey because she had been married; Miss Holroyd because she had been educated.

'Anyway,' said Mrs Turvey, 'it's a Mr Gordon Cranswick who's there. She said to ask if you knew anything about him, miss . . .'

Fenella shook her head.

'She was wondering if she'd made a mistake,' said Mrs Turvey, 'and Mr Tindall meant this Mr Cranswick to have come out here to Cleete to see him at home and that was why he hadn't gone in to the office this morning.'

'Miss Holroyd doesn't make mistakes,' changed Fenella. It was a sort of litany she had learnt from her father.

'I'm sure I hope not,' responded Mrs Turvey repressively. 'Anyhow, she says Mr Pysden is all tied up with one of his timed experiments and so he couldn't see him instead of your father.'

'Oh, dear.'

'He's someone important, she said.'

Fenella put down her coffee cup and said energetically, 'I don't like the sound of that at all.'

'There now, miss, don't say that. Your father'll turn up presently or give us a ring.'

'Did you tell her,' asked Fenella more diffidently, her head studiously bent over her coffee cup, 'that we'd told the police?'

Mrs Turvey busied herself over the stove. 'Well, I sort of hinted that I'd happened to mention it to Mr Hepple on account of me just happening to see him in the road beyond the drive when I answered the door to the postman.'

'Was she cross?'

'Not so much cross,' said Mrs Turvey consideringly, 'as a bit surprised.' She straightened herself up. 'Still, what's done is done and can't be undone.'

'No. I mean, yes. You don't think he's just gone to London or anything like that, do you?' Fenella pushed the empty coffee cup away and answered her own question. 'No, he'd have rung first thing to tell us, wouldn't he?'

She jerked her shoulder in a compound of anxiety and irritation. It was absurd to know so little about the habits of one's own parent but when you have been away from home so much and have not been back again very long . . .

'He'd have telephoned Miss Holroyd anyway,' declared Mrs Turvey sensibly, 'because of this Mr Cranswick coming to see him specially. He wouldn't have forgotten him, not your father. Not unless he's gone and lost his memory or anything like that.'

Fenella sighed. 'I can't understand it at all. It's just not like him to go off like this without saying anything to anyone.'

Mrs Turvey's mind was going off on quite a different tack. 'I do wish he'd put on that clean shirt I left out for him yesterday morning, miss. I laid it out for him special.'

'Yes, of course . . .' The laundry was one of the threads of life at the Dower House which Fenella hadn't yet gathered up into her own hands.

'I don't like to think of him in the one he had on, miss, whatever he's doing,' she said, turning her attention to the kitchen sink. 'And it wasn't for want of reminding, Miss Fenella. If I said to him once I said it a dozen times . . .'

'I know,' Fenella assured her hastily.

Mrs Turvey sniffed. 'Seemed to me that he didn't want to look smart on purpose yesterday. He put his old suit on, too.'

'The grey.' Fenella remembered that much.

'The grey with the button off the left sleeve,' retorted Mrs

Turvey, 'which I left out to take to the cleaners come Friday. Not for him to put on yesterday morning. It wasn't even in his bedroom, miss. I'd put it out on that chest on the landing that your poor mother called something funny . . .'

'Ottoman . . .'

'Ottoman,' repeated Mrs Turvey doubtfully, 'so as it shouldn't be forgotten like and before you could say Jack Robinson he goes and puts it on.'

'I know.'

'And when I said about it he said he was sorry and he'd put the other one on today.' She splashed hot water into the washing-up bowl.

'I heard him.' Fenella pushed back her chair and took her coffee cup over to the sink. 'I don't think I can manage any toast this morning, Mrs Turvey. I'm not really very hungry.'

The daily woman swept the coffee cup and saucer into the bowl of hot soapy water with a practised hand, and Fenella looked at her watch.

'Mr Osborne couldn't tell you anything, miss?'

'Not a lot,' replied Fenella.

Her father had spent the evening before with George and Marcia Osborne in Berebury because she was going out with Giuseppe Mardoni on his last evening before he went back to Italy. He'd wanted her to go out. Urged her, in fact. He couldn't have her burying herself in the country for ever. That's what he'd said. He would be quite happy, he had insisted, calling in on the Osbornes. He might even go round and keep old Walter Berry company for an hour or two afterwards.

Fenella had rung George Osborne at Berebury Grammar School where he taught physics as the boys were beginning to file into morning assembly.

'Just,' said Fenella to Mrs Turvey, 'that he told them he had someone to see on the way home.'

'Not old Professor Berry, miss, do you think?'

That was just what Fenella had asked George Osborne.

'He didn't say who it was,' the physics master had replied. 'He left us about half-past ten and he was all right then. I shouldn't worry too much if I were you. He'll turn up. And Fenella . . .'

'Yes?'

'When he does will you give him a message for me?'

'Of course.'

'Tell him that Marcia found her earring, will you?'

'George! She didn't lose Great-Aunt Edith's earrings, surely, did she? Not the emerald and diamond ones?'

'The Osborne heirloom,' he agreed solemnly. 'At least, half the heirloom. One earring to be exact. Anyway, it wasn't lost after all. She's found it again, thank goodness. Last night. After he'd gone. Tell him, will you . . .' She had heard the school bell clanging in the background. 'I must go now. Ring Marcia if you want.'

Fenella hadn't rung Marcia. It was too early. The day didn't begin for the well-dressed Marcia Osborne until at least eleven o'clock.

Nor for old Professor Berry for that matter. Between his library and his chess set he never went to bed until the early hours of the morning and he rose equally late. His housekeeper bemoaned the fact up and down the village. It was no use ringing him either yet.

Fenella took another look at her watch and said instead: 'That policeman should have had time to have rung the hospitals by now.'

'Bless you, miss, you don't want to worry about him being in hospital. If your father had had an accident in that car of his – which I wouldn't suppose for one minute that he had had, a more careful driver not being on the road – we'd have heard by now for sure. There's not two cars like that one of his this side of Calleford.'

Fenella managed a rueful smile, appreciating that Mrs Turvey was trying so very hard to be helpful. 'That's true.'

'And another thing – everyone know's that it's his.' The daily woman swilled the water round the sink with vigour. 'Cars like Mr Tindall's don't grow on trees.'

Fenella started to toy with the tassel on the end of the cord on her dressing gown. 'It's a funny thing, you know, Mrs

Turvey, but I could have sworn I heard him come in last night as usual . . .'

Mrs Turvey shook her head.

'. . . I was in bed,' persisted Fenella. 'I'd been home for about an hour and I was just in that dreamy stage. You know – half asleep and half awake – when you're certain you're going to fall asleep in a minute but you haven't quite got there . . .'

'I know, miss.' Mrs Turvey had finished the washing up now and had begun to polish the taps over the sink.

'Well, I thought I heard his car last night, like I usually do. You know how he always changes down a gear for that sharp bend just before the garage – you can't get round without, not in that car . . .'

'It wasn't built for cars, that road.'

'No,' agreed Fenella, deciding that Mrs Turvey, at least, would have thoroughly approved of the horse-drawn *carrozzas* in Rome. 'Well, with my bedroom being on that side of the house anyway . . .'

'No, miss.' Mrs Turvey shook her head. 'It wouldn't have been him. Not last night. First thing I looked for when you told me he wasn't in his room was the garage key. Your father always puts it on the hook by the garden door as soon as he comes in. Always. I've never known him not . . .'

Fenella forbore to say that she had never known her father not come home for the night either.

'I was just drifting off,' she said instead. 'I remember thinking, Oh, good, he's home, and then I turned over and went to sleep.'

'The key isn't there, miss. Must have been the night before.'

She nodded uncertainly. 'I suppose so. Unless . . .' Fenella suddenly stood stock still in the middle of the kitchen floor. '. . . unless he got as far as the garage and then something happened.'

'Oh, Miss Fenella, surely not.'

Fenella girded up the long trailing skirts of her dressing gown. 'I'm going to see.'

'Wait for me, miss.' Mrs Turvey snatched at a towel with wet, dripping hands. 'Wait for me.'

'Come on then. Hurry!'

'Now, don't you go down to that garage on your own . . .'

Fenella took no notice.

She opened the back door of the Dower House and sped across the lawn, her bedroom slippers brushing a faint trail over the dewy grass. She was closely followed by a slightly panting Mrs Turvey.

Both of them came to an abrupt halt in front of the garage doors.

'Why, miss, they're shut,' declared Mrs Turvey in manifest surprise.

'That's funny,' agreed Fenella. 'They were open. I opened them myself yesterday evening while I was waiting to be called for.'

Mrs Turvey nodded approvingly. 'There's nothing your father hates more than having to get out of the car of a night to open them himself. A real nuisance, he calls that.'

Fenella advanced.

'Now, don't you open them doors,' entreated Mrs Turvey urgently. 'Miss Fenella, leave them alone. Let me go in there first.'

She was too late.

Fenella had already pushed the garage door open.

A long low-blue car stood there.

It was quite empty.

3

Mere accident.

Two matters conspired to delay Detective Inspector Sloan leaving Berebury Police Station for Cleete that morning.

The first was a sad disappointment to him.

He wasn't going to be able to take Detective Sergeant Gelven – the staid, resourceful, and utterly reliable Sergeant Gelven – with him after all. When Sloan sent for him it transpired that Sergeant Gelven had been summoned – literally – to attend the Assizes at Calleford, the county town of Calleshire.

'To give evidence, sir,' reported Gelven regretfully, 'in one of the nastiest cases of perjury I've ever come across.'

Sloan groaned aloud.

'I'm very sorry, sir,' said the sergeant. 'I'm sure I don't know why they bother myself. The accused wouldn't know an ethic if he saw one, for a start. Not if he met it on the stairs, he wouldn't. He says,' added Gelven drily, 'that he doesn't understand the meaning of the charge.'

'I'm not surprised,' said Sloan, who knew the gentleman in question. 'I don't suppose he does. Do you realize, Gelven, that that actually could be the truth?'

'First time he's spoken it in a month of Sundays, I'll be bound,' said Gelven fervently. 'And then by accident. Perjury wouldn't mean a thing to him.'

'A real no-good boyo . . .'

'That's the ticket, sir. If you happened to need someone to

sup with the devil for you, he'd be just the man for the job. Otherwise there's not a lot he's any good for, I'm afraid . . .'

'It means that I shall have to take Crosby with me instead,' said Sloan anathematizing the unnamed perjurer under his breath. He did not relish making do with Detective Constable Crosby instead of the sergeant. Crosby was young, brash, and the perennial despair of all those at Berebury Police Station who had dealings with him.

'And why aren't you being a traffic light for Inspector Harpe?' demanded Sloan with unwonted savagery when Crosby reported to him. 'Everyone else is.'

'I don't know, sir.'

Sloan, who could guess, had told him to get the car out. 'We are about to venture into the interior, Crosby . . .'

'You mean "the hush", sir,' he said reprovingly.

Constable Crosby prided himself on being up to date with the new colloquialisms. This was one of the factors which made him unpopular at the police station.

'The hush,' he repeated. 'That's what it's called now, sir.'

'Is it indeed?' Sloan had managed between clenched teeth – before going to check that nothing was known about Richard Tindall.

Nothing was.

Not 'known' in the police sense, that is.

There was one rather odd incident on record, though, from the day before.

Odd in the circumstances, that is.

In the ordinary way there was nothing unusual about a man dropping by the police station to report traffic chaos. People were always doing just that.

Especially these days.

What was odd was that the man who had done it the day before had been called Richard Mallory Tindall.

It was Inspector Harpe who told Sloan about it.

'It was all because it was such a hot day yesterday,' he began cheerlessly. Inspector Harpe had the misfortune to be in charge of the Traffic Division of the Berebury Division of the Calleshire County Constabulary. He was known throughout the Force as 'Happy Harry' on account of his never having been seen to smile. Inspector Harpe maintained that so far there had never been anything in Traffic Division at which to smile. 'It doesn't suit me, the heat, Sloan, but it suits tar.'

'Tar?'

'The Divisional Surveyor decided to resurface the road south. You know – the one between here and Randall's Bridge.'

'I know.' Sloan inclined his head. Cleete was one of a cluster of small villages beyond there. The roads from all of them crossed the river Calle at the village of Randall's Bridge.

'Well, yesterday might have suited his tar,' grumbled Harpe, 'but the blighter forgot it was market-day here in Berebury.'

'Oh, dear.'

'Chaos,' said the traffic man succinctly. 'Absolute chaos. And every man jack of 'em who'd been grumbling about the state of the road ever since that bad frost we had back in February forgot every pothole there'd ever been while they waited to get past the steamrollers.'

'More than one?'

'Two,' said Harpe. 'Doing a stately schottische, this chap Tindall said they were, fore and aft of the tar-spraying lorry.'

'At nought miles an hour,' said Sloan sympathetically.

'That wasn't all,' groaned Harpe. 'The roadmen went and got into a muddle with their flags. Roadmen!' He rolled his eyes expressively. 'They might have been roadmen but men of the road they most certainly were not. One of them had never ridden anything stronger than a bicycle in his life. The other one apparently gets a power complex every time anyone puts a red flag into his hand.'

'How did you find all that out?'

Inspector Harpe looked gloomier than ever. 'Had a bit of an up-and-a-downer with the Divisional Surveyor, if you must know. Asked him where he got his men from. He said he couldn't get 'em from anywhere and how were police recruiting figures.'

'And then what?'

'Both these characters showed their green flags at the same time.'

Sloan grinned at his colleague.

'It wasn't funny, I can tell you, Sloan. There was this chap Tindall's car sitting in between the two advancing steamrollers. Their drivers couldn't hear what was going on – you know what a din they make – and the foreman didn't want to know, what with all that hot tar about and everything.'

'I don't blame him. Then what happened?'

'I gather Mr Tindall practically stood on his horn for a start. Then, he said, at the eleventh hour the inexorable gavotte changed into a majestic minuet.'

Sloan looked up.

'That's just what he said,' insisted Harpe, whose accurate verbal memory had stood him in good stead as a young police constable. As an inspector in charge of traffic it served only to keep him awake of nights. 'Full of dancing words, he was. He said that after that the two steamrollers crunched away from each other again – for all the world like retreating partners on a dance floor.'

'Everything but the bow and curtsy,' agreed Sloan.

'Then he dropped in here to let us know what it was like out there,' finished Harpe. 'A queue two miles long on the Berebury side. What it was like the other way, I daren't think, being market-day and all.'

'How did he complain?' enquired Sloan with interest. In his experience that told you more about a man more quickly than anything else.

'More in sorrow than in anger,' said Harpe promptly. 'Thought one of our chaps might soothe things down a bit. He hadn't said anything to the roadmen, if that's what you mean.'

Sloan decided then and there that the unknown Mr Tindall possessed that rare quality, judgement, if nothing else. 'What was he like?'

Harpe screwed up his eyes in concentrated recollection. 'Seemed all right to me. Tallish, middle-aged – you know, going a bit grey at the edges – quite active, though. Got in and out of his posh car a jolly sight easier than I could have done.' Harpe glanced down at his own portly figure: he enjoyed his tummy and his contour had not so much gone to seed as gone to pod. 'Nice car, though, except for getting in and out of.'

'One of those, eh?'

'Well, I must say I wouldn't have wanted a couple of steamrollers doing a nutcracker act on it if it had been mine. They don't give them away with a packet of tea. Anyway' – Harpe quickly reverted to his own troubles – 'I couldn't send Jenkins because he was caught up with a flock of sheep on the Kinnisport road and Bailey was out teaching school kids how to be responsible traffic-minded citizens of the future – Heaven help us all – so I told Appleton to go out there and sort things out. A pity, but there wasn't anyone else available by that time. They were all round at the Market.'

'A pity?'

'He was down keeping an eye on the Calleford road junction. That's always a bad spot on market-days. I didn't think it would make a lot of difference in the long run if that did get snarled up yesterday.'

In the event this was not so.

It did make a difference.

The obstruction of the Cleete to Berebury road and the snarling up of the Calleford junction on the outskirts of Berebury – the London road – were but two of the minutiae which were later to contribute to the building up of a complete picture of the day in question.

Sloan thanked Happy Harry and went on his way.

There was subsequently no doubt in the collective police mind that Richard Mallory Tindall of Cleete had been alive and well and in no sort of apparent difficulty at a quarter past nine on the morning of the day before – that is, Wednesday, July 16th.

Fenella Tindall had only just finished dressing when she heard a car turn in to the Dower House drive. She went straight down to the front door and answered it herself.

A well-dressed man stood there, shifting his weight from one foot to the other, barely concealing his impatience as she opened the door to him.

'Mr Tindall?' he said as soon as he saw her. 'Is this his house?'

'It is.' The man was a complete stranger to Fenella. 'But . . .'

'Will you tell him that I'm here, please?'

'Who . . . ?'

'Cranswick,' he said crisply. Everything about him was crisp: from his regulation haircut down to the caps of his highly polished shoes. He produced an engraved visiting card with prestidigitatory swiftness: *Gordon Cranswick of Cranswick (Processing) Limited.*

Fenella took the proffered business card. 'I'm very sorry, Mr – er – Cranswick. He's not here as it happens and . . .'

'That won't do, you know.' Mr Cranswick shook his head from side to side. 'Not for me. It's not good enough. Not now. I know exactly where I stand, you see, after yesterday. He must know that. He'll just have to see me now whether he likes it or not.'

'He can't,' she said.

'I must see him,' said Cranswick peremptorily. 'It's important, my dear. Very important.'

'He isn't here,' repeated Fenella.

'Where is he then?'

'I don't know.'

'Come, come, now.' Cranswick gave her a hard look. He was a squarely built, contained sort of man, with a mouth and chin which could only be described as firm. 'There's nothing to be gained by playing about. What's the matter anyway? We agreed that it could all come out today. He doesn't usually keep me hanging about like this.'

'He doesn't usually not come home for the night either,' retorted Fenella vigorously.

Gordon Cranswick stopped as suddenly as if he'd been hit.

'Not come home? That's different. Why didn't he come home? Where was he last? Who was he with?'

'Friends. Some people called Osborne. As it happens. Not that that's got anything to do with . . .'

'After that,' he interjected quickly, dismissing friends with a wave of his hand. 'Where did he go after that?'

'I don't know,' said Fenella steadily. 'Not yet.'

'What I don't like about this, Miss Tindall – it is Miss Tindall, isn't it? – is that your father promised . . .'

'He wouldn't break a promise,' she put in swiftly. 'You can count on that.'

'I had to go back to town yesterday to see our bankers and tie things up with them but he promised to see me today as soon as I cared to get here.'

'Then,' said Fenella with dignity, 'I am sure that he will as soon as he can.'

Gordon Cranswick changed his stance on the Dower House doorstep and began more pompously: 'It is a matter of some considerable importance to me, Miss Tindall, that I see your father at the earliest possible moment.' He paused impressively. 'I may say that it is important to you, too . . .'

'Perhaps,' said Fenella hopelessly, 'Miss Holroyd at his office . . .'

'His secretary? I've seen her already. She's not saying anything either.'

'Mr Pysden, then,' suggested Fenella. 'He's my father's deputy . . .'

'I know. He was too busy to see me,' declared Cranswick. 'Not that I blame him for that. He isn't going to like the new set-up and I dare say he knows it. I never have seen eye-to-eye with Mr Henry Pysden.'

'What new set-up, Mr Cranswick?'

'Cranswick Processing have made an offer for Struthers and Tindall.'

'An offer?' Fenella was visibly startled. 'For my father's firm?'

'That's what I said. What's more, I think I may tell you that it's already been accepted.'

'When?' asked Fenella faintly.

'Yesterday afternoon. That's when your father agreed to sell me Struthers and Tindall' – he brought his right fist down on his left one for greater emphasis – 'lock' – smack – 'stock' – smack – 'and barrel.'

I am i' th' way to study a long silence.   4

Twenty minutes after leaving Berebury Police Station Detective Inspector Sloan had brief cause to be grateful for the road works of the divisional surveyor.

The sudden chatter of loose surface stones hitting the underside of the police car was the only thing which persuaded Detective Constable Crosby to reduce speed – and then only fractionally – on all the journey south into the country. Sloan glanced up and noted where yesterday's tar spraying had left its mark on the road.

Crosby soon picked up speed again.

Sloan averted his eyes from the road.

Driving fast cars fast was the one thing – the only thing – which Crosby did seem to be good at, but he might be wrong. Disastrously wrong.

'Cleete's a long way out, sir,' remarked the detective constable presently, putting his foot down still farther on the accelerator.

'I've got some beads for the natives,' responded Sloan tightly. 'Mind that tractor . . .'

'Bags of room,' said Crosby easily.

Sloan ran the passenger window down and tried looking out of the side of the car instead. That let a bit of air into the vehicle, too. It was going to be another hot day like yesterday. The hedgerows flashed past.

'There isn't that much hurry,' he said more mildly, allowing his mind to drift back to his roses. He thought they were flagging a little after yesterday's great heat. June had been a disappointment from the point of view of the weather – and it had come after the latest and driest spring in a decade. So only now – in mid-July – were his precious roses in really full flower. He was nurturing a truly magnificent bloom of Princess Grace of Monaco for the Horticultural Society's Show on Saturday . . .

'Coming into Cleete now, sir. What are we looking for?'

'A man.'

'What's he done?' Crosby's view of police life was an essentially simplified one.

'Gone missing.' With an effort Sloan withdrew his mind from contemplating his roses and opened his notebook.

'Perhaps he's been abducted,' suggested Crosby cheerfully. 'Like the Duke of Calleshire's daughter who was taken away by that disc jockey fellow last year. You remember, sir . . .'

'I remember,' said Sloan repressively.

No one who read the Sunday newspapers was likely to have forgotten the antics of Lady Anthea. Or the agency pictures of Calle Castle with the drawbridge up and the portcullis down.

'That was ransom,' Crosby reminded him, 'except that the Duke wouldn't pay it. Said they were welcome to her.'

'That was dowry,' said Sloan firmly, 'except that the Duke wouldn't pay it. If this is ransom . . .'

'Yes?'

'There has been no mention so far of a letter of demand.'

'That doesn't mean a thing, sir,' said the detective constable blithely.

'No?'

'If the family have had a note asking them to leave ten thousand pounds under the blasted oak at the crossroads at dead of night they aren't necessarily going to tell us.'

'Aren't they, indeed?' said Sloan grimly. 'Well, let me tell you they aren't going to get very far if they don't.'

'Perhaps it's suicide then.'

'No note has been mentioned to me,' said Sloan austerely, 'yet.'

As far as he was concerned suicides and notes went together as inevitably as Tweedledum and Tweedledee.

'There was the river at Randall's Bridge,' Crosby reminded him. 'That was only three miles back.'

'And a railway line,' commented Sloan, who hadn't been thinking about roses all of the journey.

'Almost spoilt by choice, sir, isn't he?'

'Suicides always are,' said Sloan mordantly.

Crosby tried again. 'This chap, sir, is he a bad 'un, then?'

'I don't know that either yet.' Sloan stirred irritably: Crosby watched too many Westerns and it showed. 'I did a person check with Records before I left the Station . . .'

What was it fashionable in the business world to call bad records these days?

There was a phrase for it.

Derogatory data.

That was it.

'No joy, sir?'

'Criminal Records Office have no knowledge of him under the name of Tindall, if that's what you mean by joy, Crosby.'

The constable deigned to brake for a road junction. 'Which way now, sir?'

'We want the Dower House,' said Sloan. 'Hepple says it's quite conspicuous. It's in the middle of the village High Street and almost next door to the church.'

It didn't take long to find.

Cleete was a small village – a jumble of cottages, a shop or two, a bit of green, a public house, a garage – all set round a church. They could see the thin spire of the church as they drove into the village. After that the Dower House was easy enough to locate.

Beyond both the Dower House and the church was a rather splendid avenue of oak trees but Inspector Sloan didn't turn to see where it led to. His attention had been caught by something parked at the front gate of the Dower House.

A police bicycle.

Detective Constable Crosby brought the police car to a stop beside it with a wholly unnecessary screech of brakes, and said, 'Looks as if the Flying Squad's beaten us to it, sir, after all.'

'Constable Hepple,' deduced Detective Inspector Sloan. 'He must have come back for something.'

Police Constable Hepple had indeed come back to the Dower House for something. He advanced towards the police car in evident relief.

'It's Mr Tindall's car, sir. Miss Tindall's just found it in the garage. She rang me up about it. Said she thought we ought to know it was there.'

'It's a point,' agreed Sloan.

A man and his car weren't quite as indivisible as a man and his horse but at this rate they soon would be.

'Blessed if I know what to make of it myself, sir.' Constable Hepple tilted his helmet back. 'Doesn't make sense to me. Still,' he added fairly, 'I reckon I should have gone straight out and looked in that garage for myself, sir, first thing, but when Ada Turvey said the key wasn't in its usual place . . .'

'I take it,' said Sloan, cutting in, 'that you can't see the garage door from the house?'

He had never been one for relishing recriminations and found he was less and less inclined to it as he got older. It never did any good. That was one thing which life had taught him – but not, alas, Superintendent Leeyes – by now. His only regret was that it was one of life's later lessons.

'No, sir,' replied Hepple, mopping his brow. 'Not from the house. The garage is part of the stables now, converted like, and of course they were always well to one side of the house because of the smell of the horses.'

Sloan nodded.

There was no doubt that they were out in the country now . . .

'I've seen the car, sir,' continued Hepple. 'The keys are still in the ignition and the garage key that Ada Turvey was on about – the one that's always hung on the hook by the garden door – that's still in the lock on the garage door.'

'Nothing else?'

'A gent turned up asking for him. A business gent by the

sound of him. Name of Gordon Cranswick. Properly put out he was, from all accounts. Wanted to talk to Mr Tindall sooner than now and didn't see why he couldn't. Went off somewhere in his car as quickly as he'd come, Miss Tindall said.'

'But there's still no sign of her father?'

'Not a sausage, sir.' Hepple shook his head. 'Seems as if he just vanished into thin air after he came home and before he went to bed last night.'

' "Twixt the stirrup and the ground", too,' murmured Sloan for good measure.

'Beg pardon, sir?' said Hepple.

Sloan cleared his throat. 'Between the garage and the house.'

'That's right, sir,' said Hepple, scratching his chin. 'Least-ways, that's what it looks like.'

'Quite so,' agreed Sloan. 'We must remember that things may not be what they seem.'

This was a principle he was always trying his best to instil into Detective Constable Crosby.

He hoped he was listening.

'I can't find him in the garden, though,' went on Hepple doggedly, 'and Miss Fenella and Ada Turvey, they say they can't find him in the house.' He jerked his shoulder towards the building behind him. 'Mind you, sir, it's not all that small a house . . .'

No, it was not a small house. Sloan could see that himself. It was a very finely proportioned one, though. In fact, he had to take a second look at it before he realized quite how perfect it was.

'What they call Georgian, sir, I'm told,' said Hepple, 'on account of all the straight lines.'

Sloan nodded. There wasn't a Victorian twiddle or bump in sight. And all – as the estate agents' optimistic advertisements said – well maintained in excellent condition.

Hepple's arm described a circle. 'And definitely a big garden.'

Sloan grunted. There was no doubt about the size of the

garden. You could have lost a platoon in it – easily – let alone one man.

'Best part of a couple of acres, sir, I'd say. At least.' Hepple ran an experienced eye over the grass. 'And he could be anywhere in that orchard at the back – anywhere at all. Especially if he'd been taken ill after he got back home last night.'

Detective Inspector Sloan had no time for euphemisms so early in the morning.

He looked at his watch and said briskly: 'If he's been on a real bender he could still be sleeping it off somewhere. It's not very late in the day yet.'

'No, sir,' said Police Constable Hepple, equally firm. 'He wasn't that sort of a drinker.'

Sloan looked up quickly, realizing that he'd come within an inch of underestimating a village constable; and that would never do.

'If he had been like that, sir,' Hepple went on seriously, 'I wouldn't have reported him as missing at all to Berebury. Not until much later on, sir, anyway, when I could have been quite sure.'

'I understand,' said Sloan.

And he did.

With the warble fly and the church porch and the bicycle there went a finer discrimination – and a greater freedom – than you were able to have in the town.

It was at that moment that the front door of the Dower House opened. Inspector Sloan turned his head and saw a girl – a young woman, rather – standing there. She was framed by the classical lines of the Georgian doorway. She stood quite still as she regarded the three policemen. There was something a little unexpected about her appearance – almost foreign. It took Sloan a moment or two to pin down what it was – and then it came to him.

It was her clothes.

It was high summer in England and this girl was wearing dark brown. Not a floral silk pattern, not a cheerful cotton, nor even a pastel linen such as his own wife, Margaret, was wearing today. But dark brown. It was a simple, utterly plain dress, unadorned save for a solitary string of white beads.

He was surprised to note that the whole effect was strangely cooling on such a hot day. There was the faintest touch of auburn in the colouring of her hair which was replicated in the brown of the dress. A purist might have said that her mouth was rather too big to be perfect but . . .

Sloan wasn't a purist.

He was a policeman.

On duty.

He took a step forward.

'Have you found my father?' she asked him directly.

They were barely inside the Dower House when Mrs Turvey came hurrying along the hall, wiping her hands on her apron.

'There's a gentleman on the telephone,' she said, 'asking for a Detective Inspector Sloan. Said there was no answer from the car radio or something. Sounds in a terrible rush, 'e does . . .'

It wasn't a gentleman. It was Police Superintendent Leeyes.

'That you, Sloan? Look here, we've just had a message from Randall's Bridge . . .'

'The river?'

'The river?'

'Or the railway line, sir?'

'What are you talking about, Sloan?'

'This message, sir.'

'I'm trying to tell you it's from the church.'

'The church?'

'That's what I said, man. There's a whole lot of men working in there. They're putting in heating or something. One of them's just looked into the church tower and found a man.'

'Our man?' asked Sloan, trying to keep a grasp of essentials.

'I don't know. You'd better get over there and find out.'

'Dead or alive, sir?' It was as well to know . . .

'Dead.' The telephone line crackled and went faint. 'Definitely dead.'

'What was that, sir?' asked Sloan. 'I'm afraid I didn't quite catch . . .'

He recoiled as a great bellow came down the line. The interference on the telephone had cleared as suddenly as it had started.

'Crushed to pieces,' boomed Superintendent Leeyes.

That curious engine, your white hand.   5

Whatever time and distance record Detective Constable Crosby had set up on his way home from Randall's Bridge to Cleete he broke on the return trip from the Dower House at Cleete to the church at Randall's Bridge.

Sloan hung on to the side of his seat for dear life as Crosby cornered. Police Constable Hepple they had left behind at Cleete with Fenella Tindall and Mrs Turvey.

Sloan spotted the church at Randall's Bridge easily enough. It was sited on a small prominence beside the river, its tall tower standing four square to the world for all to see.

Crosby swept the police car round the last corner and brought it to a shuddering stop behind a lorry loaded with pipes which was parked near the lich-gate. Sloan tumbled out and set off through the churchyard. There was a small knot of men clustered round the church doorway. He noticed that they were dressed in working overalls and some still had tools in their hands. Two of the men were bending over a youth who was sitting on the grass of the churchyard looking more than a little green.

'Police,' said Sloan.

One of the men jerked his thumb. 'The gaffer's still inside. We brought Billy here out for a bit of air.'

'It was Billy what found him,' said another.

Sloan didn't need telling. He'd seen that shocked, incredulous look before. When someone had seen something not very nice, and didn't really want to take it in.

'Didn't believe him at first,' said an older man. 'Thought he was having us on. You know what apprentices are.'

Sloan nodded. He knew all right.

There wasn't a policeman alive who didn't know what apprentices were.

He made his way past them to the church door, Crosby at his heels. It was unlatched but nearly closed. He put his shoulder to it and the great oak door swung open. He stepped down into the church. At least it was cool enough in here.

The first sight which met him was of apparent disorder everywhere. It needed a second glance to see that this was organized chaos – the work of the workmen. There were pipes and boards everywhere. Some of the pews were awry and there were dust sheets over the rest.

There were two more men standing by the door which led to the foot of the church tower.

'Police,' said Sloan again. 'Detective Inspector Sloan.'

'This way,' said one of them thickly. 'Over here.'

'There's been a nasty accident,' said the other.

Sloan advanced across the nave towards them, Crosby clattering along behind him like some ghastly material *doppelgänger*.

'The door won't open above an inch or two, Inspector, but you can just see inside.' The shorter of the two men stepped back from the doorway. 'You look . . .'

Sloan looked.

Crosby, who was taller, looked too, over Sloan's shoulder – and let out a long low whistle entirely contrary to his police training in professional impassivity.

The sight which had turned Billy, the apprentice, green was a curious one.

The entire base of the church tower seemed to be full of a vast quantity of smashed marble. There was one great melange of broken white sculpture – here a foot – there a head – all heaped on the floor. This was what was preventing the door from opening more than an inch or two.

There was also an arm which wasn't made of white marble.

It was clothed in men's suiting and was protruding from under all the heaped stone. The skin of the hand was pale and bloodless and though the light was poor Sloan was in no doubt at all that its owner was dead.

Like the superintendent had said.

Definitely.

It was not all that easy to see anything else. There was a sort of ecclesiastical dimness about the inside of the tower.

'The light switch is inside, I suppose,' he said.

'It is,' said one of the men. 'Not that it would be much of a help if we got to it, would it? Look.'

Sloan's gaze travelled upwards. An empty light socket dangled under a Victorian fluted glass shade.

'No bulb.'

'Poor devil,' said the shorter of the two. He had a foot rule sticking out of his jacket pocket.

'At least,' said the other man, 'he never knew what hit him. Can't have done.' This man was older and was neatly dressed in country-style tweeds.

Sloan cleared his throat. 'Er – do either of you happen to know exactly what it was that did hit him?'

'The Fitton Bequest,' responded both men in unison.

'Quite so,' said Sloan.

It wouldn't do for the superintendent; not an answer like that. He'd have to think of something better than that for his report.

'We put it in here last week, didn't we, Mr Knight?'

'That's right, Bert,' the elderly man nodded. 'You did. Bert Booth here is the foreman, Inspector.'

'Took twelve men to move it,' confirmed Bert, 'and then we had a proper job.'

'We went through all the necessary formalities first, Inspector,' the man called Knight hastened to assure him, 'before we touched it. Got a proper faculty for moving it, advertised, and so forth. I'm glad we did now. The archdeacon would have been down on us like a ton of bricks if . . .'

Mr Knight suddenly realized that perhaps this wasn't the happiest of similes and his voice trailed away to silence.

Inspector Sloan turned to Constable Crosby. 'Get Dr Dabbe from Berebury out here as quickly as possible – and Dyson and the photographic people.'

'Yes, sir.'

'And on your way out tell that gang by the church door that if they move so much as an inch from where they are now then I'll run the lot of them in.'

'Yes, sir.' Crosby clattered away again.

Sloan turned back to the narrow slit which constituted their only view into the base of the tower. It was a bit limiting. All they would be able to do was what the archaeologists called a pre-disturbance survey. They couldn't get near enough to disturb anything. He took another look at the arm. There wasn't a lot of it to see but it told him all he wanted to know.

It was a left arm.

It was contained in a length of men's suiting – grey suiting – and from where Sloan was standing it was possible to see that there was a button missing from the sleeve.

Fenella Tindall sat straight up in her chair as Police Constable Hepple came back from the telephone, her back every bit as stiff as the Principessa's.

In a way, the ringing of the telephone bell had come as something of a relief.

She had tried sitting in the garden while Constable Hepple had plunged about the orchard and found she couldn't do it. The house itself had been hardly more restful. True, there was no one in it but herself and Mrs Turvey but the impulse to go through all the rooms all over again was very strong.

So was the desire to shout aloud for her father – to call out and to listen for an answer.

She turned her head as Hepple came into the room. 'Was that . . .'

Hepple said, 'The inspector, miss. It was a message from the inspector.'

'Any news?' She looked at him eagerly. 'Is there any news?'

'Nothing definite, miss,' temporized the policeman. 'We'll let you know as soon as we have anything definite.'

Fenella relaxed fractionally. 'Then what . . .'

'It was about your father's clothes, miss.'

'But I told you before.'

'Just checking, miss, that's all.'

'He was wearing a grey suit, like I said.'

'A grey suit . . .'

'Not his best one,' she pointed out quickly. 'Mrs Turvey says there was a patch of grease on the right trouser leg. Is that any help?'

'Not exactly, miss.' Hepple coughed.

It wasn't, either.

'Not at this stage,' he added truthfully.

'That's why it was going to the cleaners, you see.'

Hepple looked down at his notebook. 'You said something else to me about it, miss, before . . .'

'There was a button missing.'

'Where from?'

'The sleeve.'

'Which sleeve?'

'The left one.'

Hepple kept his eyes on his notebook. 'You wouldn't by any chance happen to have that button, miss, would you? You know, ready for sewing back on again after the suit came from the cleaners . . .'

Something of the colour went out of Fenella's face but she kept her voice steady with an effort. 'The button?'

'It would be a great help, miss, if we might have it . . .'

'I should like now,' announced Detective Inspector Sloan to Mr Knight, 'to take a look at the outside of the tower.'

'But what about this poor bloke?' interjected Bert Booth, the foreman. 'Aren't we going to try to get him out then?'

'How?' enquired Sloan.

'I've got plenty of men outside. You know that. They'd . . .'

'If they all heaved together,' said Sloan, 'we'd never get this door open. There must be all of half a ton of marble up against the back of it.'

Bert Booth scratched his head. 'That's a thought, guv'nor. But what about the other door? The churchyard one . . .'

The man called Knight shook his head at this. 'You wouldn't be able to shift that one, Bert. No matter how hard you pushed. You can see what's up against the inside of it from here.'

'Crikey,' exclaimed Bert Booth, 'then how on earth . . .'

'Quite so,' said Sloan sedately.

Mr Knight stared at Sloan. 'But that means, surely, Inspector, that no one can have left the tower after this happened – that he was alone in here when . . .' He fell silent.

'It does,' agreed Sloan. 'That's why I want to look round outside now.'

The heat of the day struck him in full force again as he followed Mr Knight and Bert Booth out through the church door.

Billy, the apprentice, was looking slightly less green.

'Want to tell me about it now?' asked Sloan gently.

The boy gulped. 'I was just looking, mister. That's all. And then I saw this arm sticking out. I didn't mean any harm, going in there.'

'No.'

'Honest, I didn't,' he insisted earnestly. 'When the door wouldn't open above an inch or two I looked to see what was keeping it. I didn't sort of take in the arm at first if you know what I mean.'

'Then what did you do?' Sloan wasn't worried too much about the boy. His tale would lose nothing in the telling. By evening it would be as remembered with advantages as any Agincourt story – his genuine squeamishness talked out of him and forgotten. By tomorrow he would be a hero in his own small circle.

'I didn't touch anything.'

'Except the door handle.'

Billy looked crestfallen. 'I'd forgotten about that.'

'You weren't to know,' said Sloan. 'Then what?'

'I ran and told Mr Booth and he sent someone for Mr Knight.'

It was Mr Knight who now led the way through the churchyard and round the outside of the church. It emerged that he was a retired schoolmaster and also secretary of the Parochial Church Council.

'That's why they sent for me,' he explained. 'I only live down the road. Here we are . . .'

Sloan stopped and took his first good look at the church tower. It was square and had just the one pair of double doors opening on to the churchyard. Set above the rounded arch of the doorway was a small window.

Bert Booth, the foreman, looked up at it and shook his head.

'That's not big enough to get anyone through to let us in from the other side. We couldn't even push Billy through that. He's not that little.'

'No,' conceded Sloan. The window was scarcely more than a slit to give light but not access: not even to the apprentice in his traditional role of being squeezed through narrow places.

'Typical Saxon,' Mr Knight, the schoolmaster, informed him. 'The whole tower is Saxon except the battlements at the top.'

'Really, sir?' said Sloan courteously.

If there was one thing which Superintendent Leeyes would not want to know it was the age of the tower.

'We might get a better view with a ladder,' said Bert Booth, the foreman, more practically. He disappeared round the other side of the tower.

'Saxon,' said Mr Knight again. 'Built about the time of the first bridge here.' He indicated the river flowing beyond the church.

'Randall's Bridge?' said Sloan.

'Randalla the Saxon's Bridge, actually.'

Sloan nodded. Pedantry will out.

'Before that there was a ford. The Romans used the ford.'

'Did they, sir?' murmured Sloan absently.

So the Romans got their feet wet and the Saxons didn't.

That was progress, wasn't it?

Or just history?

'We don't know the exact place of the ford, Inspector. The river bed's shifted a bit since then.' Knight inclined his head in the direction of the river Calle which ran along below them. One of the churchyard paths led down towards it. 'Two thousand years is a long time.'

'Yes, sir,' said Sloan. So was twelve hours in a case like this. He peered up at the tower.

Knight pointed. 'You can see the long and the short Saxon stonework at the corners, can't you, Inspector?'

'So you can, sir.'

As it happened Sloan hadn't been considering the Saxon stonework, but long ago he had discovered that the one thing to do with antiquarians was to let them say their piece while he thought about something else. He was thinking now about the gravel outside the tower doorway. There was a certain amount of scuffing there – about six feet in front of the doors and below the window.

'It's a common Saxon feature,' went on the schoolmaster happily, 'to have the cornerstones alternately horizontal and vertical.'

'Don't step on the gravel just there, sir, will you? I shall want some pictures taken of the gravel.'

'You only get stonework like that in the Saxon period.'

'Can you get out on the roof, sir?'

'From inside? Oh, yes, Inspector. Certainly you can. It's quite a climb up there round the bells but it can be done by anyone who is – er – reasonably agile. Haven't been up there for some time myself but there's a very good view from the top. On a clear day you can see Calleford.'

Sloan stared up at the battlemented top of the tower.

From a view to a death in the morning?

Was that what it was going to be?

He didn't even know whether the death had been in the morning yet . . .

'When would the church have been locked?' he asked abruptly.

'Eleven o'clock, Inspector. I locked it myself just after eleven. I do it every night. When I take the dog for a walk.'

'Dog?' sharply.

'Spaniel. Tessa.'

Sloan expired. 'Pity it wasn't a bloodhound.'

'She's pretty good,' protested the dog owner in injured tones.

'Did she know that he was in there?'

Knight frowned. 'Now that you come to mention it, Inspector . . .'

Sloan sighed. That was never as good as the spontaneous remark. Unprompted, that was how statements should be.

'. . . she did sniff round here. I didn't take a lot of notice at the time.'

'Here? You came this way?'

'Yes. Up from the village street by the river path.'

Sloan pointed to a cottage on the edge of the churchyard. 'Is that your house, sir?'

'What? Oh, no. That's Vespers Cottage. The two Misses Metford live there. I'm over on the other side. That house opposite the lich-gate . . .'

'Then why did you come this way at all?'

For the first time the schoolmaster seemed to be at a loss for a phrase. He cleared his throat several times. 'I – er – dropped in to the Coach and Horses actually to have a pint and a chat . . .'

'And you opened up this morning – when?'

'Just after eight. For the workmen.'

There was a heavy scrunching sound round the far side of the tower and Bert Booth reappeared. He was carrying a ladder.

'That's funny,' exclaimed Mr Knight suddenly. 'Where did you find that ladder, Bert?'

'Lying along the wall. Reckon we can get up to that window with it, Inspector?'

'But,' insisted the schoolmaster, 'that ladder shouldn't have been left lying about outside like that.'

'No, sir, it shouldn't.' Sloan couldn't have agreed with him more. Ladders left lying around were always an anathema to the police.

'It's always kept in the tower,' insisted Mr Knight. 'Always.'

Bert Booth shrugged his broad shoulders. 'Well, it isn't there now and it wasn't one of my chaps who took it out. We've no need of ladders, Mr Knight, you know that. Not on this job.'

The ladder wasn't long enough to reach the top of the tower. There was no question of that. No one could have come down from the tower by it. But it was tall enough to have reached the aperture above the door.

Bert Booth turned to Sloan. 'Do you want to have a shufti through that window up there, Inspector, or not?'

'Later,' said Sloan. 'When we've taken a cast of the gravel.'

'Like that, is it?' said the foreman.

Sloan nodded.

I know death hath ten thousand several doors. **6**

'I think, sir,' began Inspector Sloan cautiously, 'that we may have found Mr Tindall.'

As soon as Constable Crosby had returned to the church Sloan had gone to report back to Superintendent Leeyes at Berebury Police Station.

He'd got his police priorities right long ago.

He was using Mr Knight's telephone. Crosby's police car radio wasn't quite private enough for this sort of conversation. As he dialled Sloan could hear the schoolmaster pacing up and down in the other room, together with Bert Booth, the foreman.

Booth was waiting his turn to use the telephone to tell his employers – a firm of central-heating engineers in Berebury – that there had been what he called 'a bit of a hold-up'. It didn't seem to have bothered the workmen. They were settling down to another tea break – this time in the churchyard. Sloan could see them and their mugs from the window of Mr Knight's sitting room.

Crosby he'd left behind inside the church.

Not that you could very well call him a 'scene-of-crime officer'.

Not Crosby.

A familiar grunt at the other end of the line indicated that the superintendent was listening.

'We can't be sure, sir, of course, yet, but . . .'

'Too much of a good thing if not,' responded Leeyes robustly. 'A missing man and a dead one in one day in one division. This isn't Chicago.'

'No, sir . . .' he hesitated.

'Well, Sloan,' barked the Superintendent, 'are you going to tell me what happened or aren't you?'

'It's not all that easy to say, sir.'

'I may not be "Listening With Mother",' said Leeyes heavily, 'but I am sitting comfortably.'

Sloan took a deep breath. 'It's like this, sir. They're putting central heating in the church at Randall's Bridge . . .'

'What for?' The superintendent was nothing if not a realist.

'Someone left them the money to do it. Just the heating. For that and nothing else. A specific legacy in a will . . .'

Sloan could hear the superintendent muttering something cynical under his breath about fire insurance but he took no notice.

'. . . a local boy who made good,' he said, pressing on, 'in Australia.'

'Funny place to think about heating.'

'He never forgot how cold it used to be in the church when he was a lad,' said Sloan, repeating what the church secretary had told him. 'He made a small fortune out of sheep, and he remembered Randall's Bridge in his will.'

Leeyes grunted. 'Go on.'

'To get the pipes in properly the central heating people had to move a whacking great sculpture in the church – in the south aisle. A sort of monument, it was . . .'

'Was?'

'Was,' affirmed Sloan remembering the arm underneath.

There was something terrible about that arm sticking out like that.

'Well?'

'It was a weeping widow and ten children all mourning the father. You know the sort of thing, sir.'

'I do. Very upsetting they are, too,' said Leeyes. 'They don't allow them any more. And quite right.'

'This one's called the Fitton Bequest. A memorial to remember Mr Fitton by . . .'

'I should have thought myself,' remarked Leeyes, 'that ten children were . . .'

'The workmen moved it into the church tower last week,' went on Sloan hastily, 'so that they could get on with laying the pipes and so forth. On its plinth. That's a good few feet high for a start. This sculpture stood on top of that.'

'Hefty.'

'I'll say, sir. It only just went through the door.' Sloan paused. 'I'm very much afraid that Mr Tindall is under what's left of it. And if it's not him, then it's somebody else . . .'

'Who's equally dead,' grunted Leeyes, 'which from our point of view . . .'

'Just so, sir.' The police point of view wasn't everything but it was the one which they both had to worry about.

'This sculpture, Sloan . . .'

'Yes, sir?'

'What was keeping it on its plinth?'

'Gravity, sir. As far as I could see, that is.'

'Gravity.' He grunted again. 'You can't play about with that, can you?'

'No, sir.' That was true. Not even the superintendent could play about with gravity.

'Well, then, did this Fitton thing . . .'

'Bequest.'

'Bequest. Did it fall or was it pushed?'

Sloan took a deep breath. 'I'm afraid it's not quite as simple as that, sir.'

'It isn't,' demanded Leeyes suspiciously, 'going to turn out to be one of these fancy suicides, Sloan, is it? I can't stand them.'

'I don't somehow think so, sir.' It didn't look like suicide – however fancy – to Sloan. Not with the river and the railway line so hard by, so to speak.

'Firm not going to pot or anything like that?'

'Quite the reverse, sir, from all accounts. I'm told there's a character who came to Cleete this morning who swears he was told that he could buy it outright yesterday. He's still as keen as mustard from what I hear.'

'Is he now?'

Sloan heard that register at the police station all right, and added, 'Cranswick's his name. Gordon Cranswick.'

'Gordon Cranswick.'

'We'll have to check, sir, of course.'

'Of course.'

'I don't think, sir,' went on Sloan more slowly, 'that whoever is under this marble could very well have pulled the thing down on top of himself at the same time as ending up face downwards underneath it. Not easily.'

'Agreed.'

'And we can tell he's lying prone because of the hand.' Sloan was still amazed at what you could tell from a solitary hand.

'Well, then . . .'

'But if it was pushed, sir . . .'

'Yes?'

'There's a snag.'

'I'll buy it, Sloan.'

'If it was pushed . . .'

'Get on with it, man.'

'Whoever did the pushing must still be in the church tower.'

'Say that again, Sloan.'

'No one's come out of that tower since the sculpture came down on that chap.' Sloan spelled it out for him. 'They can't have done.'

'What!'

'There's half a ton of marble up against the far door – the one that leads to the churchyard.'

'The west door,' said Leeyes surprisingly.

Sloan blinked. 'That's right, sir.'

'Civic services,' explained the superintendent elliptically. 'Have to go to a lot of them.'

'Quite, sir. Well, there's nearly as much marble behind the

pair of doors which give to the church itself from the tower. No one,' he added carefully, 'can have opened either set of doors from the inside after the sculpture came down.'

'The roof?' Leeyes seized on the only alternative to the doors. 'What about the roof?'

'There is a hatch leading out on to the roof,' reported Sloan, 'but the door up there is always kept locked – anyway, it's a long way up from the outside. Too far for ladders. And the church secretary has just shown me the key of the hatch – here in his house . . .'

He had also introduced his wife to Sloan. She was a drab, complaining woman who immediately explained the need for voluntary jobs, a dog which required a lot of exercise, and any number of trips to the Coach and Horses.

Last night she had had one of her bad heads and had retired to bed early. She had seen nothing and nobody. When she had one of her bad heads she always went straight to bed . . .

Sloan wasn't worried.

When he had been over by the church tower he'd seen a curtain twitch in the window of the cottage there. Vespers Cottage, Knight had called it. Curtain-twitchers usually had something to report. He would go back there as soon as he could . . .

'I can't check the roof yet, sir,' he said into the telephone, 'because I can't get in myself, but there's no doubt that it's too high for ordinary ladders and there's no rope hanging down there or anything like that.'

The superintendent groaned irritably. 'Not another of those locked-room mysteries, Sloan, I hope. I can't stand them either.'

Fenella Tindall found it more difficult to sit still when Police Constable Hepple came back from the telephone a second time.

He had taken the button from her, measured it carefully, and then gone through to ring a number in Randall's Bridge.

That was all she knew.

That was all he had told her.

She took a deep breath now as he entered the room. 'Well?'

'Have you got any friends, miss, here in the village?'

She felt a cold shiver run up and down her spine. She shook her head mutely.

'Someone who would come round,' he continued kindly, 'to be with you today.'

'Not really. You see, I've only just come home from Italy. And I've been away so much.'

'A friend of your father's, perhaps, then, miss? Who you would like to be with you . . .'

Obediently she cast about in her mind and then shook her head again. Marcia Osborne was a friend of her father's, all right, but Fenella couldn't see Marcia's charm. It was too brittle. George Osborne was a poppet, but he would be teaching now. There was always old Professor Berry, of course. He'd be up and about by now. But she could hardly expect him to be a prop and stay. Not at his age. And Miss Holroyd – staunch, rocklike and competent – Miss Holroyd would have enough on her hands as it was.

Police Constable Hepple was saying something.

'You were out with a friend last night, miss, I understand . . .'

Fenella looked up quickly. The constable might have seemed quiet and slow but . . .

'That was an Italian friend,' she said, 'called Giuseppe Mardoni. But he's gone back to Italy. He went last night. After we'd had dinner. He had to catch a plane. A night flight.'

She was talking too much. She knew that.

To stave off the moment when the policeman said what he wanted to say.

What he had to say, sooner, or later.

'You see,' she said, 'I'm quite alone now.'

'I see, miss. Well, then, in that case . . .'

'I think,' said Fenella with a visible effort, 'that I'd rather be told anything you know now . . .'

Hepple told her.

*

By the time Detective Inspector Sloan got back to the church the real experts in death had begun to arrive.

Constable Crosby might have fancied his fast driving but it wasn't a patch on that of Dr Dabbe. The Consultant Pathologist to the Berebury and District Group Hospital Management Committee was the fastest driver in the county of Calleshire. There was no doubt about that. Strong men had been known to blench when offered a lift by him. Those who incautiously accepted them were rumoured never to be the same afterwards. The Dean of Calleford, a blameless man whose faith was seemingly as firm as that of anyone in the diocese, had once tried to get out of Dr Dabbe's moving car, wishing he had led a better life the while. The doctor's assistant, Burns, who went with him everywhere, had been shocked into silence by it long ago and rarely spoke.

Sloan greeted him inside the church.

'I'm sorry, Doctor. We've got a body here for you all right but we can't get near it. And all we can see is an arm.'

'No sword?'

'N . . . no, Doctor.'

Dabbe gave a sardonic grin. 'I was thinking of Excalibur.'

'No, Doctor. No sword.' Sloan managed a wan smile. The pathologist was always like this. He had a sense of humour fit to make your blood run cold. 'The arm's lying quite flat, actually. Not – er – brandishing anything.'

'Ah . . .' Dr Dabbe advanced towards the tower doorway. 'And all I've got is a sort of leper's squint, is it?'

'I'm afraid so.' Apologetically. 'They've sent to Berebury for some heavy welding equipment. They're going to try to cut the door hinges off from this side.'

Dr Dabbe bent down and looked into the tower through the gap in the doorway while Sloan and Crosby stood to one side and Burns busied himself with some wire and arc lamps.

'Ah,' said the pathologist again. 'And not clothed in white samite either.'

'Grey suiting,' said Sloan automatically.

'So I see.'

'Not a lot to go on, I'm afraid, Doctor. Just an arm.'

'Oh, I don't know,' said the pathologist easily. 'I've had less in my time.'

'This arm . . .' began Sloan. Once started on his bizarre reminiscences there was never any stopping the doctor.

'Had just an ear once,' Dabbe said.

'On its own?' asked Crosby, clearly fascinated.

'Lonely as a cloud,' said Dabbe poetically.

'This arm, Doctor,' interrupted Sloan more firmly. He wasn't interested in unattached ears.

'This ear was . . .'

They were spared more by a light springing to life. While they had all been talking the ever-silent Burns, the doctor's assistant, had rigged up a powerful spot lamp and focused it on the protruding arm. It more than made up for the missing light bulb. As soon as it was ready the pathologist – diverted from his ear story – applied his eye to the partially open door and gave the arm a long, long look.

'It's hairy, Sloan, so it's not a Chinaman.'

'No, Doctor.' That was the least of Sloan's worries.

'It's probably male all right.'

Sloan hadn't been worried about that at all.

Dabbe grinned. ' "The apparel oft proclaims the man", eh, Sloan? Not any more, it doesn't. But the fourth finger is longer than the first.'

'Yes, Doctor.'

Out of the corner of his eye Sloan saw Crosby glance down at his own hands and register the surprised look of one who finds that a natural rule applies to oneself as well as everyone else.

'He's no horny-handed son of the soil,' went on the pathologist.

'I was afraid of that,' said Sloan.

'But he's used his hands . . .'

'Yes.'

'The interdigital muscles are well developed. Nails well kept . . .'

Dabbe altered his stance a fraction. 'No signs of disease manifesting itself in the hand – no clubbing of the fingers, no concave fingernails. No nicotine stains . . .'

Sloan made a note of that.

'And he didn't spend yesterday sun-bathing. In fact, I'd say he spent more time indoors than outside.'

That would fit.

'No rings, wristwatch, or scars,' the pathologist continued his observations. 'A good tailor but an old suit,' he added for good measure. 'One button missing from the cuff.'

'We know all about that.'

'You do, do you? Your province, of course.' Dabbe grunted and peered more closely still. 'Can't tell you his exact age yet. The subcutaneous fat has started to go from the back of the hand. The skin doesn't look as if it's got the elasticity it used to have either.' He paused. 'Let's say not old, not young . . .'

'That would fit, too,' said Sloan.

Dabbe straightened his bent back. 'And you won't be unbearably surprised to know, Sloan, that he wasn't a mental defective either. As far as I can see from this side there are the regulation number of lines on his palm.'

'Quite so,' murmured Sloan. He could see Crosby glancing down at his own hands again. He wondered what comfort he would find there.

'Cause of death,' continued the pathologist in a businesslike manner, 'not immediately apparent. Crush injuries, I suppose, but in this job you never can tell.'

'No, Doctor.' Sloan was with him there: every inch of the way. The marble looked enough to kill anyone, but you never could tell.

Dr Dabbe took a last look through the narrow slit of open door and then straightened up again.

'A classic case, you might say, Sloan, of Death, the Great Leveller.'

I saw him even now going the way of all flesh.   7

There was something teasing about talking to a total stranger
on the telephone. A man's voice didn't tell you anything like
as much as did his appearance and his actions. Sloan had never
even spoken to the writer of the anonymous letters over at the
village of Constance Parva but he would stake his pension
that the holder of the pen would be thin and angular; spiky
and mean of spirit.

Henry Pysden just sounded cautious.

'He left here a little before six o'clock last evening, Inspector. Like he usually did. We were naturally afraid that
something might be wrong when he didn't come in this
morning. Not like him at all . . .'

'There was a Mr Cranswick over at Cleete this morning,
sir, who seems to have been expecting him to be there, too.'

'Ah,' said Pysden regretfully, 'I'm afraid I was rather busy
when he called here. On an important experiment with a
built-in time factor. On a refractory material. Sea-water
magnesia. I couldn't leave it and he wouldn't wait.'

'I wanted to ask you about your work,' said Sloan. 'What
do Struthers and Tindall do?'

Pysden hesitated. 'What we do is rather difficult to describe,
and we are – er – ah – um – a little – what shall I say? – er –
reticent about the exact nature of our work.'

'Any confidence will, of course, be respected as far as

possible,' murmured Sloan diplomatically, 'but we must know.'

'Quite. Quite. I see that.' The voice at the other end of the telephone line suddenly hurried into speech. 'Shall we say – to put it in a nutshell . . .'

'Yes, sir?' Sloan was all in favour of that.

Always.

'I think Mr Tindall would not mind my telling you that what we do is other people's research and development for them.'

Sloan wrote that down.

'Only in certain fields, naturally, Inspector. Now, about Mr Tindall . . .'

'Research and development, sir. Should I know what that means?'

The voice relaxed a little. 'Not really, I suppose. No reason why you should. Research and development – R and D, it's usually called – is carried out by nearly all big firms these days. Mostly to make sure they'll have marketable products in five years' time.'

'I see, sir.'

It was different in the police force.

Market trends in crime changed, of course. One sort of mischief often surged to the forefront – became fashionable, you might say – while another receded for a while. But down at the police station they weren't troubled by the thought of running out of work five years hence.

In any number of years, come to that.

Short of the politicians finding Utopia, of course.

Or the scientists discovering a cure for Original Sin.

Or – more probably – the millennium arriving on the doorstep of the Home Office, so to speak.

Sloan didn't think that was likely either.

Henry Pysden was still talking. He'd got an unaccented voice, a bit on the reedy side.

'The work we do can amount to almost anything, of course, but firms usually stick to their own line. So that they can use their existing plant if possible. Saves retooling – that does cost a lot of money.'

'And where exactly do Struthers and Tindall come in, sir?'

'Struthers and Tindall come in, Inspector, where you have a firm which doesn't have its own research and development department.' He coughed. 'Where one of these firms needs some specific work done – say when they've got a good idea and no facilities for following it through – then we do it for them. Or . . .' The reedy voice stopped.

'Or?' prompted Sloan.

Henry Pysden hesitated again. 'Or when it has something very secret indeed which it wants an opinion on.'

'Even,' asked Sloan, anxious to get at least one thing in the case quite clear, 'when it has a research and development department of its own?'

'Sometimes.'

'Why?'

'A lot of reasons,' said Pysden carefully. 'They may have someone in their own firm whom they are – er – ah – um – not absolutely sure about . . .'

Sloan groaned inwardly. That was a point tailor-made for any policeman to take. Even Detective Constable Crosby should be able to pick that one up for himself.

'Or they may feel,' went on the cautious voice at the Berebury end, 'shall we say they may have reason to fear – that their own internal security isn't too good. Then they would use us instead . . .'

That, decided Sloan, was going to be a great help, that was.

'Inspector, there is just one thing at this end . . .'

'Oh?'

'We're a little bit concerned about one of our confidential reports.'

'Yes?'

'One of our highly confidential reports.' With emphasis.

'What about it, Mr Pysden?'

'We can't find it.'

*

Miss Hilda Holroyd might not have wanted the police sent for in the first place. As the morning wore on, though, she positively began to look forward to their arrival.

She was having a trying time.

Besides having had Mr Tindall's visitor – Mr Gordon Cranswick – darting in and out like an urgent gadfly, there was her usual work piling up. She had already postponed the rest of Mr Tindall's appointments for the morning.

'Urgent personal and domestic reasons,' she lied gallantly into the telephone, promising to ring back later.

She had also parried the Head of the Testing Department, who had technical problems; fended off young Mr Blake, who didn't seem to have enough to do; dispatched two optimistic young salesmen who wanted Struthers and Tindall to buy brand-new equipment which would halve their expenses – or so they said; and – probably most important of all – successfully placated the office cleaner and tea lady.

'Report?' Mrs Perkins was indignant. 'I haven't seen no report.' She was a small wiry woman with the vigour of ten. She advanced down the corridor, broom rampant. 'And I haven't touched it neither.'

'We've misplaced it, you see, Mrs Perkins.'

Grudgingly. 'What's it look like?'

'Green,' said Miss Holroyd. 'It's a green file.'

Mrs Perkins sniffed. 'I never touch nothing with writing on it.'

'There would just be a number on the outside, that's all.'

'That's writing, isn't it?' said Mrs Perkins incontrovertibly.

'We had it yesterday.' Miss Holroyd did her best to sound soothing. 'It's rather an important one . . .'

'Well, it wasn't nothing to do with me.' Mrs Perkins rammed the broom on the floor with quite unnecessary force. 'But if I should 'appen to see it . . .'

'Thank you.'

'I done Mr Pysden,' said the cleaner obliquely.

'Good,' responded Miss Holroyd warmly, bearing in mind that while clever young scientists could be recruited with ease cleaners as reliable as Mrs Perkins were thin on the ground.

'Not that he noticed.' Mrs Perkins sniffed. 'He was that stuck in his experiment. If you was to say to him had I bin in I bet you he wouldn't know one way or the other. Not Mr Pysden.'

'Oh, Mrs Perkins, surely not.'

'Head that buried in his papers,' declared Mrs Perkins, 'you wouldn't credit it. Not like young Mr Blake. I should like to know when he gets any work done.'

'I'm sure,' interjected Miss Holroyd swiftly, 'that Mr Pysden's room is all beautifully neat and clean since you've been in there, anyway.'

'Well,' Mrs Perkins seemed faintly mollified, 'it's better than it was. I will say that.' She brought her broom to attention at the perpendicular and said grandly: 'If I should happen to see this green file which you've lost I'll let you know . . .'

But not even the Argus-eyed Mrs Perkins could locate the United Mellemetics file anywhere in the works of Messrs Struthers and Tindall.

Miss Holroyd and Mr Pysden met again about this.

'It would happen to be the United Mellemetics report,' said Henry Pysden gloomily. 'Of all the people I'd rather not have to tell, Sir Digby Wellow comes pretty near the top of the list.'

Miss Holroyd was sympathetic. Sir Digby Wellow was one of the country's more colourful industrialists. And vocal to disaster-point.

'Was it,' she ventured, 'going to be a favourable report?'

'No, it was not,' said Henry Pysden. 'That's what's so worrying. Sir Digby sent it to us because he thought there might be something funny going on in United Mellemetics.' He adjusted his glasses. 'And according to Mr Tindall he wasn't wrong.'

'Oh, dear.'

'It's all very awkward, Miss Holroyd.'

'We've never – er – misplaced a report before,' she said. 'You don't think – possibly – just this once – Mr Tindall took it home with him?'

'Perhaps. Not like him, though. He's never done it before. And it's against all the rules.'

Miss Holroyd sighed. 'It would be the one day when he isn't here to ask. I don't quite know what we should do next.'

'I do,' said Henry Pysden grimly. 'Get me United Mellemetics on the phone at Luston. A personal call to Sir Digby Wellow, please, Miss Holroyd.'

It was a full minute after the workmen had finished welding before those watching it could see anything at all. The inimical glare of the fierce heat had stained the vision of everyone in the church who wasn't wearing goggles.

'Here she comes, mate.'

'Easy there.'

'Watch your end, Joe.'

Joe apparently watched his end all right for – very slowly – the great oak door leading into the tower from the church started to move. Willing hands caught it and laid it down in the nave. A small shower of broken marble came spattering down with it.

Sloan stood well to one side, just looking.

So did the pathologist, Dr Dabbe.

The workmen trudged up and down the nave, seeing that the big door was safe where it lay. Already, in the way of optical illusions, it looked too big for the hole that it had left behind it. 'Not so deep as a well, not so wide as a church door,' thught Sloan involuntarily. Now where had that saying come from? His mother, probably. She was a great one for old sayings.

'What do you want doing now, guv'nor?'

'Nothing, thank you,' said Sloan, his eyes once more riveted on the arm. The solitary arm exhibited a dreadful fascination. It was thrust out through the debris for all the world like that of a drowning swimmer calling for help.

The welders looked relieved and trundled their oxygen and acetylene cylinders away. Sloan beckoned with his finger and Dyson, the official police photographer, and his assistant, Williams, both moved forward, cameras at the ready.

'A nasty accident?' enquired Dyson cheerfully. None of the pictures which Dyson took so professionally was ever pretty, but he didn't let the fact get him down.

'A nasty incident,' Sloan corrected him.

Dyson nodded and took his first picture. After the penetrating flame of the welding plant the flash of his camera's bulb seemed tame stuff indeed. He jerked his thumb. 'How did Fred get under that little lot?'

'Richard,' responded Sloan automatically. 'His name's Richard.'

He was more than ever sure now that it was.

'I don't suppose,' remarked Dyson, who was an incorrigible looker on the bright side, 'he knew what hit him. Can't have done.'

'No. Now, what I want,' said Sloan, getting down to business, 'are a couple of shots of the height of the marble piled up against the outside door over there. That one . . .'

'The west door?' Dyson obediently started to focus.

'The coffin door,' supplied Dr Dabbe ghoulishly from the sidelines.

The camera clicked, recording the marble heaped up against the door.

'Now what?' asked Dyson.

'I want some of that window up there. The little one above the door,' said Sloan, 'from the inside and the outside.'

'No one could get through that, Inspector.'

'No,' agreed Sloan, 'but it's been opened and the ladder taken outside to do it with, I dare say.'

Dyson obligingly hitched his camera up and photographed the little window, while his assistant, Williams, rigged up a tripod in the nave.

'Been reading Sherlock Holmes, then, have you, Inspector?' he asked with a deceptively straight face.

'No,' said Sloan shortly. 'I haven't. Why?'

The photographer pointed up at the tiny window.

'It's a bit like in *The Speckled Band*, isn't it? No one could get through that window there, could they, and both doors were bunged up to the eyebrows with marble, so nobody could get out through them either.'

'We'd got as far as that,' said Sloan, though he wasn't sure if Crosby had actually worked that much out yet . . .

'But something knocked that thing down on the poor chap and then vamoosed somehow. Stands to reason, doesn't it?'

'If,' promised Sloan, 'it turns out to have been a deadly Indian swamp adder, I'll let you know.'

It was common knowledge in the Force that Dyson would have gone a long way on the uniform side if only he'd had the sense to keep his mouth shut at the right moment. Perhaps that was better, though, than Crosby who didn't seem to have opened his sensibly at all so far.

'Unless he went upwards,' continued the police photographer logically, taking some pictures of the narrow stairway – more of a catwalk really – which climbed up round the tower and was lost to sight somewhere among the bells.

'If he went up that way,' said Sloan, following his gaze, 'I should like to know how he got down afterwards. It's too high for a ladder and it's a long drop without one. I don't know how you get back to earth from that sort of height . . .'

'Rapunzal,' suggested Dr Dabbe, who was still waiting on the sidelines to be able to examine the dead man.

'Batman,' offered Crosby, suddenly coming to life at last.

Sloan took a deep breath. He couldn't very well bawl Crosby out; not if the doctor was making dotty suggestions, too.

'Rapunzal?' he said, injecting the word with just enough of a note of polite enquiry as not to jeopardize the traditionally good relations between police and medicine.

'In reverse, of course,' explained the pathologist. 'You remember, Sloan, she was a maiden who was shut up in a tower by her father.'

'Really, sir?' It sounded quite a good idea to him. If more fathers shut up their maiden daughters in towers more often there would be a lot less work and worry for some members of the police force.

'She grew her hair long,' added the doctor, 'and a knight in shining armour climbed up it.'

Sloan choked.

'*Grimm's Fairy Tales*,' said Dr Dabbe gravely.

'With Batman . . .' began Crosby.

Sloan rounded on him. 'If that's your only suggestion, Constable . . .'

He stopped and gritted his teeth. Was this what was called the Generation Gap? The difference between Rapunzal and Batman?

He stopped because it wouldn't be any good saying anything.

He knew that.

He sighed. He would just have to have more help, that was all.

Real help.

Not just Constable Crosby standing two paces behind him, looking bored and making absurd suggestions, and a police photographer who was a detective *manqué*.

'This lady who let her hair down,' said Dyson interestedly.

'If you've quite finished photographing that stairway, Dyson,' snapped Sloan, 'Crosby here can start getting it checked for footprints. Just in case.'

It would be a waste of time. Sloan could see that from where he was standing. The treads were too clean. Either someone had deliberately dusted them down or they were kept that way.

By whoever wound the church clock, perhaps?

He could hear the machinations of the clock overhead as it gathered strength to strike the quarter hour above them.

There were some more flashes and then Dyson stood back and said: 'That's the lot inside, Inspector. I'll come back and take a few bird's-eye views from up top when you've finished with the stairway.'

Sloan nodded and exchanged glances with the pathologist, by now gloved and gowned.

There was a sudden change of mood inside the church

tower as Dr Dabbe advanced, totally absorbed now in the arm.

They started to wade through the piled marble towards it. There was some writing on a piece of marble at Sloan's feet. He looked down and read it. '*Defunctae . . .*'

He must have said it aloud because the pathologist, who had at last reached the arm, said, 'So's our chap, I'm afraid. Very.'

I am acquainted with sad misery.   8

The Dower House at Cleete was no more empty now than it
had been half an hour ago. There were exactly three people in
it. The same number and the same people as there had been
before. Fenella herself, Mrs Turvey, and Police Constable
Hepple.

It was true that the constable had gone through into the
kitchen to talk to Mrs Turvey, but the complement of people
within the house was still the same.

But it felt emptier.

Somehow her father's presence seemed to have left it.

Fenella hadn't quite grasped all that Police Constable
Hepple had tried to tell her. Her ears had heard all right –
there was no avoiding his slow, burred Calleshire speech – but
her bemused and bewildered mind somehow hadn't picked up
the messages from her ear. Her brain was a confused jumble
of disconnected words – sculpture – crushed – arm – button –
church.

If she had been seven years old again and at a children's
party – not the sort of children's party which children had
nowadays but the sort of children's party which they still had
when she was a little girl – then the whole of Hepple's ghastly
rigmarole could have been resolved in a hilarious game of
consequences.

Sculpture – crushed – arm – button – church.

Someone in turn would then have added the ultimate

incongruity – father. Then there would have been shrieks of laughter and everyone would have gone on to the next game. Or a kind, motherly hostess would have handed out lemonade all round.

She sat quite still.

This was no game.

And there wasn't going to be any laughter.

Not now.

Not for a long time.

She could have done with the lemonade though. Her mouth was dry and she seemed to have too much tongue. There would be some tea coming soon. The constable had said so. That was what he had gone through into the kitchen for.

A cup of tea.

The police panacea.

And to tell Mrs Turvey about her father. That was nice of him. She hadn't wanted to – didn't feel she could – start on about the sculpture and the arm and the button to Mrs Turvey just now.

At least Mr Gordon Cranswick of Cranswick (Processing) Limited or whatever it was would know now why it was that her father couldn't see him this morning. She had known – she knew – he wasn't a breaker of promises . . . not her father.

It was because Police Constable Hepple was in the kitchen that Fenella Tindall got to the telephone first. She picked it up automatically without thinking almost as soon as it started to ring.

A deep male voice asked for Richard Tindall.

'He's not here,' she said falteringly. 'Who is this?'

'Where is he, then?'

'Who is this speaking?' countered Fenella.

'Wellow,' boomed a voice that was practically basso profundo. 'Digby Wellow of United Mellemetics of Luston.'

'Oh . . .'

'I require to speak to him,' announced the caller magisterially, 'as soon as possible.'

'I'm afraid you can't.'

'Why not?'

'Something's happened,' she said helplessly. 'Something terrible's happened.'

'What?' howled a suddenly anguished voice at the other end of the line. 'Tell me . . .'

But this was something that Fenella found she could not do. She stood by the telephone, her mouth working soundlessly, tears beginning to chase themselves quietly down her cheeks as she attempted to convert tragedy into words. She was making the painful discovery – as many another before her – that to comprehend bad news was one thing: to convey it to someone else quite another. Perhaps it was because to formulate the words might somehow seem to endorse the very worst . . .

This was where the kindly Hepple found her when he came back with a cup of tea a minute or so later. He lifted the telephone receiver from her nerveless fingers, listened intently for a moment, heard nothing but the dialling tone, and then replaced it.

When Paul Blake rang from Struthers and Tindall's offices a few minutes later to speak to Fenella, Police Constable Hepple answered the call himself.

In the church tower they – Dr Dabbe and his assistant, Burns, Inspector Sloan, and Constable Crosby – began uncovering the body attached to the visible arm. It was a slow, painstaking business, each piece of marble being marked and then laid in the aisle. Little by little a crumpled figure began to emerge from under the debris of the Fitton Bequest.

Incredibly, the operation was not without its lighter moments.

'Is this an angel, Inspector?'

Sloan looked up. Crosby was cradling a curvaceous marble infant, undamaged save that it lacked an arm. Its other arm – chubby to a degree – seemed to be toying playfully with the detective constable's lapel.

Sloan gave a sigh of pure exasperation.

Crosby gave the marble a friendly pat. 'Or is it a cherub, sir?'

'Neither,' said Sloan shortly. 'It's one of the ten Fitton children. Now, give me a hand with this bit, will you? It's too heavy for one.'

In fact, it took all four of them to lift the largest piece of all from the top of the body on the floor.

'Multiple fractures, for a start,' decided Dr Dabbe, who had reached his quarry at last. 'And a ruptured spleen, I should say.'

Sloan waited. To him the man just looked like a rag doll with the stuffing gone.

'She's broken his back, all right, too,' announced the pathologist a moment or two later.

'Who has?' asked Sloan considerably startled.

'The widow.'

'Oh.' His brow cleared. 'Mrs Fitton.'

The doctor bent over the body again and Sloan had time to take his first good look round the inside of the tower itself.

It was a very high one and open right up to the bells. He could just make them out in the dimness some seventy feet above his head. Sundry ropes hung down from the bell loft. Those from the bells were neatly moored against the wall opposite where the sculpture had been parked on its plinth. A single rope secured them to the wall near a brass plaque.

Sloan picked his way across the floor to read the inscription.

To call the folk to Church in time,
WE CHIME
When joy and pleasure are on the wing,
WE RING
When the body parts the Soul,
WE TOLL.

'Nice, that, sir, isn't it?' said Crosby over his shoulder.

'He could have rung one of the bells,' said Sloan, looking back to the body, 'if he thought there was any danger. There was nothing to stop him doing that.'

Crosby said, 'So he wasn't worried, sir.'

'Not about the Fitton Bequest, anyway.'

'He could have walked out, too,' added Crosby, 'if he hadn't been happy. The tower door wasn't locked, was it, sir?'

'Between eleven last night and eight this morning it was.'

'We don't know,' said Crosby going off on a fresh tack, 'why he came here either.'

'There's a lot we don't know,' Sloan reminded him with gloomy relish, 'yet.'

The pathologist straightened up from the prone body. 'There's one thing we do know, Sloan . . .'

'Yes, Doctor?'

'He was hit twice.'

'Twice?'

'Once to make him unconscious, the second time by all the marble. That's what killed him. He didn't bleed after that.'

'How do you . . .'

'He bled the first time,' said the doctor succinctly. 'He was lying on his face then. You can see how the blood trickled down the sides of his head and dried there. Some of it dropped on the ground from his head. I can confirm that for you presently . . .'

Crosby's head came up in a challenging fashion.

'. . . from the shape of the drop,' said the pathologist, answering the unspoken gesture. 'If it's a short distance then you can work it out. The shape of the drop varies with the height it has fallen.'

'Then?' said Sloan hastily.

'Then the marble came down on top of him. After that, Sloan, all the King's horses and all the King's men couldn't have put him together again.'

'How much later?' Why was it that fairy tales and nursery rhymes were all so sinister? Tales for children. Tales you brought children up on. Never mind the violence they saw on television later on.

'Good question.' The pathologist waved an arm. 'I'll see what I can do for you there. He was hit from behind the first time and from above the second. No doubt about that.' Dr

Dabbe stopped and lifted the last of the marble – a small chip – from the back of the dead man's neck and murmured, 'Pelion upon Ossa.'

Burns gave a short sharp laugh, rather like a seal barking.

Sloan, who was never sure about the doctor's medical jokes, turned his attention back to the tower wall.

It was unexceptional enough. Beside the bell ropes were various little framed cards commemorating past bell-ringing triumphs – marathon rings of Double Norwich Court Bob Major and Treble Bob Maximus. Above them a dark time-stained board recorded some ancient parish charity.

There was no message scratched on any of the walls that Sloan could see. If the tower had been a temporary prison Richard Tindall did not seem to have appreciated the fact to the extent of writing on the walls.

Nor was there anything remotely resembling a weapon.

He said so.

'Ha,' remarked the pathologist neatly, 'if not malice afore-thought then malice afterthought.'

Sloan translated this for Crosby's benefit. 'Whoever hit him took away whatever they hit him with.'

Dabbe considered the man's head. 'Something blunt and not very big, Sloan. That's what you should be looking for.'

Crosby, in fact, wasn't paying attention anyway. He had found a small mirror and, stooping, was regarding himself in it.

'If, Constable,' remarked Sloan nastily, 'it's a question of who is the fairest of us all . . .' Now he was catching the nursery rhyme habit, too.

'They've hung it a bit low, sir,' complained Crosby.

'Spotty choirboy height,' said Dr Dabbe without looking up. He never missed anything, did the doctor. 'Now, Sloan, about the time of death . . .'

The pathologist looked at his watch. Driven by an inner compulsion which comes over everyone who sees someone else look at a watch, Sloan looked at his, too. It was almost eleven o'clock. The time struck a faint chord in his memory. Eleven o'clock. Now why had eleven o'clock mattered today?

The mayor.

That was it. The mayor was due to leave the Town Hall at eleven o'clock this morning. To do something or other that had seemed important to him, if not to the police force. Sloan tried to visualize the message he had seen for only a brief moment before he had hurried out to Cleete. It wasn't the Flower Show. He knew that was next Saturday all right because of holding Princess Grace back. If it wasn't the Flower Show, what could it have been . . .

It came to him.

The water works.

The mayor had been due to leave for the new water works at eleven o'clock this morning to declare it open and cut a ribbon or turn on a tap or something. Well, the mayor would have to take his chance at the water works today.

'Just over the twelve hours, I should say,' the pathologist broke into his thoughts. 'Give or take an hour or so either way. I might even be able to calculate the interval between the two blows. I'll get nearer the time for you later on anyway when I've done the post-mortem. Brain tissue's all the thing for timing these days.'

'That won't be difficult to get,' offered Crosby.

'We think,' intervened Sloan swiftly, 'we know where he was yesterday evening – if his daughter's telling the truth, and if he's Richard Tindall, of course.'

'Not my department, old chap, his name.' Dr Dabbe started to take his gown off. 'The post-mortem'll tell you practically everything else about the poor fellow – no secrets there – but not his name. Not yet. I expect we'll come to it in time. When babies are branded at birth with a computer number, God help us all.' He tossed his gown over to Burns. 'I'm finished here now, Sloan. Done all I can. It's all yours . . .'

Sloan didn't need telling. He looked round for Crosby. The constable had waded across to look at the plinth. 'Crosby, what . . .'

'I've found some more Fitton girls over here, sir. On the four corners of the plinth. They're a bit more grown-up than the others.'

'I wish you were,' said Sloan, much tried. 'Try reading the small print.'

'Oh, I see, sir,' Crosby looked more closely and then slowly spelled out: 'Temperance, Prudence, Justice . . . I can't quite get round to this one . . . oh, yes . . . Fortitude.'

'The four cardinal virtues,' said Dr Dabbe, who had been well brought up.

'You wouldn't know about them, Crosby,' said Sloan unkindly.

Dr Dabbe mentioned a cardinal virtue which the late Mr Fitton, father of ten, did not seem to have possessed but Constable Crosby had by now seen something else. He bent down towards the bottom of the back of the heavy marble slab and pointed.

'The plinth,' said Dr Dabbe in a suddenly cold voice. 'Look down there, Sloan.'

Sloan moved forward so that he could see.

'At the back,' said the pathologist.

'Wedges,' said Sloan. 'Iron wedges. Proper ones.'

He promptly dispatched Crosby to check with Bert Booth, the foreman, whether the workmen had put the wedges there. Somehow he didn't think they had.

'To tilt it forward?' suggested Dabbe.

'But not too much.'

'Just so far . . .'

'That something could knock the sculpture off easily . . .' concluded Sloan grimly.

'But what?'

A complete search of the floor of the tower, scrupulously conducted, produced only broken marble and a spent match. The match was under a piece of marble just inside the west door and beneath the little slit window.

Sloan felt it wasn't a lot to go on.

Dooms men to death by information.   9

'Well?' barked Superintendent Leeyes down the telephone.

'It's Richard Tindall all right, sir.'

'All right is scarcely the phrase, Sloan.'

'No, sir. Sorry, sir.'

'Well?' he barked again.

'We're doing what we can,' Sloan assured him hastily, 'but there were all those marble bodies lying in the . . .'

'Sounds like a knacker's yard,' said Leeyes more cheerfully.

'Yes, sir,' said Sloan evenly. It was all right for the superintendent sitting safely in his office in Berebury. He hadn't had to hump the marble about. The superintendent – like Hamlet – had risen above action.

'Who benefits?' Superintendent Leeyes's view of police life was in its way every bit as simplified as Crosby's.

'I don't know, sir, yet.' He cleared his throat. 'There's a lot we don't know.'

He'd said that to Crosby, too.

'The great thing,' declared Superintendent Leeyes, 'is to state your problem.'

He had once been on a Management Course and had returned permanently confused about aims and objects.

'Yes, sir.'

'In as few words as possible.'

'Yes, sir.'

'So that you know what you're doing and why.'

Goals, they had called them on the course, but he had forgotten that.

'Yes, sir.'

'Well,' he growled, 'what's your problem?'

'How the Fitton Bequest got on top of Tindall,' said Sloan promptly.

There was a long pause. Then:

'No booby traps over the door, Sloan?'

'No, sir. I checked.'

'Nothing attached to the clock?'

'Not even a cuckoo, sir.'

A voice said icily as if from a great distance: 'You know perfectly well what I mean, Sloan. When the hands reached – say – midnight they could have triggered something off . . .'

For one delicious moment Sloan dallied with the idea of mentioning Cinderella too; but decided against it. He had his pension to think of.

'There was no sign of anything, sir,' he said instead.

There had been no sign of anything at all out of the ordinary about the tower. As church towers went it had seemed to Sloan like all the other church towers he had ever known: a square of ancient architecture with an assortment of dangling bell ropes in the middle.

'What about a detonator under the sculpture, Sloan? Had you thought of that?'

'Yes, sir. We looked for signs of explosive devices. Burn marks, and so forth . . .' The superintendent never gave up. You had to say that for him.

Leeyes grunted. 'And nothing to actually prove that the blasted thing hadn't just slipped, either, I suppose . . .'

'The gang who moved it,' replied Sloan carefully, 'can't remember putting any wedges underneath it at all. They swore it was steady enough when they left it – but then they're not going to say anything else, sir, are they?'

'Not if they know what's good for them,' growled Leeyes, who was nothing if not a realist where the British workman was concerned. 'Not now . . .'

'No, sir. Not now . . .'

'So what have we got, Sloan, that's any good to us?'

'One,' enumerated Sloan, 'a dead man, who may be Richard Tindall; two, a missing report, which may or may not be important; three, some tale about the firm being sold yesterday to a man who's been and gone again . . .'

'And?'

'Some scuff marks on the gravel outside the embrasure window.'

'Anything else?'

'A ladder out of place. It wasn't in the church tower where it was usually kept. It was lying outside, and round the corner.'

'That all?'

'There was a used match on the floor of the tower which may or may not have anything to do with the case.'

'You'll have to do better than that, Sloan, for a jury.'

'Yes, sir, I know.'

'And don't be too long about it. There's something else waiting for you when you get back.'

'Sir?'

'A shoe. A woman's shoe. Size six. Part worn – just too much for discomfort, not enough to throw it away.'

'Just the one?'

'Just the one,' Leeyes said. 'The left one. It's where they found it . . .'

'Canal bank?'

'Golf course,' said that master of the Parthian shot.

Sloan groaned.

On his way back from using Mr Knight's telephone again, Detective Inspector Sloan turned aside and made his way past the church tower towards the little cottage opposite. He noticed as he went by that the scuffed gravel outside the west door had been covered over by Crosby. So had the ladder which Bert Booth had carried round from somewhere behind the tower. Not that Sloan was hopeful that the ladder would yield any helpful fingerprints. Fingerprints were for easy cases. Something told him this wasn't going to be an easy case.

His approach had been observed. He had hardly raised his hand to the knocker on the door of Vespers Cottage when it flew open.

'Yes?' said a small round woman with alacrity.

Behind her stood another small round woman.

Sloan explained himself.

So did they.

'I'm Miss Ivy Metford,' said one.

'I'm Miss Mabel Metford,' said the other.

'We're sisters,' said Miss Ivy superfluously.

'Two unclaimed treasures,' chimed in Miss Mabel.

'Quite so,' said Sloan hastily. 'I'm afraid . . . I fear that someone has been crushed . . .'

'An elm?' suggested Miss Ivy promptly.

'An elm?' echoed Sloan, bewildered. This was very nearly as difficult as talking to the superintendent.

Miss Mabel waved a hand towards the churchyard behind him and intoned: 'The elm hateth man and waiteth . . .'

'It wasn't an elm, madam.'

'Not an elm.' They nodded in unison.

Sloan pulled himself together. 'What I want to know is if either of you saw anyone about here last night or early this morning.'

Two heads shook as one.

'No one?'

'Just Mr Knight, of course.'

'And Tessa.'

'Tessa?'

'His dog.'

'No one else?'

Miss Mabel cocked her head to one side. 'There was a night fisher . . .'

'A night fisher?'

Miss Ivy explained quite kindly. 'A man with a fishing rod going down to the river. Abot two o'clock in the morning, that was.'

*

The aura of anxiety at the Dower House at Cleete had been succeeded by one of mourning. It was a house of stillness now. Hepple let Sloan and Crosby in by the back door.

'It's Mrs Turvey I want to talk to first,' announced Sloan.

But the short stout daily woman in the Dower House kitchen could no more account for what had happened to Mr Tindall than could his daughter.

'Enemies? Course not. He wouldn't hurt a fly. Ever such a nice quiet gentleman, he was, Inspector. And no trouble to no one.'

'Really?' commented Sloan, making a note.

Quietness might very well be a recommendation to a daily woman. It wasn't necessarily one to a policeman. The last very quiet gentleman with whom Sloan had had dealings had been a professional blackmailer.

He didn't suppose the anonymous letter writer from the village of Constance Parva would be noisy, either.

Very quiet, Mrs Turvey said again, especially since the mistress died, but then that was only to be expected, wasn't it?

Sloan coughed discreetly and enquired if there were any signs that Mr Tindall had been – er – contemplating marrying again.

'None,' declared Ada Turvey positively. 'He was lonely. That's only natural. You could see that he was lonely with half an eye – anyone could – that's why Miss Fenella came back – but he never seemed interested in no one else. Not after the mistress.'

'Or of – er – not marrying again – if you take my meaning?'

Mrs Turvey took it all right, and shook her head.

'What about worries?'

Mrs Turvey smoothed down her apron. 'We've all got worries, haven't we?'

'Special worries . . .'

She shook her head again. 'Not that I know of, Inspector. Just Miss Fenella.'

'What about her?'

'He was worried if he was doing the right thing letting her come back from Italy just to look after him. That I do know. Didn't think it would be good for a young girl burying herself in the country on her own. What with her poor mother being gone and everything.'

'I see.'

'She would come home,' said Mrs Turvey. 'There was no stopping her. Very attached to her father she was.'

'And to anyone else?' enquired Sloan. A girl like that wasn't going to lack admirers. 'She told us she was out most of yesterday evening . . .'

'That was with an Italian friend. Giu . . . Giu . . . something Mardoni, he's called. Mr Mardoni, anyway. Someone she knew in Italy. Over here for a few days. Took her to that new Italian restaurant, he did, that's just opened. He was going straight back to Rome.'

'When?'

'Last night. A night flight. Home by half-past ten easily, Miss Fenella said she was, so that this Mr Mardoni could get to the airport on time.'

'Is there,' enquired Sloan routinely, 'anyone else besides this Italian friend?'

Mrs Turvey sniffed and said it wasn't for her to say but there was that Mr Blake.

'Mr Blake?'

'Paul Blake. He's one of the bright boys from the master's works. Practical scientist or some such thing he calls himself. Been making sheep's eyes at Miss Fenella, he has, ever since she came home.'

Sloan made note of the name.

'If you ask me,' said Mrs Turvey, sniffing again, 'what that young man's got is an eye for the main chance.'

Sloan nodded. That wouldn't surprise him at all. Of all the manifold rules for success in this world one stood out head and shoulders above all the others.

Marrying the boss's daughter.

And the good books didn't even mention it.

He cleared his throat. 'What did Mr Tindall think?'

'I reckon he wasn't keen,' responded Mrs Turvey promptly, 'but he's got too much sense to try to stop Miss Fenella.'

'Not easily stopped?' hazarded Sloan, thinking of a pair of clear eyes and a finely moulded chin.

'She's got a mind of her own,' admitted the daily woman.

'Mr Tindall had no other problems that you were aware of?' asked Sloan formally. Daughters were, after all, the normal worries of normal fathers. They didn't usually drive the fathers to leave home.

On the contrary, in fact . . .

'Mardoni,' repeated Superintendent Leeyes after him, spelling it out. 'Signor Giuseppe Mardoni, a passenger back to Rome late last night.'

'Or very early this morning.'

'I'll get them to start checking for you . . .'

'Thank you, sir.' Dutifully Detective Sloan radioed Berebury Police Station as soon as he had something – however crumblike – to report. Not that that would be soon enough for his superior officer.

'I've spoken to Mr Tindall's general manager, too, sir. A chap called Henry Pysden. He says everything's all right over at the works . . .'

'Doesn't mean a thing.'

'. . . except that they've lost this confidential report.'

'They have, have they?'

'Belonging to United Mellemetics.'

Leeyes grunted. 'That's Sir Digby Wellow's little lot, isn't it? Over at Luston. The chap who can't keep his mouth shut.'

If the highly paid and very professional public relations people retained by United Mellemetics to keep its name before the public could have heard this they would have swooned gently. They were very gentle men altogether.

Sloan, however, knew what he meant. He forged on.

'Otherwise, according to the daughter, it seems Mr Tindall spent yesterday quite normally. Nothing apparently out of the ordinary, anyway. And the business looks all right.'

'Businesses,' said Leeyes largely, 'often look all right when they aren't.'

'Yes, sir.'

'What's his lifestyle like?' Leeyes wanted to know.

Sloan sighed. The superintendent had never been the same since he had read a book on sociology.

'Er – good, sir.'

He might have known it wasn't the right answer.

It never was with sociology.

'Try again, Sloan.'

'A nice house,' he said defensively, 'and a big garden. All well kept.'

'Ah,' pronounced the superintendent hortatively, 'the carriage trade.'

'Yes, sir,' said Sloan, who considered this – after sociology – a most unfair lapse into an earlier idiom. 'Exactly, sir.'

'Anything else?'

'His car's at home,' said Sloan carefully.

'He won't have walked to Randall's Bridge,' pronounced Leeyes immediately. 'Nobody walks anywhere these days. That's the whole trouble with our traffic system. Ask 'em to park a hundred yards away from where the little dears want to go and they won't do it.'

Inspector Sloan sighed. Once he was truly astride, dismounting the superintendent from a favourite hobby-horse became a ticklish business.

'Mr Tindall's car's here, sir,' he said firmly. 'Standing in the garage but . . .'

'The whole race'll forget how to walk soon . . .' He was well in the saddle now.

'In the garage,' repeated Sloan. It was reminiscent of a joust: tilting him off.

'That's just what I said, Sloan. He'll have gone by car wherever he went.'

'We found him at Randall's Bridge, sir.'

'Your trouble,' retorted Leeyes robustly, 'is that you aren't looking for clues in the right place. What you want to do,' he added in atrocious French, 'is to *cherchez la femme*.'

Sloan cleared his throat and said deliberately: 'Whether Mr Tindall put the car there himself or someone else put it there instead – well, I wouldn't like to have to say. Not at this stage.'

'What's that, Sloan?'

'The car, sir.'

'What about the car? I said to look for the lady.'

'I have a feeling that Mr Tindall might not have brought it back to the garage himself.'

'Why not?'

'There's a slight chip of paint off the driver's door – at the extreme edge – where it's been opened against the wall . . .'

'And?'

'And a tiny sliver of the same paint on the gardening tool which was hanging on the wall at the same level.'

'Ha!'

'Yes, sir.'

'The good old exchange principle.' The superintendent sounded almost gleeful over the telephone. 'If objects meet they exchange traces. You can't beat it, can you?'

'No, sir.' Dutifully.

'Fundamental, Sloan. The best rule in detection if it comes to that. And well over a hundred years old.'

Sloan sighed. A hundred years wasn't going to be long enough to get his points over to the superintendent.

Not at this rate.

'It looks to me, sir,' he said firmly, 'very much as if whoever brought that car into that garage last drove just a fraction too much to the right-hand side.'

'Small garage?'

'Big car.'

'Sloan are you trying to tell me he was abducted after all?'

'No, sir. Not that I know of.'

'But this car was put there last night . . .'

'Perhaps we can't prove it was last night,' admitted Sloan. 'I don't know about that yet.'

'Well, then . . .'

'Except that the car is in exactly the right place now for that chip to have happened last time the car door was opened.'

'You can tell if you didn't put your own car away yourself,' declared the superintendent didactically. 'Like you can tell if someone else has used your best fountain pen.'

'Yes, sir,' agreed Sloan, 'but whether the daughter or the daily woman could tell that for us . . .'

Leeyes grunted.

'. . . that's another matter,' pointed out Sloan. 'It isn't as if it was – er – their fountain pen, so to speak.'

'Fingerprints?'

'Crosby's doing them now, sir, and then we're going round to Struthers and Tindall's works and to see these people Osborne who he spent the evening with.' Sloan coughed. 'Any sign of Mr Cranswick at your end, sir?'

'Not yet.'

'Or the other shoe?'

'All that's come in so far, Sloan, is another of those anonymous letters from Constance Parva. Someone's just brought it in. Between a pair of tongs . . .'

This foul melancholy.   **10**

Detective Constable Crosby had just finished going over Richard Tindall's car by the time Sloan got back to the Dower House garage.

'Well, what did you find?'

Crosby was good on cars, that was one good thing.

'Mr Tindall's prints all over the place, sir. Same as on that hairbrush Miss Tindall gave us for a sample. But . . .' He drew breath impressively.

'But what?'

'But on top of them there's a whole set of glove smudges. Sir, whoever drove this little outfit last wore gloves – that's for sure.'

Sloan grunted.

'I've been over the lot,' said Crosby. 'Steering wheel, gear lever, keys, door handle, roof . . .'

'Roof?'

'You can't get out of a little number like this without putting your hand on the roof – just over the driver's door.' Crosby moved forward eagerly. 'Shall I show you, sir?'

'No,' said Sloan sourly.

The exchange principle already invoked by the superintendent applied to the driver and the car in the same way as to the car and the garage wall. Fourteen stone of detective constable must also make their mark and ruin any traces there might still be of the last occupant.

'You can't get any purchase unless you do, sir,' persisted Crosby, 'because of its being so low slung.'

'I am not so old, Crosby,' retorted Sloan, considerably nettled, 'that I have forgotten how to get out of a car like this.'

'No, sir. Of course not, sir. Sorry, sir.' He began to fumble for his main theme. 'Otherwise, sir, there's just this scrape of paint. It looks quite freshly damaged. I've got a sample from the car and another from the edge of the agricultural implement on the wall . . .'

'The what, Crosby?' Sloan mustered a little patience from somewhere.

'Spade, sir.'

'I should think so, indeed.' The superintendent could call it what he liked but as far as constables were concerned spades were spades. If not shovels.

'I've got a couple of samples ready for the laboratory people, sir.' Crosby indicated two sealed packets. 'They can tell us for certain if they are one and the same paint.'

Sloan nodded.

He wasn't worried about the forensic chemists. Their evidence was either for sure or so highly technical that the jury believed it anyway. What he had to worry about was police evidence – the evidence that juries did make up their minds about – if they made their minds up on evidence at all that is – and there didn't seem to be a lot of that about so far.

Just a dead man. Richard Mallory Tindall.

If he was Richard Tindall.

Even that wasn't absolutely certain yet.

He stood for a moment looking down at the long low blue car. The position of the car might just be evidence. He wasn't sure. His experience was that cars like this were cherished by their owners – not carelessly chipped against the wall. But a stranger not used to driving it who was bringing it into an unfamiliar garage on a dark night might not have noticed that the spade was hanging there: or misjudged the swinging arc of the really wide driver's door of a two-seater car.

It wasn't much to go on.

And he didn't like it particularly.

It smacked of a great deal too much forethought for his liking. Quick crime was one thing: this sort of calculation quite another.

He went back indoors and sought out Fenella Tindall.

'Now, miss, if you can spare me a minute . . .'

'Yes, Inspector?'

'Did your father drive in gloves?'

'Gloves? In all that heat?'

'Yes, gloves.' Sloan knew some of these late-middle-aged fast-car drivers. They wore special leather and string driving gloves and pretended all the time that they were young men at Le Mans.

The girl in the brown dress shook her head in a numbed way. 'No, Inspector. Only in winter. When it was very cold.'

'Thank you, miss. That's what I thought.'

'And not always then. He thought it was affected.'

So did Sloan.

'There's something else we could do with, miss. The name and address of your Italian friend in Rome.'

He shut his notebook after he'd written it down. 'Now, I'm going over to your father's works, but I'll be back. Constable Hepple will stay here with you in the mean time. Is that all right?'

Fenella nodded dumbly.

The police car got them to the offices of Messrs Struthers and Tindall in Berebury at a more decorous speed than hitherto-fore. Detective Constable Crosby was still at the wheel but he was thinking.

'It's a funny business, sir, isn't it?'

'You can say that again.'

'It looks as if he just stood there while someone hit him and then that ruddy great thing fell on him while he was lying there.'

'There were no signs of a struggle,' said Sloan, who had

looked. 'And no rope marks on his wrists or ankles. It looks as if he went there of his own accord, though we don't know why yet . . .'

'A bit of slap and tickle? "Stop it, I like it" stuff . . .' suggested the constable.

'In a church tower?' The superintendent had said *cherchez la femme*, too, hadn't he?'

'Nice and quiet,' said Crosby defensively.

Too quiet, thought Sloan. That was the whole trouble with the church tower at Randall's Bridge. Even Vespers Cottage was out of earshot.

'Perhaps,' continued the constable helpfully, 'someone sent him a note.'

'I dare say they did.'

'You know the sort of thing, sir,' he elaborated. '"Meet me in the church tower at midnight." Something like that.'

'Written in blood?' enquired Sloan genially. 'And finishing with "Fail at your peril"?'

'That's right, sir.' Crosby waved his hand in an eager gesture.

'You'll have to stop watching all those bad films,' pronounced his superior officer severely, though they had funnier letters than that at the police station every morning. 'This isn't a Victorian melodrama.'

'He was lured to his doom, all right, though, sir, wasn't he?' intoned Crosby mournfully.

'Yes, but there's no need for keening,' said Sloan briskly. Perhaps it was more melodramatic than he thought. 'I should say he went to the church with somebody and what you've got to do is to check at . . .'

It was too late. Crosby was already following yet another train of thought.

'"There was I,"' he mimicked in a pseudo-falsetto, very high pitched, '"waiting at the church . . ."'

'Watch it,' advised Sloan, 'or they'll be having you for the church choir. In with the boys.'

Crosby went very quiet.

'There's another thing we don't know for sure' – Sloan went back to his brief – 'and that's how the deceased got to the church tower.'

'Car,' said Crosby, who could never envisage any other form of locomotion anyway.

'It was gone by eleven if it was. That schoolmaster fellow – the one who knows all about everything . . .'

'Mr Knight,' supplied Crosby.

'Him. He didn't say anything about a car being parked by the church last night when he took his dog for a walk, did he? And he would have done, surely, if he'd seen it. A strange car would ring a bell. Especially a slap-up job like Tindall's . . .'

'Another car, then?'

'Or the deceased's car parked somewhere else. And gone by eleven. Before Knight came back that way with his dog.'

Their own car was very nearly at Berebury's Wellgate now. Sloan could see Struthers and Tindall's works looming up.

'That's your next line of enquiry, Crosby. Was there any other car which could have been involved parked in Randall's Bridge last night. Or the deceased's. And while you're about it find out what time Tindall's car really left the Osbornes, and where it went after that if you can.'

'Yes, sir.'

'And what time it got back to Cleete.'

'Yes, sir.'

'The girl said some time after eleven but she may be wrong.' That was something else he would have to go into presently: if Fenella Tindall was speaking the truth. 'And time the distance from the Osbornes to Randall's Bridge.'

'Yes, sir.'

'And Crosby . . .'

'Sir?'

'Police time, not Crosby time.'

'Yes, sir.'

'Hepple will tell you who to talk to. He'll know who is likely to have been out and about in Cleete that late.'

'Late, sir? Half-past ten?'

'That,' rejoined Sloan neatly, 'is why the country is called the hush. Didn't you know?'

As he stepped over the threshold of Messrs Struthers and Tindall's works Sloan decided one thing promptly enough. That if Superintendent Leeyes was right in saying *cherchez la femme* one thing was pretty certain: that Mr Tindall's personal secretary wasn't the *femme*. Like most ugly women she didn't show her age. She had, however, a pleasant, rather deep voice.

She stood up as they introduced themselves.

'It's usually Inspector Tetley who comes over when we want anything. We just ring . . .'

'He's Crime Prevention,' said Sloan, also a servant of the public. Fred Tetley dealt with Crime Prevention in Berebury Division and he was the only optimist on the entire strength. He was the officer who went round recommending bars here, bolts there, and alarm bells with everything.

And not one of these estimable precautions had stopped Richard Tindall from dying.

'Inspector, what news—' She broke off as a dark-haired good-looking young man in a white coat put his head round her office door. He was waving a sheaf of papers in his hand.

'Excuse me, Miss Holroyd, but I can't find Mr Tindall anywhere and I've got those heat storage results for him down from Testing now. I've just finished checking them through.'

'They were wanted yesterday, Mr Blake,' said the secretary reprovingly. 'Mr Tindall was waiting for them.'

'Sorry.' Mr Blake looked contrite – but not very.

A really handsome young man, decided Sloan, doesn't get much practice in looking abashed.

'And,' added Miss Holroyd, 'Mr Pysden wants the Patent Register.'

'Everyone always wants the Patent Register.'

'What everyone wants,' remarked Miss Holroyd astringently, 'is the United Mellemetics file.'

'Not guilty,' the handsome young man waved an arm airily as he backed out of the door. 'I did my bit on that days ago.'

Miss Holroyd turned back to Sloan. 'I'm sorry, Inspector. You were saying . . .'

That she took the bad news about Richard Tindall with no more than a catch of breath and sudden paling did not weigh too heavily with Sloan. Outward calm was deceptive. He'd learned that much long ago. She was probably one of those people who always took all news with outward calm as a matter of policy. Good secretaries were like that. She could have taught the superintendent a thing or two. He always hit the roof . . .

Five hundred years ago and he'd have been one of those who hanged the messenger who brought the bad news as an automatic preliminary to getting down to business.

'I'd better take you straight to Mr Pysden,' she said gravely as soon as Sloan had explained. 'Poor Fenella. I – we were afraid that something must be wrong when he didn't come in as usual this morning – but not as wrong as this . . .'

Perhaps, decided Sloan with approval, she was one of those people who believed that the manner in which news was received made a difference to the quality of the news.

Perhaps it did.

Sloan didn't know.

He only knew that what had happened to Richard Tindall wasn't something which could very well be relegated to the Fourth Division in the news class, however carefully invested with the commonplace.

And that it wasn't exactly Ghent to Aix stuff either.

At least, he corrected himself, it was only good news for one person. If it was murder, that was.

'We'll need to know about Mr Tindall's yesterday, miss.'

'Of course.' She was the efficient secretary at once. 'Let me see now . . .'

Richard Mallory Tindall's yesterday seen from his secretary's viewpoint emerged as apparently uneventful. He had come in a little late because of the road works, and stayed in his office until about half-past eleven doing his letters. And beginning to write a report.

'The United Mellemetics report?' Sloan wanted to know.

Miss Holroyd shook her head. 'The one which Mr Pysden is working on. The Marling Contract.'

'Then what?'

The rest of the morning he had spent seeing people.

'Seeing who, miss?' he asked patiently.

Miss Holroyd frowned. 'Mr Pysden, of course. He had his daily conference with him over coffee as usual. That's when Mr Pysden gave him the United Mellemetics report. The one we can't find.'

'You didn't see what he did with it?'

'I wasn't there.'

'Go on. Who else did Mr Tindall see?'

'Mr Blake. You've just seen him, Inspector. And then the Works Foreman. Someone from Testing ... oh, and Mr Hardy. He looks after the Patents and the legal side. I think that was all. The rest of the time he was talking on the telephone. Then he went round the works.'

Sloan jerked his head. 'Anything else?'

This was any businessman's morning of any working day.

'Not that I know of, Inspector.'

'Then what?'

'At twelve he went out to lunch.'

'Where?' asked Sloan, dead on cue. It had the quality of a catechism did this going through the meaning of everything with this quiet responsive woman.

'I don't know.' She hesitated. 'He didn't say.'

'Does ... did he usually?'

She looked disconcerted. 'As a rule.'

'I expect we can find out easily enough, miss, if it turns out to be important. Anyone would remember that car of his ...'

'He didn't take his car,' she said flatly. 'It stood out under my window all day.'

'Someone called for him?' suggested Sloan.

'He took one of the firm's vans. The old runabout.'

Sloan made a note of the number. Tracing it would give Crosby something useful to do when he had finished with the

Osbornes: well, stop him from being underfoot for a bit anyway. 'When did he get back?'

'He was here when I got back from lunch myself. Before two fifteen, anyway.'

Sloan wrote that down, too. A man could go a fair way and back in a van in over two hours.

'And after lunch, miss?'

'More telephone calls.'

'Including Mr Cranswick?'

Again a cloud passed over her face. 'Not to my knowledge. Though' – she pursed her lips – 'he said he spoke to Mr Tindall yesterday. And that, Inspector, was about all he would tell me before he shot over to Cleete.'

'We'd like to talk to him ourselves,' said Sloan mildly. 'We're looking for him now.'

That was when the telephone rang.

It wa Superintendent Leeyes to speak to Sloan.

'I've got something for you,' said Leeyes. 'You know this Italian chap who was with the daughter all yesterday evening . . .'

'Giuseppe Mardoni?'

'Him.'

'What about him, sir?'

'He didn't catch his plane. We checked at the airport.'

'This way, Inspector . . .' Miss Holroyd led the way down a corridor towards another office. 'Mr Pysden's in here . . .'

Sloan was conscious of the steady hum of power-driven machinery as soon as they stepped out of Miss Holroyd's office.

It was Henry Pysden to whom Sloan had spoken on the telephone from Cleete all right. His voice was still unaccented and reedy. He emerged as a shortish middle-aged man with thick glasses.

'Poor Richard.' He heard Sloan out and then took his glasses off and gave them a vigorous polish. 'And poor Fenella. I never thought I'd see the day when I'd be glad Maisie was dead.'

'Maisie?'

'His wife. In the church, did you say? What on earth was he doing there?'

'I couldn't say, sir.' It was one of the many things Sloan would have to find out: and soon. He hadn't gone there to read the Lesson, that was one thing for sure. 'Not at this stage,' he finished formally aloud.

'Poor Richard,' again. Pysden had obviously settled for the Book of Lamentations. 'But Randall's Bridge wasn't even his church. Cleete was his parish, though I don't know that he was much of a churchman. Not,' added Pysden hastily, 'that he wasn't a good man. You wouldn't find a better, Inspector.

And I should know. I've been with him a good many years. Longer than most people.'

'No, sir, I'm sure.' Sloan cleared his throat purposefully: the verbal obsequies would just have to wait. 'You'll understand that we shall have to make extensive enquiries.'

'Naturally.'

'About him. And about your work here.'

Pysden frowned. 'I don't know that I'm in a position to tell you much about our work. Struthers and Tindall guarantee security, you know. And absolute secrecy. All part of our service. If anything at all leaks out we stand to cover the loss. I'm afraid,' he added apologetically, 'that we may have been somewhat of a burden to Inspector Tetley since we came here.'

'All part of our service,' murmured Sloan ironically.

'That's why people come to us who feel – who fear – who may have reason to fear – that their own security isn't too good.'

'Like United Mellemetics?'

'Sir Digby Wellow is – er – most unhappy,' said Pysden. 'So are we. We've never had a – er – misplaced report before, have we, Miss Holroyd? Never.'

'Never, Mr Pysden. Until now,' she added conscientiously.

'I don't know what Richard will . . . oh, dear.' Pysden took a deep breath. 'Takes a bit of getting used to, doesn't it? That he's not going to be here to say it to . . .'

'Death's like that, sir. Now about this United Mellemetics report . . .'

'It was an important one.' Pysden looked worried. 'There was no doubt about that.'

'Industrial espionage?' hazarded Sloan intelligently.

'It happens all the time.' Pysden tacitly implied agreement and then turned to look at a large clock on the wall before peering myopically across at both police officers again. The thick lenses of his glasses somehow served to veil any expression on his face. If, thought Sloan obscurely, the eye was the window of the soul, like they said, then Henry Pysden's spectacles were a most effective curtain. 'Bound to, really, Inspector, when you consider the sort of money involved these days in that size of firm.'

'It makes a difference, sir.' Sloan would like to see the situation in which money did not make a difference.

He hadn't yet.

'It was going to make a lot of difference at United Mellemetics anyway,' said Pysden. 'That's why Sir Digby came to us.'

'He wasn't happy about something?'

'You could say that again.' Pysden took a second look at the clock. 'Either someone's judgement had gone haywire or there was some funny business going on over there. At least, that's what Richard told me yesterday. I don't know all the details myself. Mind you, it's not always as easy as you'd think to choose between the two. It's difficult to be entirely independent in your conclusions when the success or failure of your department in the firm rests on them. It could,' he finished moderately, 'be that.'

It was a point of view, thought Sloan, which Inspector Harpe in Traffic Division would have appreciated. You never won in Traffic. And nobody ever had an independent view. Not if they drove a car, they didn't.

'Or,' Pysden was going on, 'it would be a case of every now and then a chap going to the opposite extreme and forgetting that commercial firms are not university research faculties. We get a bit of that.'

So they did in the police force, too.

It drove them up the wall every three months or so.

Theorists, statisticians, psychologists, criminologists, penologists – they descended on the Berebury Police Station with monsoon regularity.

And were about as helpful.

'What firms usually want from us,' said Pysden ponderously, 'is the advance judgement of the marketplace. That comes into our work, of course. It must.'

Sloan nodded. As far as he was concerned the judgement of the marketplace should come into a lot more things than it did.

Like a value-for-money prison system.

And traffic departments costed to within a life or two.

'But what Sir Digby wanted,' said the deputy manager, 'was an opinion on the work of an employee.'

'Whether it was bad judgement or bad faith?'

'Precisely.' Pysden let out his breath in a long sigh. 'Precisely. It's always a bit tricky, you know, when it's someone in your own outfit who could be the – er – maverick. You've got to be really careful then.'

They knew that in the Force without being told.

A rogue custodian was the biggest headache of all.

They said that the chief constable had something in Latin about that pinned over his shaving mirror. Someone who had stayed in his house had copied it out and the tag had gradually filtered down through the Force.

Quis custodiet ipsos custodes, it said.

One of the police cadets, fresh from school and a cocky little beast to boot, had translated it as 'Who guards the guards.'

'And which,' Sloan asked the general manager, 'was it, sir?'

'Bad faith, I'm afraid. At least,' he qualified, 'that's what Richard told me yesterday.' There was no doubt that Pysden was watching the clock now. The hands were creeping round to half-past eleven. 'I don't know all the details.'

'You do work for other firms, too . . .'

'We do indeed.'

'I shall need to know which ones, sir.'

'And I shall need to have some authority before I give you their names, Inspector. It's all secret work, you know. Sometimes only the chairman of a particular firm knows that we're doing some work for them.'

'Like United Mellemetics?'

'I very much doubt,' said Pysden drily, 'if Sir Digby has voiced his suspicions to anyone else . . .'

They were interrupted by a bell in the far corner of the laboratory. It rang from beside a complicated structure of wires, valves, glass, and metal. Henry Pysden immediately went straight across to it and took some readings from a thermometer and two little dials. He put these on to a graph and then punched a time recorder. A cylinder not unlike a barograph moved forward with a tiny jerk and Sloan could see that this was but the latest of a long series of recordings, all neatly time-punched.

'Sorry about this, Inspector,' said Pysden over his shoulder, busy now with the apparatus, 'but it won't wait. It's a time-linked experiment. I have to do this every six hours for a week . . .'

'Bad luck, sir.'

Pysden grimaced. 'All in a day's work, I suppose, except that the day starts on the early side. Half-past five.'

'You have to get here by then?'

'No, no. I sleep here. There's a camp bed. What with the eleven thirty-one and the five thirty-one there'd be no night left if I didn't.'

Pysden had his back to them now and was bending, totally absorbed, over something which looked to Sloan like a glass lathe.

'It looks very important, sir.'

'It is, Inspector, believe me. I should say it's about the most important piece of work that Struthers and Tindall have ever done. It takes about twenty minutes each time and I can't delay it without ruining the whole experiment . . .'

'Of course, sir.' Sloan got up to go.

'You'd better ask Fenella about the other business, Inspector. I dare say she comes into a controlling interest in Struthers and Tindall now . . .'

Detective Constable Crosby's lot had been to interview the Osbornes.

It had not been a happy one.

Bad news – a far fleeter traveller even than Crosby himself – had already reached *chez* Osborne. It was a neat and tidy dwelling, modestly prosperous, and set in a good residential area of Berebury near the park. Had Crosby been older and wiser he would have recognized one of those childless marriages where one partner doubles as a child. In this case it was the wife. A tearful Mrs Marcia Osborne was prostrate on a sofa. A kindly woman neighbour was in attendance trying to comfort her.

In vain.

'Poor Richard,' Mrs Osborne kept on saying over and over again.

'There, there,' adjured the neighbour ineffectually.

'Poor Richard,' moaned Mrs Osborne.

Crosby stood well back from the sofa. Very well-dressed women frightened him enough even when they weren't crying: middle-aged women got up to look like girls terrified him at any time.

He wished there wasn't quite so much of Mrs Osborne's leg showing.

He wished he was back on the beat.

At least with a razor gang you did know where you were.

'I want George,' cried Marcia Osborne.

Detective Constable Crosby, whose Christian name was William, felt quite relieved.

'Where's George?' she demanded.

The neighbour said, 'I don't know, dear. It's the school dinner hour and they don't think he's in school.'

'Why isn't he there?'

'I don't know, dear. The school secretary didn't say.'

'He wasn't there at dinnertime yesterday either,' said Marcia Osborne petulantly. 'I want him. Now.'

'Yes, dear.' The neighbour – a resolute woman – having failed to administer psychological comfort or produce George Osborne in person conjured up something in a glass and commanded: 'Drink this.'

'Poor Richard,' said Marcia Osborne mechanically, knocking back whatever it was in the glass with surprising swiftness. 'He was here only last night. In that very chair.'

Mesmerically all three of them stared at an empty chair next to the sofa.

'Last night . . .' began Crosby, knowing that he should be taking a proper interest in last night.

'Only last night,' she echoed sorrowfully, turning to Crosby. 'It doesn't seem possible, does it?'

'No, madam,' said Crosby woodenly. 'What time did he leave?'

Richard Tindall, it transpired damply, had left the Osbornes' house at some point before half-past ten. Marcia Osborne was as vague about this as she was about the time he had arrived. About seven, she thought. At ten o'clock someone had rung for Tindall, and had asked to speak to him on the telephone. He had left shortly after that. No, she hadn't recognized the voice except that it was a man's. Business, was all Richard had said about it. Nothing more.

'He only had the tiniest drink before supper, too.' She regarded Crosby between her tears. It was a predatory look.

Whatever the neighbour had given Marcia Osborne to drink it hadn't been tiny. She hiccuped slightly. Crosby noticed that the crow's-feet round her eyes gave a sympathetic ripple at the same time. It was as far as they could go considering the amount of make-up encasing them.

'And afterwards, madam?' He cleared his throat. 'We are enquiring where everyone was last night.'

She lowered her eyelashes. 'In bed.'

It shouldn't have been Crosby who blushed: but it was.

'Mr Tindall's visit was a social one, I take it, madam?'

Marcia Osborne turned her great limpid eyes towards him and opened them wide. 'Why, no, officer. He came about George's invention. It's going to be a great success. Richard brought the good news last night.' She gulped and started again 'Poor Richard . . .'

Crosby fled.

Sloan had a list in his hand – prised out of the cautious Henry Pysden on Fenella's new-born authority – a list of Struthers and Tindall's customers.

What he hadn't got was any details of the United Mellemetics experiments.

Back in her office Miss Holroyd was explaining this.

'It's part of our system here, Inspector. We always gather

up every single piece of paper to do with a client's experiments or project and return it to the customer with our report. That way we don't have any security problems with our old files. It's bad enough with the ones we're actually working on.'

'Even scrap paper?' asked Sloan hopefully.

'Every last calculation – right or wrong – has to go back to them.'

'What about the United Mellemetics report,' Sloan enquired, clutching at a straw. 'Who wrote that?'

'Nobody. At least,' Miss Holroyd frowned, 'I didn't and I usually type all the very confidential reports. Mr Tindall might have decided against a written report. He does sometimes.'

'Why?'

Miss Holroyd sketched a gesture in the air. 'Extra security, perhaps. We don't always give written reports anyway. They can be quite tricky, you know, in this line.'

Sloan nodded gravely.

All policemen knew.

And they learnt it early.

In their line.

The hard way.

'Sometimes,' explained the secretary, 'Mr Tindall just talks to the people concerned. That way . . .' She hesitated.

'Yes?'

'A chairman can choose to use only what he wants of a particular verbal report. Bits here and there.'

'No hard feelings, eh?'

'Exactly.' She nodded. 'And that way he can't be pressed for action either. Then or later.'

'Clever.'

'Chairmen of companies,' observed Miss Holroyd in a detached way, 'usually are.'

Sloan was with her there. Anyone could be a specialist. It was controlling the experts which ran you into trouble.

Miss Holroyd coughed. 'There's another advantage, too, Inspector.'

'Go on.'

'Sometimes, when there's nothing in writing . . .'

'Yes?'

'The ideas and opinions we put forward can be made to seem to come from the chairman himself.'

'Not from Struthers and Tindall?'

'It has been known.'

'The United Mellemetics chairman – Sir Digby Wellow – is he one of those?'

'I should imagine,' said Miss Hilda Holroyd delicately, 'that a verbal report would have suited Sir Digby very well.'

'But as far as you know he didn't have one?'

'No.' She hesitated again. 'He would be able to tell you that himself.'

'He's not at United Mellemetics.' Sloan pointed to the telephone on her desk. 'I've just rung there myself.'

A chat with Sir Digby Wellow of United Mellemetics had been high on Sloan's list of priorities, and Sir Digby Wellow had left the United Mellemetics factory at Luston for an unknown destination exactly half an hour ago.

The friendless bodies of unburied men.   **12**

Constable Crosby plodded across the churchyard at Randall's Bridge. The workmen had gone back to Berebury. They had been exchanged for a posse of uniformed policemen under Sergeant Wharton. They were searching the churchyard for clues. And the inside of the church: but not the tower. The tower, Inspector Sloan had decreed, was to be left severely alone until he came back.

Crosby dutifully timed the journey from the Osbornes to Randall's Bridge and now he was making for Vespers Cottage and the two Misses Metford.

He hadn't knocked before the door flew open. He followed Miss Mabel inside, brushing against the fronds of a fern in the tiny entrance.

'Mind that,' said Miss Ivy sharply.

'It belonged to Mother,' said Miss Mabel.

'Forty years we've kept that going,' added Miss Ivy.

Crosby shrank to one side – and came up against a bamboo table bearing an aspidistra.

'The sitting room,' decreed Miss Mabel quickly.

'This way,' said Miss Ivy.

'Last night . . .' said Crosby.

'The poor man in the tower . . .'

'They've just taken him away . . .'

'In a black van.'

'We saw him go.'

'All covered over.'

'We see everything from here.'

'Did you see anything last night?' said Crosby, greatly cunning. 'Cars, for instance . . .'

Miss Ivy cocked her head to one side. 'Not see.'

'Hear?'

'We heard one, sister, didn't we?'

Miss Mabel nodded. 'We did.'

'When?'

'About half-past ten,' said Miss Ivy.

'Twenty to eleven,' said Miss Mabel.

'It came up by the church gate and stopped there for a bit,' said Miss Ivy.

'How long?'

''Bout ten minutes,' said Miss Mabel.

'Fifteen,' said Miss Ivy.

'Did you see anyone?'

Two heads shook as one.

'Too dark,' said Miss Ivy.

'Too far away,' said Miss Mabel.

'But you heard it,' persisted Crosby, looking from one sister to the other. This was worse than Wimbledon.

'We did,' they chimed.

''Specially when it went,' said Miss Ivy.

'It made a funny noise then,' said Miss Mabel.

'Funny?' Crosby's head felt like a shuttlecock. He was sitting in a wing chair which had an antimacassar bounded by torchon lace which tickled every time he moved his head. Taking statements wasn't supposed to be like this.

'Louder,' said Miss Ivy.

'We don't usually hear cars go,' explained Miss Mabel.

'Go?'

'Come,' added Miss Ivy. 'We hear them come because of the hill up to the church gate.'

'It's steep,' amplified Miss Mabel.

'When they go . . .' said Miss Ivy.

'Yes?' said Crosby reeling.

'They usually go quietly,' said Miss Ivy out of turn.

'Downhill,' said Miss Mabel.

'Home,' commanded Detective Inspector Sloan as they left the works of Struthers and Tindall at long last.

Detective Constable Crosby slipped the police car into gear and turned out of the gates and into the main traffic stream.

'And slowly,' added Sloan, settling himself down in the front passenger seat and opening his notebook.

'Slowly, sir?'

'That's what I said, Crosby. It means,' he added trenchantly, 'the opposite of fast.'

A cone of injured silence encompassed the area of the driving seat. It was practically visible.

'More people,' Sloan reminded him presently, 'are killed by motorists than by murderers.'

'Yes, sir.' Crosby slid the car at high speed round a traffic island installed not very long before at the instigation of Inspector Harpe for the sole purpose of slowing down all traffic.

'Besides . . .' Sloan hunched his shoulders forward, 'I want to think.'

As *amende honorable* went it wasn't exactly memorable but Constable Crosby's obedient 'Yessir' came up with just the right inflexion this time.

Not, thought Sloan with foreboding, that the space of one short car ride – however decorous – was going to be anything like long enough to marshal his thoughts ready for Superintendent Leeyes.

There were some things, though, which could be put in hand.

'The firm's van, Crosby. Yesterday lunchtime.'

The constable patted his car microphone affectionately. 'I've sent a message out. Anyone who saw it to let us know.'

'All Calleshire?'

'All cars, sir. After twelve yesterday.'

'So Miss Holroyd says,' Sloan reminded him. 'So she says. We don't know.'

That was the police way of thinking.

The way he should be showing this raw constable how to think.

It was ingrained in him now, or so his wife, Margaret, said. In detective work you thought in much the same way as you would pick your way across a swamp, testing for firm ground each time you took a step forward.

He didn't know if what Miss Holroyd – or anyone else in this case, come to that – said was firm ground or not yet.

It was too soon to know, though already things had been said which had sounded a tinkle of warning . . .

He'd have to sort those out, too.

'That all, sir?' Crosby enquired assiduously, steering a perilous course the while between a Calleshire County omnibus and a furniture van.

'The Companies Register,' said Sloan when he'd started breathing again. 'Then we'll have the background of Struthers and Tindall and Cranswick Processing and all these other people they're doing work for.'

'Especially United Mellemetics?'

'Especially United Mellemetics,' agreed Sloan, looking at the list. 'There's Punnett Tooling, too, and Harbleton Engineering and Marlam's . . .'

'Never heard of them.'

'And Stress Engineering.'

'Or them.'

'What about Leake and Leake?' Sloan frowned. 'That seems to ring a bell.'

'Vans, sir. They have vans. Lots and lots of them. Little green ones. You see them everywhere.' Crosby made them sound like leprechauns.

'Oh, them. I know.' Sloan went back to his list. 'Osborne is the last one.'

'George Osborne,' said Crosby. 'That'll be his invention. It's going to be a great success. Tindall said so.'

'Mrs Osborne said Richard Tindall said so,' Sloan reminded him patiently. 'How many times do I have to tell you that it's not the same thing?'

Crosby didn't answer. He seemed to be busy turning the police car down Bell Street. They were getting near the police station now.

Sloan was still looking at his notebook. 'Now, Crosby,' he went on as one encouraging a pupil, 'what is the next thing we should do?'

'Eat, sir,' responded the pupil with celerity. 'It's tummy time.'

Sloan snapped his notebook shut. He really didn't know what the Force was coming to.

Yes, Inspector, a voice agreed down the telephone from the mortuary to the police station, they had received the body from the church.

Yes, they had listed the contents of the pockets. They had done that at once because of Dr Dabbe wanting to get on and you know – everyone knew – what Dr Dabbe was like when he was in a hurry . . .

What had there been? Well, the usual.

What was the usual?

Some small change – not much. Keys – house keys by the looks of them.

Not car keys?

Not car keys.

A couple of handkerchiefs. A good boy.

A what?

A good boy. One handkerchief to use and one to spare.

'Anything else?' enquired Sloan in a strangled voice.

Nothing out of the ordinary at all. A wallet, of course. With some money. The business cards in it said Richard Mallory Tindall if that was any help to the Inspector.

It was? Good.

Anything else in the wallet?

A receipt from Adamson's in London.

Not Adamson's the jewellers?

The voice from the mortuary spelled out a famous address in a well-known London street.

Sloan drew in his breath. Adamson's were suppliers to what

crowned heads remained in the world, and their lineal successors in the matter of wealth – oil-rich sheikhs, property tycoons, pop stars, pools winners . . .

'What for?' he asked.

Adamson's didn't deal in peanuts, of course. Everyone knew that. Not even in costume jewellery when it came to the point. With Adamson's it would be for real – whatever it was. At Adamson's if it looked like gold, then it would be gold.

A pair of diamond and emerald clips, read out the man at the mortuary, made to order as per pattern supplied.

'What,' asked Sloan with mounting eagerness, 'was the date on the receipt?'

July 15th.

Tuesday. The day before yesterday.

Anything else?

Well, yes, there was one of those funny little things that looked like a small ruler but wasn't – oh, a slide rule?

Really? Well, there was one of them. And a pen and pencil, and a small diary.

The Inspector would like that sent over to the police station straightaway.

Right.

Will do.

That all? Well, there wasn't anything else.

Nothing?

Nothing. Was there anything else special apart from these clips that the inspector had in mind?

A box of matches? echoed the voice. From its disbelieving tone matches might have been as rare as emerald and diamond clips. Oh, no, nothing like that.

Not even a lighter.

A man must eat.

Even if he was a policeman.

Pangs of hunger had at last driven Detective Inspector Sloan to agree with this admirable proposition advanced by Constable Crosby, who had assuaged his own appetite minutes ago.

And a detective must detect.

Even if he was hungry.

Sloan was manfully trying to do both at once: cradling the telephone receiver between ear and shoulder, a pen in one hand and a beef sandwich in the other.

'A pair of emerald and diamond clips,' he said indistinctly, when his London call came through. 'Ordered through your Mr Lee.'

Somewhere in a heavily carpeted office in the West End of London Messrs Adamson's, Crown Jewellers, brought their Mr Lee to the telephone.

'A very nice pair of clips, Inspector,' Mr Lee began cautiously.

'I should like to know all about them,' said Sloan.

He would like to know all about the United Mellemetics file, too. And a lot more about an Italian called Giuseppe Mardoni.

'They were emerald, Inspector. Mr Tindall specified emeralds in his letter. With diamonds if we could manage it.' Mr Lee contrived to make the diamonds sound like makeweight.

'Emeralds with diamonds,' mused Sloan, taking another bite of his beef sandwich while he could.

'Mixed stones are all the fashion again,' said Mr Lee. 'It's not like it used to be.'

'Really, sir?' Sloan wondered if he should have known that.

Was it the sort of thing every good detective knew? There was no limit to those. It was Sherlock Holmes who held that every detective should be familiar with seventy-five varieties of perfume, wasn't it?

Or was it fifty-seven?

Sherlock Holmes had solved his locked-room mystery by finding a deadly Indian swamp adder in residence.

Sloan had had no such luck.

So far.

'Emeralds with diamonds,' he repeated.

'That's right, Inspector. To match some Victorian emerald and diamond earrings. To pattern, so to speak.'

'What sort of clips were they?'

'Let me see now, Inspector – how can I best describe them to you? You haven't got them in front of you, by any chance?'

'No,' said Sloan shortly, 'I haven't.'

'Well, in that case . . .' Mr Lee paused. 'They were each composed of cabochon . . .'

'Cabochon?'

'Polished not cut into facets or shaped.'

'Right,' he mumbled in between beef and bread. 'I've got that.'

'Cabochon emerald and diamond clusters . . .'

It did sound rather nice, thought Sloan, as he wrote it all down. He tried to visualize a pair of clips like that on his own wife, Margaret. He found it refreshing to call up her image in the middle of the day and was dwelling on this while Mr Lee went on talking.

'I'm sorry, sir,' apologetically. 'Might I have that again, please?'

'The clusters,' repeated Mr Lee with the esoteric enthusiasm of the expert, 'were slightly graduated and each was held and intersected by a small diamond collet.'

'Collet?' queried Sloan.

'The horizontal base of a diamond when cut as a brilliant,' said the expert. 'We just had to match the existing earrings, Inspector. Not a difficult job really. We had them to go on. Mr Tindall sent us one and we worked from that and then returned the two clips and the earring.'

'When?'

There was a rustle of paper to match Sloan's chewing. 'According to our ledger, Inspector, it was dispatched two days ago.'

'Tuesday.'

'That's right. Mr Tindall mentioned a date in his letter.' Adamson's Mr Lee gave a discreet professional cough. 'I understand a lady's birthday was involved.'

Sloan pushed the description over to Crosby who had just come in. The constable was holding a message sheet which had reached them from Superintendent Leeyes.

'It's about this G. Mardoni, sir.' Crosby handled the flimsy paper with care. The police authority economized on the quality of the paper it used and much time and Scotch tape were expended on sticking it together. 'It confirms that he was booked on a direct flight to Rome leaving London Airport at one-thirty this morning.'

'And he didn't make it . . .'

'Failed to report to either the terminal or the airport, sir.' Crosby took another look at the message sheet. 'It says here that they're trying to find out if anyone of that name caught a later flight.'

'Or G. Mardoni using any other name,' said Sloan, picking up the telephone and dialling the Dower House at Cleete.

'Me, Inspector?' echoed a Fenella as disbelieving as the mortuary attendant. 'The boss of Struthers and Tindall? Oh, surely not. Not now of all times. I couldn't possibly . . . I can't begin to think straight as it is.'

Sloan kept the receiver to his ear while she did, perforce, begin to think straight.

'I couldn't possibly . . .' she repeated tremulously.

'I don't know about the Struthers part, miss . . .' It was surprising how skilled you got at interviewing people.

'I remember that my father bought a controlling interest when old Mr Struthers died. His two daughters still have a share, I know, but not a big one.'

'What they call a minority interest?' suggested Sloan helpfully.

'That's right, Inspector. They get dividends and things.' She still sounded bewildered. 'I can't be the boss, though, Inspector. Not of the whole firm. It doesn't make sense.'

'Did your mother have an interest?'

'Yes, but what's that . . . oh, I see . . . yes. Yes, she did. And she did leave it to me.'

'If you inherit your father's holding, too, miss, I can see that you might very well be the majority shareholder.'

'Oh, dear . . .'

'Going back to last night, miss . . . When did Mr Mardoni leave you?'

'Just before ten-thirty. He brought me home and then left. He had a plane to catch.'

'He had a car?'

'He hired one while he was here. He'd arranged to leave it at the airport. You can do that.'

Sloan took down the name of the car hire firm, and asked, 'When did he come to England?'

'Last Thursday. He had business in London, he said . . . he's a civil engineer . . .'

He wrote down all the details she gave him. They would have to be checked, of course. Everything would have to be checked. That was what being in the police force meant. Check, check, and check again.

Fenella Tindall, surrogate owner, had been quite willing for Detective Inspector Sloan to have the names of all the firm's clients, Henry Pysden's caution notwithstanding.

'I shall be going back to Randall's Bridge soon, miss,' he said obliquely.

'There's no hurry,' she responded dully, 'is there? Not now.'

'I'm afraid not, miss,' Sloan agreed tendentiously.

There wasn't either. Not from her point of view. Her father was already dead. All would be still at Cleete. She wasn't beset by furies like Superintendent Leeyes and Dr Dabbe and the police photographers – all of whom were clamouring for his attention at once.

And behind them there would be the baying hounds of the Press . . .

'But I fear that we will want you, miss, to . . . we will have to ask you to look at . . . to say if . . .'

'I understand, Inspector.' Her voice was almost harsh, it was so tightly controlled. 'I'll be here when you want me.'

'It'll be at the mortuary in Berebury.'

'I won't run away.'

'We're sending a car over for you.'

'Thank you.'

Sloan cleared his throat. 'It's on its way over.'

'Now?'

'Dr Dabbe . . . he . . . we can't afford to waste any time, miss. Not in a case like this.'

'No . . .' he heard her breath expire in a long despairing sigh. 'Of course you can't.'

'Miss . . .'

'Yes?'

'There was one other thing.'

'Yes, Inspector?'

'Would you mind telling me when your birthday is?'

'In March,' she said promptly. 'It's March the twenty-ninth.'

'Did your father give you a birthday present then?'

'Oh, yes. He wouldn't forget.'

'Thank you, miss.' He tried another tack. 'Do you by any chance own a pair of emerald and diamond earrings?'

'No, Inspector . . .' not quite so promptly.

'Did your mother?'

He heard her catch her breath this time. 'Not to my knowledge.'

As soon as Sloan had rung off Fenella Tindall dialled the Berebury Grammar School for Boys and asked for Mr Osborne.

'He's not here.' A throaty schoolboy voice answered the telephone after a long delay. 'It's the dinner hour. There's nobody here.'

'Where is he?'

'Out.'

'Are you sure?'

'His car's not here,' croaked a half-broken voice.

'That doesn't mean a thing,' said Fenella bitterly.

'He'll be back by two,' offered the boy with all the confidence of the young. 'He's got a lesson with us on mass and volume.' His voice took a centaur-like leap to manhood. 'Do you want to leave a message?'

'Yes, please,' said Fenella Tindall.

*

Superintendent Leeyes was in one of his ivory tower moods.

Sloan knew them of old.

The chief constable, who had had an expensive education and who knew the superintendent very well, too, called them Aristotelian.

All Sloan, who had clawed his way up through primary and grammar school, knew was that the superintendent liked his action offstage. And all over in one day.

Within one revolution of the sun was how it would have been put by the chief constable *pace* Aristotle.

'All going well, Sloan?' enquired Leeyes briskly.

'We've got a general call out for a van and a pair of diamond and emerald clips.'

'Emerald clips?'

Sloan told him about the jewellery.

'Ha! You've got down to the grass roots, then.'

Sloan took the point dutifully.

'Murder,' enquired the superintendent, 'for a pair of emerald and diamond clips?'

'There's this missing United Mellemetics file, too, sir.'

Leeyes snorted. 'Don't say there's something our precious Sir Digby Wellow can't handle.'

'Looks like it, sir, and he's disappeared too now.'

'What!'

'His firm don't know where he is,' amended Sloan.

'So that's this man Cranswick and Wellow who've both slipped through your fingers . . .' The superintendent believed in staying on top.

'There are half a dozen firms with hush-hush jobs farmed out to Struthers and Tindall, and United Mellemetics happens to be one of them, sir.'

Superintendent Leeyes looked up suspiciously. 'These people, Sloan – Struthers and Tindall – they're not doing anything for the War Office, are they?'

Ministry of Defence it might be now. War Office it had been and War Office it would remain to Superintendent Leeyes.

'Not that I know of, sir.'

'That's something to be thankful for, anyway.'

'Yes, sir.' Sloan was with him there.

All the way.

Superintendent Leeyes's last brush with Security had seared its way into the annals of the Berebury Force.

It had been a memorable affair.

The superintendent had asserted territorial rights with all the vehemence of a mating cock robin and the Security people had – in the end – retreated, muttering into their cloaks and daggers.

'There's this funny business about selling Struthers and Tindall, too, sir. To Cranswick Processing.'

'Hrrrrrmph.'

'The girl inherits.'

'The King is dead, long live the King,' said Leeyes brutally. 'Or, in this case, the Crown Princess, I suppose.'

'She says she didn't know anything about Cranswick Processing going to buy her father out.'

'They all say they don't know anything about anything.' Leeyes pointed to the papers on his desk. 'No news of the boy friend yet.'

'Who, sir?'

'That Itie. Macaroni or whatever he's called.'

'Giuseppe Mardoni,' sighed Sloan.

That, at least, had been bound to happen.

'Don't like the sound of him, Sloan,' said Leeyes equally inevitably.

'No, sir.' Sloan hadn't for one moment supposed he would.

Xenophobia, thy name is Leeyes: all the Berebury Police knew that.

And that the superintendent belonged to the 'fog in Channel, Continent isolated' school of thought.

If there was a Channel Tunnel where would natives begin then?

'The airport people say they're doing their best at this end,' said Leeyes, poking about among the paper in his In-tray, 'and we've been stirring up the Arrivals Department in Rome. Nothing in from them yet either.'

'So all we really know,' said Sloan fairly, 'is that he didn't catch his plane.'

The superintendent had no time for the impartial statement of fact. 'Two o'clock was it that those two women saw someone in the churchyard?'

'So they say.'

'And we've no witnesses as to the girl being back at the house when she says she was.'

'No, sir.'

Leeyes leaned back in his chair. 'We keep on coming back to the daughter, don't we?'

'The daughter, sir?'

'You heard, Sloan,' said the superintendent testily. 'Presumably she stands to gain more than anyone else, doesn't she?'

'I think so, sir,' said Sloan, 'but at this stage . . .'

'And this expensive jewellery wasn't for her?'

'Apparently not.'

'She mightn't have exactly taken to the idea of it being for someone else.'

'Even so, sir . . .'

'And then there's this foreign gent.'

Sloan had thought that he would crop up again.

'Perhaps,' said Leeyes, 'her father didn't quite take to the idea of her marrying him. Most fathers wouldn't . . .'

'A touch of the "O my beloved Daddy's," you mean, sir?' said Sloan swiftly.

It was Margaret, his wife, who was keen on opera, who bought and played the records. But Sloan listened to them.

'What I mean,' pronounced Leeyes largely, 'is that seventy per cent of all murders are family affairs.'

'But not daughters, sir,' protested Sloan. 'Daughters don't usually . . .'

The superintendent waved a majestic arm. 'There was that one in America, Sloan. Don't forget her. She killed her father. And her stepmother. I forget her name.'

'Lizzie Borden,' supplied Sloan weakly, though he hadn't meant to.

It was a new idea to Fenella that she might be Struthers and Tindall now.

She stood by the telephone and consciously bent her mind to considering it. She was Struthers and Tindall. Struthers and Tindall. Anything to stop herself thinking about a pair of emerald and diamond clips and a dead father.

The more she thought about it the more she was prepared to agree that it might be so.

Struthers and Tindall.

The policeman – it must have been the quiet one who seemed to be in charge who had been on the telephone – not the young one with the gangling arms – she was quite sorry for him – he seemed to have a penchant for being underfoot without actually doing anything – that other policeman – the first one – could well be right after all. She might indeed be the owner of more shares in Struthers and Tindall than anyone else now.

If she inherited her father's holding, that is.

Emerald and diamond clips.

They obtruded into her thoughts at last – thrusting their way into her unhappy mind like an obstreperous visitor and pushing out all the other thoughts with which she had been trying so hard to fill her mind just to keep them out.

Emerald and diamond clips.

He wasn't even, she told herself, the sort of person who went in for buying jewellery. Even when her mother had been alive. She hadn't known him all her life, so to speak, without knowing that. If, she decided painfully, he had bought emerald and diamond jewellery for someone else he might equally have left the Dower House and his share of Struthers and Tindall to . . .

She would have to stop thinking, that was all.

She didn't think she could take these sort of thoughts on top of all the other news of the morning.

She wished she was back in Rome.

Everything was always on such a grand scale there – especially tragedy – that her own small problems would be bound to sink into proportion if she were able to be there. She was sure of that. Put beside the Colosseum and its horrific history surely all the Tindall family troubles would just sink into perspective as little local difficulties.

She sighed.

Fiddling little matters they might seem to be against the backcloth of Roman history but just now they still filled her horizon. What she wanted at this minute was Principessa Trallanti's prescription – a day in the Forum. That was what the Principessa always counselled for anyone overwrought or too beset by the cares of this world.

'A day in the Forum, Miss Tindall, takes the edge off the present,' she would pronounce in her own impeccable English. 'I find it never fails to restore what the French call the *sang-froid*. I don't think you have a word for it?'

How very like the Principessa to use one language and then make up for its deficiencies in another – and neither of them her own . . .

Fenella had readily admitted to the shortcomings of English idiom. Actually the young had the phrase the Principessa was looking for. They called it 'keeping your cool'. She had not told the Principessa this. Though the Trallantis were both more international than any jet set they hadn't quite caught up with the world's youth yet.

The Principessa was quite right.

That was what Fenella wanted.

A day in the Forum . . .

'Miss Tindall, I wonder if . . .'

She'd had one such day in the Forum with Giuseppe Mardoni.

'Call it a Roman holiday,' he'd said persuasively.

He was very persuasive.

A long cool spring day under a clear Roman sky with the flowers thrusting themselves out of the interstices of the broken stone; a day spent wandering from one inconsequential colonnade to another. That was the whole point, of course.

They were utterly inconsequential those stones now – but once upon a time ... Ah, once upon a time they had been important – the exact position of each of consequence to somebody.

And today ... today the stones were just like any ruins anywhere and about as important ...

'Miss Tindall' – the voice was much more firm this time – 'I wonder if I might have a word with you?'

She turned.

Mr Gordon Cranswick was at her elbow. She had no idea how long he had been standing there.

I do haunt you still.   **14**

The various instruction courses attended by Police Superintendent Leeyes left their scars in a way which would have astonished the highly skilled instructors who lectured at them had they known.

Like a sticky snail the superintendent strewed a trail of imperfectly assimilated concepts behind him: not only did they show where he had been but they were a nuisance to the unwary. The latest one which he had gone to – on business management – had proved no exception to this unhappy rule.

Whether the sophisticated ideas of big business – in this case 'management by objectives' (objectives: commercial) – could be related to the police force (objectives: law and order) was doubtful. Naturally the course organizers, well able to count potential police heads, did not harp on this point.

As the burden of their spiel lay in measurement they were – from time to time – in difficulties about this. Measurement of commercial success requires only the ability to count. The proof of the police pudding isn't always in the eating. As any Home Secretary knows, measurement of successful police work takes a judicious blend of faith, hope, and charity.

There had been one other aspect of the management course dear to the hearts of the lecturers. It was called critical path analysis and it had made a deep impression on Superintendent Leeyes.

He had tried to explain it to Sloan.

'It's a great idea. You work out the right order for everything before you start doing anything.'

Sloan had given it an ear. The superintendent was given to instituting new ideas at the police station without much warning, and it was as well to be prepared.

'Then,' enthused Leeyes, 'you don't waste time going over the same ground twice.'

Sloan had been temperate in his response. Nothing was ever as easy as that.

'All you have to do,' the enthusiast had amplified, 'is to decide what's got to be done and then work out the best order to do it in.'

Sloan put the telephone down now after talking to Fenella Tindall and tried to do just that.

It wasn't easy.

What might pass for good organization in a biscuit factory might not be the best course of action in a murder hunt.

There was a pair of emerald and diamond clips unaccounted for – a pair of emerald and diamond clips which, after all, hadn't been a birthday present for Fenella Tindall. And if the receipt in his pocket was anything to go by, last seen with Richard Mallory Tindall.

There was a secret report about United Mellemetics about which much the same could be said. Unaccounted for and last seen with Richard Mallory Tindall.

There was an unknown Italian gentleman – and you couldn't, thought Sloan wryly, have a more sinister phrase than that. He and his wife, Margaret, were conscientious visitors of museums and art galleries. 'An unknown Italian gentleman' sounded like the title of a Renaissance painting. Anyway, whoever he was he had been careless enough to miss his aeroplane last night – the night on which Richard Tindall died. Sloan wasn't sure yet whether he ought to be worried about Giuseppe Mardoni or not.

There was – or rather, there wasn't – Gordon Cranswick, notable for his anxiety to buy Struthers and Tindall as speedily as possible – an anxiety which seemed to have dated only from yesterday afternoon. Mr Gordon Cranswick would have to –

Sloan dredged up another oft-repeated phrase from the super-intendent's Management Course – Mr Cranswick would clearly have to be gone into in depth.

Sir Digby Wellow was another in some sort of unavailable limbo. No one at his firm knew where he was and the Luston police couldn't find him either. Sloan wanted to talk to Sir Digby Wellow pretty badly.

There was Paul Blake, the handsome young man who hadn't done yesterday's work to order. He was the one, Mrs Turvey had said, with an eye to the main chance. Not, Sloan reminded himself acidly, that that should be thought a purely criminal characteristic . . .

There was a man called George Osborne, missing now and not at work yesterday lunchtime either . . .

And there was Fenella Tindall, who knew who it was the emerald and diamond clips were for – or he, Sloan, Calleshire born and bred – was a Dutchman.

And over in the village of Constance Parva there was someone who was nothing at all to do with the late Richard Mallory Tindall who was dipping a pen in pure vitriol to the consternation of all and sundry, but especially the sensitive.

The mayor – Sloan unconsciously straightened his shoulders – at least he knew where the mayor and his little troubles came in any critical path analysis of explaining Richard Tindall's sudden demise.

Then there was Richard Tindall himself, done to death all alone in a church tower, his solitary end engineered at dead of night . . .

Sloan paused in his appreciation of the situation.

Engineered.

Now he came to think of it it would take someone like an engineer to arrange for the Fitton Bequest to be poised so finely that it would fall on Richard Tindall at a given time and place – like when he was lying where he had been – at a moment when there was no one there to push it over.

He noted the thought and then put his plan of campaign into action.

*

Fenella started.

'If I might just have a word with you, Miss Tindall?'

'I have to go to the mortuary, Mr Cranswick.' At least he was less peremptory now.

'Oh, I see . . .' He paused, and then waved his hand. 'I'm very sorry about – er – all this.'

She braced herself.

That was another thing she would have to endure.

Sympathy.

She wasn't at all sure that she could take sympathy on top of everything else that had happened.

Something Shakespearian came unbidden to her mind. Something appropriate, of course. He was always appropriate. That had been his genius. What was the line?

'Of comfort, no man speak.'

She found to her surprise that she must have said it aloud.

Gordon Cranswick sounded surprised, too.

'Er – quite. Quite. I apologize. I am bound to be an intruder at a time like this . . .' He sounded expectant but Fenella said nothing so he hurried on: 'In the ordinary way, you realize, I should not have bothered you. You must be wondering why . . .'

Fenella inclined her head in what she hoped was a gesture of polite interest.

'It's your father's firm, Miss Tindall . . .'

'Yes?'

'I think you should know that yesterday afternoon he said that he would sell it to me after all.'

'After all?'

He cleared his throat portentously. 'Cranswick Processing have been interested in Struthers and Tindall for some time. We had been putting out feelers and so forth . . .'

He made it sound, thought Fenella rather wildly, like an Italian marriage.

'It was a natural move at this stage in our development,' said Gordon Cranswick, oblivious of her train of thought.

(Just like an Italian marriage, decided Fenella.)

'My board were right behind me, of course.'

(Parents and all.)

'We took advice on the financial aspects, naturally.'

(They did that in Italian marriages, too. First. Naturally.)

'And the long-term prospects looked sound.'

(They didn't begin negotiations in Italy unless they were happy about the future.)

'We had – on our side anyway – already gone into the ramifications of any – er – union.'

(In-laws.)

'And our solicitors were prepared at any time to meet with Struthers and Tindall . . .'

(The honest broker?)

'It seems,' continued Cranswick weightily, 'as if the outcome would be to our mutual advantage.'

Fenella nodded.

People always said mutual when they meant that they themselves benefited and didn't mind too much whether you did or not.

'Mind you,' added the businessman, striking a cautious note, 'Cranswick Processing have some prior commitments which would have to be taken into consideration.'

(In an Italian marriage contract it would be Great-Uncle Mauro's doctor's fees.)

'As I am sure Struthers and Tindall have, too.'

(And, in the other family, Cousin Luigi who wasn't quite right in the head.)

'Of course' – Gordon Cranswick cocked his head enquiringly – 'we may not be the only people in the field?'

(It was customary in Italy to establish first whether there were any other suitors.)

'That makes a difference, of course.'

(It made a difference in Italy, too.)

She became aware that Gordon Cranswick was looking at her this time as if he expected a positive response.

'Er – I'm sorry.' She started. 'I was thinking about something else. You were saying that a marriage had been arranged . . .'

Gordon Cranswick stared at her. 'I was talking about a takeover, Miss Tindall. Of Struthers and Tindall.'

'So you were. I'm sorry.' She pulled herself together. 'My father hadn't said anything to me, Mr Cranswick, about selling Struthers and Tindall to anyone.'

Yesterday she might have had the emotional energy to have felt hurt and angry about this.

But yesterday was a long, long way from today – farther than she would have thought possible – farther than the distance from the Palazzo Trallanti in Rome to the Dower House in Cleete. Her mind could take in that difference in space easily enough. Today – the today that was so far from yesterday in time – today she found she had no more feeling to spare.

'He always said no to me,' responded the businessman frankly, 'until yesterday afternoon. Then he changed his mind and said he'd sign on the dotted line today. Must have been almost the last thing he did before . . . before . . .'

'Not quite,' said Fenella astringently, a pair of emerald and diamond clips thrusting their way back into her mind.

'Oh? Anyway, that's why I'm here. And now,' he went on, not urgently, 'I need to know with whom to deal. You do see that, Miss Tindall, don't you?'

Fenella's hands strayed back towards her white bead necklace. How had that quotation gone on? There was a passage after those words about no comfort which she remembered having to learn too.

Long ago, it was, in another existence, when she hadn't a care in the world. In a chalky schoolroom, it had been, from a woman teacher who – she now realized – probably wasn't as desiccated as she seemed – when the whole class had been as detached from life and as cosseted as young queen bees in a hive.

Their Shakespeare class had been for something irrelevant called General Education.

There was a sudden crunching of car tyres on the gravel drive. Fenella looked out of the window and saw Police

Constable Hepple going out to greet another policeman. There was a policewoman sitting beside the driver.

Perhaps, thought Fenella, appreciating Shakespeare – the real man – marked a stage in everyone's development. By the time he was relevant you were no longer young and innocent.

That play – about no comfort – had been *King Richard II*. It was all coming back to her now. She could hear the voice of the English mistress as the words tumbled back into her mind and the rest of the quotation came to her: 'Let's choose executors and talk of wills.'

That was the moment when Police Constable Hepple came in to announce that the car had come to take her to the mortuary – and found Gordon Cranswick there.

And when Gordon Cranswick insisted with something of a return to his old manner, 'I want to buy the company, Miss Tindall. Now. And I'm not going to take no for an answer. Your father said I could and that's good enough for me.'

'But, Mr Cranswick,' she said, 'how do I know that?'

The search – police fashion – of the premises of Struthers and Tindall in Berebury's Wellgate was being conducted by the portly middle-aged Police Sergeant Wharton. His team had moved from the churchyard at Randall's Bridge.

It was no different from other searches anywhere else.

Sergeant Wharton ended up staring dispassionately at the crop of incongruities reaped during it.

It was a strange harvest and some of it was not his concern.

Like the reading matter of one of the technicians in the Testing Department who was apparently cherishing body-building notions. Wharton looked the man up and down and decided he wouldn't do for the Force, not unless his subscription had a good bit to go . . .

Or the small bar of plain chocolate kept by Miss Holroyd in a drawer quite clearly marked *Carbon Paper*.

Or the crossword puzzle – nearly completed – on the desk of someone else.

Some of it was his concern.

Like the books which the firm's accountant was standing over like a stag at bay. Wharton had sequestrated them nevertheless – without being unduly impressed. In his experience accountants were given to defending with their lives figures which could be seen by anyone in the published balance sheet; and it would take another accountant to establish whether there was anything to hide or this behaviour pattern was just habit.

The photocopy was his concern.

It was of one of Struthers and Tindall's patents and it had been folded neatly inside a telephone directory in Paul Blake's room. Sergeant Wharton gave his man full marks for finding that.

And Paul Blake none at all for his vehement denials that he knew anything about it.

Overdone, Wharton thought.

The experiment on which Henry Pysden was working was his concern. On sea-water magnesia, or so he was told. Wharton followed his instructions and noted the model number and the name of the makers of the time punch machine attached to the apparatus.

There was the petty cash which the office boy had put into his own pocket. But this, he insisted, he had only done as a precaution because there were so many policemen about.

'None of that, young man,' Wharton had said with dignity, 'or I'll take a magnifying glass to that old scooter outside. It is yours, I take it?'

The youth had paled into silence and Wharton had continued his stately way.

The foreman of Testing was speechless at the interruption to work but vocal about the police, the heat, United Mellemetics . . .

Wharton had pinned him down about United Mellemetics.

He – the foreman – didn't know what all the fuss was about. He had set up some experiments on detailed instructions from Mr Tindall last week. They were to do with the strength of pipes, their tensility, testing to see how ductile they would be under certain specified conditions – that sort of thing. The tests had been duly done and the results sent back to Mr Tindall.

The next thing he knew about them was this morning when Mr Pysden was round saying someone had lost the ruddy file. That was just before they heard the sad news about Mr Tindall. Well, he, the foreman, had certainly given the United Mellemetics stuff back to poor Mr Tindall; not that he could very well confirm it now, could he?

When?

Yesterday morning. The foreman didn't hesitate. The Wednesday. Put all the workings and results on Mr Tindall's own desk, he had, himself, and if anyone was going round saying anything different he would like to be told this minute . . .

Wharton, primed by Sloan, asked at what stage Paul Blake had checked the calculations.

The foreman assumed an expression which would have been recognized the world over as that of any seasoned noncommissioned officer on being given the opportunity to comment on the efficiency or otherwise of a junior officer. He very nearly took it, then discretion raised its careful head.

'Mr Paul Blake,' he said precisely, 'came down to Testing on Monday and checked our calculations, and also some which Mr Tindall had done himself.'

Sergeant Wharton looked at the foreman man-to-man. 'Everything all right there I take it?'

'Or I'd want to know the reason why,' said the foreman comfortably.

Sergeant Wharton went back to Henry Pysden's room.

One thing was apparent from the search.

United Mellemetics might not have existed at all for all the physical traces it had left at Struthers and Tindall.

He took out his notebook and said to Henry Pysden: 'I'll begin with you, sir, if I may. I need to know exactly where you were between the hours of ten thirty last night and two o'clock this morning . . .'

That lay in a dead palsy.

15

Fenella Tindall wasn't worried about her tummy. At least, not in the way Detective Constable Crosby had been.

In her case lunchtime had come and gone unremarked by either hunger or food. If she felt anything at all it was slightly sick.

That would be the smell of antiseptic in the mortuary.

She had already forgotten everything about the journey from the Dower House at Cleete to the police mortuary at Berebury. She had travelled there in silence beside an experienced policewoman who knew better than to try to distract her with kind words.

And she had walked into the mortuary in such an aura of disbelief that it was as if she were standing outside herself as she did so – watching dispassionately as a slight girl with auburn hair wearing a brown dress and a necklace of white beads took the few steps between car and door. It might have been someone else – not Fenella Tindall at all – she felt so detached.

The mortuary attendant said: 'This way, miss,' in totally matter-of-fact tones.

Fenella followed.

As she did so a tall good-looking young man uncoiled himself from beside the doorway.

The policewoman watched impassively as he went to Fenella's side.

'Paul!' Fenella halted. 'How kind of you to come.'

Paul Blake made an awkward gesture with one hand and with the other propelled her gently along the passage after the mortuary attendant.

'Sorry about all this,' he said. 'Thought I'd better turn up.'

The white-coated figure of the mortuary attendant disappeared down the passage and through another door beyond that. The smell of antiseptic got suddenly stronger, welling up ahead of them as they followed him.

'Oh . . .' Fenella gave way to a momentary pang of surprise as she saw the white-sheeted figure in the mortuary.

Paul Blake moved up behind Fenella and murmured, 'It won't take a minute.'

'Now, miss . . .' the man lowered his voice, 'if you'll just take a look . . .'

He needn't have bothered to speak in undertones. Fenella wasn't listening anyway. She was thinking about something else.

About Italy.

She'd seen death there, but it had been different. Not clinical and antiseptic like this. Not with clean white coats wrongly speaking of life not death. In Italy death was dark and medieval. The men near it – the Misericordia – were garbed in long black robes and hooded save their eyes. It was a dress which went back to the Plague.

She took a look at the face revealed by the mortuary attendant and nodded.

'That's my father.'

She would have liked to have said it was her grandfather whom she had seen – death had added a generation to her father's face.

'Richard Mallory Tindall,' she said in as firm a voice as she could manage.

'We can go back now,' said Paul Blake.

Actually the face Fenella wished she didn't have to look at was the mortuary attendant's.

She now knew why it was those men of the Misericordia – the Brethren of Mercy – were covered all over in black except for their eyes. It meant that the bereaved saw no face round the deceased – no face to associate for ever with moments like these. It would have meant that she would have been spared the memory of the mortuary attendant chirpily steering them back to his little office.

'Just one more thing, miss, and then we're done. Little matter of his effects.'

She stirred involuntarily at the word and then remembered.

The dead didn't have possessions, they had effects.

She became aware that he was asking her to identify some objects laid out in an orderly row on a table. There was some small change, his house keys, a wallet, a few notes, a slide rule, a pen and pencil, two handkerchiefs . . .

'Sign here, miss, please, that they're his.'

She made a slight movement away from the proffered form. 'They're not all there. There was his diary. It's a little leather one. I gave it to him. He always carried it with him. Always . . .'

The mortuary attendant sucked his teeth. 'That's gone to the Inspector, miss. He wanted that double quick.'

Detective Constable Crosby handed the diary – duly finger-printed – to Detective Inspector Sloan.

Sloan took the small leather-covered book and turned to Wednesday, July 16th.

That was yesterday.

Was it only yesterday?

His eye strayed involuntarily to Saturday, July 19th. That was the date engraved on his mind.

Show Day.

He looked out of the police station window and sighed. This strong sunshine would be bringing his Princess Grace of Monaco along too soon. She was a perfect rose, of course, but if it stayed as hot as this for too long she was going to be a perfect rose on Friday not Saturday.

'If you look under Wednesday, sir . . .' Crosby was getting restive.

Sloan switched his gaze back to the left-hand page. There

was just one entry in the little oblong space with that date on it. It was quite brief.

It said: *G. 12.30.*

'That's going to be a great help, Crosby, that is. G . . .' he said ruminatively. 'G for Giuseppe, do you suppose?'

The superintendent, he was sure, was going nap for Fenella.

'Or G for Gordon?' countered Crosby brightly. 'That's that fellow Cranswick's name, isn't it?'

'Or G for Osborne?' said Sloan.

'G for Osborne, sir?'

'George Osborne. He who has a wife and an invention.'

'Oh,' Crosby subsided. 'I'd forgotten about him.'

'A good police officer,' Sloan reminded him, 'can't afford to forget anything.'

'No, sir.'

'Ever.'

'Yes, sir.'

Sloan put the diary down and moved over to the wall. A large-scale map of Calleshire hung there.

Crosby joined him. 'We know, sir,' he said eagerly, 'that he left his works at twelve.'

'Miss Holroyd said he did,' murmured Sloan, unheeded, 'which isn't quite the same thing.'

'That gives him half an hour,' continued Crosby, missing the point.

'Fifteen miles at the outside,' said Sloan.

'Twenty, sir. Surely.'

'In an old van,' Sloan reminded him. 'Not in a souped-up police car with you at the wheel.'

'Fifteen then,' conceded Crosby.

'So where does that get us?'

It didn't get them very far.

Mahomet had agreed to go to the mountain.

Police Constable Hepple had been very persuasive. Not for nothing had he mastered the art of the quiet life. And the first rule for a quiet life is to arrange for all action to take place somewhere else.

Anywhere else.

That was how it was that Mr Gordon Cranswick found himself being interviewed by Detective Inspector Sloan at Berebury Police Station. In this case 'being interviewed' was something of a euphemism. It seemed at times as if the boot might be on the other foot.

Mr Gordon Cranswick, Chairman and Managing Director of Cranswick (Processing) Limited, was not only firmly planted in one of Sloan's office chairs, but was also making it quite clear that he wasn't going to budge from there until he himself took the decision to do so. He was, in fact, very busy demonstrating the fact that when Mr Gordon Cranswick was around Mr Gordon Cranswick took the decisions, sundry police detective inspectors notwithstanding.

'Now, what is all this about?' he demanded as soon as he set eyes on Sloan.

'The death of Richard Tindall,' said Sloan mildly.

He asked Cranswick what had brought him to Cleete.

'What brought me? Tindall, of course. Well, Struthers and Tindall, I suppose, to be strictly accurate.'

'The firm rather than the man?'

'It's the firm I'm interested in. Literally. Have been for some time. Just what Cranswick needed – their sort of business would back up our sort of business very nicely.'

'Your sort of business being . . .' enquired Sloan.

'Processing.' He waved a hand. 'Oh, I know that processing covers a multitude of sins but in the case of Cranswick it means that we take a patent belonging to a customer and do the lot with it.'

Sloan was guarded. 'The lot?'

'Develop, manufacture, and market. Struthers and Tindall are primarily testers.'

'So they would go rather well with you.'

Cranswick nodded vigorously. 'We realized that when we added up what we were paying them for their feasibility studies and so forth.'

'So?'

'So I set about trying to buy them.' Cranswick sat back in his chair. 'I won't say it was easy.'

'Oh?'

'Tindall wasn't all that keen on selling at first and then his wife died and that changed things a bit.'

Sloan nodded. It would.

'And then,' the businessman stirred irritably, 'something else cropped up.'

'Tell me.'

'Another buyer.'

'Who?'

'Tindall wouldn't say. Just told me that he'd had another offer better than mine.'

'You believed him?'

Cranswick shrugged. 'Why not? I could always prove it by leaving him with it if I wanted to.'

'You didn't want to?'

'I did not. I wanted Struthers and Tindall and I knew I'd have to pay for it. It's a good firm, you know. Sound. But it wasn't going for a song.'

'So someone else wanted it, too.'

'Pretty badly, I should say, from what they were willing to offer. Still, I reckoned that if it was worth it to them it was worth it to me.'

'Quite,' said Sloan. People wrote books on political economy but in the end decisions came down to homespun yardsticks like this whatever the professors had to say. 'So in the end yours was the better offer?'

'No,' said Gordon Cranswick unexpectedly, 'it wasn't. They – whoever they were – were prepared to overbid me.'

'But . . .'

'But,' he said heavily, 'Tindall wasn't prepared to sell to them. Said he'd found out something about their methods which he didn't like and if my offer was still good he'd take it.'

'When?'

'Tuesday evening.'

'Where?'

'Ah,' Gordon Cranswick leaned forward. 'That's just it. He rang me from a call box and suggested a quiet meeting somewhere simple where nobody knew us.'

'At twelve-thirty yesterday?'

'That's right. At Dick's Dive. It's a transport café half-way down the Calleford road – on the way to Luston . . .'

'We know it,' said Sloan. All policemen knew all transport cafés in their area.

'Actually,' admitted Cranswick, sounding surprised, 'the food was pretty good.'

'It has to be,' said Sloan, 'or the customers vote with their wheels.'

'What? Oh, yes, of course . . . Well, that's where Richard Tindall told me that he was willing to cut these other people out and sell to me at my last offer and on my terms . . .'

'On your terms?'

'I wasn't prepared to be hamstrung by any silly agreements about keeping people on. I run Cranswick my way and if the Struthers and Tindall people didn't like it they would have to go . . .'

'These other people who wanted to buy, he didn't tell you who they were or what methods he didn't like?'

Cranswick's brow wrinkled. 'Not exactly but he did say I needn't worry. He'd deal with them before he left.'

'And then?'

'Then I went back to town to see my bankers and solicitors and arranged to come down here first thing this morning to sign on the dotted line.'

Sloan nodded and pushed his notebook into a slightly more prominent position. 'Now, sir, if you would tell me exactly where you were between ten thirty last night and two o'clock this morning . . .'

The next call Sloan had was from the mortuary.

Dr Dabbe was ready for him.

Being Dr Dabbe it was a case of being ready and waiting.

'I've started on some of the groundwork, Sloan. That blood

on the floor, for instance, was Tindall's all right. And it had splashed down while he was lying there. While he was alive, of course. There was no more blood after the sculpture came down. That was what killed him.'

Sloan nodded.

'I should say he was hit a yard or two short of the sculpture – say just inside the door – and then dragged across the floor until he was lying practically beneath the sculpture. As to what he was hit with . . .'

'Yes?'

'You couldn't call the edges of the wound well defined but whatever it was it was enough to knock him out – sorry – render him unconscious – got to mind my p's and q's with you people . . .'

Sloan grinned. There was English, Police English, and medical words, and nobody knew this better than the pathologist.

'. . . say something like an old sock filled with sand – I'll look out for grains of sand presently. And the blow was well aimed.'

'Just the one?'

The pathologist nodded. 'And from behind.'

'A weapon,' remarked Sloan, 'would be nice.'

'Nothing to touch 'em with juries,' agreed the doctor. 'Now, Sloan, I think you'll be interested in some mental arithmetic I've been doing. Algebra, really.'

'Oh, yes, Doctor?' Sloan was wary in his response this time. Police work was one thing. Algebra was quite another.

'You can do any equation if you know all the quantities, of course.'

'Yes, Doctor.' He agreed to that readily enough.

'You can do quite a few with one unknown quantity.'

'I'm sure you can, Doctor.'

'And you can do one or two with two or more unknowns.'

'Can you, Doctor?'

'Our equation, Sloan,' said the pathologist, waving a hand at the sheaf of papers which Burns, his assistant, was working on, 'concerns the time of death of Richard Mallory Tindall.'

'Good.'

'Our known factors are what the deceased had to eat at seven thirty last evening . . .'

Sloan nodded. That wasn't exactly blinding him with mathematics.

'. . . confirmed by Mrs Marcia Osborne, plus a drink, the time he had it, and the size of the drink.' Dr Dabbe raised his eyebrows appreciatively. 'Talk about dishy. Our Mrs Osborne's quite a stunner, isn't she?'

'I couldn't say, Doctor,' said Sloan a trifle stiffly. 'I sent my constable.'

'Bad luck. Still, you'll have to go again, I dare say. Her old man still hadn't shown up all through the dinner hour, did you know that?'

'I did.'

'Sorry. I forgot it was the close season for suspects. Your bird, of course. Where was I?'

'Doing an equation.'

'Oh, yes. Food plus time lapsed after its consumption equated to state of digestion of deceased gives you the time of death.' Dr Dabbe twiddled a pencil. 'And if that's not good enough there's the state of the brain tissue. That's always good enough.'

'Always?'

'Given these factors,' said the pathologist, ignoring this, 'all I had to do then was to work on his stomach and brain and one or two other oddments and put them down, too, and Bob's your uncle.'

'Your equation?'

'Exactly. Narrows the time of death very nicely.'

Sloan turned back the pages of his notebook to his record of his interview with the two spinsters at Vespers Cottage by the churchyard.

'Would I be very far out, Doctor, if I said it was somewhere about two o'clock this morning?'

'You would,' said Dr Dabbe placidly. 'Very.'

'Very?'

'Two and a half hours out. Give me those papers, Burns.'

Sloan stared at him. 'Two and a half hours? That means you make it . . .'

'According to my equation,' said the pathologist, still amiable, 'which Burns here has just finished checking and which I am prepared to read out in open court, I make the time of death near eleven thirty last night.'

'How near?' enquired Sloan.

'As near as dammit,' said the pathologist graphically.

He did suspect me wrongfully. **16**

There was quite a plaintive note in Detective Constable Crosby's voice.

'What I don't understand, sir, is why this guy who did it . . .'

'Yes?' It was funny, reflected Sloan, how the very word 'murderer' stuck in your throat . . .

How you didn't use it unless you had to . . .

Not even Crosby . . .

Not even now they'd done away with the death penalty . . . and they'd got the life penalty instead.

Well, the quarter life penalty. It wasn't really life any longer . . .

Sloan made himself stop thinking about prison sentences.

It upset him too much.

They'd stopped talking about them at the police station long ago.

'What about him, Crosby?'

'Why didn't he just hit him a bit harder the first time and be done with it?'

'I don't know.'

'So what this guy did then, sir, was to arrange for this great lump of stuff to fall while Tindall was lying dead to the world in the right place underneath it.'

'That's all, Crosby.'

Perhaps there was something to be said for a certain simplicity of approach, after all . . .

'So,' said Crosby, negotiating a right-hand turn, 'it's just a case of how and who, sir, then, is it?'

'Don't strain yourself, will you?'

'Oh, and why, sir?' added the constable seriously.

'Strictly speaking,' amended Sloan fairly, his sarcasm evaporating as quickly as it had conjured itself up, 'I suppose we don't really need to know why . . .'

'Don't we?'

'But,' he added sardonically, 'the jury like it.'

Sloan thought back to the bloodless crumpled figure lying on the church tower floor and wondered how much motive they were going to need to make head or tail of that.

He dismissed the image immediately.

Between them he could be sure that the cynics and the psychiatrists could explain everything.

He was a policeman and he should know that by now.

The constable was talking again.

'It'll tell us who, sir, won't it, if we can find out why?'

'I hope so, Crosby,' he replied heavily. 'I'm sure I hope so.'

There was always that. Perhaps the boy was learning something after all. Sloan scratched his chin and glanced down at his notes.

There was no help there.

They were as meagre as a Spanish anchor.

'At this rate,' he added pessimistically, 'we'll just have to ask whoever did it to tip us the wink on how he did it when we've got him.'

'Yes, sir.'

'Because – quite apart from why – I'm hanged if I know how you arrange for a sculpture to be pushed over without being in there to do it.'

'The little window,' suggested Crosby helpfully.

'The little window,' agreed Sloan. 'We've got as far as that already. Somebody put that ladder up against the wall and poked something through the window and knocked the Fitton

Bequest off its plinth and then drove the deceased's car back to Cleete.'

'But not the night fisherman at two o'clock this morning.'

'At approximately ten minutes to eleven,' said Sloan crisply, 'someone was there doing something and they were gone by eleven if the evidence of the schoolmaster and those two dotty women is to be believed and he died at approximately eleven-thirty . . .'

They would have to take Dr Dabbe for gospel – however inconvenient – because everyone else would.

'. . . when Gordon Cranswick was having a nightcap in his room in his hotel in London, Paul Blake tucked up in bed at his lodgings, Mrs Osborne tucked up in bed with Mr Osborne, which isn't evidence, and Henry Pysden kipped down at the works after doing his bit on his experiment . . .'

'. . . and Sir Digby Wellow, Giuseppe Mardoni, and Fenella Tindall unaccounted for,' finished Crosby.

Sloan looked at him with disfavour. Crosby was getting more like the superintendent every day.

'There are one or two interesting events in Richard Tindall's last forty-eight hours, Crosby, which have not, I hope, entirely escaped your attention . . .'

'Losing that file at the works,' he said promptly. 'The United Mellemetics one.'

'The purchase,' said Sloan, 'of a pair of emerald and diamond clips . . .'

'And,' Crosby chipped in, 'him deciding to sell the business to Cranswick Processing.'

'Plus the discovery that someone was trying to buy the firm by methods he didn't like. Someone else.'

'That and getting himself done,' added Crosby simply.

Sloan abandoned his train of thought. 'We mustn't forget that, must we?'

The next two reports to come in were both about the Italian, Giuseppe Mardoni.

One was from London.

The Metropolitan Police had checked as requested with the car-hire firm from which Mardoni had rented the car he had used in England. They reported that the vehicle had been returned as arranged to the airport. The time of the check-in had been just before three o'clock in the morning.

The second came from Inspector Harpe and asked Sloan to drop by when he was near the Traffic Department.

'I may be wasting your time, Sloan,' began that worthy with characteristic pessimism, 'but I thought you might like to know that two of my patrol boys turned something up about Wednesday night.'

'I would.'

'They were chatting up the blokes at the all-night garage on the Calleford road . . . they always keep in well with them . . .'

So much, thought Sloan, for all those voluntary advisers of the police who thought traffic should be separated from police work.

They forgot that man was now a motorized animal.

'The garage had a call-out to a foreign gent late last night.'

'Did they?' responded Sloan alertly. 'And what time was this, may I ask? Did they remember?'

'Course they remembered,' said an aggrieved Harpe. 'Just about half-eleven. Very excited, they said the chap was. All over a puncture.'

'He had a plane to catch,' remarked Sloan absently. 'Did you say puncture?'

'A flat, anyway. The garage didn't repair it. They just changed the wheel for him. Put the spare on and got him going again.'

Sloan flipped back through his notes. 'Couldn't he change a wheel? I thought he was an engineer of sorts – oh, no. A civil engineer.'

'Couldn't see to change a wheel,' said Harpe. 'No torch.'

Sloan sighed. 'And where was all this?'

Inspector Harpe rolled his eyes expressively. 'Need you ask, Sloan? It was where they laid the tar on the Berebury to Randall's Bridge road in the morning. It's always like this when the County have had a go at the road. Punctures and windscreens shattering for days afterwards. Nothing but trouble.'

Sloan nodded briefly. Happy Harry wasn't the only one with troubles. There was nothing easier to contrive than a flat tyre. Someone in Mets was going to have to go round to the car hire firm at the airport and check if that puncture had been genuine or a convenient alibi.

'Half-past eleven,' he said, 'and Fenella Tindall says he left her at half-past ten at Cleete. I wonder where the hour went.'

'I can tell you that,' rejoined Harpe. 'Walking along the Berebury road in the dark looking for a telephone kiosk. He'd be a good three miles from anywhere there, wouldn't he?'

'Couldn't he have got a lift?'

'That road isn't exactly Piccadilly Circus after dark now, is it, Sloan? Anyway, who's going to pick up a foreigner at that hour of the night? For all we know he may look like Sweeney Todd.'

'Machiavelli, more like.' Sloan sighed. Neither of them knew what he really looked like, though there was nothing he himself would like more this minute than a sight of Giuseppe Mardoni. 'And then he'd have to find out who to ring.'

'There was some sort of handbook in the car with addresses and so forth.'

'So he could read and speak English all right . . .'

'Looks like it.'

'I thought he might.' Sloan made another note in his book.

Perhaps Giuseppe Mardoni had become a little less nebulous now but he was still shadowy.

Everyone in the case seemed just out of reach.

Giuseppe Mardoni.

George Osborne.

Sir Digby Wellow.

At least Gordon Cranswick was more substantial now than he had been. Heaven only knew where he'd got to, now, though. Luston, probably, thought Sloan morosely, to make an offer for United Mellemetics. They couldn't keep him at the station, for all that the superintendent would like to have done. And Cranswick would know that . . .

'Perhaps the airport people will come up with something,' he said to Happy Harry. 'There's always a chance of that.'

But there was no comfort to be had from that Jeremiah.

'Makes it difficult, doesn't it?' agreed Harpe with a melancholy nod. 'How are you getting on with the Tindall end of things?'

'All I want there,' said Sloan with feeling, 'is some idea of how you arrange to kill a man without being there to do it. Half an hour after you've gone away, in fact.'

'He wasn't starved to death, was he?' enquired the Traffic inspector with interest. 'I read a book once about a millionaire who died shut up in a gymnasium with plenty of food. Starved to death. Proper mystery it was, too. What these Indians had done was to hoist his bed forty feet up in the air with pulleys and then let it down again after he'd died . . .'

The superintendent's reaction to the news about Giuseppe Mardoni was immediate, predictable, and not without glee.

'Complicity, Sloan. I've said so all along.'

'Er – who with, sir?'

'The girl, of course. She drives the car back to Cleete. He waits behind in the churchyard and pokes something through the little window and then sets off for the airport.'

'And the two o'clock trip? There was someone about then, sir.'

'A fisherman. Like those two old women said.'

Sloan didn't tell Superintendent Leeyes that he'd already sent Crosby off to see the angling people. Both lots – the Calleshire Freshwater Club and the River Calle Angling Society – to see if they had any night-fishing competitions laid on. Or if they knew if any of their members went fishing at two o'clock in the morning on Thursday.

Nothing would surprise him about fishermen.

Nothing.

And he didn't want any case of his to founder on the life cycle of the roach.

When he came to think about it being aware of the close season for coarse fish wasn't all that far from Sherlock Holmes and his seventy-five varieties of perfume.

'What about the other alibis?' asked Leeyes.

'Henry Pysden's is the only one that's cast iron. The others are a bit – er – circumstantial, sir. Even Sir Digby Wellow's . . .'

That had been something of a delicate chat.

And it wasn't what he'd joined the Force for.

Ringing a titled lady he'd never seen to ask if she'd spent the night with her husband, while Crosby set about discovering the private life of the trout.

Lady Wellow's voice had been cool. 'I heard the odd snore, Inspector. Through the wall.'

'Er – yes, of course, madam – er – milady.'

'We have separate rooms. My husband likes a hard mattress – for his back, you know. I like a soft one.'

Sloan had tapped his pencil to an old metre.

Jack Sprat could eat no fat,
His wife could eat no lean . . .

Why were there nursery rhymes everywhere he looked today?

Not that there was anything particularly childish about Lady Wellow's tone.

It was ironic, detached.

'Are you trying to tell me, Inspector,' she had said, 'that Sir Digby spent the night somewhere else?'

'No, milady.'

And so betwixt them both, you see
They licked the platter clean.

'Only trying to be sure that he spent it in Luston.'

'I see. He grunted when he took his shoes off. He always does. I heard that, too.'

'When?'

'About midnight.'

That wasn't evidence, either, of course.

Not yet, anyway.

It would be soon.

If the reformers got their way.

When a husband could give evidence against his wife and vice versa.

When you wouldn't be able to tell the Criminal Court from the Matrimonial one.

He didn't know if that was a blow for Women's Lib or not.

The superintendent had started up again. He had a piece of paper in his hand.

'The handwriting people say those letters from Constance Parva are all written by the same person.'

'So far,' said Sloan. 'They won't stay that way for long.'

There was nothing more infectious than a poison pen. Once the idea cottoned on all manner of people would be taking to it. Old scores would be settled by the dozen. Pale – and not so pale – imitations would hurtle round the village before long, seeding as fast as Enchanter's Nightshade.

'And that shoe, Sloan . . .'

'The golf course one?'

'They've found its mate.'

'Where?'

'Behind the fourth green.'

'But nothing else?'

'Not yet,' said Leeyes ominously.

The next two messages were both for Detective Inspector Sloan.

Both concerned the transport café on the outskirts of Berebury near the junction of the Luston and Calleford roads. It was called simply Dick's and all the heavy transport in the western half of the county used it. Its bumpy potholed car park was the only place for miles around where there was room and to spare for a dozen lorries and their trailers.

The first was in the form of a report from one of Inspector Harpe's traffic patrol car drivers. He had noted a small grey van parked at Dick's yesterday. The van answered to the description of the radio message issued at thirteen hundred hours. He had observed it at the transport café at about dinnertime yesterday. At about half-past twelve.

The second message wasn't couched in anything like so stately terms.

It had come from Dick himself.

In a hoarse, hurried voice.

'A bloke,' he said, 'in a car on the park. Dead. Thought he'd had a heart attack, they did. Until they saw the hole in the back of his head.'

Diamonds are of most value
they say that have passed through most
jewellers' hands.

17

Even as he crossed the car park of Dick's transport café, Sloan
appreciated what a choice spot for murder it made.

Giant articulated trailers obligingly screened the car in
which the dead man lay from the view of all but those who
passed very near. It was parked well away at the back, beyond
two Continental trailers resting on their way to Romania.

It had been the Romanian drivers who had spotted the
crumpled driver and – to their eternal credit – who had then
drawn attention to him.

'Take their numbers,' ordered Sloan automatically, 'and
everyone else's. Nobody to leave the place until I say.'

He had help this time.

Two of Inspector Harpe's men, whose patrol car was never
far from this stretch of main road, were there for the asking.
They would take all the numbers and stop anyone slipping
away from the café. At the moment it looked as if – rather
than go – everyone at Dick's had decided to stay.

They were all clustered round a large black car.

'We get all sorts here,' said Dick, the proprietor. He was
referring to the opulence of the car and its gleaming chro-
mium. 'Nowhere else to eat and park for miles.'

'Had he been in?' asked Sloan.

The café owner shook his head. 'Not that I'd noticed.'

The dead man was slumped forward over the steering wheel,
folds of flesh overlapping a tight collar, his face an unhealthy

white. Sloan went round and peered in through the windscreen. Even his best friends might not have recognized the man now – not with his glazed eyes staring sightlessly at nothing and his jaw hanging slackly downwards.

Sloan certainly didn't.

The car had a Calleshire registration number, though.

'Crosby, take this number and find out who the car belongs to.'

He turned to the watching crowd of men.

'Anyone see anything?'

Nobody answered. One or two at the edge of the crowd started to drift back towards the café.

'Anyone notice how long this car has been here?'

That was more productive.

A driver and his mate with strong Yorkshire accents hadn't seen it when they had hauled their giant load on to the forecourt.

''Bout 'alf an hour ago that would have been, mate. At least. Happen a bit more. That's us over there.' He pointed to a loaded lorry. 'Hobblethwaite Castings. T'car wasn't 'ere then.'

The time of their arrival was confirmed by Dick himself.

'Two pies and peas, wasn't it, lads?'

They nodded.

'Just finished them, we 'ad, when we 'eard there was summat up out 'ere.'

'You won't get quicker service on the road anywhere in Calleshire,' said the café proprietor proudly. 'Nobody waits long for his dinner at Dick's.'

Sloan cut this commercial short. 'Anyone notice any other private car on the park?'

Nobody had.

Crosby came back from sending his radio message about the car number and Sloan packed his audience back into the café with Inspector Harpe's two men.

Then he turned to Crosby. 'Well?'

'Hit hard on the back of the head, sir.' Crosby peered forward. 'No weapon in sight.'

'We'll search for that presently. Anything else?'

Crosby took another look. 'Was he hit here, sir? In the car?'

'Looks like it.' Sloan stared at the big car that had every-thing: including room to swing a cat. Or a weapon.

'You could do it from the back seat easy, sir. Plenty of elbow room.'

'Anything else?'

'Not very long ago?' offered the constable tentatively. 'The engine's still a bit warm.'

'It isn't the only thing,' said Sloan. The sun was getting hotter by the hour.

'Nothing else to see,' reported Crosby.

'Pity,' said Sloan. He hoped that the Superintendent's famous exchange principle would still hold good.

'And no signs of a struggle.'

'Someone he knew perhaps . . .'

Both policemen were still standing looking at the dead man when the police radio in their car started to chatter.

'Foxtrot Delta one six, Foxtrot Delta one six . . .'

Crosby went over to the car and made an answer.

The voice of the girl at the microphone in the control room at the Constabulary Headquarters in Calleford echoed nasally across the café forecourt.

'Foxtrot Delta one six . . . the car number which was the subject of your inquiry of fourteen thirty-seven hours . . .'

Sloan listened impatiently. Time and number, that was all County Headquarters cared about. That and making a record of everything.

The girl's voice droned on, oblivious of his thoughts: '. . . is registered in the name of the firm of United Mellemetics Limited, Jubilee Works, Luston, Calleshire . . .'

Fenella wondered how it was that she could ever have thought that the Dower House had seemed empty before. It was nothing then to how it felt now.

The same police car which had taken her to the mortuary brought her back to Cleete. It was inevitable, she supposed, that their route had lain through Randall's Bridge. All roads to the south crossed the river there. There was no other way. Even so she could have wished that they did not have to pass that grey square tower . . .

Why the church at Randall's Bridge anyway . . .

She shook her head ever so slightly. She knew the answer to that. Someone had told her. The detective inspector. She remembered now. It was when she was still thinking in terms of an accident.

Not an accident, he'd said, hadn't he?

When she'd asked why it was that the sculpture hadn't just slipped.

Ever so kindly he had explained that heavy sculptures don't just slip on their own at eleven thirty at night in church towers that may or may not have been locked – and that they slip more easily still if they happen to have had little wedges driven under their plinths to help them on their way . . .

The house echoed to her footsteps as she walked through it again. Her first thought was to open a few windows. Even an hour with them closed on a day like this gave the building a stuffy shut-up feeling. The policewoman had offered to stay with her but Fenella had declined. Mrs Turvey, too, had gone home. She had a husband to feed, but she would be back. Fenella knew that.

The house seemed so empty that presently Fenella began to find the feeling oppressive. She took herself out into the garden. Gardens never felt quite so empty in the way that houses did . . . there weren't objects everywhere you looked which reminded you of people who weren't there any more.

She wandered about looking for somewhere to sit. There was too much sunshine for any of the usual places. Besides, living in Italy had conditioned her to seek shade not sunshine.

She gave a short laugh to herself.

Who would have thought that so brief a time in Italy would have made such an impression on her?

She would go back.

Not straight away.

When everything here at Cleete had been sorted out.

When the police had got to the bottom of all that had happened.

When they had found out the naked truth.

Once she'd wondered why people called the truth naked but not after she'd been north to Florence from Rome with Principessa Trallanti and the children.

The Principessa had watched her enjoy Florence, take in the mellowed red roofs, the black and white churches, the sculpture and the paintings before remarking in her dry, precise English: 'Everyone, Miss Tindall, is either a Florentine or a Roman at heart. One or the other. Never both. Even Signor Mardoni.'

This last had been because of Giuseppe Mardoni. Roman to his fingertips, his frequent visits to the Palazzo Trallanti had been noticed even by the Principessa.

Much as Fenella herself loved Rome she had plumped for being a Florentinian.

'Most English people do,' the Principessa had said, unsurprised.

It was on that visit to Florence that she had seen the Naked Truth.

In a picture in the Uffizi Gallery.

A Botticelli.

The picture wasn't called *Truth*. It was called *Calumny*.

It was a painting of a mythical Hall of Justice, with an enthroned judge. Only this judge was seated between two figures representing Suspicion and Ignorance. Two other figures – Spite and Calumny – were dragging a naked figure – Truth – before the judge. Duplicity and Deceit were attempting to adorn Truth, while a grim figure – old and dressed in deep black – called Penitence – looked on.

'They're all women,' she remembered stammering to the Principessa.

But that worldly noblewoman had seen nothing out of the ordinary in that.

Nor in Penitence's mourning garb.

'But she's so . . . haggard,' insisted Fenella.

'You are still young, Miss Tindall.' The Principessa had raised a hand that was gloved in spite of the heat. 'In time you will see what penitence does to people.'

Fenella found a nice patch of shade under an old beech tree and settled herself there. She could see the front of the house from where she sat and it was as good a place as any to be while she considered what had to be done. Her father had some cousins still – they would have to be told – so would her aunts – her mother's sisters . . .

She heard a car crunch up the drive and from her position under the trees saw a man get out and go up to the front door. He seemed to ring the bell and then step back quickly and do something with his hands in front of him.

She stayed where she was.

When there was no answer to his second ring he stepped off the gravel drive and on to the grass and repeated the action.

Fenella froze into immobility.

What he was doing was taking photographs.

The Press.

He must be from the Press.

A reporter.

She watched as he made his way round the house taking pictures as he pleased. He didn't catch sight of her shrinking against the bole of the beech tree though, and eventually he went back to his car and drove off.

It must have been something over half an hour after that when another car drew up at the Dower House. She did stir herself then and walked over towards it. She'd recognized the woman who'd got out of the car. Only one woman of her acquaintance would have set out for the depths of the country in the middle of the afternoon in a heat wave so impossibly overdressed.

Marcia Osborne.

Fenella made her way across the grass as Marcia picked her steps carefully over the gravel towards the door bell. Fenella almost grinned. The gravel wasn't so rough but no doubt

Marcia's shoes weren't up to anything stronger than carpet. They never were.

'Fenella! Coooooeeeee . . .'

Marcia had seen her at last and turned away from the front door and the painful gravel towards the grass.

Now that she was nearer Fenella could take in the full splendour of her outfit. Marcia Osborne was wearing a grey silk suit shot with green which was very, very smart. Her handbag and gloves and shoes tied up with the green colour in the suit in a way that must have taken days of careful matching. The whole ensemble was topped by a wide-brimmed hat designed to make absolutely sure that not a single ray of sunshine beat down on Marcia's precious complexion.

It was the wide-brimmed hat which concealed the earrings from Fenella's view at first. Fenella herself would not have considered wearing earrings at teatime but she was not particularly surprised that Marcia had them on. Marcia was like that. And her earrings, inherited from her Great-Aunt Edith, had frequent airings.

She had nearly reached Fenella – having done the lawn very little good with the heels of her shoes on the way – before Fenella got a really good look at her.

What she saw sent a cold shiver down her spine.

Besides the earrings Fenella was wearing a pair of matching clips.

They were unmistakably emerald and diamond.

18

'Who?' howled Superintendent Leeyes. He was never a man to count up to ten anyway.

'Sir Digby Wellow,' repeated Sloan.

He was tired of saying the name now. He'd said it again and again and had been met on all sides with shocked disbelief. There was a posse of incredulous men even now on their way from Luston making all possible speed just to confirm this very fact.

Not that Sloan himself was in any doubt. Not since he'd heard who the car at Dick's café belonged to, and done a few calculations. Sir Digby Wellow must have left Luston just before Sloan had tried to telephone him there.

'Wellow of United Mellemetics?' asked Leeyes. He had come back to the news after his weekly session with the Chairman of the Watch Committee. 'The one whose secret file is missing from Struthers and Tindall?'

'That's the one,' said Sloan, adding flatly, 'and he's been murdered too.'

'This file then . . .' began the superintendent excitedly.

'Is still missing.' Sloan finished the sentence for him. 'Struthers and Tindall have turned their place upside down and still say they can't find it. I had the whole building properly searched and Sergeant Wharton can't find it either.'

'But what was in it, man? That's what counts.' Sparring with the Watch Committee chairman always made Leeyes tetchy. What it did to the chairman Sloan could only imagine.

'Your guess, sir,' responded Sloan evenly, 'is as good as mine. Or anyone else's, sir, come to that. As I said before all the paperwork – even the scrap – is kept with the file and goes back to the customer. And Struthers and Tindall keep no records. That's even part of their contract apparently.'

'Someone must have worked on it, Sloan.'

'Paul Blake and Richard Tindall himself.'

'Well . . .'

'Blake says that all he did was to check some workings that Tindall had done on the coefficients of expansion.'

'United Mellemetics must know,' said Leeyes.

'No, they don't,' countered Sloan, who had had a long telephone conversation with a bewildered deputy chairman at United Mellemetics. Edward Foster had sounded to Sloan like one of those who have had greatness thrust upon them . . . unless he had got the way he had through perpetually working in the shadow of the forceful Sir Digby Wellow.

'But . . .'

'United Mellemetics didn't even know Sir Digby had taken one of their problems to Struthers and Tindall, sir. Could have been anything, this chap Foster said.'

'He must know what sort of work they've got on the go there, Sloan.' Superintendent Leeyes always knew what was going on in his manor.

Sloan consulted his notebook. 'Foster says they've just designed a new instrument for checking the performance of a solar energy source to provide impressed current for cathodic protection of underground pipe lines.'

'Nice work,' said Leeyes cordially, 'if you can get it.'

'And another,' pursued Sloan, 'for measuring internal corrosion rates of lines.'

The superintendent took a deep breath and rapidly reduced the situation to police level. 'Sir Digby Wellow sends an unknown problem to Struthers and Tindall and Richard Tindall goes and gets himself murdered in this peculiar fashion.'

Sloan agreed.

'Then the file on this unknown problem disappears.'

'Yes, sir.' That was true, too.

'Then,' declared Leeyes incontrovertibly, 'Sir Digby Wellow gets murdered as well.'

'Yes, sir.'

There was no denying that, either. Dr Dabbe had been and gone and said the same thing about the body on Dick's café forecourt.

And muttered about the wound. The pathologist wasn't prepared to commit himself at this stage but the two head wounds had a lot in common.

'Someone arranged a meeting there,' went on Leeyes. 'Set up the whole thing, I dare say.'

'I think so,' said Sloan carefully. 'It's where Tindall met Gordon Cranswick yesterday, too.'

'After which,' remarked Leeyes with celerity, 'he came back to Berebury having told this fellow Cranswick he was willing to sell out Struthers and Tindall to Cranswick Processing?'

'So Cranswick says, sir. So Cranswick says.'

This time when he got back to his own room again there was only one piece of paper on Sloan's desk.

It was the slightly tattered critical path analysis which he had drawn up that morning after the finding of Richard Tindall's body in the church at Randall's Bridge.

He looked at it for a long moment and then laid it gently on one side.

Critical path analyses took no account of suddenly dead chairmen in company cars on the forecourts of good pull-ups for carmen.

Then he had a second thought.

It could go the same way as the normal distribution curves which had so intrigued Superintendent Leeyes the month before. He punted it across the desk and into the wastepaper basket, sent for Crosby and a car, and got down to business.

'Luston first, Crosby. United Mellemetics' Jubilee Works.'

And then back to Struthers and Tindall. Any more news from Dick's café?'

'They're still taking statements out there, sir.'

'Get some photographs for them, too. Show them one of everybody.'

'Everybody?'

'The lot,' repeated Sloan wearily. 'The mayor, too, if you like. Paul Blake, Gordon Cranswick, Henry Pysden, this fellow Osborne, that Italian . . . Interpol will get you a photograph of him – and Sir Digby, of course.'

'Sir Digby, sir? All the people at Dick's café have seen him already.'

'He didn't look like he did today yesterday,' Sloan reminded him grimly. 'His own mother mightn't have known him today.'

'No, sir.'

Nor Lady Wellow, thought Sloan, making a note.

Sir Digby wouldn't be grunting when he undid his shoelaces tonight. Somebody would have to talk to her, too, soon.

Crosby swung the police car out on to the big roundabout on the outskirts of Berebury and pulled over towards the Luston road.

There was one other matter on Sloan's mind.

'You put someone to keep an eye on those two odd old women at Vespers Cottage, Crosby, didn't you?'

'Yes, sir. Like you said. An unobtrusive watch.'

'I think they're material witnesses,' said Sloan. 'Not that I particularly want them in court for Defence Counsel to play with.'

'No, sir.' Crosby changed gear.

'And someone who could kill Richard Tindall and Sir Digby Wellow would kill them without batting an eyelid. In cold blood.' Sloan scratched his chin, recalling something. He went to lectures, too. Not as often as the superintendent but now and again. In the line of duty. At one of them he'd heard the lecturer say something about how a man killed . . .

'But, sir,' Crosby interrupted his train of thought, 'what

they saw was at two o'clock this morning. Dr Dabbe says Richard Tindall was killed at half-past eleven last night.'

'Dr Dabbe,' said Sloan tersely, 'only has to report on his findings. You and I, Crosby, have also to do a little thing called solve the case – which is something quite different.'

'Yes, sir.'

Blinkov had been the name that the lecturer had quoted. Sloan had remembered it because half the audience had thought the speaker had been having them on. Blinkov the Russian. Cousin to Inoff the Red, a billiards man had suggested derisively.

Blinkov, if he remembered rightly, had argued that the coarse murdered coarsely, the refined and delicate temperament found a way of doing the job in a refined and delicate way.

And the scientific scientifically?

Sloan glanced down at his notebook.

'Do you realize, Crosby, that all these men we've been dealing with have something in common?'

'No, sir.'

Sloan sighed. At least Crosby never pretended to knowledge that he hadn't got. Perhaps in an odd sort of way that was something to be thankful for.

'They're all clever types, Constable, that's what.' His mind went back to the church tower. 'Very clever types you might say.'

Crosby assented to this. 'That was a clever way to kill someone over at Randall's Bridge, sir. Getting that sculpture to fall on the poor chap without being in there with him to do it at the same time.'

'You can say that again.' Sloan ran his finger down the list and wondered what Blinkov would have made of it. 'Henry Pysden and Paul Blake are working scientists. We know that. And George Osborne's the physics master at the grammar school. Who's gone round to keep an eye on him when he does turn up, by the way?'

'Appleton, sir.'

'Good.' Sloan went back to his list. 'Gordon Cranswick

and Sir Digby Wellow presumably know their technical stuff seeing that they're heads of scientific firms.'

He paused.

Logic demanded that he strike the late Sir Digby Wellow off any list he was making now. But his scientific knowledge might still be a factor.

He shrugged his shoulders.

It was all very well for Dr Dabbe to give him all that guff about factors and equations. In this case he still didn't know what was a factor and what wasn't. And you couldn't do equations without any factors at all.

'Then there's the . . .'

Crosby saw a woman making for a pedestrian crossing and raced her to it.

Sloan closed his eyes. 'Then there's the Italian,' he said again. One day someone would write to the Home Secretary about the way this particular police car was driven. 'Even he's an engineer of sorts.'

'Roads,' said Crosby, 'that's what they're good at, isn't it, sir?'

'A civil engineer. That's what the girl said he was.'

'That's roads, isn't it, sir?' said Crosby.

'It is,' agreed Sloan wearily. As a sounding board, Detective Constable W. Crosby definitely lacked something.

'That,' said Crosby insouciantly, 'just leaves the mayor then, sir, doesn't it?'

Sloan folded up his notebook. 'I suppose it does, Crosby. I suppose it does . . .'

'He's a gents' outfitter . . .'

Fenella Tindall gave Marcia Osborne afternoon tea.

They carried it out under the beech tree because Fenella found the house stifling and everything at which she looked there redolent of her father. It was scarcely cooler in the garden at this time of the day but under the beech tree's shade it seemed so.

'You're to tell me to go away,' insisted Marcia from time to time, 'if you'd rather be alone.'

'Of course not,' Fenella replied wanly.

Marcia meant to stay.

Anyone could see that with half an eye.

'And say if there's anything you want doing.'

Fenella thanked her with due gravity.

That was easier than explaining that there was nothing she wanted except peace and quiet and a chance to mourn her father decently and in private. And to mourn without worrying about emeralds and diamonds, or the destiny of a small family firm which had somehow tumbled overnight into her lap.

'Sugar?' Life being what it was Fenella poured out tea instead.

Tea was something that she hadn't learnt to do without in Italy. Countless small cups of black coffee throughout the day were no substitute for tea.

'I daren't, my dear. I just daren't.' Marcia Osborne patted her wasplike waistline. 'Too, too fattening.'

Fenella kept a mechanical smile on her face. That, too, she found, was easier than changing her response to whatever Marcia said next. A veil – a black veil – was what she could have done with just now. Then she could have just nodded or shaken her head as the spirit moved her. That would have kept Marcia Osborne happy . . .

'And he was so alive and well last night,' Marcia was saying wonderingly. 'He was just as pleased about George's patent having come through as if it had been his own. They were as excited as two little boys.'

Fenella nodded at that. Her father had been a whole man – generous spirited and ready to share in other people's joys and sorrows . . .

She saw that Marcia's lower lip was trembling. 'We're all going to miss him a lot, Fenella. Poor Richard.'

Amen to that, seconded Fenella silently.

But the centre of Marcia Osborne's small universe was still Marcia Osborne and inexorably all events were seen in that particular perspective.

'It would have to happen today of all days and spoil everything . . .' she said.

'Today?' enquired Fenella bleakly.

Marcia Osborne gave up the struggle to stop her lower lip from quivering and said tearfully, 'It's my birthday.'

She started to fumble about in her handbag and at the same moment the telephone bell back in the Dower House started to shrill.

'I've got a spare handkerchief . . .' offered Fenella, getting to her feet to go indoors to answer the telephone.

'No, it's not that.' Marcia fished something out of her bag. 'It's this.'

Fenella stared. She was looking at a small presentation box bearing the name of Adamson. Marcia pointed to the matching pair of emerald and diamond clips.

'They were such a lovely surprise,' said Marcia in a choked voice. 'It would all have been quite perfect except for . . . for the other thing.'

'A lovely surprise,' echoed Fenella tonelessly.

'They match my earrings perfectly. They – George and your father – took one of them, you know, without my knowing – I never even thought – to send to Adamson's for a pattern. I quite thought I'd lost one of Great-Aunt Edith's earrings and I was really upset . . .'

The telephone was still ringing in the distance.

Marcia sniffed audibly. 'I was going to show them to you today anyway. They're my birthday present from George. Your father did all the arranging for him on the strength of the patent coming through and so that it should be a big surprise. Aren't they lovely? Fenella . . . what on earth's the matter? Fenella, stop laughing like that this minute . . .'

This is terrible good counsel. **19**

In due course the police car with Detective Constable Crosby
at the wheel trickled through the outskirts of the industrial
town of Luston. The pattern of traffic had changed from
tractors to articulated trailers and heavy lorries but Crosby
forged on. They found the firm of United Mellemetics'
Jublilee Works in a part of the town even more industrial than
the rest.

There was no doubt at all about whose Jubilee the works
were named after. However modern their production methods, the United Mellemetics building was pure Sixty Glorious
Years. And it wasn't only the architectural design – Victorian
Imperial Neo-Gothic – which dated it. The philosophy of
Her Late Majesty's reign was also well to the fore. Only in
the days of the Old Queen would the sentiment – couched in
bad Latin – *Labore et Profitas* – have been so conspicuously
carved in stone over the arched entrance.

Sloan found a good deal of un-Victorian hand-wringing
going on in the management offices.

'In fact, sir,' he reported back to the superintendent on the
telephone, 'the whole firm's running around like a chicken
that's had its head chopped off.'

Leeyes grunted.

'I don't think,' continued Sloan, 'that it ever occurred to
anyone here that Sir Digby would die.'

'One of the Immortals, eh?'

'Well, they did call him God. Or so I'm told. Behind his back, of course.'

'Did they, indeed? Well, which of them didn't like him enough to kill him? Tell me that . . .'

But Sloan hadn't been able to answer that question. From what he could make out Sir Digby Wellow had been one of those larger-than-life characters who hadn't inspired dislike so much as sheer exhaustion.

'They don't want to buy Struthers and Tindall, too, do they?' enquired the Superintendent.

'They haven't said.'

'They've got a couple of rivals if they do.'

'A couple?'

'Your friend Gordon Cranswick isn't the only one after the firm.'

'Oh?' said Sloan alertly.

'Some outfit by the name of Hallworthy's want to buy it as well. They've just rung the Tindall girl from Birmingham to say so. Made her an offer. Told her they'd been after it for quite a while. And she rang us.'

'Birmingham?'

Leeyes was irate. 'Sloan, do you have to repeat everything I say?'

'I was thinking, sir,' he said hastily, 'that Birmingham is a long way from Berebury.'

'I know it is.'

'Too far for these people – what did you say they were called?'

'Hallworthy's. The Hallworthy Small Motor Company, Birmingham.'

'Too far for them to have heard about Richard Tindall in the ordinary way.' Sloan looked at his watch. 'We missed the one o'clock news and the evening papers would scarcely have got hold of any of this yet, even if they're on the streets by now which I very much doubt.'

'Well?'

'Someone went out of their way to tell them specially.'

'Ha,' said Leeyes, 'a nigger in the woodpile?'

'More likely just a spy in the camp,' said Sloan moderately, 'but interesting. Very interesting. Tindall told Cranswick that he didn't like the other people's methods. They could be the other people and a spy in the camp could be what Tindall didn't like. And that was why he was offering it to Cranswick Processing.'

'And what,' enquired Leeyes heavily, 'have Cranswick Processing and Hallworthy's Small Motors got to do with United Mellemetics?'

'I don't know.'

Leeyes grunted. 'Well, on past performance if I were Chairman of either company I wouldn't walk under any ladders for a bit. Who's in charge at United Mellemetics now?'

'The deputy chairman's a man called Edward Foster, though I wouldn't say,' added Sloan doubtfully, 'that he's actually in charge . . .'

The unfortunate Edward Foster struck him as being like a man making a gallant attempt to steer a rudderless ship.

'The board,' Foster kept on saying to Sloan, 'the board. I've called a board meeting. To decide what to do now. We need a board meeting . . .'

Sloan was less sanguine. He didn't suppose the board would know what to do without Sir Digby any more than the works did.

'If my constable might just start to go through Sir Digby's papers, sir, in case there is any reference at all to Struthers and Tindall there which might give us a lead . . .' Crosby could keep a weather eye open for any mention of Cranswick Processing and Hallworthy's Small Motors, too, but Sloan didn't say anything about that to Edward Foster.

'By all means. Go ahead.' Foster ran a hand distractedly through his hair. 'We've already had a quick look ourselves without finding anything. I'm not surprised – and it doesn't prove anything either way. Sir Digby never put pen to paper if he could help it. You couldn't say he was one for paperwork at all . . .'

Tycoons, in Sloan's experience, rarely were.

'Or for confiding in people,' added Sir Digby's deputy painfully.

'So,' said Sloan to Crosby as he showed him Sir Digby's office, 'there's not a lot of hope of your finding anything useful here either. Seems as if the big boss played his cards close to his chest all the time. I can't say,' he added, 'that I blame him. Foster doesn't strike me as a man to exactly lean on . . .'

That was one thing that didn't happen in the police force. You didn't have anyone undermining your authority.

Not after the moment when you first stepped into uniform.

You were on your own, all right, then, whether you liked it onr not.

You and your notebook and the Name of the Law.

Crosby was still thinking about Edward Foster, Deputy Chairman.

'Probably never had a chance, sir. Not with a chap like Sir Digby Wellow breathing down his neck all the time. I'd rather have had Tindall myself from the sound of things.'

'Pysden seemed able to handle things quite well,' agreed Sloan. He pushed open the door of Sir Digby's room. It was pretty plush.

Crosby, too, took a look round the late chairman's office.

'Well, there's one thing I must say, sir. It's better to be a big bug in your own rug than a little bug in someone else's rug.'

'Quite the philosopher, aren't we?' said Sloan tartly.

There was much work – police work – to be done at United Mellemetics but Sloan proposed to leave that to someone else. There were detectives in plenty attached to Luston Division. They could take statements, note who had been doing what and where at the material times and tell him when they came up with something.

If they did.

Crosby hadn't found any mention of Struthers and Tindall anywhere in Sir Digby Wellow's room.

'Or of Cranswick Processing or Hallworthy's Small Motors either, sir.' The detective constable climbed into the driving seat of the police car and switched on the radio in one automatic movement. 'I don't know where we go from here . . .'

'Struthers and Tindall. That's where it all started . . .' He paused as a message started to come up on the radio and then relaxed again.

'The White Swan, Calleford,' announced the girl at Headquarters laconically. 'Trouble . . .'

Somewhere in Calleford Division a car would peel off its route and go and sort out the trouble at the White Swan.

'They aren't the only ones with trouble,' remarked Crosby, tapping the radio receiver affectionately. 'What about us, Doris, dear? Trouble? We've got two murders, a take-over battle, and dirty work at United Mellemetics for a start . . .'

'Their file is missing,' said Sloan. 'That's all. We don't know what was in it yet.'

'But it stands to reason, sir . . .'

'No, it doesn't, Crosby. Not to reason.' If there was a word he didn't like to hear used lightly that was it. 'Not yet.'

'Sir?'

'All we actually know about the United Mellemetics file so far is what we have been told about it and that is not evidence . . .'

The radio had started chattering again.

'Three nines call,' said the announcer. 'Injury accident at the bottom of Kinnisport Hill. CAB attending . . .'

That would be the Calleshire Ambulance Brigade having its customary race with the police boys to see who could get to the scene first.

'There is one thing we have got though,' said Sloan martially. 'One thing we've always got.'

'What's that, sir?'

'The old adage that crimes are usually committed by those who benefit from them.'

Crosby's brow furrowed. 'The daughter?'

'Among others . . .'

'Bravo Delta one three,' interrupted the radio appositely. 'Bravo Delta one three to go to Fourteen Hart Crescent, Luston. A domestic.'

'. . . she won't be the only one who benefits. There'll be others. Bound to be.'

'The Italian?' offered Crosby promptly.

Sloan sighed. He had been right about Crosby and the Superintendent. They thought alike.

'Perhaps. Perhaps not,' he said. 'There were big changes about and change doesn't always suit everybody.' He waved an arm. 'It works both ways. There are always those who gain and those who lose by it.'

'So,' said the constable, 'we're back where we started, aren't we?'

'Except,' remarked Sloan acidly, 'that instead of one dead man we've now got two.' It was difficult to know if Crosby was trying to be helpful or not. 'And not everyone will call that progress . . .'

The newspapers would have a field day tomorrow: especially if the reporters had caught Superintendent Leeyes in a combative mood, warmed up for the fray by a couple of rounds with the Chairman of the Watch Committee.

'But,' said Crosby thoughtfully, 'if Dr Dabbe is as right as he thinks he is . . .'

Counsel for the Prosecution and Counsel for the Defence would fight that out in open court – and they would phrase the sentiment better: but not much.

'. . . then, sir, we've only got one bloke with a cast-iron alibi, haven't we?'

'Henry Pysden,' supplied Sloan, 'who was working his time machine at Berebury when the doctor thinks Richard Tindall died. Sergeant Wharton is checking on the time-machine alibi.'

'Which leaves us rather a lot of people without one,' concluded Crosby.

The radio suddenly came to life again.

'A member of the public,' said Doris, the announcer, 'having it out with Traffic Warden Number Five in Berebury High Street.'

'Someone will do that man one day,' forecast Sloan, 'and I only hope that I don't have to take them in for it.'

'Near the traffic lights,' directed Doris.

'If it's nobody else's job,' remarked Crosby gloomily, 'then it's a policeman's . . .'

'He's a bit stroppy,' Doris informed the radio circuit informally.

Sloan was bracing. 'We're Society's maids-of-all-work, Crosby, and you might as well get used to the idea. There's another thing it's like . . .'

'Sir?'

'Women's work. It's never done . . .'

'Number Five isn't very happy either,' added Doris, confident that Number Five would have switched off while he dealt with a turbulent member of the public.

'Now,' said Sloan, 'Hallworthy's Small Motors of Birmingham. What we need to know is their link with Struthers and Tindall . . .'

Sloan and Crosby were so engrossed in the possibilities of this that they didn't hear County Headquarters the first time they called them up.

'Foxtrot Delta one six, Foxtrot Delta one six,' repeated Doris patiently. 'Have you got Detective Inspector Sloan on board? Come in, Foxtrot Delta one six. Constable Hepple would like to talk to you at Randall's Bridge. He thinks you should see the Captain of the Tower.'

The wizened figure standing in the nave just outside the tower in the church at Randall's Bridge didn't look like the captain of anything to Sloan. He had a bent back and a leathery face and he was called Nathan Styles.

'Caught me at me dinner, 'e did,' he said, pointing an accusing finger at Police Constable Hepple.

'Did he now?' said Sloan. 'Well?'

''Appen I had a bit of a look round for 'im like Ernie 'ere said.'

'And what did you find?' So the worthy Hepple was called Earnest, was he?

'Nothing much amiss in 'ere.'

Sloan nodded. 'That's what Mr Knight told us this morning.'

Nathan Styles dismissed the church secretary with a jerk of his shoulder. 'He's not a ringer.'

'The bells?' said Sloan. 'Is there something wrong with the bells?'

Nathan Styles shook a grizzled head. 'No, it's not that.'

'Well?'

'There's an extra rope.'

'What!'

'One too many.'

'Where?'

'Hanging down the middle.' Styles stepped forward into the church tower. It was tidier now than it had been earlier.

Sloan followed him and stared up the shaft of the tall tower.

Nathan Styles pointed aloft with a gnarled and none too clean finger. 'Up there. The thin one.'

Sloan could see the one he meant.

Hanging down was a very thin length of something. It wasn't rope. From where he stood it looked as if it could be twine.

Say fishing line.

It was black and practically invisible. Sloan took a second look at Nathan Styles. He must be pretty sharp eyed.

And know his bell tower.

'If you don't believe me,' rasped the old man, 'you can always ask Charlie Horton. He'll tell you the same. T'wasn't there when we rung Sunday.'

'I don't suppose it was,' agreed Sloan softly. 'I don't suppose for one moment that it was. Or that you've had your practice night this week yet?'

'Not this week,' agreed Styles. 'Friday's practice night.'

'It's a tidy length.'

'Seventy feet,' said the old man promptly. 'Buy the ropes by the foot we has to do so I know. Cost a lot do ropes, I can tell you.'

Sloan peered up into the dimness. 'It's too far and too dark up there to see how it's fixed . . .'

Nathan Styles jerked his shoulder upwards. 'Dare say it's hitched round one of the bell beams.'

'We'll have to get up top and have a proper look.' Sloan turned to Crosby and Hepple. 'It looks as if it comes straight down all right.'

'Shall I go up the tower, sir,' offered Hepple, 'and see what I can see from up there?'

'Not yet.' Sloan waved a hand. 'Later. There's a little experiment I want you both to do first. You, Hepple, go outside and find that ladder, and then get up to that little window from the path side. And you, Crosby, go and get hold of something that we can use to get the end of that twine over towards the window.'

Hepple crunched away. Crosby moved off down the church and reappeared a few moments later with a churchwarden's stave.

'Will this do, sir?'

Sloan sighed. Justice being, in his view, only a very short head behind godliness and rather ahead of cleanliness, he supposed it would have to.

He took the stave and held it up to the twine. With the flat head of the stave he showed Crosby how to steer it towards the little window above the outer tower door. As he did so the familiar face of Police Constable Hepple appeared at the window.

Crosby continued to walk in Hepple's direction.

Hepple thrust his hand through the embrasure and caught the twine.

'It just reaches the window, sir,' reported Crosby over his shoulder. 'Exactly.'

'I thought it might,' said Detective Inspector Sloan.

Prosperity doth bewitch men.   **20**

It was Sergeant Wharton who rang the makers of the time-punch machine being used by Henry Pysden in his experiment.

They were faintly affronted at his enquiry.

'But we guarantee that the mechanism is accurate, Sergeant. That's what it's there for. It's one of those tied to both a time clock and a personal signature.'

'Why?' enquired Wharton.

'Evidence that the readings from the experiment were taken at the right time and by the right person.'

'Does that matter?'

The man cleared his throat. 'In some types of very accurate experiment it reduces some of the room for error if one person and one person only takes all the readings. It keeps the personal interpretation element down to one, doesn't it?'

Sergeant Wharton supposed it did.

'Very important in this case,' said the voice. 'Or so we were told when we were asked to set it up.'

'Were you?' said Wharton, interested.

'Struthers and Tindall checked with us first – and that it was proof against tampering.'

Wharton coughed. 'And it is?'

'One hundred per cent,' responded the manufacturer's man unhesitatingly. 'It's got twin seals with a built-in bonus highly popular with policemen.'

'I'll buy it,' said Sergeant Wharton.

'We apply the seals and give the guarantee, and we can tell if anyone's been playing about with them – even if anyone else can't.'

'Belt and braces,' observed Wharton who was so weighty that he didn't need either.

'Buttons, too, if you like, Sergeant. We don't leave anything to chance here . . .'

Constable Crosby had an objection.

He was looking in the direction of the marble plinth.

'It'd still have missed the Fitton Bequest, sir. I'm sure it would. It's too high.'

'It could swing easily enough,' put in Hepple from his perch outside the window. 'You can see that from here. With the bell ropes tethered out of the way like they are, it would have a clear run.'

Sloan nodded briskly. 'Hepple, can you tell what happened to the end of the twine?'

Hepple squinted at the piece in his hand. 'Cut, sir, I should say.'

'Not burnt?'

The twine would have to go under a comparison microscope at the Forensic Laboratory but there was still such a thing as the naked eye. Macroscopic examination was what it was called but he wouldn't put that in his report. The superintendent was sensitive to long words.

And there was still the spent match unaccounted for.

Superintendent Leeyes had no time for loose ends either.

'No, sir,' Hepple was saying. 'It's quite a clean cut. No charring. Could have been scissors or a knife. Something like that.'

There was another thing a microscope might be able to do for them. Tell if a heavy weight had strained the fibres of the twine. You never knew with microscopes these days.

'Ah.' Nathan Styles creaking voice started up again. 'B'ain't be the length it is now that counts, is it? It's the length it was afore it was cut . . .'

'That's right, Mr Styles,' said Sloan. Crosby shouldn't need a country rustic to spell things out for him like this. 'It could have been long enough before it was cut to knock the sculpture off its plinth.'

'But why take it away anyway?' asked Crosby mulishly. 'Why not leave it there?'

'Because it'd be a dead giveaway,' said the old bellringer promptly. 'Can't you see that, lad? Stands to reason.'

'There was a good chance,' said Sloan, 'that we might miss the twine or not know what it was for.'

'It still doesn't tell us how it was done,' Crosby persisted obstinately.

'No.'

'The chap could have aimed for the sculpture from up here,' observed Hepple from the window. 'I've got quite a good view.'

'You wouldn't have in the dark,' said Sloan.

'There was that match . . .' put in Crosby.

Sloan took a deep breath. 'There's only one thing we do know . . .'

'Sir?'

'The time the twine was cut and whatever was on the end of it taken away.'

'No, we don't, sir . . .' Then his face changed. 'Oh, yes, we do . . .' he breathed. 'We do. At two o'clock this morning . . .'

'Exactly.'

'By the night fisherman those two Metford women said they saw.'

'The Metfords? Daft as coots the pair of 'em,' remarked Nathan Styles conversationally, 'especially Ivy.'

Hepple, still at the window, tilted his helmet back. 'And who would the night fisherman be, sir, if I might ask?'

'That's why he needed a rod,' interrupted Crosby excitedly, waving the churchwarden's stave about in a way not envisaged by the vicar. 'He wouldn't be able to reach it from the window otherwise and we know he couldn't get in through the doors, don't we?'

'What rod?' asked a bewildered Hepple.

'A fisherman's rod, Hepple,' explained Sloan kindly. 'To catch the end of the twine. Now we know why he needed a long rod. To hook the twine and take away whatever was hanging at the end of it.'

'Ah,' said Nathan Styles entering into the spirit of things, 'that would have been back in the middle of the tower, by then, wouldn't it?'

'It would,' agreed Sloan.

'Dead underneath the bell beam,' said the little man. 'Gravity would do that.'

Sloan nodded. It had been the superintendent who had said you couldn't interfere with gravity, hadn't it?

Aeons ago.

Or this morning.

They seemed all the same to Sloan now.

'A fisherman's rod would do the trick nicely,' said Hepple ponderously, measuring the distance to the middle of the tower with his eye.

'I suppose,' said Crosby, sounding doubtful, 'that it would have stopped swinging by then . . .'

'I think,' said Sloan softly, 'that we can take it that it would.'

Crosby scratched his head. 'You mean that's why he waited until then?'

'I do.'

'He knew?'

'I think,' said Sloan heavily, 'that he worked it out. Just like he worked everything else out.' He looked up at the window. 'All right, Hepple, you can come down now.'

Hepple let go of the twine and withdrew his arm from the embrasure. His face disappeared as he backed down the ladder. The twine – even without anything on the end of it – fell back towards the middle of the tower and then – pendulumlike – swung on through an arc towards the opposite door – the one leading back into the nave and the church proper.

Sloan stopped in his tracks.

'Crosby, did you see that?'

'No, sir. What, sir?'

'The twine, man.'

'What about it, sir?'

'Crosby, we're fools.'

'Yes, sir.'

'You didn't notice anything about the way that the twine fell back from the window?'

'No, sir.'

'It went towards the door, Crosby. The door. Not the plinth. Don't you see? The window and the sculpture – they aren't in line, are they?'

'No, sir.'

'So how did anything on the twine aimed from the window in the dark hit the Fitton Bequest?'

'Search me, sir,' said Crosby agreeably.

There was a sudden high cackle from old Nathan Styles.

'Proper mystery, isn't it?'

'You don't have to explain pendulums to me, Sloan,' said Superintendent Leeyes testily. 'I know all about Galileo.'

'Galileo, sir?'

'The chap who chucked two things from the top of the Leaning Tower of Pisa to see which got to the bottom first. I've been there.' The superintendent and his wife had once been to Italy on a package tour and they were never allowed to forget it at the police station. 'He found out about pendulums.'

'What about them, sir?'

Leeyes waved a lofty hand. 'The swing of the pendulum always takes exactly the same time whether it's a long swing or a short one.'

'Clocks,' said Sloan suddenly.

'That sort of thing,' agreed Leeyes. 'They sent him to prison for it.'

'For finding out?'

'Oh, yes,' said the superintendent grandly. 'They thought he was a dangerous chap. Had a lot of new ideas.'

'I see, sir. A bad lot.'

Sloan had so far never been instrumental in sending anyone

to prison except for having old ideas – some of them very old indeed.

Cain and Abel old.

Some older than that, too, now he came to think of it . . .

He had got Crosby to drive him back to the police station at Berebury from Randall's Bridge after all. And it was just as well. There had been all manner of messages waiting for him there.

The airport people in London had traced a passenger called G. Mardoni who had caught a plane to Schiepol in Holland an hour or so after the Rome flight on which he had been booked had left.

The next message had been more useful still and Sloan had taken it in with him to Superintendent Leeyes.

It was from the Guardia de Publica Sicurezza in Rome. They had traced Giuseppe Mardoni from a Dutch flight to his apartment near the Castelsanangelo and were holding him. Please, what would their esteemed friends the Politzei Inglesi like doing with him?

'You'd better acknowledge this quickly, Sloan,' instructed Leeyes, whose knowledge of Italian history was hazy (but whose celebrated holiday tour had included Rome), 'before they throw him in the Tiber.'

'Yes, sir.'

'Anything else come in?'

'Details of the two patents. The one which Sergeant Wharton's man found in Blake's room is an old one – registered in the name of Jonah Bernard Struthers before the war. The other is George Osborne's and that's dated yesterday like they said.' Far too much had happened yesterday for Sloan's liking.

'Appleton's still watching Osborne, I hope.'

'He is.'

'Anything else?'

'The link with Hallworthy's Small Motors. Someone's been quick . . .'

'Ah . . .' The superintendent stretched his arms in a way that was positively feline.

'Paul Blake.'

Leeyes rubbed his hands together. 'Blake, eh?'

'Hallworthy's Small Motors were his last employers but one.'

'Were they, indeed?' said Leeyes silkily, the cat-and-mouse touch even more apparent now.

'The last people he worked for were bought out by Hallworthy's a year ago.'

Leeyes pounced. 'Then he came to Struthers and Tindall and Hallworthy's tried to buy Struthers and Tindall?'

'Could be. But Tindall wouldn't sell. At least, not to the highest bidder.'

'So someone kills Tindall . . .'

'Tindall was killed, sir, but we don't know exactly how or why yet.'

'What's all this business about pendulums for then?'

Sloan shook his head. 'I don't think a pendulum would necessarily do the trick, sir. The sculpture was off-line from the window.'

'Well,' said the superintendent, leaning comfortably back in his chair, 'seeing that there's no such thing as an eccentric pendulum you'd better go away and have another think, hadn't you?'

As he walked back down the corridor to his own room a little *frisson* of cold trickled down Sloan's spine . . .

Then his head came up . . .

There was such a thing as an eccentric pendulum.

He'd seen it.

In a museum somewhere.

He and Margaret. It had something to do with the earth's gravity pulling it to one side or something like that.

But only if the cord was long enough.

Long enough?

Seventy or eighty feet. It had to be something like that.

Seventy feet! whispered a little voice in Sloan's brain.

Inspector Harpe loped by him in the corridor but Sloan didn't see him.

It was coming back to him now.

If he remembered rightly the only thing this particular

pendulum needed was a long drop and a smooth start and half an hour later it was right off course. Pulled by the Earth's gravity.

The smooth start had been important. He remembered that, too. It had to be released very carefully indeed. No jerk or push or anything like that. In fact he remembered standing with Margaret while a man from the museum came along and started it by burning away the anchoring string with a match.

By burning it with a match . . .

A match.

A perfectly ordinary match.

'Crosby!' He pushed open the door of his room.

'Sir?'

'Get me the Metropolitan Police. And quickly.'

'Yes, sir.' As the detective constable picked up the telephone he pushed two more message sheets in Sloan's direction. 'There's something in from Constable Appleton, sir. George Osborne's left the grammar school in Berebury and he thinks he's heading out for Cleete . . .'

'Is that Mets?' asked Sloan into the telephone.

'The other,' persisted Crosby, undeflected, 'is from Luston Police. They haven't turned up anything useful so far at United Mellemetics.'

'Mets?' said Sloan urgently. 'Now, look here – I want you to send someone round to a museum for me. Yes, that's right. A museum. And then I want you to put me on to someone who can explain a patent to me . . . and old patent . . .'

... I have committed
some secret deed which I desire the world
may never hear of.

21

Dr Dabbe was on the telephone and still concerned with the late Sir Digby Wellow.

'I can't add a lot to what I told you in the car park, Sloan, except that his coronary arteries weren't a lot to write home about. Good for a few more business lunches and public speeches but not all that many if that's any consolation to Lady Wellow. As to the wound ...'

'Yes?'

'It is the same in every recognizable respect,' said the pathologist in the measured terms he used in court, 'as that inflicted on Richard Tindall. The only variation is in the amount of force used. Everything points to it being the same weapon. What's that, Sloan ... do I happen to know anything about what?'

'Foucault's Pendulum,' said Sloan confidently.

The Metropolitan Police had already rung him back from London. They'd been round to the museum for him.

'Let me see now ...' the pathologist paused. 'Foucault's Pendulum ... Isn't that the one used for demonstrating the rotation of the Earth on its own axis?'

'That's the one,' said Sloan.

Explaining it to Superintendent Leeyes wasn't going to be as easy as this.

Or to Crosby.

Perhaps he wouldn't even try.

Perhaps he'd just put it into his report for the superintendent and bank on Crosby not wanting to know.

'I remember.' Dr Dabbe's interest quickened. 'Actually the swing of the pendulum stays the same . . .'

'Galileo,' put in Sloan. The superintendent would like that.

'. . . and it's the Earth which moves but, of course, it doesn't look like that.'

'No.'

His voice changed. 'I say, Sloan, are you on to something?'

'Perhaps,' responded Sloan temperately. 'It would explain the spent match we found. I couldn't fit it in with anything else.'

'How?'

'When demonstrating Foucault's Pendulum you have to set it off very carefully indeed. That's the whole secret. Without a jerk. You do it by mooring whatever's on the end – say a metal ball – something heavy anyway – to something fixed.'

'Say the bars of a small window?' said Dabbe drily.

'That would do very nicely,' agreed Sloan.

There was a man from the Area Forensic Laboratory already on his way to the church at Randall's Bridge with the sort of magnifying glass that Sherlock Holmes might have dreamt of. He was going to look at the metal bars of the embrasure window. You never knew what might have left its mark there.

Dyson, the police photographer, was on his way to the church, too.

He had been detailed by Sloan to take pictures of a length of black twine dangling from the bell beam.

'Black twine, Inspector?' he had echoed. 'You must be joking. It doesn't even smile when you say "cheese" let alone watch the birdie.'

'I have reason to believe,' Sloan told him austerely, 'that it was an instrument of death.'

'There!' cried the incorrigible Dyson in tones of mock disappointment, 'and I'd been putting my money on an orangutan . . .'

'What you usually do to set off Foucault's Pendulum,' Sloan said now to the pathologist, 'is to burn through the string which anchors it at the start of its swing.'

'So you do,' agreed Dabbe. 'I'd forgotten that bit.'

'Whoever started it off – if that is what did the trick – must have dropped the match while he was reaching through the little window.'

'Foucault's Pendulum takes time, you know, Sloan. It doesn't go out of line straight away. I can't remember the details – not my field, really. Is it something like one degree in five minutes?'

'Twelve degrees in an hour, Doctor, in London.' Sloan faithfully repeated what the man from the museum had said to the man from Mets. 'It was the question of time which put me on to it.'

'Time? What has time to do with it?'

'I think our villain wanted time. That's the only explanation which makes sense. Otherwise why kill Tindall where he did – let alone how. And why not kill him outright when he hit him the first time?'

'Good point, Sloan. Sir Digby's dead enough.'

'The usual reason,' said Sloan, 'for wanting time is to establish an alibi.'

But the pathologist was still thinking about the pendulum. 'It would be a nice calculation, Sloan. You'd take your twelve degrees an hour plus the length of your pendulum and its first swing and I dare say you'd need to know the weight of whatever you put on the end. What do you think that was, by the way?'

'Something heavy,' said Sloan. 'It would need to weigh thirty pounds at least.'

The museum had told Mets that, too.

'Then,' said Dabbe more energetically still, 'you'd have to work out how far over you must tilt your statue so that the first knock from the weight of the pendulum would knock it over . . .'

Sloan cleared his throat. 'I thought, Doctor, you said that given enough factors you could do any equation . . .'

'A hit,' cried the pathologist delightedly, 'a palpable hit. Tell me more . . .'

Sloan put the telephone back and picked up something from his desk.

'Come on, Crosby. We don't want to waste any time now.'

'To Cleete, sir?'

'Certainly not,' said Sloan militantly, striding down the corridor. 'Not now that we know that those emerald and diamond clips were for Mrs Osborne . . .'

The constable was faint but pursuing. 'Where to, sir?'

'Struthers and Tindall, of course. Where did you think?'

What Sloan had picked up from his desk had been a warrant for murder.

After he had executed it he stood in front of Richard Tindall's desk in Richard Tindall's office. On his left were Miss Hilda Holroyd, Paul Blake, and Gordon Cranswick. On his right, hastily summoned from Cleete, were Fenella Tindall and George and Marcia Osborne.

Sloan pointed to Richard Tindall's desk and said, 'Big desk, big man.' Then he waved his arm in the direction of the corridor leading towards Henry Pysden's room. 'Big desk, little man.'

He was speaking metaphorically.

They all knew that.

Henry Pysden had fought like a tiger when they arrested him. It had needed all of Sergeant Wharton's massive strength as well as Crosby's weight to take him away.

'It all began,' said Sloan, 'when an old patent belonging to Struthers and Tindall became important in a new manufacturing process.'

'Better to buy the firm,' said the owner of Cranswick Processing unabashed, 'than fork out a royalty every time we used Struthers and Tindall's patent.'

'Hallworthy's Small Motors thought so, too, sir,' said Sloan evenly, 'and they went a bit further than you did. They insinuated Mr Blake here into the firm to find out what he could to help the sale along.'

Paul Blake turned an uncomfortable red.

Fenella Tindall, who had no colour at all in her face, turned to him. 'You were nothing but a spy then?'

'However,' intervened Sloan hastily, 'neither Hallworthy's nor Cranswick Processing were prepared to give unconditional guarantees about keeping staff on and that was Richard Tindall's death warrant. He found out about Paul Blake being an agent of Hallworthy's, didn't like their methods, and so opted in favour of Cranswick . . .'

'But why?' asked Marcia Osborne. 'Why did he want to sell at all . . .'

Sloan cleared his throat. 'His wife had died and I think he guessed that he might be losing his daughter, too, soon.'

'Me?' said Fenella, two pink spots appearing on her cheeks.

'Fair stood the wind for Italy,' said George Osborne, speaking for the first time. He had a lean intelligent face and had listened attentively so far. 'That right, Inspector?'

And it was Fenella's turn to blush.

'If you inherited the firm, miss, there was a good chance that Henry Pysden might be left to carry on or at least negotiate the new sale.'

George Osborne stirred. 'Inspector, I don't quite see where United Mellemetics comes into all this.'

'It doesn't, sir. Not at all. I think we would find that there was nothing wrong with the United Mellemetics file . . ..'

'But what about poor Sir Digby Wellow . . .' that was Marcia Osborne.

'I'm afraid, Mrs Osborne, that he died in the cause of . . .' Sloan searched for the right word.

George Osborne supplied it. 'Verisimilitude.'

'Very probably, sir.'

'The file, though,' said Miss Holroyd, the perfect secretary. 'I don't quite understand about the file, Inspector.'

'It did disappear but that I'm afraid was only because Henry Pysden took it. I expect it's in the river by now. You put me on to that, miss.'

'Me?' said Miss Holroyd.

'You said you weren't present when Pysden told me he handed it over to Mr Tindall yesterday. When I went back over everything to do with that file I found that all our so-called mysterious information about it stemmed only from Henry Pysden.'

Miss Holroyd frowned. 'But he said Mr Tindall said . . .'

'Only they weren't quotes at all,' pointed out Sloan. 'The works foreman and Mr Blake here' – he looked with disfavour at the young scientist – 'both found their work on it completely routine so I checked back in case it was a red herring.'

'And it was?' Fenella was beginning to look more animated by the minute. 'You mean he killed poor Sir Digby Wellow just to . . . to . . . to lend a touch of colour to the killing of my father?'

'To divert suspicion to United Mellemetics anyway, miss.'

'How could he!' she exclaimed.

'And the copy of the patent in Mr Blake's room, Inspector?' Miss Holroyd's tidy mind seized on a second loose end.

'Another red herring. Though at that stage, of course,' remarked Sloan pleasantly, 'it still left Mr Blake here in the running for double murder.'

Paul Blake started to stutter. 'H – h – hhh – how come?'

It was Gordon Cranswick, the businessman, who answered him. 'Tindall could have rumbled you, boy, and you might have killed him to keep him quiet.'

Paul Blake's handsomeness wasn't quite so apparent now. 'I wouldn't . . .'

'We know you wouldn't,' said Gordon Cranswick briskly, 'but the inspector couldn't be sure of that then.'

'Not at that particular point,' agreed Sloan suavely.

'When then?' demanded the young scientist hotly.

Sloan cleared his throat. 'When I started thinking about alibis for the killing of Richard Tindall.'

'I hadn't got one,' retorted Blake upon the instant.

'I know.' Sloan nodded. 'Nobody had an alibi except Henry

Pysden and oddly enough his was cast iron. A signature tied up to a machine which was double sealed.'

'Copper-bottomed,' observed Gordon Cranswick, in the language of Lloyd's.

'Too much of a good thing?' suggested George Osborne more perceptively.

'Much too much,' agreed Sloan. 'Unfortunately the Cranswick takeover played into his hands.'

'Why?' demanded the Chairman and Managing Director of Cranswick Processing Limited.

'I gather that cloak and dagger meetings, exaggerated secrecy, cryptic messages, and so forth are all part and parcel of these deals . . .'

'Practically standard practice,' the businessman assured him readily.

'I should imagine this lent a certain amount of credence to any message Henry Pysden used to lure Richard Tindall to the church tower late last night.'

'The telephone call,' breathed Marcia Osborne.

'Not about Cranswick Processing, Inspector,' said Gordon Cranswick.

'No, sir.' Sloan coughed. 'Would I be very wrong though if I suggested that if Pysden had said that Sir Digby Wellow wanted to see him in that particular place and time that Richard Tindall would have believed him.'

'That clown . . .' began Cranswick and then remembered that he, too, was dead, and fell silent.

'The message only had to be believable when Henry Pysden gave it to him. That's all. Nothing else. He could have dreamed up anything he liked. From then on it was all plain sailing.'

'I should like to know how,' said Fenella Tindall steadily, 'and then I should like to go home.'

'You're coming back with us,' said George Osborne in a matter-of-fact way which brooked no contradiction.

Marcia Osborne seconded this with a nod. Her diamond and emerald jewellery didn't fit in at Struthers and Tindall either.

Sloan didn't mind. Not now.

He took a deep breath and began. 'There was one important factor which was common knowledge . . .'

'. . . that, sir, was the work being done in the church at Randall's Bridge.' Sloan had to repeat it all to the superintendent back at the police station. 'They had to advertise the moving of the Fitton Bequest – the church secretary told us that – when they got a faculty for all the changes in the church.'

Leeyes grunted.

'And it wasn't unreasonable for Pysden to suppose,' continued Sloan smoothly, 'that a pathologist would be able to work out the time of Tindall's death fairly accurately. They're getting better at it all the time.'

Leeyes grunted again.

'So any time after Evensong on Sunday Pysden rigs up his pendulum, does the calculations so that it knocks the statue over at eleven-thirty, then last night – the day before Tindall is due to sign on the dotted line – Pysden gets a message that Gordon Cranswick or Sir Digby Wellow or Genghis Khan wants to see him in the tower at Randall's Bridge – or some such tale . . . that's another point against him, by the way, sir . . .'

'What is?' growled Leeyes unhelpfully.

'That sort of message must have come from someone like Pysden whom Tindall really trusted or he wouldn't have acted on it. Catch me going to a church tower at midnight.'

'If I asked you to,' said Leeyes pointedly, 'I take it you would.'

'Naturally,' said Sloan hastily. 'Of course, sir. So Pysden waits for him in the church tower, knocks him out, and sets the pendulum going.'

'Nasty.'

'Pysden drives Tindall's car back to its garage at Cleete – which is about the only place where it wouldn't cause comment – collects his own car which he probably left somewhere in Cleete – Hepple's checking on that now –

and then hurries back to the works in Berebury to establish his alibi. He's got half an hour and it all works out very nicely.'

'H'mmmm.'

'All he had to do is come back for the lead weight.' Sloan coughed. 'And killing Sir Digby was – er – just gilding the lily.'

'Another assignation?'

'Child's play, I expect. Pysden would only have to hint at something fishy in the United Mellemetics file and Sir Digby would meet him anywhere.'

'What about the Italian?' said Leeyes gamely. 'All you've said about gain applies to him too.'

'His visit was unexpected,' said Sloan. 'Mrs Turvey, the daily woman at Cleete, told us so. And this murder was – er – calculated.'

'I always said,' trumpeted the superintendent, 'that you couldn't play about with gravity.'

'Anyway, sir,' said Sloan hastily, 'at two o'clock this morning Giuseppe Mardoni was at the airport – not retrieving a lead weight from the pendulum in the church tower with a fishing rod.'

'The girl could have done that,' suggested Leeyes: but half-heartedly.

'She's going to sell out to Cranswick after she's been advised about the value of this old patent . . .'

It was Detective Constable Crosby who disturbed them.

'No news about those shoes on the golf course yet, sir, but there are two more anonymous letters in from Cullingoak.' He grinned. 'The one about the vicar's wife is rather good, actually.'

The Superintendent's face turned a choleric shade of purple.

Crosby didn't notice. He plunged on.

'And the town clerk's on the telephone. They think it was sugar in the mayor's petrol tank this time . . .'

*

'What's he going to plead?' enquired Dr Dabbe with mild interest.

'I've heard that the defence have got a psychiatrist lined up,' said Sloan.

'Old hat,' remarked the pathologist amiably. 'Head-shrinkers and trick cyclists are on their way out.'

Sloan cocked a mocking eyebrow at the pathologist. 'Seeing something nasty in the woodshed isn't why you hit old ladies over the head after all?'

''Fraid not.'

'And what,' enquired Detective Inspector Sloan, quondam law-enforcement officer, cautiously, 'is on its way in?'

'A new version of original sin, old chap.'

'There isn't one.'

'Oh, yes, there is. It's called body chemistry.'

'What's that?'

'Chromosomes, for a start. And a lot more.'

Sloan paused for thought. 'Is that better or worse?'

The pathologist chuckled. 'Worse, Sloan. Much worse. Nobody can argue with a biochemist . . .'

Detective Constable Crosby dumped the last file of statements down on Sloan's desk. 'That's the lot, sir. Including the receipt from Adamson's.'

'Crosby . . .'

'Sir?'

'Crosby, did you by any remote chance notice anything out of the ordinary about the Osborne house when you went there?'

'No, sir,' promptly.

'Think.'

'Yes, sir.'

'Anything?'

'No, sir.'

'The mantelpiece,' suggested Sloan with heavy patience. 'Did you notice anything about the mantelpiece?'

Crosby screwed up his eyes. 'No, sir.'

'No birthday cards?' It was almost a plea.

'Oh, yes, sir. A whole row . . .' His voice faltered. 'Very pretty, they were.'

'If, Crosby,' said Sloan letting out a long sigh, 'you can't be a good example, then you'll just have to be a horrible warning, that's all.'

Last Respects

With acknowledgement to Michael Burnham, ship scientist

Ma plume pour toutes mes tantes.

The chapter headings are taken from *The Beggar's Opera* by John Gay.

Suspicion does not become a friend.

The man wasn't alive and well and living in Paris.

He wasn't living in the county of Calleshire, England, either.

And he certainly wasn't alive and well. Actually he wasn't living anywhere. He was dead. Obviously dead.

Horace Boller was so sure about that that he didn't hurry after he had seen him. Not that Horace Boller was the hurrying sort. In addition to which he was out fishing at the time and fishermen never hurry. It was a universal truth. You couldn't catch fish if you hurried. The fish didn't like it: they stopped feeding at once. Like primitive man, fish equated hurry with danger and either kept their heads down or made off. In Horace Boller's considered opinion civilized man had a lot to learn about hurrying.

As it happened Boller hadn't so much seen the dead man at first as just caught a quick glimpse of something out of the ordinary in the water. It took his brain a moment or two to sort out the message from his eye: that that which was floating beyond the bow of his boat and just out of range of easy vision could be a body. He wedged his fishing rod so that he had a spare hand and reached for one of the oars. He gave it a purposive poke and the rowing boat obediently came round so that he was a little nearer to what was in the water.

It was after that that he had ceased to be in any real doubt about what it was he was looking at. The body was floating just under the surface of the water in the way that bodies did, arms outstretched. It was apparently moving. Horace Boller was not deceived. It was, he knew at once, totally lifeless. The illusion of movement came from the water, not from the man. It was one of the tricks – the many tricks – that water played. The angle of refraction came into it, too. Boller didn't know anything about angles of refraction but he did know a lot about the tricks that water could play.

This man had been dead for quite a while. He knew that, too, at once. That conclusion was not reached as a result of a long acquaintance with dead bodies – although Horace Boller had seen some of those in his time too – but from something indefinable about the appearance of the body even at a distance.

If you were to ask him, his considered opinion would be that it had been in the water a fair old time.

There was, of course, no one about to ask him that – or anything else. It was precisely because there was no one about that Horace Boller had chosen to come out fishing today. You couldn't catch fish when the water wasn't quiet. He looked about him now. There wasn't even one other boat in sight let alone within hailing distance. That was because it was a Tuesday. Now if it had been a weekend he would hardly have been able to get his boat out into the main channel of the river for yachts and sailing dinghies.

It was this indefinable sense that this particular body had been in the water for more than a little while that made Horace Boller dismiss the idea of taking it in tow.

Well, that – and something else as well . . .

The Boller family had been around in Calleshire for a long time. Not quite in the same well-documented way that His Grace the Duke of Calleshire had been at Calle Castle but for pretty nearly the same length of time. There had certainly been Bollers living in the little fishing village of Edsway on the estuary of the River Calle for as long as anyone had bothered to look. Those who looked didn't include the Bollers. They had better things to do than go searching through old parish records – things like building boats, running ferries, making sails, digging for bait at low tide . . .

The tide still mattered in Edsway. Once upon a time – in the dim past when all boats had had a shallow draught – Edsway had been the only port on the estuary. It was always something of a natural harbour, sheltered by a lip of headland from the worst of the storms coming in from the sea – the village of Marby juxta Mare took the brunt of those – but there had never been really deep water at Edsway and now – thanks to the sand – there was less.

Its commercial fate had been sealed in the nineteenth century when some distant railway baron had decreed that Mr Stephenson's new-fangled iron road should go from Calleford to the river mouth and thus to the sea on the other – the north side – of the river. That was when Kinnisport had come into prominence and Edsway fallen into desuetude. In the wake of the railway had come another entrepreneur who had caused a proper deep-water harbour to be built at Kinnisport out of great blocks of granite shipped down by sea from Aberdeen – and Edsway had dropped out of the prosperity race altogether.

But only for the time being.

Every dog did have its day.

Now it was Kinnisport that was in decline while Edsway was enjoying a twentieth-century revival as a sailing centre. The firm sand that had choked its life as a commercial harbour provided an excellent basis for the hardstanding that the little boats needed and some safe swimming for their owners' families.

The dead man hadn't been a bather.

You didn't go swimming in a shirt and trousers. Not voluntarily, that is.

Horace Boller took another look at the man floating in the water. He might have been a seaman, he might not. The Calleshire shore got its share of those drowned on the high seas and the village of Edsway got more than its quota of them. It had something to do with the configuration of the coast and the way in which the tide came up the estuary to meet the River Calle coming down to the sea.

Bodies usually fetched up on the spit of land known locally as Billy's Finger. This stretched out into the water and – so the experts said – each year got a little shallower on the seaward side and a little deeper on the river side. The river scoured away from behind what the sea laid up at its front. The ancients used to say that Billy's Finger moved, that it beckoned mariners to their doom. The moderns – the clever ones who knew everything because a computer had worked it out for them – had said, rather surprised, that the ancients were right after all. Billy's Finger did move. It moved about an inch every hundred years, a little more at the very tip.

Horace Boller took a bearing from the spire of St Peter's church and reckoned that this fellow, whoever he was, had for once somehow escaped the beckonings of Billy's Finger. And he had done that in spite of its being the season of neap tides. Boller wasn't too bothered about that. These days it didn't make any difference exactly whereabouts a dead body found landfall. He would still – unless claimed by sorrowing relatives – end up buried in St Peter's churchyard at Edsway. There he – whoever he was – would lie in the goodly company of all those other unknown men who had been washed up by the sea.

Some had unmarked graves and some had those that were dignified by tombstones. There was a melancholy row betokening a remote naval engagement far out to sea in 1917. All those memorials bore the same inscription, 'A Sailor of the Great War – Known unto God.' They hadn't even heard the distant thunder of the guns in Edsway but the men had come ashore.

In the end.

It hadn't always been like that.

Once upon a time when drowned men had been washed ashore on Billy's Finger the men of Edsway had seen to it that they weren't found and brought to land for burial in St Peter's churchyard. They had, in fact, taken very good care that they weren't. Some antiquarian who had taken an interest in the estuary's local history had once told Horace Boller all about it.

The villagers in those days had felt that they had a big enough Poor Rate to cope with as it was without taking on the cost – as a charge upon it – of burying unknown seamen. What they used to do in olden times, this antiquarian had told an impassive Horace Boller, was to wait for nightfall and then drag the body over from the seaward aspect of the strand and lower it into the deep water the other side of Billy's Finger.

The combination of sea and river – tide and current – saw to it then that the next landfall of the dead body was in the neighbouring parish of Collerton. And thus it became a charge on their Poor Rate instead.

Horace Boller had listened unblinkingly to this recital, saying, 'Well, I never!' at suitable intervals, as he knew you had to do with this manner of man. Privately he had considered it an excellent way of keeping the rates down and hadn't doubted that there would have been Bollers in the clandestine nonburial party.

'The Overseers of the Poor doubtless turned a blind eye,' said the antiquarian. He prided himself on having what he thought was a good knowledge of the seamy side of human nature. That went with a study of the past.

'I dare say,' said Horace Boller, whose own knowledge went a little deeper, 'that they were glad to have it done.'

'Well, yes, but the law was . . .'

Horace Boller had only listened with half an ear at the time. The letter of the law wasn't one of his yardsticks. Besides he himself had found the careful study of the official mind a more rewarding business than history.

'They'd be more at home in Collerton churchyard anyway,' he had said to the antiquarian, who by then was beginning to come between Horace and the job he happened to have on hand at the time.

'Pardon?' The antiquarian had known a lot but he hadn't known everything.

'The north-west corner of Collerton churchyard floods every time the river rises,' Horace had taken pleasure in informing him. 'Didn't you know that?'

What Horace Boller was thinking about now, out on the

water and with an actual body in view, wasn't exactly the same as pushing a financial liability into the next parish but it came very near to it. What he was considering was the best move to make next – the best move from the point of view of Horace Boller, citizen and occasional taxpayer, that is.

He steadied the oars in the rowlocks and considered the state of the tide. He was always conscious of it but particularly when he was out on the water. It wasn't far off the turn and he certainly wasn't going to row a body back to Edsway against the tide. The reasoning sped glibly through his mind as he took enough bearings to mark the spot in the water where the body was floating. Already he heard himself saying, 'I couldn't lift it aboard myself, of course, Mr Ridgeford. Not on my own like. I couldn't tow it back either. Not against the tide . . . not without help. I'm not as young as I used to be, you know . . .'

Half an hour later he was using just those very words to Police Constable Ridgeford. Brian Ridgeford was young enough to be Horace Boller's son but Horace still deemed it politic to call him 'Mister'. This approach was one of the fruits of his study of the ways of the official mind.

'Dead, you said?' checked Constable Ridgeford, reaching for his telephone.

'Definitely dead,' said Horace. He'd taken off his cap when he stepped into the constable's little office and he stood there now with it dangling from his hand as if he were already a mourner.

'How did you know it was a man?' asked Ridgeford.

The question didn't trouble Horace Boller. 'Floating on its back,' he said.

'I'll have to report it to Headquarters,' said Ridgeford importantly, beginning to dial. A body made a change from dealing with old Miss Finch, who – difficult and dogmatic – insisted that there were Unidentified Flying Objects on the headland behind Marby.

'That's right,' said Horace.

Ridgeford frowned. 'There may be someone missing.'

'So there may.'

'Not that I've heard of anyone.' The constable pulled a pile of reports on his desk forward and started thumbing through them with one hand while he held the telephone in the other.

'Nor me,' said Horace at once. It had been one of the factors that had weighed with him when he decided not to bring the body in. It hadn't been someone local or he would have heard. 'But then . . .'

Ridgeford's attitude suddenly changed. He stiffened and almost came to attention. 'Is that F Division Headquarters at Berebury? This is Constable Ridgeford from Edsway reporting . . .'

Horace Boller waited patiently for the outcome.

A minute or two later he heard Ridgeford say, 'Just a moment, sir, and I'll ask the fisherman who reported it. He'll know.' The young constable covered the mouthpiece of the telephone with his free hand and said to Horace, 'Where will that body fetch up if it's left in the water?'

Boller screwed up his face and thought quickly. 'Hard to say exactly, Mr Ridgeford. Most probably,' he improvised, 'under the cliffs over on the Kinnisport side of the estuary.' He waved an arm. 'You know, where the rocks stick out into the water. Not,' he added, 'for a couple of days, mind you.'

He stepped back, well pleased with himself. What he had just said to the policeman was a complete fabrication from start to finish. Left to itself the body of the dead man might continue on its course upriver to Collerton for the length of a tide or two but then either the change in the tide or the river current would pick it up and bring it back downstream again. Then the timeless eddies of the sea would lay it up on Billy's Finger as they had always done since time began.

Constable Ridgeford, though, did not know this. He was young, he was new in Edsway and, most importantly of all, he was from the town. In towns water came in pipes.

'H'm,' he said. 'You're sure about that, are you?'

'Certain,' said Boller, although the rocks under the cliff near Cranberry Point were a long way from where he had last seen the dead man. They just happened to be the most inaccessible and inconvenient place on the coast from which to attempt to recover a body that Horace could think of on the spur of the moment.

'They'd have to take it up the cliff-face on a cradle from there, wouldn't they?' said Ridgeford, frowning.

'Oh, yes,' said Boller at once. 'You'd never get a recovery boat to land on those rocks. Too dangerous. Mind you,' he added craftily, 'the coastguards up top would probably spot it for you easily enough.'

'Er – yes, of course,' said Ridgeford.

Horace Boller said nothing but he knew he'd played a trump card. Another of the fruits of his study of the official mind was the sure and certain knowledge that owners of them did not relish co-operation with other official services. Over the years the playing off of one department against another had become a high art with the wily old fisherman.

Ridgeford turned back to the telephone and had further speech with his superior. That officer must have put another question to him because once again Ridgeford covered the mouthpiece. 'You marked the spot with a buoy, didn't you?'

'Sorry, Mr Ridgeford,' lied Horace fluently, 'I didn't happen to have one with me. I was just out to catch something for my tea, that's all.'

There were six orange marker buoys in the locker of Horace's rowing boat. He would have to make quite sure that the constable didn't see them.

'I took proper bearings though, Mr Ridgeford,' said Boller.

'You mean you could take me out there?'

'If my son came too,' said Horace cunningly. 'I reckon we could get him aboard and back to dry land, whoever he is, in no time at all.'

'I'll meet you on the slipway in twenty minutes,' said the constable briskly.

'Right you are, Mr Ridgeford.' Horace replaced his cap and turned to go.

'And,' the policeman added drily, 'I'll bring my own rope just in case you were thinking we ought to get a new one from Hopton's.'

Hopton's was the ship's chandler on Shore Street. It was

the store where the myriad of small boat owners bought the necessities of weekend sailing. Mrs Hopton had been a Boller before she married.

'Just as you say, Mr Ridgeford,' said Horace. He felt no rancour: on the contrary. Like Alexander Solzhenitsyn's hero Ivan Denisovich, he was a great one for counting his blessings. As a little later he settled his oars comfortably in the rowlocks while his son pushed the boat off from the slipway, he even felt a certain amount of satisfaction. There would be a fee to come from Her Majesty's Coroner for the County of Calleshire for assisting in the recovery of the drowned man and that fee would only have to be shared within the family.

Police Constable Brian Ridgeford settled himself in the bow and look steadily forward, his thoughts following a different tack. He wasn't a fool and he hadn't been in Edsway long, but long enough to learn some of the little ways of the Boller tribe. He had not been entirely deceived by Horace's manoeuvres, either. He had been well aware, too, that when he, Brian Ridgeford, had dropped in on Ted Boller, carpenter and undertaker for all the villages round about, on his way to the slipway, to warn him that there might be a body for him to convey to the mortuary in Berebury, this fact was not news to Ted Boller. It had been immediately apparent to the police constable that Horace had wasted no time in alerting Ted, who was Horace's cousin. Naturally Ted had not said anything to the policeman about this. While Horace was cunning, Ted was sly and he'd just promised to keep an eye open for the return of their boat and to be ready and waiting by the shore when they got back.

The two Bollers pulled steadily on their oars while Horace did some calculations about tide flow.

'Be about an hour and a bit since I left him, wouldn't it, Mr Ridgeford?' he said.

'If you came straight to me,' said the constable.

Boller turned his head to take a bearing from the spire of St Peter's church and another from the chimneys of Collerton House. 'A bit farther,' he said.

Both oarsmen bent to their task, while Constable Ridgeford scanned the water ahead.

Presently Horace turned his head again, this time to take in the state of the tide by looking across at the saltings. They were invisible at high water. Birds on them betokened low tide. 'Turn her upriver a bit more,' he commanded.

Once they reached what Horace Boller thought was the right place the drowned man took surprisingly little time to locate. Brian Ridgeford spotted him first and the three men got him aboard without too much of a struggle. The victim of the water wasn't a big man. He had had dark hair and might have been any age at all. That was really all that Brian Ridgeford noted before he helped Horace cover him first with a black plastic bag and then with the tarpaulin that was doing duty as a temporary winding sheet.

Once on dry land and safely in the official care of the Calleshire Constabulary – although still with a member of the Boller family ready to put his thumb on a fee – the body made greater speed. Ted Boller and his undertaker's van soon set off towards Billing Bridge and Berebury. Strictly speaking it was Billing Bridge that marked the end of the estuary. Some medieval men had earned merit by building churches; if you couldn't build a church, then you built a bridge. Cornelius Billing had bought his way into the history and topography of the county of Calleshire in 1484 by building a bridge over the River Calle at the farthest point downriver that it had been possible to build a bridge in 1484.

Ted Boller slowed his vehicle down as he bumped his way over it in a primitive tribute to his passenger, who was far beyond feeling anything at all, while Constable Ridgeford walked back to his own house, beginning to draft in his mind the details of his report. He wondered idly which day the coroner would nominate for the inquest . . .

Just as some men liked to toy with a chess problem so Police Constable Brian Ridgeford passed his walk considering whether he could summon a jury in Edsway – should the coroner want to sit with one, that is – without calling upon a single member of the vast Boller family to serve on it. Like countering one of the rarer chess gambits it would be difficult but he reckoned that it could be done.

Ted Boller's hearse duly delivered the unknown man to the mortuary presided over by Dr Dabbe, Consultant Pathologist to the Berebury District Hospital Group. Such minimal paperwork that the body had so far acquired on its short journey from sea to land and from coast to town accompanied it and said briefly, 'Found drowned.'

'Found drowned, my foot,' said the pathologist two minutes after looking at the body.

The company are met.   2

'Found drowned, his foot,' repeated Police Superintendent
Leeyes not very long afterwards.

As soon as the pathologist's message had come through to
Berebury Police Station he had summoned Detective Inspector C. D. Sloan to his office. Inspector Sloan – known as
Christopher Dennis to his nearest and dearest – was for
obvious reasons called 'Seedy' by his friends. He was the head
of Berebury's Criminal Investigation Department. It was a
tiny department but such crime as there was in that corner of
Calleshire usually landed up in Detective Inspector Sloan's
lap.

In any case – in every case, you might say – Superintendent
Leeyes always saw to it that nothing stayed on his own desk
that could be delegated to someone else's. That desk was
usually Sloan's.

'Found in water, though?' advanced Sloan, who was well
versed in his superior officer's little ways. He was a great one
for passing the buck, was the superintendent.

Downwards.

Detective Inspector Sloan could never remember a problem
being referred to a higher level – in their case the Headquarters
of the Country Constabulary at Calleford – if Superintendent
Leeyes could possibly help it. Sloan was, though, well aware
of – indeed, would never forget – some of those problems that
the superintendent had in the past directed downwards to his

own desk. A body found in water but not drowned sounded as if it might very well be another of the unforgettables.

'Brought in from the estuary,' expanded Leeyes. 'Someone reported it to Constable Ridgeford.'

Sloan nodded. 'Our man in Edsway.'

'He's young,' added the superintendent by way of extra identification.

Sloan nodded again. He wasn't talking about the body. Sloan knew that. The superintendent had meant the constable.

'Very young.' The superintendent at the same time contrived to make youth sound like an indictment.

Sloan nodded his head in acknowledgement of this observation too. He even toyed with the idea of saying that they had all been young once – including the chief constable – but he decided against it. Medical students, he knew, when certain specific diseases were being taught, were always reminded that the admiral had once been a midshipman; the bishop, a curate . . . Anyway it was quite true that constables did seem to come in two sizes. Young and untried was one of the them. Old and cunning was another. The trouble was that the first group had seen nothing and that the second lot – the oldies – had seen it all. The latter tended to be world-weary about everything except their own lack of promotion. On this subject, though, they were apt to wax very eloquent indeed . . .

'And,' carried on Leeyes, 'I don't know how much of a greenhorn Ridgeford is.'

The only exception to the rule about old and disgruntled constables that Sloan knew was Constable Mason. He must be about due for retirement now – he'd been stationed over at Great Rooden for as long as anyone could remember. The trouble with Constable Mason from the hierarchy's point of view was that he had steadily declined promotion over the years. More heretical still, he had continually declared himself very well content with his lot.

'I don't,' said Leeyes grumpily, 'want to find out the hard way about Ridgeford.'

'No, sir,' said Sloan, his mind still on Mason. The bizarre

attitude of that constable to his career prospects had greatly troubled Superintendent Leeyes. If the donkey does not want the carrot there is only the stick left – and there has to be a good reason for using that. Consequently a puzzled Police Superintendent Leeyes had always watched the crime rate out at Great Rooden with exceedingly close attention. Mason, however, was as good as any Mountie in getting his man. This, he said modestly, was because he had a head start when there was villainy about. He not only usually knew who had committed the crime but where to lay his hands on the culprit as well . . .

'Besides,' complained Leeyes, 'You've got to put the young men somewhere.'

'Yes, sir.' Sloan heartily agreed with that. 'And some of them have got to go out into the country.'

'As long as they don't take to growing cabbages,' said Leeyes. Constable Mason – old Constable Mason – insisted that he liked living in the country. That was another of the things that had bothered the urban Superintendent Leeyes. Another was that there really seemed to be no crime to speak of in Great Rooden anyway. The superintendent had put the most sinister construction possible on the situation but three anti-corruption specialists – heavily disguised as government auditors – had failed to find Mason collaborating improperly with anyone.

'We can't,' growled Superintendent Leeyes, his mind on Constable Ridgeford of Edsway, 'keep them all here in Berebury tied to our apron strings, can we?'

'We can't keep an eye on them all the time even if we do,' said Detective Inspector Sloan, who had ideas of his own about the 'being thrown in the deep end' approach. 'Besides, we're not wet nurses.'

That had been a Freudian slip on Sloan's part and he regretted it at once.

'This body,' said Leeyes on the instant, 'was picked up in the water between Collerton and Edsway.' He moved over from his desk to a vast map of the county of Calleshire which was fixed to the wall of his office. It clearly showed the estuary of the River Calle from Billing Bridge westwards down to the sea with Kinnisport standing sentinel on the north shore and Edsway sheltering under the headland on the southern edge, with the village of Marby juxta Mare over on the seacoast to the south-west. It was a contour map and the headland between Edsway and Marby called the Cat's Back showed up well.

The limits of F Division were heavily outlined in thick black pencil. Each time that he saw it Detective Inspector Sloan was reminded of the ground plan of a medieval fortress. Superintendent Leeyes added to the illusion by presiding over his territory with much the same outlook as a feudal baron.

He put his thumb on the map now. 'They found it about here, upstream from Edsway.'

'And downstream from Collerton.' Detective Inspector Sloan made a note. 'Is there anyone missing from hereabouts? I haven't heard of . . .'

'I've got someone pulling a list now,' said Leeyes briskly, 'and I've been on to the coastguards.'

Sloan lifted his eyes towards the point on the map where the stretch of cliff beyond Kinnisport showed. 'Ah, yes,' he murmured, 'they might know something, mightn't they?'

It was the wrong thing to say.

'It all depends on how wide awake they are,' sniffed Leeyes.

'Quite so,' said Sloan.

'I don't see myself,' said the superintendent heavily, 'how anyone can keep an eye on them out on the cliffs like that.'

'Still, they might have seen something.'

'It's too quiet by half up there,' pronounced Leeyes.

'That's true,' agreed Sloan. Mercifully Cranberry Point did not have the attractions of Beachy Head. He was profoundly thankful that those who wished to end it all did not often buy single tickets to Kinnisport and walk out to the cliffs. The rocks at the bottom were singularly uninviting. Today's victim wasn't likely to be a suicide: not if he was found in the water but not drowned . . .

'The trouble,' declared Leeyes, still harping on the coast-guards, 'is that nothing ever happens up there on the cliff to keep them on their toes.'

'No, sir,' agreed Sloan. The superintendent was a great believer in a constant state of alert. In an earlier age he would have been a notable success as a performer with a dancing bear. It would have been on its toes, all right. 'This chap could have been a seaman, I suppose.'

'Eight bells,' said Leeyes suddenly.

'Pardon, sir?'

'Sunset and rise and shine,' said Leeyes.

'Er – quite so, sir.'

'The old watch stands down, duty done,' intoned Leeyes sonorously. 'The new watch takes over.'

'The coastguards'll know about shipping, surely though, sir?' Sloan ventured back on to firmer ground.

'Ah,' said Leeyes, unwilling to impute any merit at all to a distinguished service, 'that depends if their records are any good or not, doesn't it?'

'I suppose it does.' Sloan wasn't going to argue: with anyone else, perhaps, but not with Superintendent Leeyes and not at the very beginning of a case.

'Remember,' said Leeyes darkly, 'that not everything gets reported. Especially at sea.'

There was no thick black line extending F Division out into the sea to the territorial limit but in Leeyes's view there should have been. From time to time he hankered after the autocratic authority of the captain of a ship at sea as well.

'They'll listen in all the time to radio messages at sea, though,' pointed out Sloan. 'Bound to.'

He didn't know about nothing being sacred any longer but he did know that between radio and computer nothing much remained secret for very long.

'All right, all right,' conceded Leeyes. 'They may have picked something up. We'll have to wait and see what they say.'

Detective Inspector Sloan kept his mind on essentials. 'But it isn't a case of drowning, you say, sir?'

'Not me, Sloan,' countered Leeyes robustly. 'I didn't say any such thing. It's the pathologist who says that.'

'Ah.'

'And I don't suppose he'll change his mind either. You know what Dr Dabbe's like when he get a bee in his bonnet.'

'Yes, sir,' said Sloan. The proper name for that was 'professional opinion' but he didn't say so.

'It doesn't sound too important anyway,' said Leeyes. He tore off the top sheet of a message pad and added gratuitously, 'And if it's not too important you might as well take Constable Crosby with you. I can't spare anyone better today.'

If she had happened to have looked out of one of the front windows of Collerton House at the right time that afternoon Elizabeth Busby might actually have seen Constable Brian Ridgeford and the Boller *père et fils* shipping the body of the dead man aboard the rowing boat. The uninterrupted view of the estuary was one of the many attractions of Collerton House. The trees planted by the first owner, which were mature now, had been carefully set back behind the building line so that the sight of the gradually broadening river was not impaired and yet the house itself was still sheltered by them.

If Elizabeth Busby had been really interested in what had been going on in the water during the afternoon she could have done more than just glance out of the window. She could have stepped out on to the stone terrace in front of the house and taken a closer look at the River Calle through the telescope that was permanently mounted there.

This telescope was currently kept trained on a pair of great crested grebes which had built their nest at the edge of a large clump of reeds, but it was so mounted that it could be swung easily from side to side and up and down to take in the entire estuary from Kinnisport and the sea to the west right up the river to Billing Bridge in the east.

The reason why Elizabeth Busby did not happen to look out of the window that afternoon was that she had so many other things to do. Collerton House had been built in more spacious times: times when servants were, if not two a penny, at least around for ten pounds a year all found. Now it was a case of first find someone willing to work at all in the house. That couldn't be done very easily any more – quite apart from the consideration of the expense.

Notwithstanding this there were very few rooms in Collerton House that did not boast a bell-push or a bell-pull of some description – some of them of a very ornate description – as a reminder of a more comfortable past. The only one of them that Elizabeth Busby knew for certain was in good working order was the one that had been in her aunt's bedroom. Aunt Celia had rung it when she was ill and Elizabeth had answered it – and had gone on answering its each and every summons right up until the day when Celia Mundill had died in that very bedroom.

Another reason why Elizabeth Busby was too busy to look out of the window was that she was deliberately undertaking as much hard work in the day as she possibly could. If there was a job that looked as if it could be packed into her waking hours then she put her hand to it and carried on until it was done. Even Frank Mundill, himself sunk in gloom since his wife's death, had advised her to let up a little.

'Take it easy, Elizabeth,' he'd mumbled at breakfast time only that morning. 'We don't want you cracking up as well.'

'I've got to keep busy,' she'd said fiercely. 'Just got to! Don't you understand?'

'Sorry. Of course.' He'd retreated behind the newspaper after that and said no more about it and Elizabeth Busby had gone on to devote the day to turning out the main guest room. It was too soon to be making up the beds but there was no harm in getting the room ready. Besides, giving the bedroom a thorough spring-clean somehow contrived to bring those who were going to occupy it next a little nearer.

There was some real comfort to be had in that because it was her own father and mother who were due to come to stay and who would be moving into the room. Each and every touch that she put into the spring-cleaning of the bedroom brought its own reminder of them. Quite early on she had gone off through the house in search of a bigger bedside table for her father. He always liked a decent-sized table beside his bed – not one of those tiny shelves that could take no more than book and reading glasses. He'd lived abroad for so long – usually in strange and far-away places – that he was accustomed to having everything he might need in the night right beside him.

She'd never forgotten his telling her that when he was a young man he used to sleep with a gun under his pillow – but she had never known whether that had been true or not. It had been the same night that she had lost a milk tooth. She had been inconsolable to start with about the tooth – or perhaps it had been about the gap that it had left.

'Put it where I put my pistol, Twiz,' he'd said, 'and the Tooth Fairy will find it and leave you a silver sixpence.'

'Did the Tooth Fairy find your pistol?' she had wanted to know, forgetting all about her tooth. 'What did she leave you for your pistol?'

That had been on one of her parents' rare and glorious leaves when for once they had all been together as a family. Then, all too soon, it had been over and her mother and father had gone again. By the time they came back on their next furlough Elizabeth had all her second teeth and had grown out of believing in fairies of any ethereal description. Even sixpences had been practically no more.

So today she'd humped an occasional table along to the guest bedroom to put beside the bed. She even knew which side of the bed her father would choose to sleep on. The side nearer the door. That was another legacy from years of living in foreign and sometimes dangerous places . . .

The table had been heavier than she had expected but when she came to move it she realized that Frank Mundill must have gone back to work – his office was in the converted studio right at the top of the house – and so wasn't around to give her a hand. That was after they'd had a scratch luncheon together in the kitchen – Mundill had heated up some soup and rummaged about in the refrigerator until he'd found a wedge of pâté for them both. He'd hovered over the electric toaster for a while and promised to rustle up something more substantial that evening.

'Don't worry, Frank.' She'd brushed her hair back from her face as she spoke. 'I'm not hungry.'

'Can't honestly say that I am either,' he shrugged wryly. 'Still, we'd better try to eat something, I suppose . . .'

She had given him a look of genuine pity. Frank Mundill's profession might be architect but his great hobby was cooking and it had been quite pathetic during his wife's last illness to see him trying to tempt her failing appetite with special delicacy after special delicacy. On her part Celia Mundill had gallantly tried to swallow a mouthful or so of each as long as she had the strength to do so – but the time had come when even that was more than she could manage.

'I'll have the bedroom done by tonight,' Elizabeth had said abruptly. She tried not to think about Aunt Celia's last illness. It was too soon for that.

'Don't overdo it, though, will you, Elizabeth?'

She shook her head.

Only her father and mother were allowed to call her Twiz. With everyone else she insisted upon Elizabeth in full. None of the other traditional diminutives were permitted either. She never answered to Liz or Betty or Beth or – save the mark – Bess. Peter had teased her about that once.

'Even Queen Elizabeth didn't mind that,' he'd said. 'Good Queen Bess rolls around the tongue rather nicely, don't you think?'

'No, I don't, and don't you dare call me Bess either, Peter Hinton. I won't have it!'

And now she had to try not to think about Peter Hinton either.

'Give me a call when you're ready for some tea,' she'd said to Frank Mundill that afternoon. His secretary was on holiday this week. 'I expect I'll still be up in the bedroom,' she added. 'I'm making a proper job of it while I'm about it.'

So the afternoon – the afternoon that the body of the

unknown man was brought ashore at Edsway – passed for her in hard work. It was the only way in which Elizabeth Busby could get through the days. Anyway it wasn't so much the days – they were just periods of time to be endured – as the nights. It was the nights that were the greatest burden.

They were pure hell.

For the first time in her life Elizabeth had come to see the long stretches of the night as something to be feared. The leaden march of the night hours shook her soul in a way that the hours of the day didn't. The days were easier. There were punctuations in the day. There were, too, the constant demands of civilized behaviour to be met and there were the recurring needs of her body to be attended to. She had to wash, to dress, to eat and to drink – even if she could no longer be merry. All the blessedness of a routine was there for the using.

She found rather to her surprise that she washed, dressed, and – sometimes – ate just as she had always done. She answered the telephone, wrote letters, did the dusting, and attended – acolyte-fashion – to the washing machine just as if nothing had happened.

That was in the daytime.

It was a constant source of wonder to her that after the day when her own heaven had fallen and 'The hour when earth's foundations fled' she still got through the days at all.

The nights, of course, were different.

In a world that had tumbled about her ears the nights had turned into refined torture. There was no routine about the long watches of the night, no demands on her time to be met until morning, and no requirement of her body that could be satisfied – not even sleep.

Especially not sleep.

The night-time was when she could have walked mile after mile – however weary she had been when she dropped into bed. Instead custom required that she spend it lying still in a narrow bed in a small room. The room – her room – got smaller and smaller during the night. She could swear to it.

There had been a horror story she'd read once when she was young about the roof of a four-poster bed descending on the person in the bed and smothering him . . .

She'd been of an age to take horror in her stride then, to laugh at it even. Horror in those days had been something weird and strange. Now she was older she knew that horror was merely something familiar gone sadly wrong . . . that was where true horror lay . . .

Why, she thought angrily to herself as she shook out a duster, hadn't someone like Wilkie Collins written about the bruising a girl's soul suffered when she'd been jilted? That should have given any novelist worth his salt something to get his teeth into . . .

Tell the Sheriff's Officers
that I am ready.

3

Detective Constable Crosby – he who could most easily be spared from the police station – brought the car round for Detective Inspector Sloan as that officer stepped out of the back door of Berebury Police Station.

The constable was patently disappointed to learn that there was no hurry to get to wherever they were going.

'No hurry at all,' repeated Sloan, climbing into the front passenger seat. 'You can take it from me, Crosby, that this particular problem isn't going to run away.'

The other man withdrew his hand from the switches to the blue flashing light and siren.

'On the contrary,' forecast Detective Inspector Sloan, 'I shouldn't be surprised if it's not going to be with us for quite a while.'

The trouble with Superintendent Leeyes was that his gloom was catching.

'Yes, sir,' said Crosby, immediately losing interest. 'Where to, then, slowly?'

And the trouble with Detective Constable Crosby was that he was only nearly insubordinate.

Sloan settled himself in the car, reminding himself of something he knew very well already: that Detective Constable Crosby wasn't by any means the brightest star in the Force's firmament. As far as he, Sloan, could make out, the only thing that Crosby really liked doing was driving fast cars fast. That was probably why Inspector Harpe, who was in charge of Traffic Division, had insisted that the constable was better in the plain-clothes branch rather than the uniform one.

'Call us "Woollies" if you like, Sloan,' Harpe had said vehemently at the time.

'I don't . . .' began Sloan; though there were those in plenty who did.

'But,' swept on Inspector Harpe, 'I'm not stupid enough to want that boy Crosby behind the wheel of one of Traffic Division's vehicles.'

'No, Harry.'

'First time he was tempted,' sniffed Harpe, 'he'd be after a ton-up kid.'

For Adam and Eve temptation had been an apple.

For a traffic duty policeman temptation was a youth behind the wheel of a fast car ahead of him and going faster, ever faster. The driver would be showing the world in general – but the police car in particular – what his car would do. If it was his car: ten to one it would be somebody else's car. Taken for a joy ride. Taken on a joy ride, too.

Luring on the Law was practically a parlour game.

And as Inspector Harpe of Traffic Division knew only too well, what was begun 'sae rantingly, sae wantonly, sae dauntingly' usually ended up on Robert Burns's present-day equivalent of the gallows-tree – a fatal motorway pile-up. Because, as a rule, the Law's cars could do rather better than anyone else's, and the Law's drivers were trained. They were trained, too, of course, not to respond to taunting behaviour. That training, though, took a little longer than learning to drive well.

'The first time someone tried it on Crosby,' Harpe had predicted, 'he'd fall for it. You know he would, Sloan. Be honest now.'

'Well . . .'

'Hook, line, and sinker, I'll be bound,' said Harpe. 'I'm prepared to bet good money that he'd go and chase some madman right up the motorway until they ran out of road. Both of them.'

'But . . .' Even Superintendent Leeyes wasn't usually as bodeful as this.

'Catch Crosby radioing ahead to get the tearaway stopped instead of going after him.'

'Oh, come off it, Harry,' Sloan had said at the time. 'You were young once yourself.'

At this moment now he contented himself with telling Crosby where to go. 'Dr Dabbe is expecting us at the mortuary,' he said as the police car swung round Berebury's new multi-storey car park and out on to the main road.

Crosby automatically put his foot down.

'In due course,' said Sloan swiftly. 'Not on two stretchers.'

The consultant pathologist to the Berebury District Hospital Group was more than expecting them. He was obviously looking forward to seeing the two policemen. He welcomed them both to his domain. 'Come along in, Inspector Sloan, and – let me see now – it's Constable Crosby, isn't it?'

'Yes, Doctor.' Crosby didn't like attending post-mortem examinations.

The pathologist was rubbing his hands together. 'We've got something very interesting here, gentlemen. Very interesting, indeed.'

'Have we?' said Sloan warily. Cases that were 'open and shut' were what made for a quiet life, not interesting ones.

The pathologist indicated the door to the post-mortem theatre. 'What you might call a real puzzler.'

'Really?' said Sloan discouragingly.

'As well as being "a demd, damp, moist, unpleasant body", as Mr Mantalini said.'

'Not drowned anyway, I hear,' advanced Sloan, who did not know who Mr Mantalini was. The case was never going to get off the ground at all at this rate.

'Not "drowned dead" anyway,' agreed the pathologist breezily. 'You know your Charles Dickens, I expect, Sloan?'

Sloan didn't but that wasn't important. What was important was what the pathologist had found.

He waited.

'In my opinion,' said Dr Dabbe, getting to the point at last, 'confirmed, I may say, by some X-ray photographs, this chap we've got here . . . whoever he is . . .'

'Yes?' said Sloan, stifling any other comment. The body's identity was something else that the police were going to have to establish.

Later.

'. . . and however wet he is,' continued the pathologist imperturbably, 'was dead before he hit the water.'

'Ah,' said Sloan.

'Furthermore . . .'

Even Constable Crosby raised his head at this.

'Furthermore,' said the pathologist, 'in my opinion he died from the consequences of a fall from a considerable height.'

Detective Constable Crosby clearly felt it was incumbent on him to say something into the silence which followed this pronouncement. He looked round the room and said, 'Did he fall or was he pushed?'

'Ah, gentlemen,' Dr Dabbe said courteously, 'I rather think that's your department, isn't it? Not mine.'

Detective Inspector Sloan was not to be diverted by such pleasantry. There were still some matters that were the pathologist's department and he wanted to know about them.

'What sort of height?' he asked immediately.

'Difficult to say exactly at this stage, Sloan,' temporized the pathologist. 'There's a lot of work to be done yet. I've got to take a proper look at the X-rays, too. I can tell you that there are multiple impacted fractures where the shock effect of hitting terra firma ran through the body.'

Sloan winced involuntarily.

The pathologist was more detached. 'It demonstrates Newton's Third Law of Motion very nicely – you know, the one about force travelling through the body.'

Sloan didn't know and didn't care.

'He didn't fall from the air, did he?' he asked. There had been parts of a dead body dropped from an aeroplane on the Essex marshes just after the last war. That case had become a *cause célèbre* and passed into legal history and he, Sloan, had read about it. 'We're not talking about aeroplane height, are we?'

'No, no,' said Dr Dabbe. 'Less than that.'

Sloan nodded. 'But he didn't fall into the water?'

'Not first,' said the pathologist. 'I think he hit the earth first.'

That only left fire. If Sloan had been a medieval man he would have promptly enquired about the fourth element – fire – that always went with earth, water, and air. He wasn't, he reminded himself astringently, any such thing. He was a twentieth-century policeman. 'A fall from a height,' he said sedately instead.

'Yes,' said the pathologist.

'And on to hard ground,' said Sloan.

'Hard something,' said Dr Dabbe. 'As to whether it was ground or not I can't say yet.'

'Not into the sea, though?' concluded Sloan.

That stirred Detective Constable Crosby into speech again. 'What about Cranberry Point?' he suggested. 'That's a good drop.'

'Rather less than that, too, I think,' said Dr Dabbe more slowly, 'though I can't tell you for certain yet. I'll have to have a look at the exact degree of bone displacement . . .'

The knee bone was connected to the hip bone and the hip bone was connected to the thigh bone . . .

'You can get out on to the cliff above Kinnisport,' persisted Crosby, 'if you have a mind to.'

'But,' pointed out the pathologist, 'if you go over the cliff there you don't hit the water.'

'No more you don't, Doctor,' agreed the constable, in no whit put out.

Sloan had forgotten for a moment that the pathologist was a Sunday sailor himself. He remembered now that Dr Dabbe sailed an Albacore somewhere in the estuary. He was bound to know that stretch of the river and coastline well.

'You hit the rocks if you go over the edge up there,' pronounced Dr Dabbe, thus revealing that he had already given the cliffs beyond Kinnisport some thought.

'But not the water,' agreed Sloan. That was what had saved Cranberry Point from becoming Calleshire's Beachy Head all right. 'The tide never comes in to the very bottom of the cliff.'

'Exactly,' said Dr Dabbe. 'He wouldn't have ended up in the water if he'd gone over the cliffs there.'

'Unless,' said Inspector Sloan meticulously, 'someone had then punted the body into the sea.' It might be Dr Dabbe's function to establish the cause of death; it was Detective Inspector Sloan's bounden duty to consider all the angles of a proposition. 'After he'd fallen . . .'

'Or been pushed,' said Crosby unnecessarily.

It was Sloan whom the pathologist answered. 'Yes, Inspector, I suppose you shouldn't discount the theoretical possibility that someone dragged him off the rocks at the foot of the cliff and into the sea.'

'They'd have had a job,' said Crosby roundly, forgetting that it was no part of the office of constable – detective or otherwise – to argue with an inspector – detective or otherwise – let alone with a full-blown medical man.

Sloan regarded Crosby with a certain curiosity. It wasn't the breach of protocol that intrigued him. After all, protocol was only significant in one of two ways – either in its observance or in its breaching. What he had noted was that Detective Constable Crosby – traffic policeman *manqué* – didn't as a rule take such an interest in a case early on. He wondered what it was about the matter so far that had caught his wayward attention.

'I must say, Sloan,' added Dr Dabbe, who never minded with whom he argued, 'from my own experience I can confirm that it would be the devil's own job to get in there under the cliffs with a boat to do any such thing.'

'Would it, Doctor?' Cranberry Point, then, could be discounted.

'It certainly wouldn't be a job for a man on his own,' said Dabbe, 'and the tide would have had to be exactly right.'

'And as for walking round the cliffs from Kinnisport, sir,' put in Crosby.

'Yes?' said Sloan, interested in spite of himself. Crosby was no walker. His stint on the beat had proved that.

'You'd have your work cut out to do it, sir, without the coastguards seeing you.'

If Superintendent Leeyes had been there he would have automatically added a rider to the effect that the coastguards hadn't anything else to do but look out at the sea and the cliffs. The superintendent wasn't there, of course, because he never went out on cases at all if he could help it. He stayed at the centre while his myrmidons fanned out and then reported back. The still centre, some might say; others were more perceptive and spoke wisely of the eye of the hurricane . . .

'Exactly,' said Dr Dabbe, who was fortunately able to concentrate entirely on the matter in hand. Forensic pathologists didn't have superior officers chasing them. In theory, at any rate, they pursued absolute accuracy for its own sake – at the request of Her Majesty's Coroner and at the behest of no one else. The only people of whom pathologists had to be wary, thought Sloan with a certain amount of envy, were opposing counsel in court who wanted to give the Goddess of Truth a tweak here and there to the benefit of their particular client.

Detective Inspector Sloan took out of his notebook the copy that he had brought with him of Constable Ridgeford's brief report. 'Our man at Edsway says that there weren't any clues as to this chap's name at all that he could see.'

'And none that we could either,' agreed the pathologist. 'Not to his name,' he added obscurely. 'We'll have to leave his personal identity to you people, Sloan, for the time being. Even his own mother wouldn't know him now.'

Sloan nodded. The doctor's 'we' included his own assistant, Burns, a taciturn man who rarely spoke, but who would have gone through the dead man's clothes with the meticulousness of an old-fashioned nanny. 'We'll need as much as we can to go on, Doctor.'

The pathologist started to take his jacket off and to look about him for a green gown. 'His physical identity's no problem.'

'Good,' said Sloan warmly.

'He's male,' said Dr Dabbe, obligingly beginning at the very beginning.

Sloan wrote that down. The Genesis touch, you could say. 'And how old, Doctor?'

Surely that did come after sex, didn't it? 'About twenty-three,' said the doctor promptly. 'Give or take a year or two either way.'

Sloan looked down at his notebook and wondered what came next in the pathologist's logical sequence after sex and age.

'As to his race . . .' began Dr Dabbe cautiously.

'Yes?' Perhaps a seaman from an alien country had found landfall on an English shore after all . . .'

'Caucasian,' said Dabbe, reaching for his surgical gown.

Detective Constable Crosby jerked his head dismissively. 'Oh, he's a foreigner then, is he?'

'Not necessarily, Constable.' The doctor grinned. 'We're all Caucasians here, you know.' He waved a hand at his assistant, Burns, who had just entered the office. 'Even Burns, here, and he's a Scotsman.'

'Ready when you are, Doctor,' said Burns impassively.

The pathologist led the way through to the post-mortem room.

To die a dry death at land,
is as bad as a watery grave.

4

Horace Boller had never been a man to let the grass grow under his feet. Nor was he one to share confidences – not even with his own son. Certainly not with Mrs Boller. After he had got back from Edsway with the body of the unknown man he saw it off in his cousin Ted's hearse and then stumped along to his own cottage where he proceeded to sink a vast mug of steaming hot tea at speed.

'That's better,' he said, wiping his mouth with the back of his hand. Almost immediately he got up to go out again, pushing his chair back as he did so. It scraped on the floor.

Had he known it, the dialogue he then embarked upon with his wife strongly resembled that between many a parent and an adolescent child.

'Where are you going then, Horace?' she asked, casting an eye in the direction of a saucepan on the cooking stove.

'Out,' he rasped.

'Where?'

'Nowhere.'

'When will you be back?'

'Don't know.'

Horace was nearer sixty than sixteen but saw no more need to amplify what he said than did a rebellious teenager. Mrs Boller sniffed and turned down the flame under the saucepan.

'You'll have to wait for your supper then.'

From the cottage doorway all he said was, 'Expect me when you see me.'

And that was said roughly. His mind was on something else.

If that was too soon for Mrs Boller she did not say.

There were some homes that were entirely maintained on the well-established premise that the husband and father was 'a saint abroad and a devil at home'; or it may have been that Mrs Boller had just given up the unequal struggle.

Horace, on the other hand, hadn't given up anything and was soon back at the shore pushing his rowing boat out again. The agglomeration of buoys, hardstanding, and wooden rafts was too informal to be dignified with the name of marina but that was its function. Horace poked about this way and that, and then, calculating that anyone watching his movements from the village would by now have lost interest in his activities, he steered his prow in a seaward direction and bent his back to the oars.

He was as subconsciously aware of the state of the tide as a farmer was aware of the weather and a motorist of other vehicles on the road. With a nicely judged spurt of effort he moved with the last of the tide before he turned distinctly up river and into fresh water. After a little time in the middle of the stream he let the boat drift inshore again towards the south shore – the same side of the river as Edsway but farther upriver.

It was a compound of long experience and the river lore of generations that kept Horace Boller from grounding his boat on the mud banks. He seemed to know by instinct how to pick his way upriver, and which channel had deep water in it and which only looked as if it had. It wasn't only the apparent depths of the channels that were deceptive. Some of those which looked the most promising led only to the shallows. Horace Boller, however, seemed also to know where each one went. Daedalus-like, he selected one channel and passed by another with the sureness of much practice.

Presently he found himself in relatively deep water in spite of being near the shore. This was where the river cut alongside the edge of the parish of Collerton. The churchyard came right down to the river bank and as it had got more and more full over the years the land towards the riverside had been used for graves.

It was undoubtedly picturesque and in the summertime holidaymakers would come to stroll along the bank and through the churchyard exclaiming at the fine views of the estuary to be had from the little promontory. They seldom came in the winter and never in the spring and autumn when the grand alliance of wind and water almost always flooded the whole bank and part of the churchyard.

The land was dry now and from where he was in his boat Horace could see someone tending one of the graves near the river. He bent to his oars though and carried on upstream without looking up. Presently he passed Collerton House too. Like the churchyard, its land – in this case, lawn – came down to the river's edge. There was a little landing stage by the water and beyond that a small boathouse. After that there were no more dwellings, only open fields. The main street of Collerton was set back from the church. Those who professed to understand the English rural landscape were in the habit of speaking knowledgeably about the devastation of the Black Death.

'That's when all the little hovels round the church decayed,' they would say, 'and a later medieval village grew up some distance away from the old diseased houses.'

Horace Boller, who said, 'It stands to reason' almost as often as the storybook character Worzel Gummidge, knew perfectly well why the church stood in lonely splendour apart from the village. It had been built on the only patch of remotely high ground in the parish. The houses had been built well back from the river's edge for the elementary – and elemental – reason that the other land was liable to flooding. Horace was a fisherman. He knew all about the elements.

He rowed steadily upriver for purposes of his own. He didn't stop in his progress until he rounded the last bend before Billing Bridge. Only then did he turn his craft and allow the current to help carry him along and back to the estuary and Edsway. On his way home he looked in on Ted Boller, back in his carpenter's shed after his trip to Berebury. When he got back indoors his wife asked him where he'd been.

'Nowhere,' he said.

'Did you see anyone?'

'No one better than myself,' he said obscurely.

'What have you been doing then?'

'Nothing.'

All of which was – in its own way – perfectly true.

Detective Inspector Sloan entered the mortuary and took his first reluctant look at the unknown male of Caucasian stock, aged about twenty-three years. A decomposing body was not a pretty sight.

'He's not undernourished,' said Dr Dabbe, who had led the way.

Burns, his assistant, who had brought up the rear, said, 'I've got a note of his exact weight and height for you, Doctor.'

Deadweight, thought Sloan to himself, was a word they used about ships, too. He took a look at the man for himself, automatically noting that there was nothing about him to show that he had been a seaman.

'He's not overweight either, Doctor,' he said aloud. That was something to be noted, too, these days. Would historians of the future call this the Age of Corpulence?

'Average,' agreed Dr Dabbe. 'Dark hair and brown eyes . . . are you making a note of that, Constable?'

'Short back and sides,' observed Sloan. That, in essence. would tell Superintendent Leeyes what he wanted to know. For the superintendent the length of a man's hair divided the sheep from the goats as neatly as that chap in the Bible had sorted out the men whom he wanted in his army by the way in which they had drunk at the edge of the water. He'd forgotten his name . . .

'Short back and sides,' agreed the pathologist. 'What's left of it.'

Gideon, thought Sloan to himself; that's who it was. He'd

beaten the army of the Midianites with his hand-picked men, had Gideon.

'I've been looking for occupational signs for you,' said Dr Dabbe.

'That would help,' said Sloan warmly. 'In fact, Doctor, anything would help at this stage. Anything at all.'

'You haven't got anyone like him on the books as missing, then,' said the doctor, correctly interpreting this.

'Not in Calleshire,' said Sloan. 'Not male.'

Detective Constable Crosby hitched a shoulder in his corner. 'Plenty of girls missing, Doctor. All looking older than they are. All good home-loving girls,' he added, 'except that they've left home.'

The white slave trade mightn't be what it had been but it kept going. It wasn't, however, Sloan's immediate concern. He kept his mind on the matter in hand: an unknown body. 'What sort of occupational signs, Doctor?'

'Well, he's quite muscular, Sloan. You can see that for yourself. I'd say he wasn't a man used to sitting at a desk all day. Or if he was, he went in for some strenuous sport too.'

Sloan wondered what the masculine equivalent of house-maid's knee was.

'Actually,' said Dabbe, 'there's no specific sign of a trade about him at all.'

'Ah,' said Sloan non-committally.

'He didn't have cobbler's knee or miller's thumb,' said the pathologist, 'and I can't find any other mark on his person that's come from using the same tool day after day.'

Sloan wondered what sort of occupational mark the police force made on a man – day after day. Varicose veins, probably.

'And he isn't covered in oil,' said Dr Dabbe.

Oil wouldn't have come off in the water, Sloan knew that.

As a possible cause of death shipwreck after a fall on board receded a little from the front of his mind.

'There's something else that isn't there,' said the pathologist.

'What's that, Doctor?' All that came into Sloan's mind was that ridiculous verse of everyone's childhood: 'I met a man who wasn't there . . .'

'Nicotine stains,' replied Dr Dabbe prosaically. 'I should say he was a non-smoker.'

'We don't know at this stage what will be of help.'

'Well, I hope you aren't counting on a fingerprint identification because this chap's skin's more than a bit bloated over now.'

Even the deceased's physical identity was taking a little time to put together.

'Fingernails – what's left of them – appear to have been clean and well cared for,' continued Dabbe.

'Make a note of that, Crosby,' commanded Sloan. Manners might makyth man but appearance mattered too.

'As far as I can see,' said the pathologist, 'he was clean generally.'

That, too, ruled out a whole subculture of the voluntarily dirty. The involuntarily dirty didn't have well-cared-for fingernails and they weren't well nourished as a rule either.

'And he's not a horny-handed son of the soil,' concluded Sloan aloud. 'Is that all you can tell us, Doctor, from the – er – outside, so to speak?'

'Bless you, no, Sloan,' said the pathologist cheerfully. 'That's only half of my superficial examination. I, of course, use the word "superficial" in its purely anatomical connotation of appertaining to the surface, not in its pejorative one.'

'Naturally,' murmured Sloan pacifically. The doctor wasn't in court now. He didn't have to choose his words so carefully.

'And for the record,' added the pathologist breezily, 'he hasn't any distinguishing marks within the meaning of the Act.'

Detective Inspector Sloan nodded, any vision he might have had of easy identification fading away. Even with what the Passport Office engagingly called 'special peculiarities' listed just for that very reason – to help identify a particular person – it wasn't always easy. Without them it could be very difficult indeed. 'Anything else, Doctor?'

'He wasn't mainlining on drugs . . .'

Times had certainly changed. Once upon a time drug-taking

hadn't been one of the characteristics of dead young men that pathologists looked for and – having found them – echoed Housman's parodist, 'What, still alive at twenty-two . . .?'

'There are no signs of repeated injections anywhere,' said Dr Dabbe smoothly, 'and no suspicious "spider's web" tattoos on the inside of the forearm to cover up those signs.'

An old art put to a new use.

'No tattooing at all, in fact,' said Dr Dabbe, proceeding in an orderly manner through the fruits of his superficial examination.

Detective Constable Crosby made a note of that.

'His ears haven't been pierced either,' remarked the pathologist.

Times had certainly changed. Detective Inspector Sloan decided that he was getting old. Unpierced ears were a feature that he should have noticed for himself. The Long John Silver touch was something that had grown up since he was a boy. When he, Sloan, saw earrings on a man he was still old-fashioned enough to look beyond them for the wooden leg.

'In fact, Doctor,' concluded Sloan aloud, 'he was a pretty ordinary sort of man.'

'You want to call him John Citizen, do you?' Dr Dabbe raised a quizzical eyebrow. 'There you would be barking up the wrong tree, Sloan.'

'He seems ordinary enough to me,' persisted Sloan.

'There's no such thing as an ordinary man,' responded Dr Dabbe instantly. 'We're all quite different, Sloan. That's the beauty of the system.'

'There doesn't appear,' he said flatly, 'to be anything out of the ordinary about this man.' One thing that Sloan wasn't going to do was to get into that sort of debate with the pathologist.

'Ah, but I'm not finished yet, Sloan.'

Dr Dabbe had in some respects hardly started. He beckoned Sloan nearer to the post-mortem table and tilted an inspection lamp slightly. 'You will observe, Sloan, that this man – whoever he is – has been in the water for quite a time.'

Sloan repressed a slight shudder. 'Yes, Doctor.'

'And,' continued the pathologist, 'that in spite of this the body is scarcely damaged.'

Detective Inspector Sloan obediently leant forward and peered at the supine figure.

'The lack of damage is interesting,' declared Dr Dabbe.

Sloan held his peace. If the pathologist wanted to be as oracular as Sherlock Holmes and start talking about dogs not barking in the night there was very little that he, Sloan, could do about it.

'It isn't consistent with the length of time the body has been in the water, Sloan.'

So that was what was interesting the doctor . . .

Before Sloan could speak the pathologist had removed the shadowless overhead lamp yet again. This time the beam was thrown over the deceased's left hand.

'There are a couple of grazes on what's left of the skin of the fingers,' he remarked in a detached way. 'He might – only might, mind you, Sloan – have got them trying to save himself from falling.'

Sloan tightened his lips. For all his scientific objectivity, it wasn't a nice picture that the pathologist had just conjured up.

For death is a debt,
A debt on demand.

5

Although Horace Boller had told his wife that he had seen nothing and nobody and had been nowhere he had, in fact, noticed that there had been someone in Collerton churchyard when he had rowed upstream past it. Whoever it was who was there had looked up as he drew level with the churchyard in his rowing boat but Horace hadn't paused in his steady pulling at the oars as he went by. It didn't do to pause if you were rowing against the current. Coming downstream was different. You could even ship oars coming down on the current if you caught the river in the right place.

So Horace, although never averse to a little bit of a gossip with anyone – he collected sundry information in the same way that some men collected postage stamps – had pulled away at the oars and passed by without speaking. He hadn't gone on his way, though, without recognizing the figure tending the grave by the river. Most people who lived round about the shores of the estuary knew Mr Mundill's wife's niece, Elizabeth Busby, by sight. She'd been coming to Collerton House on and off for her school holidays ever since she was a little girl. She'd practically grown up by the river, in fact, and when her aunt, Mrs Celia Mundill, had fallen ill, it had seemed only right that she should give up her job and come back to Collerton to nurse her. Had been engaged to be married, too, Horace had heard, but not any longer.

By the time Horace Boller came downriver on his return

journey, she had gone from the churchyard and all he could see from the river was a fine display of pale pink roses on the new grave.

Elizabeth Busby hadn't planned to visit the Collerton graveyard that afternoon at all. She had fully intended to finish spring-cleaning the guest room and leave it all ready and waiting for the day – the welcome day – when her parents would arrive from South America. What had made her change her mind about finishing preparing the room was something so silly that she didn't even like to think about it. She'd swept and dusted the room and moved the furniture about and taken the curtains down before she even noticed that the picture over the bed had been changed.

She had stopped the vacuum cleaner in full flight so to speak and had stood stock-still in the middle of the floor, staring.

There was no shortage of pictures in Collerton House. On the contrary, it had them everywhere. But everywhere. Her grandfather, Richard Camming, had been an enthusiastic amateur artist and his efforts were hanging in every room of the house. He was not exactly an original . . . The painting that had hung over the bed in the guest room ever since she could remember had been a water-colour of a composition owing a great deal to the works of the late Richard Parkes Bonington.

It had been replaced by an oil painting done in what his two daughters – her aunt Celia and her own mother – affectionately called their father's 'Burne-Jones period'. Richard Camming had even called it *Ophelia* and Elizabeth knew it well. The portrayal of Ophelia's drowning in a stream usually lived on the upstairs landing not far from the top of the stairs.

'He might have put it nearer the bathroom,' her own father used to say irreverently. 'All that water going to waste . . .'

Elizabeth Busby had rested her hands on the vacuum cleaner in the same way as a gardener rested his on his spade while she considered this.

She was not in any doubt about the pictures having been

changed; she knew them both too well. And if she had been in two minds about it a thin line of unfaded wallpaper under the new picture – hidden a little from the casual gaze by the frame – would have confirmed it. The size of the new picture didn't exactly match that of the old.

As soon as she had taken in this evidence – before her very eyes, as the conjurors said – she had gone out on to the landing to look there for the painting that usually hung over the head of the spare bedroom bed. It had been of a stretch of beach . . . When she got to the top of the stairs, though, to the spot where Grandfather's version of Ophelia usually hung the painting of the beach – presumably at Edsway (after Bonington) – wasn't there in its stead.

There wasn't a gap there either of course.

Elizabeth would have noticed a gap straight away. Everyone would have noticed a gap. What was there in the place of Ophelia drowning among the lilies – it must have been a very slow-moving stream, she thought inconsequentially – was a water-colour of the estuary of the River Calle as seen from Collerton House. This owed nothing to any artist save Richard Camming himself and it was not very good. Moreover it was a view that he had painted many, many times – like Monet and the River Thames.

'And not got any better at it,' decided Elizabeth judiciously. Unlike Monet.

There were at least a dozen efforts by Richard Camming at capturing on canvas the oxbow of the river as it swept down towards the sea at Collerton. This particular painting could have been any one of them. Elizabeth wasn't aware of having seen this one anywhere else in the house before but there were several piles of pictures stacked away in the attics of Collerton House and it could easily have been among them without her knowing.

She went back at once to the bedroom to check that only one picture had been changed. Over the fireplace there had hung throughout her lifetime a picture in which her grandfather had tried to capture the elusive gregariousness of the work of Sir David Wilkie – the Scottish Breughel. Richard Camming hadn't actually got a blind fiddler in the picture but there was a general feeling that the musician wasn't far away.

That picture was still there. Elizabeth was not surprised. She would have noticed much earlier in the day if there had been any change in the picture hanging over the fireplace. The head of the bed, though, was at an angle from the window and only got full sunshine in the afternoon.

She had tried after this to go back to her vacuum cleaning but her determined concentration on the mundane had been broken and suddenly her thoughts and carefully suppressed emotions were unleashed in unruly turmoil.

Abruptly she left the cleaner where it was standing in the middle of the floor and went out of the bedroom. As she looked over the landing balustrade she saw with approval the glass case reposing on a window sill in the entrance hall. There was absolutely nothing amateur about her great-grandfather's legacy to posterity. What he had left behind him had been something much more useful that dozens and dozens of indifferent paintings. Gordon Camming – Richard Camming's father – had designed a valve that the marine engineering world of his day had fallen upon with delight and used ever since.

A Camming valve had been fitted into a model and stood for all the world to see in the house built by its designer with the proceeds of the patent. But it was really paintings and not patents that Elizabeth Busby had on her mind as she passed along the landing on her way to Frank Mundill's office. The studio, with its mandatory north light added fifty years earlier by an indulgent father for his painter son, served now as the drawing office of Frank Mundill, architect. Elizabeth didn't usually disturb him there, although she'd done so once or twice when her aunt had taken a turn for the worse – not otherwise – but she didn't hesitate now.

And almost immediately she wished that she hadn't.

Another time she would make a point of not going to his office unheralded because Frank Mundill was not alone.

Sitting in the client's chair in his room was a neighbour – Mrs Veronica Feckler.

'Elizabeth, my dear,' said Mrs Feckler at once, 'how nice to see you.'

'I'm sorry,' said Elizabeth gruffly. 'I didn't know there was anyone here.'

'How could you?' asked Veronica Feckler blandly. 'I crept round the back with my miserable little plans. I was sure that Frank was going to laugh at them and he did.'

'I certainly did not,' protested Frank Mundill.

'I'm sure I detected a twitch of the lips,' insisted Mrs Feckler. She was a widow who had come to live in the village of Collerton about three years ago. Elizabeth's aunt had not greatly cared for her.

'It's just,' said the architect with professional caution, 'that it's a long way from a quick sketch on the back of an envelope . . .'

'A shopping list, actually,' murmured Mrs Feckler.

'. . . to the finished design that a builder can use.'

She turned to Elizabeth. 'I had this brilliant idea while I was in the greengrocer's,' she said eagerly. 'Dear old Mr Partridge was telling me about Costa Rican bananas – did you know that they grew bananas in Costa Rica?'

Elizabeth knew a great deal about Costa Rica, but Mrs Feckler hadn't waited for an answer.

'I said I'd have three when I suddenly thought what about building out over my kitchen.'

'I see,' said Elizabeth politely.

'And it's an even bigger step from the plans to the finished building,' warned Frank Mundill. 'Clients don't always realize that either.'

'But I do.' She turned protestingly to Elizabeth. 'Tell him I do, there's a darling.'

'I was turning out a bedroom,' said Elizabeth obliquely, conscious that she must look more than a little scruffy. Mrs Feckler was wearing clothes so casual that they must have needed quite a lot of time to assemble.

'And I was wasting your poor uncle's time,' said the other woman, sensitive to something in Elizabeth's manner. She rose to go. 'But I do really want something doing to my little cottage now that Simon has said he's coming back home for a while.' She gave a little light laugh. 'Mothers do have their uses sometimes.'

Elizabeth assented politely to this, silently endorsing the sentiment. She would be so thankful to see her own mother again. Mrs Busby hadn't come back to England from South America for her sister's funeral because she couldn't travel by air. Pressurized air travel didn't suit a middle-aged woman suffering from Ménière's disease of the middle ear. Even now, though, both her parents were on the high seas on their way home from South America. They had been coming for a wedding . . .

Frank Mundill was still studying the piece of paper that Mrs Feckler had given him. 'I'll have to think about this, Veronica, when I've had a chance to look at it properly.'

He was rewarded with a graceful smile.

'Give me a day or so,' he said hastily, 'and then come back for a chat. I'll have done a quick sketch by then.'

Mrs Veronica Feckler gathered up her handbag. 'How kind . . .'

Elizabeth Busby waited until Frank Mundill returned to his drawing office after showing her out. 'I came about a picture,' she said.

He sank back into the chair behind his desk and ran his hands through his hair. 'A picture?'

'Three pictures, actually,' she said.

He looked up.

'Three pictures,' she said, 'that aren't where they were.'

'I think I know the ones you mean,' he said uneasily.

'*Ophelia.*'

'It's been moved,' he said promptly.

'I know,' she said. Frank Mundill wasn't meeting her eye, though. 'And a river one and a beach scene . . .'

He didn't say anything in reply.

'The beach one has gone,' she said.

'I know.' He was studying the blotting paper on his desk now.

'Well?'

He cleared his throat. 'Peter wanted it.'

'Peter?' Her voice was up at high doh before she could collect herself.

He nodded. 'I knew you wouldn't like that.'

'Peter Hinton?' She heard herself pronouncing his name even though she had sworn to herself again and again that her lips would never form it ever more.

Frank Mundill looked distinctly uncomfortable. 'He asked me if he could have it.'

'Peter Hinton asked you if he could have the picture of the beach?' she echoed on a rising note of pure disbelief. 'He didn't even like pictures.'

He nodded. 'He asked for it, though.'

'That sloppy painting?' She would have said that detective stories were more Peter's line than paintings.

'Let's say "sentimental",' he murmured.

'That's what I meant,' she said savagely. 'And you're sitting there and telling me that Peter wanted it?'

'So he said.' Frank Mundill was fiddling with a protractor lying on his desk now. He gazed longingly at the drawing board over in the window.

'It wasn't something to remember me by, I hope?' All the pent-up bitterness of the last few weeks exploded in excoriating sarcasm.

'He didn't say.'

'St Bernard dogs aren't a breed that are faithful unto death, are they?' she said, starting to laugh on a high, eerie note. 'If so, he should have taken the imitiation Landseer.'

'Not that I know of,' said the architect coldly.

'That would be too funny for words,' she said in tones utterly devoid of humour.

'I'm sorry if you think I shouldn't have given it to him . . .'

'Why shouldn't he have a picture?' she said wildly. 'Why shouldn't he have all the pictures if he wanted them? Why shouldn't everybody have all the pictures?'

'Elizabeth, my dear girl . . .'

'Well? Why not? Answer me that!'

'If you remember,' Frank Mundill said stiffly, 'I wasn't aware of the provisions of your aunt's will at the time he asked me for it.' He gave his polo-necked white sweater a little tug and said, 'Strictly speaking I suppose the picture wasn't mine to give to him.'

That stopped her all right.

'I didn't mean it that way, Frank,' she said hastily. 'You know that. That side of things isn't important.' She essayed a slight smile. 'Besides, there's plenty more pictures where that one came from.'

'You can say that again,' said Frank Mundill ruefully.

'Sorry, Frank,' she said. 'It's just that I'm still a bit upset . . .' Her voice trailed away in confusion. Collerton House and all its pictures – in fact the entire Camming inheritance – had come from Richard Camming equally to his two daughters – his only children – Celia Mundill and Elizabeth's mother, Marion Busby. Celia and Frank Mundill had had no children and Marion and William Busby, only one, Elizabeth.

When she had died earlier in the year Celia Mundill had left her husband, Frank, a life interest in her share of her own father's estate. At his death it was to pass to her niece, Elizabeth . . .

'There's no reason why Peter shouldn't have had a painting if he wanted one,' she said, embarrassed. 'It isn't even as if they're worth anything.'

Mr Hubert Cresswick of Cresswick Antiques (Calleford) Limited had confirmed that when he had done the valuation after her aunt's death. Very tactfully, of course. It was when he praised the frames that she'd known for certain.

'It's just,' she went on awkwardly, 'that I never thought that his having that particular one would be the reason why it wasn't there on the wall, like it always was.'

'I should have mentioned it before,' he mumbled. 'Sorry.'

'No reason why you should have done,' she said more calmly.

What she really meant was that there were a lot of reasons

why he shouldn't have done. Peter Hinton's name hadn't been mentioned in Collerton House since he'd left a note on the hall table – and with it the signet ring she'd given him. A 'Keep off the grass' ring was what he'd said as he slipped it on his finger.

It didn't matter any longer, of course, what it was called. Elizabeth had returned the ring he'd given her – in the springtime, 'the only pretty ring time' – the one with 'I do rejoyce in thee my choyce' inscribed inside it, to Peter's lodgings in Luston.

That devotion hadn't lasted very long either.

Frank Mundill picked up the sketch Mrs Veronica Feckler had left on his desk and appeared to give it his full attention. He said, 'I suppose I'll have to go down and look at her timbers . . .'

'You will,' she agreed, her mind in complete turmoil.

Elizabeth Busby hadn't known whether to laugh or to cry. On impulse she had gone out into the garden, swept up a bunch of her aunt's favourite roses – Fantin-Latour – and walked down to the churchyard by the river's edge.

She cried a little then.

How can I support this sight!   **6**

The pathologist to the Berebury District Hospital Group was
a fast worker. Nobody could complain about that. He was
also a compulsive talker – out of the witness box, that is. His
subjects were in no position to complain about this or, indeed,
anything else. His assistant, Burns, was not able either – but
for different, hierarchical, reasons – to voice any complaints
about the pathologist's loquacity. Should he have been able to
get in word in edgeways, that is.

In fact, Burns, worn down by listening, had retreated into a
Trappist-like silence years ago. Detective Constable Crosby,
normally a talker, didn't like attending post-mortems. He had
somehow contrived to drift to a point in the room where,
though technically present, he wasn't part of the action. It fell,
therefore, to Detective Inspector Sloan to maintain some sort
of dialogue with Dr Dabbe.

'You'll be wanting to know a lot of awkward things, Sloan,'
said the pathologist, adjusting an overhead shadowless lamp.

'We'll settle for a few facts to begin with, Doctor,' said the
detective inspector equably.

'Like how long he'd been in the water, I suppose?'

'That would be useful to know.'

'And damned difficult to say.'

'Ah . . .'

'For sure, that is.'

Sloan nodded. In this context, 'for sure' meant remaining sure and certain under determined and sustained cross-examination by a hostile Queen's Counsel.

And under oath.

The pathologist ran his eyes over the body of the unknown man. 'He's been there – in the water, I mean – longer than you might think, though,' he said.

'I don't know that I'd thought about that at all,' said Sloan truthfully.

'I have,' responded Dr Dabbe, 'and I must say again that I would have expected rather more damage to the body. Something doesn't tie up.'

Detective Inspector Sloan brought his gaze to bear on the post-mortem subject because it was his duty to do so but without enthusiasm. The body looked damaged enough to him. Detective Constable Crosby was concentrating his gaze on the ceiling.

'The degree of damage,' pronounced the pathologist, 'is not consistent with the degree of decomposition.'

'We'll make a note of that,' promised Sloan, pigeon-holing the information in his mind. By rights, Crosby should have been regarding his notebook, not the ceiling.

'There's plenty of current in the estuary, you see, Sloan,' said the doctor. 'That's what makes the sailing so challenging. But current damages.'

'Quite so,' said Sloan, noting that fact – perhaps it was a factor, too – in his mind as well.

'To say nothing of there being a good tide,' said Dr Dabbe, 'day in, day out.'

'I dare say, Doctor,' said Sloan diffidently, 'that the tide'll still be pretty strong opposite Edsway, won't it?'

'If you'd tacked against it as often as I have,' replied the pathologist grandly, 'you wouldn't be asking that.'

'No, Doctor, of course not.' Sloan wasn't a frustrated single-handed Atlantic-crossing yachtsman himself. Growing roses was his hobby. It was one of the few relaxing pursuits that were compatible with the uncertain hours and demands of detection. Owning a sailing boat, as the doctor did, wasn't compatible with police pay either – but that was something different.

'The wind doesn't help,' said Dabbe, stroking an imaginary beard in the manner of Joshua Slocum. 'You get a real funnel effect out there in mid-channel.'

'I can see that you might,' agreed Sloan. 'What with the cliffs to the north . . .'

'And the headland above Marby to the south,' completed the doctor. 'That's the real villain of the piece.'

Sloan was thinking about something else that wasn't going to help either and that was the official report. It would have to note that the subject was relatively undamaged but not well preserved. It was the sort of incongruity that didn't go down well with the superintendent; worse, it would undoubtedly have to be explained to him.

By Sloan.

'There's the shingle bank, too,' said the doctor.

'Billy's Finger.' Sloan had looked at the map. 'I'm going out there presently to have a look at the lie of the land . . .'

'And the water,' interjected Detective Constable Crosby.

Everyone else ignored this.

'There's always a fair bit of turbulence, too,' remarked the pathologist sagely, 'where the river meets the tide.' It was Joshua Slocum who had sailed alone around the world but Dr Dabbe contrived to sound every bit as experienced.

Immutable was the word that always came into Sloan's mind when people started to talk about tides. He might have been talking about tides at that moment, but it was the face of the superintendent which swam into his mental vision. He would be waiting for news.

'Let's get this straight, Doctor,' he said more brusquely than he meant. 'This man – whoever he is – has been in the water for a fair time.'

'That is so,' he agreed. 'There is some evidence of adipocere being present,' supplemented the pathologist, 'but not to any great degree.'

'But,' said Sloan, 'he hasn't been out where the tides and currents and fish could get hold of him for all that long?'

'That puts it very well,' said Dr Dabbe.

'And he didn't meet his death in the water?'

'I'll be conducting the customary routine test for the widespread distribution of diatoms found in true drowning in sea or river water,' said the pathologist obliquely, 'but I shall be very surprised if I find any.'

'Yes, Doctor,' said Sloan. He wasn't absolutely sure what a diatom was – and now that the atom wasn't the indivisible building block of nature any longer he was even less sure.

Something in what the doctor had said must have caught the wayward attention of Detective Constable Crosby. He stirred and said, 'You mean that that test wouldn't have done for the Brides-in-the-Bath?'

'I do,' said Dr Dabbe. 'There aren't any planktons in bath water.'

'And,' said Sloan, gamely keeping to the business in hand, 'we don't know who he is either . . .' He had just the one conviction about all things atomic – that the only really safe fast breeder was a rabbit.

'No,' agreed Dabbe.

'Of course,' said Sloan, 'we could always try his fingerprints . . .'

'You'll be lucky,' said Detective Constable Crosby, taking a quick look at what was left of the swollen and distended skin of the unknown man. He caught sight of his superior officer's face and added a belated 'Sir.'

'We don't even know,' carried on Sloan bitterly, 'if he went into the river or the sea.'

Unperturbed the doctor said, 'I think we may be able to help you there, Sloan. Or, rather, Charley will.'

'Or,' continued Sloan grandly, 'whether it was an accident or murder.' He didn't know who Charley was.

'He didn't walk after he fell,' said Dabbe. 'I can tell you that for certain.'

Sloan made a note. Facts were always welcome.

'And Sloan, my man Burns has something to say to you, too.' Dr Dabbe waved an arm. 'Haven't you, Burns?'

'Aye, Doctor.'

'His clothes,' divined Sloan quickly. 'Do they tell us anything about him?'

'Mebbe, Inspector,' replied Burns. 'Mebbe.'

'That's Gaelic for "yes and no",' said Dr Dabbe.

'Well?'

Burns didn't answer and it was Dr Dabbe who spoke. 'There was something strange in one of his trouser pockets, wasn't there, Burns?'

'Yes, Doctor,' said Burns.

'Something strange?' said Sloan alertly.

'Show the inspector what you found, man.'

His assistant reached for a tray. Placed on it was a lump of metal almost the size and shape of a bun. It was a faded green in colour.

Detective Constable Crosby leaned over. 'If that was "lost property" we'd call it a clock pendulum.'

'I'm not a metallurgist,' said Dr Dabbe, 'but I should say it's solid copper.'

'What is it, though?' asked Sloan, peering at it. There was a lip on one side of the bun shape.

'I can't tell you that, Sloan.'

'It's not heavy enough to have been to weight him down,' said Sloan, thinking aloud.

'Agreed,' said Dr Dabbe. He scratched the metal object with the edge of a surgical probe. 'It's old, Sloan. And if you ask me . . .'

'Yes?'

'I should say it's been in the water a fair old time, too.'

Police Constable Ridgeford of Edway might have been green. He was also keen. He had noticed Horace Boller take out his rowing boat on the River Calle for the third time that afternoon and kept a wary but unobtrusive eye open for his return. If it had been a fishing trip that Horace Boller had been on then he had been unlucky because he had come back empty-handed for the second time that afternoon.

Brian Ridgeford did not have a boat. He didn't own a boat himself because he couldn't afford one; and as his beat did not extend out into the sea a grateful country did not feel called upon to supply him with one in the way in which it issued him with a regulation bicycle. What he did have – as his sergeant never failed to remind him – was a perfectly good pair of legs. He decided to use them to walk upstream along the river bank to Collerton.

As he remarked to his wife as he left the house, 'You never know what's there until you've been to see.'

'Curiosity killed the cat' was what she said to that, but then she hadn't been married very long and hadn't quite mastered the role of perfect police wife yet. She was trying hard to do so though because she added, 'It's a casserole tonight, darling.'

The only piece of good advice that the sergeant's wife had given her was to cook everything in a pot that could stand on the stove or in the oven without spoiling.

'Good.' He kissed her and got as far as the door. 'I'll be back soon,' forecast Brian Ridgeford unwisely.

He, too, still had a lot to learn.

The remark wasn't exactly contrary to standing orders. It was just flying in the face of some sage advice given by one of the instructors at the Police Training School. 'Never tell your wife when you're going to be back, lads,' he said to the assembled class. 'If you've told her to expect you at six o'clock, then by five minutes past six she'll be standing at the window. At ten minutes past six she'll have her worry coat on and be out in the street looking for you. By quarter past she'll have asked the woman next door what to do next and by half past six she'll be on the telephone to your sergeant.' The instructor had delivered his punch line with becoming solemnity. 'And the tracker dogs'll be out searching for you before you've had time to get your first pint down.'

None of this potted wisdom so much as crossed Brian Ridgeford's mind as he stepped out of the police house door.

He was thinking about other things. All he did do was pause in the hall where the hydrographic map of the estuary hung. He had to stoop a little to look at it properly.

It was a purely token obeisance.

Depths in metres reduced to chart datum or approximately the level of lowest astronomical tide meant very little to a landlubber like himself. He was, though, beginning to understand from sheer observation of the estuary something about drying heights. It was a form of local knowledge – almost inherited race memory, you might say – that seemed to have been born in the Boller tribe. Constable Ridgeford was having to learn it.

It was just as well that he had delayed his departure from the house for a moment or two. It meant that when the telephone bell rang a few minutes later he was not quite out of earshot. His wife came flying down the path after him – casserole forgotten.

'Brian! Brian . . . Stop!'

He halted.

'You're wanted, darling.'

He turned.

'They've found a dinghy,' called out Mrs Ridgeford.

'Ah . . .'

'An empty one.'

He retraced his steps in her direction.

'On the shore,' she said.

'That figures.' He absent-mindedly slipped an arm round her waist. 'Whereabouts?'

'Over at Marby.'

'Right round there?' Constable Ridgeford frowned. The tiny fishing village of Marby juxta Mare was on the coast the other side of Edsway – to the south and west. It had never been the same, local legend ran, since a Danish invasion in the ninth century.

'That's what the man said,' answered Mrs Ridgeford. 'I told him you'd go straight over there. Was that right, Brian?'

Since their marriage was still at the very early stage when it was unthinkable that she could have done anything that wasn't right – the action being sanctified solely by virtue of its having been taken so to speak – this was a purely rhetorical question.

'Of course it was, darling.' Brian Ridgeford nodded approvingly.

'Or,' she added prettily, turning her face up towards his, 'have I done the wrong thing?'

This, too, was a purely token question.

It got a purely token response in the form of a kiss.

'Where did I leave my bicycle clips?' asked Police Constable Brian Ridgeford rather breathlessly.

Marby juxta Mare was a village facing the sea. It was beyond the headland known as the Cat's Back that protected Edsway from the full rigours of the sea. The road, though, did not follow the coast. It cut across below the headland and made Marby much nearer to Edsway by land than by sea.

A man called Farebrother had taken charge of the dinghy. He was a lifeboatman and knew all about capsized dinghies.

'She wasn't upside-down when we found her,' he said. 'And not stove in or anything like that or she'd never have reached where she did on the shore.'

'Has she been there long?' asked Ridgeford cautiously. Boats, he knew, always took the feminine – like the word 'victim' in the French language – but he didn't want to make a fool of himself by asking the wrong question.

'Just the length of a tide,' said the lifeboatman without hesitation. 'We reckon she'd have been gone again after the turn of the tide if we hadn't hauled her up a bit.'

Ridgeford nodded sagely. 'That's a help.'

'No one'll thank you for letting a dinghy get away.' Farebrother wrinkled his eyes. 'It's a danger to everyone else, too, is a dinghy on the loose. No riding lights on a dinghy. You could smash into it in the dark and then where would you be?'

'Sunk,' said Ridgeford.

'Depend on your size, that would,' said the lifeboatman, taking this literally, 'and where she hit you.' He hitched his shoulder, and sniffed. 'Anyways we put her where she can't do any harm and,' he added, 'where she can't come to any more harm either.'

'Any more harm?' said Ridgeford quickly. 'But I thought you said she wasn't damaged . . .'

'So I did,' said Farebrother. 'But she must have come to some harm to be out on the loose like she was, mustn't she? That's not right.'

'I see what you mean,' said the constable. Put lost dinghies into the same category in your mind as lost children and things fell into place.

'An insecure mooring is the least that can have happened.' Farebrother picked up his oilskin jacket. He was a tall man with a thin, elongated face and high cheek-bones. From his appearance he might have descended directly from marauding Viking stock.

'I don't think that that's what it was,' said the young policeman, mindful of the dead body that he'd helped to bring ashore that afternoon.

'Anyways,' said the other man, 'she's safe enough now. She's over this way . . . the other side of the lifeboat station . . . just follow me.'

This was easier said than done. Farebrother set off at a cracking pace along the rocky sea-shore of Marby juxta Mare, so different from the fine estuary sands of Edsway, his sea-boots crunching on the stones. Constable Ridgeford stepped more cautiously after him, slipping and sliding as he tried to pick his way over the difficult terrain. Farebrother slackened his pace only once. That was when a small trawler suddenly emerged from the harbour mouth. He stopped and took a good look at it. Ridgeford stopped too.

'Something wrong?' he asked.

'She's cutting it a bit fine, that's all.'

'Cutting what?' asked Ridgeford. He could read the name *The Daisy Bell* quite clearly on her prow.

'The tide,' said Farebrother. 'She'd have had a job to clear the harbour bar if the water was any lower.'

'I didn't think you went out on an ebb-tide,' said Ridgeford naïvely.

'You don't,' said Farebrother. 'Not without you have a reason.' He resumed his fast pace over the shingle, adding, 'Unless you're dying, of course.'

'Dying?'

'Fishermen always go out with the tide. Didn't you know that? They die at low water . . .'

The dinghy that had been beached was old, weather-beaten, and very waterlogged.

'She's still got her rowlocks with her though,' said the lifeboatman professionally. 'Funny, that.'

'But there's no name on her,' noted the policeman with equal but different expertise. 'She could have come from anywhere, I suppose?'

'Not anywhere.' Farebrother looked the police constable up and down and evidently decided as a result of his appraisal to be helpful. 'The tide brings everything down from the north hereabouts.'

That hadn't been quite what Ridgeford meant but he did not say so.

'Not up from the south,' continued the lifeboatman. 'You never find anything that's come up from the south on this shore.'

That, thought Ridgeford silently, tied in with a body floating in the estuary of the River Calle.

'Especially with the wind in the west like it's been these past few days,' added the other man. 'It's a south-east wind that's nobody's friend.'

'Yes,' said Ridgeford. While Horace Boller almost instinctively knew the state of the tide, so Farebrother would be equally aware of the quarter of the wind. You probably needed to be a farmer to consider the weather as a whole. It was a case of each man to his own trade. Stockbrokers doubtless knew the feel of the market – by the pricking of their thumbs or something – and equally the police . . . Ridgeford wasn't sure what it was that a policeman needed to be constantly aware of . . . There must be something that told a policeman the state of play in the great match 'Crime versus Law and Order'. The knocking off of helmets, perhaps.

'Against the current that would be, too,' continued Farebrother, who was happily unaware of the constable's train of thought.

He made going against the current sound almost as improbable as flying in the face of nature. Had Farebrother been a carpenter, decided Ridgeford to himself, he would have said 'against the grain'.

Aloud he said to the lifeboatman, 'What about this rope at the bow?'

'The painter?' Farebrother looked at the end of the dinghy and the short length of line dangling from it. 'She either slipped her mooring or she was untied on purpose.'

'Not cut loose or anything like that, then?'

Farebrother shook his head, while Brian Ridgeford limped over to the dinghy. He steadied himself against it as he felt about in his shoe for a stray piece of shingle that had made its way into it.

'Someone'll be along soon looking for it,' predicted the lifeboatman, indicating the beached dinghy.

Ridgeford wasn't so sure about that. He found the pebble and removed it.

'With a red face,' added Farebrother.

The face that sprang at once to the policeman's mind was white. Dead white was the name that artists' colourmen gave to paint that colour. The owner of that particular face wouldn't be along *Not this tide, nor any tide,* as the poet had it, *For what is sunk will hardly swim. Not with this wind blowing, and this tide.*

'Maybe he will,' was all he said to Farebrother though. Ridgeford turned his mind to practicalities, and immediately wished that he had his reference books with him. He wasn't well up in the technicalities of the law yet. Was a dinghy washed up on the foreshore 'flotsam' or 'jetsam' or the forgotten third of the marine trio 'lagan'? More importantly, was it 'lost property' or 'salvage'?

'Anyways,' pronounced Farebrother, resolving that difficulty for him, 'we'll keep it here until the owner – whoever he is – turns up. And if he doesn't you'll let the Receiver of Wrecks and the Department of Trade know, won't you?'

'Of course,' said Ridgeford hastily. So the dinghy was none of these things. It was officially a wreck. 'I'll get on to him.'

'Department of Trade!' Farebrother spat expertly across the shore. 'Huh! Trade! I don't suppose anyone there knows the meaning of the word.'

'Well . . .' Ridgeford temporized. He was a civil servant himself now and he was beginning to find out that civil servants did know what they were doing.

'And why they couldn't go on calling it the Board of Trade beats me.' Farebrother rolled his eyes. 'At least everyone knew what you meant then. Department. Huh!'

'They've always got to change things, haven't they?' agreed the young constable briskly. He cast a long glance in the direction of the headland at the south side of the estuary. Some change was for the better. In olden times the good citizens of Marby juxta Mare used to light beacons on this stretch of coast with intent to mislead poor mariners in search of safe landfall. Golden times for the citizens, hard ones for the drowned seafarers. They did say that somewhere out to sea off the headland was the wreck of a merchantman lured to its doom by the ancestors of men like Farebrother . . .

The lifeboatman spat again. 'Things should be let alone with, that's what I say. I don't hold with disturbing things that have always been the way they are and I don't mind who knows it.'

By the time the constable got back to his home in Edsway his wife was on the look-out for him. He dismounted, undid his bicycle clips, and announced portentously, 'It's all right, love. It was just an empty boat. Nothing to worry about – it's safely in police hands now.'

His helpmeet rather spoilt the effect of this pronouncement by giggling.

'Call police hands safe, do you?' she said saucily. 'I don't, Brian Ridgeford.'

'I think it was murder, all right, sir,' said Detective Inspector Sloan into the telephone in Dr Dabbe's office.

'An accident at sea, Sloan,' boomed Superintendent Leeyes into his mouthpiece at the police station in Berebury.

Sloan cleared his throat and carried on manfully. 'He was killed in a fall from a height first, and . . .'

'Washed overboard from an old dinghy,' swept on Leeyes.

'And then,' continued Sloan with deliberation, 'put into the water.'

'The dinghy's been found over at Marby juxta Mare,' said the superintendent.

'With a copper weight of sorts in his pocket,' said Sloan doggedly.

'On the foreshore at Marby,' said Leeyes. 'Constable Ridgeford has just rung in from Edsway.'

There was a flourishing school of thought at the police station which held that the superintendent was deaf. Older hands – more perceptive, perhaps – did not subscribe to this theory. They insisted that the superintendent always heard the things that he wanted to hear all right.

'Why was it murder?' Leeyes asked Sloan suddenly.

'The fall killed him,' explained Sloan, 'and he certainly wouldn't have got into the water on his own afterwards. Dr Dabbe's done some X-rays to prove it . . .'

Leeyes grunted. 'That's something to be thankful for

anyway, Sloan. The last time Dyson and Williams went anywhere near his precious X-ray machine with their cameras I thought we'd never heard the last of it.'

Dyson and Williams were the police photographers and there had been a memorable occasion when the pathologist's X-ray equipment had silently ruined all the film in their cameras and about their persons; something they hadn't discovered until after they had shot it . . .

'The fall killed him,' repeated Sloan. 'I don't know how he fell – I don't know yet who was there when it happened' – his lips tightened as he thought about the young man in the mortuary – 'but before I'm done I intend to find out.'

'Person or persons unknown,' supplied the superintendent, falling back upon an ancient formula. 'That'll do for the time being anyway.'

'They,' continued Sloan with a fine disregard for number and gender, 'put his body into the water after that.'

'Hrrrrumph.'

'Yes, sir,' Sloan responded to the sentiment as much as to the sound. 'Exactly.'

'Don't say it, Sloan.'

'No, sir.'

'I know the dead can't walk.'

'Yes, sir.'

'What was that about about a copper weight?' The superintendent never forgot anything he wanted to remember either.

'It was a small round lump,' said Sloan. 'In his pocket.'

Leeyes grunted. 'Clothes?'

'He didn't have a lot on, sir,' replied Sloan. 'Shirt and trousers, socks and underclothes . . .'

'Sea-boots?' queried Leeyes sharply. 'Was he wearing sea-boots?'

'No, sir,' said Sloan. It had been one of the first things he had looked for. Pincher Martin had had sea-boots on. A young Christopher Dennis Sloan had been brought up on the story of Pincher Martin, and when in later life an adult Detective Inspector C. D. Sloan came across a body in the water in the way of business, the poor drowned seaman who had been Pincher Martin came to the front of his mind. Pincher Martin's sea-boots hadn't saved him from drowning. 'This chap didn't have any sea-boots on, sir. Only what I said. Shirt, trousers, socks, and underclothes.'

'Traceable?' queried Leeyes, who had not been thinking about Pincher Martin.

'Easily,' said Sloan.

'Ah!'

'In the first instance, that is,' said Sloan.

'Oh?'

'To a well-known store that clothes half the nation.'

'But after that?'

'Who's to say?' said Sloan wearily, consciously suppressing an unhappy vision of the routine work it would take to find out.

'Labels not cut out then?' concluded Leeyes briskly.

'Oh, no, sir. We were meant to think that this was a simple case of drowning – if we found the body, that is.'

'Oh, we were, were we?' responded Superintendent Leeyes energetically, forgetting for a moment that it had been Dr Dabbe who had told them it wasn't.

'This dinghy, sir ...' It was Sloan's turn to do the remembering.

'Old,' quoted Leeyes, 'but not truly waterlogged. Ridgeford's no seaman but he did notice that much.'

'Over at Marby, you said, sir ...'

'Yes, Sloan.' The superintendent's voice faded as he spun round in his swivel chair and consulted the map that hung on the wall. 'The tide would have had to take your man round the headland – what's it called?'

'The Cat's Back.'

'The Cat's Back and into the estuary of the Calle.'

'That,' began Sloan carefully, 'would mean that he would have had to have been swept out to sea first and then brought in by the tide against the river current.'

He heard the swivel chair creak as Leeyes turned back to face the telephone again. 'Naturally, Sloan.'

'Sir, Dr Dabbe says that this fellow – whoever he is – hadn't been knocked about by the tide and the river current all that much.' Sloan had meant to lead into the point he had to make with the delicacy of a diplomat but in the event he didn't bother. 'Not anything like as much as he would have expected.'

'But you said he'd been in the water quite a long while,' Leeyes pounced.

'Dr Dabbe said that, sir. Not me,' responded Sloan. The superintendent had a tendency which he shared with the ancient Greeks to confuse the messenger with the source of the news. Harbingers had a notoriously bad time with him.

'What you're trying to tell me, Sloan, and I must say you've taken your time about it, is that things aren't quite what they seem.'

'That's right, sir.'

'There's still this empty dinghy over at Marby,' said Superintendent Leeyes down the telephone to the head of his Criminal Investigation Department. 'No doubt about that.'

'Yes, sir.' Sloan got the message. 'I'll get over there as soon as I can and have a look at it.'

'Doesn't add up, Sloan, does it?'

'No, sir.'

'I don't like coincidences,' growled Leeyes.

'No, sir,' agreed Sloan. No policeman did. Sorting them out for circumstantial evidence in court could get very tricky indeed. Sloan knew – sight unseen – that the superintendent's bushy eyebrows would have come together in a formidable frown as he said that.

'Now what, Sloan?'

'I'm following up the piece of copper, sir, and Dr Dabbe's lining someone up for me to see, too, who may be able to help with something else . . . a Miss Hilda Collins.'

He did not add that that someone was a schoolmistress. Some of Superintendent Leeyes's responses were altogether too predictable.

Police Constable Brian Ridgeford was addressing himself to a mug of steaming hot tea. One thing Mrs Ridgeford – good police wife that she was trying too hard to be – had learnt well. That was to put the kettle on the hob and leave it on.

He had dutifully made his report to his Headquarters at Berebury about the beached dinghy and was sitting back considering what to do next. He hadn't forgotten that before he had been diverted over to Marby juxta Mare he had been going to walk up the river bank from the Edsway to Collerton, but before that there was his report to be written. One of the tenets at the Police Training School was that – as far as records went – the telephone was no substitute for pen and paper.

'Anything come in while I was out, love?' he asked, conscientiously pulling his report book towards him.

'Hopton's rang,' said Mrs Ridgeford, sitting back and joining him in some tea. She was still at that early stage in their police married life when handing over the message was synonymous with handing over the responsibility. Her sleepless nights would come later.

Brian Ridgeford said, 'What's up with Hopton's?' As a rule his wife gave him any messages that had come in almost before he'd got his foot over the threshold, so this one couldn't be too important.

'They want you down there.'

Ridgeford frowned. Hopton's was always wanting him down there at the store. Every time a bunch of schoolchildren had been in Mrs Hopton was convinced that they had stolen things. As far as the weekend sailors and fishermen were concerned – Hopton's prices being distinctly on the high side – all the robbery was on the other side of the counter. And in daylight, too.

'Profits down or something?' he said.

'Boys,' said Mrs Ridgeford succinctly.

So it was to the ship's chandler by the shore in Edsway that Ridgeford made his way – not too quickly – after he'd had his tea and filled in his report about the dinghy.

Mrs Hopton was vocal. 'There were two of them,' she said. 'And I had to deal with them myself on account of Hopton being the way he is.'

'What did they do?' enquired Ridgeford patiently. Mr

Hopton spent his life lurking in the little parlour at the back of the shop. He was a little man and his wife was a large woman. No doubt he was the way he was by virtue of being locked in holy wedlock to Mrs Hopton. It wasn't a fate that he, Brian Ridgeford, would have chosen either.

'Do?' she said, surprised. 'They didn't do anything.'

'Well, then . . .' Somebody had once tried to explain to his class of new constables the difference between crimes of commission and the sins of omission – the latter mostly, it seemed, to do with their notebooks – but Ridgeford hadn't listened too hard.

'Unless,' carried on Mrs Hopton, 'you count trying to make me buy something that wasn't theirs to sell.'

'Ah.' Ridgeford thought he was beginning to understand. The far end of the ship's chandlers store was devoted to the sale of second-hand equipment.

'At my time of life!' said Mrs Hopton with every appearance of remorse. 'Well, they say there's no fool like an old fool. I should have known better, shouldn't I?'

'Well . . .' temporized the policeman. The theory that all were responsible for their own actions was highly important in law. It was apt to be overlooked in real life.

'Smelt a rat, I should have done, shouldn't I,' she sniffed, 'as soon as they said where they'd found it.'

'But you didn't?' suggested Ridgeford for appearance's sake.

'Not then,' said Mrs Hopton.

'When?' prompted Ridgeford.

'Afterwards,' said Mrs Hopton, challenging him to make something of that. 'When they'd gone.'

'What made you wonder?'

'When I began to think about it.' She shifted her shoulders uneasily. 'I wasn't happy.'

'About what?'

'Them saying they found it up on the Cat's Back.'

'The headland?'

She nodded. 'Whoever heard of anyone finding a ship's bell up there?'

'It is a funny place to find anything from a ship,' agreed

Ridgeford, professionally interested. Common things took place most commonly – he knew that – but it was the uncommon that attracted most police attention. 'A bell, did you say?' He imagined that – like policemen's helmets – ships' bells had a symbolic importance all of their own.

'It's a bell all right,' said Mrs Hopton heavily.

Police Constable Ridgeford shifted his gaze in the direction of the jumble of second-hand nautical gear at the end of the store. 'Had I better have a look at it, then?'

'Wait a minute,' she said. 'I've got it safe in the parlour. My husband's keeping an eye on it for me.'

Ridgeford was a puzzled man as she turned away.

When she came back it was with a very shabby and encrusted piece of metal and he was more puzzled still.

'It's a bell all right,' he agreed after a moment or two, 'but you couldn't use it, could you? Not with that crack in its side.' There was evidence of some scraping too, from a penknife, he guessed.

'That's what I told the boys,' said Mrs Hopton. 'No use to anyone, I said, it being the way it was.'

'So,' said Ridgeford a trifle impatiently, 'what did you want me down here for then?'

'Ships' bells,' she said impressively, 'have the names of ships on them.'

'What about it?'

'They have them cut into the metal so that they last.'

'Well?' If Brian Ridgeford was any judge this one had had to last a long time.

'I was curious, you see,' she said, looking him straight in the eye. 'So I got out a piece of paper and a soft pencil . . .'

'You traced the name,' finished the policeman for her.

'Not all of it. Some of it's too far gone.'

'You traced some of it,' said Ridgeford with heavy patience.

'That's right.' Mrs Hopton was above irony. 'I traced some of it and came up with some letters.'

'Did you then?' said Ridgeford expressionlessly.

She pulled out a drawer behind the counter. 'Do you want to see them?'

Police Constable Brian Ridgeford bent over a piece of grubby paper and read aloud the letters that were discernible. 'E . . . M . . . B . . . A . . . L . . . D. EMBALD? Is that what it says?'

She gave him a nod of barely suppressed excitement. 'I know what the other letters are. Don't you?'

'No,' he said. 'Tell me.' 'C . . . L . . . A . . . R,' she said. She was speaking in lowered tones now. 'To make *Clarembald*.'

'All right then,' he conceded. 'If you say so – *The Clarembald*. What about it?'

She tossed her head. 'I'd forgotten you were new here, Mr Ridgeford.'

'Yes.'

'You wouldn't know, I suppose?'

'No.'

'Everyone else knows.'

'Everyone else knows what?'

She delivered her punch line almost in a whisper. '*The Clarembald* was the name of the ship that went down off Marby all those years ago. Didn't you know that?'

Detective Inspector Sloan had not been inside the museum at
Calleford since he was a boy.

It was situated inside an old castle that had started life under
Edward III as a spanking new bastion against the nearest
enemy, degenerated over the years into a prison, and in the
twentieth century been revived as a museum. At first Sloan
and Crosby followed the way of the ordinary visitor. This led
them past glass cases of Romano-British pottery and Jutish
finds. They turned left by the vast exhibition of stuffed birds
willed by a worthy citizen of bygone days, and kept straight
on to the main office through the Darrell Collection of
nineteenth-century costume.

There was nothing out of date about the museum's curator.

Mr Basil Jensen took a quick look at the lump of copper
and immediately took over the questioning himself. 'Where
did you find this?' he demanded excitedly.

'The River Calle.'

'The river?' squealed Jensen. 'Are you sure?'

'Quite sure,' said Sloan. 'What is it?'

'A barbary head,' said Basil Jensen impatiently. He was a
little man who obviously found it hard to keep still. 'Where
did you say you found it?'

'The river,' said Sloan.

'I know that.' He danced from one leg to the other.
'Whereabouts in the river?'

'Between Edsway and Collerton,' said Sloan accurately. The police usually asked the questions but Sloan was content to let him go on. Sometimes questions were even more revealing than answers. 'What's a barbary head?'

'I don't believe it,' declared Mr Jensen with academic ferocity. 'Not between Edsway and Collerton.'

'No,' said Sloan consideringly, 'I can see that you might not. What's a barbary head?'

'Now, if you'd said the sea, Inspector . . .'

'Yes?'

'That would have made more sense.'

Anything that made sense suited Sloan. Crosby was concentrating more on his surroundings. The museum curator's room was stuffed with improbable objects standing in unlikely juxtaposition. Two vases stood on his desk – one clearly Chinese, one as clearly Indian. Even Sloan's untutored eye could see the difference between them – two whole civilizations summed up in the altered rake of the lip of a vase . . .

'What's a barbary head?' asked Sloan again. Crosby was staring at an oryx whose head – a triumph of the taxidermist's art – was at eye level on the wall. The oryx stared unblinkingly back at him.

'A single head of barbary copper,' said Basil Jensen authoritatively, 'moulded into a circular shape.' He blinked. 'Any the wiser?'

'No,' said Sloan truthfully.

'An ingot, then.'

'Ah.'

'It was the way they used to transport copper in the old days.'

'I see.'

Mr Jensen pointed to the copper object. 'You'd get tons and tons of it like this. A man could move it with a shovel, you see. Easier than shifting great lumps that needed two men to lift them.'

'What sort of old days?' asked Sloan cautiously.

'Let's not beat about the bush,' said Mr Jensen.

Sloan was all in favour of that.

'Mid-eighteenth century,' said the museum curator impressively.

'Make a note of that, Crosby,' said Sloan.

'Mid-eighteenth century,' repeated Mr Jensen.

'That would be about 1750 wouldn't it, sir?' said Sloan. 'Give or take a year or two.'

'Or five,' said Mr Jensen obscurely. He tapped the barbary head. 'And at a guess . . .'

'Yes?'

'This has been in the water since then.' He thrust his chin forward. 'If you don't believe me, Inspector, take it to Greenwich. They'll know there.' He suddenly looked immensely cunning. 'There's something else they'll be able to tell you, too.'

'What's that, sir?'

'Whether it's been in salt water or fresh all these years.'

Sloan said, 'I think I may know the answer to that, sir.'

The museum curator nodded and pointed to the piece of copper. 'And I think, Inspector, that I know the answer to this.'

'You do, sir?'

'Someone's found *The Clarembald*.' He spoke almost conversationally now. 'She was an East Indiaman, you know . . .'

Across the years Sloan caught the sudden whiff of blackboard chalk at the back of his nostrils and he was once again in the classroom of a long-ago schoolmaster. The man – a rather precise, dry man – had been trying to convey to a class of boys that strange admixture of trade, empire-building, and corruption that had made the East India company what it was. He'd been a 'chalk and talk' schoolmaster but one rainy afternoon he'd made John Company and the investigation of Robert Clive and the impeachment of Warren Hastings all come alive to his class.

'Someone's found her,' said Jensen.

They'd been all ears, those boys, especially when the teacher had come to that macabre incident in British history that everybody knows. It was strange, thought Sloan, that out of a crowded historical past 'when all else be forgot' everyone always remembered the Black Hole of Calcutta.

'We knew it would happen one day,' said the museum curator. 'In fact,' he admitted, 'we'd heard a rumour. Nothing you could put your finger on, you know . . .'

'Ah.'

'And people have been in making enquiries,' said Jensen.

Sloan leaned forward. 'You wouldn't happen to know which people, sir, would you?'

'They don't leave their names,' said Jensen drily. 'And we get a lot of casual enquirers, you know.'

'Short, dark, and young?' said Sloan.

Jensen shook his head. 'Tallish, brown hair, and not as young as all that.'

'This ship,' said Sloan. 'You know all about it then?'

'Bless you, Inspector, yes.' Jensen started to pace up and down. 'It's perfectly well documented. And it's all here in the museum for anyone to look up. She was lured to her doom by wreckers in the winter of 1755 . . .'

'The evil that men do lives after them,' murmured Sloan profoundly.

Jensen's response was immediate. 'Yes, indeed, Inspector. We see a lot of that in the museum world.'

Sloan hadn't thought of that.

Jensen waved a hand. 'I dare say that I can tell you what *The Clarembald* was carrying too . . .'

Quinquireme of Nineveh from distant Ophir . . .

'We have a copy of the ship's manifest here,' said Jensen, jerking to a standstill. 'I dare say the East India Office will have something about it too.' He pointed to the barbary head and went on enthusiastically, 'And if she wasn't carrying a load of copper ingots I'll eat my hat. Mind you, Inspector, that won't have been all her cargo by a long chalk. She'll have had a great many other good things on board.'

Sloan motioned to Crosby to take a note.

'A great many other things,' said the museum curator, 'that certain people would like to have today.'

'Gold?' suggested Sloan simply.

Topazes and cinnamon, and gold moidores, it had been in the poem.

Mr Jensen gave a quick frown. 'Gold, certainly. Don't forget it was used as currency then. But it won't be so much the gold as the guns that they'll be going for today.'

'Guns?' said Sloan. 'Guns before gold?' He was faintly disappointed. Pieces of eight had a swashbuckling ring to them.

'They're easier to find underwater,' said Jensen. 'And if I remember rightly she had a pair of demi-culverin on board and some twelve-pounders.'

Sloan was struck by a different thought. 'Armed merchantmen were nothing new, then?'

'If you worked in a museum, Inspector, you'd realize that there is nothing new under the sun.'

'Quite so,' said Sloan.

Mr Jensen came back very quickly to the matter in hand. 'There are treasure-seekers, Inspector, who would blow her out of the water for her guns and not care that they were destroying priceless marine archaeology. Do you realize that everything that comes out of an underwater find should be kept underwater?'

'She doesn't,' observed Sloan moderately, 'appear to have been blown out of the water yet.'

'Matter of time,' said Jensen, resuming his restless pacing. 'Only a matter of time. Depends entirely on who knows she's been found and how quickly they act.'

'I can see that, sir.' There were villians everywhere. You learned that early in the police force. 'There must be something that can be done about stopping her being damaged.'

'Done? Oh, yes,' said Jensen. 'For those in peril in the sea, Inspector, we can get a Department of Trade protection order making it an offence to interfere with the wreck or carry out unlicensed diving or salvage. But we'd need to know where she was. How did you say you'd come by this barbary head?'

'I didn't,' said Sloan quietly, 'and I'm not going to.'

*

Elizabeth Busby felt strangely relaxed and comforted after her cry at the graveside. She was sure that her aunt would have understood her need to leave the house and seek out a quiet spot in the out of doors. Celia Mundill would have understood the tears too – there was a marvellous release to be had in tears. And Collerton graveyard was certainly quiet enough – it was a fine and private place for tears, in fact.

True, Horace Boller from Edsway had rowed past on his way upstream but he hadn't disturbed her thoughts at all. Perhaps this was because those thoughts were still too inchoate and unformed to admit intrusion from an outside source. Perhaps it was only because – more mundanely – she hadn't liked to lift a tear-stained face for it to be seen by the man who had been going by.

She felt much better in the open air; she was sure about that. Collerton House had begun to oppress her since Celia Mundill had died – it wasn't the same without her warm presence, ill as she had been. It wasn't the same either – subconsciously she stiffened her shoulders – since Peter Hinton had so precipitately taken his departure. There was no use baulking at the fact – no matter how hard she tried to think of other things, in the end her thoughts always came back to Peter Hinton.

She had felt at the time and she still felt now that a note left on the table in the hall was no way for a real man to break with his affianced. If he had felt the way he said he did, then the very least he could have done was to have told her so – face to face. A note left behind on the hall table beside the signet ring she had given him was the coward's way.

For the thousandth time she took the folded paper which Peter Hinton had written out of her pocket and – for the thousandth time – considered it. Its message was loud and clear. It could scarcely have been shorter or balder either.

It's no go. Forgive me. P.

There was not a word of explanation as to why a man who had quite unequivocally declared that he wanted to marry her should suddenly leave a note like that. Time and time again she had turned it over to see if there had been more – anything – written on the back but there wasn't.

There still wasn't.

She had resolved not to keep on and on reading the note – and forgotten how many times she had made the resolution. She'd broken it every day. She didn't know why she needed to look at it anyway. It wasn't as if she didn't know what it said. Sadly she folded it up again and put it away.

She sat back on her heels then, more at peace with herself than she'd been all day. There was something very peaceful about the churchyard – you could begin to see what it was about a churchyard that had moved Thomas Gray to write his elegy and why her aunt hadn't wanted to be cremated. There was something very soothing, too, about the sound of the water lapping away at the edge of the churchyard grass. Gray hadn't had that at – where was it? Stoke Poges.

Elizabeth reached over and picked out the flowers that she had brought with her on her last visit. They were fading now. That gave her something to do with her hands and that was soothing too. As she carefully started to arrange the roses in the vase she began to understand why it was that her aunt's husband had been so insistent about his wife's grave being within the sound of the water.

'She'd spent all her life by the river,' he'd said, immediately selecting the plot that was closest to the river's edge.

The sexton had murmured something about flooding.

'But she loved the sound of the river,' Frank Mundill had insisted.

The sexton had hitched his shoulder. 'You won't like it in winter, Mr Mundill.'

Architects spend at least half their working lives persuading recalcitrant builders to do what architect and client want and Frank Mundill had had to prove his skill in this field in the five minutes that followed.

'It couldn't be too near the river for her,' he had said.

'The first time the Calle comes up,' sniffed the sexton obstinately, 'you'll be on to me. You see.'

'I won't,' undertook Frank Mundill.

'And there won't be anything I can do then,' said the man as if he hadn't spoken.

'I shan't want you to do anything.'

'It'll be too late then,' said the man obdurately. 'Mark my words.'

'My wife was born over there, remember.' Frank Mundill had waved a hand in the direction of Collerton House. He introduced a firmer tone into his voice. 'She loved this river.'

His gesture had reminded Elizabeth Busby of something and she had taken herself off at that point to have a look at her grandparents' grave. That was over by the church – not far from the west door. And next to it was the polished marble monument to her great-grandparents. Gordon Camming – he who had invented the Camming valve – had made it clear that he intended to found a dynasty too. He'd bought half a dozen plots around his own tomb; the sexton hadn't hesitated to remind Frank Mundill of this.

The word 'dynasty' had started up another unhappy train of thought in her mind at the time, not unconnected with Peter Hinton, and she had drifted back to the river's edge where the exchange between Frank Mundill and the sexton was drawing to a close. By the time she had reached the two men, the site of the plot for the grave of her aunt had been agreed upon and the sexton, if still not happy about it, was at least mollified.

'She'll be content here,' she heard Celia Mundill's widower insisting as she drew closer.

Elizabeth hoped then and hoped now as she tended the flowers on the grave that this was true. It was still summer-time, of course, and flooding was a long way from her mind as she took away the last of the dead flowers from her previous visit. She sat back on her heels while she carefully picked out the best rose for the centre position. Her aunt had known she would never see this year's Fantin-Latour roses on the bush – she'd told Elizabeth so in spite of all Dr Tebot had said – but there was no reason, she told herself fiercely, why she shouldn't have them on her grave.

As she placed each succeeding stem of the double blush-pink clusters of flowers in the grave's special frost-proof vase she began to see why it was that this particular rose had been such a favourite – and not only of Celia Mundill but of Henri Fantin-Latour and the old Dutch flower painters – of real artists, in fact.

Involuntarily her lips tightened into a smile.

There was a family joke about the word 'artist'. Grandfather Camming had called himself an artist and filled canvas upon canvas to prove it. The family had tacitly agreed therefore that he must be known as an artist. Other artists – those who did improve as time went by, those whose pictures were fought over by art galleries – even those whose paintings were bought with an eye to the future – deserved to be distinguished from Richard Camming and his amateur efforts. They had been known – in the family and out of earshot of Richard Camming – as real artists.

'Poor Grandfather!' she thought. Time and money weren't what made a painter. 'Nor,' she added fairly in her mind, 'was application.' Grandfather Camming had certainly applied himself. She gave a little, silent giggle to herself. Richard Camming had cheerfully applied paint to every canvas in sight.

As Elizabeth placed the roses in the vase she was conscious of how the lively shell-pink of the centre of the flower made a fine splash of colour against the newly turned earth. She would have liked to have had that bare earth covered in stone or even grass but the sexton said it had to stay the way it was until it had settled. Frank Mundill didn't seem worried about the bare earth either. When she had mentioned it to him later he had said he was still thinking about the right monumental design and so she had left the subject well alone.

She sat back on her heels for a moment to consider her handiwork in flower arrangement. She hoped it wouldn't flood in this corner of the churchyard but you never could tell with the River Calle. The river seemed to have a will of its own. Way, way inland – above Calleford, and almost as far inland as the town of Luston – it was a docile stream, little more than a rivulet, in fact. By the time it got to Calleford itself it was bigger, of course, but it was tamed there by city streets and bridges, to say nothing of the odd sluice gate.

Once west of the county town, though, and out on to the flat land in the middle of the county – those very same low-lying fields in which Grandfather Camming had painted during his Constable period – the River Calle broadened and steadily grew into a force of water to be reckoned with. The bends in its course through Collerton towards Edsway and the sea it seemed to regard as a challenge to its strength. In spring and autumn, that is.

Her flowers arranged and her tears dried and forgotten for the time being, Elizabeth Busby rose to her feet and dusted off her knees. She decided that she would walk back to the house along the river bank. It was a slightly longer way back to Collerton House than by the paved road but what was time to her now?

She slipped out of the little kissing-gate that led from the churchyard on to the river walk feeling rather as if she had stepped out of a William Morris painting – or was it another of the Pre-Raphaelites who had been so fond of having girls stationed prettily beside a river as they put brush to canvas? Perhaps it was Millais? Not Baron Leighton, surely? She always felt a little self-conscious when she was walking along the river bank with a wooden gardening trug over one arm. At least she didn't have a Victorian parasol in the other.

It was while she was walking back along the path on the river bank and rounding the bend that matched the curve of the river that the boathouse at the bottom of the garden of Collerton House came into view.

Someone, she noticed in a detached way, had left the doors of the boathouse open.

Detective Inspector Sloan and Detective Constable Crosby made their way back to the pathologist's mortuary. They found the pathologist in his secretary's room, there talking to a squarish woman with shaggy eyebrows and cropped hair. Rita, the pathologist's secretary, was there too. She was a slim girl whose eyebrows showed every sign of having had a lot of loving care and attention lavished upon them. Dr Dabbe introduced the older woman to the policemen as Miss Hilda Collins.

'We've met before,' she announced, acknowledging them with a quick jerk of her head.

Sloan bowed slightly.

'I never forget a face,' declared Miss Collins.

'It's a gift,' said Sloan, and he meant it. For his part Sloan remembered her too. Miss Collins was the biology mistress at Berebury High School for Girls. 'I wish we had more policemen who didn't forget faces,' he said – and he meant that too. What with Identikits, memory banks, and computer-assisted this and that, the man on the beat didn't really have to remember any more what villains looked like. It was a pity.

At the other side of the room Constable Crosby was exhibiting every sign of trying to commit Rita's face to memory. Sloan averted his eyes.

'Miss Collins,' said the pathologist easily, 'is an expert.'

'I see.' Sloan remained cautious. If his years in the Force

had taught him anything, it was that experts were a breed on their own. Put them in the witness box and you never knew what they were going to say next. They could make or mar a case, too. Irretrievably. There was only one thing worse than one expert and that was two. Then they usually differed. 'May I ask on what?' he said politely.

'Good question,' said Dr Dabbe. 'I must say I'd rather like to know myself. It's in the lab . . . this way.' He led them through from his secretary's room into the small laboratory that Sloan knew existed alongside the post-mortem room. 'I called him Charley because he travelled,' said the pathologist obscurely.

'With the body, I think you said,' murmured Miss Collins gruffly.

'It was my man Burns who said that,' said Dr Dabbe. 'He found it wriggling inside the man's shirt. That was still very wet.'

'He found what . . .' began Sloan peremptorily, and then stopped.

The pathologist was pointing to a wide-necked retort that was almost full of water. Swimming happily about in it was a small creature. 'Burns said they call it a "screw" in Scotland,' he said.

As if to prove the point the creature wriggled suddenly sideways. It was a dull greenish-yellow colour and quite small.

'It's still alive,' said Detective Constable Crosby unnecessarily.

'That proves something,' said Miss Collins immediately. 'What's it in?'

'*Aqua destillata*,' said the pathologist who belonged to the old school which felt that the Latin language and the profession of medicine should always go together.

Sloan made a mental note that sturdily included the words 'distilled water'. Latin used where English would do always made him think of Merlin and spells.

Miss Collins advanced on the specimen in the glass. 'It's one of the Crustacea,' she said.

'That's what I thought,' said Dr Dabbe.

'Amphipod, of course,' announced Miss Collins. 'The order is know as "Sand-hoppers" although few live in the sand and even fewer still hop.'

There were inconsistencies in law, too. Sloan had stopped worrying about them now but when he had been a younger man they'd sometimes come between him and a good night's sleep.

'You'll find it demonstrates negative heliotropism very nicely,' Miss Collins said.

If she had been speaking in a foreign tongue, Detective Inspector Sloan would have been allowed to bring in an interpreter at public expense. And as far as Sloan was concerned she might as well have been.

The pathologist must have understood her, though, because he pushed the jar half into and half out of the rays of sunlight falling on the laboratory bench. Whatever it was in the water – fish or insect – jerked quickly away from that part of the jar and scuttled off into such dimmer light as it could find.

'We do that with the third form,' said Miss Collins in a kindly way, 'to teach them phototropism.'

Dr Dabbe was unabashed while Miss Collins bent down for an even closer look. 'The family Gammaridae,' she pronounced.

Detective Constable Crosby abandoned any attempt to record this. He too bent down and looked at the creature. 'Doesn't it look big through the glass?' he said.

'You get illusory magnification from curved glass with water in it,' the pathologist informed him absently.

Both Miss Collins and Crosby were still peering, fascinated, at the glass retort and its contents. Some dentists, Sloan was reminded, had tanks with goldfish swimming in them in their waiting rooms. The theory was that patients were soothed by watching fish move about. *In a cool curving world he lies* . . . no, that was the river in Rupert Brooke's 'Fish' but no doubt the principle was the same. There were insomniacs, too, who had them by their beds. The considering of fish swimming was said to lower tension all round.

He looked across at Detective Constable Crosby. He didn't want his assistant's tension lowered any more.

'Have you got a note of that, Crosby?' he barked unfairly.

Miss Collins said, 'It can't osmoregulate, you know, Inspector.'

Sloan didn't know and said so.

'True estuarine species can,' declared Miss Collins.

Sloan did not enjoy being blinded with Science.

'*Gammarus pulex*, Inspector,is a good example of a biological indicator.'

Sloane said he was very glad to hear it.

The pathologist leaned forward eagerly and said, 'So Charley here. . .'

'I'm not at all sure that I can tell you its sex,' said Miss Collins meticulously. She raised her head from considering the water creature and asked clearly, 'Is sex important?'

Sloan stiffened. If Crosby said that sex was always important then he, Detective Inspector Sloan, his superior officer, would put him on report there and then . . . murder case or not. Detective Constable Crosby, however, continued to be absorbed by half an inch of wriggling crustacean and it was Sloan who found himself answering her.

'No,' he said into the silence.

He felt that sounded prim and expanded on it.

'Not as far as I know,' he added.

That sounded worse.

He lost his nerve altogether and launched into further speech.

'In this particular case,' he added lamely.

Miss Collins looked extremely scientific. '*Gammarus pulex* enjoys a curious sort of married life.'

As a quondam bobby on the beat Sloan could have told her that that went for quite a slice of the human population too.

'But,' she carried on, 'you don't get the really intricate sex reversal as in – say – the Epicarids.'

Sloan was glad to hear it. If there was one thing that the law had not really been able to bend its mind round yet, it was sex reversal.

'Can you eat it?' asked Detective Constable Crosby.

Miss Collins gave a hortatory cough while Sloan had to agree to himself that food did come a close second to sex most of the time. She shook her head and said, 'Its common name of freshwater shrimp is a complete misnomer.'

In the end it was Sloan who cut the cackle and got down to the horses. 'What you're trying to tell us, miss, is that this ... this ... whatever it is ... is a freshwater species, not a sea one.'

'That's what I said, Inspector,' she agreed patiently. '*Gammarus pulex* can't live in sea water and that's what makes it a good biological indicator.'

'So,' said Sloan slowly and carefully, 'the body didn't come in from the sea.'

'I don't know about the body,' said the biologist with precision, 'but I can assure you that *Gammarus pulex* didn't.'

'Are you telling me,' asked Sloan, anxious to have at least one thing clear in his mind, 'that it – this thing here – would have died in sea water then?'

'I am,' she said with all the lack of equivocation of the true scientiest on sound territory covered by natural laws.

A little hush fell in the laboratory.

Then Sloan said heavily, 'We'd better get our best feet forward then, hadn't we?'

Perhaps in their own way policemen were amphipods too. Or amphiplods.

Gammarus pulex scuttled sideways across the bottom of the glass vessel as he spoke.

He'd have to prise Crosby away from that jar if he watched it much longer. He was practically mesmerized by it as it was.

'We'll have to go upriver,' Sloan announced to nobody in particular. He turned. 'Come along, Crosby.'

Detective Constable Crosby straightened up at last. 'We might find some Dead Man's Fingers, too, sir, mightn't we?'

'*Alcyonium digitatum*,' said Dr Dabbe.

'Not in fresh water,' said Miss Collins promptly. 'Dead Man's Fingers are animals colonial that like the sea-shore.'

Sloan didn't say anything at all.

Police Constable Brian Ridgeford was confused. He had duly reported the finding of the ship's bell to Berebury police station and had in fact brought it back to his home with him. Home in the case of a country constable was synonymous with place of work. His wife was less than enchanted when he set the bell down on the kitchen table.

'Take that out to the shed,' commanded Mrs Ridgeford immediately.

Ridgeford picked it up again.

'What is it anyway?' she asked. 'It looks like a bell to me.'

'It is a bell,' he said. That sounded like one of those childhood conundrums that came in Christmas crackers.

Question: When is a door not a door?

Answer: When it's ajar.

When was a bell not a bell?

When it was treasure trove. Or was it only that when it – whatever it was – has been hidden by the original owner with the intention of coming back for it? Not lost at sea. He would have to look that up. He felt a little self-conscious anyway about using the words 'treasure trove' to his wife.

'It's a ship's bell,' he said lamely.

'I can see that.'

'It's stolen property, too, I think.' He cleared his throat and added conscientiously, 'Although I don't rightly know about that for sure.' Unfortunately when he'd telephoned the police station he'd been put through to Superintendent Leeyes. This had compounded his confusion.

'Dirty old thing,' she said, giving it a closer look.

'I think it could be lagan as well.'

'I don't care what it is, I'm not having anything like that in my clean kitchen.' She looked up suspiciously. 'What's lagan anyway?'

'Goods or wreckage lying on the bed of the sea.'

She sniffed. 'I'm still not having it in here.'

'Mind you,' he said carefully, 'in law things aren't always what they seem.' Being in the police force gave a man a different view of the legal system. 'In law an oyster is a wild animal.'

'Get away with you, Brian Ridgeford.'

'It's true. A judge said so.'

'Oh, a judge.' Brenda Ridgeford hadn't been a policeman's wife for very long, but long enough to be critical of judges and their judgements.

'Sat for a day in court they did to decide.'

'The law's an ass, then,' she giggled.

'An ass is a domestic animal,' said her husband promptly.

She gave him a very sly look indeed. 'So's a wife or have you forgotten?'

In the nature of things it was a little while before the ship's bell was moved out to the shed and Brian Ridgeford was able to concentrate on his duties again. These centred on finding the two boys who had taken the bell into the ship's chandler in Edsway.

To Mrs Hopton, 'boy' was a species not an individual.

Of their age she had been uncertain.

Of their appearance she could tell him nothing beyond that they had been scruffy – but then these days all boys were scruffy, weren't they?

But she was convinced and Hopton – even with him being the way he was – agreed with her here – that they had been up to no good.

On being pressed to describe them she had advanced the view that one had been taller than the other.

Brian Ridgeford had received this gem of observation in silence.

Mrs Hopton had cogitated still further and eventually disgorged the fact that one of them had called the other 'Terry'.

As he picked up his helmet and made for the door, Constable Ridgeford reflected that it wasn't a lot to go on.

On the other hand with Jack the Ripper they hadn't even had a name.

'The boathouse?' said Frank Mundill when Elizabeth Busby met him in the hall.

'You'd better go down and have a look,' she said, putting her flower trug down on the settle.

'What about the boat? Has that gone?'

'I didn't look inside . . .' Her hands fell helplessly to her sides. 'I'm sorry, Frank. I should have done, shouldn't I? The trouble is that I'm still not thinking straight.'

'Don't worry.' He gave a jerky nod. 'I'll go down there now and see what's happened.'

'Anyway,' recollected Elizabeth, pulling herself together with an effort, 'I didn't have a key to the little door on the garden side.'

He turned to the drawer in the hall table over which hung Richard Camming's venture into the style of David Allan, the Scottish Hogarth. 'That should be here somewhere.' He rummaged about until he found it. 'Here we are.'

'I couldn't see if there was a lot of damage,' said Elizabeth.

He essayed a small smile. 'Let's hope the boat's all right, anyway. Your father likes his fishing, doesn't he?'

'He'll be looking forward to it,' she said. That was quite true. Her father would go straight down to the river with rod and line as soon as he arrived.

In the end Elizabeth walked down through the grounds of Collerton House to the river's edge with him.

'Vandals,' Frank Mundill said bitterly, regarding the damaged doors from the river bank. 'They must have taken a bar to the lock.'

Elizabeth nodded.

'Someone had a go at it last year, too, when we were at my sister's,' he said. 'I've already had it repaired once.'

'I remember,' she said, although what she chiefly remembered about the visits of Frank and Celia Mundill to Calleford had been that this year's one had marked the beginning of her aunt's last illness. Frank Mundill's sister was married to a doctor in single-handed general practice there. The architect and his wife Celia had made a habit over the years at each Easter of looking after a locum tenens for the Calleford couple while the doctor and his wife had a well-earned holiday. Celia Mundill hadn't been well then – that was when she had had a really bad attack of stomach pain and vomiting, though it hadn't been her first. Then she'd had an X-ray at Calleford Hospital. She'd gone steadily downhill after that . . .

'Let's go inside,' said Mundill.

He unlocked the landward doors of the boathouse and led the way in. His footsteps echoed eerily on the hardstanding inside while the water lapped at its edge. The only light came from a small fan light and the open doors. There was quite enough light though in which to see that the boat was gone.

'Thieves as well as vandals,' said Mundill, regarding the empty water.

'Nothing's safe these days, is it?' commented Elizabeth Busby, conscious even as she said it that the remark was both trite and beyond her years. She must be careful. At this rate she'd be old before her time.

'And where do you suppose the fishing boat's got to?' asked Mundill.

'Edsway?' she suggested.

'More likely the open sea,' he said gloomily.

'Unless it's fetched up on Billy's Finger.'

'We'd have heard,' he said.

'So we would.'

'No,' he said, shaking his head, 'we shan't see that boat again.'

'Pity.'

'Yes,' he said, 'your father won't be pleased.' He sighed. 'And neither will the insurance company.'

Her eyes turned automatically to the walls of the boathouse. Along them rested the family's collection of fishing rods. 'Is there anything gone from there too?'

He looked up and then shook his head. 'Doesn't look like it, does it? No, I dare say the boat went for a joy ride.'

'When?' She very nearly added 'before or after', but she stopped herself in time. In her mind she was still dating everything that happened as before or after that dreadful week of the death of her aunt and the departure of Peter Hinton.

Frank Mundill shook his head yet again. 'I don't know when. I don't use the river path all that often. I usually go the other way.'

'So do I.'

He gave the boathouse a last look round. 'There's not a lot that we can do about it now anyway. Come along back to the house and I'll ring the constable at Edsway. Not that that'll do a lot of good. Can't see the police being interested, can you?'

What at this moment was interesting the police – the police as personified by Superintendent Leeyes, that is – was something quite different.

'Ridgeford rang in,' said Leeyes to Detective Inspector Sloan across his office desk, 'excited as a schoolgirl.'

'What about?' It wouldn't do, of course. Sloan was agreed about that. Being as excited as anybody wouldn't do at all if Ridgeford was going to make a good policeman. Sometimes the very calm of the police officer was the only thing going for him in a really tight situation.

'The wreck off Marby,' said Leeyes.

Sloan's head came up with a jerk. If a certain copper ingot had come from there too, then Sloan was prepared to be interested in it as well.

'*The Clarembald*,' said Leeyes, 'wrecked by the people of Marby in olden times.'

'At least,' said Sloan, 'that's one crime we don't have to worry about now.' Idly he wondered what the exact wording of the charge against the wrecker would have been. There hadn't been a lot of call for it down at the station since sail went out and steam came in. Perhaps it wasn't even in the book any more. 'Lighting beacons with intent to deceive' didn't quite seem to fit the gravity of the crime.

'The ship's bell has come ashore,' Leeyes told him.

'Has it indeed?' said Sloan. 'Well, well.'

'As well as that brass weight you said was on the dead body . . .'

'Copper ingot,' murmured Sloan, his mind on other things. 'How long ago do you suppose *The Clarembald* was found?'

'I wouldn't know about that,' responded Leeyes irritably. 'All I can tell you is that Ridgeford's only just come across the bell.'

'I should have thought,' said Sloan slowly, 'that we should have heard, sir, if it wasn't very lately.'

Leeyes grunted. 'Good news gets about.'

'We mostly do hear,' said Sloan. It was true. The police usually heard about good fortune as well as bad. For one thing good fortune could be as dangerous to the recipient as the reverse . . . Sloan pulled himself up with a jerk. He was beginning to think like a latter-day Samuel Smiles now.

Leeyes grunted again.

'Besides, sir, presumably the coroner would have had to know if anything had been found, wouldn't he?'

'Coroners,' pronounced Leeyes obscurely, 'only know what they're told.'

'Yes, sir.'

'And all I know,' said Leeyes flatly, 'is what my officers choose to tell me.'

'Quite so, sir.'

'And that's not a lot, Sloan, is it?'

'The young man's body was put into the river where the water is fresh,' responded Sloan absently, answering the implication rather than the question.

'And if that's not enough,' continued Leeyes, aggrieved, 'we've got Ridgeford playing pirates.'

'He's having quite a day for a beginner, isn't he?' said Sloan. 'A body and buried treasure.'

'Hrrrrumph,' said Leeyes.

'He'll have to remember today, won't he,' said Sloan, 'when the routine begins to bite.'

Leeyes sniffed. 'He'd have me out there, Sloan, if he could . . .'

Sloan didn't say anything at all to that.

'Mind you, Sloan, with my background I've always been interested in the sea.'

Sloan could see where this was leading.

'Did I,' said Leeyes, 'ever tell you how we got ashore at Walcheren?'

'Yes,' said Sloan with perfect truth. Nobody had been spared that story. Recitals of the superintendent's wartime experiences were well known and were to be avoided at all costs. He didn't even 'stoppeth one in three'. Every officer on station got them.

'Bit of a splash,' said Leeyes with the celebrated British understatement favoured by men of action in a tight corner.

Detective Inspector Sloan could see where this was leading, too. In another two minutes Superintendent Leeyes would have constituted himself Berebury's currently ranking expert on underwater archaeology. And then where would they be?

'I'll see Ridgeford presently, sir,' Sloan said firmly, 'and find out about the ship's bell too.'

'And this dinghy that he keeps on about over at Marby,' said Leeyes. 'You won't forget that, will you, Sloan?'

'No, sir, I'll see about that as soon as I can . . .' But before that, come wind, come weather, he had every intention of going up the River Calle.

A little later a police car with Detective Constable Crosby at the wheel and Detective Inspector Sloan in the front passenger seat swept out of the police station at Berebury for the second time that afternoon. The driver negotiated the traffic islands with impatience and then steered past the town's multi-storey car park. Eventually he swung the car on to the open road and out into the Calleshire countryside. In a wallet on the back seat of the police car was a hastily drawn up list of everyone who lived beside the River Calle on both sides of the river east of Billing Bridge.

'There's a note of the riparian owners, too, sir,' said Detective Constable Crosby, 'whoever they are when they're at home.'

'The fishing rights belong to them,' said Sloan.

'Oh, the fishing . . .' said Crosby, putting his foot down.

'There's no hurry,' said Sloan as the car picked up speed.

'Got a catch a murderer,' said Crosby, 'haven't we?'

That, at least, decided Sloan to himself, had the merit of reducing the case to its simplest. And he had to admit that that was not unwelcome after a session with Superintendent Leeyes . . .

'Chance would be a fine thing,' he said aloud.

'Someone did for him,' said the constable. 'He didn't get the way he was and where he was on his own.'

'True.' As inductive logic went it wasn't a very grand conclusion but it would do. 'Can you go any further?'

'We've got to get back to the water,' said Crosby, crouching forward at the wheel like Toad of Toad Hall.

Sloan nodded. In all fairness he had to admit that what Crosby had said was true. All the action so far had been in water . . . He said, 'What do we know so far?'

'Very little, sir.'

It was not the right answer from pupil to mentor.

In the Army mounting a campaign was based on the useful trio of 'information, intention, method'. He wasn't going to get very far discussing these with Crosby if the detective constable balked at 'information'.

'Could you,' said Sloan with a hortatory cough, 'try to think of why a body killed in a fall should be found in water?'

'Because it couldn't be left where it fell,' responded Crosby promptly.

'Good. Go on.'

'I don't know why it couldn't be left where it fell, sir,' said the constable. 'But if it could have been left, then it would have been, wouldn't it?'

'True.'

'Heavy things, bodies . . .'

Sloan nodded. What Crosby had just said was simple and irrefutable but it wasn't enough. 'Keep going,' he said.

Crosby's eyebrows came together in a formidable frown. 'Where it fell could have been too public,' he said.

'That's a point,' said Sloan.

'And it might have been found too soon,' suggested Crosby after further thought.

'Very true,' said Sloan. 'Anything else?'

'Where it was found might give us a lead on who killed him.'

'Good, good,' said Sloan encouragingly. 'Now, why put the body in the water?'

But Crosby's fickle interest had evaporated.

'Why,' repeated Sloan peremptorily, 'put the body in the water?'

Crosby took a hand off the steering wheel and waved it. 'Saves digging a hole,' he said simply.

'Anything else?' said Sloan.

Crosby thought in silence.

'Are there,' said Sloan tenaciously, 'any other good reasons why a body should be put in the water?' It looked as if they were going to have to make bricks without straw in this case anyway . . .

Crosby continued to frown prodigiously but to no effect.

'It is virtually impossible to hide a grave,' pronounced Detective Inspector Sloan academically.

'Yes, sir.'

'And,' continued Sloan, 'the disposal of a murdered body therefore presents a great problem to the murderer.'

'Yes, sir.'

'It often,' declared Sloan in a textbook manner, 'presents a greater problem than committing the actual murder.'

'Murder's easy,' said Crosby largely.

'Not of an able-bodied young man,' Sloan reminded him. 'Of women and children and the old, perhaps.' He considered the tempting vista opened up by this thought – but unless you were psychotic you murdered for a reason, and reason and easy victim did not always go hand in hand.

The constable changed gear while Sloan considered the various ways in which someone could be persuaded into falling from a height. 'He must have been taken by surprise on the edge of somewhere,' he said aloud.

'Pushed, anyway,' said Crosby.

'Yes,' agreed Sloan. 'If he'd fallen accidentally, he could have been left where he fell.'

'Shoved when he wasn't looking, then,' concluded Crosby.

'We have to look for a height with a concealed bottom . . .'

'Pussy's down the well,' chanted Crosby.

'And not too conspicuous a top,' said Sloan.

'Somewhere where the victim would have a reason for going with the murderer,' suggested Crosby.

'He'd have had to have been pretty near the brink of somewhere even then,' said Sloan. 'That's what parapets are for.'

'With someone he trusted then,' said Crosby.

'With someone he didn't think there was any need to be afraid of,' said Sloan with greater precision. He reached over to the back seat for the list of riparian owners. He wasn't expecting any trouble from them. Fishing in muddy waters was a police prerogative and he didn't care who knew it.

Horace Boller was as near to being contented with his day as he ever allowed himself to be. As he pushed his rowing boat off from the shore at Edsway – Horace had never paid a mooring fee in his life – he reflected on how an ill wind always blew somebody good.

He would have known that his two passengers were policemen even if the older one hadn't said so straight away. There was a certain crispness about him that augured the backing of an institution. Horace Boller was an old hand at discerning those whose brief authority was bolstered by the hidden reserves of an organization like the police force and the Army – the vicar came in a class of his own – and those who threw their weight about because they were merely rich.

Horace had quite a lot to do with the merely rich on Saturdays and Sundays. The rich who liked sailing were very important in the economy of Edsway. From Monday to Friday they disappeared from Horace's ken – presumably to get richer still in a mysterious place known simply as the city.

Horace himself had never been there and when someone had once equated the city with London – which he had been to – Horace's mind failed to make the connection.

Nevertheless Sunday evenings always saw a great exodus of weekenders, albeit tired and happy and sometimes quite weather-beaten, from Edsway back to the city. The following Friday evening – in summertime anyway – saw them return, pale and exhausted, from their labours in the town and raring for a weekend's pleasure – and sunburn – in the country. Horace, whose own skin bore a close resemblance to old and rather dirty creased leather, could never decide whether sunburn was a pleasure or a pain for the weekenders.

As a rule therefore Horace Boller only had Saturdays and Sundays in which to pursue the important business of getting rich himself. This accounted for his contentment this day which was neither a Saturday nor a Sunday. Extra money for one trip on a weekday and at the expense of Her Majesty's Government to boot was a good thing; extra money twice was a cause for rejoicing. Not that anyone would have guessed this from Horace Boller's facial expression. His countenance bore its usual surly look and his mind was totally bent on the business of deriving as much financial benefit as he could from this particular expedition – as it was on every other excursion which he undertook.

He gave his starboard oar an expert twist to get the boat properly out into the water and then set about the important business of settling the oars comfortably in the rowlocks. Some weekend sailors, rich and poor, conceded Boller to himself, also threw their weight about because they knew what they were doing in a boat – but they were few and far between.

He didn't know for certain yet if his two passengers were sailors or not, although he already had his doubts about the younger man. Both men had distributed themselves carefully about the boat in a seaman-like manner and had actually managed not to rock the boat while clambering into it. They had even accomplished this without getting their feet wet, which was something of an achievement, and was connected, although his passengers did not know this, with the fact that Horace was sure of getting a handsome fee for the outing. Doubtful payers and those who were so misguided as to attempt to undertip the boatman always got their feet wet.

The question of a fee for the journey they were about to undertake was very much on Detective Inspector Sloan's mind too. The payment – whatever it amounted to – would eventually have to come out of the Berebury Division imprest account. This was guarded by Superintendent Leeyes with a devotion to duty and tenacity of purpose that would have done credit to a Cerberus.

'Take you to where I found the poor man?' Horace nodded his comprehension. 'That's what you want, isn't it?'

'It is,' said Detective Inspector Sloan, detaching his mind with an effort from an unhappy vision of Superintendent Leeyes standing like a stag at bay over the petty cash at Berebury police station. 'Can you do that for us?'

'Certainly, gentlemen,' said Horace readily, even though he already knew that they were policemen not gentlemen; Horace's usage of modes of address was a nicely calculated affair and closely linked with the expectation of future reward. 'No trouble at all.'

Sloan settled himself at the bow of the boat, reminding himself that any hassle to come over payment for their trip should take second place to tangling with a murderer. He only hoped Superintendent Leeyes would feel the same.

For the fourth time that day the boatman began to row out into the estuary of the River Calle. Detective Inspector Sloan looked about him with interest. Seeing a map of the estuary with a cross marking the spot where the body had been found was one thing, but it was quite a different matter seeing the spot for oneself. He'd have to trust the boatman that it was the same spot though – he'd tried to rustle up Constable Ridgeford to get him to come with them, but according to Mrs Ridgeford he'd had to go off on his bicycle to see to something. And so they had had to put to sea without him.

Just, thought Sloan, to himself, a distant memory stirring, the Owl and the Pussy-cat . . . except that Boller's old boat wasn't a beautiful pea green . . .

Horace Boller had bent to the oars with practised ease and was rowing in a silence designed to save his breath. Then . . .

'You're going out to sea,' observed Sloan sharply. 'I thought you'd found him farther upriver.'

'Got to get round Billy's Finger, haven't I?' responded Boller resentfully.

'I see . . .' began Sloan.

'And pick up the tide.' Nobody could be surlier than Boller when he wanted to be.

'Of course.'

'I'm an old man now,' said Boller, hunching his shoulders and allowing a whine to creep into his voice. 'I can't go upriver like I used to do.'

'Naturally,' said Sloan, crisply, nevertheless taking a good look at his watch. 'Let me see now – what time was it exactly when we left?'

'I go by St Peter's clock myself,' snapped Boller. 'Always keeps good time, does St Peter's.'

'Splendid,' said Sloan warmly. 'That'll make everything easier . . .' He settled back on to his hard seat. A warning shot fired across the bows never came amiss . . .

Presently the rowing boat did turn upriver. Rowing against the eddies was not such hard work for Horace Boller as it would have been for most other men because he came of river people and knew every stretch of quiet water that there was. This did not stop him giving an artful pant as he eventually shipped his oars and caught a patch of slack water.

''Bout here it was, gentlemen,' he said, histrionically drooping himself over the oars as if at the end of a fast trip from Putney to Mortlake against another crew.

Detective Inspector Sloan was concentrating on the water. 'How far does the tide come up the estuary?'

The boatman wrinkled his eyes. 'The sparling – they turn back half-way between Collerton and Edsway no matter what.'

'They do, do they?' responded Sloan vigorously. The habits of sparling were no sort of an answer for a superintendent sitting at a desk in Berebury Police Station.

'Always go to the limit of the salt water, do sparling,' said Boller.

'Ah,' said Sloan. That was better. Sparling must be biological indicators too.

'Only see them in the summer, of course,' said the boatman.

'Been this year then, have they?' asked Sloan, unconsciously lapsing into the vernacular himself.

'Not yet.' Horace Boller unshipped an oar to stop the boat drifting too far.

'It's summer now,' remarked Detective Constable Crosby from the stern.

'Not afore Collerton Fair,' said Horace Boller flatly. 'Sparling come at fair time.'

Detective Inspector Sloan turned his head and regarded the southern shore of the river mouth with close attention. Not far away a heron rose and with an almost contemptuous idleness put the tips of his wing feathers out as spoilers. They'd left Edsway and the open sea well behind but they could now see Collerton Church clearly upriver of them. Far inland were urban Berebury and ancient Calleford and what townspeople chose to call civilization . . .

'Do smell of cucumber,' rasped the boatman unexpectedly.

'What does?' asked Sloan. They were a long way from land.

'Sparling.'

'Ah,' said Sloan again, his mind on other things. 'Pull the boat round a bit, will you? I want to see the other way.'

The view downriver was unrevealing. Edsway itself, though, was clearly visible, as was the headland beyond. Kinnisport and the cliffs at Cranberry Point were just a smudge in the distance.

'That headland behind Marby stands out, doesn't it?' observed Sloan, surprised. Seen from nearer to, the rise in the land wasn't quite so apparent.

'That's the Cat's Back,' said Boller. 'Proper seamark, that is.'

'Funny,' said Crosby ingenuously, 'I never thought you had seamarks like you had landmarks.'

Somewhere not very far away a gull screamed.

'Take us upriver now,' commanded Sloan abruptly.

Horace Boller bent to his oars once more. He rowed purposefully and without comment out of the narrowing estuary and into the river proper. Detective Inspector Sloan, sitting at the bow, was almost as immobile as a carved figurehead at the prow. He did turn once to begin to say something to Detective Constable Crosby, but that worthy officer was settled in the stern of the boat, letting his hand dangle in the water and regarding the consequent and subsequent wake with the close attention that should have been devoted to the duties of detection.

Sloan turned back and looked ahead. Speech would have been wasted. Instead he turned his mind to studying the river banks. That was when, presently, he too saw the doors of the boathouse belonging to Collerton House. Even from midstream he could see where a crowbar had been used to prise open the lock.

Frank Mundill was soon back at the riverside. This time he had Detective Inspector Sloan and Detective Constable Crosby with him, not Elizabeth Busby. Sloan had a distinct feeling that he had seen the man from Collerton House before but he couldn't immediately remember where.

Mundill indicated the boathouse doors very willingly to the two policemen and then pointed to the empty stretch of water inside the boathouse.

'Our dinghy's gone, Inspector,' he said.

'And this, I take it, sir, is where she was kept, is it?' said Sloan, giving the inside of the boathouse a swift looking-over.

'It was.' Mundill tightened his lips wryly. 'She wasn't exactly the *Queen Elizabeth*, you know, but she was good enough for a day on the river with a rod.'

Sloan examined the broken lock and loose hasp as best he could without getting his feet wet. There was a scar on the woodwork where something had rested to give leverage to a crowbar. Every picture told a story and this one seemed clear enough . . .

'Prised open all right, sir,' he agreed presently. 'Have you any idea when?'

Frank Mundill shook his head and explained that the damage would only have been visible from the path along the river bank and from the river itself. 'I haven't been this way much myself recently, Inspector. My wife was ill from Easter onwards and I just didn't have the time.' He gave a weary shrug of his shoulders. 'And now that she's gone I haven't got the inclination.'

Sloan pointed to the fishing rods on the boathouse wall. They looked quite valuable to him. 'Are they all present and correct, sir?'

Mundill's face came up in a quick affirmative response, reinforcing Sloan's impression that he'd seen it before somewhere. 'Oh, yes, Inspector. We think it's just the boat that's gone.'

'We?' queried Sloan. The list of riparian owners had dealt in surnames. It hadn't gone into household detail.

'My late wife's niece is still with me. She came to nurse my wife and she's staying on until her parents get back from South America next week.'

'I see, sir.'

'She was out here with me earlier and we both agreed it was just *Tugboat Annie* that's gone.'

Detective Inspector Sloan reached for his notebook in much the same way as Police Constable Brian Ridgeford had reached for his. A name put a different complexion on a police search for anything. A name on the unfortunate young man at Dr Dabbe's forensic laboratory would be a great step forward. '*Tugboat Annie*, did you say, sir?'

'It won't help, I'm afraid, Inspector.' Frank Mundill was apologetic. 'That was just what we called her in the family.'

The dead young man would have been called something in the family too. Sloan would have dearly liked to have known what it was.

'The name,' expanded Frank Mundill, 'wasn't actually written on her or anything like that.'

'I see, sir,' Sloan said, disappointed.

'She was only a fishing boat, you see, Inspector.' He added, 'And not a very modern fishing boat, at that. She was one of the relics of my father-in-law's day.'

Sloan nodded, unsurprised. His own first impression had been of how very dated everything about Collerton House was. There was something very pre-Great War about the whole set-up – house, boathouse, grounds and all.

'I mustn't say, "Those were the days,"' said Mundill drily, waving an arm to encompass the boathouse and the fishing rods, 'but I'm sure you know what I mean, Inspector.'

'I do indeed, sir,' agreed Sloan warmly. 'Spacious, I think you could call them.' As he had first entered Collerton House the stained glass of the inner front door and the wide sweep of the staircase had told him all he needed to know about the age of the house. It was Edwardian to a degree. Similarly the white polo-necked jersey of Frank Mundill had told him quite a lot about the man before him. He could have been a writer . . .

'Unfortunately,' Mundill was saying, 'the boathouse is very carefully screened from the house so I couldn't have seen anyone breaking in even though my studio faces north.'

'An artist . . .' To his own surprise Sloan found he had said the words aloud.

'I'm an architect, Inspector,' he said, adding astringently, 'There are those of my professional brethren who would have said "yes" to the word artist though.'

'Well, sir, now that you come to mention it . . .'

'An architect is something of an artist certainly but he's something of an engineer too.'

A policeman, thought Sloan, was something of a diplomat.

'As well as being a craftsman and a draughtsman, of course.'

A policeman was something of a martinet, of course. He had to be.

'And, Inspector, if he's any good as an architect he's something of a visionary, too.'

If a policeman was any good as a policeman he was something of a philosopher too. It didn't do not to be in the police force.

Mundill waved a tapered hand. 'However . . .'

Then it came to Sloan where it was that he had seen the man's face before. 'Your photograph was in the local paper last week, sir, wasn't it?'

The architect squinted modestly down his nose. 'You saw it, Inspector, did you?'

'I did indeed,' said Sloan handsomely. 'The opening of the new fire station, wasn't it?'

'A very ordinary job, I'm afraid,' said Mundill deprecatingly.

In the police force very ordinary jobs had a lot to be said for them. Out of the ordinary ones usually came up nasty.

'It is difficult,' continued the architect easily, 'to be other than strictly utilitarian when you're designing a hose tower.'

'Quite so,' said Sloan.

'We had site problems, of course,' continued Frank Mundill smoothly, 'it being right in the middle of the town.'

Sloan nodded. Site problems would be to architects what identity problems were to the police, obstacles to be overcome.

'Mind you, Inspector, I have designed buildings in Berebury where there's been a little more scope than down at the fire station.'

Municipal buildings being what they were Sloan was glad to hear it.

'There was the junior school,' said Mundill.

'Split level,' said Sloan, who had been there.

'Petty crime,' added Crosby professionally. He had been there too.

'Plenty of site leeway in that case,' said Mundill.

There was precious little leeway with an unknown body. Where did you start if 'Missing Persons' didn't come up with anyone fitting the description of the body you had? The architect was warming to his theme. 'There's more freedom with a school than there is with some domestic stuff.'

Sloan looked up. 'You do ordinary house plans, too, sir, do you?'

'Oh, yes, Inspector.' He smiled thinly. 'I do my share of the domestic side, all right.'

All policemen did their share of the domestic side. 'Domestics' were what new constables on the beat cut their wisdom teeth on. It aged them more quickly than anything else.

Sloan took a final look round the boathouse, and said

formally, 'I'll be in touch with you again, sir, about this break-in. In due course. Come along, Crosby . . .'

He turned to go but as he did so his ear caught the inimitable sound of the splash of oars. Sloan leaned out over the path and looked downstream as far as he could. He recognized Horace Boller and his boat quite easily. He had to screw up his eyes to see who his passenger was. And then he recognized him too. It was Mr Basil Jensen, the curator of the Calleford Museum . . .

'Terry?' Miss Blandford pursed her lips. 'Terry, did you say?'

'I did.' Police Constable Brian Ridgeford had begun his search for a boy named Terry at the village school at Edsway. School was over for the day but the head teacher was still there. 'Have you got any boys called Terry?'

'The trouble,' said Miss Blandford, 'is that we've got more than one.'

'Tell me,' invited Ridgeford, undaunted.

She opened the school register. 'There's Terry Waters . . .'

'And what sort of a lad is Terry Waters?'

'Choirboy type,' she said succinctly.

Ridgeford frowned.

'The "butter wouldn't melt in his mouth" sort of boy,' amplified the teacher.

Ridgeford's frown cleared.

She waved a hand. 'If you know what I mean?'

Ridgeford knew what she meant. The manner of boy to whom benches of magistrates in juvenile courts – who should know better – almost automatically gave the benefit of the doubt . . .

'You probably passed him on your way here,' said Miss Blandford. 'He only lives down the road.'

Ridgeford shook his head. 'Not Terry Waters then.'

He wasn't expecting Terry or his friend to be Edsway boys. Mrs Boller would have recognized Edsway boys when they had brought the ship's bell into her shop. Children from all the other villages roundabout, though, came into Edsway school every day by bus. 'What about the others?' he asked.

'There's Terry Wilkins.'

Ridgeford got out his notebook. 'Where does he hail from?'

'Collerton.' She hesitated. 'He's not a bad boy but easily led.'

Ridgeford knew that sort. A boy who wouldn't take to crime unless the opportunity presented itself. There was a whole school of academic thought that saw crime as opportunity. Remove the opportunity, they said, and you removed that crime. If that didn't work you removed the criminal and called it preventive detention.

Miss Blandford said, 'With Terry Wilkins it would depend on the temptation.'

Constable Ridgeford nodded sagely. Who said Adam and Eve was nonsense? Temptation had had to begin somewhere. It didn't matter that it had only been an apple to begin with. It was the principle of the thing. 'Go on,' he said.

'There's Terry Goddard.' The head teacher's face became as near to benign-looking as Ridgeford had seen it. 'He's a worker.'

'Ah.'

'Not clever, mind you, but a worker.'

Everyone liked a worker. Being a worker evidently exonerated Terry Goddard in Miss Blandford's eyes from any activity the police were likely to be mixed up in. Perhaps being a worker meant you weren't idle and that removed you a stage farther from temptation. Ridgeford tried to think of some industrious criminals.

Henri Landru must have been quite busy.

In the nature of things eleven murders took time.

Dr Marcel Petiot couldn't have been much of a layabout either. He hadn't kept a stroke record of the murders he had committed but the French police thought sixty-five – give or take a few.

'That the lot, miss?' he said aloud. 'I'd been hoping for someone from Marby.'

'There's Terry Dykes.' She looked Brian Ridgeford straight in the eye and said, 'I don't know what you want your

Terry for, Constable, but I wouldn't put anything past this one.'

Ridgeford put the name down in his notebook. There was no point in asking expert opinion if you didn't take account of it. He took down a Marby address with a certain amount of satisfaction, then he asked Miss Blandford if Terry Dykes had got a sidekick.

'I beg your pardon, Constable?'

Ridgeford searched in his mind for the right expresion. 'A best friend, miss.' Bosom chum sounded distinctly old-fashioned but that was what he meant.

'Oh, yes.' Her brow cleared. 'Melvin Bates.'

Ridgeford wrote that name down too.

'Melvin Bates hangs on Terry Dykes's every word, so,' she gave a quick nod and said realistically, 'I dare say that's two of them up to no good.'

Police Constable Brian Ridgeford took his leave of the head teacher and applied himself to his bicycle and another journey to the fishing village beside the open sea. Judicious questioning of Marby natives led the policeman to the harbour. He'd find his quarry there for sure, he was told. They were always there, messing about in boats. Or just messing about. But as sure as eggs they'd be there.

So they were.

Two boys.

There had been something that Brian Ridgeford dimly remembered in his training that advised against the question-ing of juveniles by a police officer in uniform. Because of the neighbours. Brian Ridgeford squared his shoulders. There weren't any neighbours on the eastern arm of the harbour wall.

Just two boys.

They saw him coming and at the same time saw that there was no point in retreating. They stood their ground as he approached, one standing against a capstan and the other with one foot on a coil of rope.

'About that ship's bell,' began Ridgeford generally.

'Wasn't worth nothing,' said the boy by the capstan.

'The old woman said so,' chimed in the other.

'Load of old iron,' said the first boy, kicking the capstan with his foot.

'Waste of time going over there,' said his friend.

'She wouldn't give us nothing for it,' said the boy who was kicking the capstan. 'You ask her.'

'Where did you get it?' asked Ridgeford.

'Up on the Cat's Back,' replied the first boy glibly. 'Didn't we, Mel?'

'Up on the Cat's Back,' agreed Melvin. 'Like Terry said.'

'Did you now?' asked Ridgeford evenly. 'Suppose you tell me exactly where.'

'By an old tree,' said Terry.

'Near the hut,' said Melvin at the same time.

'By an old tree near the hut,' said Terry promptly.

Constable Ridgeford decided that Terry Dykes already had the makings of a criminal mentality.

'I suppose,' said the policeman heavily, 'that it fell off the back of a lorry up there.'

'No,' began Melvin, 'it was in . . .'

'There's only a footpath,' Terry Dykes cut in quickly.

Any resemblance to the tableau formed by the three of them to Sir John Millais' famous painting *The Boyhood of Raleigh* was purely coincidental. True, there was more than one beached rowing boat on the shore in the background and there were certainly two boys and an adult in the composition but there any likeness ended. In Millais's picture the two boys had been hanging, rapt, on the words of the ancient mariner as he pointed out to sea and described the wonders he had seen. In the present instance the tales were being told by the boys and Brian Ridgeford wasn't pointing anywhere. He was, however, projecting extreme scepticism at what he heard.

'So it didn't fall off the back of a lorry then,' he said.

'No,' said Terry Dykes defensively, 'it didn't.'

'Just lying there then, was it?'

'Yes . . . No . . . I don't know.'

'You must know.'

Terry Dykes shut his lips together.

'Make up your mind, boy,' said Ridgeford not unkindly. 'Was it or wasn't it?'

'No,' said Terry sullenly, 'it wasn't just lying there.'

'Well, then, where was it?' demanded Ridgeford. When there was no reply from Dykes he suddenly swung round on Melvin Bates. 'All right, you tell me.'

Melvin Bates started to stutter. 'I . . . I . . . it was in . . .'

'Shut up,' said Dykes, unceremoniously cutting off his henchman.

'All right,' said Ridgeford flatly, 'I've got the message. The bell was inside somewhere, wasn't it?' He drew breath. 'Now then, let me see if I can work out where. Over here in Marby?' They were known as 'constraint questions'; those whose answers limited the area of doubt. The best-known constraint question was 'Can you eat it?' Ridgeford allowed his voice to grow a harder note. 'And you found it inside somewhere, didn't you?'

It took him another ten minutes to find out exactly where.

Constable Ridgeford was not the only policeman whose immediate quarry lay in Marby. As soon as Sloan and Crosby left Collerton House they too made for the fishing village by the sea.

'We'll pick up Ridgeford over there,' predicted Sloan. 'And he can take us to have a look at this dinghy he's reported.'

They'd left Basil Jensen still making his way upstream.

'To see if it's *Tugboat Annie*,' completed Crosby, engaging gear.

'It would figure if it were.' He paused and then said quietly, 'I think something else figures, too, Crosby.'

'Sir?'

'I think – only think, mind you – that we just may have an explanation for a body decomposed but not damaged.'

'Sir?'

'You think, too,' adjured Sloan. The road between Collerton and Marby was so rural that not even Crosby could speed on it. He could use his mind instead.

'The boathouse?' offered the detective constable uncertainly.

'The boathouse,' said Sloan with satisfaction. 'It's early days yet, Crosby, but I think that we shall find that our chap – whoever he is – was parked in the water in the boathouse after he was killed.'

'Why in the water, though, sir?'

'The answer to that,' said Sloan briskly, 'is something called mephitis.'

'Sir?'

'Mephitis,' spelled out Sloan for him, 'is the smell of the dead.'

Crosby assimilated this and then said, 'So he was killed by a fall from a height first somewhere else . . .'

'Somewhere else,' agreed Sloan at once.

'But . . .'

'But left in the water afterwards, Crosby.'

'Why?'

Sloan waved a hand. 'As I said before graves for murder victims don't come easy.'

'Yes, sir,' Crosby nodded. 'Besides, he might have been killed on the spur of the moment and whoever did it needed time to think what to do with the body.'

It was surprising how the word 'murderer' hung outside speech.

'He might,' agreed Sloan. He hoped that it had been a hotblooded affair. Murder had nothing to be said for it at any time but heat-of-the-moment murder was always less sinister than murder plotted and planned. 'He would need time and opportunity to work out what to do.'

'And then,' postulated Crosby, 'the body was just pushed out into the water?'

There is a tide in the affairs of men, which, taken at the flood, leads on . . . No, that wouldn't do. It wouldn't have been like that at all. It would have been the furtive opening of the boathouse doors during the hours of darkness, and after the furtive opening the silent shove of a dead body with a boat-hook while the River Calle searched out every cranny of the river bank and picked up its latest burden and bore it off towards the sea.

'Unless I'm very much mistaken,' said Sloan austerely, 'the body left the boathouse at night.'

'Yes, sir.'

'Probably,' he added, 'in time to catch an ebb tide.' He, Sloan, would have to look at a tide table as soon as he got back to the police station but darkness and an ebb tide made sense.

'Do we know when, sir?' asked Crosby, who was perforce driving at a speed to satisfy his passenger.

'Some time before he was found,' said Sloan dourly, 'but not too long before.'

That was a lay interpretation of what Dr Dabbe had said in longer words.

Long enough to pick up *Gammarus pulex*.

Long enough to become unrecognizable.

Long enough to be taken by the river to the sea.

Not so long as to be taken by that same sea and laid on Billy's Finger.

Not so long as to disintegrate completely.

That would have been something that an assassin might have hoped for, that the body would fall to pieces.

Or that it would reach the open sea and be seen no more . . .

'Why did the boat go too?' Crosby was enquiring.

'I think,' reasoned Sloan aloud, 'that if a boat is found adrift and a body is found in the water simple policemen are meant to put two and two together and make five.'

That was something else a murderer might have hoped for.

'It might have happened too,' said Crosby, 'mightn't it? He'd only got to get a bit farther out to sea and he wouldn't have been spotted at all.'

Sloan stared unseeingly out of the car window. 'I wonder why he was put into the river exactly when he was.'

On such a full sea are we now afloat . . .

'Well, you wouldn't choose a weekend, would you, sir?' said Crosby.

Never on Sunday?

'The whole estuary's stuffed with sailing boats at the weekend,' continued the constable. 'You should see it, sir.'

'I probably will,' said Sloan pessimistically, 'unless we've got all this cleared up by then.'

The detective constable slowed down for a signpost. 'This must be the Edsway to Marby road we're joining.'

'Something,' said Sloan resolutely, 'must have made it important for that body to be got out of that boathouse when it was.'

The car radio began to chatter while he was speaking. 'The gentlemen from the Press,' reported the girl at the microphone, 'would like to know when Detective Inspector Sloan will see them.'

'Ten o'clock tomorrow morning,' responded Sloan with spirit, 'and not a minute before.' He switched off at his end and turned to his companion. 'And Crosby . . .'

'Sir?'

'While you're about it,' said Sloan, 'you'd better find out about the niece. And what Mrs Mundill died from too. We can't be too careful.'

'Yes, sir.'

'Now, where did Ridgeford say this dinghy was?'

'According to his report,' said Crosby, 'it's beyond the Marby lifeboat station. To be exact, to the north of it. We're to ask for a man called Farebrother.'

But hark! I hear the toll of a bell.   **12**

Farebrother was quite happy to indicate the stray dinghy to the two policemen. And to tell them that Ridgeford was down on the harbour wall.

'Fetch him,' said Sloan briefly to Crosby. He turned to Farebrother and showed him the copper barbary head. 'Ever seen one of these before?'

'Might have,' said the lifeboatman. 'Might not.'

'Lately?'

'Might have,' said the lifeboatman again.

'How lately?'

'I don't hold with such things,' he said flatly.

'No,' said Sloan.

''Tisn't right to disturb places where men lie.' Farebrother stared out to sea.

Sloan said nothing.

'Mark my words,' said Farebrother, 'no good comes of it.'

Sloan nodded.

''Tisn't lucky either.'

'Unlucky for some, anyway,' said Sloan obliquely, bingo-style.

'Didn't ought to be allowed, that's what I say.'

'Quite so,' said Sloan.

'They say there was the bones of a man's hand still clutching a candlestick down there.'

'Down where?' said Sloan softly.

Farebrother's mouth set in an obstinate line. 'I don't know where. No matter who asks me, be they as clever as you like.'

'Who asked you?'

'Never you mind that. I tell you I don't know anything . . .'

'Neither do I,' said Sloan seriously, 'but I intend to find out.'

'That's your business,' said Farebrother ungraciously, 'but I say things should be let alone with, that's what I say.' He turned on his heel and crunched off over the shingle.

Crosby came back with Ridgeford while Sloan was still examining the old fishing boat. Sloan pointed to Farebrother's retreating back. '*The Old Man and the Sea*,' he said neatly to the two constables. They both looked blank. He changed his tone. 'This bell, Ridgeford . . .'

'Taken, sir, from a farm up on the Cat's Back,' said Ridgeford. 'Or so the two boys who took it into Mother Hopton's say. I don't think they were having me on but you never can tell.' Ridgeford had learned some things already. 'Not with boys.'

'Not with boys,' agreed Sloan.

'The farmer's called Manton,' said Ridgeford. 'Alec Manton of Lea Farm.'

'Do you know him?'

Ridgeford shook his head. 'Not to say know. I've heard of him, that's all, sir.'

'Heard what?'

'Nothing against.'

Sloan nodded. 'Right, then you can stay in the background. Crosby, you're coming with me to Manton's farm. Now, Ridgeford, whereabouts exactly did you say this sheep fank was that the boys told you about?'

Few farmers can have been fortunate enough to see as much of their farm laid out in front of them as did Alec Manton. The rising headland was almost entirely given over to sheep and the fields were patterned with the casual regularity of patchwork. Because of the rise in the land the farmland and its stock were both easily visible. The farmhouse, though, was nestled into the low ground before the headland proper began, sheltered alike from sea and wind. It was in the process of being restored and extended. Sloan noticed a discreet grey and white board proclaiming that Frank Mundill was the architect, and made a note.

Alec Manton was out, his wife told them. She was a plump, calm woman, undismayed by the presence of two police officers at the farm. Was it about warble fly?

'Not exactly,' temporized Sloan, explaining that he would nevertheless like to look at the sheep-fold on the hill.

'Where they dip?' said Mrs Manton intelligently. 'Of course. You go on up and I'll tell my husband to come along when he comes home. He shouldn't be long.'

In the event they didn't get as far as the sheep fank before the farmer himself caught up with them.

'Routine investigations,' said Sloan mendaciously.

'Oh?' said Manton warily. He was tallish with brown hair.

'We've had a report that something might have been stolen from the farm.'

'Have you?' said Alec Manton. He was a man who looked as if he packed a lot of energy. He looked Sloan up and down. 'Can't say that we've missed anything.'

'No?' said Sloan.

'What sort of thing?'

'A ship's bell.'

'From my farm?' Alec Manton's face was quite expressionless.

'Boys,' said Sloan sedulously. 'They said it came from where you keep your sheep.'

'Did they?' said Manton tightly. 'Then we'd better go and see, hadn't we? This way . . .'

Their goal was several fields away, set in a faint hollow in the land, and built against the wind. In front of the little bothy was a sheep-dipping tank. Set between crush pen and drafting pen, it was full of murky water. Alec Manton led the way into the windowless building and looked round in the semidarkness. Sloan and Crosby followed on his heels. There was nothing to see save bare walls and even barer earth. The place, though, did show every sign of having been occupied by sheep at some time. Sloan looked carefully at the floor. It had been pounded by countless hooves to the consistency of concrete.

'This bell,' began Sloan.

'That you say was found . . .' said Manton.

'In police possession,' said Sloan mildly.

'Ah.'

'Pending enquiries.'

'I see.'

'Of course,' said Sloan largely, 'the boys may have been having us on.'

'Of course.'

'You know what boys are.'

'Only too well,' said Manton heartily.

'We'll have to get on to them again,' said Sloan, 'and see if we can get any nearer the truth, whatever that may be.'

'Of course,' said the farmer quickly. 'Did they – er – take anything else, do you know?'

'Not that we know about,' said Sloan blandly. 'Would there have been anything else in there for them to steal?'

Alec Manton waved an arm. 'You've seen it for yourself, haven't you? Give or take a sheep or two from time to time it looks pretty empty to me.'

'Of course,' said Sloan casually, 'the owner of this bell may turn up to claim it.'

'That would certainly simplify matters,' agreed the farmer. 'But in the mean time . . .'

'Yes, sir?'

'It's quite safe in police custody?'

'Quite safe,' Sloan assured him.

'Crosby!' barked Sloan.

'Sir?'

'What was odd about all that?'

'Don't know, sir.'

'Think, man. Think.'

'The place was empty.'

'Of course it was empty,' said Sloan with asperity. 'The bell must have been tucked away in the corner when those two boys found it. Only boys would have looked there . . .'

Murderers who thought that they had hidden their victims well reckoned without the natural curiosity of the average boy at their peril. Many a well-covered thicket had been penetrated by a boy for no good reason . . .

'Yes, sir,' said Crosby.

'What wasn't empty, Crosby?'

Crosby thought for a long moment. 'Sir?'

'What was full, Crosby?'

'Only the sheep-dipping thing.'

'Exactly,' breathed Sloan. 'Do you know what month it is, Crosby?'

'June, sir,' said Crosby stolidly.

'You don't,' said Sloan softly, 'dip sheep in Calleshire in June.'

'Left over from when you did, then,' suggested Crosby.

'No,' said Sloan.

'No?'

'You dip sheep a month after shearing. Manton's sheep weren't shorn,' said Sloan. Policemen, even town policemen, knew all about the dipping of sheep and its regulations.

'Besides, you wouldn't leave your sheep-dip full without a good reason. It's dangerous stuff.'

'What sort of reason?' said Crosby.

'If,' said Sloan, 'you have been conducting a secret rescue of the parts of an old East Indiaman you acquire items which have been underwater for years.'

'Yes, sir.'

'Taking them out of the water causes them to dry up and disintegrate. Mr Jensen at the museum said so.'

'Yes, sir, I'm sure.'

'So you have to store them underwater or else.'

'Yes, sir.'

'Wooden things, that is.'

Crosby nodded, not very interested. 'Wooden things.'

'Metal ones,' said Sloan, 'aren't so important.'

'What about rust?'

'Bronze doesn't rust,' said Sloan.

'*The Clarembald*'s bell?'

'Bronze,' said Sloan. 'Or so Ridgeford said.'

'It didn't need to stay underwater?'

'No,' said Sloan. 'It could stand in the corner of the sheep building quite safely.' He amended this. 'Safe from everything except boys.' He drew breath and carried on. 'There was another thing about what was in that sheep-dipping tank.'

'Sir?'

'Think, Crosby.'

'It was dirty, sir. You couldn't see if there was anything in there or not.'

'That and something else,' said Sloan, and waited.

Dull, a constable.

That had been in Shakespeare.

He'd thought of everything, had the bard.

The detective inspector cleared his throat and said didactically, 'A good policeman uses all his senses.'

Crosby lifted his nose like a pointer. 'But it didn't smell, sir.'

'Precisely,' said Sloan grimly. 'Like the dog that didn't bark in the night, it didn't smell. Believe you me, lad, sheep-dip isn't by any manner of means the most fragrant of fluids.'

'No, sir.'

'But I'm prepared to bet that there was something in that tank besides dirty water.'

Crosby scuffed his toe at a pebble. 'I still don't see what it's got to do with the body in the water.'

'Neither do I, Crosby, neither do I. What I wonder is if Mr Basil Jensen does.'

Elizabeth Busby just couldn't settle. She was like a bee working over a flower-bed already sucked dry of all its nectar. She couldn't settle to anything at all, not to finishing off spring-cleaning the spare bedroom and not to any other household chores either.

She met Frank Mundill in the hall as he came back from the

boathouse. He dropped the key back into the drawer in the hall table.

'I don't know why I bothered to lock it, I'm sure,' he said. 'Anyone who wanted to could get into the boathouse as easy as wink.'

'Tea?' she suggested.

'That would be nice.' He looked unenthusiastically at the flight of stairs that led up to his studio. 'I don't think I'll go back to the drawing board this minute.'

'No.' She agreed with the sentiment as well as the statement. Getting on with anything just now was difficult enough. Going back to something was quite impossible.

Presently Mundill said, 'I'll have to go along and have a word with Ted Boller about getting the river doors fixed up.'

She nodded.

'It'll have to be something temporary.' He grimaced. 'The police want the damage left.'

'Evidence, I suppose,' she said without interest.

'They're sending a photographer.'

'I'll keep my ears open,' she promised. She would hear the bell all right when they came. She had always heard her aunt's bell and her ear was still subconsciously attuned to listening for it. At the first tinkle she'd been awake and on her way to the bedroom . . .

'I may be a little while,' said Mundill, elaborately casual.

She looked up, her train of thought broken.

'While I'm about it,' he said, 'I might as well go on down to Veronica Feckler's cottage and see exactly what it is that she wants doing there.'

'Might as well,' agreed Elizabeth in a desultory fashion.

'You might keep your ear open for the telephone . . .'

She nodded. His secretary was going to be away all the week. 'I will. There might be a call for me too.'

'Of course,' he agreed quickly.

Too quickly.

She'd practically lived on the telephone while Peter Hinton was around. When he wasn't at Collerton House he was at the College of Technology at Luston. His landlady – well versed in student ways – had a pay telephone in the hall. Peter Hinton had spent a great deal of time on it. Elizabeth's eyes drifted involuntarily to the instrument in the hall of Collerton House. It was by a window-seat and Elizabeth had spent a similar amount of time curled up on that window-seat enjoying those endless chats. Politicians and business negotiators had a phrase which covered young lovers as well. They often began either their alliances or their confrontations with what they called 'exploratory talks'.

So it had been with Elizabeth Busby and Peter Hinton. Their talks had been exploratory too, as they each searched out the recesses of mind and memory of the others, revealing – as the politicians and businessmen found to their cost – a little of themselves too in the process. In some ways these preliminaries of a courtship had been like playing that old pencil-and-paper parlour game of Battleships. Sometimes a tentative salvo fell in a square that represented the empty sea. Sometimes it fell where the opponent's battleship was placed and then there was a hit – a palpable hit. After that it was an easy matter to find and sink the paper battleship and win the game.

So it was with young people getting to know each other.

One thing they found they had in common was parents abroad. His were tea planters in Assam.

What they didn't share was an interest in crime. Peter Hinton knew most of the Notable British Trials series of books by heart and took an interest in villainy. Elizabeth shied away from the unpleasant like a nervous horse.

And then suddenly she'd found she hadn't known Peter Hinton at all . . .

Exploratory talks didn't always lead on to treaties and alliances. Sometimes – the news bulletins said so – they broke down, foundering upon this or that rock uncovered in the course of those very talks. So it must have been with Peter Hinton. Only she didn't know what it was that had been laid bare that had been such a stumbling block between the two of them that they couldn't even discuss it. He'd come into her life out of the blue and as precipitately he'd gone out of it again.

She brought the tea tray back into the hall for them both. There was a little occasional table there and Frank Mundill pulled it over to the window-seat. The only trouble with being in the window-seat was that whoever was sitting there could not avoid the full impact of the picture hanging on the wall opposite. It had been quite one of Richard Camming's most ambitious paintings.

'We think,' Celia Mundill used to say to visitors to the house seeing it for the first time, 'that it's meant to be Diana the Huntress.'

'But we never liked to ask,' Marion Busby would add tremulously if she were there.

'Up to something, of course.'

'But we don't quite know what.'

They had both been fond of their father but they had loved him without illusion.

Elizabeth was able to pour out the tea without thinking about Diana the Huntress. As always when she was sitting in the hall her eyes drifted to the model of the Camming valve. It was the Camming valve on which the family fortunes had been founded. It was the Camming valve which had brought Peter Hinton into her life. He'd come from Luston College of Technology with a dissertation to do. He'd chosen the Camming valve and its influence on the development of the marine engine. What more natural that he should come to Gordon Camming's house in the course of writing it? True, Gordon Camming had actually designed his valve in the back kitchen of some Victorian artisan's cottage, demolished long ago in a vigorous council slum-clearance scheme, but Collerton House was what he had built. It was a monument to his success and as near to a museum as there was.

Frank Mundill had sunk his tea with celerity. 'I'll be going now,' he said, getting to his feet.

She nodded, her train of thought scarcely disturbed this time. In her mind's eye she was seeing Peter Hinton bending over the model as he had done the first day he came.

'We've got a drawing of it at the college.' he said when he saw it, 'but not a model.'

'It's a working model,' she had said eagerly, anxious to be helpful. 'Grandfather used to make it work for me when I was little. I can't do it, though.'

He had come . . .

She remembered now his tiny smile as he had said, 'I can. Would you like to see it working again?'

He had seen . . .

'Oh, please.'

He had conquered . . .

He'd come back again, of course, another day. And another day. And another.

What she couldn't understand was why he had gone and not come back.

She sat in the window-seat now, taking her tea in thoughtful sips. She sat there so long that the cushion became less comfortable. She shifted her position slightly, almost without thinking. To her surprise this made for less comfort rather than more. Something was sticking into her. The fact took a moment or two to penetrate her consciousness. When it did she put her hand down between the cushions. It encountered something oblong and unyielding. She stood up abruptly and snatched the cushions away. All doubt ended when she set eyes on the object.

It was Peter Hinton's slide rule and she knew it well.

'Tis what we must all come to.   **13**

Some savage breasts cannot be soothed. That of Superintendent Leeyes came into this category.

'What I want, Sloan,' he snapped, 'are results.'

Detective Inspector Sloan was reporting to him in the
superintendent's office at Berebury. 'Yes, sir, but . . .'

'Not theories.'

'No, sir.' Actually Sloan didn't have any theories either but
this seemed to have escaped the superintendent's notice.

'Have you any idea at all what's going on over there?'

'Finding *The Clarembald* comes into it,' said Sloan slowly,
'though where the dead man fits in with that I really don't
know.'

'Don't forget that he had that copper thing . . .'

'Barbary head.'

'In his pocket.'

'Yes, sir, so he did.' Sloan cleared his throat. 'But there are
a lot of other things we don't know.'

'Who he is,' trumpeted Leeyes. 'You haven't got very far
with that, have you, Sloan?'

'We have one lead, sir. The girl at Collerton House had a
boy-friend who's not around any more. Crosby's chasing him
up now just to be on the safe side.'

'There's another thing we don't know besides who the body
is.'

'Why he was set out into the mainstream when he was,' said Sloan before the superintendent could say it for him.

'Exactly,' growled Leeyes.

This was one of the things that was puzzling Sloan too. 'There must have been a reason,' he agreed. 'After all he'd been dead for quite a while and in the water too. Dr Dabbe said so.'

'And then suddenly someone . . .'

'The murderer,' said Sloan. That was something he felt sure about.

'The murderer decides to punt him into the river.'

'There'll be a reason,' said Sloan confidently. 'We're dealing with someone with brains.'

Leeyes grunted again.

'Anyone,' said Sloan feelingly, 'who can kill someone without them being reported missing has got brains.'

'It doesn't happen often,' conceded Leeyes.

'And anyone who can find somewhere as clever as a boathouse to park a body until it's unrecognizable knows what they're doing. Do you realize, sir,' he added energetically, 'that if that man Horace Boller hadn't been out there fishing that body might well have just drifted out to sea and never been seen again?'

'A perfect murder,' commented Leeyes.

'Exactly, sir.' Though for the life of him Sloan didn't know why murder done and not known about should be called perfect . . .

'The dinghy,' said Leeyes. 'What about the dinghy?'

'I think that went just in case the body was picked up,' said Sloan.

'A touch of local colour, eh?' said Leeyes grimly.

'We've examined it,' said Sloan. 'And it answers to Mr Mundill's description. I don't think there's any doubt that it's the one from his boathouse but we'll get him over in the morning to identify it properly.'

'That's all very well, Sloan, but where does *The Clarembald* come in?'

'I don't know, sir. The things from the ship,' he couldn't

bring himself to use the word 'artefacts' to the superintendent, 'that have been coming ashore . . .'

'Treasure trove,' said Leeyes, never one to split hairs on precise meanings.

'Perhaps, sir. I don't know about that yet.'

'These things then . . .' said Leeyes impatiently.

'Indicate that someone has found the East Indiaman.'

'Don't forget the diver, eh, Sloan, don't forget the diver.'

'No, sir, I haven't. This farmer – Alec Manton – has been hiring a local trawler. Ridgeford saw it going out at low tide.'

'Did he indeed?' There was a pause while Superintendent Leeyes considered this and then he abruptly started on quite a different tack. 'This height that Dr Dabbe says he fell from . . .'

'I've been thinking about that, sir,' said Sloan. Every case was like solving a jigsaw and some pieces of that jigsaw had straight edges. A piece of jigsaw puzzle that had a straight edge helped to define the puzzle. So it was in a murder case. He always thought of the forensic pathologist's report as so many pieces of straight edge of a jigsaw puzzle. And the pathologist had said that the man had fallen to his death. That became fact . . .

'Well?'

'Apart from the cliffs . . .'

'Which are too high.'

'There isn't very much in the way of a drop round Collerton and Edsway.' Inland from the cliffs the rest of the Callenshire littoral was – like Norfolk – very flat.

'He fell from somewhere,' said Leeyes, who had taken Dr Dabbe's report for gospel too.

'A dying fall,' said Sloan, conscious that it had been said before.

'But where from?' asked Leeyes irritably. 'Would a church tower have done?'

'It's the right sort of height,' agreed Sloan, 'but it's not exactly what you could call private, is it, sir? I mean, would you climb a church tower after dark with a murderer?'

'No,' said Leeyes robustly. 'And I wouldn't buy a second-hand car from one either.'

'I'll get Crosby to check at Collerton church anyway,' said Sloan, 'but what I think we're looking for is a sort of hidden drop. Remember he would have had to have been pushed from the top and then stayed at the bottom . . .'

'Dead or dying.'

'Until whoever pushed him came down and picked up the body.'

'Darkness or privacy,' agreed Leeyes.

What was it that Crosby had said?

Pussy's down the well.

It would have had to have been somewhere where murderer and victim could have gone together without comment.

Then the lonely push . . .

'And,' said Leeyes, 'then the body had to be got from wherever it fell to the boathouse. Have you gone into the logistics, Sloan?'

'The boot of a car would have done.'

'And then?'

'For the last part? A wheelbarrow,' said Sloan. 'That would have done too. It's the easiest way to carry a body that I know. And there are several around the house.'

'Not one of these plastic affairs, Sloan. You mean a good old-fashioned metal one.'

'Yes, sir.' When a man came automatically to put the word 'good' together with the word 'old-fashioned', it was time for him to retire. He coughed. 'The trouble, sir, is that there is a perfectly good asphalt path to the boathouse that doesn't show any extra marks. We've looked.'

Leeyes grunted. 'So what you're saying is that he could have been killed anywhere and brought to Collerton.'

'By land or water,' said Sloan flatly. 'With a barbary head in his pocket.' That barbary head was a puzzle. Was it a pointer to *The Clerembald* or was it to point them away from someone else?

'It's what you might call wide open still, isn't it, Sloan,' said

Leeyes unencouragingly. 'You'll have to look on it as a challenge,' he added.

'I'm starting with a search warrant for Lea Farm at Marby,' said Sloan flatly. 'There's something funny going on there.'

Landladies didn't always come up middle-aged and inquisitive. Sometimes they were young and indifferent.

'Pete?' said Ms Cheryl Watson, shrugging her shoulders. 'He was around.'

'When?' asked Detective Constable Crosby.

She opened her hands expressively. 'Don't ask me. He'll be back.'

'When?' asked Crosby.

'When he feels like it. He'll settle up for his room all right, don't worry.'

Crosby did not say that that was not what was worrying the county constabulary.

'What about his gear?' he said instead.

'Still around,' she said largely. 'And his mail. He'll be back for them.'

'Why did he go?'

Her eyes opened wide. 'He had exams, didn't he?'

'You think he chickened out?'

'A man has to be himself,' said the self-appointed representative of a different way of life, 'hasn't he?'

'I wouldn't know about that,' said Crosby.

'Examinations are the sign of a decadent culture,' pronounced the young woman. 'Always making you prove yourself.'

'A sort of initiation rite, you mean?' suggested Crosby.

'That's right,' she said eagerly.

The course at the Police Training College made a man prove himself. Or leave. It was a sort of initiation rite too. A police constable was let into the mysteries of the service at the same time as he was being sorely tried by his instructors.

Ms Watson looked Detective Constable Crosby up and down with unattractive shrewdness. 'Is Pete in trouble then?'

'Not that we know about,' said Crosby truthfully.

'There was something else besides examinations.'

'Was there?' he murmured.

'He had a bird.'

'Ah.'

'Don't say that.' She looked at him. 'No, Pete was hell-bent on marriage.'

'Was he?'

'No less,' she said. 'He was real old-fashioned about it.'

Crosby gave the absent Mr Hinton a passing thought.

'He often said he wasn't going to settle for anything less than marriage.'

'Makes a change,' said Crosby. The beat made a man philosophical about some things.

'She'd got money, you see,' said Ms Watson simply. 'Or would have one day. I think that's what he said.'

It is a truth universally acknowledged that a single man seeking good fortune must be in want of a wife in possession of one . . .

'Anyway,' she said, 'don't you worry. Pete Hinton is old enough to take care of himself.'

Crosby said he was sure he hoped so too, but he came away with a disturbing description.

Elizabeth Busby sat alone in the empty house. She sat quite still at one end of the window-seat staring at that which she had found at the other.

Peter Hinton's slide rule.

It must have slipped out of his pocket the last time he had sat there. It couldn't have been before that because he would have missed it and then – for sure – a search on a grand scale would have been instituted. If it hadn't been found, then St Anthony's aid would have been invoked. A practical young man like Peter Hinton hadn't really believed in St Anthony, but Elizabeth had done so, and gradually Peter Hinton had begun to call upon him too for lost things.

Or said he had done.

His precious slide rule would have been missed very early

on. It was never out of his pocket – it was almost his badge of office. His course at Luston was a sandwich affair – so much time at his studies, so much time on the shop floor. His shop floor employment had been with Punnett and Punnett, Marine Engineers, Limited, and it was after that when he went to the College of Technology. And much as very young doctors flaunted their stethoscopes, so the slide rules of embryo engineers were frequently in evidence.

She cast her mind back yet again to his last visit. In fact she had already gone over it in her mind a hundred times or more – searching every recollection for pointers of what was to come. She hadn't found any – their only disagreement had been about her aunt – and now she couldn't recollect either any indication that the famous slide rule hadn't been around. She screwed up her eyes in concentrated memory recall and came up with something that surprised her. Surely they hadn't been near the window-seat on Peter's last visit at all?

He'd come over from Luston to see her – it had had to be like that since Celia Mundill had begun to be so ill after Easter – on one of her aunt's really bad days. Elizabeth had been dividing her time between the bedroom and the kitchen. There had been no spare time for sitting together on the window-seat or anywhere else. In fact she hadn't had a great deal of time to spare for Peter Hinton at all but that had been simply because of her aunt's illness. She had wondered for a moment if it had been this which had so miffed him that he had taken his departure, but what manner of man would begrudge her time spent with the dying?

Because her aunt had been dying. Elizabeth had known that ever since Celia's X-ray at Easter when Frank Mundill had taken her to one side and told her that that was what the doctor over at Calleford had said. He'd brought a letter back with him for Dr Tebot, Celia Mundill's own doctor at Collerton – dear old Dr Tebot who looked like nothing so much as the doctor in Luke Fildes's famous picture – but he had enjoined secrecy on Dr Tebot as well as on Elizabeth. Celia Mundill had an inoperable cancer of the stomach but she wasn't to know.

'Not ever,' Frank Mundill had said at the time.

'But the doctor . . .'

'The doctor,' said Mundill, 'said she need never know.'

'I don't see how.'

'They call it "stealing death",' Frank Mundill had told her.

Come away, come away, death . . .

'Dr Tebot said it's not as difficult as it sounds, Elizabeth, because the patient always wants to believe that they're getting better.'

'A sort of conspiracy,' Elizabeth remembered saying slowly at the time.

'A conspiracy of silence,' Mundill had said firmly. 'You don't need to lie. Anyway, Elizabeth, she won't ask you.'

'No . . .'

'She'll ask the doctor and he'll know what to say, I'm sure.'

'I'm sure, too,' she'd said then with a touch of cynicism beyond her years.

And she had proceeded to watch her aunt decline. Severe vomiting had been accompanied by loss of weight. Abdominal pain had come, too, until the doctor had stopped it with a hefty pain-killer. It had needed injections though to stop the pains in her arms and legs. The district nurse had come to give her those and Elizabeth had been glad of the extra support.

Nothing though had stopped the vomiting or the burning pain in the patient's throat.

Or her loss of weight.

Frank Mundill had been marvellously attentive. At any moment of the night or day when Celia had said she could eat or drink he'd been on hand with something. Gradually though she'd sunk beyond that.

'She may get jaundiced,' Dr Tebot had warned them one day.

So she had. Soon after that her skin took on a yellow, jaundiced look. Celia Mundill had died too with the brown petechiae of premature age on her skin. One day she'd slipped into a merciful coma.

That, when it happened, though, was too late for Peter Hinton. He'd taken himself off by the time Celia Mundill had breathed her last. Perhaps, Elizabeth had thought more than once, he couldn't stand the atmosphere of illness – there were some men, she knew, who couldn't. Thank goodness Frank Mundill hadn't been one of them or she would never have coped. He'd been marvellous.

She sat quite still now in the window-seat, increasingly confident that the last time that Peter Hinton had come to the house they had not sat together there. They'd only met in the kitchen. Elizabeth had been waiting and watching for the district nurse while Frank Mundill was taking his turn in the bedroom beside the patient. She remembered now how difficult she had found it to think or speak of anything but her aunt's illness.

True, they'd nearly quarrelled but not about themselves.

About Celia Mundill.

'She looks so awful now,' Elizabeth had cried. That had been the worst thing of all. Celia Mundill was just a ghastly parody of the woman she had been a few short months ago.

'What about her going into hospital?' Peter had urged. 'Don't you think she ought to be in hospital? I do.'

'No!' She'd been surprised at her own fierceness. She must have caught it from Frank Mundill. 'We want her to die at home in her own bed. Besides,' she said illogically, 'she's far too poorly to go into hospital.'

'Do her eyes water?' asked Peter suddenly.

'Yes, they do. Why?'

'I just wondered.'

'There's nothing more they could do for her if she was in hospital,' said Elizabeth, still het up over his suggestion. 'We're doing all anybody could. Dr Tebot says so.'

'I'm sure you are,' he said soothingly. 'It was only a thought. But don't you go and knock yourself up, will you?'

'I'm young and strong,' she had said, and she meant it.

Now – since Peter had gone and her aunt had died – she wasn't sure how strong she was. She wasn't as young as she had been either.

She stared at the slide rule.

It hadn't been missing that last evening that Peter Hinton

hd come. She was certain about that. He would undoubtedly have mentioned the fact and gone hunting for his instrument. And he hadn't lost it that evening because they hadn't sat in the hall at all.

She shivered involuntarily.

That only left the time that he had come over – the time which she had never been able to fathom – when he had left the note and the ring on the hall table. In spite of herself her eyes drifted over in the direction of the hall table, seeing in her mind's eye the piece of paper and the circlet of metal lying there again – just as she had done the first time. She'd been carrying her aunt's tray down the stairs at the time . . .

She looked round the hallway. Surely he wouldn't have sat on the window-seat to compose the note? *Congés* deserved to have more time spent on them than that. Besides she might have come down the stairs at any time and found him sitting there and that would never have done. She rejected the notion almost as soon as she had thought of it. No, that note and the ring had been slipped on the table at a very opportune moment.

And the slide rule?

She couldn't imagine exactly when the slide rule had slipped out of its proud owner's pocket and fallen deep down between the cushions. But it had been after the last time she had seen him – and it meant that when he had last come to the house he had sat on the window-seat long enough for it to work its way out of his pocket. She sat there quite motionless for a long time while she thought about it.

Soften the evidence.   **14**

The lecturer at Luston College of Technology rolled his eyes at his first visitor the next morning and said, 'Hinton? He was another drop-out, that's all, officer. We get them all the time.'

'Do you know why?' asked Detective Constable Crosby.

'This isn't a kindergarten.'

'No, sir, I'm sure.'

'Hinton wasn't any different from all the others,' he said irritably.

Crosby said he was sure he hoped not. 'Did you make enquiries at the time, sir?'

'I didn't but the registrar will have done. He'll have had a grant, you know, and that will have had to be signed for.'

'Quite so, sir.' In an uncertain world the accounting profession was more certain than most. 'Examinations, do you think it was, sir?'

'Examinations?' snorted the lecturer. 'It's not examinations that they're afraid of. It's hard work.'

'Can you tell me when he was last here?'

'That's not difficult. It'll be here in the register.' He ran his thumb down a list. 'Hinton, P. R., was here for the first two weeks of the summer term and not after that.'

'Thank you, sir, you've been most helpful.'

The courtesy appeared to mollify the lecturer. He opened up slightly. 'He was supposed to be doing a dissertation, too, but he never handed it in. His home address? You'll have to ask the registrar for that too. I have an idea his family were abroad . . .'

Detective Inspector Sloan intended to concentrate first of all on the Mundill ménage. He began sooner than he expected when he bumped into Inspector Harpe of Traffic Division crossing the police station yard.

'Mundill?' Harry Harpe frowned. 'I know the name.'

'Demon driver?'

'No, it wasn't that.' He frowned. 'Mundill – let me think a minute.' He slapped his thigh. 'Got it!'

'Inner guidance?' suggested Sloan, not that Mundill had looked a drinker.

'Not that either.' Harpe knew all the heavy drinkers for miles around. 'He's an architect, isn't he?' Harpe nodded to himself with satisfaction. 'Then he designed the multi-storey car park last year. He got some sort of architectural award for it. I met him at the official opening. You remember, Sloan, the mayor's car was the first one in.'

Sloan had a vague memory of bouquets and mayoral chains and speeches and photographs in the local paper.

Harpe emitted a sound that for him was a chuckle. 'But he couldn't understand the principle it was built on. I heard Mundill trying to explain it to him. The mayor couldn't see why the cars going up never met the cars going down.'

'Two spirals,' said Sloan immediately, 'one within the other.'

'Mundill gave it some fancy name and that didn't help the mayor one little bit.'

'Double helix,' supplied Sloan.

'That was it,' agreed Harpe. 'Mundill told him there was a well in Italy – at Orvieto, I think he said it was – that was built on the same principle. The donkey going down never met the donkey coming up. Clever chap. Not the mayor,' he added quickly, 'Mundill.'

'It's a good car park,' said Sloan.

And it was.

'Keeps the cars off the streets,' agreed Harpe.

Sloan left Harpe while he was still thinking about the apotheosis of Traffic Division's dreams – totally empty roads.

When he got to his room Sloan picked up the telephone and made an appointment with Frank Mundill to go over to Marby during the morning to identify the boat on the beach.

He sat in front of the telephone for a long moment after that and then he dialled the County Police Headquarters at Calleford.

'I want a police launch,' he said to the officer at the other end.

'Speak on.'

'Strictly for observation.'

'If you want the drug squad you've got the wrong number.'

'I don't.'

'That makes a change,' said the voice equably.

'At least,' said Sloan, 'I don't think I do.'

'Myself, I wouldn't put anything past the drugs racket.'

'No.' That was something he would have to think about. There was probably no one at greater risk than an addict – unless it was a pusher who double-crossed his supplier. Then revenge was simple and swift.

'This launch you want – where and when?'

'Off Marby. Round the headland. I shall be sending a constable up on the Cat's Back there to keep watch as well.'

'Belt and galluses,' remarked the voice. 'When do you want this observation kept?'

'Low tide,' said Sloan without hesitation.

'Right you are. By the way,' asked the voice, 'what are they to observe?'

'A small fishing trawler called *The Daisy Bell*,' said Sloan, replacing the receiver.

Then, unable to put it off any longer, he knocked on the door of Superintendent Leeyes's office.

'Ha, Sloan! Any progress?'

'A little, sir.' Intellectuals were not the only people to be troubled by the vexed relationship between truth and art. 'Just a little.'

'Know who he is yet?'

'Not for certain,' said Sloan. He could have delivered a short disquisition, though, on the phrase 'growing doubts'.

Superintendent Leeyes waved a hand airily. 'Find out what happened first, Sloan, and look for your evidence afterwards.'

That wasn't what they taught recruits of Training School.

'We haven't got a lot of evidence to consider,' said Sloan.

But it was too subtle a point for the superintendent.

'You've got a body,' boomed Leeyes.

'Yes, sir.' Dr Dabbe's full post-mortem report had been on Sloan's desk that morning, too. It didn't tell him anything that the pathologist hadn't already told him, except that the young man had had a broken ankle in childhood, which might help.

In the end.

'With a piece of copper on it,' Leeyes reminded him.

'Yes, sir.' There were those who would call that an obol for Charon but they were not policemen. Sloan had a search warrant for Alec Manton's farm now. And he'd have to find out what Mr Jensen at the museum had been up to. Things were obviously moving in the archaeological world. Jensen had been out when he rang the museum.

'This ship under the water,' said Leeyes abruptly. 'Who does it belong to?'

'Strictly speaking,' said Sloan, 'the East India Company, I suppose.'

'Ha!'

'But . . .'

'Not findings, keepings, eh, Sloan?'

'No, sir.' Not even a bench of magistrates in the Juvenile Court would go along with that piece of childhood lore and faulty law. A roomful of lost property at the police station testified to the opposite too. He cleared his throat, and carried on, 'Under the Merchant Shipping Act of 1894 . . .'

'Been at the books, have you, Sloan?'

'A wreck is deemed to belong to the owner . . .'

Come back, Robert Clive, all forgiven.

'And if the owner isn't found?' asked Leeyes.

'The wreck becomes the property of the state in whose waters she lies.'

Full fathom five . . .

'And, sir, the goods discovered in a wreck . . .'

'Yes?'

'Can be auctioned.'

'Who benefits?' asked Leeyes sharply. 'Or does the Crown take?'

'The finder gets most of the proceeds.' The superintendent's phrase reminded Sloan of a move on the chessboard.

The superintendent looked extremely alert. 'That's different.'

'Salvage,' added Sloan for the record, 'is something quite separate.'

Leeyes's mind was running along ahead. 'You're going to track this farmer down, aren't you, Sloan?'

'Oh, yes, sir.' Alec Manton was high on his list of people to be seen.

So was a man called Peter Hinton.

Before that there was still some routine work to be done at the police station. He picked up the phone and quickly dialled a number.

'Rita, this is Detective Inspector Sloan speaking. I'd like to talk to Dr Dabbe if he's not too busy.'

'He isn't doing anyone now, Inspector, if that's what you mean.'

That was what Sloan did mean.

'Hang on,' said Rita, 'and I'll put you through straight away.'

If a girl wasn't overawed by death, then neither doctors nor police inspectors were going to carry much weight . . .

'Dabbe here,' said the pathologist down the telephone.

'We may,' said Sloan circumspectly, 'repeat may – just have a possible name for yesterday's body.'

'Ah.'

'There's a man called Peter Hinton who was last seen alive about two months ago at his lodgings in Luston.'

'You don't,' said the pathologist temperately, 'get a great hue and cry from lodgings.'

'If,' advanced Sloan cautiously, 'we had reason to believe that he might be our chap – your chap, that is – what would be needed in the way of proof?'

'His dentist,' replied Dr Dabbe promptly, 'his dental records and a forensic odontologist. You'd be half-way there then.'

'And the other half of the way?'

'A good full-face photograph that could be superimposed on the ones that have been taken here.'

'I'll make a note of that,' said Sloan.

He could hear the pathologist leafing through his notes. 'Wasn't there a broken ankle in childhood, too, Sloan?'

'So you said, Doctor.'

'Everything helps,' said Dr Dabbe largely, 'and when they all add up, why then – well, there you are, aren't you?'

Which was scarcely grammar but which did make sense.

Detective Constable Crosby reported back to the police station with what he had gleaned about Peter Hinton and the death of Mrs Mundill.

'I checked on her death certificate like you said, sir.'

Yes?' said Sloan. You couldn't be too careful in this game.

'Cachexia,' spelt out Crosby carefully.

'And?' said Sloan. Cachexia was a condition, not a disease.

'Due to carcinoma of the stomach,' continued Crosby. 'It's signed by Gregory Tebot – he's the general practitioner out there.'

Crosby made Collerton sound like Outer Mongolia.

Sloan assimilated his information about Peter Hinton too.

Soon he was telling the reporter from the county newspaper that he couldn't have a photograph of the dead man.

'We might get an artist's impression done for you,' he said, 'but definitely not a photograph.'

'Like that, is it?' said the reporter, jerking his head.

'It is,' said Sloan heavily. 'But you can say that we would like to have any information about anyone answering to this description who's been missing for a bit.'

'Will do,' said the reporter laconically. He shut his notebook with a snap. If there was no name, there was no story. It was sad but true that human interest needed a name.

*

'So,' he said, 'there's just the widower . . .'

'Frank Mundill.'

'And a niece . . .'

'Elizabeth Busby.'

'And there was a boy-friend,' said Sloan.

'Peter Hinton.'

'It wouldn't do any harm,' said Sloan slowly, 'to check on Celia Mundill's will.'

Crosby made an obedient note.

'Though,' said Sloan irascibly, 'what it's all got to do with the body in the water I really don't know.'

'No, sir.'

'And Crosby . . .'

'Sir?'

'While you're about it, we'd better just check that Collerton House wasn't where our body fell from. I don't think it's quite high enough. And there are shrubs under nearly all the windows. They wouldn't have healed.'

In time Nature healed all scars but even Nature took her time . . .

Frank Mundill was ready and waiting at Collerton House when Sloan and Crosby arrived at the appointed time.

'We've just heard about the body that they've found in the estuary,' he said. 'Someone in one of the shops told my niece this morning.'

Sloan was deliberately vague. 'We don't know yet, sir, if there is any connection with it and the boat that was taken.'

The architect shuddered. 'I hope not. I wouldn't like to think of anyone coming to any harm even if they had broken in.'

'The inquest will be on Friday,' Sloan informed him. 'We may know a little more by then.'

Once over at Marby the architect confirmed that the boat beached beside the lifeboat had come from Collerton House.

'No doubt about that at all, Inspector,' he said readily. 'It's been in that boathouse ever since I was married and for many a long year before that, I dare say.'

Crosby made a note in the background.

Mundill gave the bow a light tap. 'She's good enough for a few more fishing trips, I should say. She's hardly damaged at all, is she?'

It was true. The boat had dried out quite a lot overnight and in spite of its obvious age looked quite serviceable now.

'I suppose,' said Mundill, 'that I can see about getting it back to Collerton now?'

'Not just yet, sir,' said Sloan. 'Our scientific laboratory people will have to go over it first.'

Mundill nodded intelligently. 'I understand. For clues.'

'For evidence,' said Sloan sternly.

There was a world of difference between the two.

'Then I can collect it after that?'

'Oh,' said Sloan easily, 'I dare say they'll drop it back to the boathouse for you.'

'When?'

'Is it important?'

'No, no, Inspector, not at all. I just wondered, that's all. It doesn't matter a bit . . .'

Elizabeth Busby had hardly slept at all that night. And when she had at last drifted off, sleep had not been a refreshment from the cares of the day but an uneasy business of inconclusive dreams.

Waking had been no better.

She came back to consciousness with her mind a blank and then suddenly full recollection came flooding back and with it the now familiar sensation that she was physically shouldering a heavy burden. The strange thing was that this burden seemed not only to extend to an area just above her eyes but to weigh her down from all angles. At least, she thought, Christian in *The Pilgrim's Progress* only had a burden on his back – not everywhere.

Propped beside her bedside lamp was Peter Hinton's slide rule. She had considered this again in the cold light of day. And got no further forward than she had done the evening before. It really was very odd that Peter should have taken a water-colour painting of a beach and left his slide rule behind him.

As she had got dressed she viewed the prospect of another day ahead of her without relish. It wasn't that she wanted to spend her whole life wandering in the delicate plain called Ease, just that she could have done without its being spent so much in the Slough of Despond. She had eventually got the day started to a kind of mantra of her own. It was based on Rudyard Kipling's poem 'If' and concentrated on filling the unforgiving minute with sixty seconds' worth of distance run . . .

The whole day stretched before her like a clean page.

True, there were the finishing touches to be put to the spring-cleaning of the spare room and today was the day that the dustbin had to be put out, but otherwise there were no landmarks in the day to distinguish it from any others in an endless succession of unmemorable days.

By the time Frank Mundill had gone off in the police car to Marby she found herself with the spare room finished and the dustbin duly put out. That still left a great deal of the day to be got through and she turned over in her mind a list of other things that might be done.

For some reason – perhaps subconsciously to do with the finding of the slide rule – she was drawn back to the hall. Perhaps she would tackle that next in her vigorous spring-cleaning campaign. She stood in the middle of the space assessing what needed to be done. Quite a lot, she decided. This year's regular cleaning had completely gone by the board because of Celia Mundill's illness.

She stiffened.

She had resolved not to think about that . . .

Mop, duster, vacuum cleaner, step-ladder, polish . . . a list of her requirements ran through her mind before she went back to the kitchen to assemble them. All she needed was there save the big step-ladder. That lived in the shed and she would need it to reach the picture rail that ran round high up on the hall wall.

She dumped all her equipment in the middle of the floor

and went off to the shed to get the step-ladder. It was leaning up against the wall in its accustomed place, standing amongst a conglomeration of gardening tools and old apple boxes. She moved the lawn-mower first and then a wheelbarrow. That left her nearer the steps but not quite near enough. She bent down to shift a pile of empty apple boxes . . .

It was curious that when she first caught sight of the shoe it didn't occur to her that there would be a foot in it. It was an old shoe and a dirty one at that and her first thought was that it was one of a pair kept there for gardening. That had been before she saw a piece of dishevelled sock protruding from it.

With dreadful deliberation she bent down and moved another layer of apple boxes.

A second shoe came into view.

It, too, had a foot in it.

Unwillingly her eyes travelled beyond the shoes to the grubby trousers above them. She could see no more than that because of the apple boxes. Driven by some nameless conception of duty to the injured, she lifted another round of apple boxes. The full figure of a man came into view then. He was lying prone on the floor. And she needn't have worried about her duties to the injured.

This man was dead.

This is death without reprieve. **15**

Unlike the sundial, Superintendent Leeyes did not only record the sunny hours. There were some stormy ones to be noted too.

'Dead, did you say, Sloan?'

'I did, sir.'

'That means,' he gobbled down the telephone, 'that we've got two dead men on our hands now.'

'It does, sir,' admitted Sloan heavily. 'There's no doubt about it either, sir. The local general practitioner confirms death.'

After death, the doctor.

That was part of police routine too.

'One, two, that'll do,' growled Leeyes.

'Sir?' Sloan had only heard of 'One, two, buckle my shoe' and even that had been a long time ago now.

'It's a saying in the game of bridge,' explained Leeyes loftily. 'You wouldn't understand, Sloan.'

'No, sir.' Sloan kept his tone even but with an effort. There was so much to do and so little time . . . and something so very nasty in the woodshed.

'What happened this time?' barked Leeyes. 'Not, I may say, Sloan, that we really know yet what happened last time.'

'I should say that he was killed on the spot. In an unlocked garden shed, that is.' It was Sloan's turn now to sit in the window-seat in the hall of Collerton House and use the telephone. A white and shaken Elizabeth Busby had led him there while Frank Mundill stayed with Crosby and Dr Tebot.

'Hit on the head,' said Sloan succinctly. 'Hard.'

Leeyes pounced. 'That means you've got a weapon.'

'There's a spade there with blood on it,' agreed Sloan.

'But no fingerprints, I suppose,' said Leeyes.

'I doubt it, sir,' said Sloan, 'though the dabs boys are on their way over now.'

'Fingerprints would be too much to ask for these days.'

Sloan was inclined to agree with him. Besides there was a pair of gardening gloves sitting handy on the shelf beside the spade. Sloan thought that the gloves had a mocking touch about them – as if the murderer had just tossed them back on to the shelf where he had found them.

'When did it happen?' snapped Leeyes.

'He's quite cold,' said Sloan obliquely, 'and the blood has dried . . .'

Congealed was the right word for the bloody mess that had been the back of the man's head but he did not use it.

A red little, dead little head . . .

'Yesterday, then,' concluded Leeyes.

'That's what Dr Tebot says,' said Sloan, 'and Dr Dabbe's on his way.' Too many things had happened yesterday for Sloan's liking.

'Yes, yes,' said Leeyes testily. 'I know he'll tell us for sure but you must make up your own mind about some things, Sloan.'

He had.

'And don't forget to get on to the photographers, Sloan, will you?'

'I won't forget,' said Sloan astringently.

'Who is he?' asked the superintendent. 'Or don't you know that either?'

But Sloan did know that. 'He's lying on his face, sir, and we haven't moved him, of course.'

'Of course.'

'But I think I know.'

Leeyes grunted. 'You'll have to do better than that before you've done, Sloan.'

'Yes, sir.' Truth's ox team had been Do Well, Do Better, and Do Best. Sloan decided that he hadn't even Done Well let alone Better or Best.

'I think I've seen those clothes before, sir.' And the body did look just like a bundle of old clothes. You wouldn't have thought that there was a man inside them at first at all . . .

'Ha!'

'Yesterday afternoon,' said Sloan.

'That's something, I suppose.'

'I think it's the man who found the body.' Strictly speaking he supposed he should have said 'the first body' now.

'The fisherman?'

'Horace Boller,' said Sloan.

'The man in the boat,' said Leeyes. 'The doctor here thinks it's him too, sir.' Last seen, Sloan reminded himself, with Basil Jensen on board.

'So there's a link,' said Leeyes.

'There's a link all right,' responded Sloan vigorously. 'He's got a barbary head in his pocket too.'

'What!' bellowed Leeyes.

Sloan winced. They said even a rose recoiled when shouted at let alone a full-blown detective inspector.

'At least,' declared Leeyes, 'that means we're not looking at a psychological case.'

'I suppose it does, sir.' There was nothing the police feared so much as a pathological killer. When there was neither rhyme nor reason to murder, then logic didn't help find the murderer. You needed luck then. Sloan felt he could have done with some luck now.

'Have you,' growled Leeyes, 'missed something that he found, Sloan?'

'I hope not,' said Sloan. But he had to admit that it had been his own first thought too.

'If he was killed because he knew something, Sloan,' persisted Leeyes, 'then you can find out what it was too.'

—

'I'm sure I hope so, sir.'

'He'd have known about *The Clarembald* being found,' said Leeyes. 'A fisherman like him . . .'

'He'd have known all the village gossip for sure, too, sir, a man like that.'

'Dirty work at the crossroads there,' said Leeyes, even though he meant the sea.

It had been highwaymen who waited at the crossroads to double their chances of getting a victim. They used to hang felons at the crossroads too in the bad old days. Perhaps the dirty work had sometimes come from hanging the wrong man. A police officer had an equal duty to the innocent and the guilty.

Then and now.

'Don't tell me either,' said Leeyes tartly, 'that men explore valuable wrecks for the fun of it.'

Sloan wasn't so sure about that but he was concentrating on the bird in the police bush, so to speak.

'Boller wasn't a very attractive man,' he said slowly. 'Ridgeford said you had to watch him.'

'Are you trying to suggest something, Sloan?'

'If he knew something that we didn't know he might have been – er – trying to put the pressure on a bit.'

'Blackmail by any other name,' trumpeted Leeyes, 'smells just as nasty.'

'And it's always dangerous.' The blow that had killed Boller had been bloody, bold, and resolute. Even peering over the apple boxes Sloan could see that. That's when he had seen the bulge in the man's pocket that had been the barbary head. Boller's own head hadn't been a pretty sight. Wet red – the poet's name for blood – it had been covered in.

'Was he destined for a watery grave, too, Sloan?'

'I'm sure I don't know that, sir. All I do know is that it was merest chance that he was found. The girl – Elizabeth Busby, that is – said that she only had that step-ladder out once in a blue moon. She was going to clean the hall and that's high, of course. Otherwise . . .'

'Otherwise,' interrupted Leeyes tartly, 'in a couple of

months' time we'd have had an unidentified body on our hands, wouldn't we? Another unidentified body, that is.'

'I think someone would have reported this man as missing,' said Sloan. Ridgeford had mentioned that Horace Boller had a son with them on their first trip. He cleared his throat. 'That means whoever killed him was pretty desperate.'

'The blackmailed usually are, Sloan,' said Leeyes with unusual insight. 'Because they've always got the two things to worry about they stop thinking straight.'

'What they've done and what someone's doing to them,' agreed Sloan.

'Did he get there by water?' asked Leeyes.

'What – oh, I hadn't thought about that, sir. We'll have to see.' There were so many things to see to now . . .

'We don't want two dinghies on the loose, do we?'

When Sloan got outside again Constable Crosby was standing on guard outside the shed door talking to a worried Frank Mundill.

'What is going on, Inspector?' said the architect wildly. 'Why should this house be picked on for all these things?'

'The real reason,' said Sloan, 'is probably because it's big enough to have a shed and a boathouse that don't get used very often.'

'That's very little consolation, I must say.' He shuddered. 'Ought you to search everywhere else?'

'No, sir, I don't think that will be necessary, thank you.' Sloan had got some straight edges of his jigsaw on the board already. The death of Horace Boller – no, the killing of Horace Boller – was another piece. It might even prove to be one of the four most important pieces of all the puzzle – a cornerpiece.

Mundill ran a finger round inside the collar of his white turtleneck sweater. 'It's an unnerving business, isn't it?'

'Nobody likes it, sir,' agreed Sloan. He was glad about that. Sophisticated fraud sometimes wrung unwilling admiration from investigating officers, but murder was a primitive crime and nobody liked it. The killing of a member of a tribe by another member of the same tribe was an offence against society. And it meant that no one in that society was safe. Perhaps that was the real reason why the murder charge accused the arrested person not so much of a killing but of an offence against the Queen's Peace because that was what it was . . .

'That poor chap in there,' said Mundill worriedly.

'Yes, sir.' Sloan spared some sympathy for the dead man lying in the shed. But he carefully kept his judgement suspended. Horace Boller might have been lured to his doom by the murderer in all innocence but Sloan did not think so. There was a certain lack of innocence in Boller both as reported by Constable Ridgeford and observed by Sloan himself that augured the other thing.

'I could wish my niece hadn't found him too,' murmured Mundill. 'She's had a lot to put up with lately, poor girl. What with one thing and another I'll be glad when her mother and father get here.'

Sloan nodded sympathetically. The scientists said that a cabbage cried out when its neighbour in the field was cut down so it was only right and proper that one human being should feel for another. The unfeeling and the too-feeling both ran into trouble but that was something quite separate.

'I hope Dr Tebot's got her to go and lie down,' said Mundill.

'I hope,' said Sloan vigorously, 'that he's done no such thing.' Salvation lay in keeping busy and he said so, doctor or no.

'All right,' said Frank Mundill pacifically, 'I'll tell her what you said.'

'And tell her,' said Sloan, 'that we'll be wanting a statement from her too . . .'

As Mundill went indoors Sloan advanced once more on the shed.

Both policemen peered down at the body.

'I'll bet he never knew what hit him,' averred Crosby.

'No,' agreed Sloan soberly.

Horace Boller did not necessarily have to have been blackmailing anyone. He might simply have learned something to his advantage that the murderer didn't want him to know about.

And so, in the event, to his ultimate disadvantage.

Something that a killer couldn't afford for him to know. That alone might be enough for a man who had killed once. Appetite for murder grew – that was something else too primitive for words. Having offended against society by one killing it seemed as if the next death was less important, and the one after that not important at all. By then the murderer was outside the tribe and beyond salvation too.

'We'd better get him identified properly,' said Sloan mundanely.

'Yes, sir.'

'What, Crosby,' he asked, 'can he have known that we don't know?' That was the puzzle.

Crosby brought his eyebrows together in a prolonged frown. 'He could have seen that the boathouse had been broken into.'

'And put two and two together after he found the body? Yes, that would follow . . .'

Blackmail, to be true blackmail, had to be the accusing or the threatening to accuse any person of a real crime with intent to extort or gain any property or valuable thing from any person.

Murder was a real crime.

'But he can't have known that the body in the water had been murdered, can he, sir?' objected Crosby. 'I mean we didn't know ourselves until Dr Dabbe said so. And we haven't told anyone.'

'A good point, that.' Sloan regarded the figure on the shed floor and said absently, 'So he must have known something else as well . . .'

'Something we don't know?' asked Crosby helpfully.

'Or something that we do,' mused Sloan. 'He might have spotted that sand-hopper thing too.'

'He knew about the sparling,' said Crosby, 'didn't he?'

Sloan squared his shoulders. 'What we want is a chat with Mr Basil Jensen.'

*

Constable Brian Ridgeford was panting slightly. The cliff path – like life – had led uphill all the way and it hadn't been an easy one either. He'd left his bicycle down in the village. Now he was nearly at the top of the headland. He turned his gaze out to sea but it told him nothing. There was just an unbroken expanse of water below him. Far out to sea there was a smudge on the horizon that might just have been a container ship. Otherwise the sea was empty.

He settled himself down, conscious that he wasn't the first man to keep watch on the headland. Men had waited here for Napoleon to come – and Hitler. They'd lit armada beacons up here on the Cat's Back too as well as wrecking ones. From here the inhabitants of Marby might have seen the Danish invasion on its way.

'Keeping observation' was what Ridgeford would put in the book to describe his morning.

Watch and ward it used to be called in the old days.

It was much more windy up here than down in Marby village. He made himself as comfortable as he could in the long grass and turned his attention to Lea Farm. It was like a map come to life, farm and farmhouse printed on the landscape. He narrowed his gaze on the sheep-fold. Far away as he was he could see that the sheep-dipping tank was still full.

Ridgeford spared a thought for old Miss Finch. Difficult and dogmatic she might be but she hadn't been so silly after all. She probably had seen something happening on the headland. The theory of an accurate report book suddenly came to life. Write it down, they'd taught him . . . Let someone else decide if what you'd written was valuable or not.

He swung his glance back in the directon of the sea. This time there was something to see. Round the coast from Marby harbour was coming a small trawler. Ridgeford got to his feet and walked farther up the headland to get a better view of it. As he did so he nearly tripped over a figure lying half hidden in the grass. It was a man. He was using a pair of binoculars and was looking out to sea so intently that he hadn't seen the approach of the policeman.

'Hullo, hullo,' said Ridgeford.

The man lowered his binoculars. 'Morning, officer.'

'Looking for something, sir?'

'In a manner of speaking,' he said, scrambling to his feet.

The trawler was forging ahead. Ridgeford noticed that it was keeping close inshore and that the other man could not keep his eyes off it. Ridgeford asked him his name.

'My name?' said the man. 'It's Jensen. Basil Jensen. Why do you want to know?'

The general practitioner, Dr Gregory Tebot, came out of Collerton House and joined Detective Inspector Sloan outside the shed while the various technicians of murder were bringing their expertise to bear upon the body inside it.

'She'll be able to talk to you now, Inspector,' Dr Tebot said. He was an old man and he looked both tired and sad.

'Thank you, Doctor,' said Sloan.

'Shocking business,' he said, pointing in the direction of the shed. 'Are you going to tell the widow or am I?'

Death, remembered Sloan, was part of the doctor's daily business too. What he had forgotten was that Dr Tebot would know the Bollers. 'Tell me about him,' he said.

'Horace? Not a lot to tell,' said the doctor. 'Didn't trouble me much.'

'A healthy type then,' said Sloan. Blackmail – if that was what he had been up to – was unhealthy in a different way.

'Spent his life messing about in boats,' Dr Tebot said. 'Out of doors most of the time.'

'Make much of a living?'

'I shouldn't think so. Picked up a little here and a little there, I should say. Mostly at weekends but you'd never know, not with Horace.'

'Didn't give anything away then,' said Sloan.

'He was the sort of man, Inspector,' said the old doctor drily, 'who wouldn't even tell his own mother how old he was.' He nodded towards Collerton House. 'Go easy with the girl if you can. She's had a packet lately, what with the aunt dying and everything.'

'The aunt,' said Sloan. A packet was an old Army punishment. The 'everything' was presumably a young man who had gone away.

'Hopeless case by the time I saw her,' said Dr Tebot. 'The other doctor said so and he was right.'

'What other doctor?'

'The one over in Calleford. I forget his name now. Mrs Mundill was staying over there when she was first taken ill.'

'I didn't know that.'

'Nice woman,' he said. 'Young to die these days. Pity. Still, it happens.'

'It happens,' agreed Sloan. Perhaps they were the saddest words in the language after all.

'Pelion upon Ossa for the girl though.'

Life was like that, thought Sloan. The agony always got piled on.

'She was very good with her aunt,' said the doctor, 'but she's nearly at the end of her tether now.'

'I'll bear it in mind,' said Sloan, but he made no promises. He had his duty to do.

He found Elizabeth Busby fighting to keep calm. 'It was horrible, horrible.'

'Yes, miss.'

'The poor man . . .'

'He won't have felt anything,' said Sloan awkwardly. 'Dr Tebot says he can't have done.'

She twisted a handkerchief between her fingers. 'Who is he? Do you know?'

'We think,' said Sloan cautiously, 'that it's someone called Horace Boller.'

She sat up quickly. 'Horace? But I saw him only yesterday.'

'You did?'

'He rowed past while I was putting flowers on my aunt's grave. It's by the river, you see.'

'You knew him then?'

'Oh, yes, Inspector.' Her face relaxed a little. 'Everyone who lives by the river knows Horace.'

'He was,' suggested Sloan tentatively, 'what you might call a real character, I suppose?'

'He was an old rogue,' she said a trifle more cheerfully.

Perhaps, thought Sloan to himself, that was the same thing . . .

'What did he say, miss?' he asked.

'Oh, he didn't say anything,' she said. 'He just rowed upriver.'

If Elizabeth Busby had noticed the broken boathouse doors so would Horace Boller. It was beginning to look as if he had taken the matter up with someone and that it had been a dangerous thing to do.

'You didn't see him again after that, miss?'

She shook her head.

'Nor hear anything last night?' That was a forlorn hope. The garden shed was at the back of the house.

'No.'

'Yesterday evening you and Mr Mundill were both here?'

'I was,' she said. 'Frank wasn't. He'd gone to see someone about doing some measurements for an alteration to a house.'

Sloan wrote down Mrs Veronica Feckler's name and address.

'He went at tea time and stayed on a bit,' she said.

'And you, miss?'

An abyss of pain yawned before her as she thought about the slide rule. 'Me? I stayed in, Inspector. I didn't do anything very much.' An infinite weariness came over her. 'I just sat.'

'And Mr Mundill? When did he get back?'

'It must have been about eight o'clock. We had supper together.' She looked up and said uncertainly, 'When – when did . . .'

'We don't know for certain ourselves yet, miss,' said Sloan truthfully. It was, he knew, the refuge of the medical people too. They professed that they did not know when they did not really want to say. There was no comeback then from the patient. And it was true sometimes that they did not know, but the great thing was that the point at which they did know was not the one at which they told the patient . . .

'Not, I suppose,' she said dourly, 'that it's all that important, is it? What's important is that someone killed him.'

'Probably,' said Sloan with painful honesty, 'what is important is why someone killed him.'

He was rewarded with a swift glance for comprehension.

'For the record, miss,' he went on, 'I take it that to your knowledge Horace Boller did not come to the house?'

She shook her head.

'And that you heard and saw nothing?'

'Not a thing, Inspector.' She lifted her face. 'Not a thing.'

'Thank you,' he said quietly. 'Now, miss, there are one or two things I want to ask you about a man called Peter Hinton . . .'

Her tryal comes on in the afternoon.   **16**

At first it was impossible for Detective Inspector Sloan to tell if Elizabeth Busby was understanding the import of his questions.

She answered them readily enough.

She showed him Peter Hinton's note.

'It's in his handwriting, miss, I take it?'

'I hadn't thought it wasn't,' she said uncertainly. 'But I couldn't swear to it.'

'Did he usually sign his name in full?'

'He hadn't – that is we didn't – write much. There was the telephone, you see.'

'I see, miss.'

'It was written with his pen,' she said quickly. 'He always wrote with a proper nib.'

Later she showed him what was really troubling her. The slide rule.

Sloan regarded it in silence.

'He must have come back,' she said, 'and sat here after that last time.'

'Could he be sure you wouldn't appear?' said Sloan.

'Towards the end,' she said, a tremor creeping into her voice, 'we never left Aunt Celia alone.'

'So,' said Sloan slowly, 'if Mr Mundill was down here in the hall you would be certain to be upstairs.'

'Yes, that's right. We took it in turns.'

'I see,' said Sloan. Disquiet was the word for what he was feeling about Peter Hinton. 'And you're sure your only disagreement the last time he was here was over whether your aunt should be in hospital?'

'Disagreement is too strong a word, Inspector.' She'd recounted all the details of the last time she'd seen Peter Hinton. 'Hospital was just something we talked about, that's all. Peter kept on suggesting it and we didn't want it. You can see that, can't you?'

'Yes, miss.' He cleared his throat. 'You don't happen to know if he ever broke his ankle, do you?'

'When he was seven,' she said immediately. 'He fell off a swing. Why do you ask?'

It is an undoubted fact that, once set in motion, routine gathers a momentum all of its own.

That was how it came about that Detective Inspector Sloan and Detective Constable Crosby, standing by a dead Horace Boller, were visited by a police motor-cyclist. He drew up before them coming to a standstill with the inescapable flourish of all motor-cyclists, and handed over and envelope. Crosby tore it open.

'It's a copy of Celia Mundill's will, sir.'

Routine took more stopping that did initiative. Surely there was a moral to be drawn there . . .

'Well?'

Crosby scanned it quickly.

Routine, thought Sloan, took on a certain strength too. Perhaps that was because it wasn't challenged often enough.

'It's short and sweet,' said Crosby.

It seemed a very long time ago that Sloan had asked for it.

'She left,' read out the constable, 'a life interest in all her estate to her husband.'

It occurred to Sloan that Mrs Celia Mundill may very well have been in that delicate situation for a woman of being rather richer than the man she married. Certainly they had been living in her old family home and her husband's profession was conducted from her father's old studio.

'With everything,' carried on Crosby, 'to go to her only niece at his death.'

'Including her share in the Camming patents,' concluded Sloan aloud. Mrs Mundill, then, had seen her role as a fiduciary one – a trustee for the past, handing down the flame to the future.

'And if the niece dies before the husband, then,' said Crosby, 'her sister collects.'

'What else?'

'Nothing else,' said Crosby.

'Date?' said Sloan peremptorily. There was a time to every purpose, the Bible said. The time for writing a will might be important.

Crosby looked at the paper. 'April this year, sir.'

The time had mattered then.

In olden days men would begin their last will and testament with their name and then add the prescient words 'and like to die'. The practice of medicine might not have amounted to very much in those days but at least then patients knew where they stood in relation to death, the great reaper. He wondered if Mrs Celia Mundill had been 'like to die' in April. If so she must have known it, too, and made her will.

And presumably her peace with the world.

Crosby started to fold up the paper again.

'Nothing,' enquired Sloan appositely, 'about remarriage?'

Wills were funny things. They lay dormant for years – like the seeds of some plants – and then something would stir their testators into activity again. Old wills would be torn up and new wills would be written. Or the testator died.

Crosby checked the will. 'Nothing about the remarriage of the widower.'

A time to get, and a time to lose, as Ecclesiastes had it.

No, not that.

A time to keep, and a time to cast away.

That was more like it.

Crosby folded the will neatly away. 'Nothing for us in that.'

'It doesn't appear to change anything,' agreed Sloan cautiously.

That was the important thing with testamentary dispositions and crime.

'The widower's income doesn't change anyway,' said Crosby.

'His death would matter to the girl,' said Sloan. 'That's all.'

Crosby frowned. 'Then she would scoop the pool, wouldn't she?'

'One day,' said Sloan moderately, 'she's going to be worth quite a lot of money.' It didn't weigh against a bruised heart; he was old enough to know that.

'I wonder if that boy-friend of hers knew how rich before he ditched her,' said Crosby.

In an ordinary man it would have been an unworthy thought; it was a perfectly proper one in a police officer.

'He didn't ditch her,' said Sloan absently. He was sure about that now. 'Somebody did for him. And put him in the river.'

'Poor little rich girl.' commented Crosby. He waved the will in the air. 'What's this got to do with it all then, sir?'

'Probably nothing at all,' said Sloan. The widower's income was assured, the niece's long-term future secure. 'Money isn't everything, though,' Sloan reminded the constable. It had been one of his mother's favourite sayings. It applied – with a certain irony – to some crime too.

'Comes in handy, though, doesn't it, sir. Money . . .'

'It's only one currency,' insisted Sloan. 'There are others.'

There was fear – and hate.

With Horace Boller now it looked very much as if someone had been trading in silence. From the dead man's point of view it had been dearly bought. Sloan turned his attention back to the old fisherman. Not that looking at him was going to tell the police anything. What Sloan needed was a view into the man's mind before he had been killed.

'He found the body,' mused Sloan aloud.

'He took us upriver afterwards,' said Crosby.

'He took Ridgeford out too,' said Sloan, 'to collect it.'

'And that Mr Jensen from the museum. Don't forget him.'

'I haven't,' said Sloan drily. 'And I haven't forgotten *The Clarembald* either.'

'He could have seen the boathouse doors, too,' said Crosby. 'We did.'

'He did see Elizabeth Busby by the grave,' said Sloan. 'She said so.'

'But,' reiterated Crosby, 'Boller didn't know that the man in the water . . .'

'Peter Hinton,' said Sloan with conviction. He was sure of that now.

'Peter Hinton then had been pushed over the edge of somewhere, did he, so what was there for him to get so excited about?'

'Your guess, Crosby,' said Sloan solemnly, 'is as good as mine.'

Interviewing Mrs Boller had been an unrewarding business in every way, and now Sloan and Crosby were with Mrs Veronica Feckler. It was impossible to tell whether she knew that she was being asked to provide an alibi for a man.

'Yesterday evening?' she said vaguely. 'Yes, Mr Mundill was here yesterday evening.'

Detective Constable Crosby made a note.

'He came down after tea,' she said.

'I see, madam.'

Sloan was favoured with a charming smile. She was a personable woman and she knew it. 'To measure up my cottage, you know.'

'So we gather, madam.'

She sketched an outline with a graceful hand. 'I need another room building on. Frank – Mr Mundill – he's an architect, you know . . .'

'Yes, madam.' That much Sloan did know by now. Of the fire station, of the junior school, of Alec Manton's farmhouse and of a multi-storey car park.

That was funny.

Frank Mundill hadn't mentioned that to Sloan. It had been Inspector Harpe who had told him about that multi-storey car park. Not Mundill. Even though he had got an award for designing it.

Mrs Feckler said, 'He's going to do my extension for me.'

'How long was he with you, madam?' A thought was beginning to burgeon in Sloan's mind.

'Until just before supper.' She wasn't the sort of woman who frowned but she did allow herself a tiny pucker of the forehead. 'He left about half-past seven. Is it important?'

It was strange, decided Elizabeth Busby, how heavy one's body could feel. She had almost to drag one leaden foot after the other. And yet she weighed the same – rather less, if anything – as she had done the day before.

When the inspector had left the house to go back to the shed she tidied away the cleaning things that she had brought out into the hall. There would be no more work done in Collerton House that day. She went into the kitchen and set about making coffee. That, at least, would be something useful to do and all those men out there would be glad of something to drink.

Time – even the most leaden-footed time – does eventually pass. And in the end the body of Horace Boller was borne away, the tumult and the shouting died and the photographers and the police – the captains and the kings – departed.

Frank Mundill came back indoors looking years older. 'I'll be in my office,' he said briefly, going upstairs.

She nodded. There suddenly didn't seem anything to say any more. She went and sat in the window-seat, her shoulders hunched up and unable to decide whether or not to take the tablets Dr Tebot had left for her. He really did look as if a frock coat would have suited him, but he had been kind.

Even the hunching on the window-seat seemed symbolic. There was no leisurely resting in a chair for her today while she waited for Inspector Sloan to come back. The inspector had hinted – ever so delicately – but hinted all the same that he might have some more news for her later on and that he would return if he had.

'About Horace Boller?' she had asked.

'Not about Horace,' he had replied.

Now she understood why Dante had had a place called Limbo in his portrayal of Hell . . .

It was quite a long time after that that she picked up the morning paper. It had been lying unregarded on the hall table since it had been delivered. It wasn't that she wanted to read it particularly, just that after a certain length of time she needed to do something with her hands. Not her head. That didn't take in any of what she was reading. Not at first, that is.

There is a certain state of alertness rejoicing in the grand name of thematic apperception which describes the attraction to eye and ear of items that the owner of that eye and ear is interested in. It explained how it was that Elizabeth Busby was able to read almost the whole paper without taking any of it in at all – until, that is, she turned to that page of the daily paper which dealt in – among other things – short items of news from the sale rooms.

'Bonington Sells Well' ran the headline.

'This previously known beach scene,' ran the text underneath it, 'thought to be of the Picardy coast and authenticated as being by Richard Parkes Bonington (1802–28), fetched the top price in a sale of nineteenth-century water-colours yesterday . . .'

Above the report was an illustration of the painting. It was the same one that had hung over the bed in the spare bedroom of Collerton House as long as Elizabeth could remember. It was the same one that Frank Mundill had said that Peter Hinton had asked for and been given.

She heard the tiniest sound on the stair and locked up quickly. Frank Mundill was standing there.

'Frank,' she said at once, 'you know that picture that Peter took . . .'

'What about it?' he said.

'It wasn't by Grandfather at all. Look!' She pointed to the newspaper. 'It's here in the paper.'

He strode over. 'Let me see.'

'There's a picture of it. It was worth a lot of money.'

He said, 'Well, it stands to reason that your grandfather had some good paintings, doesn't it? To copy.'

That wasn't what was bothering Elizabeth. 'Peter asked for it, you said.'

Mundill frowned. 'He did. It's the same one all right. Look, Elizabeth, I think there's an explanation for all this but there's something I would have to show you first.'

'He hasn't been seen,' she said dully. 'The police said so. And they've asked me for a photograph.'

'Come along with me,' said Mundill. 'I want you to see something. Something to do with Peter.'

'There's no one here,' said Detective Constable Crosby.

'Nonsense, man. Try again.'

'I've tried,' insisted Crosby. 'The front door and the back. There's no answer.'

'Mundill's car . . .'

'Not in the garage,' said Crosby.

Detective Inspector Sloan took a swift look round the outside of Collerton House. There was no sign of life there at all.

'They've gone,' said Crosby superfluously.

'Where?' barked Sloan.

'And why?' added Crosby. 'I thought they knew we were coming back.'

'They did,' said Sloan gravely.

'Something's happened then.'

'But what?' Sloan scanned the blank windows of Collerton House as if they could provide him with an answer. 'And where the devil have they gone?'

'The river?'

'Not by car,' said Sloan, adding under his breath a brief orison about that. The River Calle was too near for comfort. He would rather conduct searches on dry ground . . . 'No, they've gone somewhere by car. Get on to Control, Crosby, and get that car stopped.'

Crosby picked up the hand microphone in the police car and gave his message. Seconds later it came back to him and to every other police car in the county. 'Calling all cars, calling all cars . . . Attention to be given to a dark blue Ford Zephyr, registration number . . .'

'It may be too late,' said Sloan, although he didn't know for what.

'If seen,' chattered the speaker, 'stop and detain for questioning.'

Frank Mundill drove over Billing Bridge and then gently along the Berebury road. He was quite quiet and Elizabeth didn't press him into speech. He drove carefully, glancing now and then into his rear-view mirror. What he did – or did not – see there evidently caused him a certain amount of satisfaction because he went on driving with unimpaired concentration.

She tried once to draw him out about the picture.

'Wait and see,' he said.

'Where are we going?' she asked presently.

'Berebury,' was all he said to that.

She tried once more to draw him out about the picture. 'All in good time, my dear.'

Thus they came to Berebury. Reassured by yet another glance in his rear-view mirror, Frank Mundill steered the car towards the centre of the town.

'Frank, I don't understand . . .'

'You will. I've just got to park the car. It won't be difficult. It's early closing day.'

He made for the multi-storey car park. Entrance was by ticket from a machine. He took the ticket and the entrance barrier automatically rose to let them through. He placed the ticket on the dashboard and nosed the car up to the first level. There were plenty of parking spaces there but he did not stop. Nor at the second level. It being a quiet afternoon there were no cars at all above the third level. The fourth level was empty too.

'Frank, where are we going? Why are we going right to the top? You must tell me.'

'Upward and ever onward,' he said, a smile playing on his lips now.

The car swept round the elliptical corner at the end of the building and up on to the highest level of all.

'Frank . . .'

'Soon be there,' he said, accelerating. There were no other cars in sight now – just the bare ramps and parking places. He gave a swift tug at the steering wheel and soon they were in the open air again on the very top of the car park. He pulled the car neatly into a parking bay and got out.

Elizabeth followed him.

'This way,' he said. 'Do you know that on a clear day you can see Calleford?'

'I don't want to see Calleford,' she said. 'I want to know why the picture you said Peter wanted has been sold.'

'You shall,' he said softly. 'You shall know everything soon. But first come this way . . .'

He walked away from the edge of the car park to the very centre.

'Follow me, Elizabeth. I designed this place, remember. I know what to show you . . .'

'Faster,' said Sloan between gritted teeth.

Crosby changed up through the gears with demonic speed. 'Which way?'

'Berebury,' said Sloan. There was just the one hope that he was right about that.

The constable raced the car through the gates of Collerton House. With dressage and horses it was walk, trot, canter. With a souped-up police car it was a straightforward gallop from a standing start.

'Humpty Dumpty sat on a wall,' said Crosby. 'Humpty Dumpty had a great fall.'

'Let's hope that we find the right wall,' said Sloan tersely.

Crosby concentrated on keeping one very fast car on the road. He took Billing Bridge faster than it had ever been taken before, narrowly avoiding caroming off the upper reaches of one of its stanchions.

'The car park in Berebury,' said Sloan in a sort of incantation. 'The multi-storey car park. It must be.'

'What about it?' asked Crosby, cutting round a milk float. The milkman was used to imprecations from faster drivers but not to being overtaken at that speed.

'It's the right height,' said Sloan.

'So are a lot of things,' said Crosby, crouching over the wheel as if he were a racing driver but in fact looking more like Jehu than any denizen of the race-track.

'Mundill designed it,' said Sloan. 'Two spirals round a central well. Come on, man, get a move on.'

Crosby put his foot down still farther and the car ate up the miles into Berebury. They shot through the main street and swung round into the entrance of the car park. It did nothing for Sloan's blood pressure that they had to pause at the entrance like any shopping housewife to collect a ticket and allow the automatic barrier to rise.

'Hurry, man,' urged Sloan. 'Hurry!'

Crosby raced through the gears as fast as he could; the slope of the ramp needed plenty of power. The corner at the end, though, was tighter than any at Silverstone. He took it on two wheels.

'And again,' commanded Sloan at the next level.

But they had lost speed on the way up. Crosby took the next bend more easily but at a slower rate.

'Keep going,' adjured Sloan. He had his hand on the door catch.

They reached the top floor and came out into the sunshine. The sudden glare momentarily distracted both men but there was no disguising the dark blue Ford Zephyr standing in solitary state on the top platform or the two figures standing by the parapet of the central well. One of them had his arm round the other who appeared to be resisting.

'Stop!' shouted Sloan as he ran.

The man took a quick look over his shoulder and standing away from the other – a girl – vaulted lightly over the parapet.

17

'I suppose,' snorted Superintendent Leeyes, who was a sound-and-fury man if ever there was one, 'that you're going to tell me that everything makes sense now.'

'The picture is a little clearer, sir,' said Detective Inspector Sloan. He was reporting back to Superintendent Leeyes the next morning, the morning after Frank Mundill's spectacular suicide over the edge of the parapet at the top of the multi-storey car park.

'Perhaps, then, Sloan, you will have the goodness to explain what has been going on.'

'Murder, sir.'

'I know that.'

'More murder than we knew about, sir.'

'Sloan, I will not sit here and have you being enigmatic.'

'No, sir,' said Sloan hastily. 'The first murder wasn't of Peter Hinton at all. It was of Celia Mundill.'

'The wife?' said Leeyes.

'The wife,' said Sloan succinctly. 'Frank Mundill wanted to marry Mrs Veronica Feckler.'

'Ha!' said Leeyes.

'So,' said Sloan, 'he set about disposing of his wife.'

'He made a very good job it it,' commented Leeyes.

'He nearly got away with it,' said Sloan warmly. 'He would have done but for Peter Hinton putting two and two together.'

'So that's what happened, is it?'

'Elizabeth Busby tells me that Hinton was something of a student of criminology, sir. His favourite reading was the Notable British Trials series.'

'He suspected something?'

'We think so. Hinton wanted Mrs Mundill in hospital.'

'That wouldn't have done for a murderer,' said Leeyes.

'No.'

'So Peter Hinton had to go?' grunted Leeyes.

'Exactly.' Sloan cleared his throat. 'I – that is, we – think that he came back one day and challenged Mundill.'

'And that was his undoing?'

'It was. He was a threat, you see, to the successful murder of Mrs Mundill.'

Talk of successful murders always upset the superintendent. 'Do you mean that, Sloan?'

'I do, sir,' said Detective Inspector Sloan seriously. 'It was as near perfect as they come. We would never have known about the murder of Mrs Mundill if he hadn't killed the young man too.'

Leeyes didn't like the sound of that. 'How perfect?'

'Arsenic, at a guess.'

'You can't have a perfect murder with arsenic.'

'You can if it's diagnosed and treated as cancer of the stomach,' said Sloan.

'But what doctor would . . .'

'An old doctor who has had a letter from another doctor saying that that was what was wrong.'

Leeyes whistled. 'Clever.'

'Very clever,' said Sloan. 'Each year the Mundills went at Easter to housekeep for a locum tenens. Mundill's sister is married to a single-handed general practitioner in Calleford. While Mrs Mundill was there she had her first attack of sickness. The locum – a Dr Penthwin – arranged for her to have an X-ray at Calleford Hospital.'

'But it would be normal,' objected Leeyes at once.

'Of course it would, sir,' said Sloan, 'but that doesn't matter.'

'No?'

'All that matters is the letter that the Mundills bring back from Dr Penthwin to their own doctor at Collerton, Dr Gregory Tebot.'

'A forgery?' said Leeyes.

'From start to finish,' said Sloan who had seen it now. 'Mundill writes it himself in the locum's name on professional writing paper. His brother-in-law knows nothing about it – neither does the locum, for that matter. Anyway Dr Penthwin's soon gone. Dr Tebot gets the letter which he thinks is from Dr Penthwin and starts treating Mrs Mundill for an unoperable cancer of the stomach.'

'Most doctors would,' agreed Leeyes reluctantly.

'Mundill sees that the doses of arsenic follow the course of the disease,' said Sloan. 'Peter Hinton spotted it was arsenic, I'm sure about that. He'd asked if her eyes kept on watering. That's what put us on to it too.'

Leeyes grunted. 'Mundill had long enough to look it all up in the books while he was over there.'

'He'd even,' said Sloan, 'had long enough to go through the patients' medical records until he finds a letter with the wording pretty nearly the same as what he wants.'

'Clever,' said Leeyes again. A whole new vista of medical murder opened up before him. 'Has it been done before, do you think?'

'Who can say?' Said Sloan chillingly. 'Anyway, Dr Tebot isn't going to start on fresh X-rays or anything like that, is he? He wouldn't see any need for them.'

'The nearly perfect murder,' said Leeyes.

'There was something else going for him, too, sir.'

'What was that?'

'Celia Mundill didn't want to be cremated.'

'And that suited the husband, I'm sure,' said Leeyes.

'Cremation requires two medical certificates,' said Sloan. 'Burial only one.' He'd lectured Crosby on the burial of victims of murder. A grave was the best place of all.

'The nearly perfect murder,' said Leeyes again.

'He almost spoilt it, sir.'

'How come?'

'Gilding the lily.' It was surprising how often that happened with murderers. They wouldn't – couldn't – leave well alone.

'What lily?'

'The grave, sir. Mundill insisted on his wife being buried by the water's edge where the river floods.'

'To help wash the arsenic away,' said Leeyes. He cast his mind back. 'That's been done before, hasn't it?'

'And to aid decomposition,' completed Sloan. 'I don't know how much it would have helped but I dare say he thought that if anyone got any bright ideas after he married Mrs Feckler . . .'

Leeyes grunted. 'He was going to marry her, was he?'

'He was,' said Sloan. 'On his wife's money. Financially he had nothing to lose by her death and a lot to gain.'

'That's always dangerous,' said the voice of experience.

'Mundill had a life interest in his wife's estate,' said Sloan, 'but he wanted a little capital too.'

'Don't we all,' said Leeyes.

'That,' said Sloan manfully, 'is why he sold a picture that wasn't his to sell.'

'Ha.'

'And blamed its disappearance on Peter Hinton.'

'An opportunist if ever there was one,' commented Leeyes.

'What put the girl's life in danger,' said Sloan, 'was her spotting the report of the sale in the daily paper.'

It had been a close thing yesterday.

'If it hadn't been for that, eh, Sloan, Mundill might have got way with murder.'

'I'm sure I hope not, sir,' said Sloan.

'And the fisherman,' said Leeyes. 'Why did he have to go?'

'We think,' said Sloan slowly, 'that Boller must have been trying to apply a little pressure to Mundill.'

'Why?'

'He wasn't a nice man,' said Sloan obliquely. 'He could easily have known all about Mundill's visits to Mrs Feckler's cottage. He was about at all hours, remember, and not very scrupulous.'

'He could have spotted that sand-hopper creature.' Leeyes had seen the report on *Gammarus pulex*.

'That was probably what took him upriver the first time,' said Sloan, 'but I think it may have been his cousin Ted who gave him the real clue.'

'Cousin Ted? You'll have to do better than that for the coroner, Sloan.'

'Ted Boller is the village undertaker.'

'What about it?'

'Mundill wouldn't have the coffin screwed down.' The exhumation of Celia Mundill had begun that morning. A loose coffin lid had been the first thing that they had found. 'Ted Boller didn't give it much thought but he did happen to mention it to his cousin.'

'Horace Boller.'

'Precisely, sir. It probably didn't mean anything to Horace either until he saw the girl beside her aunt's grave on Tuesday afternoon and realized how near the water it was.'

'And so he put two and two together?'

'He probably just thought he would tackle Mundill about it.'

Leeyes nodded. 'By then, of course, Mundill will have got an appetite for murder.'

'It grows,' said Sloan. That was one area where policemen and psychologists were at one. An appetite for murder grew on itself. 'Besides, sir, he couldn't risk Boller raising any doubts about Celia Mundill just when he was concentrating on keeping suspicion away from the body in the water.'

'Talking of the body in the water, Sloan, what I can't understand is why Mundill broke the boathouse doors open. That just drew attention to the place.'

'If,' said Sloan, 'anyone had found that body in there at any time without the outer boathouse doors having been prised open, they would know that Mundill had put the body there.'

'And why not leave it there, Sloan, safely in the boathouse? Tell me that.'

'Because, sir,' said Sloan, 'the girl's father was expected back from South America and he liked his little bit of fishing.

The boathouse would be the first place he'd make for. We were told that right at the beginning.'

They'd been told almost everything; it was just a matter of sorting it all out. That was all . . .

'There's another thing, Sloan.'

'Sir?'

'Those copper things that were found in their pockets . . .'

Brenda Ridgeford said, 'I still don't understand about those copper things in their pockets, Brian.'

'They were meant to put us off the scent,' said her husband in a lordly fashion, 'but they didn't.'

'You mean *The Clarembald* wasn't anything to do with the murders?'

'Nothing,' said Brian Ridgeford.

'But . . .'

'Mundill' – yesterday Brian Ridgeford wouldn't have dreamed of calling the architect anything except Mr Mundill, but today the man was reduced to the ranks of common criminals – 'simply took them from Mr Manton's farm when he was over there.'

Alec Manton was still entitled to be called 'Mr'.

Alec Manton and his amateur underwater research group had been investigating the trailings caught up by a trawler. That was how, explained Ridgeford, they had come on *The Clarembald*. They had proceeded to excavate the wreck.

In good faith and secrecy.

It had been the secrecy which had baffled Basil Jensen. When news of the great discovery was brought to the notice of an excited archaeological world the name of the curator would be nowhere to be found.

'The biggest ever find on his patch,' said Ridgeford, 'and he wasn't being allowed a hand in it.' He searched about in his mind for a parallel. 'It would be like not letting me in on an armed raid in Edsway, Brenda.'

'I don't want you in on any armed raids anywhere,' said his wife. 'Professional death comes in two ways, you know.'

'They'd got a load of those copper ingots ashore,' said the

constable, 'and we reckon Mundill spotted them one day at the farm. They didn't need keeping underwater, you see.'

The sheep-dipping tank at Lea Farm had yielded a bizarre collection of wooden objects – a sea chest, a fid bound with lead, a table, and something called a dead-eye.

'Used for extending the shrouds,' Alec Manton had explained helpfully.

Brian Ridgeford had been no wiser.

'Poor Mr Jensen,' said Brenda Ridgeford. 'Left out in the cold like that.'

'Yes,' said Brian Ridgeford uneasily. Far from leaving the museum curator out in the cold, he'd very nearly taken him into custody yesterday. 'He's waving a protection order at Mr Manton now.'

'A piece of paper isn't going to save anything,' said Mrs Ridgeford.

Constable Ridgeford wasn't so sure about that. 'With the strong arm of the law behind it . . .'

'There's ways round the strong arm of the law, Brian Ridgeford,' she said provocatively, 'I can tell you.'

'That's as may be, my girl,' he said with dignity, 'but only when the law allows it.'

'I suppose, Inspector,' said Elizabeth Busby shakily, 'that I have to thank you for saving my life.'

'No, miss, you don't.' Sloan was sitting on the window-seat in the hall of Collerton House again.

'He was going to kill me,' she said, 'because I knew about the picture.'

'Murder's a dangerous game,' said Sloan sententiously, 'especially once the novelty's worn off.'

'Poor, poor Aunt Celia.'

Detective Inspector Sloan bowed his head in a tribute to a woman he had never seen alive. Dr Dabbe was doing another post-mortem now – to make assurance doubly sure. Inquest-sure, too.

'The old, old story,' she said bitterly.

'The eternal triangle,' agreed Sloan. He'd read something

once that put it very well ... 'The actors are, it seems, the usual three. Husband, wife, and lover.' It practically amounted to a prescription for murder. Aloud he went on, 'And then murder once done ...'

'Peter ... poor Peter, too.'

'He'd stumbled on your aunt's murder,' said Sloan.

'He'd always been fascinated by crime,' she said. 'He read a lot about it.'

'It was very clever of him.'

'So he had to go, too,' she said tightly.

'He had to be silenced,' said Sloan. He coughed. 'I take it that he'd have gone easily enough to have a look at the multi-storey car park if invited?'

'I did, didn't I?' She shuddered. 'Frank sounded so reasonable and I really did think he had something there to show me. And there's no one up there on early closing day.'

Sloan nodded. He could imagine Frank Mundill being plausible. 'It was a perfect place,' he said. 'A double helix round a central light well, with a parapet at the top and a door at the bottom.'

'A door with a key,' she said.

'Mundill had a key, all right,' he said. 'And to the car park exit gate. He had done the original specification, remember. He had no problems in that direction. He had access to everything he wanted. He could come back at night for the body.'

'It all fits, doesn't it?' she said.

All the pieces of the jigsaw were there now. Sloan would have to lock them together for his report but they were there. Elizabeth Busby didn't have to know about all of them. There was no point, for instance, in her being told about the blood that they'd found inside the light well of the car park, blood that wasn't Frank Mundill's. He did need to tell her about a photograph of Peter Hinton that had been superimposed on a photograph of a dead young man in Dr Dabbe's mortuary.

And about a sure and certain dentist.

Sloan said nothing into the silence that followed his telling her.

Presently she said, 'And Horace Boller?'

'He put two and two together about your aunt.' Perhaps it hadn't been such a perfect murder after all. 'He couldn't have known what really happened. Just that there was something wrong.'

'And he paid the price.'

'He knew what he was doing, miss.' For Horace Boller anyway Sloan didn't feel too much pity . . .

Detective Constable Crosby was waiting in the car for him outside Collerton House. Sloan climbed into the passenger seat and shut the door with quite unnecessary vigour.

'A nasty case,' he said.

Crosby started up the engine.

'Three murders,' said Sloan. The only saving grace had been that a wicked man's cupidity had not succeeded . . .

'Mr Basil Jensen,' said Detective Constable Crosby, 'wants us to meet him over at Marby.'

Detection demanded many things of a man. A working knowledge of eighteenth-century ships was obviously going to be called for.

'All right,' growled Sloan. 'Get going then.'

Crosby pulled the car away from the front door of Collerton House and settled himself at the wheel. He put a respectable distance behind him before he spoke.

'Sir . . .'

'What is it now?'

'What sits at the bottom of the sea and shivers?'

In the grip of powerful emotion and with an awful fascination Sloan heard himself saying, 'I don't know, what sits at the bottom of the sea and shivers?'

'A nervous wreck.'

Harm's Way

With acknowledgement to John Imhof, *agricola*

For Gwen Powell, with much gratitude.

The chapter headings are taken from the Office of Compline.

Hurt not thy foot against a stone.   1

'There's no barbed wire,' said Wendy Lamport, looking along the hedgerow.

'That's something, I suppose,' said her companion, Gordon Briggs, grudgingly. He was verging on late middle age and difficult about almost everything.

'And,' she said, looking over into the field, 'not a bull in sight.'

'I should hope not,' responded Gordon Briggs roundly. 'There's a by-law about bulls in fields in Calleshire. It's illegal to have a bull more than twelve months old in any field in the county containing a public footpath.'

'No warning notices, either, that I can see,' carried on the girl, completing her survey of the terrain before them.

'Warning notices,' pronounced Briggs pedantically, 'have no significance whatsoever in relation to public footpaths and rights of way. You should know that by now, Wendy.'

'Yes, Gordon.' Wendy Lamport nodded. She had heard him say it time and time again. 'It doesn't stop them trying it on, though, does it?' she added.

'Landowners can put what they like on notice boards,' declared Briggs, adding militantly, 'but they can't keep us out.'

'Let them try, that's all,' said Wendy Lamport loyally. 'Just let them try.'

'That's the spirit,' said Gordon Briggs.

It might have been the spirit behind the Berebury Country Footpaths Society but their actual rallying cry was more ambiguous. 'Every Walk a Challenge' was the motto printed under the masthead on their writing paper. The challenge, though, was not usually to the walker. The gauntlet was thrown down in front of the luckless owners of the land over which they proposed to walk. If, that is, those owners of the land happened to have an official public footpath or right of way running over it.

'The stile is all right,' observed Wendy a little later. 'It's just where it says it should be on the map.' She was young enough for this fact still to come as a small surprise to her. 'Beyond the first turning after the public house.'

The Definitive Map, properly marked up, was the Society's Bible.

'North-north-west off the Sleden to Great Rooden road,' said Briggs, who had done his homework.

Barbed wire, untethered bulls, and missing stiles were just a few of the obstacles that farmers and other landowners could put in their way.

'See over there,' she said, pointing. 'There's even a sign saying it's a public footpath.'

It was the Society's ambition to have all the footpaths in the county of Calleshire signposted.

'It doesn't look,' he remarked, 'as if we're going to have too many difficulties with the walk proper.'

Gordon Briggs was not to know it at the time but he had seldom spoken less prophetically.

He and Wendy Lamport constituted a reconnaissance party for the Society's next walk scheduled for the following day. Bitter experience had taught members of the Berebury Society that a preliminary survey of the countryside before a group walk saved a lot of frustration. Armed with billhook and secateurs, the pioneers could make sure that the route was open. Nature's obstructions, though, were as nothing compared with those of man.

'Who's the farmer here?' Briggs asked as they walked forward.

'Name of Mellot,' said Wendy Lamport. Feminism and Women's Lib might have made some progress but the clerical work of the Society was still done by the women. So were the teas. The men, Greek-style, sat on the committee and pontificated. She glanced down at her notebook. 'George Mellot.'

'Any relation?'

'Who to?'

'Mellot's Furnishings, of course.' Mellot's Furnishings were a nation-wide chain of upholsterers with distinctive purple delivery vans to be seen not only in Calleshire but everywhere in Great Britain.

'I don't know,' said Wendy.

'Unusual name.'

'Could be the same, I suppose.'

Gordon Briggs looked round and sniffed. 'No sign of the millionaire touch about this place, although you never can tell with farmers.'

'Poor relation, perhaps,' suggested Wendy. She had a rich cousin herself and knew what it felt like to be on the less well-off side of the family.

He snorted gently. 'Farmers aren't anyone's poor relations these days.'

'That's true.' They had both seen too many farms in their walks for her to dispute this. Agrarian depressions there might have been in the past – she knew that the turn of the century had been a bad time in Calleshire – but the country certainly wasn't in the grip of one at the moment and this farm looked properly provided with well-kept buildings and good fences.

Gordon Briggs took another look at the map. 'And we've just come on to Pencombe Farm now, haven't we?'

'When we turned right off the Great Rooden road,' replied Wendy. 'That's when Mr Mellot's land began. The wood we've just come through . . .'

'It's called Dresham,' nodded Briggs, squinting at the Ordnance Survey symbols on the map. 'The other side of the road.'

'That belongs to someone else,' said Wendy. She hadn't enjoyed walking through the wood. In her experience there were woods and woods, and Dresham Wood had had an unfriendly feel to it. There had been a clearly marked footpath all the way through the wood but there had been branches of undergrowth growing across it, and muddy, slippery patches underfoot – to say nothing of the roots of trees laid across the way acting as snares for the unwary.

And a blackbird giving its alarm call.

She consulted her notebook. 'Dresham Wood is on Lower-combe Farm. That belongs to a Mr Sam Bailey.' At one moment while they were in the wood she had had the distinct feeling that they were being watched.

Gordon Briggs put his foot down purposefully. 'We're still on Footpath Seventy-Nine, though, aren't we?'

Walking Footpath Seventy-Nine in the Calleshire County Council Schedule was the object of their exercise – in both senses – today. If they found it barred to them by any of the time-honoured obstructions they would follow their Society's set procedure. First, a letter would be sent to the landowner, then a polite visit would be made to him, followed by a further attempt to walk the footpath and then – if all else failed – a letter of complaint would be written to the Calleshire County Council.

'It seems all right,' said Wendy Lamport cautiously.

'We're still near the road,' Briggs reminded her.

Long experience had taught members of the Society that if a footpath was going to be obstructed then the obstruction wouldn't be within sight of the road.

'That's true,' said Wendy, adding hopefully, 'Perhaps it will be open all the way.'

She was a nice girl who didn't relish confrontations with angry farmers. To be honest, she didn't think that Gordon Briggs did either but he was a passionate believer in keeping footpaths open and if that included confrontation – and it frequently did – then he would endure that too.

'And it doesn't cross a ploughed field here,' said Briggs significantly.

Wendy Lamport nodded and started to pick her way along

the hedgerow, counting her paces as she did so. Footpaths that crossed ploughed fields – usually diagonally – were an especial bone of contention. The farmer found it irritating – and expensive – to leave the footpath unploughed and offered the edge of the field as an alternative. Sticklers for accuracy like Gordon Briggs saw this as the thin end of the wedge . . .

'Six hundred years,' said Wendy suddenly.

'What?'

'This hedge,' said Wendy. 'There are five different species of tree growing in thirty yards of it.'

'What about it?'

'That means it's six hundred years old, doesn't it?'

Briggs grunted.

'Dendrochronology or something, it's called,' said Wendy inaccurately. She was vague on the figures, too. 'They say you can tell the age of a hedge by the number of varieties of species growing in it. A hundred and ten years for each species plus thirty – that's the equation.'

'Very likely,' muttered Briggs. Unlike a lot of the members of the Berebury Country Footpaths Society he was neither a naturalist nor an historian.

Wendy was still looking at the hedge. 'Isn't it romantic to think that that's been there growing like that ever since the Plantagenets were on the throne?'

'Quarrelsome lot,' said Briggs, briefly summarizing the Wars of the Roses and more than a hundred years of English history. He had no imagination. He waved an arm. 'The house looks old enough to match.'

'Where?' asked Wendy. She liked looking at old houses. 'Oh yes, I see.'

'That'll be Pencombe Farm, I suppose,' said Briggs.

'Isn't it nice?' she said warmly as a substantial brick building came more fully into view. 'And how well it nestles into the landscape.'

'Pity about the barn,' said Briggs.

The girl turned her gaze towards the farm buildings. A modern two-ridged barn in pre-cast concrete rose behind the farmhouse, standing out like a sore thumb. Soaring above the farmyard were a handful of crows. 'It is a bit – well, utilitarian, isn't it?' she said uncertainly.

Briggs shrugged. 'Farmers have got to move with the times like everybody else.' Briggs himself was a schoolmaster and hadn't changed his teaching methods in twenty years. 'I expect the old barn fell down.' He turned his attention back to the footpath. 'No problems in this field, anyway. Where does the path go after this?'

'Towards the farmhouse,' said Wendy.

Gordon Briggs nodded. Many of the footpaths they walked over were relics of those ways used simply by farm labourers to get to work in times past. If it was illogical that this should result in the world and his wife now being able to tramp over a farmer's field for all time Briggs did not let the thought trouble him too much. To him a footpath – within the meaning of the Act – was a footpath and as such it was there to be walked and thus to be kept open for posterity. Its origins – be they ancient ridgeway or a Victorian farm servant's short cut to work – were of no interest to him, any more than were the flora and fauna of the countryside through which the footpaths led him. He was a single-minded man and the only thing which interested him about a footpath was whether or not it was open to the public.

'They'll see us if we follow it to the farmhouse,' said Wendy.

'A good thing too,' said Briggs robustly. He grinned suddenly. 'It'll be good practice for seeing forty of us tomorrow, won't it?'

'Yes, of course,' agreed Wendy quickly. All the same, she knew that very few farmers relished the sudden sight of the entire Footpaths Society picking its way over their fields. Almost none of them could resist the temptation to come out and make sure that the walkers didn't stray from the footpath. As it happened, that was one of the things that the farmer didn't need to worry about. Members of the Society were meticulous about keeping to the authorized footpath. It was one of their canons. Moreover it was in the Country Code.

The two walkers advanced towards the farm. Besides the new barn there was an agglomeration of older farm buildings all set round a traditional steading, four square against the wind and the weather. Well over on their left was the drive to the farm from the highway and the village of Great Rooden.

'This is the older way,' said Wendy, pointing to their path.

'How do you know?' asked Briggs.

'It's shorter,' she said. 'And it cuts off quite a corner. The road came later, you can tell.'

'Distance doesn't matter with cars,' said Briggs with all the contempt of a determined walker. He could be quite rude to any motorist who was so misguided as to offer him a lift in his car. 'Just wait until the world runs out of fossil fuel, that's all . . .'

It was a prospect that he regarded with selfish equanimity.

'The road's higher than the field, too,' said Wendy. 'You can see where they had to build it up a bit.'

'Shouldn't wonder if they didn't get a bit of flooding down here in the wintertime,' remarked Briggs, looking at the lie of the land. 'These flat meadows look as if they might have had water in them.'

'They're certainly very lush just now,' said the girl. 'Mind you, it is high summer.'

It was in fact late June and the Calleshire countryside had an almost idyllic look about it.

'They've got their hay in,' she said.

'I should hope so by now.' Suddenly Gordon Briggs stiffened and changed his tone. 'But soft, we are observed.'

Wendy looked round. 'I can't see anybody . . . oh yes, I see what you mean.'

Standing outside the barn watching their approach was a tall, sturdily built man with a dog. It was a well-trained dog and it sat obediently at its master's heel.

'Good afternoon,' said Briggs politely.

'Afternoon,' responded the man in neutral tones.

'Mr Mellot?' said the schoolmaster enquiringly. Once upon a time you could tell what a man was by what he wore but not any longer. This man had on well-worn trousers and an open-necked shirt. His shirtsleeves were rolled well up and he had obviously been working in the barn. He had about him though an unmistakable air of ownership. 'Mr George Mellot?'

'Yes?'

'We're an advance party from the Berebury Country Footpaths Society,' said Gordon Briggs.

'Yes?' The farmer was neither friendly not unfriendly. He just stood by the barn door and waited.

'We're walking a footpath in preparation for our Society's meeting tomorrow,' announced Gordon Briggs.

The other man stirred. 'You mean you're meeting here? At Pencombe?'

'That's right,' said Briggs. 'We're going to walk Footpath Seventy-Nine on the County Survey. You needn't worry,' he added quickly. 'We shan't do any damage.'

'We always keep to the Country Code,' chimed in Wendy eagerly. Mention of the Country Code was meant to reassure farmers. Usually all it succeeded in doing was to puzzle them.

This farmer looked as mystified as all the others did.

'We fasten all gates,' said Wendy. 'And we don't light fires.'

'We keep to the path,' said Briggs, 'and don't damage fences.'

'I'm glad to hear it,' said the farmer drily.

'And keep dogs under proper control,' said Wendy.

George Mellot glanced down at his own perfectly behaved dog and said, 'I'm glad to hear that too.'

'There won't be any litter either,' went on Wendy anxiously, 'and we don't damage wildlife or anything like that.'

'I'll hardly know you've been, is that it?' said Mr Mellot ironically.

'That's right,' said Wendy with relief.

'We leave nothing behind but our thanks,' said Briggs sententiously.

'I see.' Mellot looked at them both. 'I take it that you already know the route of Footpath Seventy-Nine?'

'It's on the Ordnance Survey Map,' said Briggs. There were

some farmers who pretended not to know the route of the footpaths over their land.

'It passes the farmhouse,' George Mellot informed him, 'and picks up the stream and then goes straight across the valley and out on to the Little Rooden road.'

'Footpaths always take the easiest way,' said Briggs knowledgeably. 'No point in making the going harder than it need be.'

'I think,' said Mellot quietly, 'that you'll find it easy going all right. There's nothing to stop you.' He glanced at the tools they were carrying. 'You won't need your billhook either.'

'That's a relief,' said Wendy. 'I'm no good at cutting my way through undergrowth.'

'We keep all the paths clear at Pencombe,' said the farmer, adding astringently, 'For our sakes as well as yours.'

'Quite so,' said Briggs fussily. 'It's good farming practice.'

'It makes it easier for the boys to come in and steal my apples too,' said the farmer. 'Had you thought about that?'

'That's something quite different,' said Briggs firmly. 'That's a police matter. Don't worry, Mr Mellot,' he added, 'none of our people will take anything.'

'Except photographs,' said Wendy Lamport brightly.

'Very well.' The farmer nodded and abruptly turned back into the barn, his dog still at his heel.

'That's all right then, isn't it?' said Wendy, turning to her companion. 'We should have a good walk tomorrow.'

'We should,' agreed Gordon Briggs. 'This way, I think.'

They passed the farmhouse in its comfortable setting at the bottom of the combe and picked their way along the footpath which followed a stream. The farmer had been quite right. The way was clear – indeed it looked as if it had been attended to fairly recently. Walking along it was quite pleasant and their pace unconsciously quickened. That was when they began to realize that the day was already warm and getting warmer.

Presently Briggs looked at the map again. 'Surely this stream is part of the River Westerbrook that finishes up in the Calle somewhere?'

Wendy nodded. 'Woe waters.'

'Pardon?'

'Didn't you know?' she said, surprised. It wasn't often that anyone could tell the omniscient schoolmaster anything. 'The Westerbrook is one of those streams that only flow some of the time.'

'They're called intermittent rivers,' he informed her in his classroom manner.

'They do say,' said Wendy, 'that it only flows when something awful is going to happen.'

Briggs sniffed. 'There's always something to be woeful about.'

'If it's flowing,' persisted Wendy obstinately, 'it presages doom.'

'It's more likely,' said Briggs prosaically, 'that there's a sump under the hill at the head of the valley and when that's full and primed the river starts up again.'

Together they regarded the Westerbrook. Its shallow waters glistened in the sunshine.

'I must say it looks harmless enough,' said Wendy.

Briggs turned his gaze upwards. 'There'll be plenty of water under the hill at the moment. That's why it's flowing.'

'We haven't had so much rain lately, though,' insisted the girl.

'And when it's all emptied away,' forecast Briggs, 'the Westerbrook will dry up again.'

'Woe waters,' insisted Wendy obdurately, 'that's what they are.'

Gordon Briggs shrugged his shoulders and turned away from the stream. The two walkers soon resumed their steady pace, Wendy Lamport in the lead, Gordon Briggs a step or two behind.

That was how it came about that Wendy saw the object first. She had been aware of the crows without particularly remarking on them. There were always crows about on farms and their presence had not especially impinged on her consciousness. Afterwards she could not even remember if she had noticed the actual bird that had flown across the path just ahead of her.

What was certain, though, was that it had dropped something.

Wendy was only a few paces away from that something and she automatically looked down to see what it was.

And for ever afterwards wished that she hadn't.

As she saw what it was that was lying there she halted so abruptly that Gordon Briggs very nearly cannoned into her. He, too, stopped.

'What's the matter?' he asked.

'Look!' whispered Wendy, her face pale.

'Where?' said Briggs.

'There!' She pointed an unsteady finger in the direction of the ground.

'What at?'

'That,' she said shakily.

'I can't see anything . . .' His voice trailed away as he too saw what was lying on the footpath. 'Good Lord!'

'A finger,' she gulped. 'That's what it is, isn't it?'

'It can't be.'

'But that's what it is,' she repeated, a rising note of hysteria coming into her voice, 'isn't it?'

Gordon Briggs nerved himself to bend forward and examine it more closely. 'Yes,' he said soberly, 'I'm very much afraid that it is.'

2

'Remains thought to be human,' said Police Superintendent Leeyes more technically.

It was later that same afternoon and he was talking to Detective Inspector C. D. Sloan at Berebury Police Station. Inspector Sloan, who was known as Christopher Dennis to his nearest and dearest, was – for obvious reasons – called 'Seedy' by his friends. He was the head of Berebury's Criminal Investigation Department. It was a tiny department but such crime as there was in that corner of Calleshire usually landed up in Detective Inspector Sloan's lap.

'Constable Mason reported them,' continued Leeyes.

'Mason from Great Rooden?' said Sloan.

'None other,' said Leeyes heavily.

'There's never a lot of trouble out that way, sir,' remarked Sloan.

'There's never any trouble at all at Great Rooden,' declared Leeyes emphatically. 'Ever.'

'Not if Ted Mason can help it,' agreed Sloan. 'You can count on it.'

'Mason,' pronounced Leeyes flatly, 'is one of your "anything for a quiet life" type of constable and he sees that there isn't any trouble.'

Detective Inspector Sloan knew this too. Police Constable Mason was well known for keeping the quietest beat in the county.

'He grows prize cabbages very well,' snapped Leeyes tartly.

'He won't be pleased about human remains then, sir, will he?' said Sloan in an attempt to get back to the matter in hand.

'He isn't.'

'Still, sir,' went on Sloan, determinedly looking on the bright side, 'these remains – they could be archaeological, couldn't they? Perhaps it was an Ancient Briton.'

'It's not an Ancient Briton,' said Leeyes, adding sourly, 'You're nearly as bad as Mason.'

'No, sir?'

'It's not an ancient anybody, Sloan,' said Leeyes. 'There's still some flesh on the bone.'

'That's quite different,' agreed Sloan quietly.

'It was the flesh that worried Mason, too,' grunted Leeyes. 'Bones – old bones – you can sweep under the carpet, but not flesh. Not even Constable Edward Mason.'

'What's he done about it?'

'Marked the spot,' replied Leeyes neatly, 'and passed the buck.'

'What's he done with the finger?'

'Taken it back home with him,' said Leeyes briskly. 'At the moment it's sitting in a cardboard box in his office in Great Rooden.'

'This farm, sir . . .'

'Pencombe.'

'Anything known about it?'

'Never heard of it before,' said Leeyes.

'And the farmer?'

'George Mellot,' said Leeyes, adding gratuitously, 'Nothing known about him either.'

'Mason will know him, of course.' Sloan was confident of this. What with warble fly and the dipping of sheep and this regulation and that, country constables knew farmers.

'Oh, Mason knows him all right,' said Leeyes. 'Mason knows everyone out that way.'

'Well?'

'Mason,' said Leeyes scornfully, 'has reported that George

Mellot farms well – which doesn't tell us a lot about flesh and bones on his farm.'

'No, sir,' agreed Sloan. It told them something about the man though, and that might help. It was too early to tell. 'Has he been at Pencombe long?'

'Man and boy,' said Leeyes. 'Mason knew that much.'

'If there's a finger, sir,' began Sloan tentatively, 'then . . .'

'I know what you're going to say, Sloan,' interrupted Leeyes. 'If there's a finger there's usually a body. I know that.'

'Usually?' Sloan echoed a word he hadn't expected to hear.

'Not always,' said Leeyes testily.

Sloan cast about wildly in his mind. Test-tube babies and cloning had come a long way, he knew, but . . .

'There are exceptions,' said Leeyes.

'Sir?'

'I never have been entirely happy about Berebury Hospital, Sloan.'

'Really, sir?'

'I'm sure if we looked into it that we would find their disposal system pretty haphazard.'

'Very probably, sir.' The back doors of most institutions were not as imposing as the front.

'They've got to do something with the bits they chop off, haven't they?'

'You think the finger could be surgical waste, do you, sir?' Sloan didn't know if that was what the surgeons called the end product of an amputation but it would be bound to be dressed up as some ambiguous euphemism. There was nobody better at doing that than the medical profession.

'I don't know,' responded Leeyes, 'but I do know that we'll look pretty silly in the county if this finger turns out to have come from a man who works in a saw-mill who's only got nine left on his hands.'

'Quite so, sir. I'll check with the hospital, of course. But if it isn't one of theirs, so to speak, where should we be looking for the rest of the body?'

'Exactly, Sloan, where.' On the wall behind Superintendent

Leeyes was a vast map of the County of Calleshire. The limits of F Division were outlined by a thick black line. Great Rooden was in the south-east. Detective Inspector Sloan advanced towards the map while Superintendent Leeyes swivelled round in his chair and found a spot with his finger.

'Here's Great Rooden,' he said. 'Now, where's Pencombe Farm . . . Ah, here it is, Sloan. Just outside Great Rooden on the way to Sleden and Little Rooden.'

'Yes, sir.' Sloan made a note. Archaeologists had a special word they used for the place where they found bones and other things. It would come to him in a minute. 'Right, sir, I've got that,' he said aloud. Provenance, that was it.

'It's off the Sleden road if you're going by car.'

Detective Inspector Sloan would be going by car. To begin with, anyway. The foot-slogging came later. He said, 'These people who found it . . .'

'Two walkers,' said Leeyes. 'The girl's a bit upset.'

'I'm not surprised.'

'They were out on a tewt.'

'A what, sir?'

'TEWT,' spelled out Leeyes. 'A Tactical Exercise Without Troops.' Superintendent Leeyes's time in the Army had left him with a distinctly military turn of speech. He enlarged on the theme. 'They were prospecting for a walk tomorrow with a group.'

'So they were there by accident,' deduced Sloan. 'Nobody knew they would be coming.'

'Not even the crows,' said Leeyes.

'I don't know a lot about crows, sir,' began Sloan tentatively. Detection made many demands on a man, not all of them foreseeable.

'They eat carrion,' Leeyes informed him.

Sloan repressed a slight shudder. It was all very well to use a word like carrion. It was when you came to think about it that it wasn't nice.

'And you know what that means, Sloan, don't you?'

'Yes, sir.' He cleared his throat. 'If this finger didn't come from the hospital . . .'

'Yes?'

'Then ten to one there's the rest of the body about somewhere.'

'I wondered when you were going to get round to that, Sloan.'

'We'll have to find it.'

'You will,' said Leeyes. 'Can't have an inquest on a finger, can we? The coroner wouldn't like that.'

'No, sir.'

'Besides,' said Leeyes, 'we'd be the laughing-stock of the Force.'

'Yes, sir.' Sloan could see that that factor took an even higher priority.

'And the sooner the better.'

'Yes, sir.' That went for all detection. Cold trails made work more difficult.

'And the only man I can spare today,' said Leeyes by way of a Parthian shot, 'is Detective Constable Crosby. I know you won't like it, Sloan, but you'll have to take him.'

'Thank you,' murmured Wendy Lamport. 'You're very kind.' She put her hands gratefully round a proffered cup of tea. Even though it was a warm day she was still shivering slightly.

'You'll feel better when you've drunk it,' forecast the woman whom she took to be Mrs Mellot.

Wendy Lamport and Gordon Briggs were sitting in the farmhouse kitchen at Pencombe. It was a big room with a low ceiling and a great stove at one end. In the middle of the room was the largest kitchen table that Wendy had ever seen. Mrs Mellot's first reaction to the news about the finger had been to put the kettle on the stove.

'I never have liked crows,' she said.

'Nasty brutes,' agreed Wendy, shuddering. She put her cup down on the big table. It was made of elm wood, scrubbed white for generations.

'Never mind,' said Mrs Mellot. 'Mr Mason has taken it away now.'

'That won't be the end of it,' said Gordon Briggs with a

short laugh. He exchanged significant glances with George Mellot, and said to him, 'Will it?'

'Only the beginning, I'm afraid,' agreed the farmer. 'It must have come from somewhere.'

'I said that the Westerbrook only flowed when something was wrong,' insisted Wendy tightly.

'Somewhere near,' said Gordon Briggs implacably.

All George Mellot's responses seemed to be temperate. 'Not too far afield,' he said.

Briggs swept on. 'The crow would be looking for a quiet spot to . . .'

'Don't!' implored Wendy. 'It doesn't bear thinking about, what it was going to do next.'

'You've got to face facts,' said the schoolmaster uncompromisingly.

George Mellot, quiet and controlled at the edge of the room, nodded.

'It might have come from somewhere else, mightn't it?' said the girl tremulously.

Mrs Mellot said quickly, 'Of course.'

'I mean,' she said, 'crows fly quite a long way, don't they?'

'Not with something in their beaks,' pointed out Gordon Briggs.

'That's what our policeman said,' murmured the farmer.

'That means then,' carried on Wendy uncertainly, 'that you've got a dead body on the farm somewhere.'

The farmer seemed anxious not to catch his wife's eye. 'I'm afraid it does.'

'And what will you have to do about it?' the girl asked.

'Look for it,' said George Mellot. 'The question is where to begin . . .'

They were interrupted by a knock at the back door. Mrs Mellot went across the kitchen to answer it, saying over her shoulder, 'That'll be Leonard Hodge.'

'My farm worker,' said George Mellot.

'I sent a message down,' his wife said. 'Hullo, Len, it is you, then.'

'Come along in, Len,' said George Mellot. He explained

about the finger to a powerfully built and ruddy-faced man who stood attentively by the kitchen door.

'There's always plenty of crows about at Pencombe, Mr Mellot,' said Len Hodge immediately. He was dressed in working clothes in spite of its being a Saturday afternoon and had the look of someone who had been interrupted at something. There was still grease on his arms although his hands had obviously been hastily washed.

'I know,' said Mellot.

'But I haven't seen no body,' said Hodge, shaking his head.

'Have you noticed more crows than usual?'

'Can't say that I have, Mr Mellot.' Hodge looked round at the others in the kitchen and said, 'Hard to tell when they're always around. You get used to them being there and don't notice particular, like.'

George Mellot persisted with his questioning. 'You'd have noticed them flocking around anywhere special though, wouldn't you, Len?'

'Dare say I would, Mr Mellot.'

'So would I,' said Mellot decisively, 'and I certainly haven't.'

'Mind you—' the farm worker screwed up his eyes, 'don't forget that there's upwards of three hundred acres at Pencombe.'

'Quite.' Mellot nodded.

'And a man can't be everywhere.'

'The police will be,' forecast George Mellot. 'And quite soon.'

As he stood up Gordon Briggs ran his fingers over the vast kitchen table and said tactlessly, 'They make coffins from elm, too, don't they?'

'A finger?' echoed Detective Constable Crosby.

'That's what I said,' repeated Detective Inspector Sloan grimly.

'It's not a lot to go on, sir,' said the constable, 'is it?'

'It's a beginning,' said Sloan. All cases had to begin somewhere.

'But . . .'

Sometimes cases only began with a rumour – a mere whiff of wrongdoing, whispered behind cautious hands. Without anything as tangible as a finger at all. And as often as not they still ended up as full-blown cases too.

'There is nothing to say at this stage, Crosby,' said Sloan austerely, 'that there is any crime of any sort involved at all.'

'Then . . .'

Detective Inspector Sloan climbed into the waiting police car. 'It could be just an ordinary death.'

'It could be one of those ransom jobs, sir, though, couldn't it?' Detective Constable Crosby clambered more enthusiastically into the driving seat. 'You know the sort of thing – pay up or we'll send you an ear or . . .'

'I know,' said Sloan heavily. 'Or a finger.'

'It's been done before, sir. The Camorra . . .'

Sloan shook his head. 'I don't think so somehow. Not this time. For one thing it wasn't delivered through the post with a note or anything like that.'

'Oh?' Crosby sounded disappointed.

'It was found lying on a footpath.'

'Not the same thing at all, sir,' agreed Crosby.

'You've been reading too many books,' said Sloan briskly. 'It's probably just from some old tramp who wandered into the woods to die.'

The detective constable engaged gear and steered the car out of the police station. 'Where to, sir?'

'Great Rooden.'

Crosby groaned. 'The real sticks.' He did not like the country.

'To the police house first,' said Sloan, unmoved. 'To see what Constable Mason has to say.'

Constable Mason welcomed them to a conspicuously neat house and garden. Mrs Mason provided tea and homemade scones and a general feeling of homeliness.

'Fancy,' she said, 'a crow dropping a finger like that. You sit here, Inspector. I think you'll find that chair quite comfortable.'

'I'll need to know the names of the farmers on either side

of Pencombe, too,' said Sloan, struggling to introduce a businesslike note into the domestic atmosphere.

'There's Paul Hucham at Uppercombe,' said Constable Mason. 'He's nearly all sheep. And the Ritchies at Stanestede. That's a mixed farm. Both those farms march alongside Pencombe – to the north-west and east, that is. Oh, and Bailey is at Lowercombe on the other side of the road to the south. Mustn't forget Sam Bailey's land. A road wouldn't mean anything to a crow, would it?'

'I'm surprised that a finger did,' said Sloan.

Constable Mason shook a grizzled head. 'You'd be astonished what a crow'll take a meal off.'

'Another scone, Inspector?' said Mrs Mason.

Police wives, like doctors' wives, had to get used to mixing life with work.

'You will, Constable, won't you?' she said comfortably, passing the plate.

Crosby didn't need pressing.

'There's no one missing out this way?' enquired Sloan generally.

Mason shook his head. 'Not that I've heard,' he said. 'And I think I would have done.'

Sloan did not doubt that Mason's intelligence system was as good as any mechanical one. And his retrieval system a good deal better.

'What about wayfarers?' asked Sloan.

'We do get a few showing up from time to time even in this day and age,' said Mason. 'If the finger is from one of them we may not know for quite a while. One of the old regulars would have to fail to turn up and that might take months. We might never know.'

'It's probably,' Sloan repeated his earlier statement, 'from some old tramp who wandered into the wood to die.'

Constable Mason frowned. 'That finger may be from some old tramp right enough, sir, but it's not from a wood.'

'Oh?' said Sloan, interested.

Mason shook his head. 'Not if a crow had anything to do with it.'

There was obviously more to being a country constable than just growing cabbages.

'You won't catch a crow feeding in a wood, sir,' carried on Mason. 'They'd be too afraid of being caught by predators for that.'

Crosby's head came up from the scones. 'Well, well . . .'

'That means . . .' began Sloan.

'That means, sir,' said Mason firmly, 'that the rest of this body's probably lying on open ground.'

'Should be easy to find then,' remarked Crosby indistinctly.

'No,' said Mason.

'No?' said Sloan.

'Stands to reason, sir,' said Mason, 'doesn't it? It's been lying around for a fair old time for it to get into the state it has. I mean to say, fingers don't come off a body all that easily, do they?'

'Another scone, Inspector, or will you have a piece of cake?'

'Thank you,' said Sloan.

'So,' said Mason, 'I should say that it's already been lying around for a bit and nobody's seen it yet.'

'It could have just been put out somewhere,' suggested Crosby.

'Difficult to move if it's in the state that a crow could pick bits off,' said Mason resolutely.

Sloan was inclined to agree with him. A newly dead body was an awkward enough object to move about: a disintegrating one practically impossible.

'Mark my words,' said Constable Mason, 'that body'll be on open ground wherever it is.'

'That should make it easier to find,' said Sloan.

In the event he had seldom been more wrong.

'Pass your cup, Inspector . . .' said Mrs Mason.

'This George Mellot,' Sloan said, getting out his notebook, 'what can you tell me about him?'

Constable Mason sat back in his chair. 'He runs quite a tight ship at Pencombe. Everything done to a high standard and all that.'

'What sort of a farm is it?'

'Mixed,' said Mason. 'Mellot's old man went in for pigs in a big way but you know how it is. Sometimes you do well with pigs and sometimes you don't.'

Pigs is equal, thought Sloan to himself. Now who was it who had said that?

Mason carried on. 'The place had got a bit run down by the time George came to take over. Old man Mellot was a real stick-in-the mud.'

Sloan nodded. Stick-in-the-mud was the opposite of evolution.

'He got like Sam Bailey has got now,' said Mason. 'Too set in his ways for the good of the farm.'

'Wouldn't change with the times,' said Sloan. It was easier said than done, changing with the times, especially when those times included incomprehensible technology, computers and microchips with everything.

'There was another thing, sir,' said Mason.

'What?'

'Pencombe wasn't big enough for both of them.'

'George and his father?'

'George and Tom,' said Mason. 'Oh, didn't I say? There was a younger brother, too, wanting his share.'

Sloan geared himself to hear an updated version of the Parable of the Prodigal Son.

Mason went on speaking. 'George bought him out or something and Tom went off to do a Dick Whittington.'

It was funny, thought Sloan, that there should only ever have been one Lord Mayor of London to get into the history books. Perhaps it was because he had got into a nursery rhyme too.

'And did he?' enquired Sloan. 'Oh . . .' He answered himself. 'You don't mean to say that Tom is that Mellot?'

'Mellot's Furnishings – Upholsterers to the Nation,' said Mason neatly.

Not the Prodigal Son then, thought Sloan. More like Joseph . . .

'Best thing that ever happened to young Tom Mellot was being kicked out of the farm,' said Mason.

'Some nestlings thrive on being turfed out,' said Sloan sagely. Now he came to think of it, the name of Mellot had been in the news lately. He couldn't remember the exact connection. He would have to look it up. 'Some don't.'

All police officers knew that.

'Tom Mellot did,' chuckled Mason. 'I bet he could buy brother George out a dozen times over now if he had a mind to.'

'A piece of cake, Inspector?' Mrs Mason hadn't neglected her duties as hostess for one moment. 'I made it this morning.'

He let her finish plying them with food before he asked to see the finger. Duty, he did know, came first, but there were some things which could wait. Eventually, though, Constable Mason led the way through into his little office and indicated a cardboard box.

'I've got it here,' said Mason.

The finger had brought out the atavism that lurks just below the surface in every man. For some reason too deeply primitive to explain in words the constable had laid it on cotton wool.

'It's adult, anyway,' said Sloan, taking his first look at it and putting ransomed children out of his mind for good.

'And with a bit of luck,' said Mason, 'it might just be possible to get some prints off it.'

'Too far gone,' pronounced Detective Constable Crosby, taking a quick look and stepping back again.

'It would save a lot of time and trouble if it wasn't,' said Sloan automatically. Deep down inside himself he knew that nothing was ever likely to be as easy and simple as finding a fingerprint and a person to match it.

'Yes, sir,' said Crosby dutifully.

'And now,' said Sloan briskly, 'we'd better see about mounting a search for the body. Who can we call on out here?'

3

Brethren, be sober, be vigilant.

'This was the exact spot, Inspector,' said Wendy Lamport, pointing.

'Right, miss.' Detective Inspector Sloan stood on the footpath at Pencombe Farm where the girl had stood earlier. Presently he would get Crosby to take a sample of the grit from the path to compare with any foreign bodies embedded in the skin of the finger. That might help.

'Look,' she said, 'you can see where the other policeman put that little pile of stones to mark it.'

'Yes, miss.' Sloan had already noted the infant cairn created by Constable Mason. He looked round about him. 'Now, you and Mr Briggs were walking which way?'

'North-north-west,' answered Briggs before Wendy could speak.

'Quite so, sir.' Sloan took a quick look at the sun. 'So you would have had your backs to the farmhouse?'

'That's right,' said Briggs. 'We'd come that way, hadn't we?' He turned to George Mellot for confirmation. 'You'd just seen us.'

The farmer nodded.

'We were heading for the Little Rooden road,' put in Wendy.

'And, miss,' continued Sloan, 'you've no idea at all in which direction the crow had been flying when it dropped the – er – object?'

She shook her head. 'I didn't notice.'

'It would save a lot of time,' said Sloan, thinking of the area to be searched, 'if you had done.'

'I'm sorry,' she said simply. 'You see, we didn't know what it was until after the bird had gone, did we, Gordon?'

Gordon Briggs said, 'No.'

Sloan turned to George Mellot who had been standing silently by. He had seldom met a man more continent of speech. 'If, sir, you could just show me the lie of the land . . .'

The farmer stirred. 'Pencombe Farm runs from the Great Rooden road to the foot of the hill over there. That's where Uppercombe starts.'

'That'll be Mr Hucham's land, won't it?' said Sloan, who had done his homework quite well while he was at Constable Mason's.

Mellot nodded. 'And over the other side to the east is – er – Mrs Ritchie's farm. That's called Stanestede.'

'And behind us?' said Sloan, turning round.

'The other side of the road, you mean?' said George Mellot. 'Where the wood is.'

'Dresham Wood is Sam's,' replied Mellot. 'All that land over there belongs to old Sam Bailey. That's Lowercombe Farm.'

They were some distance from it but even so Sloan could see a man coming out of the wood. George Mellot saw him too and screwed up his eyes.

'I believe that's Len Hodge, my man,' said Mellot. 'I told him to start to look around.'

'Good,' said Sloan vaguely. Crows did not inhabit woods – Ted Mason had said so – but Sloan held his peace. It was no part of a detective's duty to inform. Together they watched the farm worker make his way over the road and on to Pencombe Farm.

'I started to look in a few places, too,' volunteered Mellot.

'That's a help,' said Sloan. Finding out how far a crow flew was high on his own list of priorities. There was a flourishing school of entomologists specializing in the study of insects and the dead. What he wanted was an ornithologist with a similar cast of mind. He turned aside. 'Have you got a note of all this, Crosby?'

'Yes, sir,' said the constable stolidly.

'It still leaves a lot of acres,' said George Mellot.

'Yours and everyone else's,' said Sloan, making a comprehensive gesture that included the entire landscape. Len Hodge was walking along the footpath to the farm now. Sloan turned abruptly back to the farmer. 'I'll see your neighbours now and we'll mount a search of as much ground as we can cover tomorrow morning.'

The farmer nodded.

'We'll need volunteers,' continued Sloan. He looked towards Gordon Briggs. 'Would your Society help?'

Paul Hucham received Detective Inspector Sloan and Detective Constable Crosby hospitably enough at Uppercombe Farm.

'Sorry about the muddle,' he said, waving an arm to take in an uncleared table, 'but I live alone and the woman doesn't come on Saturdays.'

'That's all right,' said Sloan easily. 'We just want your permission to search Uppercombe Farm tomorrow. We're looking for human remains.'

'Good grief!' exclaimed Hucham.

He was, judged Sloan, well under forty and quite good-looking in a saturnine way.

'Now if you had said a sheep,' responded Hucham when the detective had explained, 'I'd have been with you right away. The crows have a dead sheep down to bare bones in no time at all.'

'It happens then . . .'

'It happens all right,' replied Hucham vigorously. 'My shepherd has to keep his eyes open, I can tell you. That's the worst of hill country – there's no knowing what sort of silly places a sheep will get itself into.'

Sloan would have given a lot to have known what sort of place a dead man had got himself into.

Or been put.

'And if one of the flock goes missing . . .' the other man's voice trailed away.

One of the human flock had certainly done that, decided Sloan. And there was a parable, wasn't there, about the importance of the missing sheep as well as the one about the Prodigal Son?

Paul Hucham's mind was still on crows. 'You can take it from me, Inspector, that we don't have any trouble with the carcass when a sheep dies.'

'No?'

The sheep farmer said grimly, 'The birds see to that.'

Sloan nodded. There had been a horror film once, hadn't there, about birds. None of your 'pretty as a kingfisher' stuff about that either . . .

'I haven't noticed anything suspicious myself,' said Hucham, 'but there are quite a few nooks and crannies at Uppercombe and I don't get round them all, even in summer time.'

'Quite so,' said Sloan neutrally.

'But search Uppercombe by all means,' said Paul Hucham. 'I'll give you a hand tomorrow.'

Mrs Andrina Ritchie at Stanestede Farm was just as willing. She received Sloan and Crosby in a farmhouse that had been modernized to within an inch of its life.

'Look where you like, gentlemen,' she said at once. She was small and dark and attractive. 'I'll tell my man that you're coming, otherwise he'll think there's something wrong.'

'There is something wrong, madam,' said Sloan flatly. 'There's a dead body about this valley somewhere and we don't know where it is.'

'Yes, of course, Inspector. I'm sorry. That was silly of me. It was just if Jenkins suddenly saw people everywhere . . .'

'You haven't got any footpaths over Stanestede then,' divined Sloan.

'Not public ones, thank goodness. Only our own farm paths.'

'That explains that,' said Sloan. 'Now if you had a public

right of way over the farm you would probably be used to people everywhere. You haven't seen any strangers, I suppose?'

She wrinkled her forehead. 'I can't say that I have. Not lately. Mind you, Inspector, we're pretty isolated out here. It's not like being down in Great Rooden.'

'All the more reason for noticing strangers, madam.'

'Of course,' she conceded at once, 'but I certainly haven't. I'll ask Jenkins . . .'

'Jenkins is . . .?'

'Our . . . my farm worker.'

'I see, madam. You have just the one man here, do you?'

'I'm looking out for another,' she said.

'I thought,' said Sloan, digging into the recesses of his memory, 'that Michaelmas was the time for that . . .'

'Not any longer,' she assured him. 'Besides, as it happens, I need somebody extra now.'

'You do?'

She faced him squarely. 'I expect George Mellot told you, Inspector.'

'Told me what?'

'My husband has left me.'

Sloan made a neutral noise. 'No, he didn't say.'

'Walked out, gone,' she said, clenching and unclenching her fists. 'Vanished.'

'When?' enquired Sloan. He was, perforce, interested in anyone who was missing.

'June the first, it was.'

The Glorious First.

'I'm not likely to forget the date,' she added bitterly.

'No, madam.' He cleared his throat. 'Do you know why he went?'

'Her name,' she said with venom, 'is Beverley.'

'Ah.' This time Sloan made an all-purpose noise in his throat.

'That's all I know, Inspector.'

'Not where she lives?'

'Calleford.' She snorted. 'Where the market is.'

'What's that got to do with . . .'

'I thought he was at the market, didn't I?' she said.

'And he wasn't?'

'He was with Beverley, whoever she is,' said Mrs Ritchie savagely. She sniffed. 'Now, Mrs Mellot . . .'

'Yes?' Sloan was interested in anything to do with the Mellots.

'She always goes into Calleford on market-day with George. Does her shopping and has her hair done.'

'And you didn't?'

'Not always.' She drew herself up. 'Not often enough, apparently.'

'I see.'

'Meg Mellot's a wise woman.'

'Quite so, madam.' Sloan stroked his chin. 'Tell me, how exactly do you know that your husband went off with – er – Beverley?'

Her lip curled. 'He left me a note, Inspector. In the real old-fashioned tradition of romatic fiction he left me a note.'

All that Sloan knew about romantic fiction was that everything always ended happily.

Mrs Ritchie was still speaking. 'He put it in front of the kitchen clock, if you really want to know.'

Sloan did not know if he really wanted to know about the absent Mr Ritchie or not. 'Did you keep the note?' he asked automatically.

'I threw it straight into the fire,' she said. She gave him a challenging look. 'Wouldn't you have done?'

'I don't know, madam, I'm sure.' The prospect of Mrs Margaret Sloan leaving him was not one he was in the habit of contemplating.

She tossed her head. 'And I changed all the door locks. I'm not having him creeping back when he's tired of his Beverley.' She gave Sloan a shrewish look. 'Or when she's tired of him.'

Sam Bailey at Lowercombe Farm could have stood in for John Bull any day. He only needed gaiters and he would have fitted the part perfectly. He shook his head solemnly when he heard Sloan's tale about the finger.

'I don't like the sound of that at all, Inspector. It isn't natural for some poor creature to be lying out there without a proper Christian burial.' He snapped his fingers autocratically. 'Elsie, a cup of tea for everyone . . .'

It was always surprising, thought Sloan, what a comforting word 'natural' was. Natural causes and natural justice both cropped up in police work.

So did tea, of course.

'How old is this finger?' enquired Mrs Elsie Bailey anxiously. She was quite upset by the visit of the two policemen.

'We don't know for certain yet, madam.'

'Very new?' she asked quickly.

'Not very new,' said Sloan, 'but not very old either.'

'How new?' she persisted.

'Don't fuss, Elsie,' said Sam Bailey. 'It's nothing to do with us.'

'A few weeks,' advanced Sloan, 'at a guess.'

Mrs Bailey's questioning subsided.

'A finger, did you say?' The portly old farmer nodded almost to himself. 'I remember the days when there were always unknown men at the gate asking for work. Any work. None of this picking and choosing.'

'Hirelings,' said Mrs Bailey, bustling about in spite of her grey hair. 'You sit over here, Constable. The kettle won't take a minute.'

'Any of them could have gone missing,' said Bailey, his mind still on the past, 'and nobody been any the wiser.'

'I hope it's not going to be like that, sir,' said Sloan.

Sam Bailey pointed to a stick in the corner of the room. 'Mind you, I don't get about like I used to or I could have told you people whether or not there was a body at Lowercombe. Time was when I went over every yard myself. The best fertilizer there ever was was the farmer's own two feet. That right, Mother?'

Mrs Bailey nodded. 'That's right, Sam,' she murmured.

'You used to go over every yard yourself,' adding almost to herself, 'But not any more.'

'Times change,' said the farmer, 'and not for the better, I may say.'

Sloan was too wise to disagree with that sentiment.

'And as for young people today . . .' began the farmer.

Or that one.

'Now, Sam,' said his wife, 'don't you start . . .'

'Well, we don't get men asking for work like we used to do,' said Bailey, momentarily side-tracked.

'No,' agreed Sloan.

'More's the pity.'

Sloan wasn't so sure about that.

'Likely then,' deduced Bailey shrewdly, 'that this finger isn't from someone casual.'

'Naturally,' replied Sloan smoothly, 'we should be very interested in hearing about anyone who was missing.'

'No one that I know about,' said the other man. 'The milkman's your best bet for that these days.'

'True,' said Sloan. Milk not taken in was the loudest signal of the twentieth century. There would, though, have been a lot of milk bottles outside the house of a person whose body had been reduced to a skeleton.

'I don't get about like I did,' the farmer reminded him, 'but I think we'd have heard if it had been anyone local, wouldn't we, Mother?'

'We hear most things,' said Mrs Bailey comfortably. 'Good and bad.'

'We should like to search Lowercombe tomorrow, all the same,' said Sloan formally.

The farmer nodded. 'We're not all that far from Pencombe . . .'

'As the crow flies,' said Detective Constable Crosby.

'Come along in, Sloan,' said Dr Dabbe warmly, 'and – let me see now – it's Detective Constable Crosby, isn't it?'

The two policemen advanced into the office of the Consultant Pathologist to the Berebury District General Hospital.

Crosby was bearing a small cardboard box. He was carrying it before him like an undertaker with the ashes.

'I hear,' began the doctor, 'that you've got something really interesting for me.'

'That depends,' temporized Sloan.

Crosby laid the cardboard box on the pathologist's desk. Dr Dabbe gently raised the lid.

'It's not a lot to go on, Doctor, a finger,' began Sloan cautiously. 'We realize that.'

'Oh, I don't know,' said Dr Dabbe easily. 'Think about Pandora.'

'Just a finger,' repeated Sloan. Opening Pandora's box had led to a lot of trouble, hadn't it?

'Better men than I have made do with less, Sloan.'

'Have they, Doctor?'

'There was a piece of a pelvic girdle once from a well in Egypt.' The pathologist stroked his chin. 'That was all there was to go on but it turned out to be a classic case of its kind.'

'It looks a perfectly ordinary finger to me,' said Sloan doggedly. He didn't like classic cases. They were for the historians and the textbooks.

'*Phalanges digitorum manus*,' said Dr Dabbe.

'Really, Doctor?' Sloan refused to think of it as anything except a finger.

Dr Dabbe picked up a probe and pointed in turn to each bone. 'We've got phalanx prima, phalanx secunda, and phalanx tertia.'

Detective Constable Crosby got out his notebook. 'Sounds like the Three Bears to me.' He sniffed. 'All we need is Goldilocks.'

The pathologist peered at the contents of the cardboard box for a long moment and then said, 'I can tell you one thing, Sloan, and that is that these metacarpals are male.'

'That's a great help, Doctor,' said Sloan sincerely.

And so it was. Women's Lib notwithstanding, if there was crime involved then usually a dead man meant a different crime from a dead woman. It was not so much the separation of the sheep from the goats as the disappearance of the sacrifical lamb . . .

'There is still a little hair present on the proximal phalanx,' amplified Dr Dabbe, 'with masculine distribution.'

'Ah.'

'Dark hair,' said Dr Dabbe. 'That means that unless it was dyed or he was totally bald, the owner of this finger will have had dark hair on his head too.'

'That might help, Doctor.'

The pathologist bent a little further over the box. 'Dead,' he said presently, 'something under a month.'

Sloan motioned to Crosby to take a note.

'Give or take a week or two,' said Dr Dabbe.

Sloan nodded.

'And depending on the conditions in which it has been lying,' continued the pathologist.

'Quite so,' said Sloan. He was used to medical qualifications.

'I can't tell you if it has come from the south-west corner of the vineyard, Sloan,' went on Dr Dabbe, 'but I can tell you that it has been in the open air.'

'Not buried,' said Sloan.

'And not somewhere dry enough to mummify it,' said the doctor, touching the flesh with the edge of his probe. He had all the delicacy of the artist. 'In fact,' he said, 'I should say that the damp had got at it quite a bit, too.'

In its way, thought the detective inspector to himself, it was quite a virtuoso performance . . .

'That any help, Sloan?'

'Anything,' said Sloan fervently, 'might help at this stage. Anything at all.'

Thus encouraged the pathologist reached for a magnifying-glass. He peered at the end of the fingernail. 'If this is anything to go by, Sloan, you've got someone here who took normal care of his appearance.'

'The trouble,' said Sloan flatly, 'is that we haven't got anyone here.'

'Just the finger,' put in Constable Crosby helpfully.

'The rest of him will be around,' said the pathologist.

'Unless someone has discovered the perfect way of disposing of a body.' said Sloan pessimistically.

'No,' said Dr Dabbe.

'No?' Sloan raised his eyebrows.

'The rest of him will be around,' said Dr Dabbe, switching his attention to the other end of the finger, 'because this member has been disarticulated naturally.'

'Naturally?' echoed Sloan. It didn't seem the right word somehow.

'Not by an instrument,' said the doctor.

'Ah.'

'By time and weather perhaps,' qualified Dr Dabbe, 'but it hasn't been hacked off.'

'We think it was picked off by a crow,' said Sloan. Perhaps he should have said that earlier but the pathologist had got there on his own. 'The girl who spotted it said that she was aware of them flying about overhead on the farm.'

'Always plenty of crows on farms,' pronounced the pathologist largely. 'Nature's dustbinmen, you could call them.'

'Nature's detective, in this case,' remarked Crosby.

The pathologist pointed to the finger. 'I shall be very surprised if the rest of this chap here isn't around somewhere.'

Sloan took another, longer look in the box. In a matter of moments the pathologist had translated three small bones and a little skin from 'Remains thought to be human' into 'This chap here'.

'Thank you, Doctor,' he said sincerely.

Dr Dabbe wasn't listening. With infinite gentleness and care he lifted the bones from their cotton-wool bed and laid them on his desk. He peered attentively at one of the joints. 'He – whoever he was – had the very early beginnings of osteoarthritis, Sloan. Mind you, we nearly all have . . .'

Sloan had momentarily forgotten that the pathologist dealt in disease as well as death.

'Feel these chalky deposits, Sloan? That's what you would call rheumatism.'

Sloan's gaze followed the pathologist's own finger. 'Well, I never . . .'

'I'll be doing a routine test for foreign bodies and fingernail scrapings, of course,' went on Dr Dabbe briskly. 'Macroscopically there aren't any but you never can tell.'

'No.' What the medical eye did not see the medical microscope did.

'Find the rest of him, Sloan,' said the pathologist cheerfully, 'and I might be able to tell you what he died from.'

Detective Inspector Sloan took his reply straight from the pages of an early cookery book at the point where the author was advising on the making of hare pie. 'First, catch your hare . . .'

Steadfast in the faith.   4

Police Constable Edward Mason might be slow. He was also sure. As soon as Detective Inspector Sloan and Constable Crosby had departed back to Berebury with the cardboard box containing the finger, Mason told his wife that he was going out.

'On duty,' he added as an afterthought.

Mrs Mason nodded calmly. A pearl among women, she did not ask awkward questions about when he would be back or even mention supper-time.

'I'm just popping down to the Lamb and Flag,' he said, reaching for his bicycle clips.

Even then she did not comment as many a wife would have done.

'To see a man about a man,' added Mason ambiguously.

The Lamb and Flag was the only public house in Great Rooden and as such was in many respects the centre of village life – the church being only open on Sundays, so to speak. As a place where information was exchanged it came second only to the village general store and post office – but then, that was presided over by a woman.

The Lamb and Flag was a long, low, jettied timber and brick building put up in the days of Good Queen Bess and good for a few hundred years more. Constable Mason dismounted from his bicycle and propped it against the gable wall. The inn sign swung from the overhanging gable above his head. Gaily painted, the red cross of the flag carried by the lamb went back beyond Queen Elizabeth to St George and a medieval England of pilgrim routes for the faithful.

Mason did not spare the inn sign so much as a glance as he made his way inside. The interior of the pub was dark compared with the bright sunshine outside and he had to pause when he first entered to get his bearings. Usually Saturday evening was the busiest of the week, but Constable Mason, who had arrived just after opening time, found the landlord on his own.

'Evening, Vic,' said Mason.

'Evening, Mr Mason,' said the landlord, Vic Higgins.

'Nice evening,' observed the policeman, looking round. A dragon beam bisected the corner of the bar ceiling and added to the darkness of the room.

'A good time of the year is June,' concurred Higgins cautiously. He was a newcomer to Great Rooden and was still feeling his way.

Mason looked round the empty bar. 'Quiet tonight, isn't it?'

'It's an away match.'

'Ah, cricket . . .'

'They're playing over at Almstone today,' said Vic Higgins. 'That's why it's so quiet here.'

'Can't have everything, I suppose.'

'And what are you going to have?' asked the landlord pertinently.

'Nothing,' said Mason, looking pious.

'That means you're on duty.'

'It does,' agreed Mason.

'If it's about after-hours drinking,' began the landlord, 'I can explain . . .'

'It's not,' said Mason.

'What is it, then?' enquired the landlord warily.

'You had a bit of fighting in here, didn't you?'

'Oh, you heard about that, did you?'

'I hear most things,' said Constable Mason placidly.

The landlord said, 'It wasn't actually in here.'

'Outside, then.'

'Outside,' conceded Victor Higgins unwillingly.

'What was it all about?'

'Can't say that I ever knew rightly.' He started to polish a glass. 'You know what pub fights are like.'

'Tell me about this one,' invited Mason.

'Not a lot to tell,' said Vic Higgins. 'I heard it start, of course . . .'

'Where?'

'In the spit and sawdust.'

'The public bar,' said the policeman. He was standing in the private one. On the wall someone had put up another sign altogether. It said 'Whine Bar'.

'I sent them outside straight away,' said the publican. 'I wasn't having no fighting in my bar.'

'Them?'

'There were just the two of them.'

'Not exactly an affray, then.'

'Nothing like that,' Higgins assured him. 'Or I would have sent for you, Mr Mason. You know I would,' he added virtuously.

'Course you would, Vic,' agreed Mason. He paused and then said, 'There were just the two of them, I think you said?'

'I did,' said the landlord uneasily. 'I didn't think anything more about it.' He looked across the bar counter at the police constable. 'Should I have done?'

'No reason why you should have,' said Mason judicially. 'At the time . . .' he added.

'Something happened, then?'

'It might have done,' said the policeman. 'On the other hand it might not.'

'Ah,' said the publican wisely.

'What were they fighting about?' pursued Mason.

'I never did get to the bottom of the trouble,' said the landlord. 'None of my business, of course,' he added self-righteously.

'Of course,' nodded Mason.

'Anyway,' said Higgins, warming to his theme, 'I got them

both out of my bar and as far as I know they finished it off outside.'

'Did they come back?'

'They did not,' said the landlord firmly.

'Neither of them?'

'Not one ever and not the other that night.'

'And that means . . .'

'I didn't,' expanded Victor Higgins, 'see the one of them again at all and the other didn't show up here for about a week afterwards. And then he kept pretty quiet about it. Sort of crept back, if you know what I mean.' He gave a reminiscent chuckle. 'He still had a bruise.'

''Bout when would all this have been, Vic?' asked Mason casually.

The landlord frowned. 'Round about the beginning of the month, I should say.'

'And the day of the week? Can you remember?'

'A Saturday,' responded the other man promptly. 'It was a Saturday all right, and a home match.' He wrinkled his brow still further. 'I think it was the day they played Little Rooden.'

'A needle match,' agreed Mason, adding profoundly, 'The nearer the opponent, the greater the rivalry.' A grin spread over his face. 'That must be somebody's Law, mustn't it?'

'It's probably,' opined the landlord, 'why we went to war with France as often as we did.'

'A Saturday, anyway, I think you said,' commented Mason.

'I know it was a Saturday,' said Higgins, 'because this character always comes in Saturdays.'

'That's the one who's been back?'

'That's right.'

'Do you know him?'

'Sort of,' said the landlord. 'Trouble is I'm so new here that . . .'

'Tell me about him,' invited Mason.

'Big chap,' said Higgins readily. 'Works up the road.'

'At Pencombe?'

'I couldn't say about that but I know it's near because he's a fireman too.' Great Rooden boasted a retained fire brigade whose members responded to a siren call-out. 'He comes in with the rest of the crew on Tuesdays after practice as well.'

Mason was too skilled to put a name in someone's mouth but he wanted to hear it spoken all the same. 'Big chap,' he recapitulated slowly, 'probably works at Pencombe, is a retained fireman. That should be enough to . . .'

'Len!' exclaimed Higgins suddenly. 'Len Hodge. That's his name. But who the other fellow was I couldn't begin to say. I've never set eyes on him afore or since.'

'What was he like?' asked Mason curiously. 'Can you remember?'

'A real wildwose,' said Higgins. 'Properly on the tatty side. Hadn't shaved and all that.'

'Thanks, Vic, anyway. All that might be a help. You never can tell in this game.'

'They had a real rough house in the yard, I can tell you,' volunteered Higgins, more relaxed now.

'Oh?'

'We could hear them,' said the landlord simply. 'Hammer and tongs it was for a while and then it stopped.'

'I see.'

'We sort of waited for them to come back in.'

'Like they do in Westerns,' said the policeman.

'For a drink,' said Higgins, 'and a tidy up.'

'But it didn't happen?' said Mason.

'No. They must have gone off.'

'Len Hodge has got a car, hasn't he?'

'If you can call it a car,' said Higgins. 'It's a broken-down old thing.'

'Didn't you even hear a car door slam, then?' asked Mason.

'Can't say that I rightly remember,' said Higgins frankly. 'Not after all this time.'

'Can you remember who else was here that evening?'

'Can't say I can,' replied the landlord, wrinkling his brow. 'Just the usual Saturday night regulars, I suppose. We don't get all that many strangers at the Lamb and Flag.' He looked up. 'Talking of strangers, Mr Mason, what's happening at

Pencombe tomorrow? I've had a character in here asking if his Club can eat their sandwiches in my bar.'

'That'll be Mr Gordon Briggs, that will.'

Higgins snorted gently. 'It's a fine thing for a house that advertises good food.'

'The Berebury Country Footpaths Society,' amplified Mason.

'So that's who they are, is it?'

'What did you tell him?'

'That as long as they drank my beer they could do what they liked with their precious sandwiches.'

'Good for you, Vic,' said Mason absently.

'Seems they've got something on tomorrow at Pencombe.'

'They have,' said Mason briefly.

The landlord reverted to his original point. 'Like I said,' he repeated, 'we don't get many strangers at the Lamb and Flag.' He paused and said thoughtfully, 'That was what was so funny about Len Hodge having a quarrel with this one.'

'You must,' persisted the policeman, 'remember some of the people who were here the night of the fight.'

'Same folk as'll be along presently,' retorted the publican. 'Hang about and they'll be in again. Tonight's Saturday, too, isn't it?'

'The finger,' Detective Inspector Sloan reported back to Superintendent Leeyes, 'is from a fully grown male.'

Leeyes grunted.

'With dark hair,' added Sloan.

'And?'

'And nothing, sir.' Sloan tightened his lips. 'That's all we've got to go on at the moment.'

Superintendent Leeyes chose to be bracing. 'You might have less, Sloan.'

Sloan hurried on without comment. 'I've had a list of missing persons pulled.'

'Persons reported as missing,' pointed out Leeyes with academic accuracy.

'Persons reported as missing,' agreed Sloan. It was at times like these that the Police National Computer came into its own.

'With the sort of timing Dr Dabbe is talking about,' said Sloan carefully, 'there are four males unaccounted for in Calleshire and a tidy number of girls.' Time was a dimension in every police case.

'Girls will be girls,' said Leeyes profoundly.

'And that's only in Calleshire,' continued Sloan. The territorial imperative was one of the superintendent's stronger instincts. Sometimes he forgot that there was a wider world beyond the county boundary. Or even the limits of F Division.

'These four . . .' the superintendent waved a hand. 'Go on.'

'One old man from the mental hospital who wandered off.' If Sloan had to put his money on someone this would be his choice.

'They don't lock the doors any more,' said Leeyes.

'That makes it difficult to keep them in,' agreed Sloan. It wasn't only in prison that locks helped those who owed a duty of care.

'And?'

'Two loving husbands and fathers who didn't come home after work.'

'Swans mate for life,' observed the superintendent cynically. 'Very few other species do.'

'Their wives usually want them back,' said Sloan. Marriage was an honourable estate.

'They do,' agreed Leeyes, adding sagely, 'Especially after they've been gone a little while.'

'Yes, sir, I'm sure.' Sloan couldn't decide if this was a male chauvinistic view or not. He did know, though, all about the value of a 'cooling-off' period. All policemen did. It wasn't for nothing that prison was called the cooler.

'That's three,' said Leeyes.

'One young person who left home and hasn't written.'

'Only one?' said Leeyes.

'Last seen hitching his way to a pop festival.'

'If that's not a fate worse than death,' said Leeyes with emphasis, 'I don't know what is.'

'We're going to check on the loving husbands and fathers,' said Sloan. 'One was from Calleford and one from Luston.'

Calleford was the county town where the headquarters of the police force was and Luston was Calleshire's industrial town in the north – where the trouble usually was.

'Every avenue should be explored,' said the superintendent, who didn't have to explore avenues himself.

Detective Inspector Sloan recollected another avenue – a closed one, this time. 'Crosby tried to get a print.'

'From the finger?'

'Yes, sir.' Sloan was irresistibly reminded of the picture of the Cheshire Cat in his childhood copy of *Alice in Wonderland*. All that had been there had been the head. And the grin, of course. With them, now all there was was a finger. No, not the finger.

A finger.

'Well?' said Leeyes.

'No joy there, I'm afraid, sir. The skin's too far gone to take prints from.'

Leeyes grimaced. 'Just our luck.'

'Yes, sir.' It would be no good fingerprinting the houses of those missing persons that they knew about. Still less running through the records. Even if the owner of the finger had a record . . .

'This search, Sloan, that you've laid on . . .'

'All lined up for tomorrow morning, sir,' responded Sloan. 'All available men and the members of the Berebury Country Footpaths Society.'

'Nice mixture, Sloan.' He coughed. 'I'm sorry I shan't be with you.'

Sloan did not say anything at all. The superintendent's Sunday mornings were well known to be sacrosanct. They were spent on Berebury golf course.

'I'll keep in touch, of course,' said Leeyes loftily.

'Of course, sir,' said Sloan, his voice utterly devoid of expression.

'And you'll let me know if – er – anything turns up, won't you?'

'Immediately, sir,' promised Sloan. He didn't know whether he sounded unctuous or not. He certainly meant to.

'What about leads, Sloan? Have you got any yet?'

'Just the one, sir.'

'Ah . . .'

'I don't know how promising it is.'

'Well?'

'There's a neighbouring farmer whose wife says he has gone off with his lady-love . . .'

'Ha!'

'She doesn't seem to want him back.'

'Don't blame her,' said Leeyes robustly.

'She hadn't reported him missing.'

Leeyes grunted.

'That will need checking on,' said Sloan.

'Routine,' declared Leeyes. 'Nothing to touch it, Sloan.' It was his credo.

'And so will the Mellots,' said Sloan. 'We'll have to find out what we can about them. Always supposing,' he added, 'that the owner of the finger is around on their farm. Find him, sir, and we'll be a big step further forward.'

'Or backward,' said Leeyes ominously. 'Or backward.'

After the police and the two walkers had been duly seen off Pencombe Farm George Mellot gravitated to the big kitchen. His wife was busy at the stove. She looked up as he came into the room.

'Supper'll be a little late,' she said, 'what with the police and everything.'

'It's not the supper I'm worried about,' said George Mellot. He looked suddenly much older.

'No,' said Meg Mellot, brushing her hair back from her forehead. 'No, I don't suppose it is.'

'Tom,' he said urgently. 'I must talk to Tom.'

'That's always easier said than done with Tom.'

'You don't have to tell me that,' he said. 'He's my brother.'

'Well, you know what he's like,' she said. 'He could be anywhere.'

Mellot nodded in agreement. 'Anywhere.'

'Especially at the weekend,' said Meg Mellot, putting a saucepan down.

'I'll try his house first anyway,' said the farmer.

He went off in the direction of the farm office and the telephone. Hanging on the wall of the office was a large-scale map of Pencombe Farm. He paused for a long moment in front of it and then he turned abruptly and picked up the telephone. He dialled a number. And then another. Presently he went back to the kitchen.

'No reply from his house,' he said to his wife. 'And his office doesn't know where he is.'

'He's taking a real break, then,' she concluded. 'And I'm not surprised either. Are you?'

He did not answer her directly. 'I tried to speak to his personal assistant but he wasn't there either.' He grimaced. 'Personal assistant indeed!'

'Tom's a busy man these days,' said Meg moderately.

'So am I,' retorted George Mellot, 'but I don't have a personal assistant.'

'Oh yes you do,' responded his wife with spirit, 'but she doesn't get paid.'

He smiled abstractedly, his mind elsewhere.

'Now I think about it, didn't Tom say he was going off somewhere to celebrate?' she said.

'He did,' said her husband. 'His exact words were "the strife is o'er, the battle done". He was in the church choir until his voice broke,' he added inconsequentially. 'He looked like an angel in a surplice.'

'Deceptive things, surplices,' observed Meg drily. 'All the same, I dare say Tom felt he could do with a holiday.'

'After everything,' said George Mellot meaningfully.

'It isn't every day,' said Meg Mellot, 'that you beat off a takeover bid.'

'Dawn raid,' said the farmer flatly. 'That was what that was called.'

'Dawn raid, then,' she said. 'It comes to the same thing in the end.'

George Mellot nodded.

She pushed a saucepan over the stove. 'And at the end of the day Mellot's Furnishings still belongs to the Mellots.'

'And not to Ivor Harbeton.'

'That's the great thing,' said Meg anxiously, 'isn't it?'

Her husband tightened his lips into a grimace. 'It wasn't for want of trying, was it?'

She shuddered. 'It was a nightmare.'

'Horse-whipping,' growled Mellot, 'would have been too good for Ivor Harbeton.'

'Business is business,' said Meg Mellot. 'I've heard Tom himself say that often enough.'

'There are no holds barred in love, war, and business,' said George Mellot grimly.

She looked at him curiously. 'Tom certainly found that out the hard way, didn't he?'

'You would have thought,' said the farmer, 'that when a man had built up a successful business it would be safe enough.'

'No,' said Meg Mellot wisely, 'that's precisely when it's at risk. Nobody wants to buy into a failure.'

He squared his shoulders. 'Ivor Harbeton wanted to buy Mellot's Furnishings. No doubt about that.'

'He very nearly succeeded, didn't he?' said Meg Mellot softly.

'If he hadn't taken the heat off when he did . . .'

'Mellot's Furnishings wouldn't still have been Mellot's Furnishings,' said his wife flatly.

'And Tom would have been out on his ear.'

'That wouldn't have done for Tom,' said Meg.

'No, it certainly wouldn't. He's a man of action, is Tom.'

She caught something in his tone and looked. 'What do you mean?'

'Exactly what I say.' He added slowly. 'Tom isn't a man to take anything lying down.'

'George, what are you getting at?'

He voiced his thoughts unwillingly. 'I just wonder why Ivor Harbeton disappeared when he did, that's all.'

His wife stared at him.

House of defence.   **5**

'This way, everybody,' shouted Gordon Briggs, waving an arm encouragingly. 'Follow me.'

The Sunday morning had found the members of the Berebury Country Footpaths Society assembled at the point where Footpath Seventy-Nine came out of Dresham Wood and entered Pencombe Farm.

When the schoolmaster had got their attention he carried on. 'Now that I've explained to you what it's all about we can get started.'

The members of the Society were clustered round the stile on the Sleden to Great Rooden road. Gordon Briggs led the way over it.

'We're meeting the police at the farm for a briefing,' he announced.

Wendy Lamport shivered. 'I only hope I don't find anything.'

'So do I,' said her friend.

'Once was enough,' said Wendy.

'Although,' added the other girl more thoughtfully, 'if it was me lying out there I'd want someone to find me, wouldn't you?'

'I hadn't thought of that,' said Wendy. All the same she still experienced a frisson of unwelcome remembrance as she set foot on Pencombe Farm again.

The other members of the Society queued up to take their

turn in clambering over the stile off the road and on to the footpath.

Detective Inspector Sloan stood by the barn door with Crosby and watched them approach. The walkers were a disparate group. The long and the short and the tall straggled over the footpath towards the barn. The collection of men who were waiting for them there was composed of policemen who were uniformly tall. George Mellot was present, too, and his farm worker, Leonard Hodge.

Sloan waited until they had all reached the farmyard before he addressed them. He had clambered up on to the step of a fork-lift tractor to give himself height.

'You are looking,' he announced, 'for a body that will have nearly been reduced to a skeleton.' His mind drifted back to an old jingle of his own childhood that had run: 'The muvver was poor and the biby was thin, only a skelington covered in skin.'

'It may be,' he continued aloud, 'partly covered . . .'

'The Babes in the Wood,' murmured someone.

'Or,' carried on Sloan valiantly, 'it may just be lying in the open.'

Wendy Lamport looked troubled.

'It won't be in wooded ground,' said Sloan. There was something in Dresham Wood, though, decided Sloan, or Len Hodge would have not have gone there first yesterday afternoon. He made a mental note to check there as soon as he could.

'Whatever you do,' warned the detective inspector firmly, 'if you do find it, don't touch it.' If he remembered rightly, the unfortunate baby in the rhyme had fallen down the plughole.

'Dogs,' said one of the walkers in an undertone to Gordon Briggs. 'Why haven't they got tracker dogs?'

Briggs didn't answer.

'If you do find it just stay by it and shout,' adjured Sloan. 'Don't even walk about round it. That will disturb the ground.'

'Clues,' said another walker knowledgeably to his immediate neighbour. 'That will be what they'll be looking for.'

Sloan indicated the waiting members of the police force.

'Wherever you are searching, there should be a policeman within earshot.'

'That makes a change, I must say,' said another member of the Berebury Country Footpaths Society in an aggrieved voice. He had once been mugged.

'If,' continued Sloan, 'you see anything in the least suspicious you should point it out to one of them.'

'Kaarh, kaarh,' croaked a crow above his head in antiphon. 'Kaarh.'

'Is that clear?' asked Sloan.

There were murmurs of assent from the walkers.

'Now we've got to be systematic,' Sloan said. 'A haphazard search isn't going to get us anywhere.'

Gordon Briggs nodded approval. He was a methodical man himself.

'We shall take two fields at a time,' announced Sloan, 'and walk across them in a straight line.'

'It's how they find people after an avalanche, too,' said a young man in the Society chattily, 'except that then you have to poke through the snow.' He spent his holidays at winter sports resorts.

'Remember that you should keep in line,' said Sloan.

'Trust the police to say that,' remarked a natural rebel in the crowd. 'Step out of it and they're down on you like a ton of bricks.'

'And keep your eyes open for clusters of crows,' added Detective Inspector Sloan. 'There's no reason why they shouldn't still be congregating round the skeleton.'

Wendy Lamport shuddered. 'How horrible!'

'It would mean that we'd found whoever it was, though, wouldn't it?' said her friend Helen practically.

'You,' said Wendy irrefutably, 'didn't see the finger.'

'I think that's all,' said Sloan to the walkers. The members of the police team had been briefed before the others came.

Gordon Briggs thrust his way forward to the front of the

group and raised his voice. 'Remember, everybody, lunch is at the Lamb and Flag in Great Rooden at twelve-thirty sharp. If we've found – ah – what we're looking for this morning, then we'll have a shortened walk this afternoon. If not, we'll keep looking. That understood, everybody?'

There were murmurs of assent from the assembled crowd.

Detective Inspector Sloan hadn't asked for questions. The one that he had had already from Len Hodge had been difficult enough to answer.

'There's crops in some of these fields, Inspector,' he had said while they had been waiting for the Berebury Country Footpaths Society to arrive. 'They're not all just grass, you know. What about walking over them?'

In the event it had been George Mellot who had dealt with that one.

While Sloan had been marshalling his thoughts the farmer had said, 'Surely there's nowhere that you haven't run over in the last few weeks, Len? Most of the fields have had a dressing of some sort.'

'That's right, Mr Mellot,' said the farm worker quickly. 'I hadn't thought about that.'

'We can always look it up,' said Mellot, 'but I don't think that there's any field in crop that hasn't had a tractor over it since the beginning of the month. And you would have spotted a body, Len, wouldn't you, even from a tractor?'

'Oh yes,' said Hodge vigorously, 'I would have seen a body right enough, Mr Mellot.'

'You'll be able to see which fields they would be, of course,' said the farmer to Inspector Sloan.

'Yes, sir,' said the policeman. 'Thank you.'

That was a help. There were helicopters at the beck and call of the police force but they cost money. He made a mental note, all the same, that Hodge could have known where a body was for longer than anyone else.

'Maize,' said Hodge. 'It's mostly maize, of course.'

'And that was only sown last month,' pointed out George Mellot.

Sloan made a note of that.

'I don't know why we're bothering too much about walking over crops,' said Mellot with a touch of bitterness in his voice. 'One of the footpaths goes right through the middle of the largest field on the farm.'

'Maize and all?' asked Sloan.

'Maize and all.' The farmer gave a short, mirthless laugh. 'I can assure you that that won't stop a dedicated walker like Gordon Briggs, Inspector. He'll stick to his rights and lead his tribe right acrss the growing crop to prove it's a right of way. That's what they've come for, remember.'

'Footpath Seventy-Nine,' Sloan said. The Red Sea might have parted for Moses and the tribe of Israel: George Mellot's maize wouldn't give way for the walkers. They would trample right over it.

'Pioneers, O, pioneers,' said Mellot. Something of the church choir had stuck with him, too. 'That's what they think they are.'

'One abreast, of course,' added Len Hodge. 'They're not supposed to walk more than one abreast across a field in crop, are they, Mr Mellot?'

'Huh!' said Mellot expressively, as the approaching walkers had come into view. 'That'll be the day, that will.'

Now Sloan watched the Berebury Country Footpaths Society walk away in an untidy straggle towards the nearest fields. The waiting policemen went with them in a neat phalanx led by Detective Constable Crosby. Constable Mason had merged into the group but Len Hodge stood out as a big man even among policemen.

'Start on Twenty Acre Field first, Crosby,' said Sloan, 'and then the one beyond.'

'Old Tree,' Mellot informed him. 'That's what the other field is called.'

Sloan nodded briefly, his mind on an old body.

'There used to be one there – an old tree, I mean,' said Mellot, 'in my grandfather's day. It's gone now.' He jerked his head. 'They say that no family lasts longer than three oaks.'

'All the fields here have names, I suppose, sir,' said Sloan. Detection in the country was certainly a different kettle of fish from detection in the town.

'They do,' answered the farmer. 'They're all on the tithe map, of course, but they're older than that . . .'

They were interrupted by the distant sound of a siren. It had a galvanic effect on only one man. Leonard Hodge turned abruptly and ran at great speed back to the farm road. He flung himself into the driving seat of an old car already turned and facing the village, and set off with a screeching of tyres for Great Rooden.

'A fire somewhere,' explained George Mellot calmly. 'You'll hear the engine in a minute. It doesn't take them very long to turn out.'

Sloan automatically took a look at his watch. He knew all about retained firemen in country areas far from full-time fire stations.

'A barn would be burnt to the ground by the time the regular fire engine got out to us from Calleford,' said Mellot.

Sloan nodded. 'And the Great Rooden crew all come from the village?'

'They do,' said Mellot. 'They won the County Shield last year for efficiency . . . listen!' He cocked his head to one side. 'I think I can hear them starting off.'

True enough, within minutes the sound of a klaxon came over the morning air. Loud at first, the noise rapidly diminished and soon fell away into complete inaudibility.

'They've gone the other way,' concluded Mellot. Sloan's attention, though, had already gone back to the matter in hand. The searchers had fanned out across Twenty Acre and Old Tree Fields, and begun their advance over the ground. They had their heads bent and eyes down as if in response to some invisible Bingo caller. Detective Inspector Sloan and George Mellot walked over to them and brought up the rear.

'No joy, sir,' reported Crosby at the end of their first sweep over the territory. 'Where now?'

Sloan pointed. 'We'll take those two over there next.'

'Longacre,' the farmer supplied the field names, 'and Kirby's. Don't ask me who Kirby was because I don't know, Inspector.'

The mists of antiquity weren't Sloan's concern. His mind was totally on the present. 'Then we'll take the orchards,' he said. 'The grass is long enough under the trees to hide a dozen bodies.'

Presently, though, the orchards, too, had been thoroughly searched without success. And the next pair of fields. And the next.

'Nothing, sir,' reported Detective Constable Crosby.

There were cows in the field after that. With feminine curiosity they approached the searchers, nuzzling their lunch-bags and staring wide-eyed as the policemen and walkers made their way purposefully across their field.

It was obvious from the demeanour of the group that they had found nothing among the cows.

'We'll do the other side of the river next,' decided Sloan.

A purposive sweep of the remaining fields of Pencombe Farm yielded no sign of a body. By half-past twelve Crosby was reporting failure.

'Not a thing, sir, anywhere.'

'You've looked under the hedges?'

'And in the ditches,' said Crosby stolidly.

Sloan looked at the sketch-map he had made with Constable Mason's help.

'It's nearly half-past twelve, sir,' said Crosby.

'Where's Mr Briggs gone?' asked Sloan.

'He's just checking on a scarecrow.'

'He would,' said Sloan.

'A maukin, he called it.'

'All right, then. Tell everyone to knock off now and be back here by two o'clock sharp. We'll tackle Uppercombe after lunch and then Stanestede.'

'I want,' said George Mellot loudly and clearly into the telephone, 'to speak to Mr Tom Mellot, please.'

He was answered in a pronounced foreign accent. 'I am the au pair,' said a girl's voice.

'I know,' said George Mellot patiently. 'Can I speak to my brother, please?'

''E is not 'ere,' said the girl. ''E 'as gone away.'

'Where is he then?'

''E 'as gone away,' said the voice again.

'So you said.'

''E 'as gone away yesterday.'

George Mellot ground his teeth. 'What I want to know is where he is.'

'I do not know where 'e is,' enuniciated the voice in careful English.

'Didn't he leave an . . .'

'Mr Mellot and the Señora and the leetle children all go away yesterday,' volunteered the voice.

'Where did they go?' asked George Mellot.

'In the car,' explained the voice helpfully. 'And the dog also because I am no good for walking the dog.'

George Mellot heroically refrained from direct comment. 'When are they coming back?' he asked instead.

The voice brightened. 'When I see them.'

'But . . .'

'That is what the *Señora* said,' insisted the au pair. 'I remember she say exactly, to expect us when you see us.'

Paul Hucham at Uppercombe Farm had a sheep in his arms when the search party got to him immediately after they had eaten. His land climbed up out of the valley and was nearly all given over to sheep-rearing. This, noted Detective Inspector Sloan, meant that all the grass was cropped short. Searching the ground therefore should be easier.

'Where do you want to start, Inspector?' asked Hucham. He lowered the sheep into a foldgarth and came forward to meet them.

'From where your land meets Pencombe land,' said Sloan. His posse was methodically working outwards from where the finger had been found. If their search revealed nothing on Uppercombe Farm they would do the same eastwards at Stanestede and southwards at Lowercombe.

'Right,' said Paul Hucham. 'If you'll all follow me, then . . .'

This time Detective Inspector Sloan perched on a stile to address his troops.

'Keep going,' he exhorted them. 'It must be somewhere.'

This, he thought, was true. The administrator of the Bere-bury District General Hospital had waxed eloquent on the subject of surgical waste the evening before. He had insisted to Sloan that the hospital's disposal procedures were absol-utely watertight. It hadn't been the most appropriate simile but Sloan had got the message.

The administrator had even quoted the hoary old advice churned out to generations of new house surgeons by the senior consultant when excising tissue at operation.

He always, he said, told them to divide the tissue they had taken from the patient carefully into three.

'Three?' Sloan had echoed, sounding like a comedian's feedman in spite of himself. Had it always been 'Yes, sir, yes, sir, three bags full, sir,' then?

'A piece for the pathologist . . .'

One for my master.

'A piece for the coroner . . .'

And one for my dame.

'And a piece for the nurse to throw away . . .'

But none for the little boy who cries in the lane.

Sloan finished saying his own piece now to the assembled company and climbed down from the stile. Lunch-time spent at the Lamb and Flag had had a mellowing effect on the walkers. They were quite talkative now and noticeably more friendly to the policemen as they once more spread out over the fields.

'I suppose,' said one of them, a 'keep-fit' fanatic if ever there was one, 'that we're doing the same amount of walking as usual.'

'More,' said his companion morosely, 'when you add up all the backwards and forwards. Like dogs,' he added.

Paul Hucham kept with Sloan. 'Inspector, there's a little hollow in the hillside where the sheep always go for shelter. A man might have done the same thing.'

'Right, sir, we'll take a look at it, shall we?'

'I can always tell when there's a north-east wind blowing,' he said. 'It'll be full of sheep.'

But there was nothing in Paul Hucham's little hollow.

'It was just a thought, Inspector,' he said as they surveyed the dip in the hillside. 'A man might have taken shelter there too.'

Sloan nodded. Watching animals made sense. They said that if a man wanted to survive in the jungle he should watch what the monkey ate. And eat the same things.

'It was worth checking, sir,' he said. In some matters Sloan was definitely on the side of the apes and not the angels.

Paul Hucham frowned. 'I can't think of anywhere else at Uppercombe where a skeleton might be other than on open ground. There's no shelter to speak of at all up here.'

'We'll find it, sir, never worry,' said Sloan. 'Just give us time, that's all. It's not going to run away,' he added grimly. 'That's for sure.'

'No,' said the farmer. He turned. 'We'll have to cut back this way, Inspector, because of the stream.'

'Where does this one go? Down to the Westerbrook?' There was a narrow footpath running down beside the little stream.

Hucham shook his head. 'No. This flows down through Stanestede Farm. It gets bigger further down the hill. It's very important to the Ritchies there.'

'They get their water from it, do they?' In the town water came in pipes but Sloan could quite see that matters might be different out here in the country.

'Their electricity,' said Hucham. 'They've got a generator just above the farm. That's how they're able to be all-electric there without it costing them anything.'

'Nice for them,' said Sloan, householder. 'What about you?'

'I have to make do with the view,' said Paul Hucham, waving an arm. 'It's not bad, is it?'

'It's very fine,' said Sloan.

'On a clear day you can see Calleford.'

Sloan nodded and turned to look back down at Pencombe Farm set at the bottom of the valley. Below them a determined search of Uppercombe Farm was being carried on. Once he caught the sound of Detective Constable Crosby's voice borne upwards by the wind. Even at a distance he could pick out Gordon Briggs hurrying about as fussy as a sheep dog. Over on his right the River Westerbrook glinted as the sun caught the moving water. He made a mental note to make sure that the banks of the river had been properly checked. Dr Dabbe had mentioned that the finger had been somewhere where the damp could get at it, hadn't he?

'Plenty of crows up here, Inspector,' remarked Hucham presently.

Sloan turned his attention to the sky. True enough, there were crows about. Their shiny black plumage was quite unmistakable. He looked at them keenly. Any one of them could have dropped the finger in front of the two walkers. And one of them, Sloan remined himself, knew where the body of a man was to be found even if he, Sloan, didn't.

'Kaarh, kaarh, kaarh,' called a crow hoarsely.

'It must be lonely for you up here, sir,' remarked Sloan.

'The winter drags a bit,' admitted the sheep-farmer, 'until the lambing starts. After that I'm too busy to notice.'

'And then suddenly it's spring, I suppose,' said Sloan absently. He could see that the latest cast by the search party below had drawn a blank. Crosby was waving his arm and slowly all his helpers started to drift down the hillside again, this time in the direction of Stanestede Farm. Sloan turned to Paul Hucham. 'Thank you, sir.'

'Sorry you didn't have any luck, Inspector.'

'It's not for want of trying,' said Sloan. He regarded the landscape laid out below him. 'And somewhere down there is what we're looking for . . .'

'I'd rather someone else found it, all the same,' said the other man with a rueful half-laugh.

'Yes, sir,' responded Sloan philosophically. There were some jobs that society was always content to have done for it by someone else. And the police force collected quite a lot of them.

'It's all very well when it's only a sheep,' said Paul Hucham. 'A human being is a different proposition altogether.'

'That's why we're searching the land now,' said Sloan. It must have been quite a benchmark of civilization when early man had begun to bury his dead. Now he came to think of it, the act of burial was one of the things which separated man from beast.

'Of course,' said Hucham uneasily.

'We couldn't do nothing,' said Sloan as much to himself as to the farmer. 'Not once we knew.' Except elephants. He was forgetting that they too buried their fellow elephants when they died, didn't they?

'Of course not,' agreed the farmer hastily. 'That wouldn't do at all.'

They had even, Sloan remembered, his thoughts running silently on, found time to bury that chap 'whose corse to the ramparts they'd hurried'. And that had been in the heat of battle. Sir John Moore after Corunna. Never mind that not a drum was heard, not a funeral note: that wasn't what had been important. What had mattered was that the old warrior hadn't been left lying around for the crows.

Filled with new resolve, Sloan turned and took his leave of the sheep-farmer.

6

A perfect end.

Mrs Andrina Ritchie received the policemen and the walkers at Stanestede Farm. She was dressed for the town, not the country. And for Sunday, too.

'You won't mind if I don't come with you, will you?' she said to Detective Constable Crosby who had led the way there.

'No, madam,' said that worthy with absolute truth. Well-dressed women frightened him. His gaze drifted involuntarily down to her feet. In his opinion Mrs Ritchie's shoes came into the category of foot ornaments rather than useful articles. They would not have stood up to life on the farm for very long.

'Go˙ wherever you please,' she said, waving an arm to encompass the land. 'It's all the same to me.'

'Thank you, madam.' Crosby cleared his throat: he had been instructed to ask an important question. 'Do you keep pigs at Stanestede, by any chance?'

'Pigs? Certainly not. Nasty, messy creatures.' She looked at him. 'Why do you want to know that?'

'Just checking, madam, that's all.' The detective constable made a note in his book. Pigs were omnivorous. That, as Detective Inspector Sloan had carefully explained to him, meant that they ate everything.

But everything.

'We've only got cattle here,' she said.

'I see,' said Crosby. Cattle were more selective. They didn't eat everything.

'They're bad enough,' said Mrs Ritchie.

'I'm sure they are,' responded Constable Crosby, townee. Actually the police weren't interested in cows, although he did not say so. What they were worried about was pigs. Eating people was wrong but pigs did not seem to know this. Cattle did.

'Cows are always needing looking after,' she said resentfully, patting her hair with one hand. 'I'm going to give them up now that I'm on my own and go over to sheep. They're a lot less trouble.'

'I'm sure that there'll be changes at Stanestede,' murmured Crosby diplomatically.

'You can bet your life there will,' she said, tightening her lips. 'I like a weekend to be a weekend.'

So did Crosby.

'And with stock,' said Andrina Ritchie, 'it isn't.'

'No, madam.' It wasn't with crime either but he did not say so.

'Now, officer, what do you want from me?'

'Did your husband . . .' Crosby stopped and started again. 'Have you got a large-scale map of the farm anywhere?'

'In the office,' she said. 'On the wall. This way.'

She led Crosby through the house and into the kitchen. The farm office at Stanestede was in a little room off the kitchen, accessible from the out-of-doors as well. The constable stared at the kitchen. It couldn't have been in greater contrast to the one at Pencombe Farm. Here there was no welcoming fire, no vast scrubbed elm table – just a formidable collection of electric machines arrayed in clinical grandeur amid a lot of colourful formica. The whole ensemble might have come from the pages of a woman's magazine. There was no touch of the country farmhouse kitchen about it at all.

'Nice, isn't it?' said Mrs Ritchie, pausing for a moment on the way through. The kitchen was obviously something she prized. 'We have our own electricity at Stanestede, you see. There's a stream,' she added vaguely.

Crosby could pick out the stream on the map of the farm. On the fields on the maps was pencilled in the current crop, and the date of sowing, and where the cows were now pastured and where they had been.

'We're not allowed to grow too many potatoes,' said Mrs Ritchie. 'I do know that.'

Crosby wondered what else this fashionably dressed creature knew about running a farm.

'Just our share,' she said.

Against one field on the map Crosby saw written a word that he had not expected to see.

'Beg pardon, madam,' he said, pointing.

'What?'

'There.'

'Rape,' she said.

'That's what I thought it was,' said Crosby.

'Oil seed rape,' she said.

'Ah,' he said delicately. 'And what – er – sort of rape is oil seed?' Back at the police station they just had the one variety of rape on the books. Not that that saved any trouble. Hard to prove and even harder to defend: that was the problem with a charge of rape. Experienced police officers suddenly found themselves urgently needed elsewhere when one was in the offing.

'For the cows to eat,' added Mrs Ritchie.

His face cleared.

She gave him an appraising glance. 'Thought fields of rape were just another of our little country ways, did you?' she said. 'Like a maypole.'

'It's a difficult subject,' said Crosby, discomfited. That was one thing that was dinned into all police constables at their training school. It wasn't so much the 'Heads I win, tails you lose' odds that went with getting involved with the charge of rape as the 'Stop it, I like it' dialogue invariably reported by the Defence and advanced in amelioration. Even when the victim was as badly mauled as a mating mink. The dialogue reported by the Prosecution was usually as totally disconnected as the 'And he said' and then the 'And she said' sequence when the paper was turned over in a game of Consequences.

'I wouldn't know anything about rape,' said Mrs Ritchie drily. 'All I can tell you, officer, is that now I know what that person meant who said something about "Hell having no fury like a woman scorned".'

'That's the other side of the coin, madam, isn't it?' said Crosby gravely. 'How are you managing on your own?'

'Everyone is being very kind,' she replied. 'I don't know where I would have been without my neighbours. Paul and George have both been very good to me.'

'That'll be Mr Hucham and Mr Mellot, won't it?'

'I don't know where I would have been without them,' she said, nodding, 'and even old Mr Bailey said if I needed any advice I wasn't to hesitate to ask him.'

'A bit set in his ways, isn't he?' ventured Crosby. That much had been evident on one visit to Lowercombe Farm.

'You can say that again,' said Mrs Ritchie wryly. 'Things haven't changed at Lowercombe since Nelson lost his eye. No wonder Luke couldn't stand it.'

'Luke?' That was a new name to Crosby.

'His son. Luke Bailey. His father drove him too hard.' Andrina Ritchie gave a brittle laugh. 'And he drove him to drink in the end.'

'Did he, madam?' That explained an old man working long after he should have been sitting by the fireside in his slippers.

'So they say.' She shrugged her shoulders. 'I haven't seen him in years. I shan't be taking his father's advice but it was nice of him to offer, wasn't it?' She favoured the constable with a tight smile. 'Anyway, I've got a good man working for me and that makes a difference.'

Crosby agreed warmly that it did and finished his survey of the wall map.

'I think that's all I need to see for the time being, madam, thank you, before we begin our search. We'll let you know if we should find anything at Stanestede.'

Mrs Andrina Ritchie shuddered delicately.

*

If the state of his temper was anything to go by Superintendent Leeyes had not won his golf match.

'Nothing?' he barked down the telephone from the clubhouse.

'Nothing, sir,' reported Detective Inspector Sloan. 'We've searched two of the farms within our radius now and there are two more to go.'

'Dormy.'

'Pardon, sir?'

'Nothing,' Leeyes grunted. 'A crow doesn't fly all that far, surely?'

'No, sir.' How far crows flew had been one of the things that Sloan had had to find out the evening before.

'And a human skeleton is a big thing.'

'Yes, sir.'

'It must be somewhere,' insisted Leeyes. He was not at his post-prandial best. He rarely was after a luncheon taken at the nineteenth hole of the golf-course.

'Sir,' Sloan went off at a tangent, 'Constable Mason has reported that one of the men out here had a bust-up with a stranger . . .'

'Hasn't made an arrest in years, hasn't Mason,' complained Superintendent Leeyes in an aggrieved tone of voice.

'It was in the local pub,' persisted Sloan. 'It's called the Lamb and Flag.'

'Trust Mason not to . . .'

'It happened about a month ago,' went on Sloan valiantly. 'The man was all cherried-up at the time, he says.'

'What man?' asked Leeyes, his wayward attention engaged at last.

'Leonard Hodge,' replied Sloan. 'He's George Mellot's farm worker. Big fellow,' he added. It was something worthy of note. Most criminals were smaller than most policemen. Sloan didn't know if this was because policemen had to be tall to be policemen or that criminals came up particularly small but as a rule they did. A rule of thumb, that is. A rule of Tom Thumb, you might say.

Leeyes groaned. 'You'd better look into that, Sloan, hadn't you? And, Sloan . . .'

'Sir?'

'Mellot's Furnishings. You said it rang a bell.'

'I thought,' said Sloan cautiously, 'that I remembered having seen something about them in the papers recently.'

'You had,' said Leeyes.

'Because they're so well known, I suppose.'

'They've been in the news all right, Sloan.' He sounded grim.

'I thought I'd read . . .'

'This,' said Leeyes meaningfully, 'had spilled over from the financial pages.'

'That explains it then, sir,' said Sloan with some satisfaction. 'What was it, do you know?'

'An attempt to take over the firm.'

'So it was,' said Sloan, metaphorically slapping his thigh. 'I remember now. I knew I'd seen the name lately.'

'An attempt to take over the firm,' reiterated Leeyes, 'and oust Tom Mellot as chairman.'

'The brother?'

'Precisely, Sloan,' said Leeyes. 'It began,' he informed him, 'with the usual thing.'

'What was that, sir?' Sloan did not pretend to be a financier.

'Buying up Mellot's shares quietly and then not so quietly.'

'I see.'

'And then a cash offer,' said Leeyes, 'at an offer price in excess of the market price of the shares.'

'Sounds fair enough,' said Detective Inspector Sloan, simple policeman.

'Or rather,' qualified Leeyes, 'a cash adjustment and loan stock in the acquiring company.'

'I suppose that depends on how good a proposition the acquiring company is,' responded Detective Inspector Sloan, not-so-simple policeman.

'Very probably,' said Leeyes. 'Anyway, in theory they only need to get the consent of fifty-one per cent of the shareholders – it's usually less in practice – and Bob's your uncle.'

Sloan translated this. 'New management.'

'It would have been the end of Tom Mellot as chairman, anyway.'

'Would have been, sir?'

'Didn't you hear the end of the story, Sloan?'

'Can't say that I did, sir.' Something else must have become a nine days wonder in the newspaper instead. 'Not that I noticed, anyway.'

'The company doing the taking over ...' Leeyes paused impressively.

'Yes?'

'They were called Conway's Covers.'

'Were they, sir?' Sloan had forgotten the detail. 'Was that important?'

'It belonged to Ivor Harbeton, the financier.'

'But, sir,' said Sloan involuntarily, 'he's disappeared. Everyone knows that.'

The disappearance of Ivor Harbeton wasn't a nine days wonder. That had been a big news story. The Harbeton financial empire touched commercial life at many points. Ivor Harbeton's interests spread out through industry like the threadlike filaments of honey fungus. The City had been shaken by his sudden absence from the helm, and the ominous word 'Levanter' for one who cheats by absconding had been hinted at in some suspicious-minded quarters. A deputy chairman was in the saddle, making prevaricating noises. Of Harbeton himself there was no sign.

'Precisely, Sloan,' said Leeyes. 'I'm having them gather all the newspaper cuttings together for you now at the station.'

'For me, sir?'

'For you, Sloan,' said Leeyes heavily. 'Just in case.'

Sam Bailey waved his stick. 'I'm sorry I can't come with you, Inspector. I'm not the man I was.'

'That's all right, sir.'

'Once upon a time I'd have got to the top of the combe before any of you young chaps.'

'I'm sure you would, sir.'

'My wife'll set you on your way, though.' He trundled off down the hallway shouting, 'Elsie, where are you? Elsie, I want you!' When there was no response to this cavalier summons he grumbled, 'She's never around these days. Spends all her time messing about in the kitchen.' He stumped back up the hall to the policeman, chuckling grimly, 'I never missed a hunt if I could help it.'

'No, sir.'

'Of any sort.' He waved his stick again. 'This is Tuesday country.'

'Tuesday country, sir?' echoed Sloan blankly.

'The South Calleshire Fox Hunt, Inspector.'

'Ah.' Sloan's brow cleared.

'They meet at Great Rooden on Tuesdays.'

'Really, sir?' The police hunt met on Saturdays usually.

'Outside the Lamb and Flag at eleven,' said the old farmer. 'I must say they used to do a very good stirrup-cup in Rodgers's day. I don't know what the new man there is like.'

With the police it was under the railway arches at Berebury in the evening. That was where the quarry was most often to be found. And they didn't have a stirrup-cup beforehand. All they ran to was a pint or two of beer afterwards.

'They usually find quite quickly,' said Bailey.

So did the police.

'Good hunting country, Inspector, this.'

'Yoicks, tally-ho,' said Detective Constable Crosby to nobody in particular.

The rallying call of the police was 'Calling all cars'.

'From a find to a check,' wheezed Bailey.

With the police, from a find to a check meant the plaintive call sign 'I am in need of assistance'.

'From a check to a view,' said Bailey neatly. 'That's what you want, isn't it, Inspector? A view . . .'

'It would be a great help.'

'I saw you on the hill.' He grunted. 'Nothing wrong with my eyesight.'

'We drew a blank.' Sloan found himself lapsing into the vernacular.

'I knew you hadn't found at Uppercombe or Stanestede,' said the farmer, 'or you wouldn't be here at Lowercombe.'

'No, sir.'

'From a view to a death.' He looked at the policeman abruptly. 'I take it you know your "John Peel", don't you, Inspector?'

'Yes, sir.' All schoolboys kenned John Peel with his coat so gay. It was about all that most of them did know about hunting, too.

'"Peel's 'view-hallo' would awaken the dead",' quoted the old farmer chestily.

'Not this dead, it wouldn't,' interposed Detective Constable Crosby. 'You see . . .'

'Suppose,' said Sloan swiftly, 'we start with those meadows over there and then go on to the wood . . .'

Sam Bailey waved his stick. 'Go where you like, Inspector, but don't count on too much.'

'What do you mean?'

'I told you that this is good hunting country.'

'So you did, sir.'

'That means,' amplified Bailey, 'that there are plenty of foxes about.'

'Well?'

'They don't mind what they eat.' He sniffed. 'Reynard's not particular at all, if you take my meaning. If they've got at your man I can tell you they'll have made a real mess of him.'

Sloan cast his gaze over the pastoral valley of the Westerbrook and the four comfortable farms within the self-imposed – crow-imposed – ambit of police investigation. Whoever it was had said 'Where every propect pleases and only man is vile' was wrong. Nature was red in tooth and claw, too. Tooth as well as claw, you might say, if foxes as well as crows were having their way with the body of a man. It was an unattractive thought. At least none of the farmers kept pigs. That was something for an investigating officer to be profoundly thankful for. He braced himself. 'Come along, Crosby.'

Crosby squared his shoulders and went off to round up his helpers.

'Make a good whipper-in, that lad,' remarked Sam Bailey appraisingly.

It wasn't the similarity to the hunt that was to the forefront of Sloan's mind as he stood on the front doorstep of Lower-combe Farm and watched the searchers fan out over Sam Bailey's fields. It was the word 'dragnet' that he thought about. A trawl over land. Somewhere out here, little foxes notwithstanding, were the remains of a human being. There must be.

'Has he been blooded?' Sam Bailey interrupted his thoughts.

'What . . . I beg your pardon, sir?'

'Made his first arrest,' said the farmer. 'That young fellow with you.'

'Oh yes, sir.' Making an arrest wasn't what Sloan would call being blooded. Initiation rites in the police force were more rigorous than that. Breaking bad news called for more courage. So did pacing a lonely beat at two o'clock of a winter's morning when all was patently not well. To say nothing of attending a raging 'domestic' when the man was roaring drunk and the woman a screaming virago, hell-bent on exacting vengeance on her man.

On any man.

On the nearest man.

He answered Sam Bailey quite seriously, 'He's been blood-ied, too, if it comes to that.'

Sam Bailey nodded.

Perhaps, thought Sloan, that was where the line lay between the new policeman and the seasoned one. After the moment when a member of that very same public whose civil rights you had sworn upon oath to uphold hit you rather hard where it hurt. Most policemen took a different view after that.

'He's had his brush then, has he?' said Sam Bailey.

'With a villain or two,' replied Sloan.

'Doesn't look old enough to me.'

'He is,' said Sloan tightly. The Master gave the tail of the fox – the brush, that is – to the youngest member of the Hunt present, didn't he? Sloan pursed his lips. It wasn't like that in the police force. There the greenhorn got the clerical work and the kicks.

'Mind you,' said the old farmer, 'I've got to the age now when policeman get younger every year.' He looked round irritably. 'Where is that wife of mine?' He turned and shouted down the hall again.

'It happens to us all,' responded Sloan more equably. He had noticed that the walls of Lowercombe Farm were peppered with stuffed heads of foxes – weren't they called masks? They had a different set of trophies down at the police station. No more arcane, of course. Some closed files, for instance; a commendation or two from the bench of magistrates; a few kind words from a judge; more satisfying, a menace to society behind bars for a tidy while, and little old ladies able to walk through the streets at night . . . If that is what they felt like doing.

'You'll let me know, Inspector, won't you,' said Bailey, latter-day John Peel, 'if you find anything at Lowercombe?'

'You'll hear all about it, sir, I promise you,' said Sloan, preparing to stride off to join Crosby and the rest of the search party.

They were interrupted by the arrival of Mrs Bailey, who came hurrying down the farmhouse hall all breathless and flustered, taking off her apron as she advanced towards them. 'Good afternoon, Inspector Sloan . . .'

'Ah, there you are, Elsie.' Her husband banged his stick crossly on the floor. 'Where have you been?'

'In the larder,' said Mrs Bailey, putting her apron on a chair and turning to Sloan. 'I'm sorry, Inspector, not to have been here when . . .'

'Didn't you hear me calling you?' demanded Sam Bailey. 'I shouted quite loudly.'

'I'm sure you did, Sam,' Elsie Bailey said drily, 'but I had the larder door closed and it was only when I got back to the kitchen and heard you talking that I realized that someone was here.'

'I was just going,' said Sloan, not dissatisfied with his visit to Lowercombe Farm. Hounds followed a trail by scent:

policeman followed one compounded of information and observation – and deduction. If Mrs Bailey had been in the farmhouse larder when her husband first called her Sloan was prepared to eat his proverbial hat.

Unless, that is, the larder had a carpet of leaf mould. Because that was undoubtedly what was sticking to Mrs Elsie Bailey's shoes.

Have mercy upon us.

7

Police Constable Ted Mason might be one for the quiet life. That was not to say that he was not also a conscientious police officer. He was not an unclever one either. He unobtrusively absented himself from the search party working its way over Lowercombe Farm and slipped back into the village. This time he did not choose the Lamb and Flag public house as his source of information. He made his way instead to Great Rooden's village store and post office. If nothing else, as Superintendent Leeyes had remarked, he knew his patch.

He began with an apology. 'Sorry to be knocking you up on a Sunday afternoon, Mabel,' he said.

'That's all right, Ted,' was the calm reply. As the principal shopkeeper in Great Rooden Mrs Mabel Milligan was an important figure in the social fabric of the village. Being disturbed out of shop hours was part of the price she paid for her importance. 'What can I get you?'

'Sugar,' responded Police Constable Mason promptly.

Now Mrs Mabel Milligan had personally served Mrs Mason with two kilos of cane sugar and ten of preserving sugar for jam-making – strawberries being nearly ready for this – only the day before but she did not say so. 'What sort of sugar?' she enquired instead, taking it that the Sunday Trading Act was not going to be mentioned by either party.

'Ordinary sugar,' replied Mason, momentarily flummoxed.

Mrs Milligan led the way through into the darkened store and picked out a bag of cane sugar for him. 'Can't have you running out, can we?' she observed drily.

'No.' Ted Mason handed over the money for the sugar, remarking with apparent inconsequence, 'I've been at Pencombe all day, otherwise I would have come earlier.'

'They're having a bit of trouble over there I hear,' rejoined Mrs Milligan.

The constable nodded. 'There's probably a dead man about somewhere.' He did not immediately expand on this. He knew that Mrs Milligan's intelligence-gathering network was at least as good as his own and there was no point in telling her anything that she already knew.

'From all accounts,' said Mrs Milligan circumspectly, 'he's been there a tidy old time too.'

''Bout a month,' volunteered Mason. There was no secret about that.

'Dear, dear,' clucked Mrs Milligan, 'that's bad.'

'Doesn't make detecting any easier,' agreed the grower of prize cabbages.

'It can't do, Ted,' responded Mrs Milligan warmly. 'A month. Fancy that.'

'Lost any customers lately, Mabel?' The policeman was quite serious now.

She frowned. 'Charlie Gibbs – he died, didn't he? About the beginning of June, that would have been.'

'I saw him buried myself,' said Ted Mason, 'seeing as how he used to grow marrows.'

'They had a ham,' remarked Mrs Milligan inconsequentially.

The policeman nodded. The purchase of funeral baked meats came close to circumstantial evidence of burial.

'There was old Miss Tebbs, too.'

'Another ham?' enquired Mason without irony.

Mabel Milligan sniffed. 'Her nephew didn't even have a tea.'

'Always was a mean man, was Albert Tebbs, and he hasn't changed as he's got older.'

'People don't,' said Mrs Milligan sagely. 'They just get more like they were before.'

'Albert Tebbs will die rich,' forecast Mason.

Mrs Milligan's mind was on something else. 'You could say,' she murmured delicately, 'that in a manner of speaking I'd lost another customer as well.'

Police Constable Mason waited.

'Mr Ritchie.' She pursed her lips. 'You know about Mr Ritchie, don't you?'

He nodded. 'We had heard.'

'Not that Mrs Ritchie has made any secret about it. "No more bacon, Mrs Milligan," she said to me the first time she came in after he'd gone, "nasty, fattening stuff."' Mrs Milligan looked down at her own ample figure and went on: 'Myself, I must say I like a nice slice of best greenback to start the day.'

'Me too,' agreed the portly policeman absently. He reverted to Martin Ritchie. 'Gone off with a girl, I hear.'

'So Mrs Ritchie said.' Mrs Milligan tossed her head. 'Can't say I blame him for that. Nothing to come home to there in the way of home comforts.'

'She doesn't look a good cook,' ventured Mason with all the authority of a man long married to a very good cook indeed.

Mabel Milligan, no mean trencherwoman herself, waved a pudgy hand. 'She isn't. She was always buying made-up dishes.'

Ted Mason regarded her with respect. 'You know all about us, don't you, Mabel?'

'A man is what he eats,' she said profoundly.

'And you,' said the policeman neatly, 'know what everyone in Great Rooden eats, don't you?'

She squinted modestly at the shop floor. 'Can't help it, can I? You see everything from behind the counter.'

'And you don't let on, do you?' he said. Mrs Milligan had a great repution in Great Rooden for keeping her own counsel.

'I never was one to talk, Ted Mason,' she retorted briskly, 'and well you know it.'

'So that's three customers you've lost in June,' he said, changing his tack a little.

'Some you gain, some you lose,' she said cryptically. 'There's swings and roundabouts in everything.'

'No one else missing, anyway?' said the policeman.

'Nobody buying for one that used to buy for two, if that's what you mean,' she countered precisely.

'Except Mrs Ritchie?'

'Buy!' echoed Mrs Milligan richly. 'That woman doesn't buy. She only picks about. She's that keen on her precious figure that she doesn't buy proper food at all.'

'We're looking for Martin Ritchie anyway, just to check up.' Mason transferred the bag of sugar to his other hand. 'Talking of checking up . . .'

'Yes?' It was the tribute of one well-informed villager to another and she knew it.

'I hear that Len Hodge had a bit of an up-and-downer in the Lamb and Flag last month.'

'Did he?' Mabel Milligan's face was expressionless.

'It's not like him,' observed Mason.

'No,' she agreed. 'He's not a fighter, isn't Len.'

'I just wondered . . .' began Mason.

'Yes?'

'If you had heard who it was that he was fighting with.'

'Me?' she said blandly. 'Why ask me? Why don't you ask Vic Higgins? He's the landlord.'

'Because he's new, that's why.'

She shifted her ground. 'Now, how should I know what goes on at the Lamb and Flag?'

'Because, Mabel,' replied Mason cogently, 'you hear everything that goes on in Great Rooden, that's why.'

'So do you, Ted Mason.'

'No, I don't,' he said simply. 'I'm a policeman, remember. I only hear what people want me to hear.' He transferred the bag of sugar back to his other hand. 'There's some things that are kept from me.'

'Are there now?' she said tonelessly.

'If people think it's better that I don't know about something, then they don't tell me.'

'Well, then . . .'

'Which is not the same thing at all,' persisted the policeman, standing the bag of sugar on the counter, 'as telling me and trusting that I'll do the right thing.'

She nodded. 'I can see that.'

'So,' he said judiciously, 'if you should happen – just happen, mind you – to hear who it was that Len Hodge was fighting with in the Lamb and Flag that night I'd be greatly obliged if you'd let me know.'

Mrs Milligan remained impassive. 'I'll remember that, Ted.'

'Because if it's anything to do with this dead man that's around somewhere we're going to find out sooner or later anyway.'

'Course you are,' she agreed.

'And then,' insisted the policeman heavily, 'it'll be a lot easier for everybody concerned if it's been sooner rather than later.'

Mrs Milligan let him get as far as the shop door before she spoke. 'You've forgotten the sugar, Ted,' she said. 'That was what you came for, wasn't it?'

Detective Inspector Sloan let the crowd of walkers and policemen fan out over Lowercombe Farm without him. He had gone with them a little way – just until he was out of sight of the farmhouse and Mr and Mrs Bailey who were standing together at the front door. Side by side the old couple looked like Darby and Joan but Sloan kept an open mind about this. Oedipus and several schools of articulate European psychologists had had a lot to say about the lasting outcome of parent and child relationships. They were much less eloquent in their pronouncements on the long-term effects of those between husband and wife.

Perhaps it wasn't so important after all but before now Sloan had noticed that the ways of the partners opposite the forceful one of the pair often ran very deep indeed. A lifetime spent outwardly agreeing with Sam Bailey would surely have made its mark on any woman. He knew from his own experience in the Force that instant obedience was no criterion of genuine compliance – nor of anything but token subservience to an authority that it would be imprudent to challenge. Sam Bailey, crossed, would obviously be a very awkward customer indeed.

Once all the others had turned the corner from the farmhouse Sloan hung back and soon the rest of the search party were way ahead of him. That was when he turned in his tracks and made steadily for Dresham Wood. It lay behind the farmhouse, sheltering it from the hill behind and coming between the road and the farm proper. Lowercombe, being at the bottom of the valley, was in by far the most favoured position of all the farms. The River Westerbrook flowed through this land, too. It was a little fuller down here than it was higher up the hill and Sloan could see the blue forget-me-nots growing in the banks and a flower that might have been purple loose-strife not far from the water's edge.

He soon picked up the track into the wood that was obviously Footpath Seventy-Nine. There was no mistaking it – the Berebury Country Footpath Society would have had little problem in identifying their trail where it led into the wood. The way through the trees was well defined, too, although here and there young branches had grown across the route, and the odd bramble had sent out a new spur which lay in wait for the unwary. It didn't catch Sloan because he had his eyes down anyway. Leaf mould there was in plenty under the canopy of the trees but it lay to the sides of the path.

He did cast his eyes upwards a couple of times to see what manner of wood Dresham was. In the main it was oak and ash trees which met his gaze, though he caught sight of a thorn or two and a holly. As he advanced further into the wood he came across a wild cherry and he thought he saw the greenish white of a guelder rose. There was a great deal of undergrowth, too. Too much. Far too much, in fact. Sam Bailey wasn't tending his land like he should. Sloan saw several dead trees that should have been out of the wood and burnt a couple of years ago at least, and others that should have been felled in their prime for timber. Woods needed culling in the same way that herds of deer did.

At one point quite soon after he had entered the wood the footpath crossed a tiny runnel of water finding its immemorial way down to the Westerbrook – too slight even to call for stepping-stones where the path crossed it. Everyone was obviously left to pick their own way over the dampness as best they could. They had done so by stepping to one side of the path or the other and selecting the best place to stride across. There the path showed footmarks in plenty. Detective Inspector Sloan regarded them with an automatic professional interest. Mrs Elsie Bailey was short but not thin. Any footprint that she made in the soft ground would be small but deep. One look at the multitude of footmarks in the damp ground disabused him of the hope that he would find any one print without a lot of trouble – and luck. He would have to seek another way of finding out what it was that Mrs Bailey had gone into the wood for.

And Len Hodge.

Sloan penetrated further but was no wiser. There was enough undergrowth to conceal almost anything from sight from the path. If there was a woodland grave hereabouts he, Sloan, wasn't going to find it single-handed. If, though, a fox had found it first, then a finger might well have been dropped on open ground by Master Reynard, and then been found by a crow. That wouldn't be so much an ecological coincidence as the sort of chain of circumstances greatly beloved by legal counsel, for whomsoever they were acting. Chains of circumstances left plenty of room for manoeuvre in court.

He carried on, his mind a confusion compounded of chidhood recollections of the deceptively simple tale of the Babes in the Wood – if ever a case had called for a full-scale police investigation it was the nasty story of the Babes in the Wood – whatever had their parents been thinking of? – and that sinister ballad 'The Twa Corbies'. Although it had been about ravens rather than crows there was a dreadful relevance about the birds asking each other where they would go and dine today.

At one point Sloan stopped and stood still for a minute or two and listened. If his eyes could not supply him with any clues perhaps his ears could. But he was aware of nothing except the alarm call of a bird which had heard him approaching and was uttering a general warning.

He pushed on again.

The undergrowth was right up to the path now, and he could see almost nothing through it. It would need a great deal of time and men to search the wood properly.

In 'The Twa Corbies' the new-slain knight whose body had provided dinner for the ravens had been lying behind the old turfed bank . . .

And naebody kens that he lies there,
But his hawk, his hound and his lady fair.

Sloan would very much have liked to have known if the same could be said of the owner of the finger that now reposed in Dr Dabbe's forensic laboratory. He would have liked to have known – and had every intention of finding out – what it was that had brought Len Hodge and Mrs Elsie Bailey into Dresham Wood so urgently. He forged on without coming any nearer to knowing and after a while started to see the trees beginning to thin out ahead.

Through the wood without being out of it yet, he thought to himself, turning and retracing his steps back to the farmyard at Lowercombe.

The others didn't find anything on Sam Bailey's land even though they searched all over it until the end of the afternoon.

Gordon Briggs, self-appointed spokesman of the Berebury Country Footpaths Society, reported failure to Sloan with melancholy satisfaction. 'Nothing, Inspector. Not a sign of anything suspicious.'

'Somewhere,' said Sloan determinedly, 'within the radius that we have been searching is a skeleton.' A crow would not fly over a greater acreage than they had walked over that afternoon with something relatively heavy in its beak. The ornithologist had said so.

'Very likely,' responded Gordon Briggs, 'but my members haven't found it yet and neither have your policemen.' He looked rather pointedly at his watch and coughed. 'Mrs Mellot kindly said she would give us tea.'

Sloan bowed to a higher realism and when Detective Constable Crosby's team, too, gave Lowercombe Farm a clean bill of health he consented to a general return across the road and back to Pencombe Farm. There was someone else making his way back there at the same time. Just as the walkers reached the farmyard they were overtaken by Len Hodge in his disreputable old car. As the farm worker clambered out one of the walkers said to him, 'You timed that nicely, didn't you, mate? Missing all the footslogging . . .'

Len Hodge grimaced. 'Footslogging would have been easier.'

'Oh?'

Hodge shrugged his shoulders. 'A character over at Sleden thought the best way of getting a bonfire going when there wasn't any wind was to pour a can of paraffin over it.'

'Oh, a fire . . .'

'He had a fire all right,' rejoined Hodge briefly.

'Not a false alarm, then,' said someone else.

'Lost his eyebrows and his greenhouse,' said the part-time fireman succinctly.

'All burns are carelessness,' pronounced Gordon Briggs with a sanctimoniousness that must have lost him a lot of friends.

'What about the singeing of the beard of the King of Spain?' put in a mischievous walker, one of the few who wasn't overawed by the schoolmaster.

'That was politics,' said Briggs severely.

Leonard Hodge shrugged his shoulders. 'I wouldn't know anything about the King of Spain but I reckon this old boy won't touch paraffin again in a hurry.'

The group struggled back through the farmyard towards the kitchen at Pencombe. Detective Inspector Sloan fell into step beside Len Hodge. 'I've had a look in Dresham Wood, too,' he said to the farm worker.

'Then you've been wasting your time,' said Hodge, apparently unperturbed. 'Crows wouldn't go into the wood for their pickings. Too dangerous for them!' He waved an arm. 'They like open country same as this.'

Sloan looked up. As if to prove Hodge's point there were several crows wheeling about overhead.

'Always around the farmyard, they are,' said Hodge.

Sloan nodded. That was only natural.

'Plenty of pickings, you see,' said Hodge gruffly.

'Of course,' agreed Sloan. In the old ballad the new-slain knight had lain out of sight behind an old turfed bank. All such likely places on four farms had now been examined without success. Sloan braced his shoulders. They would just have to go on and look at the unlikely places then. He looked round the farmyard. George Mellot had come out of the back door of the farmhouse and was standing on the doorstep watching him approach. The crows still wheeled overhead . . .

Sloan halted and said abruptly to Len Hodge, 'Where do you keep your ladders?'

'In the barn.'

'Show me.'

Instead of advancing towards George Mellot the policeman wheeled away from the direction of the back door, and turned into the barn. There was an assortment of ladders stacked against the wall. Sloan pointed to the longest and said to Hodge, 'Give me a hand with that one, will you?'

'Sure.' Len Hodge lifted his end with consummate ease. 'Where do you want it?'

'We'll try the shed first.'

Hodge obligingly propped the ladder up against the shed wall. Sloan shinned up it, concious of George Mellot's motionless figure on the back doorstep. One quick glance from the right level assured him that there was nothing lying in between the ridges of the roof of the shed. He descended and looked round the farmyard.

'Now the barn, please,' said Sloan quietly.

Hodge helped him carry the ladder back across the farm-yard. George Mellot still hadn't moved but out the corner of his eye Sloan saw Meg Mellot had come forward to the kitchen window. Her white, anxious face was right up against the pane as she watched his every move.

'I want the ladder against the gulley,' Sloan said to Hodge, who obediently swung it up without apparent effort and then stood well back in a detached way as if to dissociate himself from the action.

The moment before Sloan set foot on the bottom rung of the ladder remained one etched on his mind as a frozen section of time. There were all the elements of a tableau vivant about it – an exhibition of individuals placing themselves in striking attitudes so as to imitate statues. In fact it was the immobility of those watching him that struck Sloan most forcibly. It was as if all three had been fashioned from alabaster.

It was a higher climb to the top of the pre-cast concrete barn than it had been to the shed roof. When his eyes drew level with the roofline Detective Inspector Sloan looked along the gutter which lay between the two ridges of the roof.

This time there was something there to see.

8

'And about time, too, Sloan,' trumpeted Superintendent Leeyes churlishly down the telephone. 'You've had all day.'

'Yes, sir.' This was undeniable.

'Well? Go on, man . . .'

'There are more human remains lying on the roof of the barn here at Pencombe Farm,' reported Sloan with concision. He was standing in George Mellot's office where the window – like that of the kitchen – gave out on to the farmyard. Detective Constable Crosby was standing on guard at the bottom of the ladder that still stood against the side of the barn but no one was showing the least inclination to go up it.

Superintendent Leeyes grunted.

'It – the skeleton, that is,' carried on Sloan, 'is lying between the two ridges of the barn roof.' There was probably a technical term for the gulley at the bottom of the two slopes – more of a gutter, really – but Sloan did not know what it was. 'There's a sort of drain there but it's not quite blocking it.'

'That accounts for the damp, I suppose,' growled Leeyes. 'Dr Dabbe said he thought the finger had come from somewhere damp, didn't he?'

'Yes, sir,' said Sloan, adding, 'The doctor's on his way over here now.' He paused and then went on significantly: 'And so are Dyson and Williams.'

Dyson and Williams were the Calleshire Force's police photographers.

'Oh, they are, are they?' commented Leeyes trenchantly.
'Yes, sir.'

'That means,' said Leeyes heavily, 'that you've found something more than bones, doesn't it, Sloan?'

'It's more of a case, sir,' said the Detective Inspector, 'of not finding something.'

Leeyes grunted again. 'Like what?'

'There is most of the rest of a human skeleton up there,' said Sloan, choosing his words with care.

'Most?' queried Leeyes sharply. 'What do you mean?'

'Not all of it.'

'Hrrmph,' said Leeyes. 'So the crows have had a bit more than fingers, have they, then?'

'It's not that, sir,' replied Sloan.

'Well,' demanded Leeyes peremptorily, 'what is it then?'

'There are other fingers missing, too, of course,' prevaricated Sloan.

'Naturally,' said Leeyes, 'but—'

'But,' he said apologetically, 'I'm afraid the head's not there either.'

'What!' exploded Superintendent Leeyes down the telephone.

'It's gone,' said Sloan simply.

'But . . .'

'There's no head there, sir.' Strictly speaking, he supposed he should have used the word 'skull'.

'A crow,' pronounced Leeyes weightily, 'couldn't have taken the head away.'

'No, sir.' That much was self-evident.

'So, Sloan, either someone's been up there since for it . . .'

'Yes, sir.'

'Or,' concluded Leeyes flatly, 'we're dealing with someone who put a headless corpse up there.'

'Exactly, sir.'

'You know what that means, Sloan, don't you?'

'Yes, sir. Murder.'

'In either case,' said Leeyes.

'Almost certainly,' agreed Sloan.

'Why has the head gone?' asked Leeyes after a pause for consideration. 'Do you know that, Sloan?'

'There are two reasons that I can think of, sir.' It had been the question that had dominated Sloan's own thoughts as he had slowly climbed down the ladder and gone indoors to the telephone.

'Go on.'

'Either it reveals the cause of death . . .'

'A bullet would tell us quite a lot,' mused Leeyes, 'wouldn't it?'

'It would, sir.'

'Ballistics have come on a lot since I was on the beat.'

Sloan coughed. 'Even a fractured skull would have put us in the picture a bit more.'

'Hankering after our old friend the blunt instrument, are you, eh, Sloan?'

'Perhaps, sir.' Something had killed whoever it was who was lying up there. There was at least no doubt about that. He paused and then he said, 'There's another reason, though, why the head might have gone, sir.'

'Well?'

'A head will most likely have had teeth in it,' said Sloan succinctly. Forensic odontology had come on quite as much as the science of ballistics.

'Identification.'

'Yes, sir,' said Sloan, clearing his throat. 'It's going to be quite a problem.'

Leeyes grunted. 'There must be clues now you've got something to go on.'

'As far as I can make out,' rejoined Sloan obliquely, 'there were no clothes up there with the bones either.'

'Naked and dead?' said Leeyes lugubriously.

'Just so, sir.'

The superintendent suddenly became very brisk. 'Keep me in the picture, Sloan, won't you? This is all very interesting.'

*

'This is all very interesting, Sloan,' echoed Dr Dabbe not very long afterwards. He, too, had now climbed to the top of the ladder propped up against the barn and looked along the roof.

'Yes, Doctor,' replied Sloan. Like the superintendent, Dr Dabbe was able to take a detached view. Sloan couldn't.

'Not so much a body as *disjecta membra*,' observed the pathologist.

'Enough for a proper inquest, though?' enquired Sloan. He didn't know what *disjecta membra* were.

'Lord bless you, yes.'

'That's something,' said Sloan. Invoking the due processes of the law relating to the dead with only a finger to show had a faintly Gilbertian ring about it.

'I'll need a much closer look, of course,' said Dr Dabbe.

'I'm having a scaffolding platform brought out from Berebury.' It had only just struck Sloan as odd that the name of the scene of the direst penalty that the law could exact had declined into a mere builders' aid.

'You'll have noticed, Sloan, that the body up there lacks the Yorick touch.'

'The head's not there,' agreed Sloan more prosaically.

'Alas, poor Yorick,' said Dr Dabbe breezily. 'I wonder where it's got to?'

'So do I,' said Sloan feelingly.

'I'm not promising anything, mind you, Sloan, but with a closer look at the body I might be able to tell you at what stage the head was taken off.'

'That would help,' said Sloan moderately.

'And how it came off.'

'So would that,' said Sloan.

'Haven't seen a true decapitation in years,' mused the pathologist.

Detective Inspector Sloan had never seen one. He resolved to be more grateful for small mercies in future.

'Pity the head's gone, all the same,' said Dr Dabbe regretfully. 'So few people are completely edentulous these days that you could have counted on there being teeth.'

'Heads are useful,' agreed Sloan gravely.

'And should be kept,' said the pathologist. 'Especially when all about you are losing theirs and blaming it on you.' He jerked his head. 'You know your Kipling, I take it, Sloan?'

'Yes, Doctor.' Now there was poet that man and boy – and policeman – could understand, though there were those who reckoned that his poem 'If' had done them more harm than good. Unrealistic goals led a man to think less of himself when he didn't reach them, that's what the psychologists said when they went on about under- and over-achievers. The Empire builders, of course, hadn't concerned themselves with the non-achievers – hadn't considered failure as a tenable proposition . . .

'There's something else that it appears not to have got,' observed Dr Dabbe colloquially.

It was another poem that came into Sloan's mind then. It was called 'The Naming of Parts'. Rudyard Kipling hadn't lived to write about that war: the war in which they had the naming of parts. It had been Henry Reed who had caught the flavour of those later times with what a man did not have.

'Yes, Doctor,' he said aloud, coming back to the present. 'I know.'

'Like the Emperor,' said the pathologist jovially, 'it hasn't got any clothes. Did you notice that, Sloan?'

'I did.' Sloan didn't know about emperors. He did know about detection. 'It's going to make identification even more difficult,' he said.

'It is,' agreed the pathologist, rubbing his chin. 'On the other hand, Sloan, it did make something else a great deal easier.'

Sloan looked up curiously. 'What was that?'

Dabbe grinned. 'The Little Red Riding Hood touch.'

'Pardon, Doctor?'

'All the better to be eaten by crows, Sloan, that's what.'

Sloan nodded his comprehension and tightened his lips. It wasn't a happy thought that someone had worked this out. There was a calculation about this crime that betokened a really determined mind scheming away.

'A proper invitation to *Corvus corone linn* to dine, is having no clothes,' remarked Dr Dabbe thoughtfully.

'There's nothing,' said Sloan, waving a hand in the direction of the barn roof, 'at all accidental about any of this.'

'On the contrary,' agreed the pathologist briskly. 'Naked headless corpses do not in my experience often get themselves on to the roofs of barns.'

'And as hiding places go,' observed Sloan judiciously, 'it is difficult to think of a better one.'

'A grave always shows,' pronounced the pathologist.

'He might not have been found,' said Sloan, 'for years and years.' He knew that there were mathematical formulae where time and distance were locked together. No one had yet put a name or symbol to the ratio but time and crime were inextricably interwoven, too. The importance of Justice seemed to vary in inverse proportion to the distance of the crime from the time it was brought to book.

There was a subject for study by someone clever, if you like. Sloan had noticed before now that the punishment of an old crime had none of the passion attached to the solving of a new one, fresh in the collective consciousness. An earlier generation of crime prevention officers had even used the expression 'hot pursuit' for newly committed crime with a special meaning all of its own.

'He might not have been found,' nodded Dabbe, 'except for a crow and a finger.'

'Quite so, Doctor.' But for a nail a battle had been lost, hadn't it?

'The rest of him mightn't have been noticed for a long time,' said Dabbe, giving the barn a critical look. 'This building is almost new. It wouldn't have wanted maintenance or painting for years.'

Even barns that did need maintenance didn't get it from a lot of farmers that Sloan knew.

'I reckon, Sloan,' continued the pathologist cheerfully, 'that you're dealing with someone who had very nearly solved the eternal problem of all murderers – the disposal of the victim.'

'That's a great comfort, that is,' said Sloan bitterly. It was all very well for Dr Dabbe to be looking on the bright side. All he had to deal with was the body and the court. He, Sloan, had to tangle with real live villians as well. And clever ones at that, it seemed.

'There's another nice touch about the barn roof as a hiding place as well,' went on Dr Dabbe, unperturbed.

'What's that?' asked Sloan. It had taken more than brains to think of the barn roof. It had taken imagination too. They were a dangerous combination.

'Sometimes with murder,' said the pathologist, 'time is of the essence.'

'Popping him up there wouldn't have taken all that long,' agreed Sloan thoughtfully.

'Although it would have been a bit of a struggle.' Dr Dabbe stroked his chin. 'I'll be able to tell you presently if the deceased was a big man.'

'However difficult it was to get him up there,' rejoined Sloan energetically, 'I'll bet it was easier than burying a body in a hurry.'

'In some ways, Sloan, it was better, too.'

'Better?'

'For the murderer.'

'Ah.' It was as well to know whose outlook you were considering.

'I don't know if you've ever tried it, Sloan, but six feet of earth takes a fair bit of digging.'

'Yes, Doctor, I know.' The growing of roses called for quite a lot of spade work.

The doctor raised his nose in the air for all the world like a pointer scenting something. 'And one usual objection doesn't apply here.'

'What's that, Doctor?'

'Mephitis.'

Sloan hunched his shoulders. There was a medical word whose meaning he did remember. 'The smell of the dead,' he said.

'If there had been one,' said the pathologist, 'and there would, nobody would have noticed it here in the middle of a farmyard.'

'True.' Some person or persons unknown had clearly been very clever indeed, he decided.

'Anyway, Sloan, burial doesn't offer everything.'

'No, Doctor?' Whose point of view was the doctor speaking from now?

'Sometimes,' murmured Dr Dabbe reflectively, 'burial preserves.'

'The Pharaohs, you mean?'

'Not them.' The pathologist dismissed the surviving remains of the representatives of several ancient Egyptian dynasties with the wave of a hand. 'They were different.'

'Ah.'

'But with inhumation burial,' said Dr Dabbe more expansively, 'you sometimes get adipocere tissue and so forth.'

Tissue of any sort was something else they had not got, thought Sloan. In quantity, anyway. He wasn't sure yet how much they did have and wasn't looking forward to finding out.

'Adipocere tissue can help,' said Dr Dabbe.

'I'm sure it can,' said Sloan warmly. There was no doubt whose side the doctor was speaking for now.

'With burial, of course,' said the doctor, 'you have less chance of concealing identity.'

'And of removing clues to the cause of death,' said Sloan sombrely.

'That, too,' agreed the pathologist. 'As soon as this scaffolding tower that you've promised arrives, and you let the dog get a proper look at the rabbit, Sloan, I'll tackle your two problems for you.'

'Two?' echoed Sloan. He didn't know how on the earth the doctor had managed to reduce his problems to only two.

'Identity and cause of death,' said Dr Dabbe neatly. 'Those are the things you want to know, Sloan, aren't they?'

*

'You won't be wanting us any more today, Inspector, will you?' The leader of the Berebury Country Footpaths Society stood squarely in front of Detective Inspector Sloan, knapsack in hand.

'I suppose not, Mr Briggs,' he replied.

The whole atmosphere in the farm kitchen at Pencombe had been changed by the finding of the skeleton. Talk had dried to a trickle and the faintly convivial mood associated with tea-time after a day's walking in the open air had evaporated. It had been succeeded by one of strain and slightly forced conversational exchanges. As if by common consent not one of those present was anywhere near the window which looked out on to the farmyard. Wendy Lamport, standing at the sink and washing up as if her life depended on it, resolutely kept her head down. Mrs Mellot, concerned and flustered, was drying up cups and saucers at speed.

'We can be going then,' said Briggs.

Sloan nodded.

'Now that you've found what you were looking for.'

'Yes,' said Sloan.

'And we can't do anything more for you anyway, can we?' Gordon Briggs still made no move to go.

'Not at this stage,' said Sloan.

Briggs looked up sharply. 'What do you mean?'

'There'll be an inquest,' said Sloan. 'You'll be wanted then.'

'Of course,' said Briggs quickly.

'That'll come later.' An inquest opened and adjourned would be all that the police could ask for from Her Majesty's Coroner for the County of Calleshire. 'You'll be told when and where . . .'

They were interrupted by the sound of breaking china.

A cup had slipped from Meg Mellot's fingers and lay smashed and broken into a dozen pieces on the floor.

'It doesn't matter,' she said rather breathlessly into the silence which the sudden noise had brought about. 'It doesn't matter at all. I'll get a dustpan and brush.'

As abruptly as it had begun the silence ended: all at once everyone started talking again.

'It was there all the time, then, Inspector.' Gordon Briggs had spoken about going but in fact continued to stand where he was, unwilling to abandon the subject. 'What you were looking for . . .'

'We think so.' Sloan was conscious of some of the other walkers stirring uneasily in the background, clearly anxious to be on their way. Like bit players in life's drama, they had acted their parts and were ready to move off stage. He was equally aware, though, that there were others who wanted to stay. Although patently no longer required by the action, so to speak, something held them there, fascinated.

'Lying on the roof.' Briggs underlined the strangeness.

'Yes,' said Sloan. Was this how Rosencrantz and Guildenstern had felt, he wondered. After all they, too, in the beginning had been unwittingly caught up in events not of their choosing.

'If you're sure that we can't do anything to help, Inspector,' murmured Briggs. Rosencrantz and Guildenstern had also gone off stage reluctantly, hadn't they?

'Quite sure,' replied Sloan more firmly than he had intended. If he remembered rightly from his schooldays Rosencrantz and Guildenstern had been a little uncertain of their roles as well.

'In that case,' said Briggs reluctantly, 'we'll be on our way, then.'

In the third form's memorable production of *Hamlet, Prince of Denmark* at Sloan's school Rosencrantz had fallen over his own feet as he moved off stage.

Or had it been Guildenstern?

'Very well,' said Sloan. With Rosencrantz and Guildenstern the action had continued somewhere else too.

'Nothing to stay for really, is there, Inspector?'

'Not now.'

'Right, then,' said Briggs. Half turn to go yet turning stay . . . No, that had been another poet altogether.

'You'll be having a proper letter,' Sloan promised him, 'thanking your Society for all its help.'

'When the dust has settled a bit, eh?' said Briggs.

'When our investigations are complete,' said Sloan formally.

'You've hardly started, have you?' said the schoolmaster. 'I can see that.'

'Let us say,' Sloan answered him grandly, conscious now that he was quoting the great, 'that we've reached the end of the beginning.'

The pestilence that walketh in darkness. **9**

'Paul, is that you?' The telephone bell had rung at Uppercombe Farm and had been answered with alacrity. 'This is Andrina.'

'Hullo,' he said guardedly.

'Have you heard?'

'Yes,' replied Paul Hucham soberly. 'George rang me.'

'He rang me too,' she said in a small voice.

'He told me he was going to,' said Hucham, conscious of sounding stifled.

'You might have let me know first,' said Andrina Ritchie lightly. 'Before he did. It would have been a little less of a shock.'

'I did think about that,' explained Hucham truthfully, 'but George was dead set on telling everyone himself. You know how he feels about being a good neighbour. He'd already rung old Sam before he rang me.'

'All the same,' she said, 'it was a bit of a surprise.'

Hucham responded to that with something approaching fervour. 'You can say that again.'

'Did he say,' she asked, 'that they think it must be some stranger?'

'No,' said Hucham, 'now that I come to think about it, he didn't say that.'

'That's funny,' said Andrina Ritchie. 'I should have thought he would have done.'

'It didn't sound,' said Paul Hucham consideringly, 'as if he'd had time to do a lot of thinking.'

She changed the subject a little. 'You can see Pencombe from where you are, can't you?'

'If I look.' Paul Hucham picked up the telephone receiver and shifted his position slightly so that he could see out of the nearest window. The view gave out over the valley.

'Can't you tell what's going on there?' There was more than a little impatience in Andrina Ritchie's voice.

'Not really.'

'You must be able to see something . . .'

'Just that there's a lot of activity down there.'

'What sort of activity?'

'Well, for one thing I can see that there are a lot of jam sandwiches about.'

'Jam sandwiches? Are you mad?'

'White police cars with red stripes round them.'

Mrs Andrina Ritchie was not amused. 'This isn't the best time to be funny, Paul.'

'No use getting strung up,' he said. 'That never does any good.'

'I must say George Mellot sounded very uptight.'

'Who wouldn't?' asked the sheep-farmer reasonably. 'Having a skeleton found in your backyard is enough to throw any man.'

'Don't!'

'Well, it's true.'

'I suppose so. And to think,' she said, 'that it might have lain up there for years and years without being found.'

'So it might,' he agreed.

'George told me that they'd got police everywhere.'

'Bound to have,' opined the sheep-farmer with calculated casualness. 'It's only natural in the circumstances.'

'That's all very well but . . .'

'I wouldn't have expected anything else myself,' he said with a touch of firmness.

'I was thinking,' said Andrina Ritchie with a fine show of indirectness, 'of going over to Pencombe to ask if I might borrow their fork-lift tractor for tomorrow morning. Jenkins could use it to lift some bales.'

'I shouldn't do that if I were you,' said Hucham carefully. 'For all you know, Len Hodge may be needing it too. Besides, they'll have quite enough to be thinking about as it is without your turning up there.'

'Perhaps you're right.'

'I know I am,' said Paul Hucham confidently. 'Added to which,' he went smoothly, 'I don't suppose for one moment that the police will let anyone move anything into or out of that farmyard from now on.'

She shuddered. 'I hadn't thought about that.'

'Mind how you go,' adjured Detective Constable Crosby.

'I've been in some funny places in my time,' responded Dyson, the police photographer, 'but this is as daft as any of them.'

'You'll be all right if you hold on,' said Crosby.

'It's all right for you,' rejoined the photographer with spirit. 'You don't have to carry anything.'

This was true. Dyson, on the other hand, was hung about with quite as much equipment as Don Quixote's attendant Sancho Panza.

'Don't let go of the ladder, that's all,' said Crosby.

'And how do you suppose I take photographs if I'm holding on to a ladder? With my teeth?'

'If you don't hold on to the ladder,' promised Crosby flatly, 'you'll fall off.'

'And if I do,' responded Dyson, 'I suppose the thing to do is to look out for the view on my left as I fall?'

'All you'll see if you do that is . . .'

'I can guess,' said the photographer bitterly. 'A midden.'

'You said it,' said Crosby.

'I can smell it from here.' Dyson advanced towards the ladder against the scaffolding tower. 'It doesn't look very safe to me.'

'It isn't,' said Crosby laconically.

'All in the cause of duty, I suppose. You can put that on

my tombstone. Make a nice epitaph. Come along, Williams . . .' Williams was his assistant. 'Got the tripod all right? I expect you want me to go first . . .'

This remark was greeted with the silence that lawyers say amounts to consent and Dyson approached the ladder that was propped up against a hastily erected scaffolding tower designed to bring the investigators level with the skeleton.

'Onward, ever onward, go,' declared Dyson, taking the first step up the ladder. It shook visibly. 'Hold it, man. Don't just stand there.'

'I am holding it,' retorted Crosby in injured tones. 'It's shaking because there isn't any firm ground for it to stand on.'

'That's a great comfort, I must say,' called Dyson over his shoulder. 'No flowers, by the way, if I should die on duty. Just send the money.'

'It won't do you any good where you're going,' said Crosby.

'Are you quite sure about that, old man? I thought money and hell were as inextricably mixed as money and living. It's the other place where they won't be bothering with trifles like money any more . . .' Dyson's head suddenly drew level with the top of the scaffolding platform and the bottom of the barn roof. He looked along the gulley at the skeleton and called down, 'Say, this chap's a bit beyond aid, isn't he?'

'Yes,' said Crosby simply.

'Talk about something nasty in the woodshed,' said Dyson, sucking his teeth sharply. 'This is a lot worse than that.'

'It is,' agreed Crosby.

'Not nice at all.' Dyson had clambered from the top of the ladder on to the scaffolding platform and advanced to the edge of the roof. He called down, 'You'd better come up, too, Williams. We'll need that tripod.'

'Hand shaking, then?' enquired Crosby pleasantly. 'Or just lonely up there?'

'You know me,' rejoined Dyson. 'Nervous as a young filly.'

Williams started to climb the ladder. Dyson had taken his first picture well before the other man got to the top. 'The trouble is,' he called down, 'unless I can get up on to one of these ridges, any view I take is going to be a bit too foreshortened for comfort.'

'You can't go on to the ridge,' called back Crosby. 'Not yet.'

'In that case,' said Dyson philosophically, 'the view will just have to be foreshortened.'

'No one is to go on the roof until it's been examined properly.' The technical problems of professional photographers didn't trouble the detective constable unduly but orders were, in any case, orders. 'There may be some footprints up there.'

'I'll photograph them too,' said Dyson helpfully, 'if I can find any.'

'If you ask me,' said Crosby, 'it's been too dry.'

'Someone must have stood up there on the roof to drag him far enough along the valley between the ridges to be out of sight,' said Dyson.

'We know that,' responded Crosby regally.

'The question is, then, did they leave any traces,' said the police photographer.

'Everything leaves traces.' The detective constable chanted Edmund Locard's Principle of Interchange. 'Whether there's anything to photograph is a different matter.'

Dyson raised his camera again and took a number of shots of the skeleton in quick succession from different angles.

'If you step back any further,' forecast Crosby from below, 'Williams here will be photographing you instead of him, whoever he is.'

'It would be a good way to go, wouldn't it?' called back the photographer. 'You must admit, Crosby, that this chap up here, whatever he's called, hasn't a care in the world any longer.'

'Which is more than can be said for the rest of us,' interposed Williams, arriving rather breathlessly on the platform beside Dyson. 'Here's the tripod.'

'And there's the subject,' said Dyson tersely.

'Blimey O'Riley!' exclaimed Williams.

'Exactly,' said Crosby.

'Do you know anything about him?' called down Dyson.

'Just the one thing,' replied Dectective Constable Crosby sedulously.

'What's that?'

'He's got no head for heights,' said the constable, putting his foot on the bottom rung of the ladder.

George Mellot and his employee, Leonard Hodge, were not in the farm kitchen with the members of the Berebury County Footpaths Society. They were standing together outside in the farmyard watching the police photographers at work on the barn roof. The policemen who had helped make up the search party had been detailed to examine the farm buildings and were now scouring the ground like so many human vacuum cleaners. George Mellot bore the sight of them poking into every nook and cranny of Pencombe Farm as dispassionately as he could. Len Hodge, though, was visibly upset.

'It's a sight worse than that scare we had last year, isn't it, guv'nor?' he said to his employer.

'What scare, Len?' George Mellot took his mind off the present with an effort. Last year seemed altogether too remote for memory recall just now.

'You must remember,' said Hodge. 'When they wondered if we'd got foot and mouth disease at Pencombe.'

'Oh, that . . .' At the time George Mellot hadn't been able to envisage worse disaster than an outbreak of foot and mouth disease in the Pencombe herd of Guernsey cows. He could now. Things were different. It was a measure of his present anxiety that he had almost forgotten the earlier one. 'That was nothing . . .' he said. The funny thing was that he meant it, too.

Now.

Hodge hitched his shoulder in the direction of the barn roof. 'Who could have guessed that there was anything up there?' he said.

'No one,' said the farmer shortly.

Hodge jerked his thumb upwards to the sky. 'And there are always crows in the yard, aren't there?'

'Always,' agreed Mellot.

'I must say,' sniffed Hodge, 'I never took no notice of them myself.'

'Neither did I,' said Mellot.

Hodge hunched his shoulders. 'You sort of get used to them being around somehow.'

'Of course you do,' the farmer said, adding carefully, 'The police aren't saying we should have noticed, Len.'

'Yet,' emphasized Hodge. 'They aren't saying anything yet, are they?'

'True.' In fact the silence of the police was one of the things George Mellot was finding most difficult of all. So far they were keeping their own counsel about everything and it was hard to endure.

'It's a bad business, all the same,' Hodge said obliquely, 'him lying up there and us working down here all the time.'

'Doesn't bear too much thinking about,' agreed George Mellot in his usual understating way.

Suddenly Hodge looked up and turned abruptly. 'Hullo, hullo,' he drawled. 'Here comes trouble . . .'

'Ted Mason,' said George Mellot. 'Back again . . .'

'Where have you been, then, Ted?' said Hodge to the policeman.

'Back home to see if there were any messages,' said the village constable.

'For a bite to eat, more like,' said Hodge.

Constable Mason looked down at his portly frame. 'Well, seeing as I was there and it happened to be there I did have a slice of cake,' he said with dignity. 'Makes a most acceptable fruit cake, does the wife.'

Hodge sniffed. 'Missed all the action, you did.'

'So I hear,' replied Mason equably.

'It's a gift.'

'It was a very good cake,' insisted Mason with the fervour of the fat.

'Some people have all the luck,' said Hodge scornfully.

George Mellot stirred. 'Does anyone have any idea at all who it is up there?'

'We're pursuing our enquiries,' parroted Constable Mason immediately. He then promptly spoilt the whole effect of this non-committal pronouncement by adding, 'Not a clue, Mr Mellot, really. Have you got any suggestions, Len?'

Hodge shook his head.

'From what I hear,' said George Mellot, 'whoever's up there is a bit far gone for clues.'

'Don't you believe it,' said Mason cheerfully. 'They're so clever these days they can even tell you what a mummy in a museum died from.'

'That's a great help, that is,' said Hodge.

'Oh, it'll take time, of course,' continued the constable largely. 'These things always do.'

'What about the evening milking?' asked Hodge.

'It'll take time,' repeated Mason, ignoring the tricky question of the evening milking. 'We know that, but I dare say we'll find out all about it in the end. We usually do.'

'Where will you start from?' asked the farmer.

'Here.' Mason waved an arm in a gesture that encompassed the policemen diligently going over the farmyard as well as the complex that was Pencombe Farm. 'Where the evidence is.'

'And then?'

'Missing persons,' said Mason promptly. 'It must be someone who's missing, mustn't it?'

Hodge nodded at the logic of this. 'Stands to reason.'

'Where do you go from there, though?' persisted George Mellot. 'A lot of people go missing.'

'Then we go into the logistics, Mr Mellot.' Mason might not be any great shakes at activity but was perfectly sound on theory.

Hodge looked up suspiciously. 'Clever stuff, eh?'

'Logistics isn't clever, Len,' said Mason. 'It's just working out how a crime was committed in the way it was.'

Hodge scowled. 'Like did he fall or was he pushed?'

'That's the general idea,' said Mason. 'And when we've worked that out,' he added neatly, 'then we go on to other things.'

'What other things?' demanded Hodge truculently.

'Like how did he get up there,' said Mason steadily.

A silence fell upon the little group. As if motivated by mesmerism all three looked upwards to the barn roof.

'That sometimes tells you quite a lot,' remarked Mason.

Neither of the other two spoke.

'Not everyone,' continued Mason conversationally, 'could get a body up on to a roof, could they? Women and children, for instance . . .'

That wrung an unwilling assent from both his listeners.

'Take a fair bit of doing,' admitted Hodge grudgingly.

'It would sort out the men from the boys,' agreed George Mellot.

'Mind you,' went on Constable Mason, 'there's always the easy way, isn't there?'

'What do you mean by that?' asked Mellot.

The policeman let his gaze drift towards the fork-lift tractor standing by the barn. 'That would get it a good part of the way up, wouldn't it? If not to the very top . . .'

'So it would,' said George Mellot in tones utterly devoid of emphasis.

'Quite surprising, really,' observed Mason, 'that neither of you happened to mention it.'

Hodge started involuntarily. 'So that's why . . .' He stopped as suddenly as he had begun.

Both men turned to him.

'So that's why what, Len?' asked Mason silkily.

'Nothing,' said Hodge, clamping his jaws together and falling silent.

'You were going to say something,' said Mason.

'No, I wasn't,' declared Hodge belligerently. 'I wasn't going to say nothing and you can't say I was, Ted Mason.'

The deeds of darkness. **10**

Psychologists insist that every normal human being needs someone who is known as their speech friend. It is with this speech friend that the details of the small happenings of daily life are regularly exchanged. In the manner of their kind these same psychologists do not indicate whether this role is always filled by a spouse but there was no doubt about that in the case of Sam Bailey.

The news of the finding of the skeleton had come to Lowercombe Farm earlier but Sam Bailey hadn't been able to share it with his wife, Elsie, because he couldn't find her. There being nothing more irritating than being the possessor of interesting news and yet not being able to impart that news to anyone, the old farmer was in a fine state of indignation by the time he did meet her. She was standing in the farmhouse hall with a bunch of flowers in her arms.

'Where have you been?' he said crossly. 'I've been looking for you everywhere.'

A lesser woman might have referred to the garden. A more distant relation might have even waved the flowers at him. Elsie Bailey, however, had been married to him for the best part of forty years.

'What's wrong?' she asked practically instead.

'The police.'

Her head came up sharply. 'What about them?'

'They've found what they were looking for.'

'Oh.' Her anxiety palpably subsided.

'George Mellot rang to tell us.' He added another grievance. 'I thought you'd come in when the telephone rang. You know I don't like answering it.'

'Poor soul.' She laid the flowers down on the hall table. 'It can't be anyone we know, Sam, can it?'

He shook his grizzled head. 'That's one thing to be thankful for. What do you want with those flowers anyway, Elsie? There are flowers everywhere already.'

'Poor George and Meg,' she said. 'It can't be very nice for them. And they've had a lot of extra worry lately anyway, what with one thing and another.'

'At least it wasn't foot and mouth in the end.'

'A herd isn't everything, Sam.'

'Troubles never come on their own,' said Bailey. That made him remember something else that had caused him to feel deprived. 'That beef we had today . . .'

'Sam, there was nothing wrong with that beef. It was the best that Hubert Wilkinson . . .'

'I know there wasn't. That's what I mean,' he said indignantly. 'I thought it would be nice to have it cold with pickle tonight and I couldn't find it in the larder.'

'I've made a pie for your supper. You like pie.'

He wasn't listening. 'And another thing, Elsie.'

'What?' she enquired patiently.

'My raincoat. I can't find it.'

'I expect you've put it somewhere and forgotten where,' she said tranquilly. 'It's not raining, anyway.'

'It wasn't there when I got back from church.'

'By the way,' she said obliquely, 'I thought you read the Lesson very well this morning. The rector said so too.'

'Huh!' snorted Bailey. 'He wants the churchyard mowing.'

'You are a churchwarden,' pointed out his wife.

'What's that got to do with it?'

'And you have got a gang mower.'

'It's been the same for forty years,' he grumbled. 'Every June.'

'Grass grows every year,' said his wife.

'Let him ask me, then,' growled Bailey.

'You've done it every year.'

'He's only got to ask,' insisted the old man, 'and I'll send someone down to do it.'

'And your father before you,' she said. 'Baileys from Lowercombe have always kept the churchyard mown.'

'Now don't start on that, Elsie. The rector can have his churchyard cut the minute he asks me.'

'On bended knee?' she enquired ironically.

'I've got my pride and he's got his.'

'Oh, Sam,' she said softly, 'you are a stiff-necked old fool and well you know it.'

George Mellot left the farmyard and went indoors with the slow heavy tread of a worried man. His wife had been standing by the window watching him approach but she did not turn round when he came into the kitchen. Instead she kept her back towards him as if afraid to meet his eye.

'Len knows something,' he said without preamble.

'I wondered,' she said.

'About a fork-lift tractor,' said Mellot flatly.

'I noticed that he'd suddenly gone all quiet,' she said.

'Ted Mason spotted it, too,' said Mellot. 'About the fork-lift tractor, I mean.'

She did turn to face him then. 'It's not like Len to be so quiet.'

'Not that Mason could have missed it,' Mellot was pursuing his own gloomy line of thought. 'Len got all uptight as soon as Mason even mentioned the fork-lift tractor, let alone took a proper look at it.'

'It must be obvious, mustn't it' – she swallowed visibly – 'that's what got . . . it . . . up there.'

'There's nothing else around,' agreed the farmer grimly, 'that would have done the job half so well.'

'Don't!'

'Any policeman could see that with half an eye. There's no use pretending . . .'

'Len did work for your father, too, when he was a boy,'

said Meg with seeming irrelevance. 'Didn't he? And so did his father.'

'Oh, he won't say anything, 'said Mellot confidently. 'Not Len. I'm pretty sure about that.'

'That's all very well but it's not going to make a lot of difference to the police, is it?' responded Meg Mellot. 'They'll just go on until they find out.'

Her husband sat down at the kitchen table and sank his head down into his hands like an old, old man. 'I know.'

'And there's another thing I've thought of,' said Meg, with lowered eyes.

'What's that?'

'Not everyone can work one of those machines, can they?'

'No.'

'It's not like driving a car. You need to know how. There are levers and things,' she said. 'I've seen them.'

'The police will work that out, too,' he said wearily. 'They aren't fools.'

'That will narrow down who can have used it.'

'That's what's worrying me.'

'And Len . . .'

'I must say,' remarked Mellot, 'that Len has been a bit difficult this past week or two.'

'Longer.'

He shrugged his shoulders. 'You notice these things and I don't.'

'He's had something on his mind, anyway,' she said. 'I could tell that much from talking to him.'

'I've never known him keep out of my way so much,' agreed Mellot. 'I haven't been able to find him half the time.'

'I would say,' said Meg slowly, 'that it was since that day he came to work with a black eye. Do you remember? And he wouldn't say what had happened. He was bruised, too.'

Mellot lifted his head in slow wonderment. 'I'd forgotten all about that.'

'Oh, George, do you think . . .' she stopped.

'That was about a month ago, wasn't it?'

She nodded. 'It was a Monday morning when he came to work looking like a prize fighter. I do remember that.'

With leaden, unwilling movements her husband slowly swivelled round to peer at the calendar hanging on the kitchen wall. 'A Monday, did you say?' he echoed hollowly. 'About four weeks ago . . .'

'The beginning of the month.' She followed his gaze as if mesmerized.

He turned quickly away from the calendar and sat back at the table again, his hands covering his eyes. 'June the fifth, that would have been. Oh dear, oh dear . . .'

'What will the police do next?' asked Meg Mellot tremulously.

'They want to talk to me.' With the hesitation of one conveying unwelcome news George Mellot added, 'And they've asked for Tom's address.'

Detective Inspector Sloan went indoors to the telephone at Pencombe Farm unwillingly. The message had been that Superintendent Leeyes was on the line from Berebury asking for a progress report.

'The situation, sir,' said Sloan, stressing the word slightly and not mentioning progress at all, 'is that the doctor is up there now with the remains and that the farmyard is being searched very carefully as quickly as possible.'

'Quickly?' Leeyes pounced. 'I don't like rushed jobs, Sloan.'

'There's a herd of cows waiting to be got into their milking parlour, sir.' If Sloan could have hung the telephone receiver out of the window the superintendent would have been able to hear the mournful sound of lowing wafting across the farmyard in eerie confirmation of this fact.

'Tricky,' agreed Leeyes immediately.

'It's long past their milking time as it is,' said Sloan. They both knew that if he kept the cows out of the milking shed and the court ever got to hear about it, the Prosecution case would be as good as lost.

Leeyes grunted. 'It's always difficult with animals.' It was a lesson learned hard and early in the police force. Every chief constable had had to deal with lost dogs in his day. And then it wasn't so much a case of every dog having its day as every day having its dog . . .

'Always,' agreed Sloan fervently. There had only been one thing worse than lost dogs and that was escaped budgerigars. Little old ladies seemed to think that these were easier to capture than professional criminals and they weren't. There was no doubt, though, that animals ranked over men in sentiment as far as the Great British Public was concerned. Always over dead men. And especially over very dead men.

'So, Sloan . . .'

'So, sir, we're going over the farmyard first.' It wasn't that Sloan was an animal lover: rather that he was a realist. There wasn't a jury in the United Kingdom that would have agreed to the theoretical requirements of Justice being subverted to the actual needs of the animal kingdom.

'And then?'

'We'll tackle the roof. We think, sir,' he added cautiously, 'that we know how the body was got up there.'

'Ha!'

'There's a fork-lift tractor in the yard.'

He was answered with an unexpected witticism. 'A means to an end, eh, Sloan?'

'Quite so,' he said, dutifully acknowledging this. He cleared his throat. 'There is a farm worker here who gives the impression of knowing more than he's telling us. Mason is sure about that.'

Leeyes grunted.

'Moreover,' continued Sloan, 'he's the man who about a month ago had a fight with a mysterious stranger in the pub here in Great Rooden.'

'Nonsense,' countered his superior officer robustly. 'You don't get mysterious strangers in villages. You should know that, Sloan. Everybody knows everybody.'

'Yes, sir.' Sloan accepted the rebuke meekly. 'I'll remember that.'

'And another thing . . .'

'Sir?'

'People don't fight people they don't know,' said Leeyes profoundly.

'No, sir.'

'There's no point in it.'

Sloan rephrased what he had said. 'He had a fight with a man nobody's telling us about.'

'That's better.'

'Tomorrow, sir' – Sloan forged on; even though today had been endless, tomorrow would come – 'tomorrow I'd like the search party back.'

'One body not enough, then?'

'To search Dresham Wood,' said Sloan steadily.

'Ah!' The superintendent's response came alertly down the telephone line.

'There's something in there, sir, I'm sure, but I don't know what.' At Cold Comfort Farm there had been something in the woodshed but here at Great Rooden whatever it was was in the wood. Sloan was sure about that. At Cold Comfort Farm it had been something nasty. It might well be something nasty in the wood here. Only a proper search would tell.

'Tomorrow,' observed Leeyes gloomily, 'may be too late.'

Sloan's mother was a great reader of the Bible and from time to time Sloan was glad about this. A working knowledge of how helpful Job's comforters had been to Job had stood Sloan in good stead when functioning with the superintendent. He didn't argue. Instead he said, 'I've put out a general call for Martin Ritchie of Stanestede. It would be nice to cross him off our list.'

'One less missing man to be bothering about,' agreed Leeyes.

'The timing's right for it to be him,' Sloan reminded the superintendent.

'It is for Ivor Harbeton, too,' pointed out Leeyes. 'Those papers about him should have got to you by now.'

'And,' persisted Sloan, 'the timing's right for whoever it

was that Hodge had a fight with. 'That was at the beginning of June, too.'

'We mustn't forget him,' said Leeyes. 'The ... ah ... the third man, you might say.'

'Yes, sir,' agreed Sloan. The superintendent's responses were a little dated these days. 'Martin Ritchie, Ivor Harbeton and the third man.'

'Unless,' said Leeyes, 'Hodge had a fight with one of the other two – with Harbeton or Ritchie, I mean. Then there would be only two men in the picture, wouldn't there?'

They said, didn't they, that the counting nursery rhymes were the oldest of all. The one Sloan couldn't get out of his mind was about pigs.

And this little piggy went to market and this little piggy stayed at home . . .

He couldn't remember what had happened to the third pig.

The parlour at Pencombe Farm wasn't an ideal murder headquarters but Sloan decided that it would do. It was a pleasant, relaxed room with a few pieces of good furniture in evidence: and there was that about the carpet which made Detective Constable Crosby look twice at the state of the soles of his shoes as he came in from the farmyard.

On a rather nice burr walnut table was a bowl of freshly gathered ligtu hybrid alstromeria and on the windowsill a skilful arrangement of old roses. Detective Inspector Sloan grew roses as a hobby and he cast an appraising eye over them, noting the varieties. He had already seen a good pure white Seagull rambler growing round the front door, and the crimson purple Gallica Tuscany Superb by the gate. This farmer's wife didn't have to devote herself exclusively to the farm – there was time and money at Pencombe to spare and it showed.

Detective Constable Crosby chose the stoutest chair in the room and lowered himself into it with care. 'What's the betting, sir,' he said 'that we're going to get the three monkeys treatment about that skeleton?'

'What's that?' asked Sloan absently. He had opted to sit on

a Knole sofa done up in an old-fashioned chintz with contrasting plain sea-green cushions. He began to open the message wallet that the superintendent had had sent over from Berebury Police Station.

'They saw nothing,' chanted Crosby, 'they heard nothing and . . .'

'I know, I know,' said Sloan morosely. 'You don't need to tell me . . .'

'And they're going to say nothing,' finished Crosby triumphantly.

'Maybe.' Sloan ran his eye over the sheaf of press cuttings which had been sent by the superintendent. They were all about the disappearance of Ivor Harbeton. 'We'll know in a minute. The Mellots are on their way.'

Crosby got his notebook out.

'It says here,' said Sloan, who had been studying one of the press cuttings in detail, 'that Harbeton was a man of medium height. See that Dr Dabbe is told, will you? And while you're about it, you might check how tall the amorous Martin Ritchie was.'

'Yes, sir.'

'You can't be too careful in this game.' That was one thing that was certain in an uncertain world.

'Shall I see if there's anyone called Beverley missing, too, sir?'

'Who's Beverley?' asked Sloan blankly.

'The girl who Martin Ritchie has gone off with,' said Crosby.

'By all means,' said Sloan warmly, 'although, of course, she may not be missing at all.'

'But . . .'

'She,' observed Sloan pithily, 'may merely have used the time-honoured phrase "Come live with me and be my love" and he did.'

'Pardon, sir?'

'Nothing,' said Sloan. 'You go ahead and check.' He stopped, struck by a sudden thought. 'She may not exist, of course. We have no evidence that she does.'

'The letter . . .'

'The letter was thrown away by the outraged Mrs Ritchie. "Cupid",' quoted Sloan neatly, ' "is a knavish lad." ' The poet might have said it first but it was a lesson learned early on the beat.

Crosby made a note in his book.

'Ivor Harbeton,' said Sloan, waving a piece of newspaper in his hand, 'was last seen on Friday, June second.'

'Three – no, more than that – four weeks ago,' said Crosby, counting them out on his fingers.

'The day that the auditors were due at one of his company's offices,' continued Sloan, reading aloud.

'Auditors shouldn't say when they're coming,' said Crosby. 'They don't with banks, you know, sir. Catches out the teemers and laders a treat.'

'It doesn't sound from reading this,' responded Sloan mildly, 'as if Ivor Harbeton is the sort of man to be bothered about a little thing like fiddling the receipt books.'

'June isn't the season, anyway,' contributed Crosby. 'Not for that. It's more of a Christmas crime.'

Sloan nodded. Teeming and lading was common among shaky club treasurers, defalcation reaching its peak during December. Nemesis usually caught up with them in January.

'I rather think,' he said drily, 'that Ivor Harbeton is in a bigger league than Christmas clubs, risky as they are too.'

'Not a petty cash man,' said Crosby.

'High finance,' said Sloan, although he wasn't at all sure what the phrase meant. The newspapers had used it more than once. And the words 'wheeler-dealer' too, but all the reporting was neatly circumspect. Peccadillo – let alone fraud – wasn't even hinted at. Newspapers were more subtle than that. 'He was prominent in City circles,' Sloan read aloud from a cutting.

Crosby snorted gently. 'And now he's decamped.'

'Let us say,' replied Sloan with precision, 'that nobody quite seems to know exactly where he is.'

'Vamoosed,' said Crosby, lapsing still further into the vernacular.

'Perhaps,' suggested Sloan, waving a hand vaguely in the direction of the farmyard, 'he didn't get very far . . .'

They were interrupted by the arrival of George and Meg Mellot. They advanced unwillingly.

'You said you wanted to see us, Inspector,' said the farmer.

'Just one or two questions about the skeleton,' began Sloan easily.

'There's not a lot we can tell you,' said Mellot.

'We didn't know anything about its being there,' supplemented his wife anxiously, her eyes on her husband's face. 'Did we, George?'

George Mellot shook his head.

'We shall need some sort of statement to that effect for the coroner,' carried on Sloan smoothly. 'For the inquest.'

'Of course,' said George Mellot at once.

It was always suprising, thought Sloan to himself, how reassuring nearly everyone found both mention of the coroner and the invoking of that most ancient of Norman institutions, an inquest.

'Naturally,' said Meg Mellot.

However ambivalent their attitude to the police, the great British public saw the coroner as an impartial enquirer: inquests were a time-honoured procedure that could – and did – happen in the best of families. And, thought Sloan, generously giving credit where credit was due, it was amazing how very above the battle the coroner always contrived to appear.

'For instance,' said Sloan, coming back to the matter in hand, 'it would be useful to know if either of you had heard anything strange at any time lately.'

Both Mellots immediately shook their heads.

'Not even,' said Sloan, 'the dog barking without a reason?'

'No,' said Mellot.

'Never,' said his wife, nervously plucking at her skirt.

'Where does it sleep?' asked Sloan.

'Outside,' replied the farmer. 'In the yard.'

'I see.' Sloan paused before he said, 'And I take it that you have neither of you seen any unauthorized persons about the farmyard lately?' When he was very small he remembered his mother – no, it must have been his grandmother – teaching him the old song 'Hark, hark, the dogs do bark, the beggars are coming to town'.

'No,' said George Mellot firmly.

All the energy seemed to have gone out of Meg Mellot. She was sitting in the chair with her hands lying loosely clasped together, palms upwards, in what the art historians called the Byzantine attitude of sustained sorrow.

Sloan reached out his hand for one of the press cuttings and said, 'Does the name Ivor Harbeton convey anything to you, Mr Mellot?'

He never did get a direct answer to his question.

The detective inspector had hardly asked it before he saw the colour drain out of Meg Mellot's face. She emitted a low moan and subsided on to the parlour floor at his feet in a dead faint.

Your adversary the devil. **11**

'I say, Calleshire,' chattered the voice on the telephone line, 'you do realize that today's Sunday, don't you?'

'Yes,' said Sloan evenly. In the police force you knew not the day nor the hour when you might be working. 'Yes, Met, I do.'

'City,' the voice corrected him with celerity. 'Not Met.'

'Sorry,' said Sloan. That had been a *faux pas* of the first order.

'You're talking to the City Fraud Squad,' said the voice. 'That's who you wanted, wasn't it?'

'It was,' said Sloan. 'I'm sorry about its being a Sunday but we've got a bit of a problem down here.'

'Speak on.'

'Can you tell me anything about a character called Ivor Harbeton?'

'You bet I can.' Something approaching a cackle came down the telephone line. 'Don't say that he's been operating in your neck of the woods, too?'

'Not operating, exactly,' said Sloan obscurely.

'But . . .'

'But there may be a link.' Perhaps, thought Sloan, that was too restrained a way of putting it. Mrs Meg Mellot had canted over at the mere mention of the man's name. And taken her time to come round.

'You'll be lucky to come off best,' said the voice frankly. 'Nobody else has that we can see.'

'Tell me,' invited Sloan. Victims often brought death on themselves. In more ways than one.

'He's clever,' said the voice grudgingly. 'I give him that.'

Sloan was not surprised. The unclever did not as a rule attract the attentions of either the Fraud Squad or the newspapers. The Bench of Magistrates dealt with them and then went home to their wives complaining about the low level of education in the country.

'An entrepreneur,' expanded the man in London, 'that's what I would call Ivor Harbeton.'

It wasn't surprising, thought Sloan, that a nation of shopkeepers didn't have the right word.

'And,' went on the voice drily, 'he's nearly always nearly legal.'

'Ah,' said Sloan. Those were the difficult cases. Give him a flagrant breach of the law any day. Justice hanging on a pure technicality didn't go down well with either judge or jury. Even less well when hanging had been the operative word.

'Quite ruthless, of course,' continued the voice in a detached way.

Ruthlessness was not an endearing characteristic. It might have been that that had made a victim of Ivor Harbeton. If he was the victim, that is. Sloan didn't know yet. What he did know was that Meg Mellot had abruptly fainted at his feet. And that her husband had gone down on his knees beside her, imploring her to lie quiet and still until she felt better.

'There's no sentiment in business, anyway,' carried on his interlocutor in the City breezily, 'but I would have said Ivor Harbeton was born without it anyway.'

'Anything known?' enquired Sloan. That was police shorthand for a lot.

'He hasn't got form,' replied the voice, 'but then generally speaking the villians we deal with in this department don't have.'

In police parlance, though, they were still villains.

'Not until the ballon goes up in a big way, that is,' said the Fraud Squad man.

'And has it with Ivor Harbeton?' asked Sloan.

'Let us say,' responded the voice cautiously, 'that we would like to talk to him. Very much indeed. And so would the people at United Mellemetics.'

'United Mellemetics?' Sloan scratched about in his memory. 'They're a big firm in the North, aren't they?'

'They are. For their sins they got taken over by Hobble-thwaite Castings – that's one of Harbeton's other companies – in April this year. With Harbeton as chairman of the board.'

'And they didn't like it?'

'United Mellemetics,' replied the voice succinctly, 'were stripped naked of every asset they held. And the money . . .'

'Yes?' Sloan was always interested in what happened to money. It was the policeman in him.

'The money was applied to financing the next takeover battle.'

'Battle.' Sloan echoed the word. The language of war sat as appropriately on the background of business as it did on that of crime.

'Well, if you want to be exact,' said the Fraud Squad man astringently, 'I should say that rapine and pillage describe what went on at United Mellemetics better, but then I'm old-fashioned myself.'

'And then?'

'Then the United Mellemetics auditors went on the war-path.'

'And found that there had been sticky fingers in the till?' enquired Sloan colloquially.

'And found themselves unable to reconcile the figures with what was left of the assets,' said the other man more technically.

'That's bad.' Even Sloan, who did not count himself as numerate, could see that.

'The fixed assets were there all right but . . .'

'But the liquid ones had evaporated?' supplemented Sloan. There was even something insubstantial about the very phrase. Liquid, indeed!

'Happens, all the time,' said the voice from the City laconically.

Detective Inspector Sloan of the Calleshire County Constabulary said he could well believe it.

'Take it from me, old man,' said the Fraud Squad man, 'and keep your money in short-dated Government stock. You know exactly where you are then.'

'Quite so,' replied Sloan non-committally. Actually he wasn't at all sure that you did know where you were with Government. Even chief constables didn't always know. Home Secretaries came in different colours. And in different degrees of dampness. Some were wet and some were dry.

'And with short-dated Government stock,' said the other man, 'there's always the Date of Redemption to look forward to.' He made it sound like the Day of Judgement.

'I don't have anything much left over,' responded Sloan quickly. 'Not with my mortgage.' This was not strictly true but money over and above and to spare in the Sloan menage was apt to be absorbed by purchases from the catalogues of specialist rose growers. He cleared his throat and asked, 'Where do you come in with the man Harbeton?'

'The people at United Mellemetics came to us when they discovered the – er – shortfall.'

It was funny how malfeasance – like death – attracted euphemisms. Shrinkage was another word that meant more than one might think.

'So we started to make enquiries,' carried on the speaker, 'and we found that two and two didn't make four either.'

'Ah.'

'By then, of course, Ivor Harbeton had gone on to his next takeover battle.'

'Mellot's Furnishings,' said Sloan simply.

'Oh, you know about that, do you?'

'Only what the newspapers say.'

'He did it through Conway's Covers, which is another

Harbeton company,' amplified the Fraud Squad man. 'Don't ask me to tell you them all. Proteus isn't in it.'

'If we could concentrate on Mellot's Furnishings . . .'

The man at the other end of the telephone line brightened audibly. 'That's easy, Inspector. When all this started Mellot's Furnishings was a well-run company with prime sites in most towns.'

'Ripe for plucking.' Sloan could see that.

'The ideal victim. Couldn't have been better, in fact. The recipe's quite easy. Take it over, sell the shop sites, lease them back to the company, and use the capital for something else.'

It couldn't, thought Detective Inspector C. D. Sloan, first-time home-owner, be as simple as that. The hassle of buying one semi-detached house in suburban Berebury had been bad enough. He said so.

'It is simple,' insisted the other man airily. 'And perfectly legal. It goes on all the time.'

Sloan felt stirred into protest. 'It's not the sort of thing to take lying down.'

A grim laugh travelled along the telephone line. 'Tom Mellot didn't do that, believe you me.'

'What did he do, then?'

The man from the Fraud Squad told him.

That was when Detective Constable Crosby materialized at his elbow. 'The doctor wants to see you before he goes, sir,' he said.

The pathologist was standing on the makeshift inspection platform, his perennially silent assistant, Burns, at his side. Detective Inspector Sloan and Detective Constable Crosby clambered up beside them. There was room – but only just – for the four of them. Dyson and Williams had finished their photography and were standing at the bottom of the scaffolding tower. Also waiting at ground level at a discreet distance was a van from Morton's, the Berebury undertakers.

'Eyes first, hands next, tongue last, Sloan,' said Dr Dabbe. 'That's what I was taught.'

'Very wise, Doctor,' said Sloan. At the Police Training

College they had had a lot to say about ears and listening but there was no need to go into that now.

'Poor Fred who was alive and is dead.' Detective Constable Crosby had not been taught anything of the kind and rushed into speech.

'Very dead,' agreed the pathologist before Sloan could say anything at all. 'Well, gentlemen, we've done all that we can up here.' He looked round from their raised vantage point. 'I must say it makes a change from a ditch.'

'Yes, Doctor,' said Sloan. Now the doctor came to mention it, most dead bodies were low-lying.

'The heights of Abraham's bosom,' said Dr Dabbe obscurely.

Sloan cleared his throat. 'What do you make of him, Doctor? For the report, I mean.'

'Oh, there's not a lot of doubt about the NASH classification, Sloan,' said the pathologist, 'unless someone removed the head for fun, of course.'

'What's the NASH classification?' enquired Crosby.

'The four options open to a forensic pathologist,' responded Dr Dabbe, waving a hand in the direction of the skeleton.

'Four?' echoed the constable.

'Four, Crosby,' snapped Sloan. The constable should know all this. 'One more than three, and one less than five.' He wasn't sure if it was a good thing that the pathologist encouraged *badinage* with constables. Superintendent Leeyes didn't.

'Natural causes, accident, suicide, and homicide,' recited Dr Dabbe.

'NASH,' agreed Crosby, nodding.

'Homicide, Crosby,' said Sloan mordantly. 'The killing of a man. Like regicide but less specific.'

'Of course,' said the pathologist, momentarily diverted. 'there are always the other four things.'

'What other four, Doctor?' enquired Sloan evenly. They weren't getting anywhere standing up on the platform talking like this, and time might be important.

'Eschatology.'

'What's that?' asked Crosby promptly. It sounded like a medical word to Sloan.

'The science of the last four things,' said Dr Dabbe.

Sloan didn't say anything at all. The doctor was going to tell them whether or not he asked what they were.

'Death, judgement, heaven, and hell,' pronounced Dr Dabbe. He grinned suddenly and tapped the scaffolding platform with his foot. 'Makes you feel you're in a pulpit, doesn't it, being up here?'

The height wasn't having that effect on Sloan, besides which he had other things on his mind. 'The finger,' he began purposefully. In his opinion philosophy could wait. There were certain practical matters he needed to set in train. And soon. 'Can we be sure that it came from this body?'

'As sure as eggs is eggs,' responded the pathologist just a whit colloquially, 'but I'll check for you properly presently.'

'Thank you.'

'Actually, Sloan, nearly all the fingers have gone, give or take a thumb.'

'The moving finger . . .' began Crosby.

Sloan quelled the detective constable with a look. The trouble was that he couldn't do that with the Consultant Pathologist to the Berebury District General Hospital Management Group.

'So,' continued Dr Dabbe obliviously, 'have quite a number of other smaller bones.' He coughed. 'And we shan't be wanting a lot in the way of canopic jars, shall we, Burns?'

'No, Doctor.'

Sloan waited for elucidation.

'They're what the ancient Egyptians used to bury the entrails in,' the doctor informed him.

'When they weren't casting them?' enquired Sloan neatly.

'That was the Greeks,' said Dr Dabbe.

'Talking of height,' Sloan reverted to an earlier topic before he got into deeper water still, 'do we know how tall this man was?'

'Burns here has done some measurements,' said Dr Dabbe. 'Haven't you, Burns?'

'That's right, Doctor.'

'And taking the length of the left femur . . .'

'That's still there, then,' said Sloan.

'Too heavy for anything short of a vulture,' said the pathologist. 'Or a jackal.'

'So . . .' The only jackals in rural Calleshire were human ones.

'So, taking the known length of the left femur, measured, of course, from the top of its head to the bottom of the internal condylar surface . . .'

'Of course,' murmured Sloan.

'. . . and applying Pearson's formula for the reconstruction of living stature from dead long bones . . .'

'Yes?'

'We can calculate that he – whoever he was . . .'

Who he was, thought Sloan to himself, was a bigger question altogether. Perhaps who he had been might be a better way of putting it. He permitted himself a sideways glance at what was lying there. A quotation drifted into his mind from somewhere. 'A rag, a bone and a hank of hair' except that there wasn't a rag left on the body and no hair either.

'Whoever he was,' repeated Dr Dabbe, 'was just over five foot eight inches tall.'

'That's very useful to know,' said Sloan and he meant it.

'Give or take half an inch or so,' the pathologist added as a rider.

'A small man, then.'

'By the time I tell the court in centimetres,' said the pathologist cynically, 'they won't know whether he was a dwarf or a giant.'

Sloan nodded in sympathy. Metrication was yet another hazard to clear thought by members of juries. 'And are there any – er – pointers at all to the cause of death, Doctor?' He had an ingrained objection to using the word 'clue'.

'None that I could see from where I had to stand,' admitted the pathologist cheerfully. 'I might be able to be more helpful, though, after we've got him down off the slopes of Mount Parnassus here and back in the mortuary.'

'Quite so,' said Sloan. He agreed that these were not ideal conditions for proper scientific examination.

'Although,' said Dr Dabbe, 'how that's going to be done, I really don't know.'

'Dead man's lift?' suggested Crosby brightly.

'You had better go down first, Crosby,' said Sloan repressively.

Dr Dabbe was still considering the skeleton. 'There's one thing I can't tell you yet, Sloan.'

'What's that, Doctor?'

'At exactly what stage the head came off.'

Sloan cleared his throat. 'It would be a help to know.'

'It didn't fall off, Sloan, that's for sure.'

'No, Doctor.' Sloan hadn't supposed for one moment that it had.

'But,' said the pathologist, 'I can tell you how it came off.'

That, too, thought Sloan, would be useful information. The police didn't have a lot in the way of hard facts yet. Crosby had started to swing off the platform and on to the top of the ladder as Dr Dabbe spoke. He paused.

'Someone used an instrument,' said Dr Dabbe.

'What sort of instrument?' asked Sloan cautiously.

'A cleaver of some kind. An axe, perhaps, or a butcher's knife.' There was a sudden change in atmosphere on the makeshift scaffolding tower. The banter had gone. Now the pathologist was deadly serious. 'And I should say – mind you, Sloan, I'm speaking without a microscope . . .'

'Yes, Doctor?' Out of the corner of his eye Sloan could see Crosby poised at the top of the ladder listening too.

'That the head came off in one fell blow,' said the doctor chillingly.

Sloan absorbed the information without comment. Even some professional executioners hadn't managed that. Something gruesome about the beheading of one of the wives of Henry VIII came into his mind. Or had it been Mary, Queen of Scots?

'An axe, you said, Doctor,' murmured Sloan. The police

needed to know what to look for. And where to start looking. Firemen had axes, didn't they? Even part-time firemen.

'I can't tell you exactly what was used.' Dr Dabbe frowned. 'Something heavy and sharp.'

'It was a clean cut, anyway,' said Sloan. Somehow 'clean' didn't seem quite the right adjective but he couldn't call another better one to mind just at this moment.

The pathologist nodded. 'Between Atlas and Axis, if you really want to know.'

It would come up as something quite different in Dr Dabbe's report to the coroner, Sloan knew that.

Dr Dabbe grinned. 'The first cervical vertebra and epistropheous, actually.'

'Does that presuppose any sort of knowledge on the part of who did it, Doctor?'

The medical man considered this. 'I dare say most farmers pick up a working knowledge of anatomy over the years, Sloan. And, of course, there used to be a fair bit of pole-axeing in the old days.' He prepared to follow Crosby down the ladder. 'My guess is that when you find the head you'll find the cause of death – unless it was a straightforward decapitation, that is.'

'Yes, Doctor.' Instituting a search for a severed head was something else to be done with all possible speed. And this time they couldn't exclude wooded land. A human agency had been involved. Unlike crows, human beings weren't afraid of predators.

The pathologist took one last look at the bones on the barn roof. 'A good thing that those crows had been properly brought up, Sloan, isn't it?'

'Beg pardon, Doctor?'

'They left something for Mr Manners, like Nanny always said.'

'But not a lot,' said Crosby, disappearing down the ladder.

O let no evil dreams be near.   **12**

'Mrs Mellot didn't say a word,' said Detective Constable
Crosby to Sloan as they walked back across the farmyard
towards the house and parlour. 'Not a word. Not all the while
I was there anyway.' He sniffed. 'Mum's the word with her
all right.'

'Actions speak louder than words,' said Sloan firmly. There
had been no disguising the swift rush of blood from Meg
Mellot's face when naked fear had struck. As Sloan stepped
over the farm threshold now something came back to him
over the years from an English lesson – something that
that arch-observer William Shakespeare had noted. It had
been in one of those plays that for some reason teachers of
English literature lingered over – he of the two parts, *King
Henry IV*.

> *The whiteness of thy cheek
> Is apter than thy tongue to tell thy errand.*

He remembered the fight scenes, too. They were really what
made it a good play for boys – and the part of Sir John Falstaff
inevitably going to the fattest boy in the class . . .

'She didn't speak, you said,' murmured Sloan to Crosby.
Something else that came welling out of his subconscious was
the wartime slogan: 'Be like Dad, keep Mum.'

'There wasn't a dicky-bird out of her,' said Detective

Constable Crosby, who had not been thinking about either Shakespeare's plays or propaganda posters. 'The dog would have barked, sir, for sure, though, if anyone else had humped that body up on the roof. That was what it was there for – to bark.'

'A watch dog,' said Sloan precisely. He'd seen a hole in a wall for a watch dog once and the phrase had fallen into place in his mind. It had been in the ruins of an abbey which he and his wife, Margaret, had visited on holiday. There had been an elliptical gap at the height of a dog exactly opposite the abbey gate and the dog was expected to bark when anyone came near. They had had a death's door there, too. For a moment Sloan had thought that the abbey custodian had been joking.

He wasn't. He'd led their party to the north wall of the chancel and pointed. 'There you are,' he'd said for all to hear. 'Death's door.'

It was the custodian's party piece and he had done it well. It was, he had explained, a door in the abbey wall which led directly to the abbey cemetery. It was only opened on the death of a monk to let the body and its cortège through for burial. All that Sloan had been able to think about at the time had been the hoary – and very irreverent – medical chestnut about the patient 'being at death's door but the doctor hoped to pull him through'. The sight had stuck in his memory all the same.

There was another phrase though – a more modern one – that was rather more germane to the present. It came straight from Sir Arthur Conan Doyle.

'"The curious incident of the dog in the night-time",' quoted Sloan from *The Silver Blaze*.

'That's right, sir.' Crosby scratched his brow. 'Why didn't the Mellots just say they'd heard Fido barking? That's all they needed to do, isn't it?'

'It may not have been true,' said Sloan mildly. There was something in the Bible about that. He quoted it. '"What is truth?" said Pilate.'

Crosby looked distinctly doubtful.

'Moreover,' pointed out Sloan, 'the body may not have been put up on the roof at night.'

'But . . .'

'We don't know for certain that it was.' Sloan tightened his lips. Actually they knew very little for certain at the moment and that was a worry in itself.

Crosby looked even more doubtful. 'If it went up there . . .'

'Was put.' Sloan corrected him at once. Life was quite complicated enough without bringing levitation into the picture – even for 'the friendless bodies of unburied men'.

'Was put up there in daylight,' said Crosby, 'and the Mellots didn't know, then that means that Len Hodge did – does know. Bound to.'

'He might have been got out of the way,' said Sloan, leading the way down the passage.

'He knows something, sir,' insisted Crosby. 'Ted Mason says so.'

Sloan nodded. An interview with Len Hodge had a high priority. But so did further words with George and Meg Mellot. He pushed open the garden door and said, 'Feeling better now, are you, madam?'

Meg Mellot nodded, her face still a chalky white. She was sitting bolt upright on the couch now but she still did not look well.

Sloan began the interview without preamble. 'I've been finding out a little more about Mellot's Furnishings.'

'Upholsterers to the Nation,' responded Crosby upon the instant, demonstrating that he was as susceptible as the next man to a good advertising slogan.

'Ivor Harbeton's company,' went on Sloan, gritting his teeth and rising above the television demotic, 'made a bid for Mellot's Furnishings at the end of April this year.'

'Conway's Covers,' said George Mellot wearily. 'That was the company that Harbeton used for the attack.' The farmer was sitting on the sofa beside his wife looking years older than he had done the day before.

Sloan continued his narrative. 'Mellot's Furnishings turned

down their approaches flat.' It was company mergers that could be compared with marriages, wasn't it?

George Mellot stirred himself. 'Absolutely flat,' he agreed. 'Tom wouldn't hear of it. The firm was his baby and he wanted to keep it that way.'

'So Conway's Covers tried again,' said Sloan. Takeovers had more in common with shot-gun weddings than with arranged marriages.

Mellot moistened his lips. 'That was at the beginning of May.'

'With a higher bid,' added Sloan. A marriage of convenience, perhaps.

'If at first you don't succeed,' interposed Crosby sententiously, 'try, try again.'

Detective Inspector Sloan bit back the first response that came into his head and said instead, 'That's just what Harbeton did.' Marriage à la mode, that was it.

'He kept on coming back,' said George Mellot dully.

His wife said nothing.

Crosby looked quite interested for once. 'And what did Mellot's Furnishings do?'

'Fought it tooth and nail,' said Sloan succinctly. The man in the City had promised to let him have copies of the series of letters to shareholders and the newspaper advertising campaign that had constituted the ammunition of war. Bid followed by counter bid. Salvo by counter salvo. Or had it really been dowry all the time? Pretty reading, the City man had said they made. Pleas for support from shareholders from the embattled board of directors of Mellot's Furnishings: bait laid in front of those same shareholders by the predatory Conway Covers board, chaired by Ivor Harbeton: appeals to sentiment: appeals to greed. He turned to George Mellot. 'I'm not boring you, sir, I trust.'

'No, Inspector,' replied the farmer with all the searing astringency of rhatany root, 'you're not boring me. I'm listening.'

'Who won?' enquired Detective Constable Crosby as if the saga had the simplicity of a bedtime story.

Detective Inspector Sloan switched his gaze from one man to the other and regarded his subordinate with a certain academic interest. Not for Crosby the majestic cadences of the Edwardian versifier whose sentiments seemed to be the hallmark of every speech on every Speech Day.

He marks not that you won or lost
   But how you played the game.

Perhaps it was as well. Takeover battles did not sound particularly sporting – or sportive – affairs . . .

'The goodies or the baddies?' asked Crosby before he could speak.

That simplified the situation still further. Crosby's interest, though, was better than the monumental indifference of the sheep in the next field at the Battle of Hastings that Sloan's history teacher had brought to the attention of the class. He had been pointing a different moral, of course. 'Always remember,' the schoolmaster had been fond of saying, 'that while one of the most decisive battles in English history was being fought out the sheep in the next field went on eating. Before, during and after the battle.' And a young Christopher Dennis Sloan had dutifully remembered, though for the life of him – then or now – he wasn't sure what to think about it.

Detective Inspector Sloan, working policeman on duty, couldn't let a little philosophy come between him and the business in hand. He said courteously, 'Perhaps Mr Mellot would like to tell us who won.'

The farmer said, 'It isn't as straightforward as that, Inspector.'

'No?' said Sloan pleasantly. 'No, perhaps not. Your brother Tom gave Ivor Harbeton a run for his money, though, didn't he?' There, for a wonder, was a cliché that filled the bill . . .

'He did,' responded Mellot with spirit. Meg Mellot still stayed silent and withdrawn.

'Bully for him,' said Crosby laconically.

Sloan resumed his role as narrator. It seemed easier. 'So Ivor Harbeton tried something different.'

'Robert the Bruce's spider,' remarked Crosby unnecessarily, 'just went on.'

'A dawn raid,' said George Mellot dully. 'That was what came next.'

Detective Constable Crosby brightened immediately. They had dawn raids in the police force: exciting, truly clandestine affairs, when hardened criminals were tumbled out of bed in the middle of the night. He said so.

'Not that sort of dawn raid,' said Detective Inspector Sloan, very nearly at the end of his patience with his subordinate. The man in the Fraud Squad had just explained to him the City's version of the tactic. It was rather different from the police one.

It wasn't very long before he found himself explaining it to Superintendent Leeyes too.

'The buyer, sir,' Sloan informed him presently down the telephone, 'starts the whole thing by building up various small holdings in the company that they want to buy.'

Like Mr Dick, Superintendent Leeyes was more interested in a head. 'It must be somewhere, Sloan,' he insisted. Some there be that have no Memorial but not King Charles I.

'Yes, sir,' agreed Sloan at once. 'Naturally.'

His superior officer's voice came testily down the telephone line. 'I hope you're looking for it, then.'

'I am in the process of making arrangements to do so, sir.' It would be the superintendent's King Charles's head if they weren't careful.

'That means you haven't started yet,' pounced Leeyes, who had not risen to the rank of superintendent by the exercising of the gentler virtues.

'Not exactly started,' agreed Sloan. 'Not yet. But it is in hand.' He tried not to sound too defensive. 'It's a matter of arranging for a special photographic survey of the area.' Sloan did not pretend to understand the technicalities of infra-red cameras but there were modern – ultra-modern – methods available now for spotting patches of land where earth had been disturbed.

Leeyes grunted. 'When I was a constable we looked the hard way with water jugs.'

'Sir?'

'You're too young to remember,' said Leeyes loftily. 'A straight line of men pouring water on the ground out of jugs as they walked forward, that's how it used to be done.'

'But . . .'

'If the ground hadn't been touched,' Leeyes informed him, 'the water ran straight off.'

'I see, sir.'

'If it had been turned over to bury something,' swept on Leeyes, 'the water soaked straight in. You're a gardener, Sloan. You should know that.'

'Yes, sir.'

'Cheaper, too.'

'We haven't defined the area that needs searching, sir, yet. Not for the head.'

Leeyes grunted unhelpfully. 'I must say a farm's a fine place anyway to be looking for ground that's just been turned. They're always having a go at it on a farm.'

'There's the wood, too, sir,' Sloan reminded him. 'There's something in the wood and the cameras aren't going to help there.' The wood was one of his worries. He shot out his wrist and looked at his watch. It was too soon for more news from Dr Dabbe. 'What we need is daylight and there won't be enough of that now until tomorrow.' Some things, though, could go ahead. He'd sent Crosby up to Stanestede Farm and put out a general alert for Tom Mellot. He could explain about Ivor Harbeton to the superintendent, too, if only he would let him.

He tried again.

'As I said,' he began smoothly, 'the buyer starts the whole thing by building up various small holdings in the company that they want to buy.'

'Mellot's Furnishings,' grunted Leeyes. 'Go on.'

'They were cast in the role of victim,' agreed Sloan.

'And the raptor was Ivor Harbeton's company, I suppose,' said Leeyes.

'Beg pardon, sir?'

'Raptors are birds of prey, Sloan.' One memorable winter the superintendent had attended a series of evening classes on ornithology. This had had two unfortunate results. He became known amoung the younger constables as the Birdman of Berebury, which was bad for discipline, and he fell out with the Town Council which had a by-law prohibiting the feeding of pigeons in public places. This was bad for everyone.

'The company doing the buying,' Sloan forged on, 'hopes that nobody will notice what they are up to.'

'Ha!'

'Sometimes,' continued Sloan doggedly, 'they even sell some of their holdings, too, to stop anyone becoming suspicious.'

'Makes larceny seem quite simple, Sloan, doesn't it?'

'Some stockbrokers won't do it,' pointed out Sloan fairly.

'And some, I suppose,' remarked Leeyes genially, 'specialize in it.'

'It is a white-collar crime,' agreed Sloan tacitly.

'Fraud usually is,' commented Leeyes at his sagest, 'unless you count the three-card trick.'

Sloan kept steadfastly to the business in hand. 'Of course they don't do the buying in their own names.'

'Aliases?' said Leeyes alertly. 'Do they use aliases?'

'They call them nominees,' said Sloan delicately.

'I call them men of straw,' remarked Leeyes.

'But,' Sloan quoted his mentor in the City of London, 'undisclosed holdings above a certain limit are not allowed.'

'Sloan,' came the swift answer down the line, 'I may have retained my youth but I have been a policeman long enough to know the difference between "not allowed" and "not done".'

'Yes, sir.'

'So . . .'

'So there comes a moment when the buyer has to make that disclosure.'

'A law, is it, Sloan?'

'A code, sir,' he said. Even lesser breeds without the law

had codes of conduct. Sometimes, of course, codes worked better than laws. Sometimes they didn't.

'So that's how this character Ivor Harbeton started to get his claws into Mellot's Furnishings, is it?'

'In a manner of speaking, sir.' Now he came to think about it, perhaps 'raptor' was the right word. 'He got his hands on just under thirty per cent of the equity,' said Sloan, consulting his notebook.

Leeyes grunted.

'That's near enough,' explained Sloan, 'to the crucial figure for going into the market early one morning for the final killing which would have given Ivor Harbeton control.' When a bird of prey made its descent out of the sky down on to its victim it was called a stoop: even Sloan knew that.

There was a short silence while Superintendent Leeyes digested this information. 'That's when he disappeared, I suppose.'

'It is,' said Sloan. 'And that's not all, sir.'

'No?'

'In the beginning Mellot's Furnishings wasn't wholly owned by Tom Mellot and his wife,' said Sloan. 'The man in the City had them look it up for me.'

'Well?'

'George Mellot and his wife put up half the original capital.'

Leeyes grunted.

Sloan pulled his notebook towards him. 'I think we may find, sir, that Tom Mellot has a half share in Pencombe Farm.'

'And I think,' said Superintendent Leeyes weightily, 'that the sooner someone has a little chat with Mr Tom Mellot the better.'

'Just one or two questions, madam, if you don't mind.' Detective Constable Crosby slipped smoothly into his professional patter as soon as the door of Stanestede Farm was opened to him. 'May I come in?'

Mrs Andrina Ritchie was obviously less used to the interview routine and visibly braced herself. 'Of course.'

'It would help a lot if we could trace your husband.' He coughed. 'In the circumstances, if you take my meaning.'

She nodded. 'I have heard about . . . about Pencombe.'

'The easiest way to trace a man,' said Crosby, 'is usually through his car.'

'His car's here,' she said slowly. 'In the garage.'

'But . . .'

'It was found at Calleford Market the next day. The day after he'd gone, I mean.' She gave him a brittle look. 'The auctioneers rang up and said they'd noticed it was still at the market and was there anything wrong.'

'So you went in and collected it?'

'George Mellot very kindly ran me over to Calleford.'

'The keys?'

'Under the mat of the driver's seat where we always left them.'

Crosby shook his head sorrowfully at the monumental folly of this practice. 'Were you surprised about the car still being there?'

'Less surprised than I would have been,' she admitted frankly, 'if our solicitor hadn't telephoned me before the auctioneers did.'

'Oh?'

'It was old Mr Puckle from Puckle, Puckle and Nunnery. He told me he had had a telephone call from Martin that morning.'

'The Friday?'

'That's right. Mr Puckle had been in court but Martin had left a message with his secretary to say he was walking away from his old life completely and would Mr Puckle see to everything.'

Crosby wrote that down.

'More like walking away from his old wife,' she said bitterly.

Crosby said nothing.

'You can't just slough off the past like a snake shedding its skin,' she said with anguish. 'Can you?'

'No, madam.' A lot of people, though, thought that you could – until, that is, they tried it and found that you couldn't. Crosby knew that. Like Christian in the *The Pilgrim's Progress*, you took your scars with you. And kept them until the end of life.

'Mr Puckle said to carry on as usual for the time being.' She snorted gently. 'As usual!'

'Yes, madam.' Solicitors didn't like action. Crosby knew that, too. The only matter that stirred them into speedy action that Crosby knew about was the making of a will. They came round pretty quickly if you wanted to write a new will. 'So . . .'

'So that's what I've been doing.' She twisted her hands together. 'It hasn't been easy, I can tell you.'

'No, madam.' The constable cleared his throat preparatory to speech. There was one question that was always more delicate than the rest. 'What are you doing about money?' he asked.

'We had a joint account,' she answered tonelessly.

Sauce for the goose and sauce for the gander, was what

Crosby called those. 'And has it been used by your husband?' he asked curiously.

She shook her head. 'Not since the beginning of June. That's the funny thing. I asked the bank especially.' Her lips tightened. 'I thought he would have emptied it, you see. It would have been just like him.'

'But he hadn't?'

'He hasn't touched a penny,' she said.

Mate and checkmate.

'Perhaps Beverley whoever she is can afford to keep him in the style to which he would like to be accustomed,' she said.

Or cheque mate.

'But the farm . . .' began Crosby aloud.

'That's a proper partnership,' she said. 'It's in both our names. All signed and sealed and everything.'

So was marriage but Crosby didn't say so.

'We were in Stanestede together,' she said, 'as joint owners, each with power to act. That was in case anything happened. That's why Mr Puckle told me to do nothing and to carry on on my own. He said Martin might come back and then . . .' Her voice trailed away disconsolately.

'It would help us if he did,' said the constable truthfully. Crosby wasn't sure how Andrina Ritchie would feel about this in the long run but the police would be very glad indeed if he did. His mind was on the skeleton at Pencombe and narrowing the field always helped. 'There's just one more thing, madam.'

'Yes?' she said. Detective Constable Crosby noticed the almost subconscious squaring of Andrina Ritchie's shoulders as she spoke to him.

'How tall is your husband?' The shoulders slackened. It wasn't the question she had been expecting, he was sure about that.

She frowned. 'Isn't it silly?' she said. 'I'm not sure. He was about five foot eight or nine, I suppose.'

Crosby wrote that down. 'I expect he took his passport with him.' A new life might well begin in another country – it wouldn't be the first time that had happened.

'Passport!' she echoed with contumely. 'Martin hadn't got a passport. You don't travel if you're tied to a farm.'

'No, I suppose you don't.' Crosby could see this. A passport, though, would have Martin Ritchie's exact height on it and Dr Dabbe would tell them the height of the dead man. And if two and two made four . . .

'A farm is a millstone round your neck,' she said.

'I can see that it might be.'

'All the time.'

'Yes, madam.' Crosby knew the formula for calculating height from a thigh bone now. He wondered if there was one for doing the same thing from a pair of trousers. Or if you used the same formula. Cuff to ankle might give you height, too, if you had the ankle, that is . . .

'You can't escape from a farm,' said Andrina Ritchie.

'Could I see some of his clothes, please?' There was a code that men's outfitters used for selling off-the-peg suits that might help too. The only letters of it that Crosby knew, though, were SP and they stood for short and portly. He didn't know any short and portly farmers.

She led the way to a bedroom furnished almost entirely in white and opened the doors of a wardrobe that extended all the way along one wall. 'Martin's things are at this end.'

Detective Constable Crosby picked out a dark suit.

'His best,' she said promptly. 'His "Sunday-go-to-meeting" suit he called it.' Her lips twisted. 'His "Thursday-go-to-meeting Beverley" suit was more free and easy.'

Martin Ritchie wasn't short and portly. Crosby could tell that at once. If his suit was anything to go by he was a well-built medium man. 'A photograph might help us trace him,' said Crosby.

Andrina Ritchie moved to a drawer and pulled out an album. 'Take your pick,' she said savagely. 'I shan't be wanting them any more.'

Crosby tucked the album under his arm. 'What colour is his hair?'

'Light ginger,' said Andrina Ritchie, 'and if it's any help he had freckles.'

'It is a help,' responded Crosby gravely.

'More in summer than in winter, of course.'

'Naturally, madam.' He fingered his notebook. 'Is there anything else that would help us to build up a picture of him?'

'He didn't have any distinguishing marks, if that's what you mean.' She examined her own manicured fingernails with studied interest.

Crosby kept silent. The heap of bones that had been on the barn roof had gone a long way past distinguishing marks.

'Except an appendix scar,' she volunteered. 'He had that.'

'Nothing – er – deeper?' Crosby hunted about in his mind for a more graphic way of putting what he wanted to say and couldn't find it.

Mrs Ritchie frowned. 'I think he broke a rib once. There was some trouble once with a bull . . .'

Crosby didn't know if that would still show or not. Dr Dabbe would find it if it did. Another thought came to him. Diamonds were for ever but gold lasted well too. 'His teeth,' he said.

'What about them?' asked Andrina Ritchie, raising a pair of finely plucked eyebrows into an arch.

'Were they all there, for instance?'

'He had a crown on one front one that he'd had knocked out.'

'Another bull?'

'A hockey match,' she said distastefully.

'Ah.'

'A mixed hockey match,' she added with dryness.

'Heroes' hockey,' pronounced Crosby. 'That's what that's called.'

'And he had a bit of a gap on one side at the back. That's all.'

'It may be enough,' said Crosby, shutting his notebook and picking up Martin Ritchie's best suit. 'You never know, do you, madam?'

The detective who went round to call on Tom Mellot's family home in a rather nice cul-de-sac in a pleasant part of London was something of a linguist. He was also both young and personable. He had in fact been hand-picked for the job – Detective Inspector Sloan had asked the Metropolitan Police to send the best Spanish-speaking range-finder they had. Kitchen range-finder, that is. He had gone to the Mellots in response to an urgent message from the Calleshire County Constabulary.

'*Buenos días, señorita.*' He had begun on exactly the right note with the au pair girl who had answered the door and within minutes he was established where he wanted to be – on a chair drawn up to the kitchen table, a dish of tapas in front of him.

Teresita Losada pulled up the chair opposite to his and expanded in Spanish in a way that would have astonished her employers who had found her uncommunicative and inclined to fall into peninsular – if not positively oriental – reveries. Warnings about talking to strangers uttered by Mrs Tom Mellot did not extend in Teresita's mind to handsome young men familiar with the argot of Cartagena. Even the mandatory mention of the dreaded word 'police' by the young man did not upset her. In her way of thinking there was absolutely no connection between this agreeable listener and the Guardia Civil, still less with the Policia Armada y de Trafico. Besides, were not the British police wonderful? Everyone said so.

'*Muchas gracias,*' said the detective with the good manners to the offer of the bowl of tapas. Teresita Losada was too young and innocent to have encountered the Cuerpo General de Policia – the plain-clothes Criminal Investigation Branch of the Spanish Police. The detective quickly found out, as George Mellot had done before him, that the au pair did not know where Tom Mellot and his wife and family were.

'They are away,' said Teresita vaguely. 'They will come back.'

'Naturally,' said the young detective in his best Spanish. 'I understand. "Le Weekend".' Too late he remembered that this was predominantly a French expression but the girl did not seem to have noticed. He steered the conversation gently away from the difficulties of getting really good olive oil in this part of London – first pressing, naturally – and instead talked about the firm of Mellot's Furnishings Limited and what had happened to them last May.

'*Esa empresa!*' exclaimed Teresita dramatically, throwing up her hands.

'Tell me,' said the detective.

'What a time we had,' she said impressively. 'You would not believe it.'

'No?'

'Always the telephone. Morning, noon, and night, it rings.'

'Ah . . .'

'And men always talking, talking, talking.'

The man from the police made sympathetic noises but did not say much.

'And me,' she said, 'me, I have to look after the childeren all of that time because everyone is so busy.' She pouted. 'To keep them from being under the feet.'

'You must have been very busy,' said the other diplomatically. 'What was all the fuss about? Did you know?'

'Business,' said Teresita dismissively. Women's Lib was not as far along the road in Spain as it was in Great Britain. It had got nowhere at all in Teresita's village. 'Men's work.' She nodded in a way that would have disappointed not a few feminists.

The personable young detective nodded encouragingly.

'Mrs Mellot she did try to explain it to me one day.' The girl got up from the table to give a stir to a dish of paella on the stove.

'Ah . . .'

'But I did not understand,' she said. The great thing about the British way of life that Teresita Losada had grasped was that duennas had no place in it. Nothing else was really important to her.

'I see.' The accommodating young man contrived to sound sympathetic.

She frowned. 'I think it was that someone wanted to take their enterprise from them and they did not want that.' In Spain, too, having and holding went together.

'Naturally, *señorita*,' said the young man fluently, 'no one enjoys losing what is theirs.' Every policeman found that out very early on in his career. He slid a photograph of Ivor Harbeton on to the table. It was a press photograph and not a very good one at that – he was certainly no hidalgo – but Ivor Harbeton had been divorced not once but three times and there was no one on hand to supply a better one. His last known address was an expensive service flat. Nothing remained there to show who its last occupant had been. 'Tell me, did this man ever come to this house?'

Teresita Losada peered at the picture and nodded. 'Yes, he came here. I saw him.'

'Many times?'

She shook her head. 'Once only.' She set a plate of paella in front of the policeman.

'When? Can you remember?'

She searched for the right words. 'Just before the end of the busy time.'

'Did you have to take the children out when he came?' he asked indistinctly between mouthfuls of paella.

Her brow puckered. 'The children were in bed.'

'He came late at night, then?'

She looked blank. 'Not particularly.'

The detective metaphorically kicked himself. He should have remembered that to a nation that starts its evening meal after ten o'clock no such time as 'late at night' exists.

'I remember,' said Teresita, 'because I had to take the dog out.'

'I see.' The paella was good.

'I do not like taking the dog out.'

'No?'

'The dog does not like me.' This was Teresita's only failing in an alien land. The judgement of a small white Sealyham terrier was not wrong either. Her employers had found her kind to children but not to animals.

The detective got back to the matter in hand. He tapped the photograph of Harbeton. 'How long did this man stay here?'

She shrugged her shoulders. 'Who can say?'

'What do you mean?'

'I did not see him leave.'

'He had gone by the time you got back to the house?'

She opened her hands wide. 'I do not know. Mrs Mellot told me when I came in that it was time for bed.'

'His car?' said the detective immediately. 'Was that still standing outside when you came back with the dog?'

'There was no car,' she said. 'He came by taxi nearly.'

'Nearly?' For a moment the young man thought he had lost an idiom somewhere.

'I saw him come,' she said simply. 'He got out of the taxi at the end of the road and walked the rest of the way. He came nearly.'

The detective nodded, satisfied. Ivor Harbeton had come to see Tom Mellot for a secret meeting then, between principals, advisers out of the way, telltale company cars left in the garage. Business battles usually came down to this in the end – an eyeball to eyeball with seconds out of the ring. It wasn't so far removed from a medieval tournament and knights jousting after all.

He finished his paella before he brought the conversation round to Ivor Harbeton again: and he did that casually. 'You dont't remember which day of the week it was, do you?'

She didn't but he didn't mind. In fact he executed a little passacaglia all by himself as he went down the garden path and said 'Ole,' under his breath when he finished his report.

'Tomorrow,' Teresita Losada had said hopefully, 'I make fabada.'

Detective Inspector Sloan regarded the suit which Crosby had brought back from Stanestede Farm for a long moment and then said confidently, 'Ernest Grimshaw will know.' He looked up. 'What time is it, Crosby?'

'Half-past eight, sir.'

'Couldn't be better,' said Sloan briskly. 'He'll be back from chapel by now. The car, Crosby. You can take me there straight away.'

'Take you where, sir?'

'Postlethwaite and Grimshaw's in the High Street.'

'That crummy outfit.'

'Outfitters, Crosby,' Sloan corrected him gently. 'Gents outfitters, to be precise.'

'They're still crummy.'

'Old-fashioned,' said Sloan. But that was an understatement and Sloan knew it. The firm of Postlethwaite and Grimshaw was among the oldest in Berebury and very proud of the fact. The last Postlethwaite had died in the Old Queen's time – they had put up black mourning boards over the shop windows on the day of the funeral, naturally – but there were still Grimshaws in the business.

'They won't be open on a Sunday evening,' objected Crosby.

'Ernest Grimshaw,' said Sloan impressively, 'is probably the only man who actually still lives in the High Street.'

'Over the shop?' said Crosby.

'His grandfather slept under the counter,' said Sloan. 'Come on, Crosby, and bring that suit with you.'

What he did not tell Crosby was that he knew the shop well. It was in Postlethwaite and Grimshaw's shop that he, Christopher Dennis Sloan, had had his first pair of long trousers bought for him. In Sloan's childhood 'going into longs' had almost had the quality of a rite of passage. As the police car swept down the Sabbath-deserted High Street he wondered what symbolic rite among growing boys had succeeded it to make the transition stage between boyhood and youth manifest to the world.

Mr Ernest Grimshaw's first reaction on seeing Martin Ritchie's suit was to feel the material between his fingers. 'Nothing wrong with this cloth, Inspector. Run of the mill, of course, but nearly everything is these days, more's the pity.'

'It's not the cloth that we've come about, Mr Grimshaw.' Detective Inspector Sloan and Detective Constable Crosby had interrupted a Sunday-evening-after-chapel cold supper of veal and ham pie that was in its way as ritual as any feast in the church's calendar.

'Mass-produced, of course,' said the shopkeeper, turning

the jacket over in his hands. 'There's not a lot of bespoke tailoring about any more.' Old Mr Grimshaw's energies were engaged in fighting a rearguard action against the multiple retail stores. Postlethwaite and Grimshaw's premises occupied a prime site in the High Street and Ernest Grimshaw knew it. Young Mr Grimshaw's attentions centred largely on trying to bring the firm into the second half of the twentieth century. He was doomed to failure in this: his father had been the last man in Berebury to stop wearing spats. 'Or good cloth, either,' continued Ernest Grimshaw, who continaully lamented the passing of palmier days. 'You don't see as much worsted about as you used to, more's the pity,'

'Things aren't what they were,' said Sloan generally. He had found that this remark usually evoked ready sympathy with anyone on the graveyard side of sixty. It should go down well with the owner of the last emporium in the town to have had an overhead cash railway. Sloan could still remember the fascination with which he had watched the little brass cylinder with his mother's money in it travel to the lady cashier in her perch in the middle of the shop and back with the receipt and the change. The policeman in him now knew how vulnerable the cashier had been. The little boy in him still saw the mechanism as something that the wonder of the space age had not diminished.

'Near the top of the range, of course,' said Mr Grimshaw, looking over the whole of Martin Ritchie's outfit with a professional eye, 'but not quite at the top.'

'What we wanted to know,' said Sloan, 'was whether you could tell us how tall the man who wore it was.'

Mr Grimshaw dropped the suit back on to the table rather quickly.

'A little matter,' explained Sloan, 'of our having the suit on the one hand and some human remains on the other.'

'Quite, quite,' said Mr Grimshaw hurriedly. 'I thought there would be – ah – a reason. It being – ah – Sunday evening and so forth. How tall, did you say?'

'I wouldn't have been seen dead in it myself,' remarked Crosby chattily.

Mr Grimshaw had already taken a quick look at what the detective constable was wearing and averted his eyes.

'How tall,' concurred Sloan pacifically.

'Let me have a look at the trousers, then.' Mr Grimshaw felt about round his own lapels for the tape-measure which lived over his shoulders from Monday morning to Saturday evening. When his hands came back empty he looked at them in some surprise. 'Where did I put my inch tape?' he murmured.

'The inside trouser leg measures thirty inches,' supplied Crosby.

'Then the wearer will have been between five foot eight and five foot nine tall,' pronounced Mr Grimshaw promptly. He looked up. 'Is that what you wanted to know, Inspector?'

'It is a fact,' temporized Sloan, 'and facts are always helpful in our work, Mr Grimshaw.' Who was it who had said that there were no problems, only missing data? At least Martin Ritchie's height was a little less missing data.

'That's off the cuff, of course, Inspector,' said the outfitter.

'Naturally,' said Sloan. It was every man to his own metaphor. He picked up the trousers.

'They would fit our body,' remarked Crosby less discreetly.

Mention of the word 'body' aroused Mr Grimshaw's professional memory. 'We used to do a steady trade in white silk stockings for laying out,' he said, shaking his head sadly, 'but there's no call for them any more.'

'You wouldn't be seen dead in them either, Crosby, I suppose,' said Sloan sourly. He thanked Mr Grimshaw and reached for Martin Ritchie's coat and trousers. 'Come on. We've still got work to do.'

The grave to be a bed of hope.   **14**

The primitive instinct to congregate can be observed in almost all animal species, not least the human variety. Sociologists have noted that this herd instinct is powerfully reinforced by exciting news of any description but more especially by bad news. The inhabitants of the village of Great Rooden did not differ from the rest of mankind in this respect and the evening of that day found many of the more curious sitting in the Lamb and Flag public house in the middle of the High Street. A regular visitor there would have found the bar unusually crowded for a Sunday evening in summertime.

As well as the members of the parish there were also quite a number of people present from the Berebury Country Foothpaths Society. They, having found the hostelry eminently satisfactory in the middle of the day, promptly repaired there again as soon as it was open in the evening to mull over the events of the afternoon. It was to them that Gordon Briggs was holding forth about the delights of the walk the Footpath Society had missed that day.

'We'll do it next week,' said one of his listeners, adding drily, 'It won't have run away.'

Briggs looked blank. A week might be a long time in politics – so it was in the investigation of murder.

'What are the police doing now?' asked someone else.

'They've gone up to Stanestede Farm,' announced Len

Hodge thickly. He was standing against the bar, well into his cups.

'Ted Mason tell you that, Len?' asked his drinking companion, who was called Arthur.

Hodge shook his head. 'Poor old Ted's still seeing to everything at Pencombe.' He took a long slow pull at his beer. 'No, I heard the young copper being told to get on with it at Stanestede.'

'That'll be Crosby,' said Paul Hucham. The tall farmer had come down to the inn from Uppercombe Farm. He had been listening attentively to Len Hodge's recital of the discovery in the farmyard. 'I heard Inspector Sloan call him Crosby.'

'He's rather nice,' said Wendy Lamport. 'I liked him.'

'He's a policeman, isn't he?' growled Hodge. 'There's no such animal as a nice policeman.'

'Ted Masons's not so bad,' volunteered his neighbour, 'though I must say I'd like to know where he gets his cucumber seed.'

'Seed!' snorted someone else. 'You can say what you like but I'm prepared to bet Ted doesn't use ordinary seed. Not for those cucumbers of his. If you ask me, he buys the chitted ones.'

'What have they gone up to Stanestede for?' asked Briggs more pertinently.

'To ask Mrs Ritchie how tall her husband was, that's for why,' replied Len Hodge.

A little silence fell.

'My round,' said a gallant soul into the conversational vacuum which followed this remark. It was always a good idea anyway to stand the drinks early rather than late. The man had learnt that in the Army.

''Bout how long would it be since anyone saw Mr Ritchie, then?' asked Arthur, finishing his glass and pushing it back to the landlord for a refill in one practised movement. 'Same again, Vic, please.'

'He hasn't been around since I don't know when,' said someone else.

'Beginning of June, anyway,' said Len Hodge.

'They do say,' put in the landlord with a journalistic concern for protecting his sources, 'that he went on market day.'

'Young Jenkins didn't see him that morning at all,' said a man standing against the bar. 'Only on the Wednesday.'

'And nobody's seen him since,' said Arthur, resuming his glass without delay. 'That I do know.' He drew the top off the beer and added carefully, 'Unless that's him up there on the roof.'

'Gone to the mortuary,' Hodge updated him, 'for that doctor fellow they had up there for to have a proper look at him.'

'A bad business all the same,' said Paul Hucham heavily, 'whoever it is. The sooner it's cleared up the better. Your governor'll be pretty put out, I dare say, Len.'

'Stands to reason, doesn't it,' said Hodge suddenly becoming very taciturn indeed. The taciturnity might have been due to the beer; it might not.

Wendy Lamport shivered. She was there with her friend Helen, drinking shandy. She said, 'I still don't like to think about it.'

'Don't, then,' said Gordon Briggs, although it was actually the only thing that any of them could think – or talk – about that evening.

'No use running away from facts,' said Hucham. He turned to the farm worker for agreement. 'Is there, Len?'

Hodge plunged his face into his beer tankard before he spoke. 'It all depends what you mean by facts . . .'

Gordon Briggs, schoolmaster first, last, and all the time, opened his mouth to begin a disquisition on what constituted a fact.

'Ah . . .' said Len Hodge's friend Arthur, infusing the expression with such overtones that Gordon Briggs was constrained to close his mouth again without having uttered a word.

'There's facts and facts, isn't there?' declared Hodge combatively.

It was the measure of the scowl on Hodge's face that Gordon Briggs did not even speak when the man made this contradictory statement. Two varieties of fact would most certainly not have been permitted in Mr Briggs's class – but then his pupils were not, in the main, well over six feet tall, accustomed to hard physical work, and standing against the bar in an attitude proclaiming a willingness to take on all comers.

The tall farmer from Uppercombe did not disagree with Len Hodge either. 'It's bad business whatever way you look at it,' said Hucham.

Wendy Lamport looked troubled. 'And it's not over yet, is it?' She looked round the circle of faces. 'I mean, someone must have done it and we don't know who, do we?'

'Not yet, miss,' said Arthur. He drank some of his beer and then said slowly, 'Leastways, I don't . . .'

Hodge turned and began belligerently, 'Now exactly what do you mean by that, Arthur Sellars?'

Even Gordon Briggs, remote and ineffectual schoolmaster, knew that when old friends started using surnames when speaking to each other there was trouble brewing. 'What matters,' said the schoolmaster in the tone which he used for quelling the Third Form, 'is whether the police know, and if they don't, they'll soon find out.'

'I do hope so,' said Wendy Lamport, nervously fingering her shandy glass.

'Me too,' said her friend Helen. 'I mean to say, it's not very nice to think about it, is it?'

In his day Gordon Briggs had taught for a whole English lesson on the abuse of the word 'nice' as an adjective and any boy who used it in his essays could expect to find an astringent comment on the paucity of his vocabulary written in red ink in the margin. This evening he let it go by without a murmur. What happened today at Pencombe came in his mind into the category of pure Grand Guignol, and the bar of the Lamb and Flag was no place for a lecture on a popular eighteenth-century French puppet theatre specializing in the macabre and gruesome. Its similarity to Punch and Judy shows was another matter to be held over for a different setting. There was, as Gordon Briggs himself frequently observed, a time and a place for everything.

'If you ask me,' said Wendy Lamport, staring fixedly into her glass, 'there's something funny in Dresham Wood, too.'

'Is there?' said Len Hodge, suddenly very casual.

'What makes you say that?' asked Paul Hucham, leaning forward attentively.

'You won't laugh, will you, if I tell you?'

Nobody laughed. They all waited instead, looking at her intently.

'I had such a funny feeling when we were going through the wood yesterday morning,' she said.

'A funny feeling,' repeated Hucham in the manner of an accomplished professional listener. It was one of the techniques of the psychiatrist's couch. Repeat what the last speaker has just said and they will go on and say more, was how the psychology text books put it.

'I told you about it, Gordon, didn't I?' she said, turning to Briggs. 'When we came out of the wood yesterday.'

Briggs nodded.

'What sort of funny feeling?' asked Hucham.

'That I was being watched.'

Nobody said anything at all. That was a technique used by radio and television interviewers.

Wendy hurried on. 'You know the feeling, don't you? I can't explain it exactly but all the time I was in the wood I knew someone was looking at me.'

'Did you tell the police about it, miss?' asked Len Hodge, his face muffled by his glass.

She shook her head.

'You can't tell the police about a feeling,' said her friend, Helen, sturdily. 'Feelings aren't evidence, are they?' It was a view shared by most magistrates and nearly all juries, and opened up a tempting by-path of discussion.

Wendy Lamport ignored it. 'It wasn't only a feeling,' she said.

All her listeners moved forward slightly, projecting increased interest in the finite.

'What was it, then?' asked Hodge, running his tongue over his lips.

'I saw a shoe by the path.'

'A shoe?'

She nodded.

'A man's shoe?'

'Yes.' She nodded again. 'It came back to me this afternoon after . . . after they'd found what was on the roof – that I'd seen it yesterday, I mean,' she went on a little incoherently, 'lying by the path.'

There was a general relaxation of tension in those round the bar.

'An old shoe doesn't amount to much, miss,' said Hodge.

'There's always things like that in a wood,' contributed Arthur.

'People throw things away,' said Paul Hucham. 'They dump stuff they don't want on my land too.'

'It wasn't so much the shoe being there yesterday,' went on Wendy slowly, 'as its not being there today.'

A certain tautness came back into the atmosphere.

'That was what I've just remembered, you see,' she said. 'That it had gone by the time we walked that way to Mr Bailey's this afternoon.'

'That's quite different,' pronounced Paul Hucham firmly. 'I think I should tell the police about that if I were you.' He looked down at his watch and downed the last of his drink. 'Well, I don't know about everybody else but I must be getting along. It's Monday tomorrow and there's work to be done in the morning . . .'

So there was for them all but Len and Arthur were easily persuaded into having another beer by Gordon Briggs and the two girls seemed in no hurry to leave the comfort and fellowship of the public house. The landlord had called 'Time, gentlemen, please' more than once before the bars of the Lamb and Flag were quite emptied of people. Unfortunately no one noticed the order in which the customers left. It would have saved the police a lot of work if they had done so.

There was, of course, the usual flurry of car doors banging and cheery calls of farewell before a country stillness settled over the car park. In the midsummer dim of night no one noticed that there was still one car left there. There was no one about either – until the next morning, that is – to see its owner lying unconscious by the side of the car.

Wendy Lamport never knew what it was that had hit her.

Our ghostly enemy restrain.   **15**

'What!' bellowed Superindentent Leeyes.

'Twas on a Monday morning, all right, but he wasn't dashing away with a smoothing iron. He was sitting at his desk in his office at Berebury Police Station wildly waving a report about in his fist. Detective Inspector Sloan had been summoned upon the instant.

'Who,' demanded Leeyes, although it was all set out for him in writing, 'has been found where?'

'Wendy Lamport,' replied Sloan tautly. There was a hymn that he dimly remembered which began 'Morning has broken . . .' It was meant to herald the beginning of a glad day. Today wasn't a glad day.

'The girl who found the finger on Saturday,' said Leeyes ominously.

'The girl,' said Sloan astringently, 'who was talking to all and sundry in the Lamb and Flag last night about there being something in the wood.'

'That was obviously a very dangerous thing to do, Sloan, wasn't it?'

'We think she was simply hit on the head from behind,' said Sloan.

Leeyes grunted. 'Easy enough in the dark.'

'She wasn't found until this morning.' Sloan had started to piece his narrative together. 'Pub people don't get up all that early.'

'It's the late nights,' agreed Leeyes. 'Well?'

'She's still alive,' reported Sloan.

'That's something,' said Leeyes fervently.

'I've just come from the hospital.' There had been a message from Dr Dabbe, too, but he would have to wait. Sloan had gone to see the doctor of the living first. The duty house surgeon at the Berebury and District General Hospital was a young man in his first year of finding out what medicine was really all about. Passing Wendy Lamport's distraught parents in the corridor, Sloan suddenly saw the attractions of forensic pathology very clearly. Those who practised it were protected from anxious relatives as well as living patients.

'Is she going to live?' growled Leeyes.

Sloan couldn't answer that. The house surgeon whom Sloan had spoken to had been altogether too guarded for his liking. The policeman, trained himself to be non-committal, had been aware of much careful picking of words by the doctor. There were not a few unfinished sentences, too, and more than one chilling mention of the word 'hope'. When doctors started talking about there always being hope Sloan knew things were pretty bad.

'Or,' continued Leeyes militantly, 'is there going to be trouble with those infernal machines?'

Sloan winced. That was another complication. These days death wasn't the only alternative to life. There was a twilight area in between comprised of tubes and oxygen and ventilators and heart pumps. In *The Ballad of Reading Gaol* Oscar Wilde's Doctor had said that Death was but a Scientific Fact but it didn't seem to be even that any more. Not if what Sloan had heard was anything to go by. Not if you were on a life-support machine, that is.

'Not trouble, sir, exactly,' he answered the superintendent with deliberation.

Wendy Lamport's doctor hadn't said that death was but a Scientific Fact at all. On the contrary. He had described death as a process, not an event . . .

'Then he's never met a murderer, Sloan, has he?' said Leeyes flatly.

'No, sir. Probably not.' Death being considered a process, though, at least explained some of the difficulties in diagnosing it these days. Sloan coughed. 'The doctor says that if there are indications of brain stem death he'll – er – pull the plug out.' He wondered if in time the phrase would succeed 'kicking the bucket' and 'going for a Burton'.

'I hope he knows what he's doing,' growled Leeyes.

'He's never seen an injury like Wendy Lamport's before,' rejoined Sloan. The house surgeon had admitted as much: but then he was a very young man.

Leeyes grunted.

Sloan had taken a look at the girl himself, recumbent on a hospital pallet, but it hadn't told him anything more than he knew already. To all intents and purposes Wendy Lamport was a lay figure suspended half-way between life and death. He had stood at the bottom of her bed for a moment with the house surgeon but it hadn't helped anything except his resolve to bring whomsoever had caused the injury to book.

'I've got a woman police constable sitting by her bed in case she speaks,' said Sloan. It was the sum total of all that the police could do at this moment for Wendy Lamport.

Leeyes laid the paper he had been clutching down on his desk. 'I don't like it, Sloan,' he said.

'No, sir.'

'It puts us into a whole new ball game.'

'Yes, sir.' He cleared his throat. 'I have to report that Mr and Mrs Tom Mellot cannot be located at the present time . . .'

'You're looking for them, though, aren't you, Sloan?'

'Everyone is looking for them,' replied Sloan with feeling. He glanced down at his notebook and hurried on. 'Various South American countries with whom the United Kingdom has no extradition treaties will neither confirm nor deny that Ivor Harbeton is there.'

'If,' pronounced Leeyes, 'neither the newspapers nor his creditors could find him I don't think we shall.' It was realism that brought promotion, too.

'And, of course,' went on Sloan doggedly, 'we're trying to

establish where everyone was when the Lamb and Flag closed last night.'

'Everyone?' said Leeyes with a graphic gesture of his free hand. 'Who is everyone? Tell me that . . .'

Sloan repressed a sigh. The superintendent had an absolute gift for putting his finger on the sore point. He marshalled his thoughts. 'George Mellot . . .'

'Where was he?'

'Taking the dog for a walk,' said Sloan hollowly.

Leeyes grunted.

'Constable Mason,' said Sloan, 'was still on duty at Pencombe Farm. He says Mrs Mellot didn't leave the building. He didn't,' added Sloan, 'get away until after closing time.' This was something which clearly rankled with Ted Mason. 'And Sam Bailey and his wife at Lowercombe . . .'

'Yes?' said Leeyes alertly. 'It's their wood, isn't it, that the girl had been talking about? Dresham or something? You're searching the wood, aren't you, Sloan?'

'Yes, sir, the men are on their way there now.' He cleared his throat. 'Sam Bailey went to bed early, or so they both say.'

'Well, they would, wouldn't they?'

'Mrs Bailey,' Sloan forged on, 'says she went for a little stroll before she went to bed as it had been such a hot day. She says her husband was asleep when she got back.'

'Could a woman have done it?'

'With the right weapon, sir,' said Sloan uneasily, 'I think she could.'

'So you are looking for two things now, are you, Sloan?'

'Two, sir?' echoed Sloan.

'Do I have to spell everything out?' Leeyes said irritably. 'Two, Sloan. What the girl was hit with and what the head of the body was cut off with.' Gordon Briggs, the schoolmaster, would have had something to say about ending sentences with prepositions but Sloan couldn't have put it better himself.

'Yes, sir,' he responded readily enough. Dr Dabbe had told them yesterday exactly what to look for in connection with the head. Or disconnection. Something heavy and sharp and slightly curved, he had said.

'You can kill two birds with one stone, then, can't you, Sloan,' said Leeyes felicitously, 'and look for them both at the same time.'

'Won't keep you a moment, Inspector,' called out Dr Dabbe as Sloan and Crosby entered the mortuary.

Sloan ground his teeth. It was always the way when he was in a hurry.

'I'm just finishing a George Bernard Shaw case,' announced Dr Dabbe.

'Pardon, Doctor?' said Sloan, a little startled.

'A Doctor's Dilemma,' said the consultant pathologist with a cheeriness wholly unsuited to his surroundings. 'I'm the only person, you know, who can tell 'em whether they had been treating the patient for the right thing.'

'I hadn't thought of that.'

'And whether they did that properly,' said the pathologist as a rider. 'Medical audits are a bit of a vogue at the moment.'

Crosby pricked up his ears at the mention of the word 'audit'. 'Old accountants never die,' he chanted. 'They just lose their balance.'

'And you, Doctor,' said Sloan, manfully rising above this, 'now tell the other doctors whether they were right or wrong in their diagnosis?' It seemed a bit late to Sloan to be of any help: like a public inquiry after a riot.

'Bless you, Inspector,' said Dr Dabbe, pulling off the surgical cap which covered his hair. 'I've always done that. That's what post-mortems are for.'

'Well then . . .'

'What's new,' said the pathologist, undoing his rubber apron, 'is that now the doctors tell each other.'

'Confession is good for the soul,' observed Crosby sententiously.

Sloan said nothing. He was possessing his own soul in patience at the moment, waiting for Dr Dabbe to come to their particular case where the surgery had been distinctly amateur. It was different in the police force anyway. There your superior officer told you if you had been wrong – and pretty smartly. He usually told everyone else, too, about your mistakes . . .

'It might be good for the soul,' Dr Dabbe countered Crosby, 'but it's bad for confidence.'

'What about truth?' Detective Inspector Sloan, well brought up by his mother, was stirred into speech in spite of himself.

'The practice of medicine,' declared Dr Dabbe didactically, 'has nothing to do with truth.'

'Pardon, Doctor?'

'The practice of medicine is a purely empirical exercise, Sloan. Truth doesn't come into it.'

Sloan drew breath to answer.

Dr Dabbe forestalled him. 'It is only here in the post-mortem room that truth and medicine come together.'

'When it's all over bar the shouting,' protested Sloan.

'Nobody should expect perfection this side of the grave,' said Dr Dabbe with a solemnity that Sloan found himself quite unable to measure.

'Here we suffer grief and pain,' chimed in Crosby. 'Across the road it's just the same.'

Sloan gave up. 'About the skeleton on the barn roof,' he said weakly.

'Ah, your chappie . . .' The pathologist stripped off his surgical gown and canted it adroitly into a basket for soiled linen. 'I can tell you now that decapitation was almost certainly the cause of death.'

'That doesn't happen every day,' said Sloan.

'No.'

'There may have been a reason for removing the head, too,' said Sloan slowly, thinking aloud.

'Yes, I think that's a proper inference.' The pathologist stroked his chin. 'I don't think a psychopath would have concealed the body so carefully. They don't care, you know.'

Sloan did know. There were two sorts of Untouchables – those at the bottom of the caste system and those who remained untouched by human feeling. He said, 'Did it – can you tell – was it taken off while the person was on the roof or before?'

'Before,' said the pathologist without hesitation. 'There wouldn't have been enough purchase for anyone to stand on the sloping roof and swing anything down on something well below them with the force that decapitation would have needed.'

'Besides,' agreed Sloan, 'there would have been footmarks.'

'There weren't any footmarks,' said Crosby.

'Then,' said the pathologist, 'I assume that the head came off on terra firma.'

'So it wasn't an afterthought,' remarked Crosby with a perfectly straight face.

Sloan turned to Dr Dabbe in despair. 'If you had a skull, Doctor, you could superimpose a photograph of a person over a photograph of the skull, couldn't you?' The observation sounded to Sloan like one of those jokes children made among themselves. If we had some bacon we could have bacon and eggs: if we had some eggs.

'I could indeed,' said the pathologist warmly.

'If the cap fits . . .' began Crosby from the sidelines.

'And if we had some clothes,' said Sloan heavily, 'we should have known better where to start looking for a photograph.'

' "The apparel oft proclaims the man." ' Dr Dabbe quoted Polonius, reaching as he did so for the jacket of his own well-cut, professionally dark and striped suit.

'Clothes are a dead giveaway,' interposed Crosby wittily.

'That will have been why he was naked, I expect,' said Sloan. Of course William Shakespeare had put it better. He always did.

'The problem from your point of view,' said the pathologist pontifically, 'appears to be primarily one of identification. All the steps taken by whoever put him on the roof point in that direction.'

'Quite so,' agreed Sloan, although he was silently following a very different train of thought himself. In artists' representations of hell people were always depicted as naked. He'd noticed it on those half-circle things above church doors whose name sounded like something to do with the eardrum. It would come back to him presently. Hell, with its naked people, was always on the sinister side. On the other side would be heaven. Angels always came up clothed. He supposed there would be an explanation for that if he looked for it. Sigmund Freud, if nobody else, would have had a suggestion. Only one, of course. Tympanum, that was what the half-circle in the church was called . . .

'And the problem from my point of view,' said the pathologist, neatly separating Church and State in Sloan's mind.

'Yes?'

'Establishing the cause of death if it wasn't decapitation,' said Dr Dabbe, 'and helping you towards identification.'

Sloan nodded. That was the doctor's exact province.

'I can't help you any further with either, Sloan,' continued Dabbe. 'The answer to both may lie in the head, of course, and that may have been the reason for its removal.'

'We're looking for it now, Doctor.'

'A sort of Salome in reverse,' said Crosby, moving to one side to get a specimen case out of his line of vision. 'Funny sort of souvenirs you keep in here, Doctor. It isn't cauliflower cheese, is it? That white furry stuff over there? No, I thought not.'

'Talking about heads, Doctor,' intervened Sloan quickly, 'there's something you should know.' He told the pathologist about Wendy Lamport's fractured skull.

He looked grave. 'That's bad, Sloan. It means that time isn't on your side, doesn't it?'

'If we hadn't found the skeleton,' said Sloan, 'she would have been all right.' It was something that was beginning to worry him. He didn't know if that was what was called lateral thinking or not. He never even knew whether it was right to replace Fate or Predestination with coincidence or even a mad randomness. His grandmother had always added the proviso 'If I'm spared' when making an engagement – just in case.

'Disposing of the body is the eternal problem of all murderers,' he said.

'No,' said Dr Dabbe. 'No, Sloan, it's not.'

'No, Doctor? What is, then?'

'Eternity itself,' said the pathologist-turned-philosopher solemnly.

'Ah.'

'Dante,' said Dr Dabbe, picking up something that looked remarkably like a stainless steel chisel and pointing it at Sloan the better to punctuate his remarks, 'had Julius Caesar's murderers devoured eternally by Satan in the bottom-most pit of hell.'

'That's different,' objected Sloan. The Last Judgement might be a sort of catch-all for police officers who had been unsuccessful in solving a crime but it didn't absolve a detective from doing his duty.

'Not really . . .'

'I shall be quite happy to settle for the dock of the Crown Court at Calleford,' said Sloan firmly. That was as far as a simple police officer needed to go: everything else could safely be left to St Peter. 'Come along, Crosby, there's work to be done.'

'Where to, sir?' asked Detective Constable Crosby, tumbling into the police car. He liked driving fast cars fast.

'Great Rooden,' said Sloan with a distinct sense of relief. Great Rooden was where the action had been and that was where the police should be: not in police stations or hospitals or mortuaries.

'Great Rooden it is,' said Crosby, engaging gear.

'Lowercombe Farm first,' said Sloan. They would go back to the Lamb and Flag too, and Pencombe Farm, but a visit to Lowercombe Farm came first.

'We're on our way,' said Crosby unnecessarily. The police car was in top gear already.

'Dresham Wood to be exact,' said Sloan. Other policemen from F Division, led by Constable Ted Mason on account of his local knowledge, had already been searching it for some time. The first thing that Sloan had done after hearing about the attack on Wendy Lamport had been to order men there. He hadn't known what to tell them to look for: he had just asked to be told if there was anything there that wasn't usual in a wood. Ten to one a comedian would report a great crested tit and expect him to laugh and he wouldn't . . .

'To the woods, to the woods,' chanted Crosby joyously.

'Crosby, it may have escaped your notice,' Sloan said mildly, 'that one of Traffic Division's unmarked cars is right behind you.'

'Lawks 'a' mercy,' croaked Crosby. The speed of the police car fell appreciably.

'I don't have to remind you,' went on Sloan smoothly, 'that Inspector Harpe takes a very strict view of unnecessary speeding by police vehicles.' Inspector Harpe was the head of Berebury's Traffic Division and was known throughout the Calleshire Force as Happy Harry because he had never been seen to smile. On his part Inspector Harpe maintained that in Traffic Division there had never been anything yet at which to even twitch a lip.

'Yes, sir,' said Crosby with unexpected docility.

Sloan made no further comment, but sat back in his seat and tried to marshal his thoughts instead.

It wasn't easy.

He stared unseeingly out of the window of the car as the Calleshire countryside went by. The summer scene was a beautiful one but his mind's eye was centred on an innocent girl hovering between life and death in a hospital bed and someone out at Great Rooden prepared to kill not once but twice and he – they – still didn't know why, let alone who. He didn't even have the beginnings of a picture in his mind of the sort of person the murderer might be.

Ruthless, of course. That went without saying. Pitilessness was one characteristic common to all killers.

Strong. Even with a fork-lift tractor getting a body up and on to a roof took strength.

Clever. The barn roof had been a good place to hide a victim. Sloan didn't doubt for a moment that the victim's head too was somewhere nobody would think of looking. They would have to search for that when they had finished going through the wood. And after that there was the weapon which had been used to hit Wendy Lamport, to say nothing of the instrument that had separated the first victim's head from his shoulders.

Even that catalogue didn't include finding who it was that had killed the man on the roof, whoever he was. Who he was was something else they didn't know. All in all the police hadn't made a lot of progress to date . . .

It transpired that Crosby, too, had been thinking. 'I suppose, sir, that that attack on the girl last night lets Tom Mellot out.'

'I don't see why,' objected Sloan sourly. It rankled a little that Tom Mellot hadn't been found. A man, his wife, two children, and a white Sealyham terrier with a black patch over one ear shouldn't have been able to have been swallowed up into the background quite so easily. 'He could be anywhere.'

Crosby hunched his shoulders over the wheel as they passed out of the thirty mile an hour limit. 'It would have narrowed the field, that's all, if we could have counted him out.'

'Narrowed the field,' echoed Sloan richly. 'Narrowed the field!' He countered simile with simile. 'Do you realize, Crosby, that we don't even know the names of the runners yet.'

Crosby took this literally. 'George Mellot.'

'His barn, of course,' conceded Sloan.

'Len Hodge.'

'He would call it his fork-lift tractor,' said Sloan drily. 'And it was his fight.'

'Sam Bailey and his wife,' said Crosby.

'Their wood,' agreed Sloan. Time would tell what was in their wood.

'Andrina Ritchie.'

'Her husband gone,' said Sloan. 'I must say she sounded as if she would have killed him if she could.'

'Tom Mellot.'

'His firm,' said Sloan.

'He'd have known his way around the farmyard all right,' said Crosby. 'He was born there.'

'And Len Hodge would have helped him, I expect,' said

Sloan. 'He'd known him all his life, remember.' Those were the people you turned to in real need. The early companions on life's journey were linked by a bond of time and place. When it came to the crunch they didn't let you down. Women were inclined to joke about the old school tie but it was a bond for all that. It didn't have to be a silk one with a crest and a Latin motto on it either. The early association was what counted, be it the council school at the end of the street not named after anyone at all, founded like as not by the stroke of a committee's pen as a consequence of some reforming Act of Parliament, or a Gothic pile set up by an English king in a moment spared from battle or politicking with the French. It didn't matter.

Or a village school that everyone's son went to.

'Paul Hucham?' said Crosby tentatively.

'He seems clean.' Sloan knew better than to absolve anyone on those grounds alone.

'He was in the Lamb and Flag last night.'

'He can lift a sheep,' said Sloan absently, remembering his visit to Uppercombe Farm. 'Not that that makes him a murderer . . .'

The search party had found something in Dresham Wood. Sloan could tell from the whole mien of the man who walked towards him as they arrived. Constable Mason wasn't able to keep the satisfaction out of his voice either as he reported to Sloan.

Nor phantoms of the night appear.   **16**

Superintendent Leeyes's response was dampening.

'It doesn't sound a lot to me,' he said down the telephone line from Berebury Police Station to Sam Bailey's farmhouse at Great Rooden.

'Someone,' insisted Sloan, 'has been living in Dresham Wood.'

All the signs were there. Police Constable Mason had taken Sloan to see them. There was a thicket not far from the water's edge that had first attracted the attention of the police. A few leafy branches had been bent over some bushes to provide a sort of shelter and round about it were more signs of human habitation. Grass had been squashed down where someone had lain and twigs snapped off.

'Found a camp-fire, have you?' grunted Leeyes.

There had been no burnt-out remains of a fire. Whoever had been living in the wood had not cooked food nor seen a winter out in the open.

'Footprints,' replied Sloan succinctly. Even now a police constable was making a plaster cast of what looked like a size eight man's shoe, noticeably down at heel. 'And litter . . .'

There were no dustbins in Dresham Wood and it seemed that no one could live without creating debris. Archaeologists fell upon Roman rubbish dumps with delight for the information they gave.

So did detectives.

'Not just someone camping out?' enquired Leeyes.

'Someone living rough, I should say,' said Sloan judiciously.

'A stake-out?'

'We found some food,' said Sloan, cradling the telephone receiver between his ear and his shoulder the better to be able to turn over the pages of his notebook. He cleared his throat and said with deliberation, 'Proper food.'

The line crackled. 'What exactly do you mean by that, Sloan?'

'Properly cooked food,' elaborated Sloan. 'The end of a joint of beef. Pieces of fruit cake. Homemade fruit cake,' he added pointedly. Constable Mason, part-time gourmand, had been most insistent about the good quality of the fruit cake: had said it was important. And so it was.

Leeyes grunted. 'Anything else?'

'Bottles,' said Sloan.

'Ah . . .'

'They weren't obvious, of course,' said Sloan. 'They were tucked away.'

'They usually are,' said Leeyes.

'Even when there is a dustbin,' agreed Sloan. The disposal of bottles was a perennial problem for real drinkers.

'It's not a crime to live rough,' observed Leeyes, 'and it doesn't mean that he – whoever he is – is a murderer.'

'It's a funny thing to do, all the same,' continued Sloan stoutly, bolstered by that piece in the Bible about foxes having holes and the birds of the air having nests.

'You didn't get him, I suppose?' said Leeyes mordantly.

'No,' said Sloan, adding a rather belated 'sir'. It was marvellous how the superintendent always managed to touch a raw spot. Ted Mason's search party had done all the right things – like throwing a cordon round the wood before they went into it. Nothing, the village constable had insisted, could have popped out without being caught. No more, he had said, than a rabbit could have escaped a harvest shoot, not if it had taken refuge in the centre of a field, that is. In the end the reaper and binder – only that had got some new-fangled name now and it wasn't even called a harvester any more – cut down all the cover and the rabbits didn't have anywhere else to hide.

'So, Sloan, the bird had flown by the time you'd got there,' said Leeyes, contriving not only to touch a raw spot but to put his underlings in the wrong at the same time. That was a gift, too.

Sloan took a resolution about not being too defensive. 'There was no one in the wood by the time it was searched,' he said without any inflection at all.

'And no one knows anything about anything, I suppose,' said Leeyes testily.

'Sam Bailey says he doesn't,' said Sloan. 'I've just interviewed him.' The old farmer was behaving exactly like James Forsyte and carrying on about nobody telling him anything.

'Hrrrrmmmpph,' said Leeyes.

'And Mrs Bailey,' reported Sloan, 'left by car before the search party arrived for Calleford. Or so her husband says. She didn't say when she would be back.'

Leeyes grunted. 'And what has Len Hodge got to say for himself?'

'The Great Rooden Fire Brigade was called out to a barn said to be on fire over at Easterbrook. That's to the north of the parish,' added Sloan, 'but it's quite a way from here. Leading Fireman Hodge was at the wheel of the tender and the crew hasn't come back yet.'

'Said to be on fire?' Leeyes picked up kernels as quickly as a sow after acorns.

'False alarm, malicious intent,' said Sloan neatly. Every service had its own short-speak and the Fire Brigade was no exeption.

'Funny time for fun and games like that, first thing Monday morning,' grunted Leeyes.

'They think it's a boy playing truant,' said Sloan. There was a world of work and school – a better regulated world than the one in which Sloan lived and had his being – in which work began on Monday morning and finished – for better or worse – on Friday afternoon.

'So we don't even know if Hodge knows about the girl, Wendy Lamport, being found yet?'

'That's difficult to say,' answered Sloan slowly. In remote villages like Great Rooden it was impossible to know who knew that. It was akin to working in a fog, not knowing what was going on around you and not being able to see who was talking to whom. And sometimes, too, hearing things and not knowing whence they came . . .

'Or about the wood being searched,' said Leeyes.

'No,' agreed Sloan. One thing, though, was certain about villages and that was that news spread like wildfire. He, a detective inspector from the far-away town, wasn't going to be silly enough to say who knew what in Great Rooden. He was prepared to bet, all the same, that everyone in Great Rooden knew that he, Sloan, was back in the parish and that Dresham Wood had been searched.

'He'll hear soon enough if he doesn't,' said Leeyes realistically.

'Yes, sir.' What Sloan would like to have known was how many people knew that someone – a man, if the footprint was anything to go by – had been living in the wood.

And for how long.

He'd told them to leave the bottles where they were. A biologist might be able to look underneath them and say how long they'd been lying there. Mould told the experts quite a lot as well. Crosby was taking some fingerprints from one of the bottles at this moment. He'd found them round the neck. Whoever had been living in the wood had not troubled with a glass . . .

'This mysterious stranger that Len Hodge had a fight with, Sloan . . .'

'I shall be talking to him about that,' promised Sloan, 'as soon as I can get hold of him. And about one or two other things as well.'

'What about the Mellots?' said Leeyes. He was like a terrier with its teeth into the seat of somebody's trousers – he wasn't going to let go.

'I'm going there now,' said Sloan, 'but I'm prepared to bet

that they'll say that they don't know anything about anything, too.'

'Clams,' agreed Leeyes reflectively, 'don't have anything on people in villages. Touch 'em and they close up.'

Somewhere at the back of his mind was something Sloan had once read and remembered. It had been written by that prescient fellow who had written about 1984 and all that: ' "Those who have the beans",' he quoted neatly, "seldom spill them".'

Detective Constable Crosby was stowing the fingerprint gear back into the police car when Sloan emerged from Lowercombe Farm, blinking a little in the sunlight. It had been dark and cool inside the ancient farmhouse. Old Sam Bailey had been pacing up and down all the while, anxiety manifesting itself as crossness. He followed Sloan outside now, like an old dog with nothing else to think about.

'What shall I do next?' he asked rather pathetically.

'Try to think of places where your wife might have gone,' commanded Sloan crisply, 'and ring her up and ask her to come back home.'

Talking to Mrs Elsie Bailey had become suddenly very relevant. He hadn't forgotten that there had been leaf mould on her shoes yesterday afternoon – had it only been yesterday afternoon? It seemed aeons ago. If he, Sloan, had acted more promptly yesterday afternoon he might have saved Wendy Lamport from being injured. He braced himself mentally: policemen had to live with such thoughts just as doctors did. If you couldn't, you didn't make the grade. Detective inspectors and general practitioners were survivors.

The grizzled farmer nodded and made his way back indoors looking more bewildered than ever, his pepperiness suddenly evaporated.

'We're going over to the Mellots next,' said Sloan to Crosby, 'to see what they've got to say for themselves.'

'A proper Teddy Bears' picnic, that was, in the wood,' remarked Crosby, slamming the car boot lid shut.

'Yes,' responded Sloan briefly, his mind on something else.

'"If you go down to the woods today",' chanted the constable, '"you're sure of a big surprise."'

'No,' said Sloan seriously. 'We knew all along that there was something in the wood. What we didn't know was what it was.'

'A man,' said Crosby. 'Not much doubt about that now.'

'He'd been there for quite a while,' said Sloan. 'All the evidence points to that.'

'The bottles and things,' agreed Crosby largely.

'Doesn't that strike you as strange?' said Sloan.

'I've never liked the idea of living rough myself,' said Crosby, opening the driver's door.

'We're walking to Pencombe,' said Sloan.

'Oh.' He shut the door.

'A man,' said Sloan, returning to the matter in hand, 'has been living rough in Dresham Wood probably for several weeks and yet Ted Mason who is said by everyone to know all about Great Rooden didn't know about him. Doesn't that strike you as strange?'

'I thought Ted's beat was so quiet he could hear the grass growing,' agreed Crosby.

'Exactly.' Sloan tightened his lips. 'It's as funny as Len Hodge having a stand-up fight with a total stranger.'

'You don't have total strangers in villages like this,' concurred Crosby, falling into step beside Sloan in more ways than one.

'A stranger who is said not to have been seen since.'

'We've got a spare stranger,' offered Crosby in melancholy tones. 'Over at the mortuary.'

'All we know,' persisted Sloan, 'is that a month ago a man was killed and last night a girl was badly injured.'

'That's not a coincidence,' said Crosby.

'No,' said Sloan reflectively, 'I don't think it is. Although I must say I don't see the connection just at the moment.'

'I wonder what would have happened if that crow hadn't dropped the finger just where it did,' said Crosby.

'Wendy Lamport would be at work this morning for one thing,' said Sloan soberly, 'and not lying at death's door.'

Justice was a purely abstract concept and was something quite different.

'It's all a bit difficult, though, isn't it?' said the detective constable.

'Complaining before you get to the stile, Crosby?' said Sloan appositely as the road between the two farms came into view.

'We still don't know anything for certain,' insisted the constable. He didn't like walking and it brought out the worst in him.

'Just that harm was done to Wendy Lamport,' said Sloan, 'and that about a month ago an unknown man was killed. That's about all we know.'

'We aren't even sure it was murder,' grumbled Crosby. 'The doctor won't put that in black and white.'

'The body was decapitated and placed out of sight.'

'Good enough for a jury, I suppose,' said Crosby, capitulating on this particular point. 'They won't go for an accident or misadventure.'

'And left naked,' said Sloan, putting a foot on the stile at the beginning of the footpath to Pencombe. Naked Truth he knew all about. She appeared in a famous picture. Naked Villainy presumably had a long heritage too. He didn't know if there was any connection but he did know that the nakedness would weigh heavily with the jury. So would the decapitation. The command 'Off with his head' was something usually reserved for the enigmatic world of *Alice in Wonderland* and Tudor politics – not the contemporary English rural scene. Naked men didn't really belong either.

Crosby scuffed at a stone with his shoe.

'After which,' continued Sloan steadily, 'nothing happened at all until the finger was found.'

That was interesting in itself. There had been no hue and cry, no missing person reported, no pleas of the 'Come home, all forgiven' variety, no welcoming lamp burning in the window at eventide . . .

Presumably the waters had closed over someone as surely as if they had never been – and yet that didn't make sense either. Someone sufficiently important to be disposed of with such care must have been very much in someone else's way. It was also, it suddenly occurred to Sloan, a case of the victim being someone whose death didn't need to be known about to achieve the outcome the murderer wanted.

Or murderers.

They mustn't, Sloan reminded himself, forget that it wasn't only in the plays of William Shakespeare that murderers came in pairs. It happened in real life, too. At the very least, whoever put the body on the roof of the barn at Pencombe would have needed a look-out. Unless it had been the Mellots, of course. And if it hadn't been the Mellots, then they would have had to have been got out of the way by somebody.

And if it hadn't been Len Hodge so would he.

To say nothing of the dog.

If the Mellots and Len Hodge had both been got out of way, then, supposed Sloan, it wouldn't have mattered very much if the dog had barked because then there wouldn't have been anyone there to hear it. In his view this did not mean that the sound had not occurred – although it had been on this very point that he had parted intellectual company with the science master at school. Sound did not exist, the old dominie had declared, unless there was an ear to hear it. Sound was merely a series of waves emanating from an action and pulsating through the atmosphere. It was the receiving ear that turned those waves into sound.

'Pencombe's further away than it looks, isn't it?' remarked Crosby mundanely.

'The walk will do you good,' responded Sloan unfeelingly. 'Besides, it's giving us time to think.' Police action was, of course, taking place as well. There was an unmarked police car shadowing Leading Fireman Len Hodge and the Great Rooden fire brigade over at Easterbrook and every policeman in Calleshire was on the lookout for Mrs Elsie Bailey and her car. Every Force in the country was on the alert for Mr and Mrs Tom Mellot, two small children, and a white Sealyham terrier with a black patch over its left ear.

'I can't think and walk,' complained Crosby.

'That's a pity,' Sloan said with more than a little acerbity, 'because there's quite a lot for us to think about.' The plural pronoun was singularly generous, he thought. To date, Crosby didn't seem to have done any real thinking at all.

'The finger being found was a bit of bad luck for whoever put the body on the roof anyway,' said Crosby.

'And for Wendy Lamport,' Sloan reminded him. There might be a message at any moment from the hospital.

Crosby kicked at another stone. 'It's not something where death has to be proved or the body wouldn't have been hidden. It must have been someone who could just disappear.'

'That's true.' Sloan nodded approvingly. The aphorism 'Where's there's a will, there's a way' could be construed in more than one fashion. And 'will' could be written 'Will' with very sinister overtones indeed. 'It doesn't appear,' he concluded prosaically, 'to be an inheritance matter.'

Crosby wrinkled his brow. 'All that trouble with the furnishing firm stopped a bit suddenly, didn't it?'

'The heat was off as soon as Ivor Harbeton disappeared,' assented Sloan. 'That was when the takeover fell through.' What he really could have done with was a quiet chat with someone who knew about these things. Stocks and shares weren't his cup of tea: he had been brought up to believe them to be one stage removed from the gaming tables at Monte Carlo and nothing had happened to him in later life to make him change this view.

'The timing wasn't all that far out,' said Crosby.

'It was dead right,' said Sloan soberly. What he could not understand was why the entire police force of the United Kingdom could not lay their hands on Tom Mellot, his wife, two children, and a dog.

'The timing was dead right for when Martin Ritchie took off as well,' pointed out Crosby helpfully. A man was on his way to Stanestede Farm to check on the size of his shoes.

'Pity his wife threw his letter away,' said Sloan. Circumstantial evidence always helped, especially when real evidence was hard to come by. And the making of marks on paper with pen and pencil was one of the most revealing actions a human being could make. There were those who could read more into handwriting than a biologist into a drop of pondwater. It was just as well the study of calligraphy was a new science. Medieval graphologists would have soon been made bonfires of for witchcraft.

'She seems to be managing all right without him at the farm,' offered Crosby.

'Spiders eat their husbands and still do well,' said Sloan briskly. To his way of thinking militant feminists advanced all the wrong arguments . . .

The two policemen turned off the footpath and walked through the farmyard towards the back door of Pencombe Farm. Crosby jerked a finger in the direction of the barn roof as they did so. 'Penny plain or twopence coloured?' he said. 'You pays your money and you takes your choice.'

'It's blood money, though, that you're paying with, don't forget,' said Sloan. 'That's the trouble.'

Police Constable Ted Mason was feeling the heat in more ways than one. The temperature was rising steadily as the morning advanced. This sort of weather did not suit a man of his stature. The pressure of work which he was experiencing at the same time was all the more unwelcome for being unaccustomed. No one could have described Constable Mason as someone who was addicted to adrenalin.

He had been put in charge of the search for the instrument which might have been used to remove a head from a body – with a strong rider that he also apply himself to thinking of where a head, too, might have been hidden, seeing how, Detective Inspector Sloan had added, he was supposed to know every inch of his patch.

Neither task appealed to a man of his temperament. One required action and the other thought. Both were anathematical to Constable Mason. His working life had been centred round the skilful referral to higher authority of anything involving any effort. Knotty problems arising in Great Rooden soon found themselves dispatched to the sub-station at Almstone. In the nature of things this was staffed by a series of young, ambitious – and newly promoted – sergeants, keen to show the powers-that-be at Police Headquarters how good they were at dealing with different matters. Points on which they were able to demonstrate their mastery of police law were sometimes even positively welcomed . . .

On the other hand, anything that had been really likely to interfere seriously with the growing of prize cabbages Ted Mason had stamped on himself and forgotten to report.

With some good cause he had long ago decided that civil rights were a purely urban nicety and he had remained untroubled by them. Essentially rural devices like man-traps might be illegal and putting the villain in the stocks no longer a fashionable punishment, but the public pillory still existed in modern guise and Ted Mason had no hesitation in using it as a weapon. A threat to tell the world at large and the village of Great Rooden in particular – and for some the two were indivisible – about a breach of tribal behaviour kept many petty law-breaker toeing the line. For those who had no fear of neighbours' tongues – and were thus almost beyond redemption – he devised more condign punishment.

Only when he couldn't think of a way of making the punishment fit the crime did Ted Mason invoke the due processes of the law. He was thus much less worried than most when the courts couldn't match the two either.

He was, in short, a believer in the white-glove treatment rather than the kid-glove variety.

As a very young constable Edward Mason had once been drafted from Calleshire to London for ceremonial duty. A uniform preternaturally spick and span had been embellished by a pair of white gloves. His training days were still fresh in his memory at the time and he remembered having been told that there had been an ancient custom for judges to be given a pair of gloves before a trial, together with a nosegay to keep the plague or something at bay. He had vaguely associated the gloves with this and had started to put them on.

'Wait a minute, wait a minute,' growled the sergeant in charge. 'They're not for wearing, lad. They're for carrying.'

Constable Mason had stammered his apologies.

'Up from the country, are you?' The sergeant, who had been of the old school, had winked mightily. 'Now hold them out and I'll show you a trick or two.'

Mason had obediently held the white gloves out in front of him while the sergeant had filled the fingers with small steel ball-bearings.

'Right, lad. Now you hold those gloves in your right hand, see? And if you have any trouble with anyone in the crowd just give them a flick with those gloves and they won't forget it in a hurry. And,' he added meaningfully, 'should the television cameras or anyone else with fancy ideas about the police happen to see you doing it, there won't be any trouble afterwards, see?'

Constable Ted Mason had not only seen but had understood and remembered. He had long ago forgotten the event that had taken him to the capital. He had never forgotten the loaded white gloves . . .

Neither the Mason theory nor practice of policing was much help to him at this moment, though. He stood at the entrance to Dresham Wood now, a mass of indecision. There were men at his beck and call but he did not know where to tell them to start looking.

An instrument suitable for removing a head might be anywhere.

So, if it came to that, might be the head.

Long grass would conceal anything at this time of the year – which didn't help.

And he didn't even know exactly what they were supposed to be looking for except that whatever it was it would have to have been man enough for the job.

Which didn't get him very far.

Automatically economical of effort, he thought before he moved.

It was the village butcher's shop which first came to mind. Hubert Wilkinson's was of the old-fashioned variety. His nameboard still proclaimed him as a butcher and grazier and time was when he had killed his own meat, but Hubert Wilkinson now hung his knives up in the shop window for all to see. If any one of them had been missing for so much as an hour, he, Ted Mason, would have heard all about it.

Somebody else who would have had a tool that would have taken off a head with ease was the old lengthman who used to keep the grass verges of the roadside cut, but he had been replaced by a gang of men from the County Council. They descended on Great Rooden once a year and did a bodged job with an undiscriminating machine. The man who knew every culvert and gulley had been pensioned off and the village was the poorer for it.

Ted Mason dismissed the garage from his mind, too. Their tools weren't sharp. Even when it had been a forge the tools of the transport trade had been stout and blunt.

He didn't allow his mind to dwell on the local doctor either for all that he did have instruments that were sharp enough for the job. Doctors had easier ways of disposing of bodies than humping them up on to barn roofs.

There was always Jimmie, the wood spoiler, of course. Carpenters had saws. He would send a man to inspect Jimmie's saws.

The minion duly dispatched, Ted Mason continued to think. Next he did what an old mentor of his had often advised and put himself in the other fellow's shoes. He tried to imagine himself with a body on his hands whose head he wanted off. He would obviously look near at hand first and for something that would not lead the trail straight back to him.

That meant using an instrument that belonged to somebody else – double bluff was for a more considered crime than this, he thought. It wasn't something for country constables to be worrying about anyway. What he was looking for was something that either would not be missed or had been replaced after use.

Police Constable Ted Mason was not an academic man and distinctions between pure and applied thought would have been lost upon him but it was not at all that long before he reached the conclusion that a search of Sam Bailey's old barn at Lowercombe Farm would do no harm.

And it was not long after that when he found an old implement that had once been used for topping sugar beet.

It was by no means as dry and dusty as the other old tools beside it in the barn.

There was something new and fancy in psychiatric circles called transactional analysis. Detective Inspector Sloan had read about it from time to time in such police journals as kept an eye on what trick cyclists were up to. It made him more conscious of the quality of the exchange he had now with George and Meg Mellot.

There was a formality about his interview with them that had been absent before. It added a new dimension to this particular interface between the officers of the law and John Citizen and his wife.

Sloan's first question had been a simple one. Even so, it had provoked a visible shudder in Meg Mellot and clearly took George Mellot by surprise.

'The size of Tom's shoes?' echoed the farmer. 'No, of course I don't know what size shoe Tom took. Why should I?' He turned to his wife. 'Do you, Meg?'

She shook her head mutely.

Detective Inspector Sloan made a note. An ambitious young Spanish-speaking policeman in London might well get his fabada today after all. 'Right, sir, then may we come back to the takeover bid for Mellot's Furnishings?'

George Mellot ran a tongue over dry lips, and said wearily, 'If you wish.'

'When your father died and your brother took his portion . . .'

'No,' said George Mellot.

'No?'

'Tom didn't take his portion,' said George Mellot, 'and he wasn't a prodigal son or anything like that. Tom just wasn't cut out to be a farmer.'

'He couldn't stand the waiting, Inspector,' put in Meg Mellot a little timidly.

Sloan turned to her for elucidation. 'Waiting?'

There were two schools of thought in police circles. One was that you got more out of interviewing a husband and wife together and the other was that you extracted more from each separately. Detective Inspector Sloan took the more pragmatic view that it all depended on the husband and wife . . .

'Farmers have to take the long view,' she explained awkwardly. 'Sometimes they have to wait for years and years to see the results of their work. It's not an overnight affair.'

'Tom likes wheeling and dealing,' amplified George Mellot. 'He enjoys having everything – er – instant, so to speak.'

'So . . .' said Sloan steadily.

'So Tom went into business.'

'With his share of your father's estate?' Business, conceded Sloan silently, called for everything instant – especially judgements.

'Not exactly,' temporized the farmer.

'How, then?'

'It was all very well in the Bible,' said Mellot tangentially, 'this taking off with your portion. I dare say all they had to do was to divide the flock of sheep into two.'

'Jacob and his sheep,' said Sloan intelligently, 'of another colour.'

Detective Constable Crosby stirred. 'Have you heard,' he asked chattily, 'about the man who practised animal husbandry until they found out and stopped him?'

Nobody took any notice of him.

The farmer frowned. 'It isn't like it was in the Bible any more.'

Sloan projected polite interest in what Mellot was saying at the same time as striving to keep his blood pressure under control with Crosby. It was not easy.

'I couldn't afford to buy Tom out,' said George Mellot, 'and he couldn't afford to get started in business without his share of the inheritance.'

'Yes, I see,' said Sloan. It was the classic dilemma. Some victor or another – he couldn't remember which – had even imposed laws of inheritance on the vanquished that required land to be divided equally among all heirs in ever diminishing holdings. Was it called gavelkind? 'What did you do?' he enquired with genuine curiosity.

'Left him as an equal partner in the farm,' replied Mellot concisely, 'and went with him as an equal partner in the business firm.'

'Using the farm as surety?' Perhaps the very word firm derived from farm: perhaps they came of common stock.

'That's right, Inspector.'

'Did it work?'

'Our wives got on,' said Mellot simply.

That would be the crux of the matter, thought Sloan to himself. Competitive sisters-in-law were the very devil. He said, 'So . . .'

'So until Mellot's Furnishings went public my wife and I owned half the equity with Tom and his wife owning the other half.'

'And they owned half the farm?'

'Still do.'

'And after the firm went public?'

'We pulled out and just kept a nominal holding for the interest.'

Sloan nodded. All that explained the prosperity at Pencombe Farm over and beyond the agricultural.

'Then Ivor Harbeton came along?'

'The big bad wolf,' said Mellot tiredly. 'We pitched in behind Tom, of course.'

'He would have needed all the support he could get,' said

Sloan. Sometime last night – he couldn't now think when – he had found time to read all about the takeover battle for Mellot's Furnishings.

'Most of the shareholders were behind Tom ' said George Mellot. 'He's got a businessman's head all right but Harbeton was offering quite a lot.'

'Would he have won the day, though, if Harbeton hadn't disappeared when he did?' Sloan leant forward awaiting a reply. This was the question that mattered.

'Your guess is as good as mine, Inspector,' said Mellot drily.

Sloan cleared his throat. 'Harbeton doesn't seem to be the only person who has disappeared.'

Mellot looked up.

'Your brother's not at home,' said Sloan. 'Martin Ritchie from Stanestede hasn't been seen for a month, and a man who has been living rough in Dresham Wood certainly isn't there any more.'

The farmer didn't seem interested.

'And someone,' added Sloan for good measure, 'hit Wendy Lamport over the head last night outside the Lamb and Flag.'

Mellot nodded. 'We'd heard about that.'

'Have you any suggestions to offer?' asked Sloan crisply.

George Mellot shook his head.

'It was your barn,' persisted Sloan.

'I know.'

'And your fork-lift tractor,' he said relentlessly. 'Our forensic laboratory have found pieces of skin on the metal.'

'Don't!' implored Meg Mellot.

'It was obvious that that would be used,' said Mellot without heat. 'There is no other way of getting a body up on to the roof. I can see that myself.'

'If it had been daytime,' persisted Sloan, 'you would have heard them. Or the dog would.'

'I know,' said Mellot tonelessly.

'So either you did see it happen or it must have been while you were both out.'

'Yes,' agreed Mellot.

'Which?' asked Sloan sharply.

'While we were out,' cried Meg Mellot wretchedly. 'We didn't see or hear anything, did we, George?'

He shook his head.

'So,' continued Sloan inexorably, 'you are saying that there was a time when you were both out when it could have happened?'

'Market-day,' said Mellot. 'We have thought about that. Meg always comes with me to Calleford. Every Thursday without fail.'

'And you'd be gone long enough for any amount of mischief, I suppose?'

'Anyone could have got a small army up on the barn roof in the time if they'd had a mind to,' said Mellot flatly. 'I can't say otherwise.'

'When you are away at the market who do you leave here?' asked Sloan, although he knew the answer.

'Len Hodge,' said George Mellot miserably.

'Them as asks no questions isn't told a lie,' said Len Hodge fiercely.

He was standing by the red fire engine which had come back to its home station in Great Rooden High Street, and was sweating profusely in his thick black uniform. The yellow oilskin trousers of the firemen must have added considerably to their discomfort on a hot day such as this and the other men were changing back into their working clothes as quickly as they could.

Leading Fireman Hodge, though, was responsible for seeing that the fire engine was left ready for its next turn-out.

'Fuel all right, Fred?' he called out over the heads of the two policemen.

'Check,' came the muffled reply.

'Hoses?'

'All present and correct.'

Detective Inspector Sloan and Detective Constable Crosby had come back into the centre of the village to await the return of the fire engine. The unmarked police car which had been shadowing the fireman all morning was parked inconspicuously down the road. The two detectives had got a warm reception from Len Hodge.

'Nevertheless,' insisted Sloan firmly. 'I have a few questions to put to you.' He was conscious that he should have made the effort to have seen Len Hodge last night – except that last night he hadn't suspected that Wendy Lamport was going to come to grief. Last night, too, there had seemed to be plenty of time in which to consider at leisure the implications of a decaying skeleton on a barn roof. Today there hadn't been any time at all.

'And I've got a report to turn in to Brigade Headquarters,' countered the farm worker truculently. The perspiration was streaming down his face. It might have been due to the heavy serge uniform and the increasing heat of the day. On the other hand it might not. 'For all that it was a false alarm,' he added.

'So have I,' responded Sloan with deceptive mildness.

'You haven't got anything on me,' said Hodge, tilting his fireman's helmet upwards from his forehead.

'And I,' said Sloan evenly, 'am not dealing with a false alarm.'

Hodge carried on as if the policeman had not spoken. 'I'm not having you pinning anything on me neither.' He thrust his jaw forward. 'I'm not saying nothing, see?'

'What we want to know,' continued Sloan in the same low-key tones, 'is whether just anyone could have operated that fork-lift tractor at Pencombe.'

'Course not,' said Len Hodge at once. 'Not without knowing how.'

'Ah,' said Sloan. It was the oldest trick in the book: starting a difficult interview by asking an easy question that anyone could answer.

'It takes time to know how to handle one of them,' sniffed Hodge. 'I will say that.'

'And a bit of teaching, I dare say,' murmured Sloan cunningly. Almost nobody could resist an empathetic opening gambit.

'Just like it does one of these.' Len Hodge patted the

majestic Dennis fire engine. 'But when you've learnt how, it'll do anything for you.'

'Such as lift a headless body up on to a roof?' said Sloan sedulously.

Hodge's face darkened again. 'If you say so.'

'Not me,' said Sloan blandly. 'It's the forensic scientists at the Home Office laboratory who say so.'

'Same thing,' said Hodge immediately.

At the right time and in the right place Sloan would have advanced the cause of impartial scientific investigation being available to defence and prosecution alike. This, however, was neither.

'If,' remarked Sloan in a detached way instead, 'it had been my tractor . . .'

'Well?'

'And someone else had used it . . .'

'What about it?'

'Even if they had tried to put it back exactly where I had left it . . .'

Hodge scowled but said nothing intelligible.

'Then,' said Sloan, 'I think I would have been able to tell.'

'You would, would you?' snarled Hodge. 'Well, let me tell you . . .'

'If it hadn't been me that moved it, that is.'

'It wasn't me that . . .' Hodge stopped and stared at Sloan.

'No?' said Sloan pleasantly. 'I rather thought it wasn't, actually.'

'Tricked me, you did, you devil,' spluttered Hodge. 'I said I wasn't going to say nothing.'

'Truth will out,' said Crosby sententiously from the side lines.

'But someone had moved it,' said Sloan, undeflected.

'What if they had?' demanded Hodge aggressively. 'It weren't nothing to do with me. It isn't my tractor.'

'When?' asked Sloan relentlessly.

''Bout a month ago,' admitted Hodge reluctantly, his eyes down.

'Isn't it kept locked?'

'Not at Pencombe.' He shrugged his shoulders. 'There's nobody about much as a rule. Besides, it's always on the go.'

'This time . . .'

'I park it in the barn,' explained Hodge. 'It just fits into a space there if you're careful. Between an old harrow and the grain drier. There's exactly enough room for it.'

Sloan nodded encouragingly. Verisimilitude was the name of what he was looking for.

'Whoever put it back wasn't careful, that's all,' said Hodge flatly. 'They caught the harrow with one of the forks. It wasn't me. I've never done that.'

'When?' Sloan would send someone to check on the harrow as soon as he could. 'Night time or day time?'

'Search me.' He turned back to the fire engine. 'It was an afternoon when I noticed it but that doesn't mean anything.'

'Did you mention it to anyone else at the time?'

'Nope.' He shook his head. 'It's not my place to mention it. It's none of my business if my governor bashes a bit of his own property.'

'Which governor, Hodge?' asked Sloan softly.

All the bounce left the man. He went down like a pricked balloon, his shoulders sagging suddenly. 'You know about Tom, then, do you?'

'We do,' said Sloan. He had been reared in the good old professional school of interrogation where there was no nonsense about not hitting a man when he was down. It was easier for one thing. He didn't hesitate to press home his advantage either by adding ominously, 'All about him.'

'Well, then . . .' Hodge turned away.

'Except where he is at the moment,' said Sloan truthfully. That, he reminded himself, went for the man in the wood, too, and for Martin Ritchie. They hadn't exactly made a lot of progress to date in police terms.

'Not a man to stand still is Tom,' observed Hodge, clambering up into the driver's seat of the fire engine. 'I've got to put this away how. Mind your backs.'

Sloan stepped aside. Minding your back was an old Army

saying. It was easier said than done in the police force. So was standing still. They had another saying in the Army that didn't do for the police at all. 'Right or wrong, stand still.' What went down well in the parade ground – make a mistake there and ten to one it wouldn't be noticed if you stood still: move and it would – wouldn't do you any good at all in the Constabulary. Standing still would be viewed by the Director of Public Prosecutions as culpable, and mistakes had very little chance of not being noticed in the sort of scrutiny applied by the likes of Superintendent Leeyes.

'Wendy Lamport's pretty bad,' said Sloan, raising his voice as the engine was started up by Hodge. Even thinking about Superintendent Leeyes *en passant* kept a man's mind on the job.

If Hodge made a reply to this it was drowned by the noise of the powerful Dennis engine. Sloan waited until it had been driven out of the fire station and positioned ready for its next call-out. Hodge climbed down again and carefully placed the door in an open position. Seconds could count at a fire.

'I said Wendy Lamport's pretty bad,' repeated Sloan firmly. He knew exactly where Wendy Lamport was at this moment and it didn't help one little bit.

'I heard you.' Hodge jerked his head. 'I didn't hit her, if that's what you wanted to know.'

'But do you know who did?' asked Sloan directly.

'No, I don't.'

'The man in Dresham Wood?' hazarded Sloan.

The farm worker's response to this was completely unexpected. To Sloan's utter surprise Len Hodge's face split into a broad grin that extended from ear to ear. 'Him?' he laughed. 'That's good, that is.'

'What do you mean?'

'Him?' he said richly. 'He wouldn't hurt a fly.' Hodge started to walk towards his own car and then paused and said over his shoulder, 'That's his whole trouble.'

'Just a minute, Hodge . . .'

It was no good. Len Hodge had driven off.

The unmarked police car which had been shadowing him

all morning waited a few moments and then drove off unobtrusively after him.

The radio of their police car was chattering away as Detective Inspector Sloan and Detective Constable Crosby got back to it. Crosby fiddled with the direction tuner and then bent forward attentively, listening hard.

'Ted Mason's found something that might have been used to take the head off, sir,' he announced, straightening up again.

Sloan nodded morosely. 'It had to be around somewhere.'

'In the barn at Lowercombe,' said Crosby.

'I heard,' growled Sloan. He had just had a major suspect laughed out of court and wasn't very pleased about it.

'A sugar beet cutter.'

'I see.' He wondered what Dr Buck Ruxton had used to cut up his wife.

'It's gone to Forensic.'

'What we want now,' declared Sloan with feeling, 'is a Peterkin.'

'Pardon, sir?'

'He found something large and smooth and round.'

'Did he, sir?'

'And showed it to little Wilhelmine.'

'Well, I never.'

'They both took it to Old Kaspar.'

Crosby kept a prudent silence at this.

'At Blenheim.'

Crosby looked distinctly uneasy now.

''Twas a famous victory,' said Sloan sourly.

'Was it, sir?'

'This isn't going to be, Crosby.'

'No, sir.' Crosby switched off the engine.

'This is going to be a disaster,' forecast Sloan. He had never thought for one moment that the notion that the man in the wood might be a murderer would be something that Len Hodge would find risible. The funny thing was the fact that it exonerated him more quickly than any amount of explanation.

'Where to, sir?' enquired the constable practically.

'I don't think it really matters.'

'Pencombe?'

'Cold Comfort Farm, more like.'

'Headquarters?'

'Perish the thought, Crosby.' There would be scant comfort at Berebury Police Station either. And at the very least the Press would be there, clamouring for titbits that he couldn't – wouldn't, anyway – give them. To say nothing of Superintendent Leeyes waiting to know why he hadn't made an arrest – any arrest – yet.

The detective constable pointed along the High Street to the village inn. 'The Lamb and Flag?'

Sloan regarded the public house with disfavour. There was something seriously wrong with the anatomy of the lamb on the signboard but he hadn't time to examine it more closely. 'Nobody knows anything there, and if they do, they aren't going to tell us.' To the best of Sloan's knowledge and belief the Lamb and Flag had been wrung dry of facts as soon as Wendy Lamport had been found. He turned his gaze back to the fire station. Did Len Hodge's laughter really let out the man in the wood? On the whole Sloan thought so. It had been so spontaneous . . .

'Sir,' said Crosby, 'have you heard the one about the skeleton?'

'What's that?' He brought his mind back to the police car with an effort.

'The one about why the skeleton didn't go to the ball.'

'No,' responded Sloan heatedly, 'and I . . .'

'Because he had nobody to go with. Get it?' asked Crosby. 'No body.'

'I get it.' Sloan's ire subsided as quickly as it had risen. If soldiers sought reputation in the cannon's mouth there was no reason why detective constables shouldn't crack a bad joke or two in a murder enquiry when there wasn't anything more constructive to do.

The trouble with this case was that all they had were the ingredients without knowing what the recipe was for. To hand, so to speak, were a naked headless corpse, a weapon, and an injured girl. Missing with varying degrees of relevance – but undoubtedly germane – was a defaulting financier, an absconding husband, and . . .

The police radio came to life again.

Crosby answered with their call sign and then listened with his notepad at the ready. 'The fingerprints on the bottles in the wood . . .'

'Yes?' At this moment Sloan didn't have a harsh word to say about computers or the Criminal Record Office.

'Known.'

Sloan perked up. They weren't totally in Indian country, then.

'Luke Michael Bailey,' repeated Crosby aloud, writing fast. 'Numerous convictions all over the country for offences associated with alcohol abuse.'

'Ah . . .' Sloan sank back in the passenger seat.

'Last known address . . .'

'Yes?' said Sloan.

'A drying-out centre for alcoholics in Luston.'

18

The engine of the police car was still running.

'Back to Lowercombe, then, sir?' asked Crosby.

'Back to the drawing-board, if you ask me,' responded Sloan mordantly. In his experience alcoholics didn't as a rule commit murder except by accident in a drunken brawl. And every alcoholic he had ever known lacked the resolution to conceal dead and dismembered bodies in carefully thought-out hiding places.

'It's Sam Bailey's son for sure,' pronounced Crosby. He wrinkled his brow. 'Now I come to think about it, Mrs Ritchie did mention that Sam had a son.'

Sloan nodded. 'And he called his wife "Mother", didn't he?' There had been a prodigal son in the offing in Great Rooden all right but it had been somewhere else. It wasn't at Pencombe Farm with the Mellots, then, where there had been a definite return of the native, but at Lowercombe with the Baileys . . .

'His mother will have been feeding him, won't she?' said Crosby. 'With what was left over from the table, I expect.'

'Better than the husks that the swine did eat,' said Sloan biblically. 'Fed, forgiven, and known again' was how Kipling had put it.

'Except that alcoholics don't get hungry anyway,' offered Crosby out of his own experience on the beat. The railway arches at Berebury provided shelter of a sort for them and had to be visited by foot constables on night duty.

'Sam Bailey won't have known about him – Luke, did you say his name was? – being there in the wood,' said Sloan confidently. Sanctuary Wood – no, that had been somewhere else. 'He's not the sort of man to kill a fatted calf is Sam Bailey.'

'At least,' said Crosby, 'we know now how Mrs Bailey got the leaf mould on her shoes. That's something.'

'Len Hodge knew about him being there in the wood,' said Sloan thoughtfully. 'That's why the first thing he did when he heard about the finger was to go over there. Do you remember?'

'To check.'

'And Mrs Bailey was pretty agitated, too, at first,' recollected Sloan. 'Until we told her it was an old finger, and then she calmed down. I reckon she took off with Luke until the search of the wood was over.'

'If,' said Crosby, his face contorted with thought, 'Len Hodge needed to check that the body wasn't Luke Bailey's, doesn't that mean that he didn't know whose it really was?'

'Well done,' applauded Sloan softly. 'Go on.'

The constable continued much more tentatively. 'The body could still have been Ivor Harbeton's and Len Hodge not have known about it, I suppose?'

'At first,' said Sloan.

'Put there by one Mellot . . .'

'Or the other.'

'Or both.'

'It could,' agreed Sloan.

'But Hodge did know about the fork-lift tractor having been moved while he wasn't there, didn't he? All along.'

'He will have known,' said Sloan patiently, 'but I dare say the fact only became really significant after the body was found and Hodge put two and two together.' The assistant chief constable who was a great man for Latin tags had a favourite one for events that followed on: *post hoc ergo propter hoc.*

'That's when Hodge realized it could have been one of the

Mellots who had done the dastardly deed,' deduced Crosby, 'and clammed up.'

'I think so,' said Sloan slowly. As well as having the wrong Prodigal Son in mind he'd probably got the wrong school tie, too. Tom and George Mellot and Len Hodge would have known each other all their lives – as well as Luke Bailey. You didn't shop your childhood companions. Nor your employer if it came to that – not if you were old-fashioned, that is.

'Finding out it was Luke Bailey in the wood then,' concluded Crosby with rustic simplicity, 'is a snake and not a ladder.'

'A snare and a delusion,' agreed Sloan gravely.

Superintendent Leeyes wouldn't have chosen either metaphor but his sentiment would have been the same.

'So we've got to begin at the beginning again.' Crosby leant forward and switched off the engine.

'Except,' said Sloan appositely, 'that we don't even know when that was.' In this game you actually had to find square one first before you could get back to it.

'A finger on a footpath,' said Crosby.

Sloan shook his head. 'That came later. The finger being found on the footpath was just bad luck on the murderer's part.'

'You can't win them all,' said Crosby ambiguously.

'The finger was just where we came in,' said Sloan. Fate had thrown a six for them to start.

'But . . .' Crosby started to say something.

'It all began at least a month before that,' said Sloan firmly.

'But what did it begin with?' asked the constable.

Sloan shrugged his shoulders. Where did murder begin? Some would say with Cain and Abel. Some – the Freudians – would say with Adam and Eve. And as for what with – that was anybody's guess in this particular case. Greed, jealousy, revenge, lust . . . A judge would instruct a jury that the motive was irrelevant – the crime was what counted and the crime was what should be punished – but motive mattered to an investigating officer all right. It usually mattered to a jury as well, despite what the judge said.

'I reckon George Mellot thinks it was Tom Mellot, too,' offered Crosby after a moment. 'If it wasn't himself, that is.'

'Not so much brother against brother as brother protecting brother,' Sloan agreed.

'With George giving Tom a helping hand,' added Crosby for good measure, 'if he needed it.'

'Maybe, maybe not.' Sloan wasn't sure.

'And Len Hodge pitching in too, for that matter.'

'That would figure, all right.'

'And Tom decamps when he gets the word from brother George that all is up.'

'That fits too.' Sloan nodded. 'So does Mrs Meg Mellot fainting at the mention of Ivor Harbeton's name.'

'The body was got up there without being noticed, remember,' said Crosby, 'or the dog barking. The Mellots could have put it up there any time they liked.'

'Either of them.'

'Both of them.'

'There was just one other time when someone else could have done that, too,' said Sloan fairly. There was a word space navigators and oil-rig engineers used for a short period of time when circumstances were favourable to an enterprise. They got it from the weathermen. 'There was a window . . .'

'Pardon, sir?'

'Market-day,' said Sloan without explanation. 'George and Meg Mellot always went into Calleford on market-day. Everyone knew that.'

'Hodge would have been there, though,' objected Crosby.

'Hodge might have been got out of the way.'

'How?'

Sloan looked along the High Street and pointed in the direction of the fire engine. The idea had just come to him. 'False alarm, malicious intent,' he said. 'He'd have answered a fire alarm.'

Superintendent Leeyes was at his most peppery. He regarded his opposite number in the Calleshire Fire Brigade as a necessary evil and didn't want to be beholden to him for anything. Firemen were useful for extinguishing fires and their heavy lifting gear certainly came in handy on occasion but in his view they ranked well below the constabulary as a public service. From time to time at the golf club he played a needle match with the Chief Fire Officer at Berebury which was very trying for all concerned as the fireman was the better player. Superintendent Leeyes attributed this to the more flexible shift system enjoyed by the Fire Service. The feeling at the police station was that he would have shot at a sitting bird, too, if he could.

'It would have been theoretically possible for that body to have been hauled up on to that roof in broad daylight on market-day if Len Hodge wasn't there, Sloan,' he barked. 'Is that what you're trying to say?'

'Yes, sir.' Sloan coughed. 'We know – and so presumably do a great many people – that George and Meg Mellot go into Calleford together every Thursday.'

'Leaving Len Hodge at Pencombe?'

'And the dog,' said Sloan down the telephone.

'Well?'

'Len Hodge is a Leading Fireman with the Great Rooden retained brigade.'

'I get you.' He grunted. 'And you want to know if they had a call-out on the first Thursday in June?'

'Any Thursday,' replied Sloan. 'The body could have been hidden until the Thursday of the week after.' The forensic scientists were not prepared to be definite to within days about how long it had been on the roof.

'The head,' said Leeyes pointedly, 'has been hidden without being found.'

'We've got the instrument that took it off,' said Sloan. His superior officer had a positive gift for putting a man on the defensive.

'No fingerprints on it, though,' he said.

'No,' said Sloan. That would have been too much to hope for. Besides, they were not dealing with a fool. Or fools.

'What was it?'

'A tool for topping sugar beet.'

'Did you know, Sloan, that stage beheading is done with a cabbage?'

'No, sir.' There were a lot of things he did not know. He cleared his throat. 'We're on the track of the man in the wood.' He explained about Luke Bailey.

'Proper biblical touch, eh, Sloan?'

'Yes, sir,' he said, his memory teasing him. Somewhere in the Bible there had been something closer to the case than the parable of the Prodigal Son but he couldn't for the life of him bring it to mind.

'That's who Hodge will have been fighting with in the pub, I suppose?'

'So it will.' Sloan hadn't got round to thinking about that.

'Didn't want him showing up there, of course. Give the game away.'

'Not when he was supposed to be lying low in the wood,' he agreed.

'Where does all this leave you, Sloan?'

'Not very much further forward, sir, I'm afraid.'

'Find out who it was up there on the roof,' adjured Leeyes for the second time, 'and you'll be nearer to knowing who did it.'

'Chance would be a fine thing,' rejoined Sloan.

'What was that?' the line crackled.

'Nothing, sir.'

'Where do you go from here?'

'I don't know,' said Sloan truthfully.

Detective Inspector Sloan walked back from the telephone box to the police car. Some calls were too private for the police radio. People talked about the freedom of the air. That meant that the air was free to everybody and there were those who could pick up the wave band that the Constabulary used.

Crosby looked up as he approached.

'The Great Rooden retained fire brigade,' announced Sloan, not without a little pardonable portentousness, 'answered a three nines call on Thursday, June first, at ten hundred hours to the village at Cullingoak.'

'Did they, sir?'

'Which is at the absolute edge of the area they cover.'

'Surprise, surprise.'

'To a fictitious address,' added Sloan, although the lily didn't need gilding.

'False alarm, malicious intent,' spelled out Crosby, 'to get Hodge out of the way.'

'They did not report back to their home station until nearly eleven o'clock that morning.'

'It wouldn't take long to start up that fork-lift tractor, run it up to gutter level, and tip the body out,' said Crosby helpfully.

'And the dog could bark as much as it liked,' said Sloan. It wasn't going to be like a certain Sherlock Holmes story after all. That was a relief. Art imitating life was one thing. Life imitating literature was quite another.

'With only the murderer to hear,' said Crosby.

'Or murderers.' They still didn't know yet how many persons there were with blood on their hands. There was altogether too much that they did not know in this case. 'We may not know who,' added Sloan grimly, 'but at least we are beginning to know how and when.'

Crosby scratched his head. 'I suppose Len Hodge might have only been got out of the way to give him an alibi.'

'We might make a detective out of you yet, Crosby,' said Sloan warmly. Being a good investigation officer called for a certain quality of mind which took nothing for granted.

Crosby squinted modestly at his toes and said, 'Hodge could have put the body up there, then answered a fire call and then damaged the tractor afterwards on purpose.'

'Nothing to stop him,' agreed Sloan. Len Hodge couldn't be said to be in the clear yet by any manner of means: nevertheless there had been a time when the farmyard at Pencombe had been deserted long enough for a body to be hidden . . .

'Doesn't get us very far, sir, does it?' said Crosby gloomily.

'No,' said Sloan. Blind alleys were something a police

officer had to get used to. Unsolved cases, too, had to be lived with as well as lived down. He sighed. 'We'd better get going, I suppose.'

Crosby leaned forward to switch on the engine once more. 'Where to, sir?'

'Back to base,' Sloan said unwillingly. There would be no comfort to be had at the police station. Worse, there might be a message from the hospital about Wendy Lamport. 'There's something else we haven't thought about, Crosby.'

'Sir?'

'If Luke Bailey isn't involved with the body,' said Sloan, 'why did Wendy Lamport get clobbered last night just because she talked about the wood?'

'Search me,' said Crosby, engaging gear.

'What happened to her wasn't an accident,' said Sloan with asperity. That at least was a certain thing in an uncertain world.

The detective constable steered the police car away from the kerb. 'No.'

'The murderer must have been around, mustn't he? To have hit her, I mean.' Anything else would smack too much of coincidence.

'Yes, sir.' They were level with the Great Rooden Fire Station now.

'He did that all right, sir.' Their vehicle drew level with the Lamb and Flag car park next. Wendy Lamport's little car was still standing there. Orange ribbons marked out the area the forensic people had gone over.

Sloan stared into the pub car park as they went by. It was funny how they all automatically fell into the way of thinking of all murderers as men, but as the lawyers said, the male embraced the female. He had an idea that the one he had been thinking about in the Bible had been female. There was a parallel somewhere that he couldn't pin down. Perhaps it would come to him if he thought about something else.

'Remind me of all who were there last night,' he said.

'Len Hodge,' said Crosby.

They had exhausted the subject of Len Hodge.

'Paul Hucham.'

'All we know about him,' said Sloan realistically, 'is that he can lift sheep. I saw him doing it.'

'So presumably can George Mellot,' said Crosby.

'To say nothing of his brother Tom,' said Sloan. 'He's younger, too.'

'And Luke Bailey,' added Crosby. 'He could have been in the car park without anyone being the wiser. Drunks have a lot of strength.' This was something else he'd learnt early on the beat.

'Spoilt for choice,' said Sloan sourly. 'That's our trouble. At least I don't see Mrs Ritchie lifting a sheep. Or anything else for that matter.'

Crosby nodded. 'Nor driving a fork-lift tractor. She doesn't even look the part.'

'All the same I must say it would have been a help to have had that note she threw on the fire.' People like Martin Ritchie could always disappear if they put their minds to it. The insurance companies knew that.

'The kitchen fire,' said Sloan absently. There had been several famous cases of disappearance. Usually there was a seven-year wait for inheritance but at least Andrina Ritchie could carry on as a full partner with the farm.

'There wasn't a fire in the kitchen,' said Crosby.

Sloan stiffened. 'Say that again.'

'There wasn't a fire in the kitchen,' repeated the constable obediently.

Sloan stared at him. 'Are you sure?'

'Dead certain,' insisted the constable, aggrieved. 'It was all electric. Everything. Not like Pencombe. There wasn't a real fire anywhere.'

'Of course! I remember now,' said Sloan softly. 'The stream gives them all the power they need for free at Stanestede.' Paul Hucham had told him that, hadn't he?

When they had been up on the hill near the path from Uppercombe down to Stanestede.

'They have their own generator or something,' said Crosby. 'She said so.'

'I do believe,' breathed Sloan, thinking furiously, 'that that might be the lie circumstantial.'

'Beg pardon, sir?'

'Something Touchstone said,' replied Sloan. William Shakespeare had struck the right note as usual.

'Who's Touchstone?' asked Crosby.

'A clown,' said Sloan crisply. 'Crosby, your notebook.'

'Here, sir.'

'Let me see exactly what Andrina Ritchie said to you when you went to Stanestede.'

'Nothing very important, sir. I told you at the time.'

Sloan turned the pages back until he found the transcript. He studied it for a full minute and then said, 'You are wrong about that, Crosby.'

'Me, sir?'

'You, Crosby.' There was an old tune that went 'It's not what you say, it's the way that you say it.' That went for what Andrina Ritchie had said to Crosby, too. 'Read it again.'

'Yes, sir.'

'We're not going back to Berebury.'

'No, sir?'

'Take the next right turn,' he commanded.

'Yes, sir.'

'And you can put your foot down.'

'Thank you, sir,' said Crosby joyously.

'I've got one or two questions to ask Mrs Andrina Ritichie.'

'Stone the crows,' said Detective Constable Crosby as he accelerated.

'Let's look to the lady,' said Sloan more aptly still.

'Sloan,' thundered Superintendent Leeyes down the telephone, 'are you out of your mind?'

'No, sir.'

'What has someone in the Bible called Judith got to do with your arresting Andrina Ritchie?'

'Not the Bible exactly, sir. The Apocrypha.'

It was immediately apparent that to the superintendent they were one and the same. He growled dangerously.

'Judith,' explained Sloan hastily, 'cut off Holofernes' head while he was in bed beside her. For the good of her country.'

'Thinking of England, was she?'

'Israel, actually.' He coughed. 'I suppose you might call her an early female activist.'

'Sloan, do I have to come to Great Rooden myself to get any sense out of you?'

'No, sir,' Sloan said hurriedly. 'I'll explain. We hadn't thought a lot about Andrina Ritchie because we didn't see her humping a headless body down to Pencombe.' In the Apocrypha Judith had carried off Holofernes' head in a basket and left the body behind.

'Somebody did.'

'Paul Hucham,' said Sloan. 'He put it on the roof.'

'Ah . . .' Leeyes let out a sigh. 'An eternal triangle.'

'I'm afraid so, sir,' agreed Sloan. 'No one suspected anything because they weren't seen together. There was no need for anyone to see them because there was a path between the two farms and anyway it's all very remote up there on the hill.'

Leeyes grunted. 'The old, old story . . .'

'They were very clever.'

'Nearly pulled it off, did they?' That was the police yardstick of a villain's cunning.

'They were very unlucky,' said Sloan temperately. 'The body might not have been found up on that roof for years. I don't suppose we'll ever find the head. And without a head and therefore without teeth when it was found it might not have ever been identified.'

'Especially with a cold trail,' said Leeyes realistically.

'Exactly, sir.' He cleared his throat. 'But for that crow dropping the finger and Wendy Lamport finding it they would have got away with murder.'

'She's come round, by the way.' said Leeyes. 'Doesn't remember a thing after bending down to put the car key in the lock.'

'That will have been Hucham,' said Sloan. 'He was in the Lamb and Flag, too. I reckon he saw an opportunity to confuse the issue and took it. In every other respect this murder was a very carefully planned affair.' He paused to marshal his own thoughts. 'I think it may well have been the decamping of Ivor Harbeton that gave them the idea.'

'Everyone knew about that,' said Leeyes.

'And Paul Hucham and Andrina Ritchie also knew of the link beween George Mellot and Mellot's Furnishings,' said Sloan. 'I reckon they decided to take advantage of it.'

'So that if there were any suspicion it fell on the Mellots?'

'Yes, sir. They had to take a chance on the heights being similar, of course, but they didn't reckon on the body being found anyway.'

'Clever,' mused Leeyes.

'Cold blooded,' said Sloan. 'I reckon they left Martin Ritchie's car at the market during the night. I don't know where Harbeton decamped to or where Tom Mellot and his wife have gone, but . . .'

'Neither do I,' interrupted Leeyes, 'but there's a white Sealyham answering to our description in a kennels at Dover.'

'A few days in France,' concluded Sloan. He wasn't interested in Tom Mellot any more. He went back to Mrs Ritchie. 'There wasn't any real reason for the woman to report her husband as missing either,' he said.

'Hucham rang the solicitor for her, I suppose?'

'He only spoke to the secretary,' Sloan reminded him. 'He rang at a time when he knew Mr Puckle would be in court.'

Leeyes said, 'Husbands do take off.'

'We ran the usual checks for him,' said Sloan, 'but I must say a girl called Beverley had a convincing ring to it. So,' he added ruefully, 'did Andrina Ritchie's attitude.'

'Nearly fooled you, did she, Sloan?'

'Truth will out,' said Sloan sedately. 'It emerged when she was talking to Crosby. I've just checked.'

'To Crosby?' echoed Leeyes. 'I don't believe it.'

'She consistently referred to her husband in the past tense all the way through the interview. It's very difficult not to, sir, if you know that someone is dead. Your subconscious takes over.'

'The court doesn't like psychological stuff,' said Leeyes.

'They'll like the bloodstains on the carpet,' said Sloan comfortably. 'I reckon she had a rubber sheet on the mattress but the carpet got splashed. Crosby's working on it now.'

Sloan went back to Crosby in the bedroom. 'I should have got the answer a long time ago.' Mrs Andrina Coonie Ritchie had been taken away tight-lipped and talking only about lawyers.

The constable was more philosophical. 'Bit of a turn-up for the book, a woman.'

'The devil is an Equal Opportunities employer,' said Sloan. At least Judith had had the good of Israel at heart when she murdered Holofernes. Andrina Ritchie had been thinking only of Andrina Ritchie.

'Now I come to think of it,' said Crosby, who was on his hands and knees on the floor, 'she was the one who told us about Sam Bailey having a no-good boyo for a son, too.'

'It was all very well thought out, Crosby. No doubt about that.' He had sent Constable Mason up the hill to arrest Paul Hucham. He hoped he hadn't forgotten how to do it. Complicity was the word he would use when he charged Hucham. The leadership lay with the lady: the mode of death demonstrated that.

'That'll be why she used the Baileys' beet topper,' said Crosby, shifting his knee.

'I should have got there a long time ago,' said Sloan. How had the rest of that old ballad about the twa corbies and the new-slain knight gone?

> His hound is to the hunting gone,
> His hawk to fetch the wild fowl hame,
> His lady's ta'en another mate . . .

Detective Constable Crosby's contribution came in verse form, too. But parody. He straightened his back and chanted, 'Red stains on the carpet, red stains on the knife, Poor trusting old fellow, cut up by your wife.'

The tune was *Red Sails in the Sunset*: the sentiment quite sincere.

'Morning, Seedy.' Inspector Harpe from Traffic Division bumped into Sloan in the corridor of the police station just after he got back there.

'Morning, Harry.' Sloan looked at his watch. It was still only Monday morning.

'Quiet weekend?'

'Not really,' replied Sloan, adding politely, 'And you?'

'Two pile-ups and seven under the influence,' said the Traffic man.

'Ah.'

'And then I come in to this.' Happy Harry waved a letter in his hand.

'What is it?'

'From the Calleshire Ornithological Society.'

'Take my advice, Harry. If it's anything to do with crows give it a miss.'

'Crows?' said Harpe blankly. 'It's not crows they're on about. It's kestrels. Seems that kestrels have discovered that their prey can't cross motorways – dormice and the like . . .'

'Well, well.'

'So they drive 'em up to the edge of the road and then catch them – using the motorway as a trap.'

'Better than using it as a race-track.'

'What? Oh yes, of course.' He looked at the letter again. 'These bird people want to be allowed on the motorway to study the kestrels . . .'

Detective Inspector Sloan had a very long report to write. 'I should send the Flying Squad if I were you.'

All Pan Books are available at your local bookshop or newsagent, or can be ordered direct from the publisher. Indicate the number of copies required and fill in the form below.

Send to: Macmillan General Books C.S.
             Book Service By Post
             PO Box 29, Douglas I-O-M
             IM99 1BQ

or phone: 01624 675137, quoting title, author and credit card number.

or fax: 01624 670923, quoting title, author, and credit card number.

or Internet: http://www.bookpost.co.uk

Please enclose a remittance* to the value of the cover price plus 75 pence per book for post and packing. Overseas customers please allow £1.00 per copy for post and packing.

*Payment may be made in sterling by UK personal cheque, Eurocheque, postal order, sterling draft or international money order, made payable to Book Service By Post.

Alternatively by Access/Visa/MasterCard

Card No.

| | | | | | | | | | | | | | | |

Expiry Date

| | | | | | | | | | | | |

Signature _____

Applicable only in the UK and BFPO addresses.

While every effort is made to keep prices low, it is sometimes necessary to increase prices at short notice. Pan Books reserve the right to show on covers and charge new retail prices which may differ from those advertised in the text or elsewhere.

NAME AND ADDRESS IN BLOCK CAPITAL LETTERS PLEASE

Name _____

Address _____

_____

_____

_____

8/95

Please allow 28 days for delivery.

Please tick box if you do not wish to receive any additional information. ☐